Filomena, Cathy, and Angela Fazzi.

Il meglio delle zie.

Mauro Martone

THE ORCADIAN FILE

AUSTIN MACAULEY PUBLISHERS™

LONDON * CAMBRIDGE * NEW YORK * SHARJAH

A CIP catalogue record for this title is available from the British Library.

ISBN 9781398442443 (Paperback)
ISBN 9781398442450 (ePub e-book)
Hardback is not commercially available.

www.austinmacauley.com

First Published 2021
Austin Macauley Publishers Ltd®
1 Canada Square
Canary Wharf
London
E14 5AA

Author's Note

Sincere thanks and appreciation to AS for the cover art. BC for the generous proofing. CG for being lavish with both her time and encouragement, as well as her masterly advice on chronology. MH for responding cheerily to my random texts at all hours regarding judicial process. And the long since retired Sicilian baker, for those late-night lashings of coffee and cannoli, wherein I was enlightened on the intricacies of the Trapani Mandamenti. You all know who you are.

"The battle against the devil, which is the principal task of Saint Michael the Archangel, is still being fought today, because the devil is still alive and active in this world."
Pope John Paul II

Prologue

There is a belief among some cosmologists, theoretical physicists and theologians that there exists upon planet earth, various portals which once were, and may still be, gateways to other dimensions. Quantum physicists refer to this notion as the superstring theory. Theologians may additionally point to written evidence of vortices and whirling wormholes connecting heaven and earth described within scripture. Examples being: 2 Kings: 2.11 and Job: 38.1, as well as Zechariah: 9:14.

Notably, Zechariah suggests a wormhole in the south from which God himself will appear at the end of days. Historians and archaeologists may also point to the material evidence at locations such as Puerta de Hayu Marca (Gate of the Gods), or even Stonehenge, as being potential interdimensional stargates. Whilst Native American tribes such as the Hopi also highlighted similar beliefs through ancient, engraved petroglyphs of whirling spirals, through which their ancestors believed that giants and reptilian beings travelled from other realms[1].

Centuries later, the Apache tradition of creation, which recalls an ancient worldly flood and belief in subterranean portals that lead to a hell-like environment deep within the Superstition mountain range, maintains this principle of interdimensional portals[2]. Scripture suggests to us that the ancient Babylonians, inspired by forbidden knowledge, attempted to decrypt a portal gateway or stargate, with which to access heaven. It also tells us that this attempt caused God to intervene and prevent them from completing the project (Genesis 11:4-9). Interestingly, the name Babylon is derived from the Akkadian plural form of *Bab-ilani*—Gate of the Gods.

---

[1] Christy G. Turner and Jacqueline A. Turner (2011) *Man Corn: Cannibalism and Violence in the Prehistoric American Southwest*, University of Utah Press. p. 463.

[2] Dorothy Vitaliano (1973) *Legends of the Earth*, Bloomington: Indiana University Press. p. 170-1.

The ancient Sumerian-Babylonian poem—The Epic of Gilgamesh, which dates to 2100 BC—is often regarded as the earliest surviving great work of literature. In the second half of this epic, King Gilgamesh decides to undertake a long and perilous journey to discover the secret of eternal life. In his search, he apparently arrived at a great cedar forest located between two mountains, one of which is named Mount Mashu that spans from the heavens to the underworld. Dr Rivkah Scharf Kluger in her book, *The Archetypal Significance of Gilgamesh: A Modern Ancient Hero*, translates the word *mashu* from the Akkadian as "twins", which suggests "two mountains".[3]

Thomas Horn and Cris Putnam, authors of *On the Path of the Immortals*, suggest that the only suitable geographic location for a cedar forest located between two close mountains, and on the route presumed to have been taken by Gilgamesh, would have been the forest situated between Mount Lebanon and Mount Hermon. Hermon meaning "taboo" or "forbidden place". Notably, in the apocryphal Book of Enoch, Mount Hermon is stated to be the place where fallen angels descended to Earth.

Today, Hermon stands in the UN buffer zone between Syrian and Israeli-occupied territories. This particular location is situated at thirty-three degrees east longitude and thirty-three degrees north longitude of the Paris Zero Meridian. The location is, of course, of profound interest to high-ranking 33-degree Freemasons who, Horn and Putnam suggest, believe this to be the precise location where the founders of their order descended to earth[4].

Today, at the foot of Mount Hermon, the caves of the Canaanite pagan god Baal and the worship shrines that were once carved into the cliffs can still be seen. One of which—the Grotto of the Greco-Roman god of chaos Pan, who was worshipped there in the time of the New Testament, is still accessible. The Romans believed that the water which flows from the grotto symbolised the abyss and death, so the large cave was known as the "Gate of Hades", where murderous sacrifices and sexual abuse occurred.

Strangely, it was also at Mount Hermon's base that Jesus Christ came with his disciples for a special Messianic revelation amid these vulgar pagan shrines (Matthew 16:16). It is perhaps interesting that he had brought his disciples to a

---

[3] Dr Rivkah Scharf Kluger (1991) 'The archetypal significance of Gilgamesh: a modern ancient hero', ed. Yehezkel Kluger (Einsiedeln, Switzerland: Damon) p. 163.
[4] Thomas Horn and Cris Putnam (2015) *On the Path of the Immortals*, Defender Publishing Co. p. 179.

place regarded at the time by Jews to be Satan's turf. It was there however that the apostle Peter proclaimed him to be the Christ, and where Jesus additionally declared to Peter: "So I will call you Peter, which means a rock. On this rock I will build my church, and the gates of hell itself will not prevail against it."

Certainly, at that time, with prostitution and a regular abuse of people and animals ongoing in attempts to tempt Pan and other entities through a portal in the grotto, this would have seemed an odd location to visit by Jesus' disciples. The disciples would surely have been conscious that Mount Hermon was deemed to be an unholy place for Jews.

Dr Michael S. Heiser, a Biblical academic editor for Logos Bible Software and Bible Study Magazine, believes that there may be a supernatural entrance to a subterranean abyss below Mount Hermon. He feels that consequently, Jesus was challenging and baiting those beyond it by choosing this precise location to make such a remark about the gates of hell being unable to overcome his church[5]. Perhaps this proposed portal is what Enoch 10:12 is referring to: "Bind them [fallen angels] fast for seventy generations in the valleys of the earth, until the day of their judgment and of their consummation."

It is again, however, within the Bible, notably in Matthew 17:1-9, where one comes across further written evidence of an additional portal at Mount Hermon—upon the peak.

---

[5] Dr Michael S. Heiser (2015) *The Unseen Realm*, Lexham Press. p. 276-85.

Chapter One

Tenerife

Forsyth awoke from a light feverish sleep. It was an overly warm December in the Canaries and the lack of air conditioning did not help. His sweat stained pillow stank of rum, or perhaps he did? Anyway, he could smell it and felt shit. The room was dark like a coffin. He lay there a moment and grabbed his bearings. His head hurt now, and he remembered that he had been drinking too much recently. His mouth was parched, and he thought about relieving it with water for a moment before he remembered where he was.

The hairdryer sound of a 50cc moped whizzed by, dulled only by a single glazed window that displayed a few twinkling stars through the blinds, but it hurt to look up. Then someone below shouted something in Spanish. He tried to think about what they had said, but the process hurt his head furiously and he quickly gave up, closed his eyes again and attempted to evade the hangover through sleep.

Shortly afterwards, he heard a scratching noise from the downstairs balcony of his fourteen-story apartment block. The old woman below, who owned the little souvenir shop along at Los Cristianos, had accidently locked her Beagle out on the balcony again before going to her bed. Then a noisy diesel lorry carrying a crate of glass bottles trundled by and so he gave up and dragged himself up from his pit.

As he crossed into his adjoining hall, he felt a dizzying disorientation for a brief second before he found his little kitchen space adjoining the lounge area and used a worktop to steady himself and begin a search for ibuprofen, which he soon located in a drawer. He took two, opened the fridge and began drinking greedily from a bottle of still water. He then took a towel to dry the cold sweat from his hair, but the process caused his head to pound, causing him to drop it.

He then noticed a can of orange Fanta on a ledge in the fridge and so replaced the water and opened the can before returning to his room and drinking half of it. He placed it on his beside cabinet, burped loudly then checked his phone. There were no messages thankfully. He returned to bed and lay there waiting for the ibuprofen to kick in.

His pillow was cold and damp, so he turned it around and received a sharp flashing pain to his temple for his trouble. He then returned to the foetal position and closed his eyes and consumed the pain. He got lucky, sleep came to him within ten minutes and this time it was somewhat deeper and less frenzied.

He dreamed of Audrey, and of the time they had gone to the safari park with her niece and nephew for the day. But instead of lions and tigers in the dangerous areas, he could see the blurry faces of his enemies watching him from behind the trees and vegetation. Audrey was oblivious of course and laughing along with the kids who were loving the experience, while he continued to look-out like a secret service agent.

Then the dream developed, as it always did, and he could see Chuck's face, then his body lying like a pile of raw hamburger meat upon the pavement. He looked around the street and could see the same blurry faces peering out from behind parked cars and nearby gardens.

An alarm began to ring on a blacked-out transit that pulled out from the kerb and drove slowly past as he stood over Chuck's carcass. He then stepped out onto the road and watched it disappear into the distance, two-faced enemies looking back at him from the small rear door windows, all while the alarm continued to ring from it.

"They must have stolen it," said a voice from the crowd gathering on the pavement.

"Oh, they are much more than mere car thieves," he had thought aloud.

Then he awoke again. He was still in Tenerife. His phone was ringing, it was light now, and the sun came through the gap in the blinds. He could see his phone on the cabinet, and so he reached out a tired hand for it without checking the call ID, and hoping it was Audrey.

He felt a little better now—no headache, the pounding had gone but the general feeling of being unwell remained. He realised he was still sweating. The hot morning sun was warming his wrist as he raised the phone to his ear. He was not fit for a long conversation, he knew that much, the thought of it would likely instigate a return of the headache.

"Yep?" he whispered with a tongue as dry as sand.

"Time to get up, Chris." It was his sister, Mel, her usual sharp tone absent as she had just woken up herself. A flash of anxiety came over him now. He pictured her laying there in bed, eyes closed, exhausted and with her fuckwitted toy boy Gary out cold beside her.

There was a lingering silence for a moment while he decided how to respond. He hadn't been out here in Tenerife long, only since they had forced him to resign from the police. He was bitter, of course, and so it felt much longer than it had been. Frustrated at a few things—his lot, Chuck's murder and him not being in a position to catch the culprits, not to mention the loss of his relationship. He was also pissed off that he had ended up here, in this dusty version of Blackpool, where drunken Englishmen were in abundance, and that he was now having to serve them in his sister's horrible little boozer—The Alba Bar.

Mel and Gary did the morning shifts and he ran the place in the evenings, six nights per week for a poxy €200 plus tips and free digs—as Gary had vacated this little holiday high rise in order to move into Mel's two-bedroom villa along the coast at Costa Del Silencio.

Not knowing anyone at first, Forsyth had chosen to work seven nights a week for extra cash and began drinking quite heavily. It was just the way it was out here: having a cold beer for breakfast alongside a manky bacon roll, seemed normal after a while.

He had been drinking way too much, more than he had ever expected. The problem was, he had started going heavy on the Cuba Libres. When Mel had asked him to start doing two morning shifts too, so that she could drive Gary to Spanish classes in Santa Cruz, Forsyth had reluctantly agreed. The extra cash and tips would help, but so far he had called in sick six out of the last nine shifts, resulting in two over-the-top rollockings from her. She had even reprimanded him recently in front of Gary and a full house of customers, and things had got so bad that he had threatened to chin Gary, who had made a bravado-fuelled scene of pretending to go for Forsyth but had conveniently allowed Mel to restrain him with her thumb.

Forsyth had laughed, walked off and gotten pissed with two Welsh blokes who were on holiday. Next day, Mel had turned up at the apartment and lectured him for what seemed like hours regarding his off the rails behaviour. They had argued, she had then slapped him and called him a failure. That had hurt but he had hidden it and lashed back at her own demons. She had cried then. In the end, he promised not to let her down again and they had hugged.

He felt sick now. Dizzy and poisoned by rum. Silence wasn't an option, however, so he took a deep breath then sighed, "Right."

"I heard you were pissed last night," she half asked. "Per texted to say you were in good form."

"Okay," Forsyth had his eyes closed again and now wanted to hang up. Per was a Swedish expat who loitered around the bar and reported everything to Mel because he wanted to take Gary's place in her bed.

"Are you hungover?" her tone was now borderline aggressive.

"Yes, and I'll be fine, thanks for calling." He hung up.

It was another beautiful Canarian morning outside and as he sauntered along Avenue la Habana in his shorts and flipflops, he could already feel the sun's warmth beginning to become painful. He swigged mouthfuls of mineral water from a bottle he had brought with him as he progressed towards the bar and caught a whiff of the familiar smell of Spanish bread being toasted from the kitchen of a hotel. He would make some toast when he arrived.

He had become quite tanned in the few weeks he had been in Tenerife and could easily pass for a Canarian if only his Spanish was better. Having forgotten to buy suntan lotion yet again, he worried somewhat about his already burnt skin for the remaining few yards. He removed his old sunglasses and examined his bronzed wrists and hands as he continued—he had removed his watch before he left the apartment and placed it in his pocket in order to allow the sun to get at the white mark it had left around his wrist.

Just then, the old porter from the Marina hotel, called out to him in Spanish, "Hola amigo!"

Forsyth smiled and waved back at him as he passed the large marble steps in front of the old hotel. Old Rafael had a taste for brandy and Guinness and often came into the bar when his shift ended to drink and chew the fat with one or two of the other Spaniards who came around—Forsyth would drink with them and exchange in the universal language of football. His issues here on the island were boredom and monotony, the booze helped with this of course, as did these guys, but he still laboured to cope with the loss of the life he had previously inhabited.

The locals liked that he knew all about Di Stefano and Puskas and could hold his own, on not only Spanish football, but football in general. Though his

Spanish sometimes let him down when he tried to emphasise a particular point, such as the beauty of Roberto Baggio's goal against Spain in the 1994 World Cup or his general dislike of Real Madrid's Sergio Ramos, but overall he got his meaning across and was well regarded by them.

"Hoy?" he called back, raising a hand to his mouth to mimic holding a glass.

"Si," laughed the old man joyfully. "Tenga un buen dia."

No wonder they were all so happy here, considered Forsyth; to wake up to this glowing prettiness every day surely impelled cheerfulness. He found the Spanish to be polite and courteous in a manner that Brits had once been in his childhood days. Yes, Spaniards were often angrier than say, the Italians, and some could be moody too, just like anywhere else, but in general, there was a pleasantness about them. There was also no sign of road rage here, nor were there gangs of louts hanging around street corners drinking and littering. Forsyth, despite his insecurity regarding his life and loss of career, now found himself smiling to himself as he walked on, waving and exchanging a few "Buenos dias" with hotel gardeners and cleaners as he passed endless apartment blocks and hotels.

As soon as he opened up the bar, he put the TV on and listened to a news broadcast in Spanish on Telecinco whilst he brushed and mopped the tiled floor. It helped him pick up the language and to think in Spanish without looking for subtitles. He then washed up the glasses and ashtrays, set up the five plastic tables with parasols outside on the sidewalk and placed the blackboard outside beside them advertising draft Heineken and a choice of bar snack for five euros.

Once all of this was done, he made himself a double espresso and some toast, and watched the news a while longer before his first customers, a couple from Leeds arrived and ordered a cooked English breakfast. Forsyth stepped into the kitchen beside the bar which had a little hatch enabling him to keep an eye on it, and started cooking. In an hour or so, Ricky the teenage party boy from Hawick, would turn up and give him a hand. Meanwhile, Forsyth cracked on with frying up sausages, bacon, black pudding, and eggs for the couple.

Ricky had come on holiday a few times and had just ended up staying on. He shared a two-bedroom apartment with various DJs and a rather foxy young tour guide with tits which would have made Barbara Windsor blush in her heyday. Forsyth knew that Ricky also sold pills to tourists and was dabbling in small amounts of cocaine in order to help him with his outgoings, as well as working here as a skivvy most days. He didn't mind. though, after all he had his own

15

demons to deal with and besides, he quite liked the lad's banter and, so long as he did not sell anything from the bar, Forsyth had no issue with him.

Once he had served up the breakfasts with coffee and toast, Forsyth perched himself back upon the bar and stared out at the palm tree lined avenue outside. There were worse places to endure a hangover, he regularly conceded. This peaceful period, when most tourists were either still sleeping or having breakfast, presented time for thought. He had considered suicide whilst back in Edinburgh – initially he could not see any way out of his predicament, but he had soon realised that no matter how hellish things had seemed, he would soon find himself in a real hell should he have gone through with it.

It was not so bad here really, and most mornings he lived a contemplative life, thinking about what had happened. How his entire world had been turned upside down, and how he had lost both Audrey and the person he could have become. He often thought about what she would be doing or whose bed she might be in. He knew that he would only be truly over her once he no longer cared about her moving on.

Maybe he could sort his head out and go back to her as she had suggested? In the meantime, he would change his line of thought by watching the chicharreros strolling by with their exotic ambiance, not unlike the cariocas of Copa Cabana.

A wet boy, around 8 or 9, Spanish, and wearing nothing but swim shorts, suddenly appeared, dripping and panting. "Hola, un Cacao por favor," he looked up at Forsyth hopefully.

He was obviously staying in the adjoining apartment block where he had run around from the pool. Forsyth nodded, reached down into a small fridge beneath the bar and beside the sink, and produced a cold bottle of chocolate milk. He shook it, removed the metal cap, placed a green straw in it and handed it to the kid who promptly left a Euro upon the bar, thanked him and ran off with straw in mouth.

Try that again without flipflops in an hour or so, and your feet will burn on the pavement, son.

"Scuse me, pal, can we get some more toast please?" called the Yorkshireman at the table.

"No probs," Forsyth went back through to the kitchen and put two slices on.

Once he had served them, he returned to the bar and considered pulling himself a cold pint of cider. He was hot enough this morning, but the kitchen was much warmer, and he knew it would perk him up for the day. Just then a Guarda Civil jeep pulled up outside; three armed guards got out and walked straight into the bar and right up to him. He wondered for a moment if they were looking for Ricky.

"Buenos dias?" he enquired to the first one, a small overweight man with a face that had endured years of sunshine.

"Buenos dias," replied the officer with a knowing smile. He then produced two pieces of paper and studied them a moment before showing them to the other two officers who were both standing beside him now with their hands on their hips.

They all nodded and then the fat one turned back to Forsyth. "Are you Christopher Forsyth?" he asked.

"I am," nodded Forsyth. He guessed that the papers had his photo on them and might be an arrest warrant of some sort, but he was hopeful that this might have something to do with a witness statement he had given to the Policia Local regarding a brawl outside the bar a few weeks previously when a tourist had been flattened by a taxi driver. Though the fact this was the Guarda Civil standing before him, and not the Policia Local, reduced the odds somewhat.

"Then I am detaining you in order that you may assist us with an enquiry." The smiler relieved himself upon Forsyth's tiny string of optimism.

"On what grounds?" he had to ask.

"Just get in the jeep, now, senor," insisted the man.

"But I am here alone, may I call my sister and ask her to come and—"

"No." Smiler shook his head. "Close the place up and come with us, please, senor."

Fifteen minutes later, they were hurtling through the resort and up to the Guard barracks at Calle Noelia Afonso Cabrera.

"You were a cop. huh?" asked another of the guards as they travelled.

Forsyth knew the routine—talk away and be friendly until you have the suspect under lock and key. He remained expressionless and looked out at the buildings and people they were passing.

"Arsehole," spat the guard.

At the barracks, Forsyth was led down several corridors of tiled marble and whitewashed walls, to a set of relatively new-styled cells. There was no processing and no searching before he was ushered into a small, empty concrete block with reinforced steel door and a small, barred window twelve feet from the ground that produced a thin beam of sunlight.

There was a stainless-steel loo without a seat in a corner but no bed or chair. Cold air blew down from an air conditioning system on the ceiling and so before long, Forsyth was feeling quite chilly. He cranked his neck up to look at the sky through the little window and saw the branches of a lovely-looking tree with green leaves and little lemons hanging from it like teardrops.

He watched this a while, entranced at the flickering shadows, which danced within the ray of sunlight which pierced the cell like a laser beam. Nature putting on an alluring display by tempting him to become despondent at his incarceration, he speculated.

All of this was a contrast to the grey interior and the familiar odour of warm sewage that he had come to recognise in Spanish lavatories. He felt as if he was chained to winter here, whilst viewing summer on TV.

He heard the echo of someone whistling along a corridor and the sound of keys and doors opening and closing. He closed his eyes and was instantly back in St Leonard's in Edinburgh, confronting all the bad apples in the custody suite again. It was funny, but he could not really remember all of the reality of what had happened back in Edinburgh. Only flashes of feelings he had at the time— anger, suspicion, frustration, shock, sadness, oh and fear, can't forget the fear.

For they had surrounded him like a pack of starved lions after they had murdered Chuck. Then they had almost destroyed his relationship with the woman he loved and now missed so much, before then allowing him to run.

Hatred too, then. Of the bitter variety.

He read the scratched graffiti upon the wall opposite him. There was not much of it and most of it appeared to be authored by someone called "Iker" who was apparently a communist who detested the Guardia and who was also deeply head over heels for a "Luna". Forsyth closed his eyes again and tried to think of pleasant memories. The 1984 Scottish League Cup Final at Hampden Park between Rangers and the defending champions Celtic. His grandfather had taken him, and there had not been much hope as Celtic had been playing well.

Fortunately, they had lost their goal machine Charlie Nicholas who had jumped ship for Arsenal in the summer while the Rangers had new kid Ally McCoist recently signed from Sunderland. It had been his first game and boy what a game, Rangers had won 3-2 after extra time and McCoist had, like Nicholas the year previously, scored the winner.

So, Forsyth sat there and recalled the day, from the moment they had caught the train to Mount Florida, that had been full of supporters wearing red, white and blue, until their supper of fish and chips from Landucci's in his grandfather's home town of Dumbarton.

With the hangover it was easy to doze off. He had no idea how long he had been sleeping but the sound of the military boots worn by the Guardia, clunking along the corridor, awoke him. Then his door unlocked, and he impulsively jumped up to face whatever was coming.

This time it was an older man with cap wearing and much younger rookie behind him, who appeared. The oldie gestured for him to come out with a peaceful nod, and so he did.

"Visitor," said the rookie who did not handcuff him but proceeded to escort him along a couple of corridors and then up two flights of stairs until they came to several green doors. They stopped outside one that had nothing written on it. The rookie opened the door and the oldie gave Forsyth a light push into the room.

Inside were two pale-looking men, mid-forties to fifties, both wearing suits and shirts without ties, although Forsyth noted a part of a tie, which did not match either the shirt or the suit of the man whose pocket it was hanging from.

These were cops from the UK then.

The old guard nodded at them and took a seat at the door whilst the younger guard remained standing beside him in the door frame.

"Hiya Chris, I'm DI Turner from Edinburgh CID and this is my colleague DS Bowie," said one of the men.

"Why have the Guardia detained me?" Forsyth remained expressionless whilst ignoring the offer of a handshake from a smirking Bowie.

"You're not being detained, you are being arrested," smirked Bowie now. He had a Dundonian accent, was quite fat and had thick blonde hair which he tried to style with wax, but which was melting now. Forsyth noted that he also had flaking skin from his head, resting on his blue-suited shoulders like teeny Manchego gratings.

"They have told me nothing." He shook his head.

Turner and Bowie exchanged a smirk, then Turner sat down too and sighed. "Look, Chris, I'm sorry to tell you this but our lot are looking to charge you with murder."

"Of whom?" Forsyth remained cool, giving little away but the jolt had sent his heart skipping, and he had to straighten his leg in order to appear unmoved.

"Yvonne Kidd," replied Turner, devoid of any obvious empathy.

"Bollocks."

"The evidence apparently says otherwise, so you can drag it out if you wish, but I am here to offer you the opportunity to get on a plane with us," Turner looked now at his sidekick, possibly for a nod of approval, and then back at Forsyth with a newly formed snidey smirk, "and get this dealt with, or you can refuse and slum it here in a Spanish cell until a judge here sends you back, mate." He shrugged his shoulders in an effort to seem indifferent.

"Are you the investigating officer?" asked Forsyth.

Turner shook his head. "Noooo, DI Calvin Bennett is, do you know him?"

Forsyth shook his head; he had never heard of him until now. He did however know this routine inside out. If he refused, he would be remanded here in some hellhole, or even worse—transported to Madrid and caged with all the Latinos at the deportation clink—Aluche until all the deportation angles had been exhausted.

It would certainly be unpleasant and he had nowhere near enough money to pay for an immigration lawyer who would, no doubt, charge by the sombrero load. Mel could not pay for one for him either, for she was barely getting by as it was, and such a commitment would be too much for her to carry whilst she steadied the ship without him.

"I'll go if you take me to my apartment to get changed and collect my passport and stuff," he finally responded.

"We'll go over for you and pick up whatever you want," insisted Turner, still smirking, "while you stay here until it is time to go to the airport."

"What time is the flight?"

"Three pm," replied Turner gleefully. "You'll be home just in time for Christmas, and they do a right good meal for detainees in St Leonards."

Forsyth did not dignify this with a response; instead, he asked, "And do I get a couple of beers at the airport?"

Turner and Bowie looked at each other again, but this time in surprise and without the grins, before Turner then shrugged. "Well, only if you promise to be a good boy."

"I promise," said Forsyth.

"Deal." Turner nodded and offered his hand.

Forsyth took it and nodded over towards the old guard. "Deal. That lot have my keys."

"Okay then." Turner then nodded up at the guard, who nodded back and promptly escorted a now stunned Forsyth back down to the cells.

"Fuck," Forsyth whispered to himself once his cell door had slammed shut. He then fell to his knees, covered his face with his hands, and cried.

They plan to totally destroy me.

Chapter Two

Anybody can become angry—that is easy; but to be angry with the right person, to the right degree, at the right time, for the right purpose and in the right way—that is not easy.
Aristotle

"He has a wife, two children of primary school ages and is the sole breadwinner, M'lady," Monty informed the sheriff, who was presently scanning the paperwork.

She wore a black robe and an old wig that barely covered her long dark hair that rested upon her shoulders. "As Your Ladyship can see," Monty proceeded, "he has no previous convictions." He gave the attractive young Fiscal a quick glance across the table, but she did not look up from her file.

"I would suggest, M'lady, that he poses no threat of flight nor of reoffending and accordingly, Your Ladyship may consider granting bail and allowing him to return to his family and job?" he urged the sheriff, who now briefly raised her gaze from her papers to acknowledge him.

The canny young Fiscal had led the way beforehand, of course, by coming across well with her initial pleadings and earning smiles of approval from the sheriff. Monty, on the other hand, had pleaded 'not guilty' on the accused's behalf and not received as much as a kindly look from above.

"My friend here," he gave a tired flick of his wrist towards the Fiscal, whilst focusing entirely upon the Sheriff, "has objected to bail as instructed by the police officers who have made these allegations."

The rookie Fiscal, who was slim and pale with long wavy red hair, had been cockily confident earlier, but would not, Monty was aware, be sure as to whether or not his claim was correct. At least not until she either spoke to her boss upstairs or to the investigating police officers again. Consequently, she remained still and tight-lipped.

Neither her boss nor the cops were available today, thankfully, and so she had come into the courtroom with an unsigned note in the file that read, "It is a petition and so you should oppose bail." Monty had not quite managed to read it from the other side of the oval table, but he had seen the yellow unsigned note stuck to the file and had experience enough to know that this fledgling was simply following instructions from above.

She was a novice after all, while he had been twenty-odd years in the game, most of them in this particular courthouse. Yet she had given little away and had done considerable damage to his client by her eloquent reporting of the incident to the court in her Mary Erskine[6] accent.

"And the police have requested that bail be opposed, M'lady, because my client did not sign a statement admitting guilt whilst in their custody." He shook his head despondently at the Fiscal who kept her gaze down on her file, searching eagerly for any info on his claim.

Sheriff Pelletier looked down at her too now and raised an eyebrow, if only to see if she was going to make a hullaballoo. "Right," she eventually said when the Fiscal stopped searching but still did not look up. "I accept the points you make about flight, Mr Montgomery." She looked down at him as he sat down again. She had deep almond-shaped brown eyes and overly large teeth that did not flatter her; however, Monty found her strangely attractive at this moment and met her gaze.

The Fiscal began playing with her pen now. She clearly needed a pee, he reckoned, which almost caused him to grin, but Pelletier might have read this as manly arrogance should she have caught him doing so.

Pelletier looked down at her again momentarily but then dragged herself back to Monty without offering the young Fiscal the opportunity to respond, as it was clearly obvious that she had no intention of doing so. "It is wishful thinking, however, to suggest that these are logical reasons to grant bail in this matter, for this is a very serious allegation." She shook her head slowly to confirm that she was not with him. "Here we have two charges of breaking and entry, into two separate properties," she read from the petition again before removing her reading glasses and sighing. "Then a game of cat and mouse played, allegedly, with the police thereafter, and over a matter of months." She waved the report gently in the air. "This suggests an inclination towards reoffending, Mr Montgomery." She leant back in her chair and read on.

---

[6] The Mary Erskine school in Edinburgh is an independent school for girls founded in 1694.

There was a brief wait then, wherein Monty could hear the breathing of both the clerk and the Fiscal. He looked over at his client, 48-year-old Derry Dryburgh, sitting in the dock between two overweight security guards with his head down as if studying his shoes.

"There are also vulnerable people who might be concerned about your client obtaining his liberty." Pelletier didn't lift her gaze from the paper she was reading. She was clearly referring to three key witnesses. "Which is particularly concerning." She asserted when she eventually looked up again. "I'm inclined to conclude that the logical contention here must be a custodial remand." She was now quite ready to lock Dryburgh up for Christmas and Monty could see that all was just about lost for him.

There was silence in the packed Friday morning custody court. Black-robed solicitors were lined up like puffins on cliff ledges on one side of the oval room, awaiting the favouritism of the Clerk of Court who arranged the calling order, based upon a whisper or wink from one of them. A Glasgow-based solicitor, here to plead on behalf of his west coast client who had been caught speeding in Edinburgh, stood little chance, and Monty noted him popping his little bald head out hopefully from behind all the puffins, to no avail.

"Stand up," demanded Pelletier of Dryburgh, and he duly complied. "Remanded in custody for seven days," she announced resolutely.

"It's alright for you enjoying the holidays with your money, eh?" Dryburgh suddenly mumbled but Pelletier could not quite make him out. Monty, however, did hear and urged him with a raised hand not to say anything else.

"You are destroying me with this," shouted the balding, moustached Dryburgh, leaning over the dock scornfully towards Pelletier.

Monty had not seen this coming and looked at the security officers, who had not anticipated it either, having not originally cuffed the prisoner. He half expected them to restrain Dryburgh now though. They did eventually pull him back and restrain him; after a moment of appearing like dazed rabbits in the headlights.

"There's a new order approaching, with new rules, when people will applaud and bow to our glory, while worthless maggots like you and her," Dryburgh nodded over at the shocked-looking young Fiscal, "will lose all your powers and self-delusional supremacies. You just don't know it yet." He was then promptly frog-marched out of a side door without another word.

Monty sought out Dryburgh ten minutes later in the bowels of the court where he had been isolated away from the other prisoners in one of the new American-style observation cells with electronic caged grills controlled from an operations desk in the custody suite.

Annoyingly, he now found him unwilling to communicate and in what appeared to be a state of shock. Monty was not in the mood for a self-destructive and unappreciative client and would not be wasting his time chasing one here. If Dryburgh could not accept defeat in today's argument and commit himself to winning the next one, he could jog on as far as Monty was concerned and find himself another lawyer.

"That's me screwed for Christmas now," mumbled Dryburgh, as a self-pitying child might do whilst beginning to calm down from a tantrum.

Monty could see that there were psychological issues here and that the guy required help, but saw no point in endorsing Dryburgh's self-pity. He saw that the guy sought sympathy and an "It'll be alright" response. Unfortunately for him, Monty was not in the mood to play mummy today. He recognised that the guy needed the "short sharp shock"[7] treatment if they were to salvage anything from this mess.

"Listen, you little shit, I'm here to help you, so if you don't get yourself together and work with me, then we will be back up here on the nineteenth of December and you really will be remanded over the holidays," he warned impatiently.

Dryburgh was now handcuffed but fortunately, he seemed to have calmed down, and despite being taken aback by Monty's tone, he nodded agreement. "Okay, yes, you're right, of course. I'm sorry," he whispered, clearly knowing what side his bread was buttered on. He was intelligent enough to know that he would lose his lawyer if he continued with the 'all suffering victim' routine.

"Well, the Sheriff might have you charged with contempt of court now," Monty pointed out, "so you need to keep calm and refrain from anymore tantrums, okay, Derry?"

Dryburgh nodded that he understood.

---

[7] A phrase used by the British government of 1979 in their manifesto, which promised to experiment with tougher borstals for juvenile criminals. The idea being that the institutions would be run by prison staff in plain clothes, as opposed to social workers, and that boys would experience a short but hard-hitting educational experience as a deterrent from any future criminal activity.

"What was all that '*the end is nigh*' shit up there about anyway?"

"What shit?" asked Dryburgh with a suitably mystified look.

"That rant?" Monty scanned him for any sign of game-playing.

"What rant? I never spoke upstairs." Dryburgh appeared offended at the very suggestion.

Monty was not entirely convinced but preferred not to dwell upon it. He was more interested in getting his client a reprieve of some sort. The truth of the matter would probably only hinder him in the process.

"Look, I'm going to arrange for an emergency psychological assessment through a friend of mine called Nancy. She's a psychologist and will interview you over this week whilst you're on remand, to see if we can show that you have been stressed out or unwell."

"What, like a looney?" retorted Dryburgh.

"No Derry, simply stressed, and this being the reason for your recent outburst and why you were stalking your ex and breaking into her property, etc. Well, we might get you a little Christmas goodwill from the court, if we can," urged Monty. It was all he had up his sleeve. He knew a few other solicitors who would be washing their hands at this point and simply going through the motions until the trial date, but that was not Stephen Montgomery.

"So, play the dafty, you're saying? And what bloody outburst are you on about?" Dryburgh wasn't so sure though.

"Precisely," Monty agreed with a cheeky wink. Nancy Kelly worked in a team of psychotherapists at an NHS centre for stressed individuals with substance addictions, specialising in schizophrenia and depression. Depending on whether it was going to be helpful or detrimental to his cause, he hoped that Nancy, an old university fling, may be able to help Dryburgh—and if he was pretending to be nuts but still convinced her, well, that would do too.

Nancy agreed to provide an independent opinion on Dryburgh that could either be given to the court or not, depending upon whether it was going to be helpful or detrimental to his cause. "It will have to be after work, Monty, but yes, sure, any evening would suit," she agreed the following afternoon when Monty telephoned her.

This had been easy enough to arrange, as whilst an accused person was on remand, HM Prison permitted them daily visits with any reasonably named persons. Monty rang the prison governor early the next morning whilst he was travelling on a bus up Leith Walk en route to his office; and secured the go-ahead.

He then pinged Nancy a text to confirm, "Tonight 7-830? Cheers."

"Fine—you better be coming too?" She half-asked in her reply.

"No prob, see you there."

That was his hopes of making a big pot of pasta soup up the spout then. He shrugged his shoulders despondently and dragged himself up to ring the bell for his stop. By the time Dryburgh was back up at court, Monty found himself armed with a favourable opinion from Nancy and written confirmation from the prison that Dryburgh had behaved impeccably whilst on remand. Monty had arranged for a suit to be handed in by Dryburgh's loyal wife who was standing by him regardless of his behaviour; and then pointed her and her kids out to the new Sheriff, a fair man named Pinkerton, as they sat in court.

Pinky resided in an age-old family home in the New Town and was generally regarded to be a good judge of others, with thoughtful ethics and occasional compassion for the accused. He was also an awfully hard-hitter of the hooded rodents who frequented the court on charges of dishonesty, narcotics and violence. Monty was additionally apprehensive however that Pinky would have been pissed off by Dryburgh's contempt of court antics, with which he had recently been charged.

Monty thus pleaded with him on his client's behalf for what many in the court felt was an overly long period. He argued that years of cannabis abuse and gambling had played its part in this soap opera and tried, quite well actually, to portray Dryburgh as an unlucky wretch who required sympathy and support as opposed to a heavy hand. Nancy's report was particularly welcomed by the Sheriff and he was ultimately persuaded by Monty's argument about these first offences being uncharacteristic and the cause of a mental breakdown.

Doubtless this new Fiscal (an older chap Monty knew quite well based upon their banter about football) withdrawing his opposition to bail, prior to Pinky's appearance, had restored Monty's hope.

"I can see that you have made commendable efforts on your client's behalf with this statement from Dr Kelly, and I also note the background matters you have brought to my attention, Mr Montgomery," the Sheriff informed him curtly. "Is your client prepared to agree to stay away from the listed witnesses?"

"Indeed he is, my lord."

Shortly afterwards, Dryburgh was granted bail under the condition that he refrain from going anywhere near the witnesses, their places of employment, or their home addresses. Trial was set for the following June and Pinky left him in little doubt about the fact that should he breach his bail in any way, he would be rearrested and remanded in custody until the trial.

Afterwards, as the security team processed his release downstairs, Monty shook Dryburgh's hand and reiterated the bail conditions. "Behave yourself and don't reoffend. By the time the trial ends, and if you are found guilty, the court will be obliged to seek a social enquiry report and we can then show that counselling and support, as opposed to a prison sentence, would be a better fit for you, Derry," he advised a somewhat relieved Dryburgh.

"But can you still win the trial?" asked Dryburgh anxiously.

"We shall give it a good go, of course, but we must cover all angles, Derry." Monty remained as diplomatic as always.

Dryburgh seemed optimistic now and more relaxed than he had been upstairs, where he had chewed his nails down to the flesh. Of course, this was common among released prisoners. Freedom had that effect on a person who had just spent a week in a smelly concrete box with a stranger's farts. The fact that he may still go down on a later date, seemed not to matter presently. "Thank you, Mr Montgomery," said Dryburgh, offering his hand again. Monty shook it, nodded and walked away.

A few minutes later, as he walked back down the Bridges towards his office, Monty too experienced a wave of relief. All the shops had festive lights and tinsel up and he would now have some time off, as it was after all Christmas. He could hear "I believe in Father Christmas" being sung by Greg Lake, from a shoe shop, and he could smell enticing hot food calling him through the cold air. The streets were busy with shoppers and as he crossed the road at the old Bank Hotel, he passed a works night out, with people hanging around outside smoking and merrily singing Christmas songs.

This was going to be his eleventh Christmas alone, and he usually felt a little troubled by all the joyful merriment that he always did his best to ignore it every year. Work always helped him deflect his focus, of course, and he probably worked harder in December than at any other time of the year. The company of his dog also helped when at home too, and as he was now off until the new year, he may possibly have felt lonely had he not had it for company.

Traditionally, when the court closed around the twenty-second, he would go home and argue with himself about whether or not to put up the tree. There had been offers of Christmas dinner of course, there usually were, from his somewhat estranged elder sister Sadie in St Austell and from old Trisha, the overly friendly fifty-plus secretary at his firm who wanted to shag him.

He couldn't be bothered with either the drive down to his sister's or her husband's endless waffling about property law though. The man was quiet at the best of times, making Monty feel unwelcome through both the silence and the gaze of his beady little eyes. That was until he had taken a Christmas drink, then his brother-in-law morphed into a lecturer in real estate. Monty had about as much interest in real estate as he had in cars—none. He never understood salesmen, nor petrol-heads either for that matter; those he had encountered had all been unable to play football; he surmised.

His seclusion at Christmas had become a tradition, and he tried to convince himself that this was the way he liked it due to his irregular head. Who was he kidding, he asked himself now as he strolled down the old tobacco merchants' lane—Carrubber's Close—quite relieved to be putting behind him the sound of Christmas and the noisy diesel engines of the corporation buses, whose tyres splattered mercilessly through icy brown slush.

He was inclined to pretend to be going to someone or other's for Christmas in order not to offend anyone who felt sorry for him and invited him along to join one of their jollies. Even one of his neighbours had suggested he eat with them only last week, which had been quite a shock to the system. "I'm having a friend around, sorry." He had lied.

Monty had been raised in the little rural village of Falkland, where his parents had owned a cottage on the edge of the village, by a stream and an old pear orchard. Every Christmas had been a family celebration with extended relatives invited over, and he could recall much merriment. Although he had not really gotten on so well with his mother, he very much missed those times and so chose not to dwell upon the past. He had created for himself then, a wall of humbug in order to combat sentimental wistfulness.

As a teenager, he had been away studying criminal law in Dundee when both his parents had died in a road accident. A frozen food lorry trying to avoid a deer had swerved into them. The driver had not seen their little white Renault coming around the bend as it had been snowing heavily on the rural country lane at the time. The poor lorry driver had been devastated, mind you. Monty had seen it in the guy's eyes when he turned up the following winter, to ask once again for forgiveness on what had been the first anniversary of the accident.

On the day after the accident, Monty had returned to the family home shortly after identifying the mangled corpses. He had sat alone with the lights out smoking the governor's Capstan cigarettes and supping his Black Label, staring at the walls through tear drenched eyes. It had been then that the poor driver had first turned up, bandaged and limping, with the need to explain himself. Monty had told him that he had instinctively done the right thing and assured him that he took consolation in knowing that the deer had survived.

"That seems important, don't you think?" he had asked the stunned man. The guy had thought that Monty was perhaps still in a state of shock of some kind, but he had nodded his agreement and they both talked a while over a dram, mostly about Monty's studies and the driver's young family.

"Well, you'll make a fine judge one day, young man," the driver had told him whilst wiping tears away with a handkerchief.

Monty had never thought about being a judge. So he had doubted the observation at the time, but he had nodded and they had shaken hands and parted well.

Sadie had been working down in North London as a nurse at the time and had driven up to arrange the funeral with him. When it was over, they had tried renting the cottage out, but Monty needed somewhere to live at the end of term, and Sadie was refusing to come home and take up a position with the NHS in Fife. She wanted to sell the place in order to improve her life down south. They had quarrelled about that over the phone and in emails over the following months until they both finally decided to call a truce, sell up and split the money. After paying his student debts, Monty had enough to buy a small flat in Dundee while he continued his studies. He then stayed put in the city and did his apprenticeship with a busy legal aid-propelled firm of defence solicitors.

A few years later, he obtained a good position in Edinburgh with an upmarket West End firm and bought a small main door flat in Leith. There he learned about the process of the Edinburgh court system, which was considerably different to Dundee's. He achieved some good results during his time with his new firm, as well as making some embarrassing slipups. It was all part of his development— the point, he believed, was to comprehend his mistakes and not to repeat them.

After a couple of years practising with that firm, the mother of his son walked into his life. She was a materialistic little enchantress who came to work as an admin manager at his West End firm. She already had a child to another bloke and so was only employed part-time. There was something of the chav about the enchantress—Monty noticed this when she pinched a pair of Armani socks from him that his sister had sent him for Christmas. The chav had assured Monty that she had been on the pill when she compelled him into bed. The rest was history, of course, and he was now an absent parent to a fifteen-year-old son who had been trained to dislike him.

Monty then moved over to a small criminal firm in the old town after the chav had created a stir in the office about her pregnancy. He had to get away from her and so he joined his current firm of court lawyers, which dealt mainly with legal aid clients. He was more comfortable with court work, it had after all been his bread and butter in Dundee. Soon afterwards he cut contact with the chav as best he could. His new firm, Hendry & Co, had offices above a nightclub on Market Street. Their location did not affect their ability to function as the club was only open two nights a week and the firm was closed in the evenings. Bizarrely, their location attracted many youthful clients, who presumably had noted the firm's telephone number down whilst queueing to enter the club.

Monty joined up just as the two partners, Arthur "Arty" Llewellyn and Russell Cuthbert, the firm's sole lawyers for the previous ten years, were looking for much-needed new blood. Fellow new boy, Ally Blyth, joined the firm at the same time as Monty. Blyth had graduated as a solicitor having been a mature student before doing his two-year traineeship with the firm. When Monty arrived, Blyth had been in the final month of his traineeship, and they had become friends from then on in.

During his time at Hendry & Co, Monty had developed both personally and as a criminal defence lawyer. He came into his own as a defender and developed a certain charm and conviction of tone which was regarded by even his most critical enemies within the court system, as highly competent. A particular habit he had been recently displaying at sheriff and jury trials was a breathless knack of breaking down even the most hostile of witnesses. There was certainly a learned maturity to Monty in his recent years, as well as a new sense of compassion, which he put down to his age. This recent understanding of human emotions and their successful management had greatly assisted him in even the hottest court cases.

There was a frost in the air now as he walked in the direction of the office, and he noticed what he guessed to be some spilled Irn Bru, judging by its familiar rusty orange colour, frozen upon the pavement at the entrance to yet another tartan touristy shop. He loved this city at this time of year, even if he frequently denied it to himself. He had resided alone in Leith for several years now with his beloved spaniel. He liked living alone and he loved Leith. His was a bright Georgian main door flat, grand from the outside, but with a cosy tenement community on the inside. His property had a rear patio door that led out to a small garden, enclosed by a six-foot almond washed wall. His neighbours were good souls, all resident owners, unlike the occupants of Leith Walk or Easter Road where most of the properties were rented out.

His main door looked out onto Leith Links, which had added a fair whack to the purchase fee, but he was glad of it. He had many friends in the area, including the female owner of a neighbouring B&B, with whom he sometimes got drunk and catnapped with. His lack of interest in anything long-term however had seen things cool and they had not exchanged as much as a text in quite a while. He didn't drink much, mind, but when he did, he frequented his local, the Alan Breck Bar, for a glass or two of Cote de Niddrie when the Celtic games were on TV.

His father had been a Celtic man, originally from New Stevenston, and had taken him for his first ever game to Fir Park, the nearby home of Motherwell football club, in 1982. They had previously sat together and watched the highlights of Celtic's 2-2 draw with Johan Cruyff's Ajax the previous week on TV, prompting Monty to plead with his father to take him to an actual game.

His father, perhaps re-energised by the Ajax result and the return from injury of Celtic's then star player, Charlie Nicholas, had relented and driven his ecstatic son through to Motherwell from Fife in his old Lada, with their green, white and yellow scarfs fluttering gaily from the windows. The experience itself had seemed amazing to Monty at a time when there were no computers or electronic gadgets and when football, whether the TV highlights on a Saturday night, or a live cup final, was the joy of most youngsters' lives.

Monty still looked back warmly at that first of many games. He recalled the walk from where his father had parked the car, outside the high rise Doonside Tower, up to Fir Park. There was a carnival atmosphere among the army of Celtic supporters lining both pavements and the bright green and white scarves and shirts were enthralling to his eyes. The songs they sang seemed exciting too, full of passion and humour. His father sang along to one or two of the more football themed ones too, which had entertained Monty further, for he had never seen his father like that before.

It had all been a joyous experience, with the dazzling colours before him, the smell of burger vans filling his nostrils, and the sounds of the many food vending generators running in tandem with the happy, optimistic buzz of the crowd.

At the ground, an endless procession of buses pulled up with more and more green and white-clad people on board, their flags and supporters' clubs names proudly displayed on the front and rear windows – The Greenock Shamrock, Davie Hay Paisley, and Johnstone No1, to name but a few. Monty recalled that it had been at that precise moment in his life that he decided that he wanted a Celtic shirt, which he duly received the following Christmas. There was further excitement outside their section of the ground with people selling tablet and macaroon bars from wooden trays, touting their wares in strange, loud voices that seemed to Monty to be part-song and part-shouting.

Then there were many stalls with people selling wonderfully coloured green, white and yellow hats, scarves and badges. His father bought him one of the popular flat caps that all the youngsters appeared to be wearing at that time, and an Irish tricolour flag on a bamboo stick that he had pleaded for, without having a clue what it represented? His father thought the hat had made him look like Andy Capp[8] and pulled it down over his eyes in jest as they queued at a food van for some lunch before the kick-off. They enjoyed bags of chips and shared a strange brown drink, which tasted like a watered-down version of the gravy that his mother would make on a Sunday.

There were waist-high metal turnstiles at the ground, which his father had simply lifted him over free of charge, as was the custom back then. Then they squeezed themselves through a forest of green and white, and onto the terracing, the roar from which was deafening and a little frightening too. Monty had been unable to see a thing due to his height, so his father pushed his way through the crowd and down to the advertising boards at the edge of the pitch, behind the goal. This was where most of the kids in attendance were to be found, and where Monty too could see everything that went on.

"Is that Pat Bonner in goals, dad?"

"Sure is, sunshine, but you wait till you see young Paul McStay play," his father insisted as they stood looking back up at the happy crowd behind them. "He's a Lanarkshire man like myself," he contended as they both turned back

---

[8] A then popular comic strip character of a working-class man. Its title was a pun on the north-eastern English pronunciation of "handicap" while the surname "Capp" signified how Andy's cap always covered his eyes along with, metaphorically, his outlook on life.

and looked longingly at the main stand where everybody was awaiting the appearance of the two teams.

Monty was not really listening, for he was far too excited, and with the Celtic end now in full flow of song, it was hard to hear anything else. He had never heard such a volume of noise in his young life.

The only time he would hear anything louder was when the teams appeared and then when each of Celtic's seven goals scored that day hit the back of the net. That was the day that he, a young footballing virgin, was swept off his feet by the dazzling display, and commenced a love affair that he would take to his grave. It had been the Charlie Nicholas show throughout, however—and not quite the Paul McStay one that his father had promised.

Charlie was the fans' favourite, Monty realised straight away. The young striker was adored by the kids around Monty who all chanted his name; he had this cool new romantic hairstyle that Monty had noticed many of the younger men in the crowd sporting too. When the prodigal young Celtic striker received a pass on the halfway line and then ran half the length of the pitch with the ball at his feet, skinning one Motherwell defender before turning another and then placing the ball into the top corner of the net with his left foot, the place utterly erupted. When Charlie ran to precisely where Monty was standing to celebrate with the crowd, Monty had found his first ever hero.

Perhaps it had been the attractively bright shirts that Celtic wore, or the fact they won 0-7, or even hat-trick hero Charlie Nicholas's outstanding performance, but there would be no other team for Monty from then on in. Afterwards in the car, when they stopped for cans of juice on the way home, Monty asked his father why the Celtic support had all been chanting "Wallace for Rangers" at the end of the match.

"That's the Motherwell manager, Jock Wallace, son," his father explained with the cheeky smile he would reserve for whenever his son asked him a question about Celtic or Rangers. "He used to be the Rangers manager and there are rumours that they might want him back."

"Who are Rangers, dad?"

"Oh, well, we can talk about them later, son, they're another team." He had winked.

Monty now dragged his thoughts back to the present, but he was still smirking though as he tried not to slip on the steep cobbled lane he was descending. He would go and see Celtic the following day up in Dundee, he decided as he held on to a newly installed and freezing metal hand rail that ran down the old lane. Perhaps he still followed the team as a tribute to his father? Then again, perhaps it was something else entirely? Something that offered a link to the sentimentality of his past? Regardless, one thing was sure, Celtic was more than just a sports team to him.

He was relieved to walk through the glass doors and into the warm office. Everyone was packing up for the holidays, in an upstairs room he could hear some of the staff having a festive drink together. It was a tradition wherein everyone brought something to eat and drink and someone put on a Christmas CD. Mostly, the lawyers chewed the fat with the admin staff for a short while before the place was locked up for a fortnight.

Thankfully, Monty was not on call throughout the vacation period and he was glad of it this year. He went straight to his office upstairs where he momentarily embraced the old storage heater as if it were a long lost relative before then checking the messages on his desk. He signed a few documents, including a new legal aid application for Derry Dryburgh, before carrying several files down to the front desk and dumping them upon a sour-faced female named Maud. She was obviously pissed off about having to man the desk whilst everyone else was upstairs having a knees-up.

"Merry Christmas," she said with a mousey smile.

Monty nodded and waved and was making to leave by the front door when Arty Llewellyn appeared at the top of the stairs in a grey Prince of Wales suit, holding a half-eaten sausage roll in one hand and a mobile phone in the other. "Not coming up for drinky-poo, Monty?" he called down.

Arty was the nice guy out of the firm's two partners; slightly older, more experienced and a much better lawyer than his partner, Russell Cuthbert. Monty got on well with him because of his exceptional knowledge of Scottish football and his invaluable legal tips, which flowed in abundance. He turned his gaze away from the sleety snow now, which he could almost touch beyond the glass door, and smiled up at him, "Not this time, Arty, have a good one." He winked.

"Aye, please yourself, son, I'm going home soon too, for if I eat any more of these, I'll be unable to move." Arty waved the sausage roll at him, and crispy flakes of pastry descended down the stairway like beige confetti.

"Merry Christmas," repeated Monty as he exited out onto the street now.

He would go home, have something to eat and then get an early night so that he could get up early the next day and drive up to the game. It was cold, so he decided to cut through Waverley Station rather than walking around by the street, not that it was any warmer in the station, mind, but he would at least remain somewhat dryer. Ascending the Waverley steps onto Princes Street, he was glad to see his bus coming along past the Jenners department store. He fetched his bus pass out and took his place in the queue under the plastic shelter.

As usual, the town was mobbed with traffic, Christmas revellers, and shoppers. Though it seemed hardly as busy as previous years, he considered as he waited for his bus to take its turn behind three others. This was most likely down to the effects of internet shopping and the home delivery services of all the major superstores. He was wondering how long the iconic Disney Store at the bus stop would remain open, just as his bus finally arrived and opened its doors.

The bus windows were all steamed up tonight and he was tempted to write something in the steam as he took an empty seat. There were kids laughing upstairs where they usually hung out, up the back. Teenagers mainly, who were usually bored, and consequently quite often mischievous, and who were a tad merrier as Christmas approached, still possessing a child-like anticipation of presents and/or fun. It was after Christmas however, when the fun had expired, that the thug-like behaviour and violence would reappear in some of them, as Monty knew only too well from his years as a defender.

Downstairs, where Monty was, old and young passengers alike were staring at their mobile phones. Up the back were a couple of Poles, quietly sitting and sipping cans of Polish lager, and a few women were seated with young children along the aisles. Monty wiped the condensation from his window and watched the ant like people outside scurrying about their business without a care for one another.

Leith Walk was quieter. Quieter than Monty could remember. Few people shopped on the Walk these days, only the post office seemed to be busy—often too busy, Monty considered as the bus passed it. The bloody queue sometimes reached the outside pavement and parking was a nightmare. Not so long ago, when life in this city was a little less stressful, people could park up and go into a post office, or grab a haircut, without being tapped for cash by the council.

He thought about jumping off now and nipping into the Turkish store at the foot of the walk, to pick up something nice to cook for supper but that would mean walking the rest of the way in the sleet in his brogues and potentially contracting frost-bite, so he remained seated as the bus continued on and down

Constitution Street before then heading along Queen Charlotte to Leith Links where he and two females got off.

As he arrived home, he received a boozy festive text from Ally Blyth who was en route to the airport to spend Christmas with his wife and kids in New York. Monty quickly replied and then slipped his phone back in his coat pocket and unlocked his front door to allow his dog access to jumping all over him. Ten minutes later, when they had cuddled and wrestled, and garden pennies had been spent, both master and pooch were sunk upon the large sofa opposite the TV, watching the news over peanut butter sandwiches and hot tea.

There was much commotion around UKIP leader Nigel Farage and his issues with the European Union, followed by news of US President Obama and the alleged hacking of Sony Pictures by North Korean hackers. After a few minutes, Monty yawned at some drama on HBO before dozing off on the sofa.

He was behind on sleep and so did not wake until 9pm. The dog was curled up asleep alongside him and his legs and his neck ached from having been forced against the arm of the sofa. The TV had turned itself off, but the two lounge lamps were still on; the dog had cleaned his plate for him and was now squeezed between his ribs and the back of the sofa. He moved his neck slowly and suddenly realised that he really needed a piss.

Afterwards, he spent a while having a wash and brushing his teeth before then looking out a fleece from a cupboard in the long hall that led to the front door. As he found a pair of trainers to chuck on, the dog appeared at his feet, yawning and stretching in what was a familiar routine of excitement and preparation for their walk. Monty pulled a woolly hat over his head and began putting a dog coat on his faithful chum, who pranced about excitedly despite his master's protests and appeared to be rejoicing at the difficulty he was having.

It was snowing lightly when they finally stepped outside and paused while Monty locked the door. They then headed across to the Western Links. Monty had a tried and tested technique of thoroughly scanning the entire area for people or other dogs. Despite the weather, it seemed peaceful enough and there were no footprints to be seen on the snow so he unleashed the dog, who set off on an exploration of the many trees as they followed their usual route across the football pitches towards the Eastern Links.

Once they reached the eastern half of the common, Monty kept his eyes out for foxes and drunks who often passed through this area at night. The dog would chase any foxes and put two fingers up to his recall, whilst drunks alternatively tended to try to bond with it and cause Monty to approach and engage in small talk with them, which he was not in the mood for tonight. Almost instantly, he noticed the outline of a person sitting on one of the benches along by the old allotments forty yards to his left. It seemed strange in this weather to find anyone doing anything other than merely passing through on their way to somewhere warm. Monty felt a chill and rubbed his hands together whilst keeping an eye on where the dog was.

As he walked into a section of the green that enabled him to see the person through a ray of light coming through the branches of two oak trees beyond the bench, Monty noticed that it was a man with a Peruvian hat who had what appeared to be a little terrier dog sitting in the snow at his feet. Monty thought the poor thing would be cold and that, if not exercising, the bloke should take himself and his dog home.

As he came level with the bench, Monty could make out a small glow, possibly from a mobile phone, which lit the man's distinctly welcoming and amused face. Then he sensed movement and looked down at what he was sure was a fox and not a terrier. There was a gap of a few seconds as Monty stopped walking and stood staring motionless at the creature in order to confirm that it was indeed a fox. Once he had looked a while, he turned and whistled for his dog.

"Do not be afraid," the seated man called over to him.

Finding the dog, Monty walked towards it and put the lead back on its collar.

"I'm not afraid," he called back, with a chuckle in order to make the man see that he was not at all scared. "I just don't want him to chase your fox." He looked up and smiled.

"Oh, this little fellow is not mine," smiled the man, looking down and stroking the fox, which leaned its neck affectionately against his hand. "He's just a friend."

Monty couldn't believe what he was seeing. He often brought a few custard creams or tit-bits for the allotment foxes and one or two now stalked him and the dog as they walked the Links at nights, and he thought perhaps he recognised this one, but, of course, he could not be sure.

"I think I've seen this one before, he's lovely but I'm afraid my dog will try to chase him if not on the lead," he found himself saying, still somewhat bewildered at this strange encounter.

"No, he won't." The man motioned at the dog, which was also sitting now without a care in the world. "And like I say, there is nothing for you to be afraid of," replied the man.

Monty nodded slowly, but he was confused and wondered if this was at all real.

"And yes, you have seen him before," the man seemed to read his thoughts. "He says you often give him a bite to eat in order to prevent him crossing the roads in search of his supper," he declared, as cool as you like.

Monty's jaw dropped now for a moment; his warm breath appeared like puffs of white mist before his face. He quickly composed himself though, in the dawning realisation that either this strange character was stalking him, or he was losing his marbles. He had seen similar examples in court over the years, and despite the lingering intrigue that delayed his feet for a moment, he then bade the guy a cheery "Well, goodnight then," and trooped back the way he had come. When he eventually reached his house, he looked around to see if he had been followed before quickly opening the door and then locking it up behind him and switching on the alarm system.

He pondered this bizarre experience for a short while in the kitchen as he sipped at a glass of water, while the dog enjoyed some freshly cut apple. Then they went to bed and, regardless of the experience, were soon both dozing off.

Monty had barely closed his eyes when he sank into a deep sleep, briefly losing command over all that he comprehended. Then along came an unseen guide whom Monty felt beside him now. He sensed that it was most likely an angel. He was in some ancient Greek place. Doric-style pillars supported a chalky rotunda stone wall, the ceiling of which was hand-painted with images of warrior women fighting men and olive trees sprayed in blood splatters. It was more than a dream though, he sensed.

It was the city of Athens and the year was—what did it matter? He was in a circular place built of stone blocks with similar stone benches encircling a centre stage below. There were several long white and blue draperies behind the stage, which hung from wooden beams on the ceiling and dropped all the way to the floor. Upon these were embroidered images of olive branches. On the walls between the draperies were brass lamps, which provided an artificial light from a wick fuelled by animal fat. A crowd of around one hundred men sat upon the stone blocks, observing and laughing at a tall, handsome, green-eyed male who was standing in the centre.

The man was chatting to them about another older man who was seated before him. Monty sensed by the chitons and sandals worn by the audience that these were surely ancient times and strangely enough, he was not surprised by this at all.

He was also not surprised to discover that he understood the tongue being spoken either.

The seated older man, who was the subject of discussion, seemed somewhat scruffy compared to the others; he was short, balding and had a disordered grey beard. He was also barefoot, unlike everyone else, his head was hanging slightly, and he leaned heavily upon a wooden stick, which he was using as a staff.

There was another older male seated in the centre of the hall, slightly off-centre, who appeared to be some sort of judge and who wore a blue himation that was bordered with a gold strip across his left shoulder, and gold-coloured sandals peeking out from beneath it.[9]

"This is the evening trial of Socrates in 399BC," whispered the unseen guide.

"Behold," gestured the tall, green-eyed male in the centre, his handsome features illuminated by the lamps as he gave a dramatic sweep of his arm causing a flickering shadow in the shape of a dragon to flash across the walls too quickly for anyone to see clearly (but Monty had seen it), "the bare-footed atheist with his sturdy crutch and endless theories," declared the green-eyed man with a suspiciously charming leer upon his face.

"This arrogant specimen not only questions everything, the gods, this city's ancestors, and her laws, whilst also making up his own false deities, but he additionally admits to having studied the literature of the convicted Anaxagoras too," the green-eyed man announced with a striking elegance and confidence.[10] "He believes that he alone knows the wisdom of the world that he is so privileged to inhabit. And that he alone knows what is wrong with the rest of mankind. Of course, his contemptible defence is that he is in fact providing knowledge to our youths." He gazed up at those watching from the benches. "This is particularly alarming in this case, because he preaches that the thunder of the gods is not in fact an act of the gods at all."

---

[9] A type of cloak or shawl.

[10] Anaxagoras (510-428BC) was a Greek citizen who served in the Persian Army after it invaded Greece. Years later, as a resident of Athens, he was convicted of a charge of impiety for claiming that the earth was flat and that it floated upon a bed of hot air that occasionally overheated, which caused earthquakes.

There were several murmurings at this.

"No; instead, he bases his belief upon the fact that because his fat stomach rumbles whenever he is hungry, then the rumbling of the heavens must similarly be man's undertaking," he explicated.

There were now hoots of contemptuous laughter at this absurdity from the audience.

"Thus, he has no belief in gods and instead elevates man to the roles of Zeus and Apollo themselves," he continued hardheartedly. "And by projecting his disciples to practise such blasphemous elevations of grandeur, he is corrupting our youth and bringing the wrath of the gods upon our city state." He paused now for a moment to search the faces of the men seated before him. "Upon your sons," he murmured at them knowingly.

There were plenty of heads nodding in agreement now.

"Any man who says there are no gods must simply die." He shook his head and showboated now, robe over wrist as he gracefully turned on his heels and glided back across the stone floor to retake his seat opposite Socrates.

Socrates chuckled to himself before then sluggishly looking up and over at the green-eyed speaker, "And yet you, Orcadius, accuse me of being an atheist who creates gods?" he replied, causing considerable laughter and applause among a section of the men below Monty. "Can a man believe in wine without believing in grapes?" he asked, just as eloquently as his accuser.

The green-eyed man appeared infuriated by his error. His face slowly reddened, Monty noticed, and his fists tightened in annoyance.

"See how his irritation overcomes him, Stephen," the unseen guide pointed out quietly in Monty's ear. "Read the file, for this is his weakness."

What file?

The green-eyed man stood up again now; he was over six feet tall and very well built. He stared down at Socrates for a moment with a look of utter wickedness, before finally sweeping his red himation across his shoulder and striding back over to address the audience once more. His leather sandals purposely applauding the stone floor and dragging out the moment like a trapeze drumroll.

Then he paused and faced the benches, and with left hand on hip and right hand raised towards the roof, he shook his head at them all. "Do not become spellbound by his honeyed words, citizens, for this blasphemous wretch," he gestured a hand stained by injustice down toward Socrates, while assuring his audience, "is more of a threat to Athens than any Persian spy." He appeared to Monty to have a talent for convincing others. His tone was well-mannered and earnest and seemed to entrance them.

"We all remember the traitor Alcibiades, do we not?" The green-eyed man now paused to allow this particular name to sink in, and when the mumbling began to build up again among the spectators before continuing, "Who was his teacher?" He nodded knowingly at them whilst slowly pointing a thin white finger down toward Socrates.

There was some applause from a section of the men seated directly to Monty's left.

"And how can we ever forget Charmides[11], a tyrant of the thirty?" The man shook his head now with dramatized disgust at the mere mention of the name. "And who was his teacher?" Again, he stretched one manicured nail down towards Socrates, whose head was bent downwards again.

"SOCRATES," several of them crooned along now.

"Citizens, should you not stop his contagious corruption of our youth right now, the gods will curse not only you and your families, but will most certainly punish the entire city itself," he firmly vowed.

There was some silence now as this was considered. A few men whispered among themselves in groups, but it was generally quiet. Monty could hear trickling water and turned to look over beyond to where the judge was situated. Behind him there was a small wooden stage and upon it he could tell that the whole proceedings were being timed by a water device of sorts.

He also sensed that this was Socrates' time to speak but that the green-eyed man had previously used up his own allocated time and was now taking up Socrates' time. "See how he steals the equally allocated time from Socrates," whispered the unseen guide. Monty thought the guide's voice somehow seemed familiar.

But then suddenly, everything seemed to fast-forward somehow and another man was reading out the verdict of the audience,

"Two hundred and sixty-three against Socrates, and two hundred and thirty-four for him. There were four abstentions," he declared.

Socrates chuckled and shook his head again.

---

[11] One of the thirty tyrants who ruled the city of Athens in 404 BC after her defeat to Sparta in the Peloponnesian War.

"Come now, Stephen, you must return to the world of the slumbering spirits," urged the unseen guide, and Monty realised it was the voice of the man with the fox who had been on the Links. Regardless, he nodded slowly but kept staring down at Socrates. An ugly, scruffy little man, sure, but fascinating nonetheless. *He took the verdict well*, thought Monty, for Socrates sat there smiling and gently waving his thanks at the audience.

22 December 2014

The alarm on the bedside table went off at midday but Monty still had to drag himself out of bed. A week of late night reading and writing had caught up on him; he now felt quite recharged however. Before taking a shower, and whilst waiting on the kettle to boil, he sat down in the kitchen and tried to remember the dream; it was slightly hazy though. He then went on his laptop and searched online for Socrates and discovered that the ancient philosopher had been found guilty and put to death after a trial in Athens in 399 BC. The man who had led the inditement against him was named Orcadius, who apparently then disappeared shortly after the trial to travel to Mount Olympus on Cyprus.

The green eyed man?

When the kettle boiled Monty closed his laptop and made a brew. Shortly afterwards, whilst standing in the shower, his eyes closed under the warm water that massaged his crown like thousands of little fingers before pouring all over him, he recalled the dream more clearly and went through it all. He wondered if it meant anything.

What file?

He had often wondered about dreams, despite rarely remembering any of his own. Once, he had dreamed that he was eating a spider that was calling on him not to do so, only to then wake up and find a spider's leg in his mouth.

He could make no sense of this though by the time he was drying off. Then he recalled the strange scenario with the fox and the man on the park bench the previous evening. That had been quite odd too and, despite the bloke having only radiated a friendly vibe and there having been no obvious threat, Monty had abandoned the walk because of the overall peculiarity of it. After throwing on some jeans and trainers however, he forgot about it all and looked out a long-sleeved Celtic shirt and dark fleece to wear. The fleece would easily hide the football colours as he walked to the stadium from where he intended to park his car, as well as keeping him relatively warm throughout the match.

Dundee was a dangerous town, he knew from experience, and he had seen many strange incidents in his time as a football supporter, so he would hide his colours. He fed the dog some Weetabix with warm water before opening the patio door for it. Then he sat down at the little kitchen table with a bowl of bran flakes whilst the dog pottered around the garden.

He checked his phone between mouthfuls of cereal. There were three text messages from friends who were aware that he was now officially on holiday for Christmas and were offering festive drinks. One was a drunk friend who owned a used furniture store who was only texting because his younger Cambodian wife had binned him now that she had her visa and he was home alone supping beers and in need of someone to shoot off to Pattaya with in search of her replacement. He had been texting for a while now, usually when half-cut, hinting at the joys on offer in Thailand.

Another was from a married female dentist who had been a friend of a Facebook friend and who knew his ex. She seemed keen to play, Monty reckoned, but he didn't fancy her, and so was always short and courteous with her in his "I'm washing my hair tonight" replies. He'd thought she had given up until this new probe into his availability.

Both were ignored.

The last text was from his sister. Silence was not an option there, he knew, so he considered what to say to her over the time it took to finish his cereal, but he kept being smothered by thoughts about the strange man on the Links with the fox.

He was the unseen guide in last night's dream.

He sat a while and took some sweet black tea as he considered everything. Was he really going mad? He could hear the dog sniffing around in what was left of the snow outside, so he fetched a poo bag and took a step out onto the patio. It was frosty and there was a bright sky above; he guessed that he would be cold up in Dundee today. He then checked the sports updates on his phone— all the games were still on. He picked up the poo, binned it, washed his hands, then put on a second pair of socks.

"I'm away to the football, pal, be good," he said to the dog as he was getting set to leave. The hound looked up at him, disappointed. He locked the patio door, gave the dog a dental chew and helped himself to a small bottle of spring water from the fridge before stepping out of the front door onto the crunchy snow.

The drive up to Dundee took around an hour and a bit. He travelled via Perth while listening to Babyshambles most of the way. As he came alongside the great River Tay, he found himself singing along to *Farmer's Daughter*:

You've been travelling on that dusty road
Come break some bread with me!
With your wife and donkey on a dusty road
Now break some bread with me!
Now come and rest your head with me!
When asked to choose between this and that
Hmmm, I'll take the former
I'll take the former every time!

"And there was me thinking that all the good sounds were Satanic," he grinned to himself.

The Tay was always stunning but now, with the white dusting of snow along either bank, it was even more vivid. He wondered if perhaps he was experiencing a little reconnection, no matter how briefly, with all-encompassing nature. The landscape made the trip seem more meaningful than just a trip to see a football match. This was an added bonus, like the usually excellent Dundee pies that would be on sale at the match. The city of Dundee had always stocked Wallace mince pies and Fleming's of Arbroath steak bridies, which Monty had practically lived on during his student years.

He reckoned that when it came to pies and bridies nowhere else compared; although Bain's of Stenhouse in Edinburgh made outstanding pork pies that were, most irritatingly, always sold out by midday. Monty decided he would grab a pie at the game, and he put his foot down whilst licking his lips. The car responded with a deep whirr and carried him onward towards Dundee.

When he arrived and parked off the Hilltown neighbourhood, he had a little time to find a ticket for the match. He had intended walking down the Dens Road to wait for the supporters' buses because they were usually a good source of spare tickets. However, he noticed a few hooped shirts through a window of a pub he was walking past so popped in to see if there were any touts selling them there. There was a little old bloke in a bonnet sitting among a group of friends at a round table in a corner, who waved him over when he called out. The guy looked like he had been on the Pat Lally[12] all night, chuckled Monty to himself, but he approached him anyway.

"I've got two for the main stand son at £22.00 each," said the half-canned pensioner over his whisky.

"Cheers, I'll take one if that's okay?" smiled Monty.

Twenty minutes later, he was in the stadium and in a queue for one of those pies. Such was his tradition, despite not thinking much of the watered-down Bovril that accompanied his pie (he never had throughout the years, mind). It was like eating duff at Christmas or buying a bottle of aftershave on the plane whenever he went on holiday—just a sentimental tradition. He thought about this as he took his turn to be served at the little kiosk. Everyone has their own traditions of course. Passed down from father to son and mother to daughter over the generations. It happens here, abroad and across the world, he considered. Perhaps this is how religious beliefs are passed on?

Tradition incorporated into lifestyle by one age group and passed to another. It seemed daft to him now because man was designed to be individual and free to choose his own path, rightly or wrongly. When he was finally served a pie, which he proceeded to smother in brown sauce (which his father would certainly have frowned upon), he decided to get himself a hot chocolate instead of a Bovril.

The game itself was something of a disaster. Monty found himself perched beside a fat idiot in the stand who wouldn't stop shouting, even at half time.

After the game, as the crowd descended the steps in the main stand, Monty was forced to listen to all the so-called experts among them with their varied opinions on the Celtic manager and his use of the four strikers available to him. Some were in favour of a Guidetti/Griffiths partnership while others insisted that Stokes and Griffiths should be the preferred pairing.

"What we are needing is another Bobo Balde to beef up the defence as that Cifti was bullying our defenders all day, by the way," groaned one Glaswegian.

"A big striker who can run with the ball like a train," shouted another.

"Aye, like Hartson was?" A female with a Dundonian accent shouted back from behind Monty.

"He couldn't run, hen," scoffed another Glaswegian.

"Well, a guy like the Brazilian Ronaldo, he was like a bloody express train, and strong too," said a young Highlander.

---

[12] Pat Lally: Glaswegian slang for "Swally", meaning to swallow alcohol.

"Aye, and how do we afford someone like him, pal?" a Fifer growled in response, clearly impatient with the slow progress towards the exit.

"It's that ponce Biton in the midfield," an elderly Irishman with long grey whiskers and a bonnet turned to murmur to Monty, "he doesn't know the concept of what Mr Stein called 'putting on your overalls and doing a shift'."

"Cork?" asked Monty, trying to place the brogue.

"Tipperary, son," the old man said before they spilled out onto the street and were separated by the crowd.

Just as well, really, because Monty disagreed with all these experts. Personally, he was a fan of the old 4-4-2 formation, with two attacking wingers. It was the Celtic way, wave after wave of attack down either flank and two strikers lurking with intent in the box. He believed that the best way to defend was to attack and that wingers were the key to success.

He was too young to have watched Celtic's greatest ever player, the winger Jimmy Johnstone, nor his adversaries at Rangers, Jim Baxter or wee Wullie Henderson, but he had seen videos of Johnstone tearing teams apart, such as the English champions Leeds United and Real Madrid. He had also seen Johnstone live once however, in a charity match against Manchester United when the player had been in his fifties. The wee man had only gone and lobbed the United keeper from just over the halfway line to score, and Monty had been mesmerised by him. The problem was that thousands of other punters had their opinions too and listening to their tuppence worth like this had always been part and parcel of the match day experience.

As he walked down towards the Dens Road, he thought about the potential wingers that the club had missed out on over the years, such as the brilliant Bobby Connor, who would have fitted in perfectly, Ray Houghton and wee Pat Nevin, who had both grown up idolising Jimmy Johnstone. Monty had watched Nevin doing keepy-ups on the trackside at Hampden whilst a substitute for Scotland in the 1980s, and knew then and there that he could have filled the Jimmy Johnstone role for Celtic.

He sighed despondently at what might have been and reluctantly listened to the opinions of the other experts among the crowd as they all walked on. Just then, Monty's gaze flicked across the bobbing heads before him and caught a glimpse of a familiar, smiling face, looking back at him. The face called over to him, "Did you forget Damien Duff?"[13]

Monty looked around him to see if anyone else was the target of this bizarre question, but before he could confirm or not, the face was lost among the other countless heads descending down the street towards the buses. It took a moment or two until Monty was able to place the face as that of the man with the fox that he had encountered on Leith Links last night.

"What the hell?" he heard himself say out loud.

This, on top of the strange behaviour of that fox, was too weird to ignore—creepy even.

He felt a shiver once or twice as he crossed into the Hilltown and continued to look around to see if the guy was following him. What with the crowds, he was unable to tell, so he kept walking amongst them towards where he had left the car. Once he arrived at it, he did another full circle to see if the guy was anywhere to be seen.

This is nuts.

He then quickly jumped in and locked all the doors.

What the fuck is going on?

He decided to travel back via Fife this time. There were cameras on the Tay Bridge and he supposed there would be a record of any vehicle that came after him; however, as a precaution, he did three full circles of the roundabouts at both ends of the bridge in order to shake off anyone following.

Once he had covered a few miles through the Fife countryside, he relaxed a little. He shrugged it all off again as a most unusual fluke. He must have been thinking too much about the incident last night, and hence obviously mistaken someone else, who must have been calling over to someone in the crowd near where he had been walking.

Just keep telling myself that.

By the time he had reached the outskirts of Glenrothes, he felt relaxed enough to swing by Kirkcaldy and pick up some fish and chips from an excellent little fish bar he knew called the Jolly Friar that was much better than anything he could ever find in Edinburgh. When he arrived, he parked up right outside the place. Unlike Edinburgh, there were no silly traffic restrictions, thankfully. There

---

[13] Damien Duff: Irish international football winger who was a former Lourdes Celtic youth player who went on to star for Blackburn Rovers and Chelsea.

48

were a few people in the queue, and so he joined them. When it was his turn to be served, there was only an elderly lady left behind him.

There were two females serving and they both called "Next" at the same time, like drones.

"Single fish and two pickled onions please," said Monty to one of them.

"Fish and chips please, hen," said the old dear behind him.

The female serving Monty quickly picked up the last fish on the range and asked him if he wanted salt and vinegar on it.

"Sorry, there's no fish left, dear. I can put one on for you though," the other female informed the old dear.

"No thanks, I need to get my bus in a minute, so I'll just leave it," smiled the obviously disappointed elderly female, who then slowly turned to leave.

"That's okay, dear," Monty put a light hand on her shoulder. "You have the fish," he insisted.

The two servers looked at each other, presumably unused to such unselfishness. Monty read their confusion. "Manners cost nothing," he smiled at them. "I'll take a single King Rib instead and leave out the onions please," he nodded for them to proceed.

They did as they were told and he received smiles back from both of them. The old woman then thanked him kindly and then went to pay for her supper.

Afterward, as he was approaching the car with King Rib under arm, the fox man was leanng against a bus stop beside it.

"That was very kind of you, my friend," he said knowingly to Monty with an infectious grin.

Monty stopped dead and straightened up before dropping his still-wrapped supper on the pavement.

"Who are you?" he asked somewhat open-jawed at this irrationality standing before him. For he simply could not understand how on earth this person was standing here.

"I'm Jophiel, but most folk call me Joe," the man said warmly and his adorable child-like smile instantly relaxed Monty a tad.

"Why are you following me? How did you hear what was said in the chip shop, and how did you read my thoughts in Dundee?" The lawyer in him now surfaced and urged him to question this madness.

"Who says you're being followed?" asked Joe, as he stepped forward and picked up the package of food. "Have you considered the possibility that it's you who have instinctively followed me?" he asked, offering Monty the parcel. His smile was so warm and penetrating that despite his concerns, Monty found it impossible not to smile back.

But he finally replied, "I don't believe you," promptly getting back into his car, without taking his food with him, and driving off.

After a while, he had stopped looking in his rear-view mirror and thought about going to the police but then he checked himself.

They would tell me to get lost as they have enough on their plates on a Saturday night, and besides, no crime has been committed as yet.

He could see himself trying to explain to the desk officer that he thought the ancient Greek philosopher Socrates had something to do with it all. "This is nuts," he laughed aloud as the miles went by along the coastal route back to the Forth Bridge. Perhaps he could phone a friend when he got home though, for advice. He needed to share this with someone. Then he considered that he may be going mad. One thing was for sure, he would not be taking the dog out late at night again until he had established some sort of understanding of this situation.

Once back in the city, he made straight for home. He looked around again once more as he parked and locked up the car, and then again before opening his front door. There was a teenager cycling on the pavement on a BMX bike who almost rode straight into him, but Monty neatly moved aside: "Idiot," he twisted his neck and shouted at the kid, who did not bother to turn around or apologise.

After all this, and his growing concerns, Monty was in no mood for his excited dog, who jumped all over him as he quickly turned to close and lock the front door. He knew that none of this had anything to do with the dog, and that it was only displaying its usual joy at his return, so once he had secured the property, he checked himself, then leaned down and gave his pal a big bear hug.

"Sorry buddy, I missed you too, but something weird is going on," he told it.

Later, once he had eaten something and let the dog out, he settled down onto the sofa for a while. He considered calling someone, anyone really, just to share this and to obtain an opinion from. Any feedback would do, because he was now quite uncomfortable, bordering on worried, about the strange timing of these bizarre sightings.

He had to think over his initial alarm however, because he had to come to some sort of understanding of what on earth had happened over the last 24 hours.

He thought about it a while over a third cup of tea while the dog had some tinned sardines and pasta. Intuitively he sensed that the fox man was not stalking him, and remembered that the vibes he had got from him were not at all hostile. More like an old friend sort of feeling. Yet they had never met. No, there was something paranormal about all of this, and this was what niggled at him now.

He then found himself thinking about the Derry Dryburgh case again. He had not understood all the waffle that had poured out from his mouth in court, but somehow, he wondered if it had anything to do with all this?

Should I call him on his mobile and see if he gives anything away by his tone?

At that precise moment, a text came through on his phone. When he checked it, however, there was no sender's number. He opened it with cautious intrigue:

"You managed your hair-dryer treatment of master Dryburgh very well and obtained the compliance required. It is not easy to growl a man into submission, you are evidently skilled in your field. Does that make you a good man, though, Stephen? Talented, yes, but are you a good soul?" it read.

Monty sat up and looked around the room before then slowly falling back into the sofa. This was freaking him out now. He placed the phone down on the coffee table and wondered if it was the fox man.

Then, when he spontaneously picked it up again with the intention of reading it again, he discovered that it had been deleted.

What the...

Chapter Three

We are being run by maniacs for maniacal ends and I am likely to be put away as insane for expressing that.
John Lennon

Mallorca

It was just after two in the morning and she was tired, having been awake for the last 31 hours. Most of this time she had spent arguing with her lover, trying to persuade her to make various calls to the stage designer of a newly announced tour by a well-known musician in San Diego. Hours of arguing had been relieved by only a couple of short breaks for food and sex. Her partner had crawled to bed both mentally and physically exhausted, her mascara running down her bruised cheeks.

Luna had very much craved to join her but remained awake now despite her fatigue. Even now as she sat in the pitch dark, there was no danger of her dozing off, for anticipation and excitement devoured her. A hidden enthusiasm, which had been active within her for days now, hummed deep inside her and ensured that slumber could not develop.

She had been instructed not to leave the engine running so without the air-con the temperature was a bit hot both inside and outside of the vehicle. She put the window down to have a cigarette but the mosquitos were attempting to feast upon her uncovered wrist, so she took several long draws of her Marlboro and then pinged it out onto the dusty ground of the car park, which was scattered with fallen pine kernels.

She had been told to expect the fallen one between two and three in the morning, but that this might change, and so to stay put until he eventually appeared from the portal. The car park outside the Caves of Drach[14] was still, and pitch black at this time. There was no moon tonight and the velvety darkness about the place ensured that she could see very little. The only sounds were of the crickets in the distance and the occasional Vespa passing by the old Monte Verde hotel fifty yards away on the main road. She was not scared. She possessed little fear of anything.

There was some fear now in this darkness. A fear of confrontation with whatever might appear from the other realm tonight. Though it was easy for her to ignore this possibility and place the concern to the rear of her beautiful mind; for she had long ago mastered the art of doing so.

Luna occasionally felt that a lack of fear might be a weakness. She was, after all, of witch blood and could track her ancestry to those giant men of legend who once roamed Bashan in the time of Og[15]. She was naturally brave when it came to any threat of violence and was both as fast and as strong as most fit young men. She also thought much quicker than them and knew the art of violence well enough.

Her speciality was not violence, though. Rather, she tended to use her stunningly attractive good looks to seduce a target. Usually a politician or scientist, depending upon who her masters chose. Her kiss was exceptional, adaptable and accompanied by a variety of flavours, released depending upon the unlucky bastard that she set her scope upon.

Personally, she had little time for men, or mankind in general, for her black heart was set upon her masters' cause. Tonight, she had left her current pet, a female executive of a well-known record label, in a tranced sleep in their villa in Porto Cristo while she took her car and attended to the present matter in hand.

On the front passenger seat beside her was an envelope with a UK passport and some additional ID in the name of Oliver Farquharson who, it stated, was born in Scotland. Beside this was a single flight ticket from Palma to Edinburgh for 05:10 am that morning. She had not looked inside the unsealed envelope and knew nothing more than that. She had been instructed to drive her passenger

---

[14] Catalan: Coves del Drach, Spanish: Cuevas del Drach - the caves of the dragon. Located in Porto Cristo on the island of Mallorca, the ancient subterranean caves, with Lake Martel deep within them, are considered by some experts to date from the Miocene Epoch.

[15] Og of Bashan was described in Deuteronomy (3:11) as their king and was the last of the Refaim race and a descendant of the Nephilim.

directly to the airport the moment he showed up. What she did know was that her passenger would be appearing through an ancient portal inside the caves.

Luna cared not for who or what was to be her passenger, only for their common cause: *Ordo ab chao*[16]. For her horde was feverishly engaged upon the creation of disorder and the subsequent cry from all of humanity for order. It was the hope of her breed that the cost of such order would be the handing over of earthly control from men to her masters, who might, in turn, ensure that her bloodline seeded the earth, instead of man.

Nevertheless, she knew from bitter experience that there were some formidable challengers to her hopes, and so she sat quite alert now, listening for the sound of a pine kernel being stood upon or of bats scampering away from anything approaching. Her kind were close though, close to completion of the plan, and she could almost smell victory.

Suddenly, the rear door to the Merc opened and the fallen one entered and sat inside. He stared at her through the rear-view-mirror. She had not heard him approach and she needed a few seconds to relax again.

"Greetings, my lord," she said via the mirror before gently handing him the envelope.

He was handsome, of course. All she could really make out were his green eyes and the outline of a somewhat chiselled, Nordic-looking face. His hair was shoulder length and straight and he wore a denim jacket and dark corduroy trousers. He took the envelope from her tenderly and briefly examined the contents.

"Proceed," he said softly in a distinctly Scottish brogue that he immediately felt would require a slight linguistic adjustment.

She started up the car and its wheels began crushing pine kernels as it exited the car park. The town was almost dead as the black Merc cruised through it and then onto the Ma-4020 in the direction of Manacor. At Manacor, she turned onto the Ma-15 and put her foot down for the airport. She chose not to look at the mirror again and worked hard at controlling her thoughts, well aware that her passenger was freely able to read them.

She did not mind the silence: she was enchanted by the scent of amber that escaped from him. She was hopeful that he would allow her to taste him. This

---

[16] Translated from the Latin as "Order out of chaos". The motto of the masonic 33rd degree to be attributed to the Masonic Supreme Council of the Ancient and Accepted Scottish Petite at Charleston.

was often bestowed as a form of a tip by some dark lords to her kind. A drop of his blood would probably place her in a short form of ecstasy, perhaps even a momentary lapse of control, but the aftershock would be an accumulation of either considerable strength or wisdom. She had tasted it once before in Africa and lost her sight for over an hour afterwards, yet her reward was that she could now read men's minds.

"What is your name?" he asked her as they passed signs for Vilafranca de Bonany.

She was a little surprised at this, yet pleased, but hid it as best she might, and answered quickly enough, "Luna, my lord. My father worshipped the angels of your choir on the moon, my—"

"Silence!" he snapped with an incongruous grin that she missed. For he was toying with her now. "Only speak when spoken to. Understand?" He warned her.

"Yes, my lord," she replied without turning around or looking in the mirror.

There was further silence for a moment before he spoke again. "I know why you were given that name. Tell me, child, what say you in regard to where humanity has collapsed here?" he asked her impishly.

Yet because she held passionate convictions regarding this, she replied quickly, "People are addicted to self-adulation and care only about their appearance to others," she said. "Self-preservation before morality is their preference, my lord," she added.

"Ah, but were they not always this way inclined, dear Luna?" he asked her.

"Previously, they had Yahweh leading them to some extent, but now they worship themselves, my lord," she responded shrewdly. "This makes them incompatible with the planet and this is why the planet and the beasts are being destroyed," she added as an afterthought.

There was an ominously long-drawn-out silence before he responded. "And is the enemy close to defeat?" His fingernails were lightly tapping his window.

"We have the initiative now, my lord, of that I am sure," she replied.

"Hmm. Interesting, Luna. Interesting." He sat back and closed his eyes for the remainder of the journey.

He had no time for her type. To him, her Nephilim bloodline was so distant that she was more a talking monkey than any hero of old. Regardless, those who actually managed the sides in this particular conflict paid little attention to the cannon fodder who pontificated from the side-lines.

"Silence is of the gods, only monkeys chatter[17]," he eventually sighed as he searched for self-patience.

She understood precisely what he was referring to—that humans talk too much—and so wisely remained quiet.

He could swat her like the fly she was at the end of the journey and feel absolutely nothing. If anything, there would be pleasure in the act. He dared not though, for there would no doubt be complaints from her lot, the so-called auxiliaries, and he would face a recall and a reprimand.

Instead, he kept his eyes shut and remembered the past. He thought of the Heracleidae heroes of old[18], and how, from his observations, they had seemed more angelic in appearance and mannerisms than anything within the so-called auxiliary force here today. The Heracleidae would never have been so presumptuous as to state that the game was almost won. Their logic was based purely upon a divine understanding of reality. Whereas these things here—well, they were all monkeys with theories. Even the angels themselves had been weary of the old bloodlines back in the day. Not so these remaining offspring, it seemed. These auxiliaries would be the serfs of tomorrow, he knew, but in the meantime they could embrace the cause and do the work required.

When she arrived at the drop-off point at the airport fifteen minutes later, she pulled over, got out and opened his door for him with her head bowed.

He swiftly stepped out and walked away without another word or a tip. She controlled her disappointment and watched him disappear into a group of tourists who had recently been dropped off by a German package tour company, before turning to get back into the Merc. As she did so, she noted eight deep scratches on the glass panel that separated the driving cubical from the rear of the vehicle, and despite the warm night, a sharp chill came over her and she trembled a little.

***

It was daylight when the BA flight crossed over the Mallorcan cliffs and the Mediterranean Sea below. The fallen one, now calling himself Farquharson, looked out eastwards at the white and lilac clouds, and then down at the endless sea below. A sea that had hosted this struggle since the outbreak, and long before the great flood. He thought of that unpleasant journey on the little corbito from

---

[17] He quotes Buster Keaton here.

[18] The ancient Greek descendants of the demigod Heracles (Latin: Hercules).

Tyre to Brundisium long ago and of how the limitations of the Kertamen rules had forced those entities who were released from incarceration, on missions such as this, to travel from state to state in such a manner.

Yet this was a little better than a corbito, he supposed. What the Greeks would have done for a few EasyJet's back in Sicily in 413 BC, he smiled as he recalled the desperation of the sick and injured left behind at Syracuse.[19] The local auxiliaries had had little notice of his own appearance in Porto Cristo tonight. The next available flight had only had second-class seats available, but they had booked him two together for comfort. There was a male couple seated in the row in front with a very loud and moody six-year-old child they had adopted. One of the parents was wearing a clerical dog collar and kept standing up to get stuff out from the overhead luggage compartment for the kid.

The fallen one sensed that this monkey was an attention-seeker, as he had not removed his work wear, even whilst on holiday. The other humans aboard should have been able to see this too, but they were too focused on themselves. This cleric kept looking at everyone onboard, grinning and hugging the aisle with little shoulder shifts, and even winked at someone across the aisle.

He was loud too, and the fallen one dragged his eyes away from the sea below and took him in. He could see who he was easily enough. He could also sense that this talking monkey was moving slowly into the early stages of Othello Syndrome. He then considered the other parent now as he too stood up wearing a red polo shirt and took the brat to the toilet. He was a thief, a thief who worked in the Law Society of Scotland and who had attempted several times to get himself on reality television.

---

[19] In 415 BC, the Greek naval superpower that was the city state of Athens invaded Sicily by sea with a large expeditionary force that anticipated a quick victory. Having become bogged down by heavy fighting early doors at Syracuse on the east coast, the Athenians ended up fighting trench warfare for two years. By 413 BC, thousands of Athenians lay sick and wounded in the trench camps while the supply fleet was destroyed in naval conflict.

Forty thousand fit men abandoned the injured and fled into the Sicilian countryside in the hope of a rescue fleet arriving from Athens. These men soon surrendered, however, and died either as slaves in Sicilian quarries, or through thirst and starvation, or by execution. Those abandoned in the trenches were left to die a slow death by both their countrymen and the Sicilians.

All very auspicious, right enough, but if they did not settle down for the remaining couple of hours of the flight, the fallen one might well spell-bind them and the brat in the most unpleasant way, he considered.

He had never coupled with a monkey, had never seen the need other than to display rebellion to Yahweh (which he had already declared aplenty in heaven, so there was no point in practical demonstrations). Even at the time of the fall, when so many of the others had done so, he had found the primordial beings more appealing. He had tortured and murdered plenty of the monkeys, though, but those bloody days seemed so long ago now that he dropped the thought from his amazing mind.

He looked out of the window again and down at the sea. The same sea that Odysseus had once been pin-balled across, in his idiotic quest to return to his love—Penelope.

She hadn't even been that hot.

This sea had seen so much occur over the ages. And of course, he himself had searched it for years, for his own dear one. He again found himself recalling a time when crossing it had been a lot more demanding than the relative luxury he was experiencing now in the clouds. A time without budget airlines and stewardesses.

He stared down a while at the silky water below and studied the occasional rising surf that appeared here and there upon it. It was an infinite desert of dark blueness that could erupt into a storm at any moment, and which concealed so much below its surface.

"Ceto[20]," he whispered, whilst staring long and hard at it.

----

[20] A mythological primordial female sea being who, in the Orphic tradition, was born from the void of Chaos and is portrayed as a shape-shifting deity who gave birth to the three Gorgon sisters.

Chapter Four

Repetition of small efforts will accomplish more than the occasional use of great talents.
Charles Spurgeon

Midsummer, AD 160

The vortex transported the Dragonfly from beneath the icy spring of *Caesarea Philippi* at Mount Hermon on the Golan Heights. Despite the brownish-grey shades of dusk that were beginning to consume the bright blue sky, the air was still warm when he appeared. The area was busy with taverns and brothels all full of travellers, farmers, artisans and two hundred Roman soldiers on leave from Antioch in Syria-Palestina.

Among this crowd were around thirty drunken cavalrymen of *II Adiutrix* who had decided to stop over for some jollities on their way to their new posting at Nikephorion across the Euphrates on the Mesopotamian front. The Parthians[21] had been engaged in off-and-on skirmishes with Rome ever since they had drawn Marcus Severianus, the former Governor of Cappadocia (Roman Turkey) into the unpredictable terrain of Armenia a few weeks previously and slaughtered his force. Severianus had obviously not read his Xenophon[22].

---

[21] The term "Parthia" is a continuation of the Latin "Parthia" and Old Persian "Parthava", which was the language of a North Iranian dynasty that not only re-established much of the former Persian empire lost to Alexander the Great of Macedon 496 years previously, but was said to have halved the world with the Roman empire in AD 165 after winning various military victories against Rome. (Andrew Smith. Justinus: Epitome of Pompeius Trogus (Book 41).

[22] The Greek General Xenophon led 10,000 Greek mercenaries into a Persian civil war on behalf of one faction and lost a battle that left them on a bloody retreat from what is now modern-day Iraq, through the mountains of Armenia to the Black Sea.

The pompous horsemen of *II Adiutrix*, however, were letting loose before being sent to police the empire's frontier against the incredibly efficient Parthian cavalry in the Badlands across the Euphrates. These young men were struggling to hold their wine during their brief stay here at Pan's grotto. Twice, they had caused drunken dramas with off-duty legionaries on leave from the front, who were quick to throw punches at them.

This evening, though, the cavalry had learned the hard way and so were instead targeting the Ionic Greek-speaking slaves whose job it was to refill the wine goblets and to manage the animals that were being abused in the name of the deities beyond the grotto spring. Both soldiers and cavalry were now eating and drinking together, with other travellers and revellers arriving in pockets, having slept away the hot afternoon in the shade elsewhere.

The whores who served the visitors were screaming as usual, some in banter but many in pain. There were Jews here too, the Dragonfly observed all of this as it surveyed the scene from a rock above the grotto. The Dragonfly had been here on the surface many times previously in order to play a tune from a familiar song book, and after such a long incarceration it always took a moment to survey the scene. This old entity was what modern men might consider to be a law specialist, and soon enough it would be too busy for such indulgences as observing the monkeys below.

For this was a being that had a job to do. A being that had galloped upon dragons, escaped the great flood, and crooned with the bards on the shore at Troy. Now it observed some of the men below again, men who were busy profiting from the ongoing pagan commerce, scurrying around after money like the talking apes they had always been.

Nothing new here then.

To the left, where slave children were running around dressed as little animals and nymphs, were a group of Sumerian herdsmen, all drunkenly shouting at each other about money for whores. To the right were a group of travelling Jews who had stopped by to soak up the seedy pagan produce on offer for an hour or two before moving back down the road. The Dragonfly cared nothing about such ironies; it was neither amused nor pleased by them. Instead, it was thinking about whether to head straight for Mount Lebanon and the port of Sidon beyond, or south, to Tyre.

Suddenly, it flew down to around an inch from the rocky ground below and hovered over to where some slaves were feeding Roman horses that were penned in an old corral beyond the brothels. The Dragonfly then shifted into the form of a man, wearing the robes of a Roman equestrian, and he touched the dusty soil in a pair of fine leather sandals.

A young Cypriot slave turned around and approached him.

"Saddle up one of the best horses, boy," he ordered the teenager in perfect Koine Greek.

There was no pause for reflection from the youth; his defenceless spirit was instantly seized by an overwhelming force that was so beautiful, intrusive and evil that it consumed him. He complied without any fear of the consequences that would inevitably follow when a hungover Roman officer came looking for his horse in the morning. The boy simply did as he was told, while the man, who appeared to be in his fifties with light brown hair and green eyes, waited patiently.

When the horse was ready, the fallen one took the reins and mounted without another word and galloped off down the dusty track in the direction of the port of Tyre. The grey mare went at a fair pace along the old merchant road; she was a fine specimen from Gaul that had ended up on its way to the Euphrates with the cavalry.

He did not allow her to slacken or rest for the entire three-hour journey though; instead, he dug his nails into her neck throughout. She was on her last legs when she carried him into the port at Tyre, and as he dismounted, he struck her with his fist on her right eye, which caused her to stagger and fall against a wall. He then strode on towards a little trading corbito[23] moored at a busy pier, on foot.

As he walked confidently up a timber plank onto the ship, a pleasant sea breeze made the little lamps of castor berry oil that were hanging around the ship's edge swing back and forth. The seamen would use these to signal other ships in the dark, to avoid collisions. He noticed a large, engraved ornament of a winged figure on the stern post according to the Mediterranean custom. He was pleased to read "Apollo" on a plaque beside it.

The single sail was red, like on most Roman ships, and was attached to a central pole on the upper decking, which could seat around eighty souls. He stepped onto it with an arrogant swagger and approached a small timber galley

---

[23] A little Roman merchant's vessel with timber hull, mast and helm that could hold up to eighty tons.

61

upon the poop-deck where six men were eating bread which they were dipping into a bowl of garum[24].

"Who are you?" asked a chubby one with a mouthful of bread on display.

"My name is Quintus Junius Rusticus," smirked the fallen one in perfect Latin.

"And?" the fat captain demanded in his Alexandrian twang.

"You will sail this ship immediately to Brundisium[25]!" ordered Rusticus.

There was some smirking among the men now at this.

"We are heading to Alexandria with a cargo of garum in amphorae below, and some pilgrims who will be boarding in the morning. After that, we carry grain to Cyprus then return here," the fat captain stated plainly before turning away and continuing with his meal.

"You will set sail now," Rusticus whispered and exhaled an unseen vapour from his lungs towards them all. Within a second or two, they had all abandoned their meals and begun preparing the sail for their departure.

Despite ingrained concerns at undertaking this open sea voyage which would feature no land to cling to, this land-clinging captain bawled at his men, including a young Syrian galley slave, to hurry up the preparations, which included bringing bags of oranges aboard as a floating water substitute in case of an emergency. As well as some amphorae of pine syrup to be placed in the hull, tucked in with blocks of dried cow intestine, which, combined, would be used as a waterproof sealant for any small hull cracks which could appear at sea.

Rusticus sat down on the deck and watched them all running around. He hated them for their simplicity and because they were confined to a limited perception of their surroundings. Just then, the galley slave, a boy who looked around fourteen years old, approached him with a basket of oranges and offered him one. He took it and removed the skin with his teeth, which he spat overboard and onto the pier. "What is your name, boy?" he asked as he devoured the fruit. He enjoyed surface foods from time to time but was only eating out of boredom now.

"Thaimallos, my lord," mumbled the lad.

"You have Sumerian ancestry," Rusticus informed him casually.

"An orphan from Damascus, my lord, and a slave from birth."

---

[24] A much sought-after Roman fish sauce.

[25] A Roman sea port on the heel of Italy and the main Italian staging post for maritime transportation to Greece, Turkey, and the Levant.

"You did not know your mother?" he asked the boy with a trace of curiosity.

"No, my lord, only that my mother was a slave and my father unknown," replied this pale boy with brown almond-shaped eyes and dark brown hair that appeared lightened from so much exposure to the offshore sun.

"I smell it in your blood," smirked Rusticus as he consumed the orange flesh. The boy seemed quite confused. "And you're Akkadian!" Rusticus told him as he now licked his fingers and, for once, he was not lying.

"Akkadian? Do you mean from Persia, my lord?" the lad asked, still puzzled.

"Your people were from Mesopotamia," Rusticus said with a sigh. As he spoke, he noticed a double-masted Roman freighter, a naval ship, that was arriving at the entrance to a large harbour only a discus's throw away. The red sails had the Roman version of the Greek mythological god Apollyon sewn on them in white. He noted too that the mastheads on the freighter had strengthened brass fittings. The last time he had been here the monkeys were still using iron fittings and trying to figure out how to circumvent the corrosive effect of iron on timber. The image of Apollyon carved upon the freighter's stern also appeared now; however, his view of it was blocked by crew members bringing stones aboard and placing them on deck to hurl at any pirate ships that might try to rob them at sea.

"Who be your gods, boy?" Rusticus looked up and asked.

"Mithras and Apollo, but sometimes Roman gods with other names," replied the boy, who only really prayed to the corbito's deity for safe voyages at sea.

"Ah, Apollyon. Christ called him the 'prince and power of the air', but you should know him as Apollyon," smirked Rusticus.[26]

"Christ?" the boy asked.

"Just another pretender to the throne," sighed Rusticus.

The crew finished packing the garum amphorae above the ballast of the stern, which was twelve feet in height. They had cushioned each amphora individually with multiple green papyrus branches. The captain examined the hold, still under the angelic spell but also with a vague trace of regret that he would not be travelling to Alexandria to trade some of his garum for precious Egyptian wheat.

The floor of the hull's hold was given over to ballast and then tiled over. Under the tiles were timber holes to allow seawater to escape. Bilge water was such a problem that the least able of the crew was often detailed to stand by and observe it.

---

[26] Ephesians 2.1-2.

All preparations made then, the captain gave the order to set sail and called for the boy to come down to paste some heated pine resin onto any emerging cracks in the hull timber, and to keep an eye on the bilge water. They headed out to open sea with a good land wind behind them. The helmsman skilfully but slowly steered them through the part of the harbour they had been moored in by guiding tillers which were linked to the two rudders, but once out at sea they were soon travelling at six to eight knots due to their light cargo. In the evening, Rusticus sat undisturbed and watched how the few passengers all made up shelters to guard them from the spray on the stern side where they then shared their bread, wine and fruit among themselves.

There were Roman families with shrieking children, some Italic Spaniards and several pilgrims who had taken the opportunity to return from Palmyra to Italy, to whom the captain had hurriedly sent word of his voyage. The crew ate together in the little galley, a stew of octopus, onions, and olive oil with some bread. The boy was sent out to offer a plate of it to Rusticus, but he simply shook his head and dismissed him. He had been staring at the sea for hours as if searching longingly for something.

Later, the crew hung up their hammocks in the hull and offered one to the fallen angel, who again declined with a shake of his head. It was bad enough having to complete this mission in the form of a man, which was demanding enough, as Christ would doubtless confirm, but to sleep beside these talking apes would be intolerable. Instead, the age-old entity sat away from them all in a sheltered spot on the lee of the galley where no spray landed and where the creaking of the hull seemed distant and less irritating. From there, he looked out to sea and prayed to the Prince of the Winds to control the dangerous Meltemi[27].

Regardless, in the night, they very suddenly entered a gale that dragged them into watery canyons with hilly waves that soon began crashing down upon the deck, and consequently, two or three people were lost overboard. Rusticus held onto the mast throughout the madness which would engulf them for several hours. He knew that should he go overboard; he would have little choice but to shapeshift into a shark, which would render his mission a failure and force him to return prematurely to his incarceration.

---

[27] The Meltemi were famous etesian winds of antiquity that blew from west to east across the Mediterranean. From May to September, they could be lethal to large vessels, never mind little corbitos.

These were the ridiculous rules of the Kertamen: rules that he would accept should this storm not relent, he considered with a frown as they crashed over one giant wave after another, lunging forward as the salt spray covered the deck. Rusticus looked up at the sky throughout, smiling as a boxer does after taking several punches, at Yahweh[28] and his elements. Twice, he fell to his knees and endured the pain men felt; once he was even convinced that a wave was taking him, but he held on with all his human strength.

The suntanned crew slid rapidly around, securing anything of value as the ship plummeted down and up the soaking valleys while the passengers held on for their lives.

Rusticus heard many accents attempting to scream out commands above the roar of the sea, but the rain hammering the deck and the howling wind, which frequently lashed it with salty water, made it near impossible for anyone to hear. At one point it seemed as if the little corbito was done for as it rose up one mountainous upsurge and then plummeted down into a wet trough before somehow steadying itself and then being blown along a wet valley by the fury of the winds, which propelled it at a quite ferocious speed towards a petrifying climax.

By sunrise, everyone, including Rusticus, had bellies full of salty water and muscles which were aching and exhausted. Rusticus was lying in the prow clasping to a rope that had burned his hands raw when the morning sun forced him to open his eyes. He ached like a man and had the thirst of one too, but he felt cold and wet still and his head hurt terribly.

He got up onto one elbow and looked around with squinted eyes at the now calm sea stretching out beyond. The galley slave boy had survived the carnage too, by finding a little space in the hold to weather it out. He turned up with an amphora of fresh water. Rusticus spewed up some sea water first and then drank some from it.

Then he staggered down to the galley where, despite his chill, he sat in the shade to rest. He drank deeply from another vase and then poured the rest of its contents over his head before hurling it away without a care for anyone else or how much drinking water have survived.

A galley slave soon began cleaning up around him and then made a fire on a tray with some dry wood from the hull. Soon he was preparing hot water for the

---

[28] God of the Old Testament and of the Israelites.

65

remaining passengers and crew to drink in order to warm them up. Rusticus just sat there, waiting for the journey to end.

That afternoon, they sighted Cyprus off in the distance before catching a favourable breeze which took them to the coast of Crete by the following morning, and without further incident. The captain wanted to moor at Crete to replace the lost drinking water and food that had gone overboard in the storm. He did not ask his strange passenger for permission, however, somehow sensing that doing so was best avoided, and so he pressed on for the rugged coast of Sparta, which the vessel clung to over the following couple of days. Thankfully, with further favourable land winds, they surged on and up through the Ionian islands to Corfu in no time at all.

There, as they prepared to enter the Adriatic and make the crossing to Italy, the boy returned to ask Rusticus more about his ancestry.

"Why do you care, boy?" Rusticus asked him contemptuously.

"Interested, my lord," replied the boy, who looked down in shame.

"Pray to Apollyon, Cernunnos, Osiris, Saturn, Satan or whatever you wish to call him, to relieve your curiosity then, boy; I am no teacher of monkeys," he told him with his eyes closed. "Away now, or I'll put you overboard," he warned with such chilling assertion that the boy's heart skipped a beat and he duly bolted.

The following day, they spotted seagulls above the boat looking for food, and a few hours later, land was sighted. The little corbito, ignored by the marine patrol who usually floated around the approach in a frigate, glided into the Roman harbour of Brundisium, which is shaped like a stag's antlers. There was a surprisingly fast order of entry, not dissimilar to aeroplanes in modern times awaiting their call to approach the runway for take-off. It was half-past three on a surprisingly dull Adriatic afternoon with slow winds, and the place was hectic with people hurriedly loading and unloading ships.

The noises of the screaming slave dockers, who were doing most of the loading and unloading around the bay, echoed out to sea. From a distance they looked like one long caterpillar with many legs, carrying amphorae and military equipment from tunics and belts to weapons and tools, as well as crates of wild animals and personal belongings. The shouting was matched by the screaming legions of seagulls circling above, ready to dive down for any scraps which might appear.

Rusticus walked down to where the crew were getting ready to toss a rope or two over to the pier at the waiting dockers and officials. He observed them all smiling at what they saw as potential prey—another little merchant ship.

"Those materialistic Alpha apes standing up there," he whispered to the boy, "on their patch every day, waiting for their lifetime ship to come in, know deep down that their ship has never left port," he told him. The boy understood almost exactly what this strange man meant by this.

"Ahoy there!" roared a docker before a crew man chucked him up a rope. Then after a slight bump or two, the corbito was securely fastened to iron props on the pier wall.

Rusticus moved quickly up a timber board onto the pier and simply waved his hand and blew out towards an approaching pack of clerks and a customs official seeking to ask him some questions about himself, the corbito, and her cargo, for *tetare*[29] purposes. The men inhaled his breath and were instantly turned away and oblivious of him, in the manner that most men are when spirits are present.

He passed them all without hindrance thereafter and proceeded along one of the long piers that dominated the twin-branched bay. There, another group of officials argued among themselves and with some Italian sailors employed by a family firm in possession of a state contract to transport grain and Indian spices from the Red Sea ports, about the transportation of an Illyrian auxiliary cavalry across the Adriatic to Dalmatia.

"It is not in my brief to have to troop those Dalmatae over there, particularly not without upfront payment!" shouted an Italian seaman to one wig-wearing official who was making a great show of reading a bunch of notes on papyrus while thinking up some official retort that would put the fear of death into this uppity sailor. Most of them, officials, sailors and a couple of auxiliary officers, all turned to look at Rusticus now as he approached, but he simply blew in their direction too, causing them all to turn away, unmindful of him.

As he stepped onto a stoned road beyond the port, he walked right into the waiting Illyrian cavalry group, around a hundred and fifty men and their horses. They were pitched up and awaiting transportation across the Adriatic. Alongside some other travellers, he passed among them as they ate, drank and played dice along both sides of the road. At the end of the group their horses were all tied up to mule posts. He approached and helped himself to a fine charger, blowing upon

---

[29] A Roman maritime custom tax for merchant shipping.

the sleeping officer who was supposed to be minding the beasts as he did so. He then galloped off at speed along a short track and then onto the stoned Via Appia Traiana, which had been constructed long after Rusticus's last visit to this anthill.

Back at the corbito, a tall, freckled official enquired of the now bewildered skipper as to the nature of his visit to Italy. "Honestly, I can't remember," the captain replied with a befuddled look across his face. He soon came to his senses, however, and quickly sent the boy as a runner to the warehouse of C. Peticus of the Peticii import and export company along the pier, to offer them the garum he had brought with him in the boat. He also asked the customs officer to wait ten minutes or so. People were milling everywhere and soon the official was aboard seeking to inspect the cargo, while state spies loitered around listening to every word and scanning every face.

Rusticus was pleased to be away from the monkey pen as he pressed the horse to a full gallop along the coastal highway. Conscious that the beast would not endure the three hundred miles at full pelt, he reluctantly stopped at one of the roadside taverns a few hours later, near Canosa on the older stretch of the *Via Appia*. Here he demanded a clean room from the little female who was serving wine, bread and fruit, and requested that the horse be stabled and fed too.

After sunrise the next day, he dragged the beast out by its mane, mounted it and was back on the road at a full gallop without paying a sesterce to the tavern. He charged past various travellers on foot and in carts for most of the day until mid-afternoon, when he reluctantly allowed the beast to slow to a walk and take water from a skin he had stolen from the stables, before pushing the poor thing on again in the evening.

That night, he lodged at another, larger inn near Capua, where he helped himself to a fresher horse and galloped off again before sunrise at full speed, but the horse soon became lame from the uneven stones on the road, so he abandoned the beast and jogged a while until he came across another one. This successor horse collapsed beneath him near Aricia in the hot afternoon sun a day and a half later, leaving him to walk the last sixteen miles to Rome.

Only a few other people travelling upon foot and a few groups with mules passed him, but he resolved not to steal a mule to carry him into the city because he recalled that Christ had entered Jerusalem on a mule. Instead, he walked on in his sweaty tunic and robe, an older-looking man with sandals that he was unused to as a consequence of his long absence from the surface; he cursed his aching legs and the uneven stones as well as the talking monkeys who had laid them down so idiotically.

At either side of the road approaching the city were summer meadows covered in flowers and herbs. He could smell the sage bushes, which were well fed by the multitude of streams that never over-ran the land or formed swamps, for the slopes of the land drained off the water so that they were not absorbed into the Tiber.

He soon passed under the Arch of Drusus on the outskirts of the city before arriving at the grand old Porta Capena[30] shortly afterwards. The Caelian Hill rose above and beyond the Servian wall, and he was surprised to note so many scroungers loitering around the entrance area. The emperor needed to chuck the whole lot of them in with the big cats, he thought as he gave the evil eye to any who dared to approach him. One or two tried but were instantly astounded by his gaze and, cringing, immediately retreated.

The gate was manned by twenty or so praetorians and one or two officials who were taxing everyone trying to enter. One poor Jew was receiving twenty lashes from a bulky Germanic-looking praetorian as a punishment for not declaring some jewellery in a hidden compartment of his cart, while his wife and children sat with their heads in their hands listening to his screams[31].

Christ had not screamed in pain when also in human form.

Rusticus blew and waved his hand at the Romans on the gate as he approached them, making them instantaneously unconscious of his presence. However, he did stop and whisper in the ear of a prefect who was questioning a teenage boy of North African appearance and his companion, an older female from Spain. They both held baskets and had been attempting to exit the city to pick herbs for the lad's father, a retired auxiliary soldier who was now a tavern-keeper on the Aventine:

"He is a runaway slave, and that is his master's mistress who he has manipulated into his plan to flee to Carthage with," Rusticus lied to the prefect. Of course, they were doing nothing of the sort, but they were sure to be detained now and their day ruined; he smirked.

"I don't believe you," the prefect then snarled at the youth before punching him in the face.

---

[30] A grand old entry point into the city located within the Severin Wall at the Via Appia.
[31] The first-century AD Roman writer Juvenal spoke of Jewish beggars congregating at this gate (Juvenal, 3.10-16).

Rusticus chuckled as he passed through the gate to the south side of the ancient city. Immediately to his right, he saw a few men with litters, so he hailed one over to rest his weary legs and feet.

"Villa Rusticus on the Esquiline," he told both men as they lifted him up and he settled down on the cushioned base.

"Right you are, sir," snapped the lead carrier, and off they went at a slow pace through the crowded, humid streets.

After a while, Rusticus heard flutes playing, and a Libyan voice pleading over the music that he was not preaching Christianity and had merely been bartering over some nectarines with a street merchant. Rusticus popped his head out of the curtained litter and saw a large group of *vigiles urbani*[32], some armed with wooden batons and knives, dragging a still-protesting man with curly hair away.

"Why are the *vigiles* out in large numbers at this time of day?" Rusticus called back to the man carrying the rear of the litter.

"Been like that the last few days, sir," the man replied in an obvious Aventine brogue. "The Christians have been burgling houses and rioting after dark, so there has been a ban on them gathering in groups throughout the day."

Rusticus smirked, sank back into the litter and crossed his arms behind his head in delight, for that man had not been in any group. The bullying would not be restrained by technicalities then, he mused as he rested his eyelids.

"The arrest of their religious leader—Justin—has got their robes in a twist, I daresay," offered the carrier now.

"Always up to no good, sir," piped up the front one, as they pressed onwards.

"Ever since Lucian had a go at them in his piece about that chap who set himself alight and died at the Olympic games,"[33] added the one at the rear.

"Aye, they don't have a lot of friends in either Athens or Rome," laughed the other.

---

[32] Night watchmen of the city who kept a lookout for crime and fires.

[33] Possibly a reference to the second-century AD Syrian rhetorician—Lucian of Samosata—who was known for his comic monologues as well as an ancient work of science fiction *A True Story* (Latin: *Verae Historiae*). The litter carrier may be referring to Lucian's attack on the Christians in his satire *The Death of Peregrinus* (Latin: *De Morte Peregrini*).

"Shut up now, the pair of you," Rusticus barked. He just lay there grinning with his eyes closed and his nostrils open. What a city this was, he could smell everything, and he despised mankind as a consequence even more.

Half an hour later, they walked through an unpolished gate of African red cedar, opened by a seven-foot-tall Greek with a dagger in his belt. They proceeded into a Hellenistic-Persian styled garden with a central path leading down through some shrubbery and herbaceous plants towards a modest villa with terracotta roofing and a large frontal stone patio. There was a view from the gate down the hill to some grander properties, but, beyond a small statue of Apollo that stood at the edge of some steps down to the patio, the house was enclosed by tall walls lined with chestnut trees.

Rusticus stepped out of the litter just as a tall, completely bald eunuch suddenly approached and knelt before him to touch his feet.

"Greetings, Dominus," he said with bowed head.

Rusticus left this hybrid Nephilim on his knees and turned to the two litter carriers standing beside him. He blew in their faces and instantly, the two men picked up their litter and began walking back to the raised garden and down the pathway without a sesterce for their efforts.

Rusticus entered the house, passing a female slave who bowed her head and offered him a bowl of water to drink. He ignored all the staff who appeared in the atrium and walked past the hand-painted walls that bore an image of an impressive peacock preening itself beside a fountain of whirling blue water.

Paying no attention to the artwork, he headed straight for the study, closing the door behind him. The black magic that had brought him here in the form of Junius Rusticus would only last for a few more days: he had to read up on legal matters immediately and instigate judicial proceedings as quickly as the cobra strikes.

There was a stone desk before him, beyond which was a window with glorious views down over a smaller rear peristyle garden with Doric columns down one side of it and leading to a gapped patio with a view of the Flavian amphitheatre beyond. On the desk were piles of papyrus, at least thirty scrolls in a box, and several wax tablets with notes regarding the matter at hand. He sat down at the desk, called for some honied wine mixed with water, and began reading the notes.

"Will I instruct cook to prepare a meal, Dominus?" asked the tall eunuch, who reappeared with a jug of wine, some of which he poured into a goblet.

"Fine. And send a runner to Asinius Hortensius on the Palatine Hill and have him inform the emperor that I am ready to proceed to litigation against the prisoner tomorrow morning," replied Rusticus without lifting his gaze from the notes. The eunuch nodded and swiftly departed to carry out the instructions.

Hortensius was a former governor of Egypt, and presently a well-regarded secretary to the emperor, Antonius Pius. The daily maintenance of the empire was far too much for Pius, so he divided much of the work among a select group of trusted administrators who, along with the hierarchy of the current Pretorian guard, had his ear.

A while later, as it became dark outside and the eunuch served a plate of pan-fried sea-carp, garlic potatoes and honeyed dormice, Rusticus finally lifted his head from a scroll, sniffed the food and nodded at the eunuch.

"Take the fish away," he said with such an expressionless countenance that the eunuch had not a clue as to whether his master was angry or not. For Rusticus had unfathomable eyes of green and such a cold gaze to go with them that they gave very little away.

"Yes, Dominus, shall I bring some meat instead?"

"No. This will suffice. Prepare me a bath and have robes laid out for me to wear in the morning."

"Yes, Dominus," nodded the hybrid, who had been made a eunuch for being too presumptuous with another entity once upon a time in Pergamon.

Rusticus watched him leaving and then picked at the mice and potatoes before pushing the plates away and pouring himself more wine. The notes he was reading contained a background on the Christian community of Rome and statements from so-called witnesses who claimed, perhaps for a coin or two, to have seen them doing this or that. Most of it was a crock of shit, of course, so Rusticus focused upon several books on Roman law, including some relevant extracts from the endless bureaucratic drivel of Gaius Plinius Caecilius Secundus (Pliny the Younger). Sighing at the prospect of yet more Pliny, who was known for his limitless jabbering, Rusticus sat back, sipped some wine and began reading again.

Later, when two slaves appeared and hurriedly lit the oil lamps in his study as darkness approached, he raised his head for a moment, then turned and looked out of the window. He could smell evil nearby, but that was not uncommon in this city at this time. The slaves removed the plates from the table and left as quietly as the moth now sitting on the window ledge.

72

The eunuch then reappeared at the doorway, bearing a scroll. "Dominus, there is a message from Asinius Hortensius," he said gently and with head bowed.

This eunuch had seen many fallen angels appearing as men, women and animals over the years since his youth in Thebes[34]. He was a direct descendant on his maternal side of the biblical Nephilim king Og of Bashan. He had seen many a shapeshifter; some were talkative, some resented the mission they were on, and others—well, some others so detested the human species that they struggled not to be unkind even to his hybrid line. This one however, he thought, appeared morose and keen to get on with his brief.

The eunuch had been sent to work as the butler to the house of Quintus Junius Rusticus in Rome only a few weeks previously, and was instructed to be prepared at any time to receive a fallen angel who had shapeshifted into Rusticus. Experienced as the eunuch was in this business, as soon as all the drama with the Christians had erupted with the street protests and the arrest of their leader Justin, he anticipated the arrival of his new shapeshifting master at any time.

When he discovered that his human master had disappeared the previous morning without a word, the eunuch knew that a replacement would turn up at any moment. He also knew the rules and restrictions of the Kertamen, so when he spoke again, he did so delicately: "There have been angels in the city urging the Christians to feed and befriend the wild dogs that roam the streets in packs, Dominus. So, if you were thinking of walking to the trial tomorrow via the colosseum, we may need to send guards with you," he suggested.

Rusticus raised his head in interest now. He knew that should any dog attack him, as they nearly always would attack his kind, he would most likely shift from a man into another form and slay them, thus rendering his mission a failure.

"Yes. Arrange a litter and armed guards then," he replied coldly as he reached out his hand for the message scroll.

It was a jovial note from Hortensius, in which he confirmed the emperor's pleasure at this news and added that the emperor's adopted son Marcus Aurelius would reside as judge over proceedings in the Centumviri court at ten in the morning.

Rusticus was invited to present an *actione in rem* against the Christian school of Justin and the leader of said school as well as the actual property itself, all on

---

[34] Now known as Luxor, in Egypt.

behalf of the so-called state. It was the *princeps* who really got the spoils of any success though.

"Arrange my bath and my bed. I do not wish to be disturbed until nine, when I shall breakfast in my study and then depart by litter at nine-twenty-five," he instructed the eunuch, who nodded and departed.

Rusticus sat for a while and beheld from the open window the motionless garden, which echoed a tranquil peacefulness on this warm summer evening. He cared not for peace, however, and was still annoyed at his dilemma of being incarcerated and only free for the purpose of this trial, which he considered to be something of a chore. Just then, the sound of a female slave being beaten by her incredibly angry mistress arose from an adjoining property beyond the garden wall and entered through the window like a refreshing breeze. He closed his eyes and smiled at this for a moment, before getting up and walking through to his bath.

He slept reasonably well despite having to endure things from within the body of an older human on an uncomfortable bed. Throughout the night a slave girl stood by the side of the bed fanning the man she supposed to be her naked master with an ostrich feather to cool him from the stifling humidity of the summer night.

The next day, Rusticus was surprised by how refreshed he felt as he sat in the study again, eating a peach and some cold ham for breakfast. He initially sat on the desk, looking out of the window, watching the sun beaming down upon the seven hills of the eternal city, which were partly shaded by the many Italian pine trees that stood upon them like little umbrellas. But he soon became irritated at the little birds that nipped around gaily from garden to garden, singing and enjoying the properties of the Esquiline in the beautiful morning sunshine, so instead, he sat on a chair with his back to the window and finished his food.

The litter journey to the Centumviri court, which was held in the Basilica Julia in the Forum, was an uneventful one which took around ten minutes. Rusticus had been stuffy under his linen tunic and toga and so fanned himself with an ivory fan as they descended the Esquiline. The Forum had changed since he was last there, having lost its thriving Republican-era commercial character to become instead a formulised monumental zone under these blasted emperors. Eventually, having been carried along the old sacred way and around to the almost seven-hundred-year-old Temple of Saturn, or Kronos, as the Greeks had previously called the Prince of the Winds[35], Rusticus stepped out and bowed in front of it. He had specifically instructed the slaves to bring him here so that he could bow to his prince.

The Basilica Julia was next to the temple, and he was beginning to walk towards it when he heard his name being hailed from the direction of the Temple of the deified Vespasian. When he turned around, he saw a man jogging towards him carrying several scrolls and parchments. It was the young Verginius Rufus Pollio, a well-known lawyer from Pompeii, who was suspected by Rome's satanic choir of working with the other side.

"So, they have sent another Son of Disobedience to ensure that old Rusticus contends a good case then, eh?" Pollio, quite out of breath, pulled up and quieried.

Pollio had somehow been able to recognise that this wasn't really Rusticus standing on the steps before him.

"Either that, or something had been whispering in his ear?"

Regardless, this was irrelevant to this Rusticus, but the mockery within Pollio's words was duly noted and would not be tolerated long. "Go now to your client, Pollio, or I shall personally visit your children tonight and rip their livers out with my hands and force you to eat them," Rusticus coolly smiled down at the still-grinning lawyer, who now immediately stopped smiling.

An abrupt chill came over the Pompeiian, and he took a cautious step back, terrified at the cold stare being projected upon him like a flashlight on a burglar. Pollio could be in little doubt now about what exactly was stood there before him.

"See you in court then," he nodded nervously now before scurrying away up the marble stairs, with his head lowered and a slight shiver, despite the warming sunshine.

Rusticus watched him scampering up and into to the court and made a mental note to arrange this monkey's murder with his pupil, Marcus Aurelius, before he departed this irritating dimension.

"Insolent meat bag," he mouthed to himself as he leisurely followed him up the stairs.

Although this particular case was not entirely a civil quarrel of the type which the Centumviri typically dealt with, it was not unusual for high-profile criminal

---

[35] A term that Jesus Christ used for a supernatural spirit who leads the fallen angels— Satan (Ephesians 2.2).

matters that are led by the state, to be played out within a civil grievance. A farmer, for example, might be attacked by the state via a civil writ against his estate, as it was often simpler to ensure the destruction of said farmer and his property by attacking him using this process. To raise such an action was tantamount to a criminal proceeding, but a losing defendant would end up as the property of the state and be sentenced to death as well as having their property or wealth seized. So, an *action in rem* within the Centumviri, with a head of state sitting as judge, suited the state, as there was no hope of a jury (something that everyone was entitled to in any other criminal proceeding).

The building itself was vast and pleasantly cool inside, which was a relief in the summer months. A huge, marbled space opened out under several Corinthian pillars, each as wide as three men and as tall as a battleship's masts. This marble labyrinth provided much-needed confidentiality for scheming lawyers to hide and to conspire with clients and witnesses.

There were two upper levels with various porticos that were home to the shops and offices of the *argenti distractors*—the Argentarii[36]—and some food-eating areas. Regrettably, though, the courtroom walls were as thin as plasterboard, and with certain lawyers opting frequently to play up to the crowds in attendance there was rarely any time for quiet reflection.

Rusticus exhaled another resentful sigh as he entered and then advanced into the interior, which echoed with many footsteps and heavy doors creaking and closing. Around eighty armed praetorians were dotted around the lower foyer, as well as over in a doorway where he detected twenty of them hanging around. He headed directly for them.

Suddenly, he was rudely approached by an older court official, a feather pusher whom he instinctively understood to be a disciple of hell—Publius Quintilius Fuscus, who smiled at him. "Welcome my lord, praise the Morning Star and Prince of the Winds himself for gracing us with your presence," declared Fuscus joyfully.

Rusticus simply stared at him with an expression as plain as Fuscus had ever seen.

---

[36] The Roman bankers and moneylenders who, in AD 204, during the reign of Septimius Severus, would build the Arch of the Argentariorum in the city. Today, there are several drilled holes throughout this monument, thanks to treasure hunters who hoped that the *Argentarii* had hidden treasure within.

"I can reveal that Verginius Rufus Pollio of Pompeii is assisting the accused in judicial process my lord," announced Fuscus. "Pollio should not be underestimated due to his persuasive oratory skills, and his history of inspiring and motivating the crowd," he then pointed out.

"I shall conclude matters rapidly," snapped Rusticus before moving off in the direction of the praetorians.

Fuscus was confused, and reluctantly skipped around to the front of Rusticus again, blocking his path. The fallen angel stopped and fought down a fiery desire to blind the man there and then.

"But my lord, Rusticus himself publicly declared only last week that the examination of the Christian man would take two days," Fuscus mumbled, inflating a confused expression across his chubby sunburned face.

"Fuck off, Fuscus, and don't presume that you can approach me offhand. Nor, for that matter, should you ever question my command of this pathetic undertaking," Rusticus quietly snarled at him. He then leaned down and whispered in Fuscus's ear: "Do you understand, you talking monkey?"

"Yes, yes, forgive me, I merely—"

"Fuck off now and instigate some gossip among the other lawyers and the crowd in my courtroom, regarding how simple this case will be for me as *praefectus urbanus*," he ordered before softly pushing the fat scribe away and walking on.

Fuscus understood his instructions but not how all this would be achieved without a long dramatic performance by Rusticus. Regardless, it was all he could do to muster the strength not to bow to this being in front of so many watching eyes, instead opting to nod before turning and heading for the advocates' room in order to sprinkle the seeds of hearsay.

Rusticus then approached the praetorians who were gathered around a large, polished oak door. He quickly declared who he was and demanded to see Marcus Aurelius, who was presiding as magistrate over the trial. A bulky-looking tribune with a couple of scars across his nose and lips from his time as a centurion in the army went inside, closing the door behind him, only to return a few seconds later and nod for Rusticus to enter.

"Quintus Junius Rusticus," the tribune saluted as Rusticus entered the small marble room where his former pupil, Marcus Aurelius[37], lay on a cushioned couch having his right foot massaged by a slave. It looked a little swollen to

---

[37] The adopted son of then-emperor Antonius Pius and former pupil of the real Rusticus.

Rusticus, as he sniffed the eight German bodyguards who wore their long hair and beards traditionally and who all looked over six feet tall. Each of them carried German-forged swords and daggers, and eyed Rusticus suspiciously.

He switched his attention first to another door, which presumably led to the courts, and then down to the centrepiece of the room—a rectangular marble table laden with fruit on jewel-encrusted golden plates.

Rusticus smiled unceremoniously and gave a little courtesy to his old pupil. "Hail Marcus Aurelius," he said with convincing affection.

Marcus looked up and smiled at his old teacher. "Sorry about this Rusticus, old boy; I've a muscle tear in my foot from hunting last week, hurts like buggery, you know," he exclaimed cheerily.

"If you send your slave to fetch the arnica montana plant from near Ostia, my prince, and then eat a mouthful with every meal as well as rubbing the leaves and stem upon the foot, it will relieve you," suggested Rusticus.

Marcus sat up. "Never heard of it. but thank you, I shall try it," he said before then clicking his fingers, forcing a blonde slave girl, around 20 years of age to scurry off and see to this.

"Rusticus, by the gods, it's good to see you here!" exclaimed Marcus. "It has been a few months now; the dinner at Latium, I recall?" Rusticus nodded. "Well…I jolly well missed you, don't you know?" insisted Marcus.

"How is your father, our beloved emperor?" Rusticus felt obliged to point out which father he was referring to.

Marcus stood up and slowly approached the table now, where he stopped and gazed down at the fruits on offer. There were oranges and grapefruit from Spain, black grapes from Etruria, apples from Gaul and peaches and nectarines from Sardinia. Finally, he helped himself to a peach and nibbled away at it, beckoning Rusticus to help himself.

"He was up and about yesterday," he then mumbled. "Apparently he took a short swim, so we are all optimistic that the gods are assisting in his recovery," said Marcus unconvincingly.

"I shall sacrifice to his health as soon as this nasty business is concluded, my prince," lied Rusticus convincingly again, whilst gently shaking his head to decline the fruit.

"Well, it's a damnable situation, this business, quite frankly," groaned Marcus as peach juice trickled down his fingers like blood from a cut. "Lucius[38] and I have been invited down to Formia for a wedding at Senator Tiberius Pompeianus's place tomorrow. His wife Caecilia Plautia is an old friend of our mother, of course, and I should have preferred to have set off this morning as opposed to this evening, in order to spend time with them." Marcus washed his hands in a large marble bowl of water with rose petals floating on it.

Just then, the praetorian tribune entered the room again. "The governor of Sardinia, Gaius Cornelius Asiaticus, is outside requesting a moment, my prince," he declared with another salute.

"Tell him to make an appointment through Asinius Hortensius," said Marcus. The tribune bowed then left, gently closing the door behind him. "Lucius left this morning with his whole entourage and my wife, but because he will doubtlessly spend the whole journey chin-wagging about the bloody Parthians, I suppose I should be content to follow at a distance," he giggled to Rusticus, who in turn forced a grin in response.

These apes are tediously primitive.

"But I suspect this business is going to drag on all day, and I do so awfully despise travelling overnight." Marcus poured himself some water mixed with lemon and orange juice now into a silver goblet with a boar relief engraved upon it and offered it to Rusticus, who again politely declined with a shake of his head.

"In that respect, sir, I think I can assure you that should you instigate proceedings presently, I can present and conclude the case within half an hour at the most," he spoke now with such a confidence that no one in the room doubted him.

"Half an hour?" exclaimed Marcus. "Jupiter's mercy is with me," he told one of his German guards, who did not flinch. "But the bugger will surely have us here all day twisting and turning the matter, Rusticus? For I heard that this Justin chap and that fat Greek—Crescens, the Cynic—debated for eight hours in the colosseum, of all places, only last month; not to mention the damn witnesses— which there are forty-two, you know." Marcus looked at his scribe behind his guards for confirmation, and a crouching elderly fellow checked some notes and quickly looked up at his master.

"Forty-eight, my prince," he replied.

---

[38] Lucius Verus, adopted brother of Marcus Aurelius and adopted son of the then-emperor Antonius Pius.

"Regardless, my prince," insisted Rusticus, "I have the formula and will apply it to finish him off easily and quickly. Then it will be for you to sentence him." Rusticus gave Marcus a knowing, convincing nod.

"By the gods, Rusticus, I tell you what, if you can pull it off and have us out of here in a jiffy then I won't forget it when I am granted the imperium," Marcus promised him eagerly.

"It is my honour to please you, sir." Rusticus gave another pathetic little bow.

"And, if he does surprise you and tongue-twists away at you, I shall ask the Furies[39] to punish every bloody Christian in the empire while I have this Justin crucified slowly in the open sun. Righty-ho, let us proceed then, what?" Marcus, now full of enthusiasm, rubbed his hands together.

"Just one more thing, sir," urged Rusticus.

"Oh yes?" replied Marcus, forgetting his pain.

"Virginias Rufus Pollio."

"Why yes, he has volunteered to assist this Justin character when no one else was prepared to touch the case."

"An irritating little character who has no place in this city, assisting this ungodly sect of Christians against the state. I should urge you to consider arresting him after the case is heard—for blasphemy against the gods and of course the emperor," proposed Rusticus.

Marcus smiled, not so much in agreement at this, but more at what he considered to be the humour within the suggestion. "Not sure about that, Rusticus. Domitian soiled the courts with his damned interferences, and I personally think that all lawyers should be at liberty to operate freely." With that, he chuckled and patted Rusticus on the back before making his way out of the side door, closely followed by his entourage of German brutes.

Rusticus was not happy about the pat on the back or the refusal, but he gritted his teeth and exited via the other door where the praetorians were all still hanging about. He then strode purposely across the polished marble foyer towards court number IV.

We'll see.

The courtroom was about the size of a modern tennis court, and as its centrepiece was a large, cushioned chair with a foot stool for the magistrate, in this case Marcus Aurelius. To either side were bronze busts of emperor Antoninus Pius and his predecessor, Hadrian. Two oak tables with chairs stood

---

[39] Roman mythological chthonic (subterranean) deities of vengeance.

80

opposite each other in the centre, with clay cups and jugs of water upon them. At the end of the room was another desk with official scribes sitting ready to read and take notes.

To the side of the room, beyond a waist-high red rope of velvet with golden threads neatly sewn along it, where five praetorians stood, were at least a couple of hundred observers including quite a few lawyers who crowded the front seating area behind another thicker and well-worn rope, while everyone else was packed into a small portico which led outdoors.

All eyes turned to Rusticus in his toga and tunic as he entered the room and headed for the praetorians, who seemed to recognise him. Perhaps they were regular court guards, he thought as they lifted the rope to gain access to one of the tables. Opposite sat the accused Christian known as Justin, and beside him Pollio, who made every effort to read his notes with his head lowered while Justin stared right up at Rusticus.

Justin was surprised that Rusticus carried no notes and had no assistants. Rusticus sensed his confusion immediately and so gazed over at his prey with a brilliantly convincing smile, and studied him closely.

Justin was early sixties in years, with warm brown eyes and short dark greying hair in the Roman fashion but with the beard and robes of a Jew. Born and raised in Flavia Neapolis,[40] Justin was a product of a Roman father who had married a Greek in Alexandria, where he had been on the staff of Rome's official overseer of Egypt's grain production. The family had prospered and retired to an estate in the new Flavian city of Flavia Neapolis in the late nineties.

Rusticus could see the Greek in him as he scanned and smelled him. The notes of the real Rusticus and his spies, which this fallen one had gone over the previous night in the study, contained views about Justin's Greek maternal blood, and in particular his abominable championing of a Christian logos. The real Rusticus had regarded this as proof that Justin was surely no Roman. Certainly, his nose was of the old Hellenistic line which Rusticus thought might have been Ptolemaic in origin, but there were too many other scents in the courtroom presently, and so his ability to realise the origin of human blood from its scent was limited.

---

[40] Modern-day Nablus, which lies north of Jerusalem in the North Bank. The city was in the region referred to in the bible as Samaria, and was named Flavia Neapolis by the emperor Vespasian in AD 72.

Justin continued to stare back at the so-called man before him, mind racing and eyes twinkling with understanding. Both of them continued to stare at each other, Rusticus maintaining a smirk throughout. Suddenly a noise captured everyone's attention as a tall set of bronze doors opened behind the throne and a large group of praetorians entered and began taking positions around the court.

"All rise!" shouted a new praetorian tribune, who proceeded to list all of Marcus's honorific titles before the man himself came in wearing a friendly smile, and waving firmly at the audience before taking his seat.

Gradually, Rusticus and Justin's mutual gaze broke off as Pollio spoke to Justin and handed him a note to read. Rusticus stood up, bowed to Marcus, then strode up to the bar and gently leaned his human arse upon it. He waited for Marcus to speak and commence the matter, but instead Marcus merely waved him on with a casual flick of his wrist.

Rusticus took a moment to scan the crowd first: there were all sorts here, listening in and many excited smiles could be spotted, just as in the crowds at Saturnalia[41]. There were various lawyers present, many plebs, a few moneylenders and even a senator or two. The ears of the city were clearly listening.

"My prince, I bring before the court today an accusation of an abuse of citizenship, an attempt to pervert the population of Rome and to blaspheme the gods, and a direct insult to Caesar himself as Pontifex Maximus[42], by the Samarian known as Justinian the Christian." Rusticus spoke to Marcus, rather than to the crowd, which was the normal practice.

"Who do you represent in this case?" Marcus asked him.

"The people of Rome, my prince." Rusticus gestured gently to the audience now as if he were introducing an operatic act in the theatre. There was considerable clapping at this from the plebs, and one or two cheers from Fuscus's toadies among them.

---

[41] The annual festival of Saturn, where gifts were given within families and where slaves dressed up as their masters and were served food and wine by their owners families and enjoyed parties as well as a large public banquet. This reference here may be towards the jovial crowds and carnival atmosphere of what the Roman poet Catullus called "the best of days".

[42] Pontifex Maximus was an honorary title (high priest of Rome) that was given to some emperors, including Antonius Pius.

"Stop that!" Marcus frowned and shook his head at them, and they fell silent again, only too aware of the points of several praetorian gladiuses within close proximity. The praetorians wouldn't hesitate to cut down anyone who crossed the line by disrespecting Marcus Aurelius.

"What say you, Justin?" Marcus asked, looking at Pollio however.

"My prince, my name is Verginius Rufus Pollio and I am assisting Justin the Christian today in his denial of this overly harsh allegation," pleaded Pollio.

Marcus nodded in understanding and turned to Rusticus and again flicked his wrist. "Pray continue, Rusticus."

Rusticus's dark charisma had kicked in now. He felt the admiring and excited eyes of all the monkeys upon him filling his soul with yet more confidence.

"Are you Justin the Christian, born in Flavia Neapolis to one Roman parent and another Greek?" he asked Justin across the floor.

"I am," replied the accused.

"And are you now a citizen of the city of Rome?"

"You are implying that as a citizen of the empire, I was not always a citizen of Rome," replied Justin.

"Regardless," Rusticus smiled at this and shook his head to brush it aside, "have you now decided to reside as a citizen within the city of Rome?" he pressed.

"Yes," replied Justin.

"And are you aware that we Romans believe our deities helped to create this holy city?"

"I know your mythological beliefs, and I respect them fully and—"

"Silence. Your answer is yes, then," Rusticus told him before looking at Marcus, who nodded approvingly.

"Thus, you are well aware that we are an exceptionally religious people and that this is our capital city, a profoundly religious capital city in an empire that spans from Caledonia to Persia?"

"Yes, I understand the customs and traditions of Rome. My own father was born and raised in the city," replied Justin.

"Yet regardless, you, a half-breed with citizenship, chose to misuse your liberty by moving into our holy city and preaching of your God, a deity whom you insist is the only true God." Rusticus looked at the crowd now and received the applause and calls he sought. "Then you founded a school for Romans, not simply Christians but Romans, whom you proposed to convert to the religion of this so-called God you call Jesus?" Rusticus asked him so matter-of-factly that Justin shivered at the coolness of this old warlock's tone. "The attempt to run a school in Rome, is, I contend, a blatant challenge to the gods of Rome, as well as an attempt to turn Roman citizens away from them," Rusticus barked at him now.

"My Prince, does my honourable friend here intend to call any witnesses to substantiate this claim that Justin urged pupils at his school to abandon Roman gods, or does he propose that none is required?" Pollio cut in here to ask Marcus.

"The Christian God is a single deity, although they claim that his supposed son walked the earth a while," Marcus replied.

Pollio remained silent. "As did Hercules and Achilles," shouted a voice from the crowd, a comment that had Rusticus up and looking around for a face.

Marcus then continued: "As such, any Roman converting to Christianity and studying at this chap's school is quite clearly disowning the gods of his ancestors. So no witnesses are required dear Pollio, and I suggest that part of the claim against your client is almost proven, unless of course your client cares to speak further on this matter?" he politely asked of Pollio.

Justin stood now. "I teach about the logos, my prince, and my beliefs in it," he said.

"Your beliefs?" put in Rusticus, which in turn had the crowd nodding and humming.

"Belief in God and about the philosophical connection between atheism, immorality, and disloyalty to the Empire, which Christians, Jews and pagans should all understand and reject," offered Justin as calmly as he could, and with an honesty that surprised Rusticus.

Even Peter the fisherman had abandoned the truth under pressure. Truth however, was a risky tendency within a Roman courtroom.

"It may seem trifling, my prince, but to teach Christianity in Rome, regardless of how small and smelly the building may be..." (this raised considerable laughter, which Rusticus ignored) "...could lead to consequences which are tantamount to religious abomination and an alien sect gathering momentum within our glorious city. Indeed, one that desires to pollute nature whilst spitting on our gods. I need not remind you, my prince, of how the gods protected this city and ensured our glory," he pointed out.

"Precisely!" nodded Marcus, confirming unofficially that Rusticus had proven the first part of his claim.

"A lack of respect for myself I can excuse in my learned friend," Rusticus said, looking at Pollio, "but a lack of respect for the people of Rome and for the most glorified emperor himself, well, this is unacceptable," he smirked as he advanced all over the younger Pompeiian, who was now red-faced, whilst the crowd cheered and clapped, as though hapless fighters were being savaged by lions.

Justin, however, remained calm and tranquil and stared at the ungodly enemy before him who was mesmerising everyone, including Marcus. Pollio was aware that to many men, Rusticus was regarded as having the same standing as a statesman and philosopher. He was presumed not only to be a defender of truth, but also an investigator as well as a scientific philosopher who sought justice. At that moment however, he felt his career slipping away from him and his secret Christian faith stumble. He looked at the bubbling crowd in search of the angel who had urged him to take this case on, but could not find him.

He also needed to wipe a trickle of sweat from his cheek, which he did with his toga. He looked again but found only hostile faces staring back at him and despaired at the matter-of-fact directness of Rusticus's argument, which obviously did not require any convincing witnesses so long as Marcus was judge. Pollio was well aware that the public were supposed to view the Roman judiciary as a champion of truth, ethics and priestly political science. In this sense however, it was a judiciary in crisis, as the public, or at least the plebs, regarded the Centumviri court as something of a theatre where entertainment was on show alongside snacks and drinks, not to mention exploitation and enslavement, while justice be damned.

The days of Cicero are obviously long gone.

The judiciary had long since lost its patrician origins and ethics of the *Mos Maiorum*[43]. These days the bar was open to all citizens of a growing empire owing to the need to manage its vast resources. Pollio had not carefully considered the consequence of assisting this poor man and losing the claim. He had written proof that Crescens the Cynic had paid several witnesses to claim falsely they had heard of evil goings-on within Justin's school, but Rusticus was bypassing this by not calling any of them. First blood to Rusticus, then, as he openly pissed upon Pollio's entire defence.

---

[43] The *Mos Maiorum*, "the ways of the ancestors", was a moral code from which Republican Romans derived their social norms. It was the traditional concept of Roman conservatism and was distinguished from, but in dynamic complement to, judicial law.

"The fact that many of Caesar's predecessors are regarded as deified gods, decreed as such by the senate, adds further insult to the injuries which you throw at us Romans, Justin." Rusticus shook his head in disappointment while Fuscus's cronies made clamours of assent among the audience.

"*Kalumniator*!"[44] came one clear shout from the crowd now.

Rusticus scanned the crowd; his gaze, which was as quick and sharp as a bird of prey, rested upon the golden face of a beautiful, dark-haired angel wearing a senatorial robe. For a moment, he was nervous and looked around to see if there were other immortals among the monkeys; as he still could not detected their scent due to the crowd. He knew very well that a mere angelic touch is often sufficient to set things in a commotion that could potentially spread throughout the crowd like a good joke, which in turn helps to influence judgements.

He assured himself, however, that this case was a done deal, and so he raised his hand towards Justin, who was seated before him. "Are we, the descendants of the gods and the greatest race on earth, going to tolerate this Samarian frequenter of Oedipean banquets[45]?"

Of course, Marcus was not incorruptible but he was principled to some extent, hence Rusticus's attendance in court today in order to run the case as opposed to just executing Justin; and Rusticus was confident that even the crowd, regardless of any angelic support, would not sway the verdict. Suddenly, though, he was dragged back into the proceedings by the sound of Marcus's voice.

"Have you anything else to add to this?" he asked Justin.

"Only that I have never intentionally insulted Caesar, my prince, and that indeed I wrote to him to explain that we Christians live peacefully, pay our taxes, and contribute to our magnificent empire," he calmly replied. "I admit to

---

[44] There was no official prosecution service in Roman courts. In order to discourage frivolous claims, individual prosecutors who were unsuccessful, would be branded with the letter K on their forehead and receive the same punishment which they had sought for the accused who had defended the claim.

[45] The Romanized North African forensic orator, Cornelius Fronto, a teacher of Marcus Aurelius, did a public speech which was in part directed against Christians. In which, he produced the terms, "Thyestean banquets" and "Oedipean intercourse", referring to the Greek mythological characters—Thyestes and Oedipus. Fronto cleverly linked the Christian community in Rome with cannibalism and incest. The latter being one of the few sexual iniquities that most Romans held issue with. Rusticus understands well, the popularity of the derogatory remark of "Oedipean banquet", which was regularly shouted at Christians in the build-up to this trial.

debating philosophy with Crescens the Cynic, over whom I won the public debate, my prince, which is possibly why he has instigated this false claim against me here today," he added, somewhat despondently. He paused before continuing: "I only worship my God in private, and I believe that by displaying morality and compassion to both my betters and those worse off than myself, I will gain his favour."

With those words, he shook his head and sat back down again as there was nothing more to say. Marcus studied him for a moment, with a measure of curiosity and even perhaps a little awe at such faith, unfaltering even now when his life was on the line.

Had not Pliny the Younger written to Trajan about how decent these strange people were many years ago?

"Given the absence of any credible defence today, and this admitted preoccupation with a Judean deity, who apparently could not protect himself from crucifixion and the humiliation of having to carry his cross through the streets under the crack of a Roman whip, I suggest that Justin fully deserves the death penalty," said Rusticus, raising his eyebrows at the crowd.

His words rippled through them for a moment before some cries of "Yes!" and "Hear, Hear!" bounced off the walls.

Rusticus smirked, cocksure, at those who had remained impartial, before shrugging and sighing with fake forbearance. "However, let us examine the facts of his guilt somewhat further," he told them. "There is a statue of the Roman god Apollo high up there." He pointed at a naked statue of the deity positioned above the door by which Marcus had entered the court. "Go now, bow and pay worship to the great god Apollo before every Roman present here," he proposed to Justin, knowing that he would not.

"I shall not," replied Justin firmly, and with such bravery that even the praetorians admired his steadfastness.

"And there," Rusticus pointed to a statue of the divine Augustus above the door by which he himself had entered the courtroom. "Go and bend your knee in worship to that great Roman god and emperor," he urged, smugly.

Again, Justin refused and replied that he had only one God, and that Jesus was his son. At this statement, there was considerable laughter from the crowd.

"Closing speeches, gentlemen?" proposed Marcus now with a yawn.

"The people rest, my prince," declared Rusticus haughtily as he sat down.

At this, Pollio stood and threw all his oratory skill into a ten-minute speech on Justin's innocence and his religious beliefs but, despite his aptitude, all was lost, and it showed as Marcus yawned twice throughout.

Then, Justin stood for a moment and praised the Lord before stating that he was prepared to die for his belief in the one true God. When he sat down again, there was a moment's silence as everyone absorbed his words. Such bravery, such confidence and such desire to do right by the deity who, he believed, loved him enough to receive him.

Marcus then addressed him: "You have openly preached obedience to the Christian god—Yahweh, and his demigod son, Jesus the Nazarene, who was executed in the reign of Tiberius Caesar. By doing so you have publicly called for an end to the worshipping of the gods of Rome and of the emperors themselves." He paused to let these words sink in among everyone gathered. "And you publicly began a school for Romans to enrol in and to be brainwashed with your blasphemous treason." He sighed with genuine regret at what he was about to say next. "I find you guilty in the entirety and sentence you to death by beheading," he added without any satisfaction. "Your property and possessions shall go to the public treasury and your family shall be sold into slavery."

"My prince, can I suggest that he first be tortured and forced to provide the names of all his so-called students, so that they might also be executed as blasphemers and potential threats to the state?" proposed Rusticus who half got off his seat and bowed.

"Very well, but let there be no further arrests among innocent Christians regarding this claim," Marcus told the court, and the officials wrote down his final decree.

Marcus then departed with his team of blue-cloaked praetorians and when the door was swung open, Rusticus noted that the German guards had been standing just outside listening to everything. Two Praetorians then approached to place Justin in chains so that they could transfer him to the cells at the Capitoline, while Pollio stood, shook his hand and apologised for not being able to save him.

"He targeted my faith," replied Justin. "You could not have defended me any better, dear Pollio. God bless you," he said, standing up and allowing himself to be chained before then being led away.

"You're lucky I didn't pursue your arse too, Pollio," Rusticus looked up and informed the young lawyer.

"Fuck off, you fallen reject," snarled Pollio back at him.

This angered Rusticus considerably, not least because he had never been spoken to by a human like this before. It was also, in essence, a fairly accurate affront, and this burned deep inside him, but he did not take the bait. Instead, he got up and quickly left the court and walked straight out of the building with teeth gritted. His slaves were waiting outside in the Forum at the foot of the steps, soaking up the heat among a long line of litters. Spotting him descending towards them, they immediately hurried and set the litter down before him.

"The Porta Capena," he told them as got on. They were surprised at this, as they half-expected to be taking him home or to eat and drink somewhere, but they proceeded via the Capitoline and across it towards the wall. At the gate, they set him down and he ordered them home and then walked past all the officials again, blowing in a face or two here and there before walking a half mile down the road.

Quite a few people were travelling this way so he stepped into some trees which shadowed the fields to his left and made his way deeper under their canopy. He was about to shapeshift into an eagle and fly south towards the sea when the tree branches began to blow uncontrollably. He suddenly sensed a presence beside him, and quickly turned to see who or what it was.

"That was tantamount to murder," said the beautiful angel standing before him. It was the one who had been in the court earlier, now wearing a hood over his head.

"That is the nature of the contest, brother," replied Rusticus tensely, awaiting any sudden move from his foe.

"Then you murdered another fourteen men for good measure," snarled the angel with deep fury in his eyes, the flames within were evident and spellbinding.

"Yet it was in THEIR court and by THEIR laws that this was achieved," smirked Rusticus, whilst casually shrugging his shoulders.

The angel did not respond, simply remaining there, frowning back at him. Rusticus stared back too, mentally inviting the angel to make a move. If he did so, the victory would be even greater for the dark side. After a moment or two, Rusticus became fed up wasting what valuable time remained. He knew he had three days left to return to Pan's grotto and he intended to enjoy the rest of that time.

He was protected by the rules of the Kertamen, of course, and he would carry on regardless as a consequence. So, without further ado, he shifted into a beautiful eagle and lifted himself upwards, his wings flapping and clipping pine branches as they lifted him up, up and out of the wood. Once clear, he glided upon a cool wind to the south.

The angel standing below observed him flutter out of the canopy but did not pursue. Instead, he walked back out of the wood and onto the road among the many travellers entering the great city of evil.

Chapter Five

Once the game is over, the king and the pawn both go back in the same box.
Italian Proverb

Monty awoke around the back of nine in the morning. The dog was sprawled out beside him and it instinctively began yawning and stretching its legs in anticipation of breakfast.

"Okay, boy, let's get up." He dragged himself up, groaning at the usual stiffness he endured due to not having replaced his mattress for four years. He had bought the current one on eBay for *only* £160 and found it to be luxuriously comfortable initially, but then it had quickly become as stiff as a timber raft, and his joints ached most mornings now. This was part of the ongoing problem with modern society, he knew—too much convenience shopping online.

He stretched as he opened the blinds and groaned somewhat at the process before swaying through to the kitchen where he continued to groan as he bent down for the dog's bowl. He then served up the hound's breakfast, before attempting some home-improvised Tai-Chi, which he found often relieved the stiffness, whilst the kettle boiled.

"It's not old age, son," he told the dog, which was only interested in its cereal. "It's that damn mattress," he groaned as he lifted his leg up to waist height and stretched it.

Feeling a little better, he sat down to a mug of Lavazza and a slice of honeyed brown toast. When he had finished, he chucked on a fleece and some sneakers and took the dog out for a walk across to the Links. He felt safer in daylight for some reason—witnesses and all that jazz; but he kept a sharp eye out for the fox man.

He kept checking his phone as they walked. He was questioning whether or not he could possibly have imagined the previous evening's strange text. He knew deep down that he hadn't, though, and so he scanned the whole western Links suspiciously as they progressed over the road and onto the eastern side.

Despite the cold, the Links were busy with dog walkers and joggers as usual, causing him to somehow feel slightly safer.

Halfway along he bumped into two females with a Jack Russell and a glum-looking rose boxer that was obviously fed up hanging around in this climate as its owner nattered away with her chum. Both women tended to stop everyone, including Monty, for a chat whenever they could, but they really just wanted a good moan about anything and everything to do with the council's management of the Links. Today, it was the council's recent decision to start charging for the uplift of garden waste that had gotten on their wick.

The younger of the two, an ugly hippy type with brown Dr Marten boots, lime-coloured laces and rabbity looking teeth in her late forties, was particularly aggrieved about this. Her name was Sally and she was a roll-up smoker who spent her days watching lifestyle television and trolling MSPs on Facebook. She would often just appear and start chewing the fat about anything with anyone, and Monty had begun to dread her regular "Yoo-hoos" whenever he took the dog out at this time on weekends.

"It'll just result in people dumping garden waste across the city, I tell you," she whined. Monty drew up politely and stood listening and nodding. He would give her the usual two minutes out of polite courtesy, before making his excuses. "I'm thinking of taking the council to court over the unemptied bins here on the Links too," she insisted quite vehemently and pointed over to a bin which was overflowing. "I mean, if we tolerate all this, they'll start charging us for domestic waste and recyclables too." She was not for stopping today.

God spare me from amateur lawyers, groaned Monty to himself, clicking his heels together to stop them from freezing but also to indicate that he would soon be on his way. All three dogs, having greeted and sniffed each other intensely, wanted to get going again too, so Monty simply smiled and agreed with her as he always did. "Well, they need to pay for their trams somehow, Sally," he shrugged with a grin, before moving off again with a friendly wave.

"Catch you later then," she called back as she checked his arse out.

"Not if I see you first, deary."

"Sally?" The boxer dog's owner wanted her chum to return to the chat.

"Huh…?" Sally finally turned around.

Once Monty arrived at the pear orchard beside the old embankment, he let the dog off the lead and played ball with it for a while, receiving a few hellos from passing joggers in the process. He then took a couple of slices of bread from his pocket, broke it up and fed the sparrows which occupied the hedgerows, and that kept their distance before then diving down like World War II Stukas for the crumbs.

Oh, to be a bird.

The walk back to the house was uneventful. He wondered if his stalker would suddenly appear from behind a tree or a bush, as he continued to monitor everything and everyone. He asked himself again, as he had several times since returning from the football yesterday, whether or not he should drop into the police station and brief them on what he had experienced.

Yet, as always, he knew they would just shrug and suggest that he come back once the bloke had actually committed a crime. That was if they didn't question his sanity first. He had once gone into Leith police station to report seeing what he suspected might have been dangerous green powder left around popular dog walking routes. He had informed one tall smirking uniformed officer that he suspected something potentially sinister. The guy had told him that the police had no capability to test the powder and that he was too busy to discuss Monty's concerns further. "Come back if your dog eats it and dies, pal," had been the advice.

Lesson learned.

Outside the house, Monty had a notion to pop out to IKEA and treat himself to a new mattress for Christmas. He could pay for it to be delivered and then hopefully, he would no longer feel like a geriatric on getting out of bed every morning. As he contemplated this, fumbling for his keys, he sensed someone approach to his right and instantly turned to look up.

"Morning, chief. I'm Ronnie Charnley," said a cheerful male voice with an accustomed slow eastern Fife drawl.

Monty located his keys, and then straightened up and faced the man. He was in his late thirties and quite fat in the cuddly Friar Tuck mould, with gingery blond pork chop sideburns and, once he removed his tweed bonnet to offer his hand, Monty saw that his hair was short and fair. "Okay?" Monty shrugged his shoulders, wondering what this was about, as he took his hand and shook it.

"Hello, fella." The guy then bent down and patted the dog before straightening up again.

"What can I do for you?" Monty politely cracked a smile to hide his growing suspicion. The guy was wearing a waxed green country jacket and dark brown cords with expensive tanned leather brogues which appeared to have some grass stains on them.

"Well look, Mr Montgomery, I'm sorry to bother you like this, but I'd be obliged for a minute or two of your time while I try to explain," said Charnley courteously. He seemed genuine and quite humble enough. A friendly oaf type of bloke perhaps, and one who now bowed his head to emphasise how sorry he was for door-stepping Monty.

"Fine, go on," replied Monty as the dog sat down upon the pavement and had a scratch.

"Have you ever heard of Lundin Links in Fife?" asked Charnley.

Monty squinted his eye lids a moment and nodded. "I think…yes, I've driven through on my way to Largo?" he slowly recalled.

Charnley nodded keenly. "That's right, sir. It's a wee village on the coast between Leven and the hometown of Robinson Crusoe—Lower Largo."

Monty nodded, for he remembered having visited the house where Crusoe (aka Alexander Selkirk) had been born on a trip to the beach in Largo as a kid. He now also recalled that the fish and chop shop there had been called "The Man Friday" after another character in the Crusoe book.

"A few yards back from the beach, there's a golf course," explained Charnley. "On that course there stands a former stone circle, very similar to Stonehenge but with only three stones remaining, between thirteen and eighteen feet tall."

This was news to Monty, and he instinctively felt somewhat attracted to the variety of scenarios that Charnley might be leading to now. "Right. I didn't know that, Ronnie," he nodded with a smile, revealing a slight curiosity.

"Do you know anything about Stargates?" asked Charnley.

This took Monty by surprise. For some reason, he had always had an interest but knew truly little about them, other than there might be supernatural doors somewhere, possibly between star systems or even galaxies, that he had either read about somewhere or seen on the History Channel. "Not really," he replied, shifting his weight on to his other leg.

Charnley was about to go on when Monty received a text on his phone. The loud sound of a judge's gavel hitting polished wood was enough to freeze proceedings. "Sorry," Monty said, reaching into his pocket and quickly opening the phone to read the message.

"It's the movie *Stargate* that you are thinking about, Stephen. You can trust Ronnie, and IKEA can wait until tomorrow."

Monty's heart skipped a beat and he almost dropped the phone from his hand as if it were a red-hot stone. He took a breath and quickly calmed himself before re-reading it twice over as Charnley stared at him enquiringly.

Monty finally looked up and searched Charnley's face for any sign of recognition, but all he saw looking back was a confused individual with a slightly concerned expression.

"Everything okay?" asked Charnley.

There was something discharging from him, a strange sense of integrity and honesty which Monty felt but did not quite begin to see. His dopamine sensual receiver was detecting a pure sense of goodness oozing from within this Charnley guy. How Monty was able to identify it was beyond him. People generally don't access their full senses and can only detect a fraction of the discernible range all around them. Man is thus handicapped, unlike other beings. His palate, in particular, is often restricted to the spiciest or bitterest aspects, whilst his perception of scent is eighty-five per cent redundant. Monty was receiving Charnley's odour in full now, however, and his stomach had pleasurable butterflies fluttering around as if it were rejoicing.

It was as natural an experience as a eureka moment born in a mind. The closest Monty had ever come to such a realisation before was perhaps when his nose detected an aroma of garlic being cooked in butter, causing his brain to register that something nice was developing.

"I just got a text from no number, telling me to trust you and mentioning IKEA. Going to IKEA to buy something was a thought only in my head." He shook his head now and then looked at Charnley with a mystified expression.

Charnley nodded. "Yes, I've had that. I can explain further."

"But how does this person know about IKEA?" Monty demanded.

"I don't know that, but I can tell you what I do know." Charnley still appeared concerned at Monty's obvious confusion.

Monty looked around the street and then back over towards the Links for some evidence of a logical explanation. He could feel his heart beating faster. Concern returned now too as the fox-man came back to mind.

"There's been a man with a fox," he said, looking around. "I'll be honest," he sighed and turned back to face Charnley. "I thought he might have been some kind of ghost or something," he confessed, shaking his head and smirking nervously. Charnley remained silent and impassive. "Well, he's been stalking me around Scotland." Monty looked around the street again.

Charnley shook his head now. "Not got a clue who that was." He offered a compassionate smile. "But if I tell you what I do know, we can speculate on it together, Mr Montgomery?" he suggested.

Monty checked his phone again; the text was once again gone. "This is fucking nuts." He shook his head.

"Aye," nodded Charnley softly, looking down at his own shoes in the snow.

"Right—do you want to come in off the street for a cup of tea, then, as the dog's getting cold?" asked Monty.

Charnley looked up with the look of a child being served an ice cream sundae. "Oh, I'd love a brew, Mr Montgomery, if you're offering."

"It's Monty. Call me Monty. Come on then." Monty now unlocked the door and let the dog in before taking his lead off and then ushering the politely hesitant Charnley in behind.

Charnley drank sweet black tea and did not say no to the biscuit tin, helping himself to two Jaffa Cakes and a chocolate digestive.

"Okay, so what's going on here, Ronnie?" Monty patiently asked as he sat down with a coffee and checked his text messages again, but there was nothing new.

"Right, you accept that there's something strange going on then?" Charnley asked politely.

Monty nodded with a mouthful of coffee. "That much is crystal," he finally said. He was relaxed now somehow in this guy's company.

Trust but verify however.

There was certainly a belief that Charnley was a genuinely safe fellow. The dog seemed to trust him too, and for Monty this was a considerable factor.

Charnley helped himself to another Jaffa Cake and dipped it in his cuppa. He mismanaged this, however—due to the milk-less tea being hotter than normal, half of the biscuit ended up floating around until it resembled a Maitake mushroom. After a brief delay wherein he considered whether or not to salvage it whilst scalding his fingers, he duly attempted and failed to retrieve it, burning a finger and thumb in the process.

"Well," he said after giving his fingers a few sporadic blows of air, "I was a van man for Semi-Chem in Fife ten years ago," he said before now helping himself to a Hob-Nob with his unburned hand and dipping it in his tea for a much shorter duration.

Monty nodded, also helping himself to a Hob-Nob and nibbling at it like a rabbit. He knew only too well that if he dipped this king of British cookies into a hot beverage, it would melt the buttery cookie, which he much preferred to have dry, like a cheesecake base.

"I don't drive, never have," Charnley went on between crunches. "I was a happy-go-lucky type of bloke, Monty," he explained cheerily. "An orphan brought up with relatives and mismanaged by unworthy types." He shrugged his shoulders, still cheerily though. "I left home at sixteen, worked in an old folks' home in Pittenweem, where I met Brigette, my wife of twenty-five years," he continued.

"Right."

"Brigette's dad was a resident at the home and so we met there, and two weeks later I moved in with her in St Monans. Been with her ever since. She's twenty years older than me, like, and it looks like I might need to become her carer one day."

"Right, Ron, but about this problem…" Monty, of course, had not wanted to sound rude, but he could see that this guy was doing a Billy Connolly and running from one matter onto another. Monty wasn't sure that Charnley possessed Connolly's ability to double back to the original point though, and nor did he have the patience to find out.

"Sorry, I do get lost," conceded Charnley. "Anyway, I moved on job-wise a couple of years later and became a van guy with Semi-Chem," he said again. "So, this meant that there was me loading and unloading the van with a driver," he explained.

"Right?" Hob-Nob now finished; another mouthful of coffee followed.

"Well, my point is, Monty, that after several years working the same driver, we became quite close and I was really happy with my work, which is rare, you know." Monty placed his mug back on the table and nodded. He couldn't really say the same. "So, it would have taken something amazing to make me give it all up."

"Sure." Monty wondered if Charnley might have been under the thumb at home, and that his daily escape with his driver buddy might be a therapeutic relief for him.

"Well," continued Charnley, "one day I received, right out of the blue, a text similar to what you've been receiving with no number, telling me to apply for a vacancy for a groundsman at the Lundin Links golf course." He said with an astonished expression.

Monty crossed his legs in expectancy, for Charnley was getting to the gist of things now.

"Now, I knew bugger all about golf, Monty. I mean, I'd roamed my local course looking for wayward balls as a kid, but the role wasn't something someone like myself would be considered for, surely?"

Monty didn't want to seem rude, so he half shrugged but remained mum.

"I just ignored it, and like yourself, found that the text then deleted itself somehow. When I got home, Brigette mentioned that she'd seen a vacancy at that same golf club in the local paper and urged me to apply for it," said Charnley. "Now, she knew better than anyone that I knew nothing about golf, Monty, and so I couldn't believe she was urging me on." He shook his head. "It couldn't be a coincidence? Anyway, nothing I said about being totally out of my depth when it came to golf convinced her. We actually ended up having an argument about it. Resulting in two days of me making my own dinner." He continued to shake his head at the recollection.

"So, what was the job?"

"Head groundsman on nineteen and a half thousand per year," he stretched forward to stress. "I was only on thirteen back then as a van guy," he pointed out.

"Okay, so what happened?"

"I filled in an honest application to please her after I'd received another text from Mr no number, which also disappeared after I'd read it," he said. "I mean, I took pains to explain that I had no experience whatsoever with golf or as a groundsman, and yet, lo and behold, I was called to an interview within a couple of days."

"Did you tell your Mrs about the strange texts?"

Charnley scrunched his lip. "Aye, and she didn't believe me, but I did mention it to the three men at the interview."

"And?"

"Nothing. They had the same oblivious attitude as Brigette, which seemed very strange to me, Monty." He waved his finger.

"Of course," agreed Monty. "And then?"

"So, the buggers must have been on drugs, I reckoned at the time, as they only went and gave me the bloody job, didn't they," chuckled Charnley.

"Really?"

"And I'm still there ten years later, while every error I made—some very costly to the club, by the way—was accepted and quickly forgotten about as if it didn't happen." Monty shuffled in his chair. "Two weeks into the job, I received another anonymous text telling me to be at the standing stones on the course at nine that evening."

Monty leaned forward now. "The standing stones?"

"Ancient stones on the golf course, like Stonehenge," replied Charnley.

"Right." Monty had never heard of them.

"It was July and still light enough, so I turned up a few minutes early and had a smoke, as I was quite nervous about who this person was," explained Charnley.

"And what happened?" Monty was impatient.

"It's hard to explain, but everything went strange. It was surreal, like—well, did you ever take hallucinogenic mushrooms as a kid?" Charnley seemed somewhat embarrassed to ask.

Monty had. Once, aged seventeen, at a beach party by Tentsmuir Forest in summer while visiting relatives near Tayport. There had been around fifty people there at the time, some of them his age and some older. There had been a generator providing the music and a large fire around which people were drinking, smoking and pill popping, whilst others danced in the shadows of that great forest. Someone had given him a couple of hundred mushrooms with thin stems and little nipples upon the caps. He had moulded them up in his hands into three little balls and swallowed them with mouthfuls of water.

He was soon running around on his own in the forest for hours, laughing endlessly, until some random female had turned up with cigarettes, and then he and others had watched her wave the lit end of one of them in the darkness, creating a sort of comet trail, for the rest of the bizarre trip.

He now looked at his cup upon the table for a moment and recalled how, afterwards, when the girl and himself had sat on a sand dune looking out at the Tay estuary as the sun began to rise, he had realised that although he was still brilliantly under the magical influence he was no longer tripping in that other magical place where he had just spent the night. He longed to return to it as the sun appeared, and before she had kissed him. "Yes, once upon a time," he nodded at Charnley thoughtfully.

"Right, do you recall how the whole experience seemed like a trip into a different reality of sorts?" Charnley chuckled now that he knew he was not the only one of them to have undergone this alternative voyage into psychedelia.

Monty understood the point here. For at the precise moment that the female, someone named Cornelia maybe, had appeared beside him with the cigarettes, he had laughed and exclaimed loudly to her, "So you're here too?"

"Yes, it provided a logical analysis to the unfathomable mystery of life, for just a brief moment, but then it was lost when the drug wore off," he replied half in jest, half in seriousness. He was unsure which was more appropriate.

"I immediately felt that I was in a different reality." Charnley shrugged his shoulders and looked at Monty for a sign of understanding.

"Without doubt," agreed Monty, thinking back to his surprise at the girl entering his reality at the time.

"There seemed to be a different sensitivity, a completely different consciousness of realism, to what I had previously experienced." Charnley was aware that he could not explain the experience fully to anyone who had not been there too. He had tried again and again to do so to his partner, and always found it impossible.

"Okay, and?" asked Monty.

"And then an angel appeared."

"An angel?" Monty had not seen this coming.

"Yes." Charnley nodded at him.

"How did you know it was an angel?" After all, it was surely possible that Charnley had been hallucinating.

"Because he told me through telepathy, and it was clear to me that he was as he said."

"Riiiigggght," Monty spoke very slowly as he considered this. "Go on," he urged.

Sensing some doubt, Charnley tried to explain, "In that situation, the timeless experience that I was visiting, I could see the truth quite clearly," he said. "As clearly as the colour green on your mug there." He pointed at Monty's Celtic mug.

Monty detected no fraudulence in the man. If anything, he was overcome with a growing sense of trust in him. He had sat down with many a liar in his time as a criminal solicitor, and although it was virtually impossible to determine whether someone was bullshitting him, he liked to think he had a knack for instantly disliking and/or distrusting a bad apple.

"How so?" he asked now.

Charnley shrugged again. "Okay, let me tell you a joke," he urged.

"A joke?" Monty wanted to take a look at his watch now but found that he could not as he was quite riveted by all of this.

"Indulge me?" Another cheery shoulder shrug now from Charnley, who then seized the moment it took for Monty to agree with a smile to take, then drown, another Hob-Nob in his tea. "An Irishman, Englishman and a Scot all turn up at a restaurant for a chef's vacancy," he mumbled with his mouth full. Monty nodded. "The owner shows them a knife, a potato and a lettuce." Monty smiled in eagerness. "He asks them individually which of the three is the odd one out." Charnley continued to demolish the cookie.

"Okay." Monty nodded again.

"The Scot and the Englishman both state that the knife is the odd one out as the other two are vegetables." Charnley grinned at him before giving the Jaffa Cakes the once-over again. "Anyway," he dragged his gaze back to Monty now, "The Irish guy replies that it's the lettuce that's the odd one out because 'you can make chips with the other two'," he smirked. Monty smiled. "But the Irish guy wasn't wrong, Monty."

Monty nodded. "That was just how he saw things," he replied.

"Correct," said Charnley. "Everyone sees something different from the person next to them, even in this reality of ours, but in that precise moment I was in a different mode of sensitivity entirely and I promise you Monty, I knew he was telling me the truth because I could feel it." Monty believed him.

"Okay, Ronnie, but what's this got to do with me?" he asked, still rebelling against his instincts.

"They've asked me to ask you to return with me to meet someone," revealed Charnley now.

"Eh, what? Where and who are they?"

"At the stones, Monty," persisted Charnley.

"At Lundin Links?" Monty was a little concerned now. He did not understand why, it was perhaps all too surreal.

"The stones are a stargate," Charnley then revealed.

"What?"

"Aye, turns out that was why I was given the job; they made it all happen so that I could be the secret gatekeeper," he explained.

"Gatekeeper?" Monty did not know what to make of all of this.

"Look—I'm a good man, Monty. I don't steal, gossip or want to be something that I'm not." Charnley seemed genuinely uncomfortable with self-praise. "I wasn't very religious, but I knew the difference between right and wrong and was quick to show compassion and forgiveness," he went on. "I also went out of my way to feed my animal neighbours and to help them as best I could. But more importantly, they said I had a connection to the earth because I liked to plant and sow things as well as my habit of picking up bits of plastic from anywhere."

"They?" Monty repeated the question despite knowing that Charnley was referring to angels.

"The angels," confirmed Charnley.

"Have you met a few?"

"No, just that one, but they text me, just as they did you."

"Was that person following me with the fox, and at the football yesterday, an angel then?" Monty already knew the answer.

"Haven't got a clue. All I know is that I received a text instructing me to tell you to come, and that you're not to be scared," shrugged Charnley again.

Monty still wasn't sure about all of this. What if this was a demon thing and not an angelic one? "What's your role as the gatekeeper then?" he asked.

"I can't really go into that, other than to say that it's a ritualistic process and something involving nature that I must see to twice a year in order to maintain the power field around the hidden gate," explained Charnley.

"So, have other things come through this gate, then?"

"I believe so, Monty, but I haven't seen anything since my first experience with the angel."

"How do you know it's not a devil or something else manipulating you?" asked Monty.

"I'd thought a bit about that at the beginning, Monty, yes. I read that the devil had apparently shown Christ certain things and tried to mislead him too, so yes, of course I thought about whether or not I was also being bullshitted." Charnley looked down at the oak pattern on the table as he recalled his initial reservations.

"It's a fair question to ask yourself," shrugged Monty.

"But then I was shown enough to convince me otherwise, Monty, and that was the end of that," Charnley assured him firmly.

"Such as?" Monty was gasping to know but he concealed it well.

"Can't say, Monty. But I know, I just know."

"Did you go through this gate thing, Ron?"

"No—well, I can't say…but it's not like that." Charnley shook his head now as if to a child who was enquiring about a bucket of gold at the end of a rainbow. "Some angels have movable portals, I think. The static gates are old-school doorways to different places. It's too hard to explain, Monty, but no, I didn't need to travel through the stargate that I maintain. Any road, if it were the other side that was involved, they wouldn't get someone like me to do their dirty work; they would honour one of their own human disciples." Charnley shook his head convincingly.

"Perhaps they would take a perverse pleasure in having a good bloke polish their crockery?" shrugged Monty again, still fighting the urge to fully trust Charnley.

"In that case, why am I not required to commit sins, then, and encouraged only to be forgiving and decent towards people?" asked Charnley. Monty had no swift answer to that one. "No, Monty, like I say, I just know. Look you have nought to fear. If a bad entity wanted to harm you, it would do so now in your house, mate, and there would be no need to bullshit you into travelling to the stones," Charnley assured him. There was silence between them for a moment as they both thought about things and finished off their cuppas.

"Can you tell me anything else about these beings, or even the stones? You're asking me to trust a stranger who I've only just met, to take me to go and await the arrival of an angel, or god knows what, at an ancient portal?" Monty smirked at the lunacy of it all.

"I can't really, Monty, I'm not permitted to reveal the things I've experienced or been shown, but I can say that I've been blessed with happiness, and several times good things have happened to me and mine." Charnley seemed at pains to assure him. "I still have my job, my health and hopefully a future beyond this world," he surmised. Monty raised an eyebrow at this, and he considered things a moment before Charnley spoke again. "The stones themselves are located virtually at the foot of what they call a mountain, but what you and I would refer to today as a hill."

"So, you've had conversations with them in English?" asked Monty.

"Yes—well, no," Charnley smirked as he realised that he had been conned into answering the question. "It's just that I can understand. Let's leave it at that." He continued to grin warmly, and Monty could still feel the goodness pouring out of the guy. "And at the sea, only a stone's throw away, there are clear solar and lunar associations in the original design of the stones," explained Charnley. "Why don't you have a look online?" He now gestured towards Monty's tablet on the kitchen worktop.

Monty reckoned this was a good idea and was in the process of doing so when he noted the dog resting his head on Charnley's knee. This was rare, he considered as he turned the thing on. He soon found a quote from an archaeo-astronomer—an Alexander Thom, who apparently visited the stones in the 1970s and found them to hold cosmological significance.

It was clearly an important site, so placed on flat ground that there was plenty of room for geometrical extrapolation. The alignment is seen to indicate the setting point of the Moon at the minor standstill. Trees and houses now block the view, but as the new large-scale OS maps are now available it is possible to construct a reasonably accurate profile of Cormie Hill. In good visibility, a large tumulus could have been seen on the Moon's disc, and the tumulus shown on the Ordnance Survey happens to indicate the upper limb when the declination was (ε-ι-Δ). When the Moon set on Cormie Hill, it rose on the Bass Rock, and was (ε-ι). We see how the stones were so placed that the lower limb just grazed the Rock when the declination is...

"Sounds creepy to me, Ron," said Monty, stopping and turning to Charnley, but before Charnley had a chance to respond, Monty raised his index finger to his lips and bid him to hush as he picked up his mobile phone and searched, found and then quickly called the Lundin Links golf club.

"Hello. Lundin Links Golf Club?" Answered a cheery person on the other end.

"Hi there, can I speak to a Ronnie Charnley—groundsman?" asked Monty.

"Mr Charnley is on his day off today...may I ask who..." Click, brrrrrrrrr. Monty hung up. He had withheld his number. He then searched, found and rang the Lundin Links police station, giving Charnley a wink for his patience.

"Hello, Lundin Links Police Station, Sergeant Coutts speaking," said an older male voice.

"Ah, hello there, this is Ralf Roberts from the Procurator Fiscal's office in Edinburgh."

"Uh huh. I mean, yes, sir." The cop sounded like he had just shat himself.

"I'm doing a check on a potential jury member. May I ask you if you've heard of a Ronnie Charnley, by any chance?" Monty was gambling on the small-town local bobby giving away any hint that Charnley was a known villain, if indeed he was known as such, rather than doing the right thing and verifying whether he was actually truly speaking to a fiscal on the other end of the line.

"Eh, well, yes, he is the green keeper at the local golf club, sir, and a good man," Coutts let out before he commenced considering passing the phone over to his inspector in the next room.

"I see. Thank you." Monty quickly hung up again.

"Who was that?" Charnley asked.

"Lundin Links plod."

"That will be Coutsy. He's a right wanker who'd shag his auntie if he got a chance," sighed Charnley.

"He gave you a reference," smirked Monty.

"He's honest enough." Charnley winked back at him.

"Yep."

But obviously not the brightest.

The two of them then stared at each other a brief moment.

"And if I do go with you over to Fife," sighed Monty with raised eyebrows, "how do I know that something isn't going to happen to me? Such as me being dragged through this bloody gate of yours, hmm?"

"Oh, don't even think that, Monty, please," urged Charnley who was clearly offended at the notion. "Like I said, pal, if the dark hoard wanted to do anything like that, they'd just do it here and now. I think that guy with the fox that you encountered might have been an angel, but perhaps he was called away or was unable to persuade you? So, now they're determined to communicate with you this way," he suggested.

"It's still hard to accept all this though, Ronnie," Monty spoke honestly. "I mean, why me? What interest can I be to these...these angels?"

"Why not?" Charnley seemed genuinely confused.

"Well, I'm not even religious, nor am I a particularly interesting or useful person." Monty considered himself to be somewhat miscast for all this. "I mean, I'm just a struggling lawyer without a wife, and with a kid I don't see and a shitload of criminals who I lie in court about in order to win them their liberty so that they can reoffend."

"Was David not a shepherd's son? And was Peter not a fisherman?" Charnley looked at him as a father might a son and Monty was again encouraged by the genuine goodness which continued to radiate from this guy's presence. He knew enough about Christianity to know who David and Peter were. One of them had been required to lead the flock whilst the other one had been sent to fish for men. Even so, Monty was unsure as to why anything as grand as an angel would seek anything from him. He was not even a QC, nor was he ever likely to be a judge or even a lawyer with any influence. He could not fight, had been useless in relationships, and spent the majority of his life arguing for a living, so why him?

"You must instinctively sense whether this is or is not the right thing to do," Charnley then told him.

He was right; Monty did feel drawn to making the journey to Fife regardless, and he instinctively felt that Charnley at least meant him no harm. Of course, he had reservations, and the obvious fact that this was all very mysterious provoked fear in him of the unknown. Yet, perhaps due to the whole drama with the fox-man, he felt a strange pull towards further exploration of this matter.

Charnley was spot-on about that at least. It would not be clever to decline and then forever be keeping an eye out instead for the fox-man, who could read minds and turn up anywhere willy-nilly. Plus, he knew only too well that not knowing the facts would drive him nuts for years. Besides, if there was any trouble, he could probably deal with Charnley, and if there were any nasty entities intent on doing him any harm, Charnley was right, they would do it anyway no matter where he was. No, he should go and face this, he reasoned.

"To attend to this request would be an example of faith, Monty, believe it or not, and there's nothing more loved than faith, you know," offered Charnley.

There were a few more moments of silence between them as Monty went over it all again in his mind, and of course found no convincing case for not going, other than a nervous apprehension which was fused in part by tension.

"It's not faith, Ron, more curiosity," he eventually said. He picked up his phone again and proceeded to text his sister: "Hi, don't ask or text back, but I'm heading to a golf course in Lundin Links at Fife. To some strange standing stones with a stranger named Ronnie Charnley who works at the golf course there, and to meet a potential new client. If I don't call you in four hours, call the police in

Edinburgh, not Fife (they will contact Fife police and keep them on their toes) and tell them about this text and that I might be in trouble. Thanks sis."

He then turned his phone off to avoid the guaranteed call she would be trying to make, and coolly eyeballed Charnley for a second or two. "I'm a black belt at karate," he felt obliged to lie.

Charnley shrugged and shook his head in mock confusion. "You won't need that to batter me if you feel the need to, mate, I assure you." He smiled again.

"Right then, I take it I'm driving my car over?" asked Monty finally as he considered looking out an old baseball bat that he had picked up on holiday years previously but knew he would never find it without turning the place inside out.

"That would be good Monty, aye, as I got three buses here. Mind if I have another Jaffa Cake first?"

Chapter Six

The distinction between past, present and future is only a stubbornly persistent illusion.
Albert Einstein

The drive over to Fife was unhindered by the usual traffic tail-back, possibly because so many people were busy with late Christmas preparations. So they made good time, and once they had crossed over the Forth Bridge, Monty asked Charnley for as much intel as possible on his personal experiences with these stargate visitors.

Charnley initially remained evasive, and as they headed eastward towards Kirkcaldy Monty suspected that his otherwise cheery passenger had been given instructions not to discuss the subject. He decided to press him regardless, and to his relief, Charnley did go a little bit into his take on the meaning of it all.

"I look mainly to scripture for guidance myself, Monty, and I reckon that there's some sort of heavenly dispute going on," he said, arms folded and resting upon his belly.

"Over what, though?"

"Over us." Charnley nodded his head slowly as if to convince himself of this theory too. "I suspect that there are portals all over the planet that contain, or keep out, various entities, both good and bad," he explained.

Monty said nothing but was all ears as they cruised along past the old mining towns of Cowdenbeath and Lochgelly. He had been to Cowdenbeath once before when he was a kid with his father, to witness the Celtic scrape a victory in the old League Cup. Charlie Nicholas had come on as a late sub that day and poached a goal to see them through, but Monty never forgot the scare the Fifers had given them at the old stock car racing ground.

Even as late as the 1980s, the town itself had retained a pre-war vibe, he recalled. Men in bonnets, shops selling boiled sour plums and tackety boots; it had all seemed like another world to him. Then there had been his experience after the match when they had queued in a fish and chip shop that had wartime posters on the walls for Bisto gravy and cocoa. The place had looked as if Ronnie Barker or David Jason should have been serving in it[46]. Another thing he would never forget about that visit was that the old chippy had offered its customers red puddings, which was quite different to Edinburgh where fish and chip shops sold only black, white, and haggis puddings.

Charnley went on now, despite seeming a tad uncomfortable: "Some of these portals provide access for angels to enter this world, whilst others are for—who knows what? My own experiences are purely of goodness though, and, as I said, angels."

"We hope," said Monty with a growing fear that he gulped down as they got nearer.

Charnley gazed at him warmly with a cheeky smile. "It'll all be well, don't worry."

"So, is heaven on the other side of this portal then, or as you say, other dimensions?" Monty pressed him regardless.

I can't believe I'm actually having this conversation.

"As I keep saying, so much more than that, and I still don't have an inkling myself, really."

"Yet you're convinced about the angel stuff, aren't you?"

"A hundred per cent convinced. I've seen God's love as well as receiving his communications, Monty."

"Such as?" Monty turned left onto the Leven Road as they reached Kirkcaldy but had to slow down for an articulated Tesco lorry that was reversing in order to deliver to a local store.

"Such as my prayers being answered and interventions on my behalf time and again," assured Charnley who certainly looked as if he believed what he was saying.

"Lucky you," replied Monty sarcastically. Like many other people in need, he had tried prayer in the past and hit the proverbial brick wall every time.

"Maybe it didn't go the way you wanted for a reason?" suggested Charnley, reading his thoughts. It was, after all, the most common complaint from atheists who lived their lives without the friendship of God, but who still tended to turn to him when they urgently wanted him to do something for them.

---

[46] Two British actors who played a shopkeeper and his nephew in the BBC classic, *Open All Hours*.

"I'd like to know what that might be?" Monty thought aloud as the lorry finally got out of their way and he was able to put his foot down again.

"I'm sure you can ask whoever they send to talk with you today, mate, and get some answers." Charnley gave him a small yet unexpectedly comforting pat on the shoulder now.

There was silence between them for what seemed like an ominously long time. Both men fell into their thoughts about things and speculated on what was likely to develop. The countryside was opening up ahead of them like a thick white cover of snow patches sewn together with old stone walls and the occasional woodland or cottage. They could have been in rural France. The farmhouses in snow-covered fields on either side of them along the rural road were offering free-range eggs, festive trees and logs for sale on home-made signs.

Monty remembered a childhood holiday to Burgundy. It had been during a warm summer, but the landscape was not too dissimilar to this. He missed those days very much now that he was alone; any pleasure he had felt at this nostalgic scenery soon faded however and gave way to the loneliness he frequently felt at this time of year. He had never really thought much about God or religion throughout his life, apart from when he had been questioning him over his parents' death.

He now brushed his fingers slowly back through his hair and sighed; he knew he needed a haircut. He thought of all the families enjoying passed-down festive traditions and felt a slight twang of regret that he was not picking up a nice noble fir tree himself that he could dress with his kid beside a glowing fireplace, whilst the smell of cookies being baked in a kitchen filled their nostrils. He had often been encouraged to leave a carrot and a glass of milk out on the doorstep when he had been a kid on Christmas Eve.

His parents had allowed him to open one present on Christmas Eve, and that tradition had remained for a while. No matter how moody or stubborn he had been as an adolescent, he had still been excited by that tradition until his parents had died. On Christmas mornings at church, which Monty usually found uninteresting and dull, all the kids would receive a present from the church upon departure, handed out by choirboys. Because of this, Christmas Day had been the only day in his life that he had cared for the church or God.

He had stopped attending church at the age of eleven when has father had jacked it in. It was probably fair to say that religion had faded at that point in his life. His mother and sister had continued to attend regularly though. Then, after the death of his parents, he had been angry. He'd blamed God for everything and often told him where to go. From then on, he had decided that self-preservation would be prioritised and God, if he existed, could do one.

There were only a couple of other cars passing in the opposite direction while the falling snow increased as they progressed onward. A tractor appeared from a lane bearing a sign which read "The Convent of Poor Clares" before cutting off along a little hedge rowed track that appeared to lead up a little brae towards a large farmhouse. Monty slowed to let it pass and noted the smile the female driver gave him in appreciation.

"A random smile can be considered a form of charity too," mused Charnley who had also noted it.

Monty did not respond. One thing he was sure of was that he had remained a righteous man at least most of his life, though he knew it could also be argued that he made a living from crime, and was thus perhaps even evil? But he had rarely wronged anyone, and reminded himself now that he had been quite happy running his life with a certain morality, the lines of which he had drawn up himself, rather than any so-called entity who allowed cancer to flourish, and evil bastards to wage wars with bombs on kids. He detected a whiff of resentment building up now, so he put the foot down harder despite the snow.

Off to meet my maker, am I?

He had always been naturally compassionate and, he liked to think, fairly honest with others. He gave buskers something if he had it, as well as homeless people. He loved animals and hated crime in general, which was why he practised law. Was he, in part, righteous? He would never dare to presume so, he had after all shagged more than his fair share of women. Yet despite this fear he was experiencing, there was now also a growing sense of belief in something.

A recognition of his high standards?

Maybe he subconsciously sensed from time to time that he was being observed by something up high, which possibly might be an example of faith. Hence he did what he perceived to be moral as a consequence? He preferred not to investigate these thoughts, however; it was far easier to ignore the instincts, and just put it all down to a sense of human integrity instead.

He was not sure what he had gotten himself into here, though; not entirely convinced that Charnley wasn't being misled, or that angels, God, or the like, were going to appear from some fancy doorway and enlighten him now. Nor was he persuaded that nothing horrible might occur. Therefore, he was nervous and becoming rather scared. Scared in that bizarre, magical way, the way a child experiences fear when being driven to its first day at school—when the magical butterflies dance around the tummy and that crazy blend of nervousness and excitement combine.

Back when he had been a student, coping with the sudden death of his folks, he had tried praying again. Praying for relief from his sadness and the daily pain he was secretly enduring. This had, of course, failed, and he had questioned God many times thereafter. How can you claim to love me, yet put me through all this whilst I am in the middle of a degree? How can you create the earth and the sea, yet not have the power to help my parents? What kind of God are you? Didn't you want to help them? What's your game? Do you enjoy playing with my emotions?

After he had dragged himself through university, all he had to go on regarding the existence of God had been his education and experiences, and he did not have much credibility in those areas. What was new here was that he was being pressed to rely on his instinct, as opposed to faith, and this was something else entirely, he considered.

The fact he had experienced the appearance of some kind of paranormal goings-on over the last couple of days had obviously moved the goalposts slightly and was perhaps why he was unsure now. Did he instinctively want to believe? He could not say. Regardless, he knew he needed to deal with this shit, and find out what the hell was going on, one way or another.

"You see, I reckon we're probably in the middle of a really important point of this game of cards, Monty." Charnley spoke up quite calmly and bang on cue, pulling Monty out of his musings. He unconsciously slowed down now and took it easier on the increasingly twisting road, his tyres cutting through more and more icy slush in the process. "End times, some folk call it."

"Not sure I believe in all that crap, Ron," replied Monty, still resisting.

"Think about it, mate," urged Charnley. "How else can we explain all the insanity that's going on in the world? Libya, Egypt, Syria, North Korea, Yemen and Ukraine? The list goes on."

Monty shook his head as he had difficulty with this argument: "Go back to the eighties and you had the Falklands, South America, Afghanistan, North Korea, Grenada and most importantly, the Cold War," he pointed out.

"That wasn't as insane as the current madness, Monty; this also involves Syria where all the big players are getting involved, including Israel and Iran, mate," replied Charnley.

"So?"

"Well, Syria is geographically important when you consider any references to the end times within scripture," reasoned Charnley.

"There's been conflict there for decades, Ron, remember the Six-day War?" Monty pointed out and shook his head pessimistically.

"But now people are rude, common manners are dying, and compassion is about as common as a red squirrel," argued Charnley insistently, before despondently adding, "We're lazy, and we pursue social media adoration more than we do morals or, dare I say it, any of the Ten Commandments. Not to mention child abuse cults who operate within the highest levels of society. Do we need any more pointers, mate?"

"Those cults were always around, Ron."

"There's a rise of open Satanism within the movie and music industries too, as well as a leaning towards the elite establishing control over our food chain and the regulation of medicine. These issues should be ringing alarm bells for us." Charnley shook his head now to disagree with any personal doubts he himself harboured.

Monty felt the man's conviction, and in a sense, it lifted and excited him further. Could there really be a God, the God of the Hebrews and creator of both good and bad angels? Charnley certainly seemed convinced, but was that in itself convincing?

"Then there's food. Everything is smaller, less chocolate, fewer prawns and everything tastes shit!"

Monty laughed and nodded, for this was certainly a fact of living in austerity thanks to the Labour Party's wars and overspending policies. "What's the size of a chocolate biscuit got to do with the end times, Ronnie?" he asked as they took a sweeping bend down onto the costal road which runs east along the Firth of Forth.

"All part of a miserable time," scoffed Charnley. "Then there's parking, the cost of fuel, and the mind-numbing traffic congestion due to over-population and the lazy management of local authorities, not to mention there being no trade or industry left today for young people, who are all running around in hoodies with their social media tools in hand."

"And that's all evidence that we are living in the end times?"

"It's evidence of unhappiness and strife, mate. Life was good ten or twenty years ago," replied Charnley.

"Well, a lot of things have gone downhill; I'd agree with you there."

"Tsunamis, birds falling from the sky, bees under siege, foxes and badgers forced to live in the cities and towns where they're often run over for fun by wannabe murderers, polar bears, dolphins, whales, elephants and rhinos being murdered and brought to the brink of extinction?" he exclaimed with hands stretched out to emphasise the point.

Monty had no answer to any of this; these things were all a disgrace.

"Then there are the rain forests and global warming, and of course, who can forget our special curse upon the planet—plastic!" Charnley hissed contemptuously.

A better point.

Yet none of this proved that we were created by a supernatural intelligent entity or that the Old and New Testaments were factual guidelines to the said being. Ironically, however, it was for the reasons that Charnley argued that some people held on to a tiny particle of optimism about the existence of a moral and forgiving God who might rescue humanity before it destroyed the earth.

"Let's have some music or something," suggested Monty, switching on the car radio. Richard Ashcroft was singing his epic and captivating "Check the Meaning" with its warming horns, funky instrumentals and dark strings. Monty discretely turned it up on his steering wheel button:

And when the city sleeps we go walking
We find a hole in the sky and then we start talking
And then we say "Jesus Christ, Jesus Christ,
Jesus Christ, Buy us some time, buy us some time
Hear what I'm saying
Can you hear what I'm saying?"

Monty and Charnley exchanged a quick glance at one and other before they both smirked and looked back out at the road without a word exchanged. The soulful electric piano combined with those deeply moving horns as the snow landed upon the window but unfortunately, the song was reaching its end and so, rather than listen to adverts, Monty changed the station.

The SLP leader, the fascist Colin Anderson-Forbes, was talking now: he was being interviewed outside the Rotunda Casino by the Clyde in Glasgow. He was banging on about some poor Labour MP who had done something or other that perhaps she should not have done.

"So, are you saying that Miss Hill should stand down as the Labour candidate for Glasgow West?" asked the female interviewer.

"Absolutely. The people of Scotland are going into this general election with a requirement of faith in the candidates who are asking for their votes. If Miss Hill, in her previous life as a single mother, lied to the benefit agency about the flatmates living in her then home, regardless of how many years ago this was, then yes, this was dishonest and fraudulent and she must resign both as a candidate and as an MSP," stated Forbes disapprovingly.

"Even if she were to repay any monies and even though she has since done a good job as an MSP in her later life?"

"Well, look, it's a criminal offence to commit benefit fraud and frankly, if an election candidate is found to have done so, then they're not fit to stand for parliament regardless of whether or not they can do a good job, because they'll also have been deemed to have covered up a criminal offence." Forbes allowed a dramatic pause for this to sink in with the listeners before continuing: "Only last week she denied it all again, so if it turns out that she was lying to her constituents, that clearly shows a lack of desire to atone as well as a lack of judgement and honesty," the eloquently spoken Forbes pointed out.

"So, little festive goodwill from your party to Labour then?" teased the interviewer. Forbes remained silent. "What would you say to those who are calling for leniency and for Jo Hill to remain in office regardless of whether or not she fibbed when she was a teenager?" the interviewer pressed him.

"Bah humbug!" replied Forbes, and Monty could almost see the man's smirk. For he hated him and everything that his party represented. He began fiddling now with the radio knob, trying to find a tune, but there were only male singers who sounded as if they wanted to be female vocalists, so he gave up and turned it off.

Maybe Charnley had a point; all the music these days seemed to be crap too, with a general lack of guitar, sax, piano and lyrical talent. In three hundred years from now, will the historians of the future look back and regard "Star Trekkin'[47]" in the way Mozart is acknowledged today? He considered this with a silent chuckle.

"And the rise of that Nazi bastard here in Scotland," groaned Charnley now, who was gazing out of his window at a hilly, snow-covered field where a few Clydesdale horses huddled together in their winter coats, their distinct white markings almost camouflaged in the snow flurry.

"Who will you vote for in the summer then, Ron?" asked Monty, though he guessed it would be the Scottish National Party.

"The Greens, probably," replied Charnley. "I used to be a Labour man, but they're just a joke whenever they get into power, whether it be in London or Edinburgh." He turned and sighed with disappointment.

Monty had always voted Liberal Democrat, but for too long now the party in Scotland had employed a mouse with no presence as its leader. No other party interested him these days, so he tried to keep away from politics. However, much to his annoyance, the recent referendum and now this pending general election had often dragged him into sporadic natters on the subject. "Maybe you're right about the bloody end times then, Ron," he sighed.

"I am mate, I am." Charnley patted him again on the shoulder.

They pressed on along a long winding country road that curved and dipped regularly. Again, Monty found himself admiring this organic shire, despite his apprehension at what lay beyond. The scenery now seemed to him like something straight out of a James Herriot novel. The foliage and hedgerows, all covered in frosty glitter, emphasised the season along both sides of the road. He suspected that there would be a warm fire going in a Herriot-themed pub somewhere nearby, no doubt serving soup and crusty bread. Perhaps though, this was no more than the proverbial city slicker's notion of a drive in the sticks?

They soon entered into the pretty little village of Lundin Links, and Monty impulsively touched his phone in his front trouser pocket with his right hand. He could turn it on at any moment, he reminded himself. There were lawyers in that phone, one or two police officers and two or three gangsters who all liked to think that he was their buddy. There was help on standby, he assured himself as the butterflies kicked off again.

---

[47] "Star Trekkin'", performed by The Firm. The song was written by John O'Connor, Grahame Lister and Rory Kehoe, as a tribute to Star Trek. It was released in 1987 and went on to become a UK number one hit.

On their left they passed a line of detached homes with driveways before Charnley told him to turn right into the golf course car park, located next to a complex links landscape with open burns and strategically placed bunkers along it. There was an impressive long sandy beach running to the south of the course with frosty grey views out to the river Forth and the East Lothian coastline beyond.

There were no other vehicles in the carpark, though the clubhouse lights were on. Monty realised the snowy ground had probably put all the golfers off. When he got out of the car, the bitter sea air hit him like a slap on the face. The gulls shrieking above were headed inland to freshwater burns and streams where potential lunch was to be had.

"There'll be a few folks around for a festive drink later and the place will get busier," Charnley said as he urged Monty to follow him out onto the fairway.

They walked across the course for a few minutes, their feet crunching on the thin snow, and the salty air chilling their lungs. They then headed across and onto the ladies' course, at which point, with only woodland and fields off in the direction of a nearby hill, the stones suddenly appeared before them like giants. There were only three of them left now; one was around eighteen feet high and all of them appeared strangely shaped and placed. It was obvious that there had been more here once and that they had all been part of a circle. Monty noticed the markings on the natural stone bases as they approached.

"Impressive, aren't they?" Charnley asked in between deep icy breaths, whilst rubbing his hands together in a pointless attempt to generate heat.

"Indeed," gasped Monty with Stonehenge in mind, his breath sweeping out before him like cigarette smoke.

As they arrived and took a close-up look, Monty noted that the stones were covered in greenish grey moss like barnacles and that there were no other footprints upon the snow around them. They were alone and so he gazed back the way they had come, and saw that there was no view back to, or from, the clubhouse either.

"Look there, see that?" Urged by Charnley, Monty looked over and could see that there appeared to be a smooth curving dip upon the summit of a large hill around a mile away to the north which gave the impression of a large green arse sticking out. "See how we're aligned directly to that dip at the hill summit..." he said, still pointing at the dipped channel which resembled a hilly buttock, before he then turned, "...then beyond to the sea," he grinned as he pointed south towards the Forth, "and then over to the Bass Rock."

Monty could see the alignment for sure, and guessed it would be linked by sunlight at a certain time of the day or year. Yet he wondered more now about where the other stones had gone, and—more pressingly—what was going to happen next?

"This was a circle once," said Charnley. "A tomb was found here a long time ago but it was believed that later, Vikings settled around here and pulled most of the stones down." Stamping his feet on the ground to prevent his toes from freezing, Monty studied the alignment again. He listened and tried to concentrate as Charnley continued the lecture. "Though I have it from a reliable source that prior to that, Roman marines based at Cramond in Edinburgh in the reign of Septimius Severus[48] navigated around the east coast and landed here, where they engaged in a fierce battle with a Pictish tribe." Charnley winked and tapped his nose knowingly.

"Is that what the angels showed you?" asked Monty, but Charnley moved on now, grinning as he did so.

"After the Romans defeated the Picts here, they destroyed most of the site, as they believed it had been built as a shrine to the Picts' gods," he revealed.

"Okay," Monty nodded as he saw that it was not far, perhaps a four-minute walk back to the beach, so the Romans would have possibly been able to surprise the natives.

"They dragged, then sank, most of the stones in the sea and burned whatever wooden structures were here at the time. Severus then mysteriously fell ill and died soon afterwards," he added ominously.

Monty could now clearly see that Charnley was no simple van driver's boy; that was for sure. The guy was clearly not academically educated, but he knew his stuff and could talk about it in great detail. This raised the question: had the angels shown him such things?

---

[48] The Libyan-born Roman Emperor Septimius Severus arrived in Britain in AD 208 and proceeded to strengthen Hadrian's Wall before pressing into Scotland, where he re-garrisoned abandoned Roman forts at Cramond on the River Forth and at Carpow on the River Tay. His conflicts with the Maeatae Caledonian tribes were supported by thousands of soldiers, sappers, and craftsmen, as well as by a strong naval fleet and maritime supply line, which ran south to the Roman town of Eboracum (modern-day York).

"So, what happens now then, Ron?" he asked, clicking his heels together and wishing he had brought his gloves.

"I expect there'll either be a message coming through to one of us, or someone will come through the portal," replied Charnley, with a look that suggested pure guesswork.

"Well, I'm not hanging about here as—"

And then, BOOM…it was as if a room full of gas had just been ignited. Instead of fire though, there was an engulfing of something else entirely. Something extra-dimensional and non-threatening. Monty was lifted up by some sort of relaxing force which felt like an invisible current. He could feel his chest, ears and throat pop as he floated on his back in the centre of the circle some four feet from the ground.

"Help! Ronnie, help me please!" he tried to scream but found that he could not.

"You will do as you are instructed," he heard a firm male voice say in his head, and he knew that it was not his own, nor was it Charnley's for that matter.

He was then carried away and passed over.

Charnley, who had fallen to his knees at the precise moment that the warm bubble of whatever it was had swallowed up the area surrounding the stones, now looked up towards the circle. Monty was gone, and the snow was melting within the circle zone as if a car with a running engine had been sitting there.

Suddenly, his phone message alert beeped and he fumbled about for a second or two before finding the bloody thing, then fumbled further and dropped it in the snow twice before finally opening it with frozen fingers. It was from nobody, again.

Wait back in the clubhouse for him, he will not be long. Then you may go home, it read.

As soon as he read it, he stood up. Some snow stuck to his knees and shins, so he brushed it off and attempted to reread the message, but he found it had vanished without a trace. He took a second to look around him and then directly back at the circle. There was no sign of anyone. Some jackdaws flew low at chest height across the fairway towards some nearby woodland, but that was the only sign of life. He could hear some crows perched high in the woods observing him. He then turned and headed back towards the car park.

Monty saw everything he had been thinking about throughout his youth and adolescence, and he saw everything that those around him in those times had thought and said about him. All these sensations and all the information came to him simultaneously. Then he saw everything he thought and believed in now, as a man, from his politics, his football team, his favourite food, drink, music and even preferences in women. In other words, he saw everything about himself both now and before, instantaneously.

This made magic mushrooms seem like a walk in the park.

There seemed to be no sequence of time. There was no need for an emotional concentration now, though his sensitivity was thumping, and his body consciousness was outstandingly brilliant and quite beyond his human comprehension. He realised that he had hitherto been comprehending reality not as it is, but as it had been prior to now. He then seemed to travel in this moment, to a cold, hard place and his shoes clicked as they touched a polished marble foundation.

"Wow!" he gasped, as he realised that he was standing in what appeared to be some sort of fancy building. There were several paintings across the four small walls of the whitewashed room he now found himself in, and there was a large glass display of sculptures and busts before him. He was momentarily stunned, of course. His body shell throbbed pleasurably, and he soon realised that the lights on the ceiling were bright. Maybe this was an art gallery? There also appeared to be exit signs and a "No Smoking" notice in what he thought might be Russian, but he could not be sure.

"You're right enough, Stephen," came a friendly voice from behind him. He instantly turned around. He had done his best to remain prepared for anything. His anticipation of the possibility of anything at all developing had helped him to keep as calm as possible at the vital moment.

He now saw before him a tall, handsome man with short curly hair and deeply beautiful green eyes. He looked somewhat Greek in origin and was dressed in a creamy, almondy-coloured cotton shirt without buttons and similar baggy trousers. On his feet were brown slippers and he was wearing two watches on both of his wrists.

Monty did not step back, though he knew not why. He seemed to control his fears and simply stood staring back at this person.

"This is a museum in Moscow," said the man with an endearing smile. Monty felt a natural comfort and trust towards him, as if he was in the presence of an old friend or sibling—a kind of faith reserved only for those he was sure really cared about him.

"And you?" he asked him, very faintly.

"My name is irrelevant to you. I am an angel of the Lord your God, and I am of the choir of Powers," replied the angel.

"Okay," replied Monty very slowly, not knowing what the choir of Powers was or what it represented. Then, at that same moment, he noted a reference being stamped into his internal memory corridor: "Ephesians: 6.12." A lightbulb moment, which he knew he would never forget. He would investigate this further when, or perhaps if, he returned to the other place from whence he had come.

"We are a particular type of angelic choir, one whose presence you should consider yourself most privileged to be in," smiled the angel.

Monty said nothing. He believed that all of this was really happening, but a small niggling voice in his ear was generating a little doubt about whether or not it was some sort of manipulation.

"Are you going to continue listening to him?" asked the angel, still smiling as he now casually leaned upon a four-foot Doric column with a bust of someone resting upon it.

"Who?" asked Monty.

"You know who that is whispering doubts in your ear, don't you?" asked the angel. Monty shrugged. He took a quick glance around the place again; it was definitely a museum. "Will you trust me, Stephen, and stop listening to him?" the angel asked telepathically, and Monty now realised that this was the voice he had first heard back at the stones.

"You mean it's the devil whispering doubts in my ear?" Monty asked him vocally.

The angel laughed, and it was instantly infectious, so Monty laughed with him. The angel then stepped forwards and placed his hand upon Monty's left shoulder. "He doesn't like that title" said the angel. "You were gifted with instinct upon your formation. Use it now to determine righteousness from corruption," he urged.

Monty understood now. This Power angel had intervened because the messenger angel—the one called Joe, with the fox back in Edinburgh, had not quite fulfilled his brief with him.

"Close. Jophiel was required elsewhere and upon deliberation, you now have the honour of a half-hour lecture from myself before you are safely returned, enlightened I may add, back to your realm," stated the angel, reading Monty's thoughts.

121

"May I ask why I am receiving this honour, sir?" Monty asked, as curious as always and despite being well aware that he should perhaps only speak when spoken to.

"Are you aware that God is your creator?" asked the angel.

Monty nodded. "Yes, sir." He realised he was no longer doubting this now.

"Are you aware that there are such beings as fallen angels?"

Another eager nod, though he knew truly little about any of that stuff, frankly. "Yes, sir."

"Well, some of them consider your kind to be no more than talking monkeys who pollute the realm in which you reside," the angel told him. "And accordingly make it their business to persuade man to destroy himself and his world."

"I follow," replied Monty, well aware that this was the gist of it. There were so many questions to be asked, though, such as why this was allowed to happen? "I've never sought your approving judgement, angel, nor God's if I am honest, but I'm sorry if I offended by not thinking about him. I have no wish to offend nor to anger anyone, and if I have done, it has been entirely unconsciously. I hope any offence won't last long and that I can do whatever it is that you want from me," he assured, but he was thinking more along the lines of:

If there is a God all along then why has he allowed so-called fallen angels to attack mankind?

"Relax, Stephen; this is not a reprimand," replied the angel with another pat on the shoulder, reducing Monty's anxiety, which, after all, could not be hidden from an angel. "Again, this is not relevant," the angel added cheerfully. "This freedom to think and then to presume to understand and question matters is precisely why they hate your species so much," the angel told him, having read his thoughts again.

"Then why would a talking monkey like me receive this honour now?" asked Monty. The angel studied him for a moment, amused by the audacity of his cynicism. "I apologise for my sarcasm, sir, excuse me." Monty quickly backtracked, but the angel smiled warmly at him.

"Some of my choir think those who hate men are quite mistaken, Stephen, and we desire to help man and prevent them from destroying you and your world."

"Only some?"

"Yes. Some of the others simply obey the commands of the Lord your God regardless of whether or not man is endeared to them or not," explained the angel.

122

"To answer your question," he continued, "it's not a question of your intelligence. Whether you're a talking ape or not, although I personally believe that you're a fine lawyer, as it happens. It's rather more about the purity of your soul and what percentage of it is not corroded. You, my friend, are not short of goodness, you don't commit great evil, and your sins, though they are plentiful, are potentially rescindable," he clarified.

"Do you know," he went on, "I am informed that you don't even backstab or gossip; that's rare in your generation, Stephen. It's apparently very common to disrespect a person behind their back in your time," he pointed out with obvious regret, before then pausing and speaking again. "Yet you don't participate?" the angel observed with an expression of joy upon his beautiful face.

Monty tried to think now, aware that his thoughts were being broadcasted. How strange that felt. The angel had got to him with this point too, about not backstabbing; he had not seen that coming and needed to think privately. So, he gave up and answered slowly and truthfully instead: "I've never believed that it's cool to gossip or backstab," he almost mouthed.

"No, indeed," the angel laughed now. "You didn't even laugh at that poor disabled boy whom most of your school friends sniggered at in the swimming pool back when you were ten."

"I can't really remember, where was—"

"No matter." The angel waved away the question with perfectly manicured hands and nails. "Let us make haste now," he stretched out a hand for Monty to take, which he duly did.

"Why send Ronnie, and not simply knock on my door yourself?" Monty asked as they walked across the marble floor and through an archway into a small gallery with oil paintings upon the walls and very old, darkly polished floorboards that did not whine under their combined weight.

"Because you responded poorly to Jophiel and you were, shall we say, a little uncomfortable with him, so it was better that Mr Charnley came and settled your nerves by explaining things a little to you first before I intervened to persuade you further," replied the angel as they crossed to the far end of the small gallery. "Rest assured, young Stephen," he added playfully as he closed in upon one framed painting in particular. "My lecturing style is somewhat funkier than what you experienced as a law student."

Monty could not help but smile. His stomach was full of excitement and despite a little apprehension and surprise still tingling throughout his body, he knew this was an experience that he had to try to accept and relish while it lasted. As they stopped at a particular image on the wall, the angel released Monty's hand. Both of them then studied the piece for a precious moment of contemplation.

The brass plate beneath it read: "*Moscow Burning* by Ivan Aivazovsky, 1812," in Russian, English and French. The beautifully dark image was of precisely that: a burning Moscow in the background beneath a dark, smoke-filled sky, and with a straggling line of Napoleonic troops retreating out of the city in the foreground along a river bank.

"Napoleon Bonaparte invaded Russia in 1812," explained the angel without taking his eyes from the piece.

"Yes, I think that's the only thing I know about him: like Hitler, his army had a hellish time with the weather in Russia." Monty dimly recalled some TV drama or other from some point in his life that had highlighted this, but he had never studied history so was otherwise uncertain.

"Correct," nodded the angel. They continued to explore the piece with their eyes for a few seconds in silence.

"Are we really in Russia?" Monty thought to him.

"We are observing shades of earlier happenings," came the telepathic reply.

Monty did not want to dissect that remark just yet, for he was still trying to protect his thoughts from being read; however, the fact he only partly understood what the angel was suggesting embarrassed him slightly.

The angel had some pity for the poor fellow; after all, it wasn't every day that a human was asked to soak all this up and remain as steady as Monty was. Instead, the angel decided to lay out the painting's background for him. "Both Hitler and Bonaparte ordered the largest armies ever assembled in their respective generations to invade Russia," he explained. "Both broke peace agreements with Russia when they did so. Both then successfully punched their way to within a few miles of Moscow," he recalled without taking his eyes from the smoke-filled image hanging before them.

"Hitler's army stood only a few miles from the city and could have taken it, but for some reason he ignored the opportunity to take his rival's ancient capital and instead swung his forces south towards a defeat at Stalingrad, which would then instigate his overall destruction. Bonaparte went for Moscow, however," he pointed out cheerily, "And his Grande Armée of six hundred and eighty thousand was practically destroyed thereafter."

"By the Russians?" Monty was guessing that Moscow must have been for the French what the city of Stalingrad had been for the Germans.

"No," the angel shook his head. "Here is knowledge, Stephen." He looked Monty in the eyes with his own glowing green pupils, leading him somehow to turn away and look back at the painting. "The Russians evacuated the city a week before the French arrived. The origin of the great fire thereafter, as you see depicted here"—he flicked a hand out at the painting—"has never been determined." He grinned impishly.

"There's much artwork representing the great fire, but stories vary as to just how it was started. The French claimed that the retreating Russians started it to leave them nothing by way of supply or shelter. The Russians claimed that the French started it out of savagery and spite, at having to retreat due to dried up supply lines. Most Russians didn't know who started it so they naturally blamed the French, who then mysteriously began a very silly retreat from Moscow back to France, in what would be one of the worst winters in a century."

Monty nodded, recalling in his mind's eye images of soldiers with big hats like the ones that used to adorn the old Nestlé Quality Street chocolate tins on Christmas mornings in his childhood. He could see the images of the retreat now, but the frozen soldiers were not wearing red uniforms like the Quality Street ones; rather, they wore the blue tunics and grey coats of the Grande Armée; and many who collapsed in the snow in that chaotic retreat had their coats striped from them by their freezing colleagues.

"Only thirty thousand men made it back to France alive, Stephen," said the angel grimly. "And that was also the beginning of the end of Bonaparte's existence, too."

"So, what happened?" asked Monty. Despite knowing very little of all of this, or military matters in general for that matter, he knew it would have been much wiser for the French to have wintered in Moscow and either resume a supply line or retreat in the spring.

"Well, the French don't know either. They blame the Russians, as one might expect. Some historians even argue that fires were started across the city by French troops cooking or trying to stay warm, and that they burned out of control." The angel shook his head at this despondently.

"Are there no witnesses?" The lawyer in Monty popped up now, raising a smile from the angel, who turned and faced him for a brief moment before returning his gaze to the painting.

"A French officer of the old guard wrote afterwards that there appeared to have been a mysterious celestial second sun, or a great fireball, as another of his fellow officers called it, that appeared over the city and then struck it," revealed the angel.

"A fireball?"

The angel shrugged his shoulders and smiled softly as he studied the image before him of the incredible fire. "He wrote that many French soldiers went down with sickness in their multitudes and began to develop sores in the days thereafter," he told Monty, who was now utterly fascinated. "And also, that some officers had their hats and hair melted to their heads, as well as many horses with riders just disappearing in flames.

"One Russian soldier who claimed to be in the city wrote that he had seen several missiles raining down from the sky, and that he saw people simply evaporating. But most who witnessed the outbreak of the great fire died. Much of the present thinking of historians is based upon the hearsay of those Russians who were within a two-hundred-mile radius of the city that night, for they observed the glow of the fire and passed down this story in various forms over the years."

"Some fire," Monty thought aloud. It looked hellish from the artwork before him. He then suddenly became aware of several black lines painted across the smoke-engulfed skyline of the painting, which appeared to be dipping down towards the city from the sky.

"What are those lines?" he asked, pointing. He half expected the reply to be that they were debris being blown upwards from the fires, yet the short, straight black lines were coming down from the sky like giant black arrows, as opposed to going upward.

The angel seemed pleased that Monty had finally noticed them, and grinned playfully. "What do you say they are, young Stephen?" he asked.

Monty hadn't a clue, and once again didn't want to be mentally observed whilst in thought. So, rather than sound silly, he just spoke honestly again, "They look like missiles. Is that what the French soldiers suffered from—some kind of radiation?"

"Well done. It's an interesting painting that not many of your generation will ever look at or think about," the angel told him.

"But angel, how is that possible? Can you explain it to me?" Monty was really confused because, as far as he knew, which admittedly was not a lot, the

Napoleonic wars were not fought with air to surface nuclear-powered weapons of any capacity.

The angel now turned and faced him. He was slightly taller and broader than Monty and, well, he absolutely shone with fitness and perfection. Monty felt the power and radiance now; it sunk into him and warmed him more to the entity who was sharing this enlightenment with him.

"To answer that, we must first briefly explore Bonaparte; come, follow me this way," he now thought into Monty's head, and they were soon walking across the wooden floorboards again and on through another large golden painted archway on the left, which had another sign in Russian above it that Monty could not read, and a fire extinguisher on the floor beneath a phone on the left-hand wall.

For a brief moment, he wondered if he was about to meet Napoleon as they entered another parquet-floored room, although this one was quite different. It looked like an old classroom, as it contained around twenty old wooden school desks with as many kids wearing period costumes seated at them. There was straw on the floorboards and an old mildewy smell to it. At the far end he now noticed a bewigged teacher with a grey shoulder-length wig with side curls, such as an English judge might have worn in days gone by. This was utterly surreal—Monty felt as if he was looking into an old person's outdated suitcase of memories. The scene appeared to be the 1700s, he presumed—was this Bonaparte's school?

The black-robed teacher pointed to some numbers and symbols chalked upon a large blackboard with a wooden cane. Above it was written:

Theorie der Parallellinien

Monty hadn't a clue about maths, but he guessed this might be an algebra class.

"A study of the fifth postulate in Euclidean geometry," smirked the angel.

"What?" asked Monty in puzzlement.

"Indeed," chuckled the angel. "I personally never had much interest in it either."

"So, which one is Napoleon?" Monty dared to ask.

"There." The angel pointed at the smallest child in the class, who looked miserably unhappy for some reason. He had a round face and straight, dark hair which covered his ears.

Monty thought the child looked out of place among the other mostly taller, fairer boys, who all seemed to more interested in the blackboard then he was.

"Precisely," said the angel, who had read Monty's thoughts. Monty turned to look at his guide.

"You see, this is the King's military academy for the children of the elite. There are Bourbons[49] sitting in this room presently." He shrugged blasély.

Monty presumed that the Bourbons were an elite French family but instead asked, "Why does Napoleon look so unhappy?"

"Yes, you are quite right," replied the angel peevishly. "Look at him, a little Corsican dwarf compared to the other thoroughbreds here," he sighed. "He speaks with a Corsican accent too, which in this period is deemed to be more of a strange Italian twang than regional French," he explained. "This little fellow is about as French as Macaroni," he smirked.

"So, the other kids picked on him for being Corsican?" asked Monty.

"That, and the fact that he was on a King's scholarship, as he was quite poor," replied the angel, still looking over at the little boy.

"Just as if I'd gone to Eton then," reflected Monty to himself, but the angel read his thoughts.

"Much worse. Interestingly, though, young Bonaparte began to realise that he was special in some strange way, and even now as we see him sitting there, he is mentally concentrating upon a strange extrasensory awareness which suggests to him that he is destined for something big," explained the angel.

"So, what's going on in his head?"

"A force is developing within him, one that will go on to elevate and anchor him to the summit of chaos, but he is only at the point of trying to understand what is happening to him, at this point." Monty wondered what this could be, and again the angel read his thoughts. "He has been chosen by dark entities to lead their cause on earth."

"An Anti-Christ?" it now became apparent to Monty that he had already heard this claimed somewhere.

---

[49] The House of Bourbon was a European royal house of French origin. The dynasty once held thrones in Spain, Sicily, Naples, Parma and France. It is likely that the angel is referring to the Princes de Conde here, who were a cadet branch from an uncle of Henry IV or even of *Princes de Conti*. Both the Condi and Conti branches were noble French families who played a role in the pre-French Revolution political affairs of state at this time under Louis XVI.

"In a way. At least, that was what Nostradamus predicted him to be and Tsar Alexander I named him as such. The approaching revolution seemed perfectly set up for him because the terror and chaos that followed provided him with an opportunity to lead and produce an unbelievable sequence of military successes. Thus he became an Emperor of Europe and Egypt within a fairly short period of time."

"Yes, but the Anti-Christ?" Monty was startled for a moment. Napoleon was the so-called biblical son of Satan who would bring about great misery upon the earth?

"Certainly. The famines and massacres he instigated across the continent convinced many respected English writers of the time to consider him as such," confirmed the angel.

"And what do you say?" asked Monty.

"I am only here to educate; it's for you to make what you will of the lesson. Come, now." The angel turned and smiled at him again.

With that, he took Monty's hand again and led him around the little wooden desks and across the classroom, quite unseen and unheard by either the boys or their teacher. Then on through a small wooden door into what appeared to be Napoleonic Cairo, judging by the hats and uniforms of the soldiers. Monty saw that he was now standing upon a stone balcony looking out towards the ancient pyramids of Giza; the evening breeze was warm and filled with the odour of cooking and spices.

"In the period we are visiting, he now leads the French army and has invaded, defeated and assumed control of Egypt, despite stating to the directory in Paris only a few months ago that invading Egypt was an 'impossible' proposal," explained the angel.

Monty gasped at the magic which had brought him here. He could see the outline of the three great pyramids, appearing purple and brown in the evening sun beyond the old city's buildings and mosques with their tall towers. There was undoubtedly something magical and extraordinary about this view, and he was quite overwhelmed by it. The fading sun caressed his face like a mother's touch, and he could smell the heat of the old buildings, which felt familiar and relaxed him somehow. He could hear the full throbbing noise of the old city at mealtime below too, but it seemed distant.

"Why?" he asked the angel without removing his gaze from the mysterious sight beyond and above the roof tops of old city. He belatedly noticed bright

French tricolours raised upon several of the finer buildings below, having been initially enchanted by the sight of those three strange pyramids sticking up into the dimming sun. The city seemed layered from here, brown, then burnt orange and then—above the pyramids—grey, a grey that merged with the sky as paint does with water.

"They asked him this when he first changed his mind, to which he replied that he had learned something after his military successes in Italy against the Austrians, but he did not reveal what that had been," said the angel mysteriously. "There, look at the little general." He indicated towards a large building across the road from where they were standing. Monty scanned the building and there, on a balcony directly below them, was Napoleon himself in a loose white shirt, sporting a ponytail, and accompanied by several other men in European civilian clothing.

"The British Royal Navy have attacked and destroyed the French fleet," explained the angel, "so his force is now stranded in Egypt without a supply line. One of his officers wrote in his diary at this time that Bonaparte spent no time regarding his stranded army and instead appeared to be searching for something out amongst the ancient sites."

"What are they doing?" Monty asked him as he looked down upon the men below. They all appeared to be going over some rudimentary astrology charts which were raised upon improvised painting easels.

"Bonaparte was drawn to Egypt, and by this point now, he believes in his superiority over all other men and so he searches for some clue to his destiny here in this land."

As Alexander the Great had done.

"The men with him below," the angel indicated down towards the civilians who all appeared to be engrossed in their notes, "are a selection of leading French scientists, mathematicians and historians who he brought with him to help him locate the certain thing that he searches for."

"What is it he is searching for?"

"The same thing that the Templers were searching for under the Temple Mount almost seven hundred years earlier, Stephen," replied the angel, who was now looking southwards beyond the citadel to where the Ottomans had once expanded the city towards Memphis and the green Nile delta. He then turned his gaze back and outwards upon the city below. "Consider what his options are for leading his army out of this place," he urged Monty, who was still partially in a state of shock. "Bonaparte has a vast desert and hostile forces beyond to the east." He raised a hand eastwards to show the rather jumbled Monty where the east lay.

He then turned westward, where vast sand dunes could also be made out beyond the city. "To the west, he faces yet more desert followed by a draining coastal march across North Africa, only to find himself once again at another ocean and in need of a very long bridge to take him over to Spain." Monty could see the dunes beyond rising above clutches of palm trees at the outskirts of the city. They seemed to stretch on endlessly in line with the darkening sky until they became blurry to his eye.

"The sea lies to the north, where the British fleet are waiting to pounce," pointed out the angel. "Could there be a fourth option for the little Corsican, hmm? A suicidal march south down the Nile in search of nothing, perhaps?" the angel shrugged his shoulders. Monty at least knew his basic geography and had holidayed in Luxor once upon a time, so he had a grasp of Bonaparte's dilemma.

Why would he go south?

The angel read his thoughts again and spoke: "Quite," he smiled, reading Monty's thoughts again, before then returning his gaze down upon Napoleon and his group below. "Unless he seeks divine knowledge, as Alexander the Great had done before him, he can't march south[50]," thought the angel.

Just then, Napoleon swiftly moved across the room below towards some notes that lay upon a large marble table. He frenziedly wrote something down with a quill, then walked back over to a chair at another corner of the room and sat down with arms crossed and one foot impatiently tapping the floor. The civilians at the table all leaned over to read whatever it was he had written and began looking at each other in confusion. "Inside the pyramid!" Napoleon shouted. "That is where it is!" He now stamped both his feet.

Off to the corner of the large apartment in which the Frenchmen were studying their charts, Monty could see two moustached French officers, who

---

[50] Alexander the Great of Macedon, having recently defeated a large Persian army in Turkey in 333 BC, advanced west against Persian-administered Tyre, Gaza, Israel and then onto Egypt instead of taking the obvious strategic choice of advancing straight across the Euphrates towards Babylon and then onto Persia and her Asian territories. Strangely, by going west, he delayed this endgame by two years and instead went off with his closest companions for several months into the desert, to obtain knowledge from the oracle of Ammon.

were the only other military men in the room. They were slouched on large cushions smoking hookah and not paying much attention however.

"That lot are smoking hashish and don't have a clue about whatever it is those learned gentlemen are trying to figure out over there," said the angel. A former Mameluke[51] slave was engaged in keeping the two officers cool by standing over them with a large fan of ostrich feathers. Monty reckoned he could do with some of the same as he felt a trickle of sweat roll down his back.

"All the while, Bonaparte, in his belief that he is a Messiah, directs his mental concentration fully upon his hunt for something mystical, instead of focusing upon his stranded army who will remain here on his crusade indefinitely." The angel spoke with a slight hint of contempt, Monty noted. They observed the scene for a while longer. It was clear that Napoleon was far more concerned with figuring something out with these civilian experts, than he was about his army's plight.

"Are fallen angels guiding him, then?"

"Yes, they were, but more accurately, they sowed the seed in his mind so that the seed would grow and do their work for them." Monty thought he at least partly understood and thus nodded. "He now thinks he understands himself and so pursues the voice in his mind, which is directing him towards becoming the new Charlemagne," explained the angel.

"Yes." Monty got the drift, despite not knowing who Charlemagne was.

"Before he lost the fleet, he'd been preparing the shattered and much disturbed French public for his reign by sending cartloads of Egyptian booty back to Paris on the ships, along with some propaganda art of himself as, among other things, a conquering pharaoh," chuckled the angel now.

"I take it he brought his own artists with him too?" Monty asked, and the angel nodded cheerily.

"Let's go and see his hunting methods, shall we?" prompted the angel as he once again took Monty's hand and led him from the balcony back through the door that they had previously come through. They soon found themselves out in

---

[51] After the collapse of the Western and Eastern Roman empires, Arab caliphs unwittingly created a force of considerable power in the Middle East by strengthening their armies over the following years through acquiring slaves from the former Roman and Parthian (Persian) controlled lands. These multicultural slaves spoke their own version of the Turkish language rather than the Arabic of their owners and became known as Mamelukes (from the Arabic *mamluk*, 'owned').

the open sand beside the Great Pyramid. It was obviously another time of day, now judging by the Egyptian sun, which was much hotter. Monty could feel his sun on his head as they began to walk towards some rubble and a stone wall, which lay ahead between them and the pyramid.

His emotions were all over the place as they proceeded, partly by the overwhelming impression of his first view of the Great Pyramid itself, which was simply breath-taking against a backdrop of the bluest sky he had ever seen. Then there was fusion of fear and adrenalin generated by the sight of a handful of French light infantry on boundary picket duty, hanging around the crumbling wall. They were all wearing white cotton pants and half-wains, with light cotton blue tunics designed with the heat in mind, although these troops often complained that they suffered from cold during the night as a consequence.

As they advanced towards the soldiers, the angel turned to Monty with confidence. "We shall interact with these infantry pickets. Have no fear, they will see us as two superior French officers of the Grenadiers and will never threaten us," he calmly assured.

Monty did not question this; nor, despite his fluttering stomach, did he disbelieve the angel. Rather, he hoped that his divine guide would at least defend him from a bayonet should anything go wrong. Then, as if on cue, the steel bayonets glistened brightly at the end of the up-pointed French muskets, just as they both approached.

Monty still had no clue as to why he was here, or where this was all going. He had known from the off that he should simply comply regardless, of course, but he figured that this did not mean that he should not remain alert and on his guard throughout the experience. He carried on walking in the scorching heat towards an approaching French sergeant who stopped just before them. He was a sunburned, moustached fellow who stood to attention and saluted them both.

"Stand to attention for the officers," the sergeant shouted back to his comrades behind him in provincial French.

"Sah!" he then addressed the angel. Monty realised that the fellow was speaking in a district dialect which seemed to be a cross between French and something else, but he found he could fully understand him. He had no idea how this could be as he had been hopeless at French in school, learning only a little of it from an afternoon spent in a haystack with a randy Canadian student named Li Ming.

"Good afternoon, sergeant," replied the angel with a lazy salute.

"Afta-noon-sah!" roared the sergeant. The other men behind him now were also all stood to attention.

"At ease," commanded the angel calmly, at which the sergeant saluted again "Sah!" before relaxing.

"Tell this young lieutenant here," the angel indicated to Monty, "what happened here recently with general Bonaparte and his party, sergeant," he gently ordered.

The man immediately turned to face Monty, who stared back, trying to measure his reply, and any sign of dishonesty from him. "Well, erm, he went inside the Great Pyramid, sah, with a large group of civilian specialists in tow from the universities in France," stated the sergeant nervously. His eyes flicked back and forth between Monty and the angel while a bead of sweat poured down a scarred cheek.

The angel immediately reached into a pocket and handed the fellow a white cotton handkerchief. The poor man was stunned by this gesture, for never before had such a high-ranking officer as a major handed a grunt like himself a handkerchief. He hesitated.

"Take it," smiled the angel, and the sergeant nodded and saluted again.

"Thank you, sah!" he snapped. He then stood with it in his hand, unsure whether it was to be used or not.

"Then what?" asked the angel.

"Well, sah, they remained inside for three full days and nights and only come out this morning," the sergeant informed Monty. Monty nodded at him, unsure what else to do.

"And what did he say?" asked the angel.

"He was asked by another officer, who had been waiting outside, what had occurred to keep them inside for three nights, sah," the fellow explained.

"And?" Monty heard himself ask.

"And general Bonaparte replied that he could not say as he would not believe him, sah," the sergeant shook his head in trepidatious concern at how this bizarre tale might be received.

"Thank you, sergeant," replied the angel. "Go back to your chums and forget us." He then raised his hand up towards the sergeant's chin line and clicked his fingers.

The sergeant about turned and returned to the others, who all began talking amongst themselves again. Monty lingered for a moment to observe them, but none looked back gain. It was as if they had never existed.

"Come," the angel beckoned him to return along the short sandy track to the doorway that still stood there, completely out of place upon the sand.

"What did he find in the pyramid?" asked Monty as they walked.

"Or rather, what found him?" replied the angel.

As soon as they walked back through the doorway, instead of arriving back in the classroom from where they had come, they both stepped onto a stone pier at a harbour. Gulls screamed overhead as several black teenagers in long robes ran along, carrying trunks, baggage and supplies towards a Maltese fishing boat tied to some moorings.

There was a pleasantly cool breeze now and the sun was far less powerful than it had been at Giza. Monty looked around and detected a North African or even a Greek vibe, judging by the odd Doric columns behind them in what appeared to be a distinctly Mediterranean city. However, the group of Napoleonic French officers and civilians gathering around a long gangplank leading up to the boat suggested that perhaps they were still in Napoleonic Egypt.

"This is Alexandria," said the angel reading his thoughts again. "Bonaparte is abandoning his men here to rot while he sails back to France on the only boat he can muster," he declared as he led Monty along the pier.

"Will we be characters again?" asked Monty somewhat enthusiastically, having enjoyed his role as a French officer.

"Alas, no," replied the angel smiling. "Let us just listen to master Bonaparte here for a moment," he urged as they approached the crowd gathered around the plank.

Two civilian gentlemen were walking at a pace ahead of Napoleon as he strolled towards the ship with his hands clasped firmly behind his back, Monty was suddenly able to hear and understand what was being said as he came to rest beside an older gent with a grey moustache who was wearing a green cotton tunic.

"But…General Bonaparte, may I please ask you to reconsider and allow me to travel with you"—A tall ponytailed and bespectacled gent carrying a leather folder of sketches was appealing to Napoleon. Monty was sure the bloke would trip in the large-heeled and buckled mules that this generation favoured.

"No, Oliver," interrupted Napoleon. "You must remain and continue the search for Alexander's tomb," he informed the downhearted looking man, who blew his hooked nose with a handkerchief.

"But I—" Oliver was beginning a protest when a cavalry officer pushed him aside in an obvious rage.

"Damn your impotence, you blasted mathematician, no means no!" he bellowed at him.

Bonaparte then stepped onto the timber plank, paused a moment, and turned to the collection of aides and commanders. "I saw this moment in my dreams. Soon I shall march on Asia upon an elephant with a turban upon my head, holding a new Koran, which I shall compose to fit my needs[52]," he declared.

Everyone, including Monty and the angel, stood there in silence. Only the sea and the gulls were to be heard during the little Corsican's proud walk up the thin plank of wood to his destiny.

Just then an older, husky, posh voice from behind spoke very quietly, but most of them heard his musing well enough: "Now we are abandoned."

One or two of the officers in front of Monty and the angel casually turned around with cheeky smiles. The moment passed and as the little ship gradually exited the harbour through the fishing boats that the British had not destroyed; all present waved their farewells to their diminutive general who stood upon the prow in his grey coat, white breeches and black hat, his right hand resting within his partially unbuttoned white waistcoat. He appeared to stare straight over towards Monty.

"Can he see us?" Monty asked telepathically.

The angel stood there and smiled back at Napoleon. "Only as a man can see the green reflection of the fox's eyes in the dark of night," he said, before turning and taking Monty's hand again. "Come, let us return to the question of his bizarre retreat from Moscow now."

They then walked back along the age-old rock pier. Monty could hear trumpets from the shoreline ahead, but he looked back at the departing ship for a moment. The little man continued to stare back at him in the distance.

---

[52] It is unclear whether or not Napoleon stated this on the pier to those he left behind upon his abandonment of his troops in Egypt; however, the remark has been attributed to his written memoirs. See *Memoirs of Napoleon Bonaparte*, Volume 1, by Louis Antoine Fauvelet de Bourrienne (his private secretary), edited by Colonel R.W. Phipps, late Royal Artillery, 1891.

"So, he's being instructed by fallen angels to abandon his men here?" queried Monty.

"You might think that, Stephen; I can only show you the event. It's for you to decide, but I will assure you of one thing. He would have required some very powerful assistance and knowledge to have made it from here, even to Malta, never mind as far as France, without Nelson's Royal Navy intercepting him," assured the angel.

"The angels of the wind?" asked Monty, again half recalling something he had read or heard somewhere.

"You know your stuff," smirked the angel with a slight hint of sarcasm. "He wouldn't even have escaped from Elba without assistance from what men will later refer to as 'the paranormal'," he added as they approached a doorway at the end of the pier.

"Back to Paris to take over France and make war all over Europe?" Monty was not finished yet and dug his heels in a moment.

The angel obliged him and smiled warmly to confirm that it was fine to ask some more questions. "Paris is in chaos in the aftermath of the revolution. Terror reigns supreme. Bonaparte is in submission to the secular force that now controls him and is blowing him back to Paris, where everything has been conveniently set up to await his arrival," he explained. "Works of art depicting him as a messianic saviour are now being displayed all across Paris and the process of turning his Egyptian disappointment into a propaganda triumph has already begun. In short, the stabilising hero of Egypt shall return to find his path clear for a coup." He patted Monty on the shoulder.

"So, a military coup within a political coup then?" Monty thought aloud as it all dawned on him. Extremely dangerous, of course, considering that the quick matter of an appointment with the guillotine was so common in those times. To instigate any sort of coup at this stage of revolutionary chaos in France required a huge level of daring and confidence; a mystical confidence, even.

"Yes Monty, a confidence similar to that displayed by Alexander in his approach against Persia," the angel confirmed with a knowing grin.

"What found him in that pyramid?" Monty needed to know.

"It will be for you to form a view on that once you learn more, but at this stage you may care to say that he experienced an epiphany that changed everything," replied the angel.

"Was he looking for the Ark of the Covenant?"

The angel appeared to consider this for a moment, or perhaps even to be silently conferring somewhere. He soon responded warmly, however. "You may be right to consider that Bonaparte was pursuing some sort of mystical advantage to use in his pursuit of world domination." He nodded. "I cannot, however, confirm that he sought the ark itself; simply that arcane knowledge was believed to be hidden in various locations by believers and it was this which he sought."

"So, he could have been searching for a dark magic?" Monty stretched the last word because he was unsure of whether or not he was on the right track or not.

"You mean something like Solomon's ring when you use the term magic?" the angel teased him.

Monty guessed that Solomon was a biblical figure from the Old Testament, but he knew nothing about him or of any magical ring. The angel thus fleetingly expressed sadness at his confusion.

"Oh well, something for you to Google later, Stephen," he replied with what seemed like paternal affection, his goodness and reliability shining out and urging trust. "Shall we?" he then gestured with his hand towards the doorway beyond.

A moment later, they were back in the parquet-floored art gallery, the angel leading him back to Aivazovsky's *Moscow Burning*.

Again, they stood looking at it. Those bizarre black missiles coming out of the sky were very strange. For Monty, they looked like sticks of liquorice, falling down upon a burning city. More chillingly, they also looked like missiles carrying who knew what in their tips; indeed, could they even have had nuclear heads? Leaving aside the technological timeline that did not make rational sense, he knew that modern weapons would explain the deaths of so many, as well as the reported symptoms of the French troops thereafter.

"These missiles weren't Napoleon's, then?" he sought clarification.

"No," smirked the angel. "He was able to use the arcane knowledge he was given to become the greatest battlefield commander of his generation, and then to become a new Roman Emperor blessed by the Pope himself, whom he despised, I might add, but no. If Bonaparte had possessed the firepower seen here, he would never have toiled at Borodino[53], and would certainly have used it again at Krasnoi or even Berezina[54]."

"So, are these missiles yours then?" Monty felt like he was displaying a lack of faith by not being quite sure that they were.

"All I can say is that Bonaparte, and the dark force steering him, were obligated into overplaying their hand and glided into the most disastrous military defeat in history—up until that time, anyway—the winter weather did more damage than any Russian guns ever could." The angel winked playfully at him now. He then studied Monty a moment and read in him a potential to become entangled in a pointless consideration of why all this had occurred. "Do not try to understand why it is that not all barbaric threats to the planet are checked, Stephen," he warned him, still playfully though.

"Intervention only happens under certain circumstances, at least on the part of the Lord. Admittedly, the dark horde have tended to abuse the rules in the last couple of centuries, but as far as I and many other members of the holy choirs are concerned, rules are the key to holiness because they are set by the architect himself," he said in a friendly enough tone, but now with a piercing stare. "Concern yourself only with the theme itself, Stephen, as opposed to whether the theme can be enhanced or bettered," he insisted.

"I understand," nodded Monty. He saw the point. He knew that he lacked the intellectual intelligence required to understand the background to these extra-dimensional events, and that the only requirement being made of him here was to accept that there was an ongoing struggle between angels that he was— possibly—being dragged into. The point, of course, was that while he was a mere

---

[53] The Battle of Borodino took place in Russia in 1812. Both French and Russian forces suffered heavy casualties, exacerbating the logistical difficulties that Napoleon encountered in the Russian campaign. The exhaustion of the French forces, and the lack of information on the condition of the Russian army, persuaded Napoleon to remain on the battlefield with his army instead of ordering the kind of vigorous pursuit he had deployed in previous campaigns.

[54] Two other battles that took place respectively before and during the horrendous retreat from Moscow during which thousands of French died both upon the battlefields and throughout the following nights' frozen temperatures. At Berezina, the remnants of Napoleon's army were famously engaged in battle while attempting to cross the Berezina River to continue their escape.

human, he was created in the image of God and thus was designed to be free and individual, and to explore and think for himself.

"Man lost his image of God after Eden, Monty," explained the angel. "His faculty of reason, however, remains, and can either reunite him with God, or destroy him."

"And regardless of man's reasoning process, he is entirely free to come to any conclusion he wishes?" asked Monty.

"For as long as the individual is in the game," nodded the angel.

"The game?"

"The Kertamen," grinned the angel.

"The Kertamen?"

"It's an ancient term meaning a contest or struggle between the angels and the fallen ones."

"Similar to the Cold War then, with man being, say, Poland, who was stuck in the middle between the east and the west?" asked Monty curiously.

The angel knew he was not being cheeky here but once again could see where this was leading. "It becomes arrogance when man thinks he can improve matters that he knows extraordinarily little about. It's rather more about whether or not he accepts his situation, or continues to challenge the system."

"I accept that God is my creator and that you and others are doing exactly as the bible says," conceded Monty.

"Yet you are still to read the bible fully." The angel mused thoughtfully on what he deemed to be the cringeworthy respect that many humans offer up in order to please. "You haven't experienced enough magic today to be convinced, surely?" he smirked at Monty.

Monty remained silent. He would read the book properly and in full over Christmas if he got out of this in one piece, that was for sure. The angel beamed a great smile at him as he read this intention.

"Man still has his assets and a special place in God's affections, Monty, and there are always occasions when messengers like myself are sent forth to assist chosen men to apply their faculty of reason in the correct manner. Often it's necessary to show them a little, as I have done today with yourself, and so that they may understand that they have misread things," explained the angel knowingly. "Anyway," he continued, "now that you've been shown a little indication of how it might be that the dark horde intervenes with certain people at the highest levels, let me show you yet another case of intervention by both sides, but at a much lower level."

For Monty, this whole experience was obviously scary, but the fear and caution he felt in his stomach were somehow overwhelmed by an excitement that exploded from deep within him. Seeing Napoleon had naturally been something that could, if misunderstood, have freaked lesser people out, but the sheer enchantment and virtuousness which flowed out from the supernatural presence before him, deep into his soul, seemed to drown his anxiety.

The angel offered his hand again. Monty took it enthusiastically.

Chapter Seven

To become truly great, one has to stand with the people, not above them.
Charles de Montesquieu

The angel led him over again to the same door that had previously led to Napoleon's classroom. Monty was full of anticipation as the butterflies returned and the warm air beyond the portal hit him straight away as he entered a packed-out public square—no, to be more precise it was an open area, with Roman-style buildings towering above and around on all sides and a couple of hundred people standing within. He instantly recognised that some sort of public event was occurring; sensing the eagerness of the crowd waiting patiently in this paved precinct, which seemed to be about the length and width of several football parks.

Steep hills rose behind large buildings on three sides of the zone, he felt stone under his shoes, and detected the heady mix of incense, meat being fried and human sweat upon the warm air. He looked to the angel for information.

"This is ancient Rome in the summer of 80 BC," smiled his celestial guide.

It was warm despite there being a breeze, and the sun was radiant above cloudy blue sky. Monty felt overdressed compared to the crowd around him, who generally wore dark tunics made of coarse materials. Some donned capes of similar cloth, and there were some slaves dotted amongst these people, wearing robes and holding parasols over their wealthy masters.

Monty realised that these ancient people around him were plebeians[55], and he now understood that he had been mentally enlightened by the angel as he could now see and understand everything that was going on.

He could see dye imported from Lebanon in the robe of one of the wealthier people shaded under a bright orange parasol, and knew that it had made a journey from Leptis Magna to Syracuse in Sicily, before then passing the corrupt customs clerks at Ostia and up the Tiber by a mule-drawn barge to the market place in Rome. He could see the fake counterfeit dye produced in Rome itself on the

---

[55] A lower Roman social class.

stolas of many of the women here, some attractive, some not, and found that he understood their whisperings too, much of which was in gutter Latin.

"You have the gift of enlightenment for the duration of our short stay here, Stephen," explained the angel, who seemed less formal to him now as he led him through the excited crowd towards a central area.

Monty saw that large sheets of cloth had been erected upon timber frames at all sides of the square. He understood now that in Republican Rome, criminal court trials were heard mainly outside in summer and that these vast frames acted as partitions between the public hearings. Ahead of them, towering above one particular partition, stood a great cliff: Monty knew that it was the Palatine Hill, the summit of which was the home of the current elite and where future emperors would reside. "This is the Roman Forum,"

"Quite, Monty," the angel spoke up as he smoothly led him on an unlikely path through the buzzing crowd. "Acquaint yourself with the matter at hand," he urged as they arrived at the open centre.

"This is the *peroration*[56] part of a criminal court trial?" Monty thought again. He tittered a moment to himself, for he had never studied a word of Latin in his life and found all of this to be the most brilliant madness.

In the open space before them sat one hundred men of the *patricii*[57], all wearing white togas made of Egyptian linen, except for one or two wearing silk, which had arrived long-haul via the Silk Road. He was now able to spot such things as simply as he might the number on a London bus. All these clean-shaven, crisply chiselled men seemed to be between thirty and sixty years old and all had short-cut hair brushed forward; some even wore wigs to cover baldness, which looked vaguely comical to his modern eye.

"Forget them; look at the case itself," urged the angel, charmed at the process of a human trying to cope with such a unique gift of vision.

A magistrate was seated on a throne of sorts, set slightly above the one hundred seated men. Monty understood that this grey-haired, woodpecker-

---

[56] The closing speeches of both the prosecuting and defending advocates in a Roman criminal trial. Usually, these lasted up to twenty minutes and were timed by a water clock.

[57] Aristocratic class—the patrician families of the late Republic were the ruling elite who claimed a blood linkage to the first one hundred fathers (*patres*) appointed by the mythical founder and first King of Rome, Romulus. By the time of the early imperial period, however, many patrician houses were in serious decline.

beaked man, would pass sentence once the men had judged the case. "This is the case of Sextus Roscius being heard and he is accused of *patricide*[58]," he measured silently to himself.

The angel continued to smile, for Monty did not yet know how to hide his mental analyses, and of course, he would not learn the art of how to do so presently either.

"And the background to the case?" asked the angel now, moving things along.

Monty studied the scene. In the centre of the court were two wooden tables facing each other. Seated at one were two men in tunics, one older than the other. The younger man, a dark-haired fellow, was talking to the older looking man, with brown hair.

"That is Sextus seated there, he pointed at the older man, and that is his young lawyer, a twenty-seven-year-old named Cicero who has put his entire future on the line by representing Sextus," Monty spoke aloud but only the angel could hear him. He felt quite hot now and the first trickles of sweat began to appear on his temple.

He was in the process of removing his fleece, but the angel stopped him, smiling warmly so as not to alarm his charge. "Leave it on, for we may have to leave suddenly."

There was a sudden burst of laughter from the crowd gathered behind one of the large partitions, and the breeze in this crowded pocket spread an unpleasant waft of incense mixed with vegetable-infused farts. This was bad enough, but the slave standing next to Monty, a tall, red-headed Celtic female, smelt of sun-dried urine.

On the left were some wooden benches where more observers sat. These people appeared to be of higher stock and most were laughing and talking amongst themselves while all and sundry waited for Cicero to speak.

"And?" asked the angel now, getting back to the lesson.

"Cicero is young and risks everything he has upon this case," replied Monty, still surveying the magical scene before him. "He has been warned and threatened, and by still taking Sextus's case, he has acted a little peculiarly," he half said, half suggested.

---

[58] In Roman law, this was the charge rendered against a person accused of murdering their own father. The term derives from the Latin word for father, *pater,* and the suffix *cida*, meaning killer or cutter.

"He was urged to take the case by my choir," revealed the angel.

"But he's not aware of this." Monty knew, but sought confirmation.

"No." The angel shook his head.

Monty was struggling to understand. "It's a case that many others would have refused due to the likelihood that the charge is undefendable, and because of the dark power that I sense is behind the prosecution."

The angel nodded slowly, continuing to stare at the prosecutor seated behind the table opposite. Monty followed his gaze. He saw a small fat man with a curly red wig and a toga, dyed yellow by saffron which had been brought from Persia alongside six tigers on a merchant vessel made in a Cypriot shipyard.

"Too much information!" he gasped in excitement. "Why does it do that? I don't need to know all about the tigers and the details of the journey or the ship!" He was becoming frustrated at the amount of data he was uploading.

"Don't knock it, kid. Moving on—and him?" The angel patiently urged him to ignore the overwhelming knowledge he was dealing with, and to home in on the matter at hand.

"That's the prosecutor, Drusus Publius Erucius, whose whole case is based upon false testimony and fraud," clarified Monty as he read the intelligence that filled his mind like an open tap. "Erucius is evil. He's a puppet of a Greek slave with power…no, no, a former Greek slave…" Monty corrected himself. "One who has wormed his way up to form a powerful connection with the dictator Sulla[59], and who is now using his new-found power to extort wealth from Romans."

"What else?"

"Well, this former Greek slave—Chrysogonos—is effectively a gangster with a foot in Sulla's camp. He uses this connection to blackmail wealthy Roman citizens, and in this case had the accused—Sextus's father—murdered and Sextus charged with the murder." Monty was shocked by this and shook his head.

There was shouting from another court beyond the screen, and laughter could be heard from some observers high up on one of the cliffs, who were leaning upon the railing of a crowded gallery that bore blue painted pillars and a timber-roofed frame with vines twisted around the beams.

Monty looked up, squinted his eyes under the sun, then continued, "The accused's father owned thirteen farms and since the arrest of his son Sextus here,

---

[59] Lucius Cornelius Sulla was a Republican general who marched on Rome, took the city and established himself as dictator in 81 BC.

145

Chrysogonos has purchased all the farms for the price of only a couple of educated slaves."

"Like you buying Edinburgh Castle for two thousand pounds, Monty," said the angel.

"So Chrysogonos wants this court to finish the job for him by finding young Sextus guilty of his father's murder, and permanently getting him out of the way," Monty surmised.

"Correct, and Chrysogonos was able to purchase the farms for such a low price because he sent a team of armed enforcers to make sure that no one else bid for them at the auction, which he himself had instigated by murdering Sextus's father," nodded the angel.

Monty now had a flash of a fat man in his fifties with short brown hair being stabbed repeatedly by several men outside a stable somewhere. "So, why is this young Cicero guy representing a man who is surely going to be convicted because of this Chrysogonos?" he asked, realising that all the finest advocates in Rome had initially refused the case before Cicero had been offered it.

Monty also knew that the punishment for anyone found guilty of this crime was to be forced into a sack with a dog, a snake, and a cockerel, which was then firmly seamed up and tossed into the Tiber River. For Cicero, the odds that he too would be murdered should he conduct a decent defence of his client were clearly high. If he dared to mention Chrysogonos himself, it might be the end of everything he valued, including his family. Yet should he lose the case, as he was expected to do, mainly because of the pile of fabricated evidence and an older, more experienced advocate in the form of Erucius up against him, his future career would be severely hampered.

"He has already dragged the name of Chrysogonos into the mix," the angel declared, as they both shifted their gaze to a chunky man standing among ten or twelve lictors at the southwestern corner of the court among the onlookers gathered behind Erucius' desk.

There he stood. Not very tall, yet exceptionally muscular and with long hair in the Greek fashion. He was bronzed, wore a fine leather military tunic, and stood with his hands behind his back and his weight arrogantly pressed upon one leg. Chrysogonos looked every bit the thug that he was known to be, and some of his lictors looked very threatening too. Monty could see that half of them were armed with daggers under their tunics; he immediately understood them to be former soldiers. and one was even a freed Dacian gladiator who stood seven feet tall with arms like tree trunks, and hands which Monty reckoned looked tough enough to crack open coconuts.

"Because of Cicero's sense of injustice and ethics?" shrugged the angel. "Cicero is a decent enough fellow despite his belief in false gods. So, we utilised him to counter the dark power fuelling Chrysogonos."

"But the accused isn't a believer either, so why the intervention?" Monty thought he had a valid point here.

"Not quite an intervention; I would describe it more as an opposition, for as I said, Cicero is defending with his own ability, not mine or that of any other of my choir." The angel grinned at this now and placed a comforting arm around Monty's shoulder. "Tell me, what else do you see?"

Monty stared at Chrysogonos a moment longer; the group certainly looked nasty, and he noted that they were all staring menacingly down towards young Cicero, who understandably looked stressed and under pressure as he sat there scanning a pile of notes upon the table before him. This whole scene was really not so different from one found in a Scottish criminal court, thought Monty.

He also noted the sole magistrate, who was now pretending to be reading something while he decided to either commence the court, or to go and empty his bowels, for his stomach was rumbling and tumbling from the underdone seagull and pint of Spanish garum that he had consumed earlier.

The one hundred *quaestores* (judges), seated in five rows of seats beneath him were a sitting jury on criminal matters of bloodshed, similar to Scottish solemn procedure. There was also the prosecutor (whose role it was to present proof—*probabilis causa litigandi*), and the defenders, as well as several clerks of court waiting eagerly upon the magistrate, whose title was coming through to Monty as *praetor urbanis*.

Sensing that the similarities between Roman and Scots law would be a whole other pot of information for Monty to plunge into, the angel decided to steer him along: "Watch the unsubtle prosecutor now, Monty," he said as he motioned merrily towards Erucius, seated at his own desk and looking pleased with himself for some reason.

This fat-necked, bewigged conspirator now tapped his own right ear with an index finger, which immediately signalled to several men, in the crowd behind Monty and the angel, to call out loudly that Sextus was a murderer who deserved to be placed in the sack.

"Quite the poisoned dwarf, then," sneered the angel contemptuously.

"And Chrysogonos?"

"He has giants' blood in his veins; it is faint, true, but the evil flows easily enough within him," the angel sighed. Both of them studied the burly Chrysogonos again. He was trying his best to look menacing as he loitered around in an attempt to intimidate everyone present, from slave to magistrate. He kept focusing menacingly upon Cicero and poor old Sextus Roscius, who remained seated and was looking down miserably at his hands. Sextus knew the fate awaiting him, and Monty could see that he had very little hope of being absolved by the judges. If there were a few butterflies evident within Cicero's gut, Monty could sense that Sextus was hosting an absolute swarm.

The heat was becoming intolerable, and Monty reckoned that advocates here must rush cases in order to escape it, which suggested further unethical proceedings. "It's silly having the court outside," he thought.

"Yes, yet another judiciary in crisis," smirked the angel.

"I wouldn't want to live in this time, angel, nor would I want to practise Roman law." Monty now realised that if the prosecutor failed to prove his case, according to Roman law he would be branded a false accuser by having a K tattooed upon his forehead, and as a consequence, his career would hit the proverbial brick wall. "A judiciary where corruption flourishes and where power-hungry men pursue wealth and reputation through legalised murder," he added somewhat contemptuously, whilst continuing to stare in the direction of Chrysogonos. He had no idea where this opinion came from, but he was now processing an overflow of general knowledge much faster than he had done minutes earlier.

"The problem with this hybrid bully,"—the angel also sized Chrysogonos up as he spoke—"is that he lusts after more and more power and wealth. This, of course, was eventually his undoing," he said thoughtfully, with obvious knowledge of how this story panned out.

"Because he can't stop?"

"Because he can't stop. Correct," nodded the angel without taking his almond-shaped green eyes off the Greek hybrid.

A general hush fell as the magistrate placed his documents in the hands of a little bald clerk beneath him, cleared his throat, which was still quite salty from garum which had been watered down with sea-water, and gestured with a lazy wrist movement for Cicero to proceed. The young advocate, with his thick black hair cut short and lightly oiled, stood up with a smile upon his friendly, round face. This was it: his moment to make or break his future. Monty thought Cicero had the face of a shepherd forced to sell his sheep. He also seemed to be a good actor, considering Monty could feel Cicero's worry and apprehension and hear his heart pounding; there was clearly no stage fright.

Then, to his utmost surprise, Monty could see the fluttering butterflies in Cicero's stomach as if a high-tech image highlighter machine was scanning him; and he gasped and exchanged a quick look with the angel.

"Young Cicero has not eaten since the previous evening?" smiled the angel at the magic which was creating the visual sensation.

"Go for it, lad," Monty heard himself saying aloud, stimulated by this opening act like a football supporter witnessing his team stage a cup final fightback. Only the angel heard his words and was amused by the passion aroused in his human pupil.

"You were well selected, Stephen," he told him telepathically.

Just then, Cicero was approached by a clerk of the court who first apologised to the magistrate with a nervous bow, then scurried over to hand the young advocate a note from an anonymous source, urging him not to "mention the Greek by name".

Cicero knew this was a last-gasp plea from some well-wisher or other, possibly even someone within his own family who feared for his life after the trial. Cicero read it twice before casually walking over and handing it to another clerk, who ran over and handed it to the magistrate. The latter quickly read it, shrugged his shoulders and handed the note back again. When it was returned to Cicero, he casually passed it to the first judge on the lower row and quietly asked him to read it and then to pass it on among his fellow judges.

Cicero's Roman accent was quite well-to-do, with only a hint of the rural south, a slight twang that a city-raised Roman might have detected. Educated in Rome itself, he was by now well on the way to mastering Latin prose and oratory, to the extent that when it came to eloquence, even at this relatively young age, he was already quite possibly unrivalled.

Monty could see Cicero's uniqueness oozing from him now, for it positively glowed. He could also see that he had been commissioned by the lady Caecilia Metella Balearica, a formal Vestal Virgin with her own house and staff. She was, like Chrysogonos, well allied and powerful, and she had particular connections with the wives of both Sulla and Pompey as well as an immensely powerful brother, who was also well connected to Sulla.

Her support of the young Sextus Roscius had so far been unchallenged physically by Chrysogonos' thugs. Instead, Chrysogonos had tried to murder Cicero after pressurising every other advocate in the city into declining the obviously poisoned chalice.

While waiting for all the judges to read the note, Monty instinctively looked up towards a road that led up the Capitol Hill. He saw the Portico Deorum Consentium at the offices of the judicial clerks above, and there she was, Caecilia of the Metelli, leaning over with an orange in her right hand. She was cheerfully watching the show in the company of several of her toadies, whilst various well-dressed slaves acted as fan bearers and bodyguards to her group. Monty understood that all these slaves were discreetly armed and quite prepared to go toe-to-toe with Chrysogonos' thugs should the need arise.

It seemed to Monty that the situation really was volatile here, with two powers wrestling each other over the matter of Sextus Roscius and his estates. Bullying, extortion and murder pitched up against a sly benefactor and her young, inexperienced lawyer—the risk-taking Marcus Cicero.

This would not end well for somebody.

"The very fact you are not sure which way this case might go is a display of optimism not held by the crowd, Cicero, or his client, Monty," laughed the angel.

"Optimism?" asked Monty.

"You understand what is being asked of Cicero," replied the angel. Monty silently chuckled at this; the angel was, of course, quite right, that this was like watching your team playing away at the Nou Camp against Barcelona after having two players sent off in the first five minutes.

Yet, there is always hope?

"Which is why you have been chosen, Monty," divulged the angel.

"For what?" Monty silently asked. Fear and excitement in his voice.

"Patience. We shall come to that soon enough," nodded the angel.

All eyes were on Cicero now. The young middle-class advocate spoke directly to the judges, his voice loud and polite, profoundly eloquent and brilliantly friendly considering that most other lawyers of this period simply tended to bootlick to the elite and grovel their defences across to the judges. "I imagine that you, my lords," he told them, "may have, over the course of this demanding trial, considered why it may be, that I, a young advocate with neither the experience nor skill of, say, my learned friend over there," he paused and gestured an open hand at the seated Erucius and smiled over at him. Erucius lightly scratched his own nose at this, but the group of people behind Monty and the angel, instantly applauded, with one man even shouting "Hear-hear", which caused ripples of laughter around the square, with even the *vigiles urbani* who were policing the entrance of an adjoining court joining in.

"...am standing here on behalf of Sextus Roscius?" Cicero turned back to the judges now. "Or why it is that so many of Rome's most eminent orators and noble advocates of the laws have rejected the case?" he cheerfully added. "Or even, why it may be that those learned advocates have refused to accept payment and to represent a Roman citizen in his legal defence against the unrivalled evil and wickedness being applied to rob him of his ancestral home and mortal life." He continued to smile at them warmly...*what an actor he was*, thought Monty.

Cicero's chilling words were also heard across at the Senate steps where one or two of Sulla's puppets stood watching.

"It is because they are scared, my lords," nodded Cicero knowingly. "Scared of the same evil befalling them too, an evil directed by that man standing over there." Cicero suddenly dropped the act and turned and pointed straight at Chrysogonos.

"The former Greek slave," he almost spat, careful not to mention the man's newly freed Roman name of Cornelius, which was Sulla's family name.

There was a considerable reaction to this among the crowd, including some exaggerated gasps and even some cheering from the weaker men. All of the judges looked over at Chrysogonos, and one even shook his head at the young Cicero, with a wide smile across his face.

"Yes indeed, my lords," Cicero nodded over towards Chrysogonos, who glared viciously back. Monty recognised his weakness, Chrysogonos knew only how to scare and murder, and this was written all over his scowling features for all to see; he could not do battle with words.

"For it is this Greek,"—Cicero pointed at him again—"who was freed from servitude by the honourable Cornelli family as a consequence of having served against the enemies of the citizens of Rome, but who now, having been freed and given Roman citizenship, has abused this great honour by conspiring to murder Roman citizens." Cicero turned back to stare down upon Erucius, who was sitting there with a look of endurable condescension.

"And it is this false accuser here," Cicero raised a finger towards the prosecutor now, "who has the audacity to think he can drag the honour of the Republic into this Greek's sordid conspiracy by disgracing the virtue of our laws." He casually leaned back onto one leg now, grasping his toga with clenched fist upon his opposite shoulder.

The court is hanging upon his every word.

"I am aware that you judges, my lords, have been exceptionally patient throughout this trial and consequently, I shall borrow your ears for only a few moments more," assured Cicero. "I shall tell you exactly what has occurred here, why my client should be absolved, and how by his absolution, the virtue of our Republic shall be defended against the elevating lust of an orientalist Greek."

"Wow," thought Monty. He had not seen this coming; having reckoned that the only defence open to Cicero would be to target the lack of evidence and very delicately touch upon the conspiracy. This was something else entirely. This was nationalism being stoked here.

And it just might work.

There were many murmurs among the crowd and a fair deal of clapping from the porticos of the Capitol. "*Cui bono,*" shouted someone from somewhere in the vicinity.

"Indeed," smirked Cicero, his head down in imaginary thought, slowly treading the Carthaginian stones between his and Erucius' desks. "Who would benefit from the murder of this Roman citizen's father?" he casually thumbed behind him at Sextus.

"So Roman courts are about good acting then," Thought Monty.

Suddenly, Cicero stopped dead, then twisted around like a rock star in order to look up at the judges. "Well, let me put it to you, my lords,"—he raised a knowing eyebrow at them—"that Sextus Roscius Senior was murdered in the city of Rome and I have previously proven to the court that his son here, Sextus Roscius Junior, was over sixty miles away, busy running thirteen farms across thirty-one miles of countryside. He,"—he twisted again and gave another flick of his wrist towards Erucius—"invites you to convict the son of the murder victim regardless because it benefits the plan of the Greek. And he wants you all to conspire with him to help this Greek."

He scoffed at the very audacity of the presumption, hand on hip, arm raised and toga held firmly. Monty could sense his fears, though—an electrical sense of arguing for his life was clearly propelling him—but by God, this Cicero was a talent, this was obvious.

Erucius raised his hand and scratched his nose again, causing the same group of hired hustlers who were dotted about behind Monty to boo loudly.

"Enough of that," the magistrate snapped at the crowd. This was clearly a warning to be taken by Erucius.

Cicero seized upon this good fortune. "As you can see, my lords, it has taken an honourable magistrate here to limit the awfulness of this wicked disrespect." He again flicked a limp palm out at Erucius, who now shifted in his seat uncomfortably and shook his head. "Perhaps this is how they conduct legalised murder in Greece, my lords, but it is not how our Roman law works, and the virtue of Roman law will counter the bad form on display here from this prosecutor who acts on behalf of his Greek pay master," he measured sharply.

"An outrageous allegation!" snapped Erucius, who jumped up and made a hullabaloo by pointing furiously at Cicero. "You are out of order, Cicero, and attempting to mislead this court," he growled, launching sprays of saliva across his desk.

"You have stated here in your closing speech that a Roman citizen is guilty of murdering his own father and should be sewn into the sack, Erucius," snapped the magistrate. "Cicero is also entitled to deliver his own thoughts, so sit down and we can all listen while he does so." The flustered Erucius turned stupidly and exchanged a look with Chrysogonos. The latter was clearly feeling fidgety by now too and kept looking around the court at all the Roman faces, searching for friends and foe.

The judges did not miss this, and neither did Monty, who could see something dark and evil looming from within the Greek: something that was evidently an ambitious spirit within him. Suitably encouraged, Cicero moved swiftly to close his case for the defence.

"My lords, the only evidence that the prosecution have offered here in response to conceding that Sextus Roscius junior was many miles away from the murder scene comes from his two cousins. Both are men with zero credibility, as we all learned from their evidence. Indeed, their false evidence asked us to believe that Sextus somehow arranged the murder of his father from a distance." He shook his head, and Monty and the angel noted a few nods of agreement among the crowd. "Yet they cannot tell us anything about this plot, or who may be involved." Cicero stretched his arms out and feigned surprise, which earned him a ripple of muffled sniggering around the court.

"The basis of the prosecution case then is that apparently these two cousins heard Sextus Roscius say that he wished his father was dead several weeks prior to the murder." He held the spotlight now, turning slowly to the crowd and making a face of confusion. "Perhaps they can tell us who they think murdered Alexander of Macedon next time?" He earned himself further ripples across the court at this. "On their evidence alone, Sextus should be absolved, my lords." He nodded confidently at the judges.

Still winging it.

"Yet, bear with me a further moment, my lords, while I explain why it is that the two cousins are lying to this court," he politely pleaded, with an elegant dip of his neck and a swan-like swoosh of his arms.

"This guy should be on the stage," joked Monty telepathically.

"He is," replied the angel, who was also entertained.

"Upon the arrest and charging of Sextus Roscius, who was so inappropriately removed from his bed, on his farm, in the middle of the night, these said two cousins turn up and instantly take over the various farms owned by the family." Cicero spoke merrily as if building up to some sort of joke or other, which of course captivated everyone, even Erucius and Chrysogonos.

"Then, within a further twenty-four hours…and months before this trial, I might add,"—he now shook his head distastefully towards Chrysogonos—"all the farms and estates were seized by the state because Chrysogonos had been given a position of authority by Sulla, along with his freedom." He mentioned the dictator's name again, but he had to play it this way.

Quite the gambler, aren't you son.

"An authority he has been abusing, and thus not only has he disrespected Rome's judiciary, but he has also betrayed the generosity of the honourable Lucius Cornelius Sulla, by using his gifted position within our glorious Republic to murder and steal from Roman citizens." At this point, Chrysogonos turned and left along with his toadies, and one or two people shouted out goodbyes in mock Greek at him, which provoked some clustered laughs among the equestrian benches.

"He used this newly gifted authority to attract bit-part pawns into his vile plans, like those two country bumpkin cousins, who each managed one of Sextus Roscius senior's farms for him." Cicero shook his head in mock disbelief and disgust before lifting his nose as if he had just caught a whiff of the Aventine sewers. "Chrysogonos offered them ownership of two farms each in return for playing along." He paused to let this sink in around the court.

"They have both admitted to this court that the farms' new owner gifted two each to them," smirked Cicero, who leaned for a moment on Sextus's chair. "And we can take from their simple rustic personalities that it was not they who approached Chrysogonos first," he said, which caused even a few judges to smirk, knowing of course that Cicero himself hailed from the countryside. "Rather, it was the cold, calculated, power-hunting Greek who approached them as he needed them to run these new estates for him, as well as the ones he would gift them. A man who fought against his own Greek people for Rome, who now comes in and hopes to slaughter our ancient Roman traditions and laws. Well, even if his sense of loyalty is in question, our Greek certainly plays an aggressive and productive game of Kertamen, does he not," he turned and asked the crowd, who responded with nods of agreement and contemptuous shakes of their heads.

"Well, was it any surprise to learn that Chrysogonos immediately purchased all the estates owned by Sextus Roscius Senior, the rightful inheritance of Sextus Roscius junior," he patted his client's shoulder. "He even had the audacity to send a group of armed thugs to intimidate the auction process to make sure that he would obtain the properties for around about—nothing!" He now laughed at his own mock surprise, earning first the laughter of the crowd but also the applause of the growing crowd of observers up on the Capitol.

"However, due to being the rightful heir to these estates, as well as coming from a respectable Roman family, Sextus Roscius would not just die, and has since obtained the support of various other Roman citizens who seek to help the poor fellow here by at least obtaining a fair trial process for him, as opposed to a fall down the gallows stairs," he pointed out. "His liberty from arrest until this trial was maintained through the influence of some of his supporters, who have little doubt of his innocence," he declared, and Monty wondered if Cicero intended to lean upon the credibility of the *Metelli*. "And, as I have said, I appear to be the only advocate willing to stand up and defend this innocent Roman citizen from the disgusting villainy I have outlined," Cicero reminded the court.

Sextus wanted to cry as he felt the remaining seconds of his life ticking along with his quickening heartbeat. His tunic was of a light-yellow, which was by now wet with sweat, and his toes throbbed from constantly being squeezed into the soles of his leather sandals. He squirmed in his seat and wondered if he could bear the tension much longer. He suddenly felt sick when a waft of honied dormice being chargrilled nearby filled his nostrils.

"So, my lords," Cicero pressed on, "as you can see, Chrysogonos, who has already stolen this man's father and his rightful property, has a dilemma. A dilemma that he wants this court to fix for him—Sextus Roscius." He patted

Sextus on the other shoulder now, sighing deeply. "Chrysogonos is keen for this court to find my client guilty, and then to throw him in the Tiber"—he turned slowly to the crowd and shook his head despondently—"securing the name Chrysogonos on the deeds of all those farms. But, if you grant this Greek tyrant what he seeks, then it will be fair to say, judging by the man's theft of various other properties in Italy, that his evil lust for our property will not end there."

With these words, Cicero looked around the court, slowly shaking his head and raising his voice for the crowd up on the porticos. "Oh, yes," he nodded eagerly, "for this Greek lusts after much more, you know. And his evil will spread until the wolf himself knocks upon your own doors." The point he made was received by every single judge, even the eight who had been bribed by one of Chrysogonos' contacts, with the chill Cicero intended.

"Kill that Greek bastard!" shouted someone from afar who was hidden behind the canopy.

"A Greek slave, by the gods, surely not?" shouted a distant prophetic female voice up on the Palatine, but again she was hidden from view. Monty sensed the *Metelli* family purse behind her, of course.

"I ask you, learned judges: is the honour of our age-old traditions, as well as the very future of our Republic, not in your hands today?" Cicero asked the judges. Monty saw that several of them were nodding and smiling down at the young advocate. "I also ask you, honourable judges of Rome, is this not a case of Saturnalia gone mad?" Cicero had his left hand on his hip, leading with his right—and the crowd all burst into sporadic laughter.

One beaky-nosed geriatric judge two rows from the front nodded along to calls of, "Hear, hear," and "Well said, Cicero," from the observers upon the Capitol.

"For, if we tolerate this, it will be Rome herself next," Cicero alarmingly promised all those present. He looked around the court for a moment, soaking in the smiles, before returning to the judges. "I do without being ordered what some are constrained to do by their fear of the law." He quoted Aristotle at them before adding, "This Greek former slave obviously thinks that there is no need to fear Roman law." He smirked over at Erucius, who just shook his head back at him. "I respectfully ask you to show this Greek former slave that a Roman court will always protect its own against any barbaric lust to steal from them."

Cicero closed on that simple chord, and it seemed that regardless of the argument having nothing to do with preventing Chrysogonos from taking the estates, he was banking everything upon using the injustice of it all to persuade the court to spare a free-born Roman citizen's life by putting it before the greed of a non-Roman.

He bowed and then purposely returned to his seat beside Sextus at the desk, and took a deep breath of what he hoped was an air of considerably more accomplishment than he genuinely felt. Applause rang out from the Capitol, however, and then also from within the crowd; even a wolf-whistle or two could be heard. There was a fair bit of whispering amongst the crowd now that Monty could hear and, to his considerable pleasure, he found that he had the mental capacity to turn each voice up and down in his head according to his fancy.

He listened keenly to some of the judges, who were whispering in each other's ears, though there were not many of them. Most were keen to disguise how they voted on the wax tablets before them, which they turned upside down and held close to their chests. This way they could lie with confidence if Chrysogonos' thugs, or even Sulla's for that matter, ever came calling and demanding to know which way they had voted.

The time it took for the clerks to count the wax tablets twice was around fifteen minutes, then the magistrate counted them before returning to his seat. Everyone spoke to whomever was standing beside them about the potential verdict. Monty and the angel merely listened and observed. Meanwhile, Sextus Roscius leaned into Cicero and whispered nervously, "Your closing speech was a bit short, wasn't it?"

Cicero continued to stare at the judges regardless, searching their patrician features for clues. He too was nervous, of course, and Monty could hear his heart pounding above everyone else's. Cicero breathed slowly through his nose; he believed that he had persuaded them that a Roman citizen, regardless of his standing, should stand above any Greek.

He knew the price of defeat though. He would probably face nocturnal assassins should he have to travel across the city for any purpose at night, and this may even be the case should Sextus be absolved. He had, of course, decided to leave the city with some friends, family, slaves, and several armed bodyguards, to stay at a relative's estate near Frusino. There he would lie low and hope that Sulla did not take any offence at the method of his defence of Sextus Roscius.

"I mean, I thought you might have mentioned my connection to Divine Ceres[60]," Sextus mentioned nervously to him.

"We don't need all that religious fudge here, Sextus." Cicero turned and patted his wrist gently. "It won't make a blind bit of difference to these buggers, not when they all believe that they are descended from the gods anyway." He turned to observe the judges again, who were all staring at the crowd, perhaps attempting to sense the pending reaction to the verdict, which was about to be declared.

Monty really wanted water now; his lips were parched and strangely, he realised that he also needed to pee.

"But you—well, it was a short speech, not a full twenty minutes?" Sextus piped up again.

"I had to aim for a certain chord, Sextus, and I sense that my aim may have been true," Cicero turned and whispered confidently to him. "Regardless, our defence lies within the audacity of the conspiracy, so time is of no consequence to us."

"I don't want to die," Sextus said with an involuntary shiver, and Cicero poured him a cup of watered wine that his secretary had left in a jug for the purpose of steadying the nerves.

At this point, the Magistrate returned to his seat and looked back down, first at Erucius and then over towards Cicero, before clearing his throat and speaking stridently: "Absolved!" he declared.

The whole court began applauding, and there were several cries of joy from upon the Capitol. Sextus sank down upon the desk and breathed an enormous sigh of relief while Cicero stood and took a bow in front of the judges.

Monty turned and smiled at the angel. "I fair enjoyed that!" he admitted.

"Come, let us return." The angel took his hand and led him back through the lively crowd towards the strange doorway. "Come on!" he urged joyfully.

Monty felt complete trust in this entity, as well as the beginnings of joy. He quickly scurried after the angel through the doorway and back into the Russian art museum with the parquet floorboards again.

"Wait—what happened then?" Monty protested, tugging on the angel's hand.

"Sextus escaped the death penalty, of course, as a consequence of his acquittal, yet he didn't get any of his estates back, sadly." The angel told him.

---

[60] Greek and Roman mythological goddess of agriculture and the harvest.

"Sulla had them all seized for the state," sighed the angel, searching Monty's mind for his reaction.

"Bastard."

"A compromise of sorts," said the angel. Monty did not understand and shook his head accordingly. "Well, he allowed Sextus to continue to live, and had Chrysogonos hurled from a ship two days out of Crete, where he thought he was being sent to exile on an estate he owned there. Three nights later actually," he revealed. "He drowned within minutes."

"Yes. but how was it a compromise?" Monty still couldn't see it.

"Sulla had known what Chrysogonos was up to. Cicero dared to publicly attack the freed slave in the big gamble we observed, but he wisely refused to drag Sulla into it, for very practical reasons. Cicero had defeated Sulla's puppet, and the city accepted this, whilst also pointing out that it was an insult to Sulla, who had given the Greek his freedom and the honourable gift of citizenship. Sulla was spared the discredit but he was clearly obliged to turn upon Chrysogonos. He might well have had Cicero murdered too, but his mind was turned in another direction by certain entities."

"Cicero was not godly, so why did he risk everything there for Sextus?" Monty needed to know.

"In order to achieve greatness, he knew he needed to do it by doing the right things," smiled the angel. "Which was precisely why we chose him, of course." He winked.

"And what happened to Sextus?"

The angel released Monty's hand and motioned him to walk back over towards Aivazovsky's painting. "Sextus was whisked out of Rome by the *Metelli* family to their large olive estates near Pollentia on Mallorca[61], where he managed one of them."

"And his family?"

"Sulla allowed his family to join him," shrugged the angel.

---

[61] Quintus Caecilius Metellus was Consul in 123 BC and later received a proconsular command, defeating the pirates who had plagued the Balearic Islands of Mallorca and Menorca and received a Triumph for this in Rome as well as the honorific title of "Balearicus". He established two Roman towns—Palma and Pollentia—in Mallorca and by the time of the trial of Sextus Roscius in 60 BC, the Metelli family still owned vast olive estates across the Balearics.

So Cicero had purely been defending the man's life, not winning him back his property, considered Monty with a hint of sadness.

"Away from the gloom and subservience of Republican Rome, and the darkness of Bonaparte's support team, do you now have a clear understanding of how it is that both good and evil are involved in an age-old struggle?" asked the angel, quite casually.

"Yes, in part I am, but..." Monty hesitated, "I think I'm beyond understanding it completely."

"Quite," smirked the angel as they halted in front of the painting again.

"I hadn't really believed in God, because all my persuasive powers of reason told me not to, because he either did not exist, or he was long gone," Monty explained by thought. "Yet, by giving me a taster of all this wonderful stuff, I now have a new optimism in him."

The angel studied the painting some more as he softly thought back at Monty: "You don't know him. That is why you're not happy in life. You justify this by arguing that you're firstly an academic, and thus have done well, then that you're an officer of the law who protects the deprived and the damaged from the unjust few." He shrugged, continuing to take in the dark image of Moscow burning in front of him. After a moment, he continued to explain: "Yet you know only too well that that argument is entirely dependent upon ignoring the harsh reality, which is that you also defend guilty individuals whose crimes often bring out anger, disgust, irritation and general distaste in your heart," he pointed out.

Monty said nothing. Instead, he smirked and exhaled through his nostrils whilst turning to look at other paintings nearby. He recognised Van Gogh's vibrant, layered brushstrokes and the control of colours that Monty knew still appealed so much to his own generation, who hung prints of his work upon the walls of their modern homes.

"Rules have been compared to cobwebs, in that whilst they may prove sticky to little flies, they often allow the wasps to wriggle through," offered the angel.

"Not all of the Scottish legal system is flawed, angel," Monty eventually submitted.

"I am familiar with your law," replied the angel. "But, let us return to the point, which is that you don't know God because you tell yourself that because your world is not a perfect place, there can't be a God. Or, that he should intervene and use the power you think he should have to prevent all misery and suffering. I'm right, am I not?" he asked.

"I suppose I have considered these issues," replied Monty, nervously now, unsure whether to declare his apologies and new-found commitment to God or not.

"He is not understood by the human concept of reason, nor is your simple deliberation of the actuality sufficient to enable you to understand why, how, who, or where he is," explained the angel patiently.

"And the point is?" Monty thought across to him.

"The point is that God created you and your world, and that regardless of things you cannot understand, he is good and cares very much about you." The assurance offered to him was wholehearted, and Monty believed it, but was struck by spontaneous emotion. The angel paused and allowed him to regain control.

"And—this struggle between angels and demons—what is it that they are fighting for?" Monty asked as calmly as he could, whilst touching his eyes with his cuffs.

The angel suddenly handed him a glass of iced water: "You are still thirsty." Monty hesitated, looked at the water, then trusted and drank deeply before gasping and thanking the angel. "The dark beings do not love your species, Monty, and they do not think that mankind is fit for anything better than servitude, and in some cases, abuse."

Monty placed the glass on the floor and nodded that he understood that much at least. "And so, a contest of some sort is being played out?" he asked.

"More a struggle, with points being proven and disproven," replied the angel.

"And? I mean, what precisely do they want?"

"To bring about polytheism, it is necessary to destroy Christianity, both within society and her so-called morality," grinned the angel knowingly.

"How are they able to do that, just by placing their people in power everywhere?"

"Well, in part, yes. But also by destroying old principles, firstly by making faith seem unfashionable and straitlaced, and then by slowly changing laws and implanting new traditions that are gradually accepted as the norm," the angel explained, so nonchalantly it seemed as though it were all as simple as making a cup of tea.

"Such as?" Monty knew this; he had seen and commented upon the decay of society, like everyone else his age, but it had always seemed easier to ignore it and to plod on.

"Making aliens the reality and killing religion or the worship of God in the process." The angel winked again, as if amused by Monty's sudden understanding of the process. "Slowly, the old biblical morality is attacked and then erased, by subtle little changes such as the selling of alcohol on the Sabbath. That was never allowed, even as recently as the 1990s." He shook his head in sadness. "And the time will come soon when twenty-four-hour supermarkets are no longer restrained from selling it after the current 10pm restrictions." He smiled again.

"Why would that be so wrong?"

"Watch and see for yourself," smirked the angel.

"Like alcopops or cheap cider, is it about polluting the youth?" Monty tried to guess.

The angel looked at him and sighed with forbearance. "It's about disrespecting a holy day and sticking two fingers up to God—nothing more," he whispered while knowingly tapping his nose with his index finger. Monty nodded; he had never appreciated the football being changed from a traditional Saturday afternoon to a Sunday to appease TV broadcasters who paid millions of pounds for the rights. "The opposition have now become self-assured, so their arrogance is everywhere to be seen through their abominations," the angel told him.

"Openly on public display. Business logos, public services and particularly through music and cinema, to name but a few of their favoured billboards. People no longer consider this behaviour to be abnormal in your generation." The angel shrugged again. "Oh, they sigh at it, yes, but they accept it all too readily, and thus the paranormal has become the normal in your era." He eyeballed Monty a moment, allowing this to sink in.

"Why though? It can't simply be to stick two fingers up at God, surely?" Monty questioned their objective.

"No, you miss the point," sighed the angel again. "It's to see man put two fingers up at God by neglecting the Sabbath, which of course is one of the ten commandments," he insisted. "Thus showing that man being gifted absolute liberty was a mistake, as he will inevitably be lured away from his creator, as easily as flies are from the cow's back to the dropped pat," sighed the angel.

"And yet he won't stop these angels from misguiding people?" Monty pointed out.

"That would defeat the purpose and yes, he has done just that at times despite the rules of the contest."

"Then why is this struggle allowed to continue?" Monty asked on behalf of his species.

"The struggle is necessary and you cannot begin to understand why this might be, but it's because man's intellect is primitive. What matters," insisted the angel, "is that mankind avoids the bait."

"Which it's obviously failed to do so far," suggested Monty cautiously.

"Precisely," nodded the angel. "Yet the ultimate point is whether or not mankind is corruptible enough to destroy itself."

"Why was Cicero chosen by you if he was a pagan, then?" Monty was curious.

"Because he was fit for purpose and had a moral soul, not to mention the fact that Chrysogonos was an abomination who could have changed the course of history otherwise," replied the angel, somewhat amused by this sudden change of subject. "Today, in your era," he went on, "the fallen guide their disciples into factions whose objective it is to herd mankind into a single world government. As I say, they are no longer subtle about it either, and their actions are quite evident. I am sure you must have noticed this yourself?"

"I see things, angel; sure, we all do. Whether we register them or not is a different thing, and personally I always thought it was all about greedy people trying to rule the world." Monty had never considered that higher entities were pulling the strings in an age-old struggle over mankind.

"There are always others behind the men and women pursuing power," cautioned the angel, reading Monty's thoughts again. "Soon, they hope to unlock Pandora's box of quantum physics and end their need for an ego-driven slave race," he warned.

"But why me, angel? Why are you revealing all of this to me?" Monty needed to know the answer, as this question had been eating away at him like a guilty conscience ever since he had first viewed the Aivazovsky painting of Moscow falling.

"I want to offer you a deal, Stephen," the angel smiled at him.

"You do?" Monty had been hopeful of this in the last few minutes now that hindsight was in play.

The angel laughed and it was instantly infectious. Monty could not help laughing too, in a wonderful moment of joy between them. It seemed an electric connection, one which was as moving to a human being as, say, the joy experienced at the birth of a child, which persuaded him further that this was, indeed, an angel of the creator standing before him.

"That is precisely why this undertaking is for you, wouldn't you agree?" chuckled the angel.

"Perhaps…" Monty was cautious still of what the deal might entail.

The angel placed his hand on Monty's shoulder, just as Cicero had done to Sextus. "You have seen examples of how, sometimes, interventions occur, both great and small, by both good and evil, Stephen. This can happen regardless of a person's faith, belief, or general opinion. It is not always possible to intervene. Indeed, it is almost always impossible, for reasons you can never understand. But I want you to assist me in an intervention," revealed the angel, with a joyful expression across those marvellously chiselled features.

"Okay." Monty was enthusiastic enough.

"A good man is stranded behind enemy lines, and I want you to come to his aid," explained the angel.

"In what way?"

"By representing him in court, my boy!" laughed the angel again.

"Is that all?" Monty was quite surprised that this was all there was to it.

"Yes," grinned the angel.

"Okay," smiled Monty, feeling somewhat relieved.

"And if you do this, and sin infrequently, and worship the Lord for the remainder of your life, you will be admitted into our domain," added the angel with considerable pleasure.

"You have a deal then," Monty quickly offered his hand, which the angel shook firmly.

"You are from a time where disputatious people are driven to take issue with anything and everything and an era where selfishness comes before courtesy. This, of course, creates frequent arguments and a great need for practised masters such as yourself." The angel sighed despondently. "This is a result of your geniuses and officials putting their faith in so-called men who pursue self-glory and power, as opposed to the worship of God. You live in a time Stephen, when men believe that all the glory of their past were achieved alone, and they assume this without any consideration of nature's architect in their calculations.

"So, in their arrogance they begin to worship these so-called men and their financially designed logic. For the occult fingerprint is appearing in increasing areas of your arrogant society and people's behaviour would have turned heads only twenty years ago," he pointed out. "Now though, the paranormal is fast becoming the normal, and the general bitterness pervading society is one of the symptoms of this collapse of order."

"So much for the recession and austerity being behind it all, then?" Monty half joked.

"There are not many like you, that is for sure. Not many who put obsolete notions of ethics and honour before a lust for affluence," insisted the angel with a warm, knowing look in his eyes that promised friendship and loyalty.

Monty took the point, of course; he had always believed that he had chosen to practise law because he was one of the good guys. He had known for years now that his imperfect childhood sense of justice being automatic was far-fetched and quite adrift from the reality of the legal system. Genuinely, his initial intention upon entering the field of law was to help to address growing inadequacies by defending individual liberties. It was fair to say that money had never been the be-all nor end-all for him, but he could not help but wonder whether the angel was over-valuing him somewhat here.

"And that is why you are so well qualified to defend this innocent man on the Lord's behalf," said the angel, reading his thoughts quite matter-of-factly.

"I see...I think?" Monty was not quite sure.

"Because you do not instinctively lust after the role, nor indeed are you convinced that you are good enough for it," laughed the angel, and once again, it was such an infectious laugh that Monty could not help but join in. No one had brought such a reaction out in him in a long time.

"Yet the facts that you are both moral and considerably more compassionate than many others of your era are the deciding factors—which you should consider to be rare assets," the angel assured him now with a comforting arm around the shoulder again.

Monty did not know what to say to that, so he asked: "What is he charged with?"

"Murder," sighed the angel with a sudden straight face.

"Murder? But I am only a solicitor; I can't represent him," Monty wanted to shout in protest but instead, with obvious forbearance, he thought it across telepathically.

"True, but you will play the all-important wing-man role to an advocate, whom only you will be able to persuade to take the case," assured the angel, taking in the painting again.

"Who?"

"Never mind that; you start by trying to get the case binned at the Sheriff Court stage, and then if necessary, bring in the QC to take the case in the High Court," insisted the angel.

"And what if we lose the case?" asked Monty. After all, did he need to win to get his promised pass into heaven, or was the offer a reward for just participating?

"You're being asked to help us because some limited intervention has been authorised. In return, you will be considered for eternal life and your previous sins may not be held against you," confirmed the angel. "It is a rare honour and one which usually rewards the helper. However, if you prefer to question your fee for such a case, then perhaps it is best that I allow you to return to your dimension presently, and wipe your memory of this experience." He stared straight into Monty's eyes.

"I'm only establishing the facts being put to me, angel; you will grant me that and be patient with me—after all, I am—well, my whole life seems to have changed as of today, and my realisation of God and Satan, the meaning of the cosmos and all that, has been shaken and turned upside down," mitigated Monty.

The angel, seeing that he was being truthful, nodded and smiled at him: "I understand, but you need to act swiftly as your time here is coming to a close. Will you believe and worship God as your creator and spiritual guide, from now on until your passing day?" asked the angel, his face expressing the love that a parent's does to a child.

"In my own personal way, yes, I will," replied Monty.

"And will you take this commission in the hope of pleasing the Lord?"

"Yes." Monty knew that this was the priority, sure, but he also hoped for an eternal life. Who wouldn't?

The angel saw this hope in him and recognised it for what it was—faith. "Then return now and find that everything will fall into being without any further effort," he told him.

"So how will I know who…" Monty asked whilst gazing around the bright and clean gallery room. A painting of a bearded man hung upon the wall opposite and beneath it stood a tall tropical plant in a brass pot.

"It will just happen," assured the angel. "Make use of Ronnie Charnley; he will prove helpful and is a good soul."

"But wait, will I see you again?" Monty was thinking along the lines of some sort of divine hotline or angelic handler, particular seeing as he was being asked to manage a potential murder trial against the fallen entities and their Nephilim disciples.

The angel nodded. "Not me, but another of my choir will provide you with guidance," he laughed that endearing and soothing laugh again.

All Monty had to go on was knowledge and instinct, and he recognised that he was witnessing an out-of-this world experience as well as a chance to rectify something personal. He must not become starstruck or overwhelmed by it all, he thought. He instinctively wanted to trust this being, this guide…and sensed that he must seize this unbelievable opportunity while he could, and trust something that for the majority of his adult life he had refused to acknowledge even existed.

"And what if I had respectfully declined your offer?" he politely asked without fear.

"Then the struggle would have continued without you and you would have returned to what you feel is your life."

Monty waited a moment… "Can I really make a difference?"

"Dark energy and matter will continue to come through to your world regardless, but you will help mankind to stand up to it," confirmed the angel.

"But why do these things want to destroy mankind? And if they have powers akin to those that you obviously have, angel, what use can I possibly be?" Monty pressed, regardless.

"You will be helping us to prevent the rise of a dark power, one that is not always visible to human sight, and that has been trying for many years to destroy moral values and principles," clarified the angel again.

"Well, I don't think I can play much of a part in this production." Monty spoke as he felt, and this was, at least, more appreciated by his guide. "But I have been enlightened and shall worship God now, and if I can do even something small for him, I would be honoured to try," he said, with a touch of pride.

"Splendid!" The angel beamed with joy and lightly patted Monty's shoulder again. "Even the smallest act of piety is another brick in the wall of mankind's defences," he said. "And as long as there is piety in the land, the land will prosper and the people will be glorious, as the last three centuries have shown for your country, Stephen. Yet when man and his posterity reject the authority of the Lord by abandoning him for the enterprises of the occult, the land will be overwhelmed by evil and all the so-called achievements which men are so proud of, will be buried in insignificance."

"Sold!" said Monty. He knew what side he would take; he always had; it had simply been a case of not being sure that there were any sides to choose from. He now recognised that there truly were, and of course he would back the right horse.

A silence fell as the two beings shook hands slowly and firmly, with only Monty's breathing to be heard. "I'll do it," he thought before looking up at the beautifully carved ceiling frieze, which reminded him of the old Victorian Smith's tearoom around the corner from his house in Leith.

Was this really happening? He knew the difference between reality and a dream, he had always thought. There was magic at play here though—no, this was no dream…this was a baptism.

"Of course, I'll do it," he laughed again. "Will I need to be baptised, then?" he half joked to himself now.

"I do believe that you will at some point," smiled the angel, reading his thoughts. "Do you have any more questions?" he asked warmly.

"Plenty," smirked Monty, and they both smiled again.

"Well, prepare a list of them and ask the mentor who appears," said the angel merrily as he put a loving arm around Monty's shoulder and slowly walked him back towards the portal.

"Can I meet Jesus Christ?" Monty suddenly asked as they arrived back at his original point of entry into this dimension.

"If you earn the right to, yes, you can. All people can," the angel stared into his eyes now, those wonderful green eyes feeding him the truth.

"Goodness, that would be interesting." Monty shook his hand again for a final time.

"Walk back through the way you first came, and when you arrive back at the stones, head back to the clubhouse and find Ronnie Charnley. He will have something for you." He lightly patted Monty again on the shoulder before ushering him back through the strange doorway.

Monty was immediately subjected to a dizzying disorientation as he entered.

"God bless," thought the angel to him as he passed back over.

Chapter Eight

We took care of Kennedy.
Sam Giancana

Monty walked back to the car park without glancing back at the stones. He was initially oblivious to the icy wind that came in from the sea as he was deep in thought. After a few yards however, he was gradually roused by the salty air which was beginning to numb his forehead. He had been preoccupied by thoughts of what this was all about and how it was going to develop. He felt privileged and excited to be invited onto this mission, but it was all a lot to take in. He strode on purposely across the snow-covered grass like a king amongst men, whilst the barren and snow dusted trees to his left, bent over like courtesans thanks to gusts of wind from the sea. Their frosted branches appearing like pipe cleaner figures who were honouring him. He wondered if any deities were watching him now and found himself shivering more; for Egypt and Rome, the wind was painfully bitter.

He tried to ignore it though and to think back to his recent encounters with the angel; after all, if they were prepared to transport him to other dimensions in order to persuade him that he had been wrong all along about God, and that he should join their bizarre struggle, then he should not concern himself with a head-chill, he told himself. Truth is he was really excited, and for the first time in his life, felt blessed. So he fought off the chill by ruminating about this as he approached the club house. He had, after all, just been in the proximity of both Napoleon Bonaparte and Marcus Tullius Cicero, and couldn't help purring at his luck.

What did I do to deserve that?

The snow on the carpark crunched beneath his feet; having hardened slightly throughout his recent adventure. He checked his watch—two hours had passed. There was only one other set of footprints visible—Charnley's.

Charnley was waiting inside at the bar with a glass of water for him. "Your thirsty then?" he grinned as he passed it along the bar, whilst sipping from a cup of tea. The clubhouse lounge was empty apart from a cleaning lady who passed through carrying a little Henry vacuum cleaner. A barmaid with brown curly hair and a pierced nose sat looking down at some paperwork in a kitchen area beyond the bar and out of earshot. It was warm thankfully, thought Monty, but he was indeed thirsty and thanked Charnley for the water.

"How did you know I was thirsty?" He gasped after necking half the glass.

"Another of those strange texts," grinned Charnley.

A radio was on. There was a discussion ongoing about the general election. Monty suggested that they go over to a half-circled leather booth in a far corner of the large lounge. As they both crossed across the thick green carpet towards it, they listened to the people on the radio discussing the use of Twitter by the election candidates. A young female with a husky voice was pointing out that Twitter was going to play a big part in next year's election because it helped "remove the suits and introduced the real Cameron's and Miliband's to the electorate."

As they approached the booth, Monty looked out of a large window at the sea. It was choppy and appeared to be a dark grey like an old anvil, but with smudges of white and brown surf. "Cameron writes long texts on Facebook, but my generation don't care to read long texts," giggled one very camp teenage male radio guest.

"Yeh, I heard a few people say that," laughed an older female. "So, is it just simpler for modern society to read Twitter then?" she queried.

"Yes but some politicians use Twitter to just broadcast press releases, which is not something that I am particularly interested in reading," replied the camp guy.

"I agree," pipped up another teenage female with a Dundonian accent now, "I think I'm just more inclined to listen to a real person, as opposed to a candidate who uses social media to blast slogans and rally calls at everyone," she announced merrily and before giggling like a school girl.

"I would say that the SNP are doing OK with their Twitter posts," pointed out another young male now who had a bit of a lisp and seemed quite serious.

"So you guys want to feel the real person as opposed to the suit?" asked the older female host.

Charnley spoke now as they sat down. "So, what happened?" he asked before taking an unsteady sip of his tea. They both had a fine view of the icy sea through a blue velvet curtained window, which reminded Monty of how cold it was outside. Thankfully, there was a radiator beneath it that pumped warmth out under their spacious round table.

"I was enlightened," he replied thoughtfully. He could feel himself beginning to unwind and relax now. Charnley smiled. The radio in the background seemed distant as the rhythmic sound of the wind beyond the double-glazed window dominated before gradually becoming hypnotic.

There was a dark oak framed oil painting to the left of the window of a golf course, but it did not appear to Monty to be this one. There was another frame next to it, a watercolour, hanging above another dark timber shelf with a small Royal Doulton golfing character jug upon it. This one was of an early Victorian gentleman playing golf somewhere. It was a strain on Monty's neck to look over at it so he returned his gaze to the elements outside and sipped what remained of his water.

"So, they removed your blinkers then mate, did they?" asked Charnley before then wearily having a quick peek back across the empty lounge.

"I met an angel in a museum in Russia and well..." Monty paused and shrugged, "he didn't tell me his name."

Charnley nodded as if this was the most natural thing in the world.

"He took me to see Napoleon Bonaparte and then afterward, to a legal trial in Rome." Monty scanned Charnley's face for any sign of prior knowledge, but there was none; the man's nutty looking smile betrayed the fact that he was as bewildered as Monty was.

"What happened?" Charnley wanted to know, eyes feverish with excitement.

"Well, I was enlightened on the struggle between good and evil and how both sides have used people as pawns across time, regardless of who they are, or what their standings are," explained Monty.

"The light shines in the darkness and the darkness has not overcome it?" stated Charnley with a cheeky smirk across his chubby face.

Monty thought that with his rosy cheeks, Charnley looked like a fat garden gnome, and so nodded and sipped some more water.

"And?"

"And I was asked to help someone who is going to be, or has recently been, charged with murder," shrugged Monty.

Both of them considered this for a moment and gazed out at the sea beyond. A female newsreader was on the air now.

"And the newly appointed Scottish Labour leader Jim Murphy, who has the job of dragging his party off its knees and into an election battle with both the SNP and the SLP, has been talking with our Alison Hastings," she announced before Murphy's familiar West Coast voice then came on and began talking about a repeal for alcohol at Scottish football matches.

Monty considered this a moment while watching the grey waves rising under the fading light outside. The sleet filled wind appeared to be maddening the sea and the sky was quickly darkening now too. Quick look at his watch—4 pm. The traffic back to Edinburgh would probably still be smooth, he hoped.

"They will never allow that again surely?" he thought aloud.

"What, booze at the football? No, I doubt it," agreed Charnley.

"And the Scottish Conservative leader Ruth Davidson has previously called for a review into the ban on alcohol at football matches too," the field reporter pointed out to Murphy.

"Well, never mind all that," gasped Charnley, a tad surprised at how seemingly casual Monty appeared to be. "What did you say?" He wanted to know.

Monty turned to him slowly and smiled, "I bought into the whole shebang and agreed."

Charnley nodded slowly as it had always been clear to him that this was the only logical option.

"God, creation and all that," nodded Monty as he polished off the last of the water.

"And what is the objective then? I mean, is there an end game regarding this murder trial, etc?" asked Charnley.

The radio suddenly switched over to another station playing old Christmas music now. Dean Martin's *Marshmallow World* now filled the lounge.

"That will be them starting dinner soon," said Charnley, taking another look around again but there was still no sign of life. "Anyways, the end game?" He turned again to Monty.

"Peace on earth," grinned Monty. "Now what is it you are supposed to have for me?" he asked.

Charnley took yet another quick glance behind him—all clear. He then carefully reached into his inside jacket pocket and produced what appeared to be a cork from a wine bottle. "Here," he offered it to Monty.

"What is it?" Monty hadn't a clue as he reached out and took it. It certainly felt like a cork in his hand and sniffed at it but there was no wine stain or scent upon it.

Charnley took yet another annoying glance behind him before leaning over the small table at Monty and whispering, "Rub it with your thumb twice. It's something they designed just for you," he urged. "It will supposedly only respond to your touch, Monty."

Monty rubbed it lightly and cautiously with his thumb. Instantly, it became a small glowing blade of sorts. The handle of which grew perfectly into the palm of his hand. "Wow!" He opened his mouth and gasped. It seemed small, the length of a machete perhaps, but it was very impressive on the eye.

Charnley's jaw dropped too. He had not seen it in this form before.

It did not appear to be made of any kind of metal substance, rather it appeared to be formed from some scintillating substance unknown to him. It seemed to be moving as a flame might. Yet it was sparkling blue in colour, and then—almost clear as if diluted with water.

Monty did not feel fear, or anything else other than calmness and reassurance when holding it. Somehow, he began gradually to sense that it was a living organism, or as if it were an additional limb or muscle which was attached to him.

"Don't wave it about in here, for goodness sake," Charnley urged before taking yet another concerned look behind in the direction of the bar.

Monty double tapped it without thinking, and as he had somehow anticipated, it instantly returned to being a little cork between his finger and thumb. "Wow!" he whispered as excitedly as a child who had just been given its first bike. He then quickly placed it in his jacket pocket.

"Apparently, they forged it for you from something called Anarama and it will cut through any material," insisted Charnley.

"And it only responds to my fingerprints?" asked Monty.

"I think so, well, more your touch." Charnley shrugged his shoulders. "That was all I was told when it appeared at the stones a few days ago," he said.

"Told by text?" asked Monty.

"Yes but of course, it deleted itself afterwards, didn't it?" Charnley shook his head. "A similar weapon to that once carried by the far-archer himself," he pointed out.

"The far-archer?"

"Apollo from Greek mythology, Monty." Grinned Charnley. "Apollo apparently favoured the bow but the text said he also had a blade similar to that," he shrugged and indicated towards Monty's coat pocket.

Monty was somewhat familiar with Greek mythology, though the little he knew about the Trojan war had come from movies. "Apollo was the god of Troy?" he asked.

Charnley nodded. "Yep, Apollo, or Apulu, as the Umbrians knew him," replied Charnley.

"The Umbrians?" This was all going somewhere obviously, but Monty was somewhat surprised to be learning about it from this dark horse here; what else did Charnley know?

"An ancient Italian people with Greek heritage, who were, after various wars, eventually overrun by Rome and then incorporated into the Roman Empire," explained Charnley.

"How do you know all of this then, mate?"

"It was all in the text, Monty, and then I researched it a bit more." Charnley shrugged again. "But the point is," he took another glance around before leaning forward again and whispering, "Apollo had the first prototype of your new toy."

"So, it is a weapon then. Why do I need a weapon, no one said I was required to fight?" Monty was a tad concerned at the idea of brawling like Achilles and Hector.

We know how that particular clash turned out between the demi-god and Human.

"You are required to defend yourself from those that would harm you for helping the good guys in this matter, Monty," Charnley corrected him.

"Am I likely to be killed?" Monty asked ever so calmly.

"No. You are protected by angels now, and that is why they gave you that tool." Charnley shook his head.

That's a contradiction.

"How can I trust you?" Monty considered that he might be being misled by evil entities here, just as easily as being recruited by angels.

"Having doubts now despite what you just experienced?" Charnley smiled at him and there was a moment of silence between them before he spoke again. "Get to know your enemy, Monty, try Revelations 9:11," he suggested.

Monty took a mental note to check up on it later. He looked outside again at the darkening sky. "Okay, shall we move on now, I want to get going," he said.

"Right you are then, squire." Nodded Charnley. "My number is logged in your phone back in your car," he said.

Monty didn't bother asking how that was possible considering he had locked the car before leaving.

"If you need me for anything, anything at all, even if you want me to move in with you as support throughout this matter, just ask." Charnley shrugged, but this only worried Monty further as to what on earth might lay in store.

It's not from earth though, is it.

"Just call me and I'll drop everything here and come over to Edinburgh within a couple of hours, Monty," assured Charnley.

"Thanks. I'll certainly keep that in mind," murmured Monty. He needed to get away and drive, for only then could he think things over and establish some kind of preparation plan for whatever was about to develop. "Shall we go?" He slowly stood up.

"Okay. I'll find my own way from here then, Monty. Good luck and God bless," agreed Charnley, standing up and shaking his hand.

Monty then headed back past the bar and out the adjoining exit. He could feel the cork in his pocket as he crossed the car park towards the car. "This is insane," he told himself as he unlocked it and got in. He checked his phone. "Charnley" was indeed logged into it. He leaned back a moment and sighed. It really all was a hell of a lot to take in this. He googled "Revelations 9:11" and read, *They had as king over them the angel of the Abyss, whose name in Hebrew is Abaddon and in Greek is Apollyon (that is, Destroyer).*

Monty had not known that any Greek mythological deities were referenced within a biblical context. Was Apollo a fallen angel then? "Know your enemy" had been Charnley's advice. It was all so sudden and dramatic though, and accepting all of this might take a while. He started up the car, checking for any sudden surprise passengers to appear in his rear-view mirror as he slowly pulled out across the snowy gravel and back out onto the coastal road.

Throughout the drive back, which was more awkward due to a sudden snowstorm and ever-increasing darkness, he kept a relatively easy pace with the radio off. He had the heating on, but the snow on the bonnet before him made him feel cold and he did shiver a little.

Or was that fear?

He was not sure. He didn't feel troubled nor was he disturbed by his experience today, rather he was confused and still in shock. The whole experience rotated within his mind as he drove.

Why me?

Is there another meaning?

Why do I deserve this honour? For it is an honour, we have established that?

Why do I deserve this grace then?

How can I possibly help?

One thing he was certain of was that the spiritual tone in his life had completely changed—big time today. And then it began—a lightbulb moment. Gently initially, just a subtle notion of understanding. A developing theory perhaps; and then within a few minutes—an insight.

Monty sensed that his thoughts were being energised by something, a spirit—a good spirit. This immediately instigated a pleasant boost of confidence and recognition that the fact he could now see clearly out of the car window despite the heavy snowstorm, was also a part of this mystical honour. He was also conscious about the simple things that some people take for granted, such as the basic ability to breath unassisted.

My thinking has changed.

Should praise follow now?

Was he asking himself, or was he talking to the spirit? Was he even asking God? Everyone would think he was nuts if he spoke of this. This thought made him smile to himself as he proceeded westwards through the coastal village of Kinghorn.

"Thoughts are purified by the spirit so you understand the realism."

Praise is the key then?

"Genuine praise changes everything."

We shall see.

"Indeed."

As he crossed back over the Forth Bridge, there was less snow fall and he could easily make out the lights of both North and South Queensferry. The new multi-million-pound bridge known as the Queensferry Crossing, set to open in 2016, stood out to his right, though it would no doubt become delayed as per Edinburgh's tram project. They were making progress though, he noted. Enormous support pillars had been erected in the river below and the builders were slowly working each section across to them, one by one.

Isn't man a clever creature?

Unexpectedly, he noticed something bright from the corner of his left eye; he looked out over the area between himself and the Forth Rail Bridge and there, looping playfully in the air around 30 ft from the dark water beneath, was a light. The increasing wind suggested that a gale would arrive soon, yet the light, which Monty thought may be round, about the size of a football, continued to loop, swoop down and then glide across the unyielding surface of the water below.

He gripped the steering wheel tightly and put his foot down in order to get across the bridge as soon as possible.

What the hell is that?

He watched now as it began to rise into the grey sky again, before then swooping back down and out across the rocky shore of North Queensferry where the salty surf was beginning to crash against the stone dock which shielded the western side of the little harbour. Icy gusts were ushering the growing waves on like a war drum—determined not to dwindle in the face of battle. The object appeared to have the ability to hover and then move off both slowly and at an incredible speed in all directions without any restriction to the elements. Monty noticed a gull struggling to avoid being blown into the beautiful yet treacherous water beneath but the airborne light had no such issue.

He looked in his rear-view mirror, just to see if he could see if any other drivers were also witnessing this strange phenomenon, but it was impossible to tell due to the snow and the permanent sun visor, for the dog, on the rear window which he hadn't bothered removing since summer. He was scared now though. He hadn't a clue what on earth this object was, only that it was certainly not influenced by the weather. Indeed it seemed to even be playing in the gusty chaos.

Perhaps it was one of the baddies?

His heart pounded as he drove across to the southern side of the crossing and just then, he could have sworn that he had seen the light drop at an incredible speed into the water beneath and not reappear.

He watched his speed as he drove into Edinburgh despite instinctively wanting to hit the accelerator and get as far away from the river as possible. He was growingly anxious for his wellbeing now and began to think about pulling over at the Barnton and calling up his old client—Jimmy Lazarini.

Giacomo "Jimmy" Lazarini was a native of Gambettola, south of Bologna, who immigrated to Liverpool in 1980 where he married an Italian publican's daughter. He had been handy with his fists from his school years onward, so had no problem finding regular work as a night club bouncer and then later, as a maître d for a privately-owned casino in Manchester. It had been in 1984 when Jimmy had first met Remo Scarfo, known around the casino circuit as "Ronnie from Zeebrugge".

Other than this, little had been known about Scarfo, who had used a fake passport and address when taking out his membership, and he always paid in cash too so he left no electronic fingerprints either. This had not been an unusual practice in casinos in those days, with punters keen to keep their losses secret from their banks and better halves.

Scarfo had turned up alone a few times a month and played heavy on the roulette, tipping the waitress who brought him his soda water and lime every hour with ponies[62]. Most of the regulars liked him and of course as a fellow Italian, he had become friendly with Jimmy. Scarfo always seemed to be just passing through on business. Originally from Scotland, and consistently evasive whenever anyone enquired into his private life, such as old Mrs Chung who would sit alongside him at the tables for hours on end because she thought he was lucky. His cover story was that he owned a hotel somewhere.

If he had, Jimmy guessed that it was nowhere near wherever Scarfo claimed it to be. For Scarfo liked to fudge, and Jimmy detected this about him early doors though he never questioned nor tried to suss him out because Scarfo's business was his business. It just happened to be that his business was being a vital linkman in a heroin supply line for Edinburgh's Cattaneo crime family.

Aneillo "Wee Neil" Cattaneo's father had been the youngest of three siblings who had all been successful business entrepreneurs on the east coast of Scotland from Berwick up to Fife, and as far west as Falkirk. Traditionally, they had dominated the east coast's ice cream manufacturing since the 1960's. These days however, most of the brothers' descendants were sitting landlords of catering and hospitality properties. A spoiled silver-spooned generation who had turned their noses up to the kind of hard work that the three old timers had once endured. Some of these descendants still ran the family restaurants, fish and chip shops and guesthouses, whilst others had amusement arcades and one or two fish factories. A couple of branches, including Wee Neil's clan, had broken off from

---

[62] Twenty-five-pound casino chips. British soldiers serving in India had created the term to refer to an Indian 25 rupee note because the number 25 appears similar to a horse's head and tail.

178

the catering route and ventured into the nightclub and private sauna industries in the mid-seventies.

By the time his father had died in 1977, Neil had moved into the private casino domain as a cover for his growing heroin enterprise. His two younger brothers—Nicodemo (Nicky) and the stuttering Gerardo (Gerry)—had been his trusty wing men in what had become a highly lucrative, though traumatic few decades. Nicky had managed the Casino, the saunas, night clubs, and strip joints, whilst keeping a firm handle upon the large team of muscle who policed the doors for him.

Having handpicked them all, he felt secure and he also had access to a handy reserve force too with which to shield his brother's drug enterprise from any threat of violence. Muscle had always been the key to success and security when it came to the business of big heroin distribution.

On the other hand, Gerry, who officially owned a scrap yard in Leith, remained in the shadows whilst he secretly orchestrated the business strategy. He was bright and ran the show for his elder brother via a buffer man—another Italian within the clan who passed on the instructions to everyone. The buffer man dealt with a trusted ten-man crew, who in turn all had specially selected and trusted friends (known as players), who helped distribute the heroin in particular areas. Each one of the ten could call upon the accumulated muscle that Nicky retained, at any sign of trouble.

The success, at least financially, had been instant. The chosen system had overcome the frequent quandaries of supply and maintained a steady profit over a couple of decades. The real key to Wee Neil's success however had been his refusal to over stretch his reach, unlike his Scottish rivals, and to patiently perfect the security arrangement by establishing a trustworthy crew over the years. The financial returns were washed within legitimately owned businesses, while bungs and bribes were required to be both generous and regular in order to maintain the operating system.

One of the greatest successes they experienced had been when a customs security crew in Aberdeen had, for a two-year period, turned a blind eye to the staff of a sub-sea vessel connected to the oil industry, who took regular shore leave. The bribery payments to said customs crew had been high, but the amount of heroin which had come ashore as a consequence throughout that period of grace, had been colossal.

By the eighties, the crew's hold on the Leith docks began to sway with the general decline of commercial shipping and ship building. Neil had established an influence over the dockers unions but when the last yard closed in 1984, a new main supply line had to be established through Corsican suppliers on the continent, and this was all now managed by none other than Scarfo. Scarfo's role had been to maintain the relationship with the Corsicans in France as well as to manage the receival and transportation of the product by land through the UK to Scotland.

The more he frequented the Liverpool casino where Jimmy Lazarini worked, the friendlier the two men had become. Scarfo had often noted how well Jimmy would deal with any trouble in the casino, and so one day he offered him the opportunity to earn some extra cash by assisting him in his role for the Cattaneos.

Jimmy had agreed and was stunned to be given a grand in cash just for going along with Scarfo to meet some people one evening. He then received five grand for joining Scarfo and three other men, whose identities had remained a secret, on a yacht off Porthcurno in Cornwall where they all fished out eight large packages of heroin which had been dropped two days earlier by a small engine private plane from France. The packages had been weighed down and sunk by large sacks of salt attached to them.

The salt had slowly evaporated in the water over a couple of days, causing the packages to pop back up and reappear on the surface again. This technique worked for a while until the Royal Navy spotted the fifth drop and realised the scam. They then hung around and fished up the packages themselves when they eventually resurfaced. Jimmy wondered why Scarfo didn't just buy a redundant Russian submarine and run the shit from the continent to wherever they wanted to transport it to.

"The Navy can detect submarines, particularly ones owned by cowboys like us." Scarfo had laughed. Then one day, Scarfo just disappeared never to be heard from again. It was soon obvious to Jimmy that something unforeseen had occurred and despite having been kept in the dark about the origins of the continental suppliers, as well as where the dope ended up, Jimmy had overheard enough over time to suspect that Scarfo had gone over to Europe to meet his suppliers.

Had they potentially murdered him?
But why would they?

He could only guess—Scarfo had maybe betrayed or stolen from the wrong people? Jimmy had little option but to just wait and see if any news would come to light whilst getting on with his job in the casino. Regardless, for the next month or so he kept one eye over his shoulder in anticipation of either the cops or some guy with a knife or gun turning up. The only person who did turn up sniffing around however, was a guy from Edinburgh named Davie Haig, who had been sent down by Gerry Cattaneo's buffer man. Haig started asking questions one night in an upstairs room of the casino, named the green room, which contained two crap and three blackjack tables.

Haig had started out playing blackjack for a while in the room, never splitting cards against anything higher than a six, and never sitting on the end box where his every move would have faced the tuts and sighs from the clique of regulars. After three nights of this, he had begun fishing for information among the members, talking about his "mate" Scarfo. No one knew anything however but one punter, a blonde cougar whose voice rasped of years of fag smoking, mentioned this to Jimmy in passing on the stairwell.

So, Jimmy kept an eye on Haig, a blonde man in his mid-forties with a pointed nose and skinny frame. Jimmy did not mention anything to the management and studied the new man with the Scottish accent. He wondered if Haig was a cop at first, but instinctively soon sensed that he was a villain, and potentially the northern buyer of the heroin whicht Scarfo had once drunkenly admitted to Jimmy was "headed north".

If Haig was fishing for his missing supplier, then Jimmy sensed that there may be a possible opportunity for himself here, though he knew he would have to play it cannily. That night he went to the Manchester address which Haig had written down on his casino membership application—it was a bogus one. A Bangladeshi family lived there and had done for years apparently. Jimmy did have a phone number for Haig, whether it was genuine or not was another toss of the coin. He could not be sure that Haig would turn up at the casino again for a fourth night of cards either, but his instinct convinced him not to call the number and to just wait and see.

Thankfully, the following evening, Haig turned up at the casino again. This time he played roulette at a busy table downstairs, where he shouted out small £5.00 call bets around zero and the neighbours for a couple of hours, winning himself few hundred quid. The pit-boss, however, changed the croupier and put on an older spinner who continually hit Tier, and so Haig began to slowly lose his winnings. After a while, and just before he lost everything, He began fishing again among the variety of punters at the table, regarding the missing Scarfo. Again, no one knew anything.

Shortly afterwards, he went upstairs to the restaurant and ordered himself a steak and a half carafe of red wine. Once he had finished his meal, he went to relive himself in the lavatory and it was there that he found himself face to face with a tense and aggressive-looking Jimmy Lazarini. "Why are you looking for Ronnie from Zebrugge?" he wanted to know.

"Are you Italian?" inquired Haig as cool as a cucumber.

"Yes; so?"

Haig did not reply; instead, he merely scanned the 6 ft lump before him.

"Scarfo is my friend," added Jimmy, whilst meeting Haig's gaze.

"Was he now, big fella?" Smiled Haig as he turned away to wash his hands.

"Yes, we are friends and I help him out from time to time."

"Is that right? What do you help him with then?" Haig's eyebrows lifted as he turned to dry his hands on the wall dryer and study Jimmy in the mirror.

Jimmy did not answer. "And you?" he asked instead.

"I'm a friend too," smirked Haig, turning around to face him.

"From?"

"Tell you what, think we need to meet for a cuppa away from here," suggested Haig.

"Okay," agreed Jimmy and he passed Haig a card with his number on it, before both of them left without exchanging another word. They did not speak again for the remainder of the evening in the casino either and Haig left after another hour of unproductive roulette.

They met for coffee the following afternoon. After an evasive start, both men relaxed and explained themselves. Within a week to ten days, Jimmy was back working for Wee Neil Cattaneo's Scottish heroin enterprise, which was known simply as "The Edinburgh Outfit" by Haig. The Outfit had first appeared around the once busy Port of Leith docklands in the mid-seventies and bullied their way to gaining control of the Dockers union. By the end of that decade, it was said that they had the power to pull every docker off the loading piers at any time of day or night.

Money had been made, of course, but by the eighties, the docks were at deaths door, fruit, spices, and oil, had begun to be transported by planes and lorries, so the Outfit had no other choice but to turn the zone into a red-light district. They may have only gained control of the docks at the tail-end of an era, but the eighties had brought in a new market for them to latch on to instead—smack.

Jimmy had impressed them from the off, and Haig's research into him had revealed that he was a hard man who had indeed been helping Scarfo with the supply line for a while. The Outfit initially positioned Jimmy into a three-man team headed by Haig, who were based in a Bristol holiday let, and who were tasked with searching for the missing Scarfo. Jimmy had shown himself to be quite adept at this too, when he had suggested to Haig that from overhearing some of Scarfo's boozed up calls, they might like to look in the Torquay area for a hotel that served Italian food which Scarfo might own. He explained that he had also heard Scarfo shouting in French at someone called 'Laurent' over the phone once.

It took another few days of calls to find Scarfo's "Seabreeze Hotel" in Torquay and another twenty minutes to locate this so-called Laurent guy who, it turned out, happened to be the hotel manager. Everyone suspected that Laurent was involved in the link with the Corsicans and so Haig had wanted to go in heavy and interrogate him, but Jimmy felt that could blow any chance of a link-up with the Corsican suppliers. Instead, he persuaded Haig to offer Laurent £10,000 to set up a meeting with the Corsicans.

A bold and presumptuous move, sure, but Jimmy was now guessing that Laurent was a key link man in the continental supply chain. Haig agreed and went along with the notion and thankfully for Jimmy, within a short period of time, the Outfit re-established the supply line with the Corsicans and subsequently had considerable success in transporting the product within bars of soap and tins of sardines driven over from France.

Thereafter, Jimmy had helped out the Bristol team, who had the unenviable job of managing the new supply line. They had all suspected the Corsicans regarding Scarfo's disappearance, but money talked of course in this business, and besides, the Corsicans denied any knowledge of Scarfo's whereabouts. Privately Neil Cattaneo suspected that Scarfo may have tried to cheat the Corsicans somehow and that they had murdered him for it, but what was important to him and the Outfit itself, was that they were getting rich on this newly re-established supply line.

Consequently, both parties proceeded to do business together and over the course, a highly prosperous connection was maintained. Impressed by Jimmy

Lazarini's input, the Outfit invited him up to Edinburgh to meet Gerry Cattaneo's bag man—Fiore ("Gentle Fifi") Bompensiero, at his little Greek taverna—"Polynikes" on Elm Row.

"Neil's wife is Greek, so Fifi was ass licking when he opened up his taverna," joked the unknown guy who had collected Jimmy from Waverly in a transit van and driven him down to Elm Row. The reality, however, was that Fifi had realised that the main source of clientele available to him in the Elm Row area, came in the form of theatre goers and that most of the various Italian, Gurkha, Indian and Thai restaurants in the immediate vicinity were all offering theatre specials whilst trying to get the upper hand on each other.

Fifi had recognised that what had been missing had been a Greek joint, with slanted terracotta tiles outside to give it a rustic appearance, and offering boozy plate smashing musical nights where people could carry on the theatrics when spilling out of the theatre. He had been right, of course, and Polynikes had positively thrived.

It had been at this original meeting that the Outfit had offered Jimmy the role of Maître d at their Edinburgh casino, with a wage of £30,000 per year and an upfront welcoming cash bung. He would also receive another £25,000 per year in further bungs for a side-line role as a violent enforcer for the Outfit. This was organised crime personified and the fruitful offer had been difficult to refuse. Jimmy soon learned that the Edinburgh Outfit was nothing like the traditional mafia as such.

Not quite Black-Handed[63] by nature, rather they were a close-knit crew, managed by a small hierarchy. They had no connections nor structural similarities to the Mafiosi operating in Sicily whatsoever. Nor were they comparable to the Camorra of Naples, nor the Calabrian 'Ndrangheta factions. Rather, the Outfit was a small and enigmatic heroin enterprise with various side-lines in prostitution, shylocking, extortion and the palm-greasing of officials.

Jimmy accepted the offer. He used the cash to put a down payment on a home in the Craigentinny area of the city. It would be there that he would bring his young family north to begin a new life in Edinburgh. The fact that Edinburgh

---

[63] The Black Hand (*Mano Nera* in Italian) was established in Naples in 1750, but is later referred to extortion rackets among Italian and Sicilian immigrants in New York city in the early 1900's. These criminal syndicates targeted fellow Italians whom they sent letters to threatening violence if money was not paid. The dreaded letter was usually decorated with the image of a black hand.

had one of the largest Italian communities in Britain had appealed to his wife who was a loyal companion anyway but who supported wholeheartedly her husband's decision. By the mid-nineties, having proven himself as an endearing and loyal asset, Jimmy was given control of the runners who pushed smack in the Clermiston and Broomhouse neighbourhoods of the city. He soon gained himself a reputation as a ruthless enforcer who, in addition to his Casino role (which had earned him the nickname of 'The Waiter' within the Outfit), was often called upon to deal with local thugs who tried muscling in on the trade or who occasionally crossed the line in the Outfit's saunas.

By 2003, Jimmy was recognised as a high earner for the Outfit and so when he decided to open up a couple of florist shops and give up his casino role, Nicky Cattaneo personally met with him and asked him not to leave the firm. Jimmy had assured Nicky however that he remained loyal to the Outfit, and that his interest in the floral business was a completely separate project that would not conflict with the Outfit's interests. Nicky had grudgingly accepted this at the time and then gave Jimmy control of the Outfit's heroin interests in both Fife and Dundee, which were large operations and quite demanding.

Much to Nicky's disappointment, however, this plan did not slow down Jimmy's interest in the floral industry and within a year, thanks to the arrival of his brother from Emillia-Romanga, he had opened up another six outlets across Edinburgh. Slowly, over the following couple of years, Jimmy brought in a few other guys from Emillia-Romanga who spoke his Romagnolo dialect, which was perfect for keeping other Italians ears out of the conversation.

Nicky had niggling concerns about Jimmy's ambitions and at one point, suggested to his older brothers that Jimmy was a ticking bomb that was going to blow up in their faces. In particular, Nicky had stressed that Jimmy had more power than any of the Outfit's other players and that at the very least, he should be demoted and contained.

Gerry Cattaneo had not agreed to this however, as he secretly believed that his brother was simply jealous of Jimmy's success in the field, not to mention his reputation as a hard man: "Besides, it's better to keep him close than to behave like these fucking Scots villains who murder their own guys out of paranoia and greed," he had argued.

Of course, Nicky had taken this as a direct dig at himself by his brother. In the end, the matter was soon brushed aside however as all heads were turned elsewhere when a particularly aggressive group of Somalians appeared in the city and started muscling in on the Outfit's heroin racket. These guys had a particularly good product supplied to them by a Kurdish source, who was a puppet of a very well organised and incredibly powerful Georgian supplier. The Edinburgh Outfit weren't aware of any of that though, and so had to deal with the threat on the street regardless. A conflict quickly ensued which saw automatic assault weapons brought into the city for the first time, and which became game changers.

The Somalian invaders had driven up from England in an old BMW one night and pitched up inside a Southside pub, wherein a fence, connected to the Outfit, was known to frequent. The fence made a call and within a short space of time, a blue van pulled up outside the pub and six masked men burst inside with the loaded assault rifles and emptied them everywhere, killing no one but maiming three Somalians and an innocent woman who was being chatted up by them.

Jimmy had led the assault team and it was all over very quickly. A fourth Somalian, however, was dragged away in the van and tortured in a flat in Granton before then being thrown from another moving vehicle outside an African owned internet café on Nicholson Street. Local press reported that the tortured man had lost six fingers and three toes and that he had a bag of heroin stuffed into his mouth.

Shortly after this, a group of steroid popping Albanians appeared on the scene and tried to extort protection monies from various Edinburgh saunas. When the Outfit heard of this from an independent owner of a sauna who paid them for protection, Jimmy wondered if the Albanians might be connected to the Somalians and if there was a puppet master south of the border who was pulling the strings of both factions. Regardless, he hunted the Albanians down and attacked them, again wearing balaclavas, in what ended up as a pitched street battle.

Jimmy's brother was slashed through his balaclava and received stitches from a discrete doctor afterwards in a house in Merchiston. Baseball bats, and knives were all used this time, and it had been a touch and go battle until Jimmy had finally drawn a revolver and shot two of the Albanians in their legs. At that point, the rest of the Albanians had dropped their weapons. They were all then brutally pounded with baseball bats thereafter and the following day, a car wash in Longstone, which had been the Albanian's base, was burned to the ground whilst the on-duty attendant had both his hands smashed to pieces with a claw hammer. Police discovered him on the pavement with his maimed hands and his head drenched in the massage oil used in the saunas the Albanians had attempted to extort.

"This was a particularly vicious assault on a foreign national simply doing his job to provide a better life for his family, and now he might never work again. Subsequently we would appeal to any members of the public who may have seen anything—anything at all—to come forward and call us on this number in absolute confidence," said a cop on the television that evening. Police would later admit on a local radio station a fortnight later that there were no suspects. Somehow they had failed to connect the arson attack to the hospitalisation of several Albanian men the previous evening either.

Despite some violent resistance in one or two areas from local dealers operating as subordinates of Glaswegian firms, Edinburgh's heroin trade was under the control of the Outfit and things settled down again when the rogue dealers were offered a superior product at a better rate. It had not been long until Jimmy's crew, who were nicknamed the 'Pie Crew' by the rest of the Outfit, due to their Dundee operation, obtained a firm hold over the majority of heroin in Dundee, Fife and the west side of Edinburgh. Throughout the mid to late nineties, they milked the city's poverty-stricken schemes under the cover of fast-food deliveries, for hundreds of thousands of pounds. As a consequence, the Outfit were able to continue to make vast bribery payments to police and corruptible council officials in order to proceed relatively unhindered in their new enterprise—construction.

The pie crew were never broken up by the Outfit, despite Nicky Cattaneo's desire to do precisely that, and they remained a loyal and highly lucrative branch of the firm. Then in 2012 Wee Neil Cattaneo died naturally in his sleep and his brother Gerry surprised everyone by deciding to call it a day and move full time to his holiday home in Frosinone with his fortune. Nicky Cattaneo would step in as chief executive of the Outfit, but on the condition that he would begin to dismantle it and eventually extricate himself too. Nicky agreed to sell off the majority of the family property portfolio, to wind down the casino business, as well as the saunas and clubs, though he insisted on continuing to manage the Outfit's heroin interests whilst this process was ongoing.

Of course, this was never going to be good news for Jimmy, who sensed a mounting tide of trouble headed his way. He had first anticipated waves coming from Nicky's direction a while back of course and so had prepared for impact.

First, he voluntarily withdrew from the Dundee and Fife business, which was then taken over by one of Nicky's trusted guys for a while. Jimmy on the other hand had begun focusing upon gathering his own small crew in Edinburgh, which did not include any Frosinone Italians from the Outfit. Instead, he gradually surrounded himself with a small sprinkling of Romagnolo speakers from Emillia-Romanga, all of whom had either grown up around, or were related to him. Privately, he prepared all these guys for a schism with the Outfit and this led his guys to gradually look down upon the Frosinone Italians as country bumkins. None of this was lost upon Nicky Cattaneo however.

"That specky little *contadino* is going to Judas us as soon as his arse is in the driving seat," Jimmy had predicted of Nicky long before Wee Neil had died. "*Sono sciacco?*" he had shaken his head. "Nicky will make a move against us as soon as Gerry steps on the fucking plane."

By then, Jimmy had a legitimate floral chain across Edinburgh named "Ottova Via", which was doing well financially—employing forty staff, hence his new nickname among his own crew, "Jimmy the Gardener". Most of the stock was delivered from Holland on long haul lorries, and due to a need for freshness, these lorries arrived regularly, which enabled perfect cover for supplementary interests.

Jimmy then became a silent partner in another legitimate enterprise— "Merchiston Heating and Air Conditioning"—who obtained contracts for various hotels and construction sites. As a consequence, he took on a young Sicilian business student named Calògiru Profaci who had gone from part-time dish washer to head waiter at Jimmy's younger brother—Sam's, restaurant in Linlithgow. The kid had been at university and was not only computer savvy but was a cunning little fox who had various successful marketing theories. It had been Profaci's general reliability alongside the fact that he too had been quite handy with his fists, that increased his value in Jimmy's eyes.

Jimmy had been served a few times by the kid in the restaurant and had chatted to him in passing. He had also heard good things about him too after Profaci had done some casual work for the pie crew outside of the restaurant sphere. Sam Lazarini certainly trusted the kid and got along well enough with him, so Jimmy was not entirely surprised when his brother recommended Profaci to him when he was looking around for someone to come into the florist chain. The switch from restaurant to flowers meant a pay raise for Profaci of course, and money talked after all, but more importantly, despite his Sicilian dialect being had to follow, he had been given a rare opportunity to become close to Jimmy Lazarini.

"The chefs call him 'Seagull[64]' but I call him 'Carlo'," Sam Lazarini had laughed. "I know he isn't one of us etc, but he is reliable and loyal, Jimmy," he had assured his older brother at the time. The kid was indeed loyal, and he soon become a useful support tool for Jimmy over a period of time and who eventually came to trust Profaci as much as any of the Romagnoli.

Over the next couple of years, Profaci contributed to the success of the florist chain and its expansion into Livingston, Falkirk and Stirling. He settled in well enough and before long was renting his own flat on Marionville Road. Jimmy had been aware that Profaci's family had some vague connection to a *Mafiosi* clan in Palermo; so was not entirely surprised when the kid turned out to be competent when grasping the criminal nature of the business which was now paying his rent.

Jimmy had been impressed enough by Profaci's evident application and loyalty from the beginning, and so began involving him in most aspects of his business. "Soon they will be calling you 'Teacher's Pet' instead of 'Carlo'," he joked to the kid.

"I prefer Charlie," Profaci had boldly countered at the time.

Things couldn't have gone better for Profaci. Jimmy's wife had often praised him to her husband too, and none of the other pie crew had a bad word to say about him either. Jimmy had allowed the kid into the inner workings of his crew, with one eye upon establishing a potential friendship with Profaci's family connections back in Palermo where yet another narcotic supply line was probable. Over a relatively short period of time, the smart-thinking Profaci was able to expand the floristry business even further with some old-fashioned marketing, which Jimmy had not utilised previously. This was achieved through a formula Profaci termed "Delicate Coercion".

He would identify a small profitable business property, say a newsagent, whose leaseholders or owners were making a hash of things financially. Then he would step in and offer financial relief and/or physical protection from

---

[64] A "Seagull" was originally a derogatory slur used by the Outfit throughout the 1970s in reference to newer Italian immigrants who were fresh of the boat. The term originated from the established Edinburgh-Italians inability to understand the dissimilar dialects, particularly the much faster-speaking Sicilian ones which seemed to just fly over their heads like the city's seagulls.

choreographed threats from selected actors whose roles and scripts had been created by Profaci. The next stage was to step in as a partner before then progressing to the final stage, which was that one way or another, the business partner would gradually be brought to the point of giving up due to either extreme stress and/or debt.

This was achieved by setting the partner up with a multitude of financial, legal and traumatic nightmares. If that didn't do the trick, and the partner tried to be strong and swallow the pressure, then over the course of time, one or two of them had been run over by speeding vehicles as they crossed the road, and/or mugged, stabbed and hospitalised, which ensured that they had been unable to run a business thereafter.

Jimmy was pleased with the kid's old school Sicilian expansionism, which would deliver several small businesses into the jaws of the Ottova Via chain, either in their existing form, or as florists across the central belt. All narcotic money which Jimmy was now bringing in on the back of the break-up of the Outfit, was then washed through this new business and young Profaci used his educational skills to manage an electronic system of control over all the new assets. "The admin guy, that's what we'll call you, kid," Sam Lazarini had suggested one afternoon on the golf course.

"I prefer Charlie, thanks," had been the cold reply again from Profaci.

About a year later, Jimmy spent a while locating a new heroin supplier in Holland. A trusted friend in Antwerp had finally put him in touch with a Turkish supplier whom he met twice, once in Amsterdam over coffee and then later in Dresden where he was shown the product and had it explained to him how the Turkish/German crew was transporting the product from Turkey into Europe. The first run into Scotland had gone well and so it developed into a successful monthly venture. Once safely in the UK, the product was transported by two runners, through two separate routes, into Scotland. So, by the time Nicky Cattaneo took control of the Edinburgh Outfit, Jimmy was on his eighth run from Amsterdam.

Jimmy previously decided that the best way to deal with any demands or threats from Nicky Cattaneo, would be to ignore him. After all, the Outfit was hardly a mafia family and Jimmy had not been sworn in by any oath of loyalty to his former benefactors. Rather, it was more like a gym or a golf club scenario wherein one could relinquish his membership at the drop of a hat, at least that was how Jimmy saw it. Despite this, Jimmy knew that Nicky was going to be like a fish in the Sahara now, desperate and panicky and that he might react like a cornered fox. He decided that he would always offer Nicky his friendship and undertook never to go against him unless Nicky struck first. If Nicky targeted either Jimmy or his family, then that would only confirm what everyone already knew—that the man's greed and ambition was a threat to everyone.

Nicky saw himself as a modern gangster who liked to hang out in his 1950's basement jazz bar most evenings, wearing tight white jeans and Gucci loafers without socks. He only drank champagne and sniffed coke from the naked bodies of the fun girls who worked in the clubs. It was obvious to most that Nicky intended his short term reign of the Outfit to be one where fear shielded his hedonistic lifestyle. Jimmy never saw himself in a similar vein of course; he so hated the term gangster and he much preferred sweet Asti to dry French fizz. He viewed himself as just another fragment of what he regarded to be a perpetual circumstance—the narcotics industry.

Jimmy knew that his approach to being independent of the Outfit required a much different approach to his days as an enforcer for them. He also understood that a man can lead out of a fear of his ability to display violence, but that in the end, it takes wisdom and craftiness to be a proficient leader of men.

Jimmy believed that if a leader was to prosper at the pinnacle of any small organisation where there was no jealousy or whispering among the workforce, there would be less chance of treachery. He was not convinced however that Nicky Cattaneo saw things similarly. On that note, Jimmy had been sure that the biggest threat to his new independent heroin enterprise, was from either a telecommunication leak or from internal treachery. An attack from outside his crew could usually be dealt with, but one from within was a different and potentially fatal conundrum.

So, for Jimmy Lazarini, there would now be a preference on conciliation and loyalty from the inside out. He now had several years of experience under his belt, from the Scarfo years, to this recent split from the Outfit. Clearly, being a nice guy was the best way to fashion a protective shield for any kind of effective enterprise, particularly from the tribulations of jealousy and betrayal that he recognised to be more of a threat than anything else. Secrecy was key of course and conflict undesirable; such policies would be the essence of the Lazarini business model.

Personally, Jimmy had no desire to murder Nicky. That was all far too Scottish a method for him, and besides, he still had loyalty and appreciation towards the Outfit guys for improving his life for the better. He now lived as a Scot and had financial security and a property in Scotland; the Outfit had provided him with all this. Another reason he had not desired conflict with them was because they still had considerably more muscle as well as influence among the Edinburgh establishment. Similarly, any conflict with them would have been very much in the public eye of a comparatively small city, and this would have brought excessive attention upon both firm's business interests.

With those considerations in mind, Jimmy focussed his selling zones in areas not controlled by the Outfit. He had also not been naive enough to believe that this serene and courteous approach meant that the gesture would be reciprocated by Nicky Cattaneo, of course. After all, the Cattaneos were of *Latini*[65] origin, and those Romans had ancient form for turning upon their friends in the pursuit of power.

In the end though, Nicky would be diagnosed with terminal cancer only a few months into his reign and quickly ended up in a hospice before he had a chance to turn his attention to Jimmy's crew. When he died soon afterwards, Gerry Cattaneo reluctantly returned to Scotland and stepped in for an intermediate period, but he was emotionally crushed by the loss of his two siblings and had absolutely no stomach for the darker side of business any more.

Jimmy attended Nicky's funeral and had a drink with Gerry afterwards. The man had seemed manically depressed to him as well as quite frail. There was no surprise then, when soon after he had buried his brother, Gerry Cattaneo returned to his mountain villa in Frosinone, leaving the family law firm to sort out the sales of most of the Outfit's assets. The Dundee racket was handed over to a local Dundonian enforcer named Hugh McMoodie. The McMoodie family had been violent Cattaneo associates for years. The Outfit still supplied the product, which the McMoodies bought from them and subsequently functioned independently.

---

[65] The ancient Latini and Hernici tribes once occupied the territory of Valle Latina, south of Rome (*Latium Vetus*). The Roman historian Livy tells us that after around 600 BC, the leading families of the Alba Longa mountain settlement in the Latium region, were forced to immigrate into Rome and were incorporated as Patricians and resided on the Caelian Hill area of the city; namely the *Julli*, *Sevilii* and the *Geganii*.
All of Latium was eventually integrated into Roman rule by 338BC and throughout both the Republican and Princeps eras, several patrician and plebeian figures were connected to the region. Including Cato the Elder, Cicero, Juvenal and Gaius Octavian (later the emperor Augustus Caesar).

It was said that from thereon not one guy from the Outfit ever stepped foot in Dundee again though it was still their heroin which polluted the city.

By 2014, the shrinking Outfit was rapidly winding down its narcotics interests. What was left of it was mainly being run by "Gentle" Fifi, who played golf with Jimmy a couple of times a year and who had a good relationship with him. Fifi was known throughout his unwinding of the Outfit's illegal interests, for his preference for diplomacy, tolerance, and peacekeeping. Around the time of the Scottish Independence referendum, Fifi had faced a criminal court trial when he had slapped a teenager who had been abusive to an entire queue of cinema goers one evening when Fifi had been out with his family. The teenager and his chums were just hoody wearing chavs who had caused the cinema staff to call the cops due to their threatening behaviour.

However, Fifi had taken exception to one of them being disrespectful to a female standing in the queue and had words with the kid who then responded by threatening him, and so Fifi duly slapped the brat in the face. Thirty minutes later, he was banged-up in a police cell charged with an assault upon a minor.

The following eight months saw Fifi endure considerable stress upon both himself and his family while the legal proceedings dragged on. In the end, he was acquitted and had been particularly impressed with the solicitor that Hendry & Co had allocated to represent him—Monty. Fifi had sent Monty a case of Dom Perignon after the verdict. Shortly afterwards, upon the golf course, Fifi endorsed Monty to Jimmy Lazarini and explained that the only reason he did not now have a petty criminal record was thanks to Monty having gone the extra mile to get his acquittal across the line.

Shortly after this, Jimmy hired Monty to represent his wife in the District Court against an allegation of using a mobile phone whilst driving. Monty managed to get the case deserted *pro loco et tempore* at the pleadings diet, which spared her from a potential points-ban on her licence that would have hindered her role in the floral chain. Jimmy had been highly appreciative of this and had rung Monty up personally to express his gratitude.

Over the course, Monty's firm then began to receive calls from various street level Scottish drug dealers facing criminal charges which varied from possession to violence, and who asked directly for Monty. Most of whom would end up receiving positive legal results as a consequence. In gratitude, Jimmy told Monty once that should he ever require any assistance of any kind, he was simply to ask. "If anyone ever bothers you, threatens you or even if you just need an MOT for your car, call me," he had insisted.

Monty knew well enough who and what Jimmy Lazarini was from word of mouth around the court circuit, so he understood this to have been an offer he should never forget. As he drove now into the Barnton neighbourhood of Edinburgh, relieved to leave the antics of that flying light behind him for a moment, he reflected that this discord between angels was nothing less than ridiculous. It was obviously creating a chaotic environment for the whole world and this had clearly been the case for centuries.

There was no chance of him now worming his way out of things though, not now that he had been whisked off his feet and dragged into the heart of the madness—He was still excited and feeling blessed but after that performance at the bridge, he was now also experiencing worry, frustration and anxiety. He was well aware that he was now required to be on his guard from here on in, otherwise, why else had he been given this magical weapon in his pocket?

He felt about for it now as he sat at some lights, once his fingers located it, he felt as reassured as any person who might be searching for their passport on route to the airport, but who then finds it in a pocket. He considered that he might well be being paranoid of course, but that did not mean that there was not going to be airborne enemies trying to hurt him, he reasoned. It might not hurt to explore further protection as a safety net, he figured. He considered calling Jimmy Lazarini now. He bit his lip though, what would he say to the guy?

He could hardly tell him any of this. Then the lights changed, and he turned left along Whitehouse Road, past the Royal Burgess golf club before then turning right along Gamekeepers Road, he suddenly pulled over behind a skip by the kerb. He thought about it again. He had witnessed some really strange supernatural activity on the bridge earlier, on the back of having been stalked by an angel with a fox and then transported to Napoleon Bonaparte's world by yet another angel.

Hardly being paranoid, am I?

He started to scroll through his phone until he came to the name Jimmy Lazarini. He then sat there for a moment looking out of his window at a squirrel sitting on a frost-covered wall across the road, eating what may have been a rich tea biscuit. He remembered that it was Christmas time, a time for family, and that Jimmy would probably be busy wrapping up his kids presents or something, but just by making contact, Monty sensed that he would feel a little reassured psychologically.

One thing he knew was that if he was going to survive this chaos, he needed to think sharply and apply his own instinctive measures. Wasn't that why the angel had chosen him after-all? It was perhaps selfish to call Jimmy at this time of year, but after all that he had experienced today, Monty felt inclined to touch base with the guy at least. He pressed call.

Jimmy Lazarini was slouched upon a lounger by the circular mosaic pool of a whitewashed villa in Lanzarote which he was renting in order to escape both the commercialism and cold this Christmas. His wife was out buying food for Christmas dinner with the kids. He was hot now, having been in the same position upon the lounger for more than thirty minutes, wearing only his trunks and a pair of shades. He considered whether any hitman who was to walk across the terrace now, would aim for the little gold crucifix which was resting upon his chest, or his head? Then he thought for a brief moment that a gold crucifix was perhaps a bit rude, vulgar even? Wouldn't Christ have pulled it off him and suggested that he sell it and give the proceeds to the poor? But then he asked himself, what did he know about such things.

Sono prete?

He decided to take a cooling dip in the pool now but before he could move, his phone rang out on the table beside the glass of Martin Codaxs Godello that had been part of the welcome hamper the owner of the villa had left. Jimmy read the caller ID and wondered why Stephen Montgomery of Hendry & Co was calling him now.

"Hello?" he eventually accepted the call.

"Hi there, this is Stephen Montgomery here."

"Hi Perry[66], how are you?"

Monty forced a chuckle. "Yes, I am fine, thanks. Nothing to worry about but I was wondering if you could pop into the office in the New Year, in order to go over some of the things we discussed the last time we spoke?" The last time they had spoken had been in Monty's office almost a year ago but Jimmy recalled exactly what had been said.

"Sure, I'm in the Canaries for Christmas but will be home after New Year," replied Jimmy.

---

[66] Presumably a banterous reference to the 1960's American TV legal drama, "Perry Mason".

195

"That will be fine, how would the second week in January suit?"

"Sure, I'll sort something out once I'm back and make an appointment with you."

"That would be perfect, thanks."

"Listen Perry, is everything okay, do you need someone to come talk to you now?" asked Jimmy.

"Yes, all is well but no, no, it can wait and I will look forward to seeing you in January," assured Monty.

"Okay, no problem. Well, have a good Christmas then, Perry son." Jimmy wanted to get in the pool now before he burned again as he had last year in Cuba when he had fallen asleep on a beach.

"Thanks, I shall, cheers and Merry Christmas to you and the family," said Monty before hanging up. It had been obvious to him that Jimmy had not forgotten his offer of appreciation, hence the proposal to send someone now. This was reassuring. He restarted the engine and drove off in the direction of Leith.

It's all psychological, this.

After a quick dive into the cool water, Jimmy wondered if the friendly little solicitor was in some sort of trouble. He liked the kid, he was certainly a talented brief, that was for sure and he knew that he would help him as best he could; he had given his word that he would, and his word was good. This was an era where people habitually gave their word and did not follow through with it thereafter; Jimmy Lazarini was not like those people. Besides, it was always wise to keep a talented criminal lawyer close, particularly in Jimmy's line of business.

There were far too many people who didn't keep their word these days, he sighed. Hadn't the female he had waited thirty-two minutes to speak to on the phone yesterday, made assurances about their first-class seats on the plane out here? Yet his family had been forced to take second class seats due to her not doing precisely that which she had promised to do. Jimmy thought about this again now as he did a slow doggy paddle across the cool, ducking his face under the water to cool it.

When he reached the metal pool steps attached to the side, he pulled himself back out and onto the warm mosaic tiles. He then dried himself a little, opting to leave his hair wet in order to keep cool, before heading inside in search of a snack to keep him going until his family returned. He checked the hamper stuff that was now in the fridge—butter, eggs, bread and five types of Canarian pate.

"*Sono barbone?*" he sighed, before closing the fridge again. Instead, he took a banana from a fruit bowl and returned to the poolside to peel it.

Chapter Nine

Reading is that fruitful miracle of a communication in the midst of solitude.
Marcel Proust

The route eastward from Cramond to Leith shadows the river Forth across the north of the city. The salty wind was carrying a thick sleet inland which resembled a spray of cola slush as it landed upon the car windscreen. Monty turned the heating up; the car engine had cooled during the call to Lazarini. Upon reaching Lower Granton Road, Monty switched the radio on, and after a fruitless search wherein he only came across Christmas songs, or irritating adverts, he finally tuned into a local news station.

A husky female voice, perhaps Aberdonian, said: "And now our political reporter Angus Falkner is enjoying a snow shower down in Jedburgh." She chuckled. "Where he has stumbled across another indication that the whistle has indeed blown on the 2015 UK general election campaign trail," she cheerfully announced.

There was a little chuckle now too from Angus, before he got on with his report: "Yes Heather, it is certainly snowing heavily down here in the Scottish Borders, where a snow plough has just past us," he groaned, sounding genuinely cold. "What listeners can't see behind me however," he continued, "and as you quite rightly suggest, Heather, is that the Scottish Conservative Party has indeed kicked off their 2015 national election campaign," he declared whilst a loud car horn went off a few times in his background.

"That's not the crew getting in the way of the snow plough, is it, Angus?" asked the overly cheery Heather. More laughter followed now between these two for a moment before Angus finally got on with his report.

"Erm no, that was something else," he chuckled. "But yes Heather, I am standing here in Jedburgh under a large billboard image of a road stretching out through green fertile countryside and with the slogan, 'Let's Stay on the Road to a Stronger Economy', blazed across it."

"So, to be starting things off now then, five months before polling day, have the Tories pulled off a master PR stroke, Angus, or is everyone instead focusing upon Christmas and not really interested in this sort of stuff at the moment?" asked Heather.

"Yes well, certainly, people are busy doing last minute shopping and travelling around of course Heather, but that is precisely why the Tories have gone with this tactic, as they hope to get their message across whilst people are out and about," contended Angus.

"So, what is the point being made on these campaign billboards then, Angus?"

"Well Heather, the Tories will say that they came into power in 2010 and were forced to clean up a large financial deficit that they inherited from the Labour Party, and that they had no alternative but to install austerity measures for the good of the country," explained Angus. "However, they are arguing now that in the five years that they have been in office with their coalition partners— the Lib Dems, they have plugged the financial hole and significantly reduced the deficit," he pointed out.

Heather may have nipped off to the loo judging by the prolonged silence at her end?

"This is quite a simple, yet highly effective point being made here by Mr Cameron," Angus continued regardless. "And the point is that his party has done a good job in dealing with the financial crisis thus far, but that the repair job is still a work in process." He paused briefly. "So, the Tories are arguing that the country should allow them finish the job," he concluded.

"Well, is there any sign that the other political parties are to follow suit then, Angus?" Heather was back.

"Yes, we can anticipate an explosion of posters and TV adverts over the next few months, but apart from Labour arguing that Tory cuts are extreme and unnecessary, in a bid to persuade the voters to recall them to power, so far there has only been the SLP in Scotland who have begun a radio and press campaign at this stage," confirmed Angus.

"So, at this early stage, Angus, is there any indication as to where the voting battleground will be?"

Angus didn't need to think about this. "Well, obviously the economy, as we are witnessing here with these billboards, but also the growing concern of the British public regarding immigration and healthcare, I should expect, Heather," projected Angus.

Monty fiddled with the tuner again, he was fed up with politics. Settling instead for a smooth-talking Welshman who sounded as if he was wearing a black polo neck and about to present a jazz band, but who was instead actually hosting a carol service from some cathedral somewhere. Monty imaged him to be in his late fifties, grey-haired, and smoking a cigarette.

"Here we have the Gustav Holst version of *In the Bleak Mid-Winter*. Which, of course, is based upon a poem by the English poet Christina Rossetti, written sometime before 1872," declared the old smoothy.

Monty listened to the choir as he drove into Leith; thinking a little more about today's events and what it all meant for the future of mankind. His life was going to have to change now, that was for sure. If only everyone could experience what he had experienced today, there would be a good world and probably an end to such barbaric acts as murder and child abuse, he considered.

I'd probably be redundant then though.

He tried to stop thinking about it and to just listen to the music for the remainder of the drive. When he did finally pull up outside his house, he could see that the lights in the building a couple of doors along were still on. The corner property had once been an old Victorian grocery shop which had then become an impressive tea room in the Edwardian period. It still had its pleasing Georgian ceiling with remarkable frieze, which had been crudely painted over in purple by the help-centre for minority females who now occupied the place.

The centre had been based here for a few years now and Monty noticed over time that there were more and more East European females attending the evening classes on offer. Immigration was like that—an ever-changing face of people. They were all part of Leith's history of course, from the sailors and wanderers who had anchored centuries ago at the old Port, to the great Irish community who once occupied the slum tenements of Easter Road and Leith Walk in the Victorian era right up until the renovations of the 1960s. Then there had been the Sikhs, the Italians and the Cantonese, who had all made Leith their home from the 1920s onward.

Monty knew that this immigration process had been precisely what made Leith the multicultural, good-humoured working-class community it had always been; although he conceded that it was a changing place these days. There was now a growing East European population, and there were more Poles than any other immigrant community. Some of the remnants of the once thriving Sikh community who had formally been a part of Leith's fabric, could still be found drinking in the local pubs from time to time, though the majority of these families resided in more affluent neighbourhoods these days.

Additionally, many Mirpuri and Kashmiri Pakistani families had settled in Leith too in the early seventies, unlike dissimilar migrants from Faisalabad and Lahore, who had arrived from northern England in the eighties, and who spoke a very different dialect to the Mirpuris, and who had settled mainly in the west of the city in the old concrete jungle which was the Wester Hailes housing scheme. Leith had also been home to a small sprinkling of Afro/Caribbean settlers, who had been resident since Queen Victoria's reign.

Nowadays, however, most of the Mirpuris, Italians, and Cantonese, had also moved out of Leith to more affluent neighbourhoods such as Craigintinny and Gilberstoun, whilst South Indian Hindus and East Europeans have gradually replaced them in the endless tenements. This vibrant passing of the baton was highly evident here in the help-centre, thought Monty. He would occasionally pop in to give legal advice to the staff and was on good terms with them, so he had witnessed the demographic transition over time.

One member of the staff—a female named Mehreen, who didn't have a Leith accent, more of an uptown brogue, and who had hazel coloured shoulder length hair, was on the reception. She was apparently Kashmiri, and had a milky complexion and almost permanent smile. As Monty crossed the road, which was now under a few more inches of snow, he watched her through the window chatting to a darker Indian female. He felt drawn to her at times, but he was always too busy to talk to her and so nothing had ever happened on that score. He decided to pop in and say hello. She was slightly chubby, but he didn't mind that and she had been endlessly flirting with him over the previous year. Perhaps he had shown little interest because the scenario was all a little too close for comfort; what with her practically working next door to his home. If he got involved and it all went tits-up he could hardly disappear, could he. He had never met a woman that he had wanted to give a spare key to his personal zone anyway and having someone working on his perimeter, was equally off limits. Good manners, however, were not—he decided to pop in and say hello. "Hey, working late again, I see?" he said cheerily as he entered the warm reception area.

Mehreen turned away from the Indian lady she had been chatting with and positively beamed at him. She looked pretty tonight, her teeth were whiter than the snow upon his fleece, and the Persian features which some Pakistani females have, looked radiant. "Hi Stephen, yeh, it's the Christmas coffee and cake gig downstairs for Maggie's writing class; how's you?" She flashed those teeth at him.

Ahh...It's the Christmas party night out afterwards and she done her hair and is wearing make-up.

"Not bad, a bit busy with Christmas, etc. so I won't keep you," Monty now focused upon the shelves behind her. "I just wondered if you guys still keep some religious books here for your clients?" he asked. He recalled that they had a few copies of the religious books of most faiths.

"Yes?" She was slightly confused now, but continued to smile and gaze at him. Monty was not beautiful in her eyes, more average-looking, but with an attractive kindness about him that constantly caused her love strings to glow whenever they conversed.

"You wouldn't have a Bible I could borrow by any chance, just for a few days?" He gave her his best smile now.

What's that scent she's wearing?

She went into a metal cupboard behind her and began a lazy search. Monty slowly approached her desk in anticipation. Then she found something and turned and quite deliberately stuck her cleavage out. "*Foods of Ghana* or *Traditions of Romania*?" She teased with both books in her manicured hands, of course she stretched her wrists out to expose her tight-fitting Monsoon blouse, the little blue buttons of which positively looked as though they were about to burst as her creamy breasts bounced to attention. She grinned satisfaction as his coolness floundered momentarily and he was forced to pause very briefly, before shaking his head.

"Okay-dokey." She turned around and continued to search, before then turning back again, slowly, with both hands at her waist this time in order to press home those assets once more. "*King James* or *NIV*?" She smiled, taking him in as she always did. He could smell the perfume more now, and as always, he couldn't help admiring her lovely hands.

"King's will do, Mehreen, thanks." He gently took it from her. "Is it okay if I keep it for a few days?" he asked while avoiding her gaze.

She whispered seductively that this would be fine. "We close up tonight for Christmas and are open again on the 8th of January," she announced happily.

"That's fab. Well, have a merry Christmas, Mehreen," he said before turning on his heels like Fred Astaire and sharply exiting through the old glass door that still had its antique bells above. He heard her shouting some festive tidings as he stepped onto the crunchy snow again, but he did not turn around. He did want her, there was no doubting that, or at least his cock did, but it was a dangerous proposal, he kept reminding himself, and thus, she was off limits.

That was the discipline. He had learned the hard way with the chav. The dog was pleased to see him as he walked in the door but instead of engaging with it as he normally would, Monty did a full sweep of the house first, checking all the windows and doors and even turning the garden lights on to scan the white quilt of snow which covered the handkerchief sized lawn and patio for any footprints. Relieved to find none and everything else in order, he put the kettle on before then going down on his knees to greet his little friend. "We are in a bit of a pickle, lad," he said, "but let's get the dinner on anyway." He smiled as it wagged its tail joyfully.

He made a cup of tea and then some toast with brown bread which he buttered and then lightly covered with marmite. He had disliked Marmite as a kid but had developed a taste for it in his later years. He ate it whilst heating up some penne, which he then added a tin of pilchards and some grated carrot to, before then serving it to the dog. The pilchards had come in their customary tomato paste, which irritated him slightly because he had to waste time rinsing the stuff off the fish; and he wondered a moment why it was that he no longer saw pilchards in brine anymore. He occasionally bought sardines or mackerel for the dog, however he tended to end up eating the mackerel himself and so it was usually either lamb, pilchards or vital organs for his little Springer.

Later, when he had locked up and gone to bed, he switched his phone off and placed it on the bedside table alongside the cork that Charnley had given him. There was a little peach coloured lamp on the table, that did not go with the rest of the room, now which comforted him. The dog also seemed to appreciate it too and was soon snoring away upon the floor beside him, so he adjusted his pillows into a reading position and opened up the Bible. He was soon caught up in it and found himself enjoying it from the off. He raced through Genesis, Exodus and Leviticus within an hour or so, and was halfway into Numbers before he began to feel sleepy, and so he reluctantly put it down beside his phone, yawning.

He then lay down and stretched his back a little before reaching out to turn off the lamp. The dog, being a gun dog, would alert him to anyone standing outside the window or front door, never mind actually inside the property, so Monty felt relaxed enough to drift off. Before he could however, he lay there thinking about what he had just read for a moment. It was certainly a brilliant read, there could be no doubt about that.

At times, it was almost as if the reader was being introduced to God through the stories and their meanings. The Bible was revealing to him a deity who was not all softness and affection, but one with human like feelings such as anger, jealousy, and love. He seemed to be a deity who could be persuaded by a human to change his mind. Monty noted that Moses had persuaded the Lord to turn away from his anger and not to destroy the Israelites in Exodus. This God could be angry, just like any human could, but despite his anger, he could also be persuaded to show leniency, which intrigued Monty, who had spent much of his working life trying to persuade Sheriffs to do likewise.

He had often judged Sheriffs on how hard they hit his clients in sentencing, or how they tended to respond to a plea for compassion. Like everything else, there were fair ones and harsh ones. He closed his eyes now. This God character was also quite funny at times too, he considered, recalling what could also be perceived as God taking a sort of huff in Numbers (11:18-20) when he declared that the Israelites would be eating quail until it came out of their nostrils. Regardless of the chuckle that Monty had had when reading that, he knew that the point being made was about appreciation and gratitude for what we have.

Do people appreciate what God gives them today, or do they prefer to blame him for everything that they do not have?

A car drove past the window outside with overly loud music playing. Monty recognised it straight away and listened to it as it proceeded down the street—it was the Stones:

I saw her today at the reception,
In her glass was a bleeding man
She was practiced at the art of deception
Well, I could tell by her blood-stained hands.

You can't always get what you want
You can't always get what you want

You can't always get what you want
But if you try sometimes, well, you just might find
You get what you need.

His eyelids opened again.

Coincidence?

There was certainly an endearing humour to be found in learning about this God fellow who had once apparently sat down and eaten humble human food with Abraham at Mamre[67]. By his own admission too, he was a jealous and vengeful God. Hadn't he allowed the murder of the three thousand by the Levites to take place after the Golden Calf incident? And had he not also given Miriam a skin disease in Numbers (12.10) because she had gossiped about Moses marrying a Cushite[68].

Monty considered that a common slip-up some people make when dismissing the idea of God's existence, is the notion that if he did truly exist, he must be an ever generous, loving and protective deity; thus presuming that because not everything on earth is perfect, he cannot truly exist. Monty saw now that this God, the God he was now sure existed, was misunderstood due to a basic lack of scripture reading. At least that was how he might explain his own previous lack of understanding. It seemed to him also, that another misconception was that a generous and loving God would automatically forgive those who disrespected him, or his commandments.

For I am a jealous God, punishing the sin of the parents to the third and fourth generation of those who have hated me.

---

[67] Mamre is today part of the city of Hebron but in Old Testament times, it was a hill that looked south towards the city from the north. The Bible says that God appeared there with two angels who were being sent on down to the ancient city of Sodam to save Lot and his family before the city was destroyed, but that all three were persuaded by Abraham to first sit awhile and receive the meagre refreshments that his wife, Sarah, cooked for them (Gen 18:1-5).

[68] Scholars have varied opinions on where the land of Cush was, but the evidence suggests Nubia, Ethiopia or Somalia and there is also reference to the Cushites being of a darker skin than the tanned Israelites in (Jeremiah 13:23). The Roman/Judean historian Flavius Josephus, in his *Antiquity of the Jews* (1.6-2), says Ethiopia.

Monty would have refused to believe in, nor worship such a vengeful deity, but he now realised that such logic would in itself have been an acceptance of the very existence of God. Up until now, he had told himself that he did not believe in a creator or supreme being. Now that he knew that his entire belief had been based upon a paradox, he felt differently. He had never hated God, rather he merely questioned his existence.

Now that he recognised that he had been mistaken, he felt a little relieved to have this opportunity to serve and potentially be redeemed. There were those who do hate God, of course, or think that they do, Monty was aware, but hate was such a strong sentiment. Could a person really hate their creator? People become angry when they lose a loved one, or a material object, but to blame God for that, Monty now realised, was muddled logic based upon a misunderstanding of what God can or should be doing. Monty now saw that God was not to blame for the terrible things that occur; evil exists for sure, but he is certainly not the perpetrator of it.

Monty had previously heard about the power of prayer, and he now suspected that good people of faith could obtain God's kindness through prayer. He also imagined that some so-called God-haters were in trouble for both their contempt and their evil acts, which brought them directly into conflict with this deity. Monty wanted to sigh but instead he yawned, this was all so weird and even a little confusing; as well as exhausting. He needed to sleep and so allowed himself to quickly drift off.

He had been asleep for an hour or so when he became conscious of being awake again and staring up at the ceiling. He was unsure of where he was, he felt as if he had just come from somewhere but did not know where. Then he heard the dog snoring beside him; having sneaked up onto the bed again. He felt its warm body with his hand now and realised precisely where he was. He had been dreaming, he sensed, but he could not recall anything about it. Though he just knew that he had dreamed something.

He closed his eyes again and tried to reminisce but he was drifting off again. He now sunk slowly back into the depths of unconsciousness, his command over everything he understood as rational was temporarily resigned. He was then rudely pulled out by a loud voice shouting his name; it was similar to that early morning wake-up for school voice of his father's which had gotten more and more irate after every call. Then he remembered his previous dream, or at least a part of it. Questions came now, questions about God, and Monty's understanding of him, or at least his previous understanding of the white-bearded, lightening throwing folklore, compared to the jealous, angry and sympathetic God of the Old Testament that he was now becoming acquainted with.

"Stephen," his father called out again.

Monty could sense him now, he saw his father's outline and familiar white shirt as if he were a painted impression—a coloured silhouette, like oil paint on canvas but without any glow or light—just an impression or shadow.

"Never mind that, why are you alone again at Christmas?" The voice demanded to know.

"I have my dog."

"Yes, and a fine little fellow he is, but a person should be with other people too at this time of year. The point being that people who spend the majority of their year being self-absorbed, come together at this time of the year to celebrate the saviour's day." His father's voice seemed gentler than Monty remembered.

"I don't really have a family anymore, dad," he replied. It was partly true enough.

"Then you should be helping those who are in the same boat as you but who would appreciate company at this time of year son. Befriending, doing charity for others, that is how you should be spending your time, so spare me your gibberish self-centred excuses." The old boy was still as flippant as he had always been.

"Okay." Monty seemed to know this contact was surreal, yet automatically accepted the point being made.

"And what say you now about the creator?" Asked his father.

"You first," insisted Monty. The fact that his father had never been particularly religious perhaps influenced this impertinent reply.

"Always the smart-arse lawyer, aren't you? Well, not with me, son. Answer the question." His father was having none of it.

"Well, I don't know him very well yet, but he comes across as almost human, in the sense that he displays some of the emotions we possess," replied Monty.

"Such as?"

"Anger and vengeance."

"And?"

"Yet only towards those who cross him and who put two fingers up at him."

"And?"

207

"And it seems to me that he desires to be man's friend, to spend time with men, face to face even, but that in some cases, mankind has rejected him by refusing to believe in him and following the Darwinian bandwagon," considered Monty.

"So you still have more to learn then, son."

"Yes." Monty knew this to be true.

Then the dream evolved into nothing, at least nothing that Monty would remember. He duly sank now into an unfathomable lightness. Yet he could still sense the sleeping entity—the dog, beside him. A loyal and loving creature that was completely prepared to die in defence of its master. There was a deep bond between them both and this comforted and enabled Monty to sleep easily despite all the excitement and nervousness.

He awoke early as usual and quite regenerated, sprung up with a childlike burst of energy. He intentionally reduced his momentum upon reaching the bedroom door and then gracefully slowed down to a stroll as he reached the hall and headed through to the front door area to check for mail. There was a letter the size of a laptop upon the vibrant art nouveau tiles. A large brown envelope that seemed too large for the letter box, but there was no sign of any damage to the envelope itself to suggest that it had been forced through.

He checked the three front door locks and then the alarm panel upon the wall but there was no sign of a breach. He duly whistled for the dog who promptly arrived. "Go on, son, check the house," he urged and the little spaniel began doing what all gun dogs like to do—search for a scent. Deep down, Monty knew that this was another supernatural occurrence and that if anyone had been in the house during the night, both the alarm and the dog would have been onto them— even a ghost.

His thoughts were confirmed two minutes later when the dog returned having located nothing abnormal, so he finally bent down and picked up the envelope. It seemed light enough, though Monty knew a file of sorts when he felt one, and so he slowly walked through to the kitchen and put it down upon the table. His name was written in blue pen across the envelope but there was no address nor postage.

He decided to relax a moment and just feed the dog some Weetabix and warm water first despite the urge to open the envelope. First he switched the kettle on and began making himself some green tea and a slice of brown toast. The retro radio came on with the multi-plug—Radio 4 and the distinctively smooth and familiar voice of Colin Anderson-Forbes being interviewed outdoors somewhere, now filled the room:

"Well, the people of Scotland can vote for a party which ensures that the economy grows, whilst creating employment and reducing taxes for the majority of low earners," he promised.

"And what about the fact that Labour are promising the people of Scotland precisely the same concessions, but without what one MSP has referred to as your party's 'poisonous narrow-nationalist agenda'?" asked an elderly male with a restrained Morningside accent.

"Well, Scottish Labour have zero credibility when it comes to what they actually campaign on and then how they then behave when in office, and I believe that the Scottish electorate have no intention of being fooled by them again," asserted Forbes. Monty could picture his irritating smirk.

"So, your festive message to the people of Scotland, Mr Anderson-Forbes, is not to believe in the false promises of Labour but to place their faith in the Scottish Liberation Party?"

"My message to the people of Scotland is firstly, have a very merry Christmas, a wonderful New Year, and then yes, to follow their instincts in the election," confirmed Forbes.

Over in the studio, the correspondent, who was unaware that Forbes had removed his microphone and walked off, began to ask another loaded question but Monty unplugged the radio. He leaned on the bunker awaiting the toaster to pop, and once again became momentarily lost in thoughts of the previous day's drama. His body buzzed in the way it had directly after giving his first ever power-point presentation at university, or first speech in court as a trainee solicitor. His heart and soul no longer slammed against each other as they had when he had first encountered the angel yesterday.

It had been as if someone had organised a surprise school reunion for him or something like that, and then afterward, once the initial astonishment had lessened, there remained a butterfly effect within his stomach which was stoked further by the peculiar appearance of this envelope.

The toaster sprung the toast, causing him to snap out of thought. He stood back and proceeded to butter the toast. He poured some boiling water into a mug and dropped a tea bag in. He then fed the dog before taking a seat at the table. He stared at the mysterious package for a moment; only the sheer pleasure of the freshly buttered hot toast delaying the instinct to open it. When he had finished, he opened it, and found that it contained a tattered leather dossier, tied in the centre by two thin leather twines which reminded him of the laces on his moccasins. He slowly untied them with the trepid anticipation of a teenager removing lingerie for the first time.

Inside were thirty or so A4 sized sheets of creamy expensive paper, with writing in black ink upon them. The first page was titled: "The Orcadian". Monty relaxed a little now; he realised that there was no threat to himself and that this was some sort of angelic message. He began reading, and in the same manner in which he read legal files—twice over before then taking notes:

Dear Stephen

As you know, the island of Orkney is located just off the coast of northern Scotland. Recently there was an archaeological discovery on Orkney that has been regarded by experts as mind-blowing[69]. Here is a quick briefing on precisely why they have come to this conclusion. Feel free to check with the ever-useful Google, and then when you are finished with it, leave the file back on your porch area then close the hall door behind you please.

D.

Who on earth was D?

Monty blew on his tea now before cautiously sipping it. Orkney was a place he had never visited. He could feel the dog lay down by his feet, which was again comforting, and so he relaxed further and read on. The file explained all about a Neolithic temple complex which had recently been discovered on Orkney, and which archaeologists were considering as 'mind-blowing'[70].

---

[69]The mysterious Neolithic religious temple complex found recently upon the Ness of Brodgar on Orkney is thought to be dated from around 3300 BC - predating both the Egyptian pyramids and Stonehenge. The nearby standing stone circle, known as the Ring of Brodgar (2500 BC), is comparable in size and sophistication to Stonehenge, though with a more mystical and windswept backdrop due to it being situated upon a thin isthmus between the freshwater loch of Harray and saltwater loch of Stennes.

[70] Archaeological work began on the temple precinct in 2003. The site is around the length and width of five football pitches and is characterised by architecture without parallel in northern Europe. Unlike other Neolithic sites, there are also various decorated

It revealed that the zone itself had once been a mysterious place of worship for an ancient group of sophisticated individuals. A community who possessed arcane knowledge given to them by a being who resided among them for parts of the year, and who they worshiped as a deity within this temple complex.

As Monty flicked through the notes, he came across three aerial images of the mysterious isthmus which seemed to be pointing out to sea. He was minded of the mysterious alignment of the hill and stones in Fife which had seemed to connect across the sea to the Bass Rock. He read on for about thirty minutes, got up and let the dog out into the garden, then returned to learn that this being had removed female humans from other locations around Britain and positioned them on the islands where he mated with them and created a subject line of Nephilim. The offspring continued to breed among themselves and became a maritime community who traded their skills and goods, initially with mainland Scotland, but then also with the rest of Neolithic Britain.

A fine example of this is the Neolithic stone circle at Stonehenge in Wiltshire, which is predated by the remarkable Ring of Brodgar[71]. Monty studied the three images of the Orkney stones, and was quite taken by the third one—an aerial view which resembled a location set from a Star Wars movie. He half paused for a moment and wondered whether, from the angle of the photograph, the site had been some sort of alien landing zone.

Were aliens actually angels and/or the fallen? Anyone familiar with the accounts of the witnesses at Fatima, may wonder.

Monty shrugged and continued to read on. The file informed him that there had previously been an ancient portal at Brodgar, one which accessed other dimensions including "the land of lost spirits", which was apparently an abode where incarcerated entities remained, "for now". The being who had once been

---

buildings and stones with geometric motifs, as well as pavements and a sacred religious complex which once had perimeter walls.

[71] The Ring o' Brodgar stones on Orkney stand upon a remarkably windswept, sloping, green plateau between two lochs—the freshwater Loch Harray and the saltwater Loch Stennes. The circle itself is around 104 metres wide, but the location makes this conceivably the most remarkable of all the Neolithic henges. Notably, the site is considered by archaeologists to be dated around 2500 BC, whilst the first bluestones of Stonehenge are thought, by carbon dating, to have been raised later between 2400 and 2200 BC.

worshipped on Orkney, had been a fallen angel, "whose names were older than the sea itself." Having first arrived through this portal in the days after the great flood, he set himself up as a god; as the other fallen angels had previously done in Mesopotamia, the Mediterranean, and Egypt.

This entity was one of the original rebels who had defied God and who had thereafter been defeated in the first war of the heavens. At the time of his dwelling upon Orkney, he would often shift into an amphibious sea dweller who, in part, imposed his authority upon the other sea creatures within sixty miles of the archipelagos. He was then deified by both them and his hybrid human offspring on the land. He taught his descendants new approaches to farming and engineering, whilst also encouraging them to pursue maritime expansion.

His litter worshipped him as Odonyses—Lord of the wind and sea. In turn, many of them received the gifts of sorcery and arcane knowledge from him. As a result, the group were able to travel to and trade with the rest of Britain. Over the centuries, these Neolithic Orcadians established colonies up and down mainland Britain. However, the file explained that Odonyses was forcibly removed from Orkney by a small group of fallen angels, the leader of whom was later to be known as Mercurius by the Latins.

The issue had been over the female sea demon Ceto. Ceto calmed the fierce currents between the islands and the mainland, enabling safe crossing for the Orcadians, as well as providing them with regular supplies of oysters, mussels and haddock, which she herded into the shallows. She had also regularly confused pods of whales by guiding them into mass beach standings. This had provided the Orcadians with luxury supplies such as oil and flexible whalebone—the plastic of antiquity.

Additionally, Odonyses brought cattle from Crete for them, as well as sea eagles from North America which he had enslaved as the protectors of his hybrid brood. In the end, he went too far by forcing them to worship not only himself but Ceto too, as united deities of the wind and sea; hence the ring of stones being located between both fresh and salt water lochs—representing the division between water and air. This had angered not only the angels of God but also the fallen angels too, who agreed to deal with the matter. Odonyses was then confronted by Mercurius, before later being imprisoned along with several others of his kind, in the depths of hell following a second angelic war.

A rush of dread now overpowered Monty again, just in time to bind with his remaining scepticism, but he read on regardless. He learned that the temple complex bore all the hallmarks of the rituals of the occult having been practiced there for many years after the departure of Odonyses. Human sacrifice had been rife however, despite there being no trace of any human remains found by archaeologists. The reason for this, Monty read, was that the victims had been transported through the portal to the depths of another dimension, where they had been sacrificed and gorged upon by demons.

Apparently, Odonyses possessed the power to shift into many creatures but the sea deity that he loved and tried to deify—Ceto, had not. When Odonyses had made her a magical cloak of eagle feathers however, this had enabled her to walk upon the land and to travel through the portal to different realms with him. Mercurius had clashed bitterly with Odonyses over this and forcibly removed him from Orkney. The following second war of the angels had seen the portal permanently closed and Ceto flee into the sea again to hide from the victorious angels of God whom she had sided against.

When the rules of the Kertamen had been established thereafter, various incarcerated entities, including some fallen angels, were granted certain freedoms to return to this dimension to work within the new rules and on behalf of their dark lord. Certain specialists in a multitude of fields were among them, many of whom were allocated various missions wherein they would conspire against mankind. These assignments were always time-limited and party to the rules, of course. Once the allocated time was up, these entities would return to their incarceration.

Odonyses, the file insisted, should from now on be referred to as "The Orcadian," as he occasionally returned to this realm to argue both law and politics on behalf of his master who sought to provoke the deprivation of mankind.

Monty took a deep breath as he turned over the final page now. Upon which he read the following words: "It is the Orcadian who shall run the legal case against your innocent client, Stephen. Do not underestimate him—ever!"

Monty shivered whilst gently closing the file. What the hell was this? How on earth was he expected have any chance of pulling off a result against a bloody fallen angel who represented the devil himself in court? He felt fear now—real fear. He could imagine this Orcadian character reading his thoughts in the court room and constantly being one step ahead of both himself and the defending counsel, who was also quite unlikely to be overly enthusiastic about this fact.

How do they expect me to explain all of this to counsel?

He thought about how he was going to persuade anyone at all into buying into any of this, never mind whomever he would be sourcing to lead the defence. He imagined the Orcadian being a smooth talker, learned, and would turn up at court upon a dragon with several heads, whilst applauded by an admiring horde of evil trumpet playing thugs and a bloody flyover by the Red Arrows or something. His heart sank.

"God help me." He exhaled with an abundant lack of enthusiasm. Regardless, his legal instinct kicked in anyway and he began to go over the file again, searching for any of the Orcadian's weaknesses whilst trying not to dwell upon his pressing concerns. Yet the more he read, the more he realised that there was none evident, apart from an obvious desire for human women and some sort of sea bint called Ceto. Monty eventually sat back and wondered if he might ever go for another swim in the sea again.

"What's to be done, son?" he sighed down at the dog whilst closing the file a second time and slowly massaging his forehead with his fingers. The dog, still under the table, had not understood so accordingly did not move. It was Christmas Eve, of course, and Monty suddenly realised that he should try to change his routine, as he had recently been advised to in his dream by his father. "Christmas shopping then," he thought aloud before getting up and heading for the shower,

That's a start

Half an hour later, as he drove out towards the Kinnaird Park retail complex with the dog, he decided to try not to dwell on things and to try and savour the pleasure of buying gifts for others. It was impossible to go shopping in the city in this day and age where parking was around £6 quid per hour and where there were endless roadworks and a hunting pack of parking attendants looking to extort those who dared to run the gauntlet. At least this way he could escape the hassle, and besides, there was a pet store at Kinnaird Park too as well as a Marks & Spencer store, so he now reminded himself that he would be picking up something nice for his Christmas dinner.

On the drive he noticed plenty of last-minute shoppers, mainly men mind but a few females here and there too, who had nipped out for more Sellotape and other bits and bobs. Everyone did seem so happy and excited, he thought. It truly was a wonderful time, he conceded. There were hardly ever any crimes committed on Christmas Eve in Scotland, probably because everyone was cheerfully looking forward to what was to come. Even the neds who regularly hung around the Lochend garage were nowhere to be seen, most of them all at home wrapping up gifts or organising drugs for that evening's festive ding dong.

In Monty's experience, it was always two or three days after the trainers had been unwrapped and the chocolate selection boxes consumed, that the hoodies with knives returned to the streets again. On a large billboard at the Portobello junction, he noticed an advertisement for the newly released movie—Exodus Gods and Kings, with an image of Christian Bale. Monty stared at it a while as he waited at the lights. He vaguely knew the story of the biblical exodus across the sea which God had parted in order for the Israelites to escape the Egyptian pharaoh and his army. He decided to go and watch it over the holiday period and to read up on it again before doing so.

That's a start too.

He had left the file upon the entrance area as instructed. He wondered now if it would be gone by the time they got back. He could recall when he was very young and his father had left out a glass of whisky and a carrot for Father Christmas and his reindeer every Christmas Eve. For a brief moment, he wondered now if there were actually any angels creeping around at night who wouldn't mind a tipple being left out?

He smirked at his own simplicity though— more likely humans would help themselves first.

Maybe that would be another start then?

Kinnaird Park was busy but he got a parking space easily enough outside Argos. He wondered how many of these Christmas shoppers believed in Christ, never mind any other deity? How many of them would even give their neighbours a card this year? He recalled when he had been a kid, all his neighbours had exchanged cards, and even chocolates or wine. His best friend Lewis's mother had always brought round some home baked cookies and a bottle of mulled wine—which his parents had hated.

"Changed days, son," he told the dog as he removed the key from the ignition. "Won't be long, buddy," he promised.

First, he popped into a sports shop where he bought trainers, a football and some football boots for his son. Then he picked up a card at Clintons and borrowed a pen from the counter assistant to write it out to him. He then walked across the car park to a cash machine and withdrew £300, which he placed in the card. At that moment, his phone rang…it was Sadie.

"Hello bro," she said merrily.

"Hi, Merry Christmas," he made the effort to seem pleased to hear from her.

"And to you." She was surprised that he had not blanked her call. "What are you up to?"

"Just picking up some food for the house and getting Sasha some doggy treats." He couldn't be arsed discussing his son with her as it would just turn into another unqualified lecture on parenting, and then inevitably—the usual fight.

"So, what are your plans for tomorrow then, hun?" she asked.

"Working from home on a big case that I am behind on sadly," he lied, and he knew, that she knew, that he was.

"Well, we are sorry you decided not to join us, but will it be okay for me to ring you briefly tomorrow while you're having a coffee break?" She always called when she was half pissed at Christmas and he always took her call out of sentimentality, despite preferring not to.

"Sure, I might even take a brandy with you, Sadie." He smiled, glad to sense that the call was winding up.

"Right you are then, Mr." She knew the score; it was time to let him go. "After the Queen's speech then?"

"Aye, that will do," he agreed.

"God bless then, Stevie," she said.

"And to you, sis, give my love to everyone," he replied before turning his phone off just in case anyone else wanted to pass on any more compliments of the season.

He walked over to the large pet warehouse and bought the dog one of those stuffed pheasant toys that it loved so much. The bugger would tear it to shreds in a few minutes mind, but he fair enjoyed the process. He grabbed some pigs' ears too whilst he was there and then joined the irritatingly long queue of other pet owners who were buying gifts for their furry friends.

He noticed a former client of his as he waited, one Jenny Henderson aka Jenny Ha[72]—a persistent shoplifter, back street trickster and junky. She was

---

[72] The slang name for an 18th century Edinburgh landlady-Janet Hall. The old licencing law of 1699 had forbidden the employment of women in tavern's, cellars and drinking shops as being "a great snare to the youth and occasion for lewdness and debauchery". It was then challenged and severed in 1749. A woman who kept a tavern of the character

eyeing up the guinea pigs and rabbits which were on display in a large wooden pen. Monty could see her urging her male companion, a skinny looking unkempt lad who resembled the Rodney Trotter character from the Only Fools and Horses television comedy series, to steal one. Monty left his place in the irritatingly slow queue now and casually strolled over towards them both. "Hi Jenny, admiring the rabbits?" he asked her.

Jenny looked up in surprise. She appeared overly haggard for her young age and her naturally wiry ginger hair, which was partly bleached blonde, was becoming less so thanks to several days of grease. She was even sweating a little now despite it being chilly outside. It was obvious to him that she was rattling for her next fix and had decided that one or two of these furry critters would just about pay for it. "Oh, hello Mr Montgomery." She brushed her hedgy hair back with her hand in an attempt to tidy it up. Her teeth were dark yellow turning brown, and when she smiled, Monty could see that a few were going black.

"You're not thinking of pinching one of them, are you?" He smiled at her. "I wouldn't want to see you locked up in a cell over the festive period," he said.

"Who is this?" Her sidekick demanded to know.

"This is my old lawyer eh," she told the Rodney lookalike who then smiled too, revealing hardly any teeth at all.

"You couldn't spare us a tenner for a power card, Mr Montgomery, could—" but before she could finish her sentence, Monty handed her a £20 note that he had in his pocket.

"Try to eat, Jenny, and keep out of trouble," he urged.

"Cheers," she replied gleefully before then striding off purposely toward the exit, whilst her more polite lacky gave Monty an interesting quarter curtsy before jogging after her.

Monty knew she would probably go and buy a bag of heroin with it, but at least he had probably saved an animal's life, he reasoned to himself as he rejoined the queue again. Afterward, he nipped into Marks & Spencer and picked up a couple of sirloin steaks, some chestnut mushrooms, a portion of potato dauphinoise and some milk chocolates. He contemplated treating himself to a scarf or something, but he had one already and couldn't see the point.

No point in going overboard with the jollities .

---

of Jenny Ha's pub was termed a "Lucky", e.g., a "Lucky Ha", the title signifying a "Guidwife".

Back at the car, which the snow had covered like icing on a cake, the dog was pleased to see him regardless as he wiped it away with his hand. "Hello buddy, I got us some steaks for tomorrow," he told it as he fastened his seatbelt and turned on both the radio and the heater. There was a woman talking in what Monty suspected was a church service somewhere, perhaps a festive carol service?

"And so, at this time of year when everyone is buying gifts for one and other, indeed gifts that may have no use after the holidays, can we think about how to trim the expenses and give more meaning to our gifts?" she asked her listeners whilst Monty drove out of the park and headed westward towards Gilmerton.

"We can turn to Luke 11:9-13," she suggested, her voice echoing slightly as if she were in a cathedral.

So, I say to you: Ask and it will be given to you; seek and you will find; knock and the door will be opened to you. For everyone who asks receives; the one who seeks finds; and to the one who knocks, the door will be opened.

Which of you fathers, if your son asks for a fish, will give him a snake instead? Or if he asks for an egg, will give him a scorpion? If you then, though you are evil, know how to give good gifts to your children, how much more will your Father in heaven give the Holy Spirit to those who ask him!

"We can bring our loved ones into the light, and into the power of prayer," she then suggested. "For if we believe that prayer is a glorious gift, then this is an example of strong faith, is it not?" she asked.

Monty grinned at this because oddly enough, he had picked up the only religious looking card he could find for his son, one with an image of a donkey and co looking down upon the new born Christ in his manger. Suddenly a BMW cut in front of him, causing him to break sharply before it then sped off left towards Newton Village. Monty got quite a fright but impulsively checked to see if the dog was alright; which it was thankfully. He turned the radio off again and drove on regardless, if not more warily.

Taking the back roads over to Gilmerton because they usually saw less traffic, he was headed for his son's maternal grandparents house, though he drove slower now. The boy's mother didn't live there anymore of course, Monty hadn't a clue where she stayed now and he didn't want to either. This was why he picked up and dropped off the kid at the grandparents' place whenever he saw him.

The visits had become less frequent nowadays as the child had become a teenager and preferred to do his own thing, but Monty knew that the chav reinforced her one-sided tutoring of the boy both regularly and strenuously. Hers was a biased curriculum, based upon disappointment and miscalculation; the essence of which was an anti-Monty agenda. Blend all that up with the little shit's evolving teenage attitude, and a general lack of respect for anyone older than himself, then there was little surprise that the father-son relationship was about as far away from the Walton's as it could get before there was no relationship[73].

The old part of Gilmerton was a bit of a rabbit warren and it always took Monty a minute or two to find his bearing no matter how many times he had been here. Eventually he recognised the street from the multitude of garden gnomes in one particular garden at the start of yet another identical row of houses. He pulled up outside the grandparents' house, noting that the old boy's green Toyota was parked in the drive. He got out and took the gifts up to the door and tapped it twice gently. The blinds twitched and then after a long pause, the door was opened by the old boy.

"Aye aye, Stevie," he said as he raised a pipe to his mouth and struck a match to light it.

"Hello Bill, I'm just dropping off these for the laddie." Monty placed the bags on the step and took a step back to make it clear that he was not hanging about.

"Fine. I'll make sure he gets them then," replied the old boy, who made an effort to look away as he bent down to pick them up.

"Cheers, have a nice Christmas," Monty now found himself saying, but he then quickly shuffled away.

There was no reply, of course, it was beyond the old bastard to exchange season's greetings with him. The point now was that at least Monty had been polite. The old man would be too concerned about whose gifts the boy would prefer now, but Monty couldn't care less about all that pettiness, so long as he had maintained his own dignity. On the drive home, it snowed heavily, and he

---

[73] *The Waltons* was a 1970's American TV show that aired for nine seasons, about a loving family living through the Great Depression of the 1930s. The signature scene at the end of every episode was when the lights went out at night and most of the family bid each other a goodnight.

decided to stop at the Inch Park and run the dog before it got too heavy to do so later on.

There were no other footprints upon the pathway which led into the park but the snow was falling in abundance so that might have counted for nothing. The dog scurried off ahead, exploring the woodland whilst Monty kept his eye out for anyone or anything. He fiddled with the cork in his jacket pocket as they took in a couple of laps of the park, hoping that if he were to encounter the paranormal here, in this bright Christmas card scene, it would be the fox man as opposed to the Orcadian or any other unholy bastard with mischief in mind.

Fortunately, the only thing to interrupt their flow was the dog doing his business which Monty duly bagged and binned before they completed their final lap. He noticed that their prints had been covered up by the falling snow by the time they had returned to the car park. Then by the time they had crawled home through the roads which needed ploughed, the snow had stopped, and lay motionless, covering everything from cars to bus stops. Monty was pleased to see some families on the Links making snowmen together.

"Why can't families be like that every day of the bloody year, eh?" he asked, but the dog was looking forward to his daily treat and simply looked up at him with expectancy. This made Monty grin and he was further cheered by the fact that there was a parking space right outside his front door. "Right, let's go," he said, grabbing the shopping, eager to get in and get the kettle on.

Once inside the front door, he noted that the file had gone. He had left it precisely where he had found it. In its place lay a blue envelope with what he guessed might be a Christmas card in it. It was obviously delivered after the postie had been, so Monty guessed that it might be from a neighbour. The dog patrolled the tiles in a quick couple of little circles, sniffing the ground, before finally heading over to the hall door and sitting down to wait for access to the carpeted hall. Monty locked up first before kicking his snow-covered shoes off and hanging his coat up. He took the cork out his pocket and held it in his free hand as he opened the hall door with his other, keeping alert as he walked confidently down the hallway.

"Go and see, boy," he commanded as he reached the lounge and as usual the little gundog was off inspecting every nook and cranny of the property while Monty looked out of the patio doors to see if there were any footprints in the garden. Somewhat satisfied, he then opened the doors and let the dog out to do an inspection of the garden whilst he got the heating and kettle going. He chucked the food in the fridge and got the milk out, sighing as he remembered that he had forgotten to pick up more.

At this time of year, when he had been a youngster, his mother would usually have filled the house with smells of her baking. Particularly on Christmas Eve when she had made cherry sponge and shortbread that would be cut into large thick squares and which were a meal in themselves. He smirked as he allowed himself a brief moment of nostalgia now as he waited on the kettle to boil. It was unusual to receive cards at home at Christmas time because the only ones he mainly received were at work, and he left those there. Sure he got one from Sadie every year, but hers always came late in the New Year.

He opened this one. It was not one from a Christmas pack, he noted, rather it was from Oxfam and had a picture of a Spaniel, like his, feeding a lamb with a bottle of baby milk in its mouth. So this one had clearly been hand-picked as well as hand delivered. He opened it up and instantly noticed a mobile number written beside Mehreen's signature:

"Merry Crimbo, Stephen. I hope it's a good one. If you find yourself at a loose end over the holidays and fancy a Festive drinky poo, gives a text. X."

Well, well, well, Monty raised an eyebrow. She was going for it again and she wasn't shy, was she. He had a big smile glued to his face for a moment or two as he made a brew and took out a dried pig's ear for the dog. He soon had the patio door closed again, and the lounge was warming up nicely. He was glad to relax on the sofa, this was the real beauty of the festive period, he kept telling himself—the chance to relax. He turned his phone back on and began to read the Bible again with the *Lawrence of Arabia* tune on the telly in the background. There seemed something comforting about a classic cinema score going on in the background at this time of year. It relaxed the dog too, otherwise he probably would have gone away to eat his pig's ear in the kitchen or hall.

Monty soon became cosy as he sipped his tea whilst the dog snuggled in between his legs on the sofa. He read through from Deuteronomy to Judges and then leaned back and considered that the Bible itself could be considered better than anything Dickens or Homer had ever produced. At precisely that moment, Monty experienced his second paranormal happening of the day. It was nothing major, but it was still something nonetheless, he believed. For at the precise moment that he had been thinking that the Bible was a better read than Dickens, etc., he looked down and noticed that he had come to Deuteronomy 32:4, which

221

shocked him[74]. He decided against dissecting the ins and outs of how this might have come about.

Is someone or something reading my thoughts, or even directing them?

Instead, he decided to go with the flow and savour what was becoming quite rewarding after only twenty-four hours—newfound enlightenment. It was just like those magic mushrooms he had taken when he had been a kid it had been safer back then to just go with the flow of the trip, as opposed to questioning or struggling against the experience.

After a while he put the book down on the coffee table and watched the news. There was more waffle on about the general election and a Labour pledge to enforce the fox-hunting ban, etc. He soon dozed off for half an hour before his phone on the table rang.

He jerked himself up and leaned over to see who it was. *Chicken Run* was on the TV now and the dog was watching it with interest, he noticed. It was his boss—Arty Llewellyn. "This could be kick-off time?" he told the dog who was completely glued to the animation.

"Hello?"

"Stevie, its Arty." Arty had the proverbial—I'm sorry to have to chuck this at you, mate—tone.

"Yep?" Still half asleep.

"Russel is down with the flu at his place in Aberlady and he canny even take a call, never mind be on call." Arty sounded like he didn't believe it either but was backing his partner regardless.

"Fine." Monty shook his head but deep down he knew things were all coming together.

"I'm sorry, Stevie, I know it's Christmas but you'll have to go on call. What with the courts being off. There hopefully won't be anything much for you to do but keep your phone on 24/7, just in case St Leonards custody suite call you, okay mate?"

Mate?

"It's fine, Arty, I'm just at home with the dog so no worries, nothing planned."

"Good man, Stevie, well, I'll get Russell's wife to bell you as soon as he is over it, mate."

"No probs, Arty, have a good one."

---

[74] Deuteronomy 32:4 points out that God's work is "perfect".

"Right okay, Merry Christmas, mate." …click brrrrrr.

Mate?

Russel Cuthbert had been the on-duty solicitor for the firm over the festive period, having drawn the lowest card in Llewellyn's office one rainy afternoon back in November. To be fair to him, he had drawn the low card for the last three years so Monty didn't really grudge him it. It just meant he couldn't have a drink tomorrow, which he was not much fussed about anyway. "Right fine. Let's get dinner sorted then."

He pulled himself up off the sofa and went through to the kitchen where he found a Chinese takeaway menu and stood giving it a once-over. He tended always read the menu before going for the same old chow Mein and boiled rice, or the calorific duck in plum sauce with chips. He decided to go for something else for a change, seeing it was Christmas and he had earned a treat.

He phoned up and ordered a beef curry, fried rice and chips. He was told that it could be up to an hour. They always said that though and it was usually no more than thirty minutes, so he opened the chocolates he had picked up earlier and had a couple while he boiled the kettle again. At that moment, his phone rang again, it was his friend and fellow solicitor—wee Mikey Pritz who still worked for the Stafford Street firm where the chav fished for sperm donors.

Monty used to play five-a-sides on Tuesday nights with Pritz for a long time after he had moved on to his present firm, but once Pritz had started seeing a friend of the chav's, Monty gradually wound down the friendship. He knew his kid's mum well enough, and seriously disliked her for her materialistic, classless and dishonest nature. Her setting up of her friend with Pritz, was no coincidence, and it would not be long until she was attempting to get updates on Monty through the willing-to-please-for-a-pair-of-tits—Mikey Boy.

Monty still saw Pritz at court from time to time these days, but was thankful that they were usually both too busy to chat, though they occasionally exchanged texts, and since neither played football anymore either, Monty was able to severe the connection without totally ostracising someone whom he would have to see in court regularly.

"Hi," he answered reluctantly.

"Hiya, Stevie lad." It was a fake tone; Monty knew now for sure that this was something to do with her.

"Hi Mikey, how's it going?"

"Oh not bad, I just wound up that Sheriff and Jury trial last week and have been on a break since," Pritz smirked down the phone.

"I heard that, Mikey, well done." It was clear Pritz wanted to disguise the real reason for this random contact by supplying some self-admiration as the starting point.

They talked a while about the case. A serious assault on a barman in a Grassmarket boozer which had entailed Pritz's client being bottled over the head by a female barmaid before he then had laid into her and broke her jaw. There had been no glorious defence of Pritz's guilty client however, rather the case was binned halfway through the trial. After a cagey cross examination of the two key witnesses in the morning, who had then been instructed by the Sheriff not to be in contact with each other over the lunchtime recess. The reason being, they were contradicting themselves in their statements and also when giving evidence in the dock. The pair were then caught on camera in each other's company during lunch break. So, the case was duly deserted by the Crown.

They then talked football a little; Pritz was a Hibs fan and an Everton admirer, before then doing the "*what are you up to for Christmas*" routine. Finally, Pritz came to the point.

"Stevie, I've had my Mrs nagging in my ear tonight about her pal who is moaning in her ear."

Your Mrs? At least he was prepared to put it all down to the woman.

"Right?" Monty played along before some female shouted out in the background at Pritz's end:

"I'm not nagging, whose nagging?" Which was partly to publicise the fact that she was no longer living in a flat in Sighthill, but had now moved into Mikey boy's Stockbridge flat.

"Anyway Stevie, the thing is, she is moaning about you handing in presents or something for the laddie today that weren't wrapped up, etc., and now he has seen them," said Pritz.

Monty was silent, then Pritz felt he had to say something more, "The granny had to wrap them up or something."

"Well, that's perfect, mate, as she does such a good job at it. Cheers." Monty then hung up. He couldn't turn his phone off though as he was now on call.

Thankfully, Pritz didn't call back though. A short while later, however Monty then received a couple of festive texts from Ally Blyth from work, who commiserated about hearing that Monty was now the on-duty brief over

Christmas. Then shortly after that, yet another text—a boozy offer to jump a fast black up to Mountcastle to have a "festive drinky poo" with old Trisha from work.

"On call Trish, sorry. X," he duly replied just as the doorbell went with his Chinese food.

Chapter Ten

Be not forgetful to entertain strangers, for thereby some have entertained
angels unawares.
Hebrews 13:2

Monty was up, showered, sipping decaf coffee by 11AM and started on the chocolate and clementines thereafter. Eating them on Christmas morning had been a tradition of his since his childhood. He was only partly conscious of the psychology involved now however, but not to do so seemed unthinkable. Of course, if questioned on the subject, he would have denied caring about such sentimentality. He just maintained the tradition in order to dispense with the niggling aches of his self-isolation. Christmas morning was the best part of the day, and sure, it would be nice to hear the sound of kids opening their presents etc, but then Monty didn't want kids in his life after midday, so he didn't dwell upon it too much. This way he at least felt that he was not missing out on all the tradition.

He was enjoying watching Nigella Lawson on the TV presently. He fancied the pants off her like every other bloke his age. She was quite seductively conjuring up some late-night festive snacks from leftover turkey etc. Regardless of the fact that he would not be having turkey today, nor any of the trimmings, he almost felt part of her festive vibe, simply by tuning in to her show.

His phone then rang out abruptly and he dragged himself away from the culinary goddess momentarily and reached over to the coffee table for it. It was a withheld number, he had to answer it because it was potentially the police. "Hello, Stephen Montgomery speaking."

"Hi dad." It was his son.

"Hi son. Merry Christmas." He sat up and smiled.

"Merry Christmas, dad. Thanks for the money and the footie stuff." The lad was as glum sounding as ever, but this was new, he never usually rang on Christmas Day; Monty was pleased.

"No problem, I hope you buy yourself something nice with it."

"Yeh, I'll get the bus into town tomorrow for the sales and get stuff, thanks." There was the sound of a movie, possibly Toy Story, on in the background.

"Good. Well, if you fancy meeting up for an Indian or something, we could go for dinner over the holidays?" Monty heard himself say.

"Okay, that would be good, yeh. The day before New Year, I come back from visiting mum's friend in Inverness, so that would be good?"

Monty wondered if the "friend" was a guy? But he reminded himself that he didn't care. "Can you give me a ring on the 29th then, son, to confirm the time and the place?"

"Perfect, dad. Thanks again, speak to you next week, and Merry Christmas." The lad seemed cheerier now.

Later, when Monty returned from a walk along Portobello beach with the dog, he got the steaks out, some baby potatoes, which he rinsed and then began peeling. He had some cooked chicken in the fridge too that he took out and picked at whilst the potatoes boiled on the stove. He gave more of it to the dog however and wished for a moment that he could have a couple of glasses of plonk whilst he waited on lunch. It was always the same, he sighed, when he can have a glass he didn't want it, and when he can't, he wanted one.

His phone received a text now—it was Charnley.

"Happy Christmas, Monty."

Monty replied and actually wrote more than he might have to anyone else. Then just as he was sending it, the door went. "Who can that be?" He looked at the dog. He kept the dog behind the hall door however, in case there was any kind of trouble as he did not want the little fellow getting hurt. He had no spyhole regrettably. He had been meaning to have one installed in this relatively new front door.

Hand in pocket—fingers on cork—he opened the door and saw an olive-skinned man standing there. A man with a pleasant smile and warm friendly eyes. He was wearing an old-fashioned grey hooded duffle coat and a red knitted woollen scarf around his neck. He was holding a tin foil covered tray in his left hand and Monty sensed instantaneously that this was someone special. This guy radiated a peaceful calming energy that reassured Monty that he was either an angel, or something better.

"Are you the Orcadian?" Monty asked in all seriousness. Though unable to lose the smile which had appeared upon his face, nor the inner joy that this person was causing.

"No. So fear not, Stephen." Smiled the angel.

Monty instinctively gestured for him to enter and took a step back. The dog was watching all of this through the art deco stained-glass hall door, and was up wagging his tail excitedly, which Monty noted with interest.

"Welcome." Monty said to this clean-cut and gentle seeming person.

"Thank you kindly, Stephen, allow me to introduce myself," the angel reached out his right hand. Monty took it and they gently shook. Monty also noted that the fellow's hand was as warm as his own despite it being cold outside, "My name is Dai and you're quite correct; yes, I am an angel."

"Thanks for coming then." Monty seemed briefly star-struck with a joyful and friendly smile but he felt as relaxed and calm as he might have been should it have been a childhood friend door stepping him now.

"And this beef Wellington," said the angel with a well-to-do Edinburgh accent, and he handed Monty the tin-foiled tray, "is our Christmas dinner; only needs warmed up," he chuckled merrily before then producing an unlabelled bottle of what Monty thought might be red wine from within his overcoat. "Ta-da!" The angel positively beamed.

"Let's go through then," chuckled Monty as if he had already had a glass or two.

"Don't worry," said Dai telepathically, as he bent down to pat the incredibly happy little dog when Monty opened the hall door. "You won't receive any calls for work today, so you can have a glass or two." Which surprised Monty momentarily and caused him to take a step back and away from the angel. He then took a deep breath and stepped back again.

"Okay." – Still beaming.

"Ah, trust. A good start." Dai stood up and winked as he removed his overcoat. Monty saw that he was tall, well-built and had the appearance of a man who was around the same age as himself.

"Do you want me to put this in the oven and put some veg and potatoes on, Dai?" Monty asked, quite spellbound as Dai hung his coat up in the hall.

"Now you're talking. Potatoes would be lovely as well as that turnip you have in the fridge," replied Dai cheerily as he sauntered into the kitchen.

Monty was still somewhat shocked but he got to peeling and then boiling the potatoes and turnip. During which time, he conversed with Dai about the particulars of the angel's presence here.

How was it possible? How did this conflict between angels work?

"Mostly, my choir appear as men to humans," explained Dai, who casually leaned on the worktop whilst Monty began mashing the turnip up. "We do so because it is a familiar form to human beings; as is appearing with wings too," he conceded with a shrug to himself.

"Because that is how humans relate to you, but are you saying that this is not your true form?" asked Monty.

"Correct, Stephen. We are beings from another dimension and if we were to appear to humans in our natural form, I'm afraid that would be beyond your comprehension, and so quite pointless," said Dai very patiently.

"And the fallen ones?" Monty queried whilst adding salt, pepper and some butter to the turnip.

"They also tend to appear as humans because they usually also have reasons for being accepted by humans, but in some cases they prefer to frighten, hurt, and even to possess humans, and so they may shape-shift and use other forms," said Dai wearily now as he turned to take in some travel magnets on the fridge.

Monty had of course, never experienced anything as wonderful as this before, apart from his inter-dimensional trip via the Lundin Links stones. He was now, as he had been then, quite enchanted, though on this occasion he was completely relaxed and comfortable with what he sensed, felt, and saw. He wanted to chuckle at it all but instead, as he then began making up some gravy with some old stock he had frozen, he asked, "Which raises the obvious question of why this is allowed to all take place?"

Dai swung around accusingly. "Ask your question properly." He smirked. Monty knew the angel had read his mind.

"Okay then." He smirked back. "Why does God let this go on instead of ensuring that evil does not flourish?" he asked whilst focusing on the food and attempting to maintain a note of passing enquiry.

Dai smiled and helped himself to a chair at the kitchen table.

"Humans have the gift of free will, Monty," he said. If he noticed the disdain in Monty's thoughts, he did not show it. "The Kertamen is essentially a dispute over that," he explained.

"But why can't more energy be directed upon saving people from bad things?" Monty instinctively felt that this was the key to it all really, cancer, paedophilia, violence, etc.

"Because humans have free will, Monty, they have to ask for help and even then, more often than not they have to deserve it," replied the angel with a rigidity that took Monty a little by surprise.

"It is like hot soup being handed out by the Salvation Army tonight in a snowy corner of South Leith, there is not enough for everyone, particularly not for those who don't deserve it," suggested Dai in the friendliest of tones now.

"Well, what about cancer or the holocaust, Dai?" asked Monty, quite undeterred as he checked upon the Wellington in the oven.

"Neither of which are God's doing, Stephen. As I said, humans can choose to pray for intervention because they have free will, but many only pray when they need something. Consequently, my choir will never interfere unless we have been instructed to do so."

"But that is my point, why aren't all prayers answered?" Monty shrugged.

Dai shook his head in a 'kids today' manner. "Whether or not we are instructed to intervene, is all down to both the character and the faith of the individual praying as well as availability." He shrugged back—still smiling.

"Availability?"

Dai nodded but was silent for a moment—clearly a theatrical pause for contemplation. "Like I said, Stephen," he finally sighed, anxious at the lesser minds of men, "intervention with regard to man's behaviour is not always possible on an *ad hoc* basis."

"Yes, but evil intervenes to save or help its own, doesn't it?" Monty decided that the Wellington was heated up enough now and so took it out and began carving it up.

"Yes, occasionally, but they are punished for it, Stephen," assured Dai.

"I'd like to think so, Dai." Monty turned to look down at the angel now who was sitting back, quite relaxed with the dog sitting upon his lap, which he was stroking lightly. Monty had never seen the dog like that with anyone else before.

I'm not sure about people who don't like dogs, but I trust a dog who doesn't like a person.

"We are just messengers, Stephen, like an Uber delivery driver if you like"

"You only go where you are sent then?" Monty nodded. He was not sure himself if he was being sarcastic or whether he was simply understanding the reality.

There was a flicker of a grin on the angel's pale but beautifully carved face like a defective lamp bulb. He could not read Monty's sentiment because Monty had not known it himself. "Sometimes we messengers intervene to help man without him ever knowing, and sometimes we too are reprimanded for doing so."

Monty smiled politely and quickly made up a bowel of pilchards mashed with kibble for the dog. "We can have our steaks tomorrow." He looked down and told his quite contented pet.

"Despite not being gods, nor having the power to prevent all evil from operating here, we do influence your agriculture, fertility and from time to time, save lives," advised Dai. "There have been many incidents wherein we have prevented children from being knocked down by traffic, drowning, or falling from heights to their deaths," he said.

"But let me tell you something, Stephen," he added, "prayers which voice complaints and grievances, are useless," he revealed.

Monty was confused.

"Man has free will, and it is better to request help when he prays, rather than tell us about the evil injustices ongoing within his dimension instead; for we know all about them already." Dai shook his head now. "We can only respond to specific requests for assistance that are authorised from above. To obtain such an intervention, faith is would be an important key."

Monty understood and nodded.

"And every time we intervene without authorisation, we are reprimanded," clarified Dai.

Monty felt that he had to ask. "So, many prayers are not answered then?"

"Correct." Dai nodded now as the dog jumped down to have its dinner.

"Why not?" asked Monty.

"Well, that's a decision made upstairs, but rest assured, there are always reasons. Which, of course, makes your question irrelevant. Do you understand this, Stephen?"

Barely.

Monty served up the buttery flaky pastry covered beef onto two plates with mash and turnip which he duly drizzled with gravy. "People struggle to accept that God doesn't end all suffering around the world, regardless of whether those suffering are deserving of it or not," he said softly.

"I understand that," Dai read his thought, "but the question of, why does God not do this or that, is irrelevant because he is God. The utopia that men seek, can only be achieved through pleasing God, and not by any survival of the fittest mentality," he replied telepathically.

"People whose prayers go unanswered, lose faith," said Monty plaintively.

"All he wants is to be worshipped and loved above anything else in your life," insisted Dai. "Questioning him, or his reasoning, whilst blaming him for things he has not done, are not the tools required to propel a person along the road to sanctity."

Monty served up the two plates of food and poured two glasses of the wine, then he went back over and produced a bottle of cold spring water and two more glasses which he half-filled with ice.

"If you have faith, place your trust in him, be grateful and not too demanding. Then you'll see him open up doors that you never expected to be opened," continued Dai, still smiling as he spoke. "Thank you very much," he then said as Monty served him and then poured them both some water.

"So, faith and appreciation in return for being able to breathe?" asked Monty.

"Faith, and appreciation of every day wherein you can view the trees blowing, or the cut grass that you need to love so much when playing football—yes," chuckled Dai. Monty sat down and they both toasted their glasses.

"Unconditional worship then," offered Monty with a hint of sarcasm.

"Unconditional love, shall we say," offered Dai before sipping some of the deep red wine.

Monty thought the Wellington smelt outstanding but was too deep into this conversation to mention it. "And ignore our free will by not asking questions?" he asked.

"No, you can always ask for enlightenment, Stephen. But know that God knows when to educate a soul. What was it that Christ said again?" asked Dai playfully, for he knew Monty had not got as far as the New Testament yet. He spared him the spotlight moment and went on before he could reply. "Do not let your hearts be troubled. Trust in God and also in me," he quoted.

Monty nodded that he understood this, and he knew that he was accepting of it now. He simply sought to understand things. He raised his glass at Dai again. He never tasted the wine in restaurants—that was such a bourgeois charade, and always told the waiter instead to just pour. He sipped at it now. It was deep and smooth with what Monty thought was a cherry flavour as well as a hint of something else that was highly pleasant but that he could not place.

"Wow. That is delicious," he gasped before taking another mouthful.

"Indeed," agreed Dai. "It's Etruscan," he said before his lips touched his glass.

"Etruscan?" Monty was unfamiliar with the term.

Dai replaced his glass and blessed both their plates. "The Etruscans were a civilisation who dominated in Italy long before Rome had their day, around 900 BC," he explained. "They were mainly located in cities in an area known today as Tuscany."

"Around 700 BC however, they perfected the art of wine making after being influenced by the Greeks in the archaic (orientalising) period. The technique had filtered through from Shiraz in ancient Persia," he revealed as they both began eating.

The food was exceptional, Monty realised upon tasting his first mouthful. "Mmm…and what happened to them?" he asked between more mouthfuls.

"They fought wars with a developing Rome over hundreds of years and were finally absorbed by the Romans around 100 BC," explained Dai merrily.

"Were you there at the time of any of that Dai?" Monty quickly asked before filling his mouth with some more of the juicy wine.

"Yes. From time to time during the rise of Rome, I was occasionally in Etruria," replied Dai thoughtfully as he too munched away.

"Were you involved in a conflict with fallen angels back then?" asked Monty.

"In a way, yes." Nodded Dai.

"As in the Kertamen?"

"Correct!" Dai seemed pleased that Monty had noted the term.

"Well, the wine is outstanding, Dai, and the Wellington is superb too." Monty raised his glass again and took another taste.

Dai raised his glass. "When Christ turned the water into wine, which incidentally, was not what his abilities were intended for, he made a lot of my choir smile with that move." He clinked his glass against Monty's. "And it was men who invented wine," he added cheerily before drinking some.

"Here is to the Persians then," giggled Monty now, for the wine was strong stuff. "But I do take the point about faith and the power of praying," he pointed out.

"And the Wellington comes from an oven in a country house kitchen near here in the 1930s."

Monty raised an eyebrow at this.

Time travel is the mode of transportation for angels; why then can't wrongs be righted?

233

"But you're right, if we all loved God, we probably wouldn't sin as much," he said instead.

"If all humans loved and obeyed God, regardless of the frequent attempts by the opposition to lead them astray, then it would be a peaceful, compassionate world, where violence and mistreatment would be a rarity," replied Dai, ignoring Monty's real thoughts.

"And illnesses such as cancer?"

"The cures to most illnesses are available now Stephen, but because people are easily misguided by the dark side to primarily focus upon wealth and self-adulation, they are not always visible."

"So creation itself is an ongoing process which requires us to create a perfect utopia here on earth, wherein empathy, compassion, and appreciation for the finer things in life, are the keys to prosperity?" queried Monty.

"Precisely. If government funds were redirected towards an investigation into such matters, the answers are there to be found by any God worshipping society," said Dai.

The angel seemed to be enjoying the mashed potatoes: "Very nice, Stephen," he said.

"Butter, prunella cheese and a dash of cream if you have it," chuckled Monty at the bizarreness of it all. Albert Finney could then be heard singing from the TV in the lounge.

Scrooge?

"Yes Stephen. Albert Finney as Scrooge," smiled Dai as he tucked in, "that's the best version of Dickens' *Christmas Carol*, I'd say, but you prefer the old Alistair Sim version, don't you, I think?" he said, reading Monty's mind again.

It had been the closing performance by Finney in the film however and so the news soon came on. Monty excused himself, nipped through and turned the channel over to another film and then returned. "Sorry about that, Dai, but the news can be depressing and today is a day for happiness," he pointed out.

"Hear, hear." Smiled Dai and he raised his glass and took another mouthful of wine.

They both listened in silence with cheerful anticipation now. It was a film about Joan of Arc.

"I would rather die than do something I know to be a sin, or to be against God's will." The female actress could be heard shouting.

Monty and Dai exchanged a look momentarily. Dai stopped chewing the beef in his mouth.

"Did you do that?" asked Monty suddenly; wondering at the coincidence.

"You did it, my friend," replied Dai truthfully, and then they both grinned. "The holy spirit is clearly with us," he then declared.

"That was quite something," said Monty.

"Yes, that was God's will, Stephen." Beamed the angel jubilantly as he now chewed his food.

"Why me then, Dai?" Monty was coping well with all of this drama, and the potential outcomes, but the one thing that niggled away at him was why any manufacturer of his species, would consider him, Stevie Montgomery, worthy of a starring role in what was nothing short of a theological epic?

"That would be another irrelevant question, Stephen," chuckled the angel. "It is best that you accept things as they are and not spend your precious time and energy wondering why God acts in certain ways," he suggested.

"The concept of your DNA is similar to mine and to our cosmology Stephen," he warned. "But there are more differences than similarities, so it is natural that there are things you cannot understand. But that you should simply accept; for that is faith in a nutshell, Stephen."

Undeterred, Monty continued to obtain a better understanding. "DNA is a key clue to creation, isn't it?" he asked with the same cheeky grin he gave witnesses he was cross examining in the dock.

"DNA could very well be an example of obliteration," was Dai's expressionless reply.

"How so?" Monty sensed a chill from him, but he had to know.

"The cosmology is all about potentials, Stephen," explained Dai, "where the heavens catch fire and clash into one and other—creating annihilation, but the principle material remain, and so there are undeveloped seeds left for new heavens," he said.

"So, order is a key then? God's cosmos I mean?"

"Yes. A notion of one supreme eternal being, and an accompanying portion of order. Anyway, the point is, there are things you should just accept and not challenge," assured Dai.

Fortitude in defiance of philistinism?

Yes something like that Stephen.

After they had eaten their meals, they chatted a while about the war in heaven before heading through to the lounge where they sat sipping the wine. Monty had brought the chocolates through and placed them on the coffee table between them both. The film was still on and it was only 2 pm, Monty noted.

One thing was for sure however, Monty knew that he had to savour these valuable moments but not only enjoy the experience, but also seize the opportunity to dig up more on this Orcadian character.

"So, you read the file then." Dai read his thoughts again.

"I did." Monty nodded, sipping from his glass.

"What is your take on it then?" smiled Dai.

"I recognised the stone circle connection as a link to my own experience over in Fife, and I think that they are some sort of stargates," said Monty. "And also that hills, or mountains even, are involved in some way?"

"Let's call them doorways," suggested Dai as he leaned forward and helped himself to one of the chocolates. "Have you ever heard of any of the ancient native North American people?" he asked with a casualness which seemed remarkable to Monty.

"Like the Apache and the Sioux?"

No.

"Long before them, there were the ancient Anasazi, who lived 2,000 years before Christ," said Dai once he had finished his chocolate.

Monty shook his head, guessing that the Anasazi were from the caveman era.

"Well, they were a pueblo living people, yes," confirmed Dai. "A people who built their homes high up into stone mountain faces in order to protect themselves from supernatural enemies," he explained.

"Supernatural?" asked Monty.

"Well, the Anasazi drew inscriptions on stones which still exist today and which display a spiral vortex with a supernatural being coming through it." Dai let Monty take this in a moment as he helped himself to another chocolate before continuing telepathically:

And those drawings also show small five-toed human feet running away from some larger six-toed feet beside the spiral vortex.

Monty remained silent, suspecting now that Dai's point must be that there was a connection between these North American rock carvings and the mystical stone circles in Scotland.

"And the Navaho too," mused Dai, "they also carved images of spiral doorways. All of these North American carvings match the descriptions of the whirlwind entries of various divine entities within the Bible; which you will learn in due course when you read yours fully." The angel winked at Monty now playfully.

"Their pueblos were discovered deserted, and some human experts suggest that they just left one day and migrated south?" grinned Dai with a knowing shrug of his shoulders.

"So, the Anastasi, in around 1500BC, apparently just vanished overnight. Yet they left behind such travel necessities such as salt, which they traded with as currency?" Dai raised his shoulders again, inquisitively now.

"Salt would have been an invaluable necessity for a long journey because it not only preserved meat, and healed wounds, but as I say, was their main trading currency," he pointed out.

Strange then?

Indeed, Stephen. They also left their tools.

"So, were they all killed or enslaved and taken through a portal by rogue angels?" Monty was wondering whether fallen angels were still doing this sort of thing today?

"My choir are not here to upgrade humanity's consciousness of reality, Stephen. I cannot give you all the answers, as you have the gift of free will and will be judged upon how you figure things out independently. As well as why you come to your conclusions, and how you treat others of course, but it is not my place to lead you into a conclusion. I can only help you to see things through your own free will, contrary to the opposition who tends to blur men's views of reality."

"So, they disappeared then, these Anasazi?" Monty asked.

"Their name, the Anasazi, means enemy of the aliens. Interestingly, they had ancient traditions; one in particular was that that they were formerly a tribe of old who had fought giants." Smirked the angel.

"Giants?" asked Monty, accepting Dai's process of skipping questions that he preferred not to answer.

"Yes." Nodded the angel.

"As in same as the giants of the Old Testament, etc.? As in Nephilim?"

"None other," replied Dai, gently, yet congratulatory, as a primary school teacher to a pupil who had just figured out how to spell a word.

That would explain the cliff Pueblos then. They were trying to keep out of the way of attacks by carving out homes high up on cliff faces.

"So, either they were all murdered, or they went through the stargate, or doorway, etc.?" deduced Monty.

"You decide what you will from the things I tell you, Stephen, but I will not give you all the answers you seek, nor for that matter will I lie to you," promised Dai with sincerity showing in his eyes. Monty saw now that this being opposite him here was so uncontaminated and earnest that his own inferiority echoed shamefully.

"Were some evil beings able to travel through these doorways even after the great flood then?" He managed to ask whilst attempting to understand and explore all the theological possibilities.

"You are trying to figure out how the magic works, Stephen. Well, you will need to make your own conclusions on that." Dai winked at him.

"Why though, why can't you help me by just answering my questions, Dai?"

"Some questions cannot be answered because it is not necessary for you to understand. All that is necessary is for you to love your creator. Thus, Stephen, they become irrelevant questions that I will not provide you with an answer to." Smirked the angel.

"Why though?"

"Moving on." Dai gave him an absent wave.

"Why?" Monty felt as if he were in court now, and had little fear, at least not when in the pursuit of the truth.

Dai looked him over with a curious grin. "Jacob wrestled with the angel, eh[75]," he smirked. There was a protracted silence between them both now for a moment before Dai eventually laughed again—that infectious laugh of his—the merriment returned.

"I can see why they sent the Orcadian now." Dai eventually nodded intuitively. "You're quite good, aren't you, Mr Montgomery?"

Monty nodded back conceding defeat, so much so that he simply leaned back on the sofa and lazily raised a hand to apologise, before then changing the subject. "So, what is the point regarding these lost Anastasi people then?" he sighed.

"That there are certain places on this earth that are, or were, doorways. One of which you have travelled through I believe," said Dai.

---

[75] Genesis 32:22-32.

238

"Yes." Monty drank some more wine and helped himself to a chocolate.

"Some fallen angels, and first and second-generation hybrids, are temporarily released from their incarceration and allowed to reappear in this dimension to participate in the Kertamen," explained Dai.

"What about third and fourth generation Nephilim then?"

"Those bloodlines are also here in your dimension, but they remain permanently above the surface and free; it is only the first- and second-generation heroes of old who are incarcerated, along with certain other evil entities connected to their cause."

"Heroes of old?"

"Yes—the first- and second-generation Nephilim who were known in antiquity as demigods."

"What, you mean, like the half gods of Greek mythology?" asked Monty thinking of Achilles or Aeneas[76].

"You know your Homer then." Nodded Dai.

"So, who are the bloodlines who are now operating freely on earth today then?" asked Monty.

"Secretive cliques who are involved in everything that's blasphemous and evil," replied Dai.

Hardly an elaborate reply.

Monty could make quite a few guesses as to who they were likely to be, but he focused instead upon the facts. "So can the ones who are incarcerated, but who are regularly allowed into this dimension for certain missions, all come here at the same time or only individually?"

"No, they have a quota, as do my choir, and in general it is only specific individuals in specific fields, who are selected to come and operate in a mission here," assured Dai.

"What if they come through and don't go back?" Monty's scepticism betrayed his growing dread at being shepherded into a bout with these magical beings.

"The Kertamen has a code of conduct, just as both the legal or medical professions do, Stephen," insisted Dai.

"What if?" Monty was persistent.

---

[76] The Greek term for a demigod was "hermitheos". The prefix "Hemi" translating as "half" and "theos"—god. The Latin equivalent was "Semideus", "half deity".

"They would be removed; as had happened to the Orcadian at Orkney," replied Dai.

"Do tell?" urged Monty as he supped at his wine.

"He had returned from his incarceration after the flood for what was supposed to be a short time," Dai calmly explained. "He went AWOL however, and instead of hiding, he arrogantly pitched up for a short while on Orkney," he shook his head.

Why Orkney?

"He hid from the known world on Orkney yes, but not from God who sees everything. It was rather, his own though, who were ordered to fetch and return him to his incarceration."

"Where could he have hidden?"

"There are one or two deep cave systems that the eyes of men have never seen," replied Dai.

"Where?"

"Underwater, in the Pacific and Southern Oceans actually."

"Then why is he allowed out again now, and to batter me in a courtroom?" Monty urged Dai for a justified explanation for this ridiculousness.

"Because there was another outbreak of conflict between his hoard and ours and after they were defeated again, many more of them were incarcerated," explained Dai, calm as ever. "Lucifer was then granted the right to select any of them to participate in the Kertamen, lest he not claim the contest be unbalanced."

The notion of a contest at all, was what people can't understand?

Dai read his thoughts and telepathically responded, "And nor are they supposed to, Stephen. Man has free will yes, but the whole argument is about whether he decides to think that he himself is the creator and that only he knows best, or that God is his lord and creator."

Again, there were a few seconds of silence as they both took deep mouthfuls of the delicious wine. The dog, curled up on Dai's lap now again, yawned as he stroked it gently.

"And the Orcadian usually gets the legal gigs then, does he?" asked Monty with a tad of sarcasm which was duly laughed away by Dai.

"Sometimes, yes." He liked Monty and could see that he liked to win, but that he was overly concerned about losing in court too. "Despite his previous act of breaching the Kertamen, and despite a severe punishment for his unauthorised abominations at Orkney, he is still regularly selected by the opposition as a specialist in certain issues, including all of man's laws in general." Dai sighed with an obvious tone of deplorability.

Monty did not reply, instead he sipped more of the wine, savouring the taste while continuing to be oddly relaxed. Of course, there was a desire in him to just refuse to do it and hope that they get someone else in. Regardless, he said nothing.

"And he is not just being released now," assured Dai. "He has been released many times since, and was in Scotland again, as early as the year 1649 when he took the vessel form of a man named Walter Bruce of Inverkeithing[77]. Bruce chose to become a minister in the church so that he could legally murder hundreds of innocents accused of witchcraft," revealed Dai.

"The witch laws were an endemic across Britain that were under the judicial jurisdiction of travelling Assizes and local *ad hoc* theological courts in any town wherein a church minister would sit in judgement of the accused persons." Dai raised his eyebrows at Monty suggestively.

"Bruce's talent for discovering sorcerers and compelling confessions from them in his perverse court," he continued, "shocked even the Kirk hierarchy who sensed his kill rate was abnormal. So, the Orcadian has been practicing his skills within this dimension, and in this corner of it in particular, quite often since he had his moment in Orkney."

"Where is he imprisoned now?" Monty was curious.

"Where do you think?"

"Beyond in another dimension that is accessed near a mountain or hill?"

The Bible certainly refers to several mountain based portals, does it not, and the Lundin Links stones are somehow connected to a nearby hill.

The angel shrugged. "That theory is not just an Abrahamic one, for instance did you know that the ancient Anasazi believed that there is a sacred mountain in America that has a supernatural doorway too?" he asked.

"No?" Monty shook his head.

---

[77] Walter Bruce was a Kirk Party Minister of Inverkeithing in Fife in 1649. Bruce pursued, tried and then judged many alleged witches and healers, whom he accused of sorcery. Many victims from Inverkeithing, Aberdour and Burntisland, were then tortured and burned alive.

"Throughout the history of the earth Stephen, from Olympus, and Athos in Greece, to Ida in Turkey, Kailash in Tibet, Fuji in Japan, Ausangate in Peru, and Taranaki in New Zealand, humans have regarded mountains to be sacred. Take for example, the Temple Mount in Jerusalem," he offered, "all three Abrahamic faiths believe that it is a sacred place, do they not?"

Monty supposed the angel was right enough and nodded cautiously. The fact was he just didn't know enough about such matters yet and so could do little more.

"Mountains are key to the inter-dimensional gateways you will find referenced in your Bible Stephen." Grinned Dai. "The information available to you within it may or may not influence your overall conclusions," he added. "More importantly, regarding the Orcadian, the Bible refers to mountains as places where transportation from other realms is possible; such as Enoch at Herman, or Nimrod at Babylon and his arrogant attempt to create a tower which would connect earth to heaven," he pointed out. "Or Moses at Sinai where he talked with God in the same way that we are sitting here talking now." He smiled.

"And Abraham?" Monty had read his Genesis, of course[78].

"Indeed." Dai raised his glass.

"I am still learning these things, as you know, I knew nothing about these stories," explained Monty. "Prior to recently when I borrowed a Bible and began reading it," he shrugged, "But I can see now that mountains are linked to these doorways?" he agreed.

"Well, there are other clues out with the Bible or even the Abrahamic religions, Stephen, for across this planetary dimension, or solar system as your astrologers prefer to call it," Dai shrugged his shoulders, "there are many anomalous megalithic structures around the world which suggest supernatural design and construction, which date to the pre-flood time before God's patience with the early Nephilim and their fathers ran out," he pointed out.

"So, by siring these Nephilim, the fallen angels committed a genetic abomination against the laws of God?" asked Monty.

"Indeed. They played at being God, so he flooded the earth and killed off the hybrids whilst incarcerating others along with fallen angels," confirmed Dai.

"And now man is doing the same by cloning and mixing DNA?" guessed Monty.

---

[78] Genesis 22:1-19.

"Yes, to a certain extent there are a broad range of inter-species entities being created for supposed medical purposes. One need only read the available British Medical Society report entitled 'Animals Containing Human Material', particularly page 15." Smiled Dai matter-of-factly before drinking some more wine.

Monty went over and took a little notebook out of a drawer in a Victorian writing desk in an alcove at the other side of the room. He then returned and sat down again. "Are you okay with me taking notes?" he asked.

"Certainly. Can I ask, do you know what a mule is, Stephen?" asked Dai.

"A cross between a horse and a donkey?" guessed Monty who could only think of the beast ever being mentioned in some old western movies he had seen.

"Correct. Yet, as per the centaurs of old, who also did not have the adequate chromosomes either, the mule cannot reproduce and thus, is genetically imperfect," declared Dai[79].

"A centaur is a creature from the *Clash of the Titans* movie or something like that, right?"

"Indeed." Laughed Dai.

"So, the old Greek myths refer to gods, who are really fallen angels who set themselves up as gods?" Monty scribbled away.

"Correct." Nodded Dai.

"And the so-called hybrid children of the heroes of old, like Hercules and Achilles, etc.," Monty was now sponging his mind of everything he had ever picked up from watching Jason and the Argonauts as a kid and then Disney's Hercules with his own infant son. He understood now. "So, only a species created by God can be deemed perfect, as it is only his magic which enables perfection?"

"Correct." Snapped Dai.

"Which was why he flooded the earth but saved Noah, who is described in the Bible as being…perfect?"

Dai clapped his hands very slowly. "Bravo, excellent, young Stephen," before adding in an American accent, "Aint choo cleva." Whilst smiling warmly.

---

[79] Latin Centaur (Greek Kentauros): A hybrid creature from ancient Greek mythology which had the upper body of a human being, and the lower body and legs of a horse. It was suggested by the ancient Greek Poet, Nonnus of Panopolis, who was born into a large Greek community in Roman Egypt, that the Centaurs were created in Cyprus by the Greek deity-Zeus.

Monty laughed at this and they toasted each other again. Both of them were enjoying this pleasant time together. Both feeling an appreciation of each other and for Dai, this was certainly not a chore.

"But the Greeks simply took on the legends of old Mesopotamia[80], as well as Egypt and Phoenicia. All of whom were familiar with the old dragon and his fallen hoard long before Homer came along," Dai pointed out.

"You are correct however, in linking the mountains to the DNA issue, Stephen," he conceded. "Did you know, for example, that the Mayan deity, whom they called *Bolon Yokte' K'uh*, was believed by them to guard the DNA of giants in an underworld cavern beneath a sacred mountain," he asked but did not wait for Monty to reply.

"Or that the Afrikaans term for the Drakensberg mountain range in South Africa, *Drakensberge*, translates as the 'Mountains of the Dragons'?" he asked. Again, he did not pause for a response.

"Or that the ancient Aztec believed one particular mountain to be sacred to the understanding of spirituality? And that it was named *Coatepec*, which translates as 'Mountain of the Serpents'?" Finally, he paused and allowed Monty to write this down before continuing.

"Or perhaps you had heard that the Apache consider Mount Graham in Arizona to be a supernatural place where a doorway to the spiritual world exists?"

Monty shook his head; how could he know any of this?

"Well, the Vatican moved up there and set up long range telescopes in 1984[81]," revealed Dai.

---

[80] Perhaps a reference to the ancient Sumerian poem—The Epic of Gilgamesh, whose mother goddess, Inanna (approx. 4,500 BC), becomes the Akkadian goddess Ishtar (2,334 BC) when the Akkadians rule Sumer. Ishtar is represented in Mesopotamia by her star, later referred to in the Roman age as the Venus star. The Ishtar/Venus star is still represented today within some masonic temples.

More publicly, Rosslyn Chapel in Scotland, has an axis with two wavy lines wrapped around the top like the serpents on a medical caduceus as well as several carvings of serpents and of Cherubs (said to be the children of Venus in Roman mythology), while there is further apparent reference to the orbital geometry of Venus and her star, as well as a pentagonal window at the top of the building that is aligned with the ray of the Sun on the Autumn equinox.

[81] Mt Graham in Arizona, also known as *Dzil Nchaa Si'an* by the Apache, was removed from the boundaries of the San Carlos Apache Reservation and placed in public domain

Monty shook his head again. "Why, what were they looking for?"

Dai stuck with the Apache angle however. "Well, the federally recognised Apache tribes bitterly opposed this and legally challenged it—failing, of course."

Monty accepted that Dai was not going to answer certain questions and so moved on. "Mountains or hills are key then to these supernatural doorways, beyond which are prisons and other locations such as heavens?"

"Well done." Dai nodded at him. "Even Buddhists have sacred mountains, you know." He now skilfully swirled the swine around in his glass. "One in particular—Mount Jiuhua in China, which has many shrines and temples upon it—is where Buddhists believe the bodhisattva guards over those incarcerated in hell," he said.

"However, there are gateways on flat terrain too, but they are newer editions and fewer by number, as you should have noted from the Orcadian file," he then pointed out.

"It's all very hard to take in, Dai," said Monty as the bigger picture, which appeared to be continuously changing, developed in his head.

Dai laughed as he read his thoughts. "Yes, but you should not waste energy analysing why it is that you are receiving this info, Stephen. You have the gift of free will and thus must either accept or reject it," he insisted in a jolly tennis racket manner.

"Yes perhaps, thanks to you, the Internet and the Bible, but I never grew up with a Bible and well, I can't help wondering if I am going to be judged one day on the part of my life prior to this, well this enlightenment?"

"I know. Yes you are but you have to realise that how you live your life from now onward, will have a greater influence upon how you are judged," insisted Dai—looking for recognition on Monty's face. "Look, I am here to help you with this present challenge Stephen," he assured whilst sensing Monty's plummeting confidence.

"Chin up, old son, you have been blessed by upstairs and it looks like you're getting a pass because you have something to offer. So, don't worry, and just embrace this blessing," Dai urged convincingly. Not only was he highly convincing, but he radiated a sense of honesty and empathy which was as

---

in 1873. This action, which did not recognise the Apache belief that it was a supernatural mountain, set the stage for a legal struggle by the recognised Federal Apache tribes years later when in 1984, the Vatican selected Mt Graham as a site for an astrological observatory base. The Apache were unsuccessful.

apparent to Monty as the lingering smell of the Wellington. This relaxed him and pumped some confidence in his own ability.

Perhaps there is an advantage to being underestimated.

Reading his thoughts, Dai spoke up now, "The Orcadian wont underestimate you Stephen, but he has certain restrictions and there are rules which he must abide by. Should he break them, his mission will be forfeited, and myself and others will appear and remove him back to his incarceration where he will be punished severely."

"Is my cork/sword thing any use against him?"

"No, not really, but it will protect you from the hybrid bloodlines who serve him throughout his mission here. It is those disciples of Hell whose souls you can send to Hell with one swipe of your weapon." Nodded Dai knowingly. "And as for your talent, which will be required as a support pillar for Mr Daily, you underestimate yourself considerably." He tut-tutted.

"Daily?"

"Yes. You will win the day by seeing to it that Mr Dailly has the required tools with which to defend your client."

"Mr Dailly?"

"Yes. Mark Dailly," confirmed the angel.

"Mark Dailly QC?"

"Indeed, Mark Dailly, the Queens Counsellor."

"But my firm uses old Angus Pentland or—"

"Others. Yes, I know, but it will be Mark Dailly this time." Nodded Dai assuredly.

"But I don't even know him. He was a Fiscal years ago and he tore apart my defence of a client." Monty recalled Dailly, a former Procurator Fiscal who was now a defence QC.

"And you're thinking that the great QC won't consider breaking up his diary for a mere court mouse like yourself, should you even get past his secretary?" Grinned Dai.

"Bang on," confirmed Monty, raising his glass.

"Well, that is who you will approach to argue the case for the defence regardless, and it will be so," insisted Dai, who tapped his smoothly sculpted nose with his index finger. "So stop worrying and start accepting things," he urged.

"Is Dailly one of your guys?"

"No, not quite." Dai chuckled at this, ever amused by man's simplicity. "He isn't a bad old stick and he does possess a good amount of fair-mindedness and morality."

"Fine, but you can deal with my bosses who prefer using Pentland," insisted Monty.

"Faith, Monty." Dai tapped his nose again.

Magic?

"Of sorts."

"This Orcadian is a sorcerer, isn't he?" asked Monty.

"That's one way of describing him, Stephen, yes," confirmed Dai.

"Was Christ a sorcerer then too?" Monty heard himself ask.

Dai appeared to be taken by surprise by this. Though Monty sensed that the angel had already anticipated the question. "Sorcerers do not use magic to persuade men to embrace morality, Stephen," replied Dai flippantly.

There was an awkward moment of silence between them.

"Does a sorcerer attempt to persuade people to live righteously so that they can be judged favourable by God? No, because sorcerers have no interest in reforming sinners; Christ, on the other hand, set an example to mankind of the best way to live their lives through his actions," said Dai in a somewhat fatigued tone.

"Okay but he had magical powers, did he not?" Monty again chose his words carefully.

"Indeed. That does not make him a sorcerer however."

"Understood." Nodded Monty.

Just then his phone rang. He looked at the Edwardian clock on the fireplace—3:30 pm, he had forgotten the Queen's Speech.

"It's Sadie, go take it in the bedroom, I shall wait here and watch some of this Caribbean Pirates comedy," insisted Dai before Monty accepted the call.

"You can still listen." Smirked Monty as he picked up his phone and casually headed out and along the hall as relaxed as a Carioca[82].

"I won't," promised Dai telepathically.

Sadie was half cut already; she would usually down a few bucks fizzes in the morning and then would have had a couple of glasses of wine whilst preparing

---

[82] Resident of Rio de Janeiro. Some travel experts have suggested that it is rare to see a Carioca with an angry face, as they are mostly living without the built-up stress that other city dwellers endure.

Christmas dinner no doubt too. The conversation was relatively short though, because both siblings were merry and simply going through the motions, eager to return to their respective guests. They had their first giggle in years when she told Monty all about a slight mishap she had had with her turkey. She sensed a change in him today too, a change from the normal vagueness that he regularly dispensed. She was both surprised and happy about this.

When Monty returned, he poured both himself and Dai some more wine. He was stunned to find the bottle full again and so he looked down at Dai in surprise. The angel merely winked up at him. "Sorcery," he whispered.

Monty didn't reply, instead he sank back down upon the sofa again with his glass and took another mouthful before placing it down on the coffee table and retrieving his pen and pad again. "What can you tell me about this dark side's agenda, and are they wining this Kertamen thing you spoke about?" he asked.

"It is a struggle, akin to a cold war conflict where both sides are restrained to certain extents," replied Dai.

"But there has been violent conflict, right?"

"Yes, but not whole scale since Troas," assured Dai.

"What's Troas again?"

"Troy to you, Stephen," explained Dai with a straight face now. The recollection of that war was not pleasant, so he changed the subject. "Let us discuss the Orcadian now, shall we?"

Monty nodded. "Are they winning this cold war?" he asked.

"In this instance, they have taken a strategic initiative, yes, but they have neither out witted us, nor have they secured their objectives," replied Dai.

"May I ask why they hate us humans so much, Dai?" pressed Monty.

"They see you as talking apes who, by being given free thought and free will, are not only destructive, but arrogant beyond contempt. In short, they see you in the same way some people might regard a starving fox—vermin," explained Dai.

"I like foxes," argued Monty.

"As do I, but there are many of your species who enjoy killing and torturing them, I can assure you," pointed out the angel.

"So how does my defending this client help the side of good in the bigger picture of worldly affairs then?" Monty was still struggling to see how small fries like himself, or the guy he was being asked to represent, were relevant to the grand scheme of things.

Constantly patient with Monty's want to understand, Dai took a deep breath. "There was a covenant made once between angels and men, and we do not leave good men behind enemy lines, Stephen," he assured.

"So, this is the fallout from a previous drama then?" Monty guessed, and by the sound of it, it didn't sound like one that had gone entirely to plan.

"Indeed. We can go over all that when you have met your client and have obtained a grasp of the case. Let me just say that what is important here, is that innocence be protected, and do not concern yourself with the guilty, for there is too much sin for us to punish them all, their punishment will come in the end by a greater authority than myself; our concern should only be for the innocent party in this matter."

"When will I get the call?"

"Soon, so let us discuss the Orcadian now," urged Dai again.

"Right," Monty agreed. "So we know that he is a sorcerer, presumably he is also deceptive then?" He knew the answer but was just confirming it anyway.

"Worse. Lying to him is like breathing to you. A liar is a liar, and in a way, most men can soon detect that particular trait in an individual, whilst somebody who speaks mere portions of truth, in order to veil their deceptiveness, is an artist of desolation, Stephen," confirmed the angel knowingly.

"The Orcadian has many names and just as many tricks to go with them," he pointed out, "one of which being that he is not simply just an artist, but rather that he is a master of his art," he said chillingly.

"Can he use those tricks against me?" Monty was thinking that if he could, then that was surely checkmate and they might as well turn out the floodlights before they even kicked off.

"Not most of them, and he cannot hurt you," assured Dai. "Plus, the opposition are eager to convict your client through the rules of the Kertamen, and then have him die in prison thereafter. Which is why the Orcadian has been called upon, to ensure that the job is done within the rules as no human, nor even a hybrid with Nephilim blood can be relied upon."

It seemed to Monty that both sides had a toxic co-dependency upon each another, but he reminded himself that because he didn't know what else angels did in their daily lives, it was unfair of him to presume that they only busied themselves with humans and this earthly dimension of his. "But can I cope with him in a courtroom, Dai?" He had to ask.

"We shall, Monty. We shall," promised the angel.

"What magic can he use on me then? As in, reading my mind, etc.?"

"He is forbidden to use anything like that in the court scenario, but if he does, even for a moment, he will be seized, and the matter will have been forfeited by him," assured Dai.

"So, what can he use then?"

"Only a brilliance in arguing legally. You and Daily will be given a helping hand, so try not to worry, and instead relish what will be a highly regulated and privileged challenge."

Relish?

"And outside of the courtroom?"

"Outside of that theatre, it is indeed different—good point," conceded the angel. "He has many tools to use whilst in Edinburgh, should he call upon them."

Not sounding good, this.

"Such as?"

"Both human and hybrid disciples of hell, particularly the hybrid Orcadian bloodlines, but that is why you have a weapon in your pocket, even now." Smiled Dai sympathetically.

"Ronnie Charnley and I are also here to help you, of course," he added, "and there are others who can be called upon should they be required, rest assured."

I'm not assured.

"Oh, I think that they are required, Dai," replied Monty as he wrote down a few more scribbles to himself without looking up at his smiling guest opposite.

"The Lord will make peace with you, Stephen, simply for trying your best in this matter, which is a wonderful blessing for you," promised Dai.

"And I now recognise that, but I still want to be effective against this guy, and I worry that he will be too much for me," insisted Monty.

"Know this Stephen; all luck has a hint of magic in it," said Dai with a persuasive coolness.

"Fair enough," conceded Monty—who was he to argue with an angel about lady luck.

Luck of the devil?

"Dailly will be on home ground in the high court building and he is an exceptionally talented lawyer. Whereas you have learned your trade over the years in that Akeldama, that is the Sheriff Court[83]. So, with Dailly as the defence and midfield, let it be so that you are the striker in the penalty box."

Akeldama?

"The opportunity is here for us you to apply a tactical advantage whilst the opposition gaze is concentrated upon their clever little strategy, for that is their weakness, they cannot see beyond their own talent and thus stoically fail to see the effectiveness of others."

"So, he believes that he is not a baddie then?" smirked Monty nervously.

"He is no different from most humans in that respect, the difference is that, when faith, morality, empathy or even law and order are applied, they tend to frequently harness their bad sides whereas he struggles with doing so," confirmed Dai.

"The Orcadian however is evil by nature, and the weakness of all evil is that it believes it is worthy of success, hence it has false aspirations of magnificence," he explained.

"So what are his other flaws then?" Monty couldn't see how any of this assisted him.

"You." Grinned Dai. The air of confidence that came out from him now was overwhelming though. Emotionally transmitted in a similar manner to a love-at-first-sight experience—like an enchanting perception detected by an unknown radar. Monty just believed him, plain and simple. He smiled too now, lightly shaking his head at his own doubts.

"Other weaknesses that the Orcadian has," Dai pretended to have to think about this—simulated posturing with finger on chin etc, "Hmm well, he has zero empathy in him, so no consideration for the suffering he causes."

"Not really a weakness though, is it, Dai?" suggested Monty, still taking notes.

"Of course, it is, lad," exclaimed the angel now. "If they have no empathy for other beings, they will spend most of eternity alone, unloved, untrusted and hunted by their own, whilst quite unable to realise their true worth. Because after time, their emotional deprivation will eventually cause them to turn firstly upon their own hybrid offspring, then themselves," he promised merrily.

---

[83] Akeldama (Field of Blood) is the name of an ancient field outside of Jerusalem where, according to Acts 1:18-19, Judas Iscariot's stomach exploded after his betrayal of Jesus Christ. The soil of the field is known today for its deeply red clay content. Dai is perhaps referring to a bloody professional field here.

"They claim that they came here to gift mankind technology, energy, and to remedy misery, but they lie, Stephen. They have abandoned their heavenly estates in order to harvest the earth and to destroy mankind, but they will destroy much more than just men if left unopposed."

"So, do you and this guy have a history then?" Monty wondered.

"No, not quite an 'Ahab and the Whale' scenario, but I have encountered him previously, yes," confirmed Dai.

"And so how come all his human disciples are all working for him? I mean can't you just convince them in the manner that was done with myself?" Queried Monty.

"The ancient Orcadians have his blood in their veins, and all of them abandoned the islands long ago and spread out across the planet. Each of them teaching their offspring the secret doctrines of their ancestry, and so, they do not care to be taught nor indeed blessed in the manner that you have been, Stephen."

"Yes, but there must be clean blooded humans conspiring with this mob too, in order to do all the leg work and brain washing, surely, Dai?" insisted Monty, whilst looking up at him.

"Wealth and a desire to be adored, is supreme in the affairs of the humans who have rejected God. So much so, that they now call Lucifer god. A lust for capricious power, Stephen, is precisely what makes them work unwillingly for the opposition. They are, if you will, held in a form of spiritual bondage. Again, these people are blind to themselves becoming lost in insignificance."

"Well, I think there are a few of them in this town, Dai, and I have probably met them in court." Sighed Monty.

"There are good and bad in this town, like any other place, but right now the dark hoards are increasing their power, and that is why you are one of many decent souls being unleashed against them," said Dai.

Decent soul?

Monty wanted to chuckle at this, but the angel was so convincing, he had bought into it. "So how do I recognise these disciples of his who are pure blooded humans then?" he instead asked candidly.

"They are obvious to you even now, Stephen," assured Dai. "Who do you say they are?" He grinned.

Instinctively, Monty guessed, "The masons?"

"Well, that is for you to say, Stephen. I couldn't possibly comment other than to ask, what was it De Gordian brought back from the Temple Mount in

Jerusalem and hid at Rosslyn in that masonic replica of Herod's temple that they now call a chapel?"

Who?

"No matter, Stephen, as I say, that is for you to consider at a later date. What we can agree upon is that all his disciples are linked to arcane knowledge conjured up by the Morning Star."

"The Morning Star?" Monty scribbled all of this down in a strange shorthand that he would probably struggle to read later.

"A reference to the Mesopotamian goddess Ishtar, as well as being linked with Christ in the Bible." Dai poured some more of the wine for them both. "Though, if the Ishtar connection is to be considered further, then you would find that she was once known by the Latins as Venus, and of course the light of Venus coming in the morning blah-de-blah." He measured with apparent impartiality as he lounged back and smelled the ancient wine in his glass.

Meaning?

"And of course, Lucifer himself is referred to in Isiah 14:2 as the 'Son of the Morning'," he cogitated.

Monty knew extraordinarily little about the masons, other than that they were a secret fraternity which flourished amongst his profession. Whether or not their craft was such a grey eminence that proceedings in some court cases were no more than outward shows, he could not say. He had however, heard of people in civil litigation, who had given off little signs in open court, signs indeed which one or two lawyers had later joked about later in the lawyers' room thereafter. He did suspect that his boss, Russell Cuthbert, was a fully-fledged member of the fraternity, due to his comments and interests.

"So the Morning Star is another term for the devil? And are you saying that the masons are disciples of his then, Dai?" he asked.

"Most masons know nothing, Stephen, and must resort to their own suppositions regarding what it is they are involved with. The first three craft degree members soon learn that there are no absolute answers, and that in the case of 'The Great Architect of the Universe', the deity whom they are all presented with at the ritual of exaltation process, they have no comprehension as to whether this is actually the Christian God of the Old Testament, or another god entirely," explained Dai.

"Do they refer to him as the Great Architect then, and not God?" asked Monty, still taking notes.

"Well, it is only within the higher stratums of the craft, such as the Knight of the Brazen Serpent and above, where an understanding of the true name of this 'Great Architect' is partly understood." Grinned Dai.

"What is the name?"

"Jah-Bul-On," replied Dai.

"What does that mean then?"

"Jah is the Hebrew term for God, as in Jahweh from the bible. Bah refers to a fallen entity named Baal, whilst On, refers to another one named Osiris," explained Dai between sips of wine.

"So, God, Baal and Osiris then?" Monty sought to clarify the translation before taking a supp at his own.

"There are no 'ands', Stephen; it is best understood within a three-syllable format, Baal-Osiris-God; thus to these individuals, they believe they are one."

Monty let this sink in a moment. "Meaning Baal and Osiris are pagan deities, or fallen angels, and so these two fallen angels are being claimed to be one god?"

"Precisely." Nodded Dai.

"But the majority of lower craft masons don't understand all this?" Monty couldn't believe that they were all Satan worshippers.

"Correct. They won't have a clue but as I suggested, perhaps those above the Royal Arch degree might think they understand. At least not all of them will have studied those passages fully, but the further up you go, the more will be understood. The craft itself attracts all sorts, Stephen, most of whom, upon being initiated into their mystagogical fraternity, have little serious understanding of the hieroglyphical, astrological, numinous symbolism and rituals which they encounter," stated Dai.

"A society filled with individuals pursuing self-elevation, and who do not fully understanding what they are involved in?"

"Not so different from some churches, Stephen, when you think of it," insisted Dai. "One might suggest that some leaders of Christian and Jewish teachings are only in their positions for the sake of a little prestige too." Shrugged Dai.

There was another moment's silence whilst Monty considered this.

Blind guides and brood of vipers.

Monty looked up from his notes as Dai's words telepathically entered his mind.

Matthew 23:15-33.

254

"I haven't got to that part in the Bible yet," said Monty, but he got the point. "Quite."

"But they can't all be Satanists surely?"

"No, not all of them, at least not that they are conscious of it," confirmed Dai.

"And what about this Osiris/Baal then?"

"Osiris still plays the Kertamen, whilst Baal no longer exists." Shrugged Dai, avoiding any self-remembrance of the death of that particular entity; for it still distressed him to recall the affair[84].

Monty sensed that Dai did not want to elaborate on the Baal thing, so he made a note to look it up later, then sat back with his glass and thought for a moment. He remembered Russel Cuthbert had been boasting one day in the office to his secretary, about there being a masonic hospital in Hammersmith where only masonic patients were treated. Monty had fancied Cuthbert to have been simply blowing off more waffle about all the so-called trumps he held in his pocket, in order to woo the poor girl. Cuthbert was like that, loud and boastful.

Monty couldn't help wondering now if Cuthbert was a Satanist though. He was certainly cold at the best of times, regularly stone-faced and appeared bitter though buyable. He was disliked by many of the other Edinburgh lawyers due to his air of superiority and arrogance. Plus, the bugger never gave out Christmas cards to the other employees, nor did he buy his secretary a gift either, unlike all the other lawyers in the firm—not even a poxy box of Maltesers. Of course, this was no proof that he was a Satanist mind, but if he was, then Monty might have to leave soon.

"Are they really Satanists then, or simply naive people mistaking fallen angels for gods?" he asked now as he polished off his glass of wine.

Dai shook his head and drank some more too. "It is no mistake, Stephen," he insisted thoughtfully, "as I say, most crafts know nothing of the reality but the specialised ones, such as the cult lodge that we shall call—The Inner Circle, in Fairmilehead, well they are quite different, Stephen, for they are Satanists whose hierarchy understand quite a lot more than other lodges, and who answer to Nephilim masters across the globe."

Now we're getting to it then.

---

[84] Baal was slain by Dai and three other angels in the previous novel—*Kertamen*.

"Allow me to quote some written words attributed to Albert Pike," proposed Dai. "Pike was a Grand Commander of Scottish Rite Freemasonry in the United States. If you research this Stephen, you will find that Pike is alleged to have issued the following instructions to various Scottish Rite Supreme Councils.

That which we must say to the crowd is—we worship a God, but it is the God that one adores without superstition. To you, Sovereign Grand Inspectors General, we say this, so that you may repeat it to the brethren of the 32nd, 31st and 30th degrees—the Masonic Religion should be, by all of us initiates of the high degrees, maintained in the purity of the Luciferian Doctrine."

Monty had a clear vision in his head now of a suspected masonic linesman raising his flag against Jorge Cadette at Ibrox Stadium back in the 1990's when he had scored a goal for Celtic against Rangers that may have seriously dented Rangers march to nine championships in-a-row.

He quickly changed his thought: "Well there are plenty of them at the pillars of the establishment in Edinburgh, so this is obviously really alarming," he said.

"As the Russians say, the fish rots from the head down." Nodded Dai.

They sat in silence for a further moment. The news was on the TV now. Labour's Ed Balls was apparently accusing the Tories of having an 'extreme and ideological' approach to spending cuts, stated a female news desk reporter.

"Even on this day of all days, the Lord's day, the general election takes precedence over God and family," sneered Dai disapprovingly.

"It does my head in, Dai, honestly." Sighed Monty. "The referendum almost caused the two leading partners in my firm to split the firm up and start their own separate companies," he said and he shook his head at the absurd triviality of it all. Like most people, he had had enough of politics after Indyref. He could see however that the pending general election was in danger, at least north of the border, of developing into a re-run of the referendum drama, and that all the bitterness from it was set to return.

"Democratic mandate and all that jazz." Grinned Dai.

"Suppose." Monty refilled his glass.

Just then his phone rang again. He leaned over the coffee table and picked it up; it was Charnley.

"He is trying to delay the inevitable," thought Dai to Monty.

"The inevitable?"

"Charnley's Mrs insistence that they play charades," chuckled Dai knowingly.

Monty chuckled too—he quite believed that. "Hello, Merry Christmas, Ronnie, how's things?"

"Happy Christmas, Monty. Aye, not so bad." Monty could hear Elton John's *Step into Christmas* in the background as well as loud female laughter.

"Having a nice time then, Ronnie?" he asked.

"Aye well, she's got me doing charades, so I thought I'd escape with my Drambuie here and give you a ring, mate," chuckled Charnley.

"Have you eaten yet?" asked Monty.

"Not half." Laughed Charnley now. "We just finished and this is the bit I hate. I just want to have a kip on the sofa now, do you know what I mean?" His laugh was deep and hearty, like the Santa Claus who had visited Monty's school when he was a child.

"Me too, but I have an angel here talking to me," said Monty.

There was a long pause down the line now, though Monty could hear Charnley breathing, as well as the ongoing music and laughter.

"Right then, Monty, I best not interrupt that. Get back to that and I'll call you back later." A surprised Charnley eventually gasped, before briskly hanging up.

Monty down looked at the screen on his phone. "Strange man that," he smirked.

"Aye, but he is your most loyal friend in the whole world right now," Dai assured him.

Monty looked up at him now, the radiance from the angel's eyes was convincing, whilst his voice urged truth. The whole truth and nothing but the truth.

"Okay." He sluggishly nodded.

Chapter Eleven

Since it is morally justifiable, I have only to consider the question of personal risk. Surely a gentleman should not lay much stress upon this though, not when a lady is in most desperate need of his help?
Arthur Conan Doyle

Boxing Day 2014 07:09 am

Monty awoke from a deep sleep. The wine had been intense, and his cheeks were blushed now as he propped himself up onto one elbow. He released a deep yawn, then surveyed the room with wet eyes in order to confirm that the bedroom door was still closed and that nothing had entered through the night. Satisfied he sank back and yawned. The dog would have alerted him if there had been unwanted guests of course, but then again considering the magnitude of this new threat, perhaps not. The pooch had creeped up onto the bed during the night and was still curled up and at ease beside him. He stroked its ears and lay there staring at the ceiling a while. Slowly, he began remembering his dream now—it had been as if he had once again been in another dimension.

He could recall having been on some sort of a train where only spirits were the passengers. He had been travelling to meet someone, Mehreen perhaps?

Of course it wasn't her, why are you even thinking about her?

He shook his head and sighed to himself now, no not her. He recalled that he had apparently acquired some light flannel cream-coloured trousers for the train journey however, and he supposed that he might have looked rather dashing in them. He could remember now, he had walked through a space which had resembled a train carriage but which had also felt more akin to a 1950's American diner, wherein he had sat down.

At which point he had become aware of a warm and wet sensation seeping through his new trousers, before the familiar smell of shit had reached his nostrils. Instantly, he had jumped up to check only to discover that he had been sitting on a runny, rusty coloured diarrhoea which had contained much sweetcorn.

At which point the voice of an English female had come across a speaker above: "Ladies and gentlemen, please be aware that the rules of the Kertamen convention do not permit participants to use magic within their allocated settings. On the other hand, profanes are fair game." She declared quite matter-of-factly. Monty had not understood this at the time of the dream, but he was re-evaluating now. Had she possibly been referring to the Orcadian having his powers restricted during his time in this dimension? And what or who were profanes?[85]

A carriage door had revolved, and a tall gaunt figure stepped into the scene. The being had seemed more reptile than human, perhaps a blend of both. It had then bounded towards Monty and as it closed on him Monty had noticed it was wearing black leather biker boots and a red tunic with an Assyrian styled breast plate made of what appeared to be a dark leather which was finely embroidered with fine gold stitching. Somehow, perhaps due to the enchantment of the dream, Monty had recognised the breast plate, and also spotted what he now recalled to be the image of a roulette wheel engraved upon the centre of it.

The being was bald too, with scaled creamy skin across its skull, which appeared almost human in shape. It also had a bony Mohican protruding out from its centre crown and down the cranium. It had deep, opaque green eyes which betrayed both envy and anger. Its strange skin stretched from broad shoulders into bony wings upon its back, similar in design to a bats, Monty was now recalling it all quite vividly. "My hands will be tied in the courtroom, child," it had hissed at him in English.

"Who are you?" Monty slowly mouthed back in shock.

"Even so, things won't be smooth sailing," it continued with a contemptuous bitterness.

Monty had remained standing still before it.

The creature leaned forward now and smelled him inquisitively. "I was one of the crocodile kings who built what you apes call the sphynx," it said softly but with a hideous smile which revealed a circular suction cut mouth which ringed razor sharp yellow teeth inside.

---

[85]Etymology: From the Latin profanes, *pro*-before, *fanum*-temple, meaning unclean and non-religious people before the time of Solomon's temple. A term favoured today by Freemasons for non-Freemasons, whom they feel lack esoteric knowledge.

"Answer the question. Who are you?" Monty had demanded despite being repulsed by the creature's mouth which now bore a resemblance to a sea lamprey.

It laughed at him though. "They have selected well, I see, but regardless of the restrictions that provide a life-line for you when in my presence, you will wish you were dead soon enough, Montgomery," it leaned forward again and murmured tenderly to him as if he were a child. Monty had smelt death upon its breath and recoiled, repulsed as well as concerned.

The female voice on the speaker above then returned: "It is permitted that such bad form may be invoked upon you by this being, but know that the Holy Spirit is observing, and so he can not harm you. Accordingly you may leave this dream at the next stop," she appeared to be speaking directly to Monty. The train then noisily slowed to a halt, Monty took one last look at the creature, its nose had no cartilage nor nostrils, just two holes, but it's eyes were penetrating and revealed fury. Monty had then slowly stepped out of a sliding exit and onto a concrete platform.

He could not recall any more of the dream, perhaps it had simply ended there on the platform and he had slept on peacefully. He was glad now that it had been a mere dream however, but he did sense that he had encountered the Orcadian. He felt quite rough now too, probably from the ancient wine he had sunk with Dai last night.

On the lash with an angel last night—really?

They had talked into the late evening about the Kertamen, and about an Edinburgh cop named Chuck Kean, his side-kick Chris Forsyth, and some covert operation that they had been on. These two cops had apparently been looking into allegations, made by the late lawyer—Leo Frazer, about a paedophile cult.

"Weird!" Monty now heard himself say. His mouth was dry and so needed to wet it. He thought about getting up and opening the bedroom door, so he leaned over and felt for the corkscrew and was comforted to feel it still there. "Think we might need to buy a couple of crucifixes too, buddy." He sighed at the dog who was now thumping its tale upon the duvet in anticipation of its breakfast.

Monty dragged himself up and went along to the kitchen where he filled the kettle up with water. He turned the kitchen radio on and yawned—a poshly spoken female was discussing something about the American civil rights movement in the early 1960's with an elderly male whose accent was a strange cross between German and New York, on Radio Four.

"In Noo Yoik at that time, vee all believed in him. His vay of talking to normal people like myself, vas different to his predecessors," he said.

Monty, however, began was recalling his encounter with Dai the previous evening and this strange story about Chuck Kean and his death. Dai had explained all about a paedophile named Irvine Stroker, and Kean's use of him to dig deeper into the allegations made by the bent lawyer Leo Frazer, before Frazer was also murdered. Monty made some toast and lightly buttered it before giving a slice to the dog, then he poured the kettle into a cup with a single green tea bag. Dai also explained that Stroker had been forcibly injected with an overdose of heroin which had been laced with battery acid, on the same day that Kean had been gunned down on Portobello high street.

Monty sat down at the table to eat his toast. The female on the radio: "Well, let us briefly listen to his 1961 address to the American Newspaper Publishers Association in the Waldorf Astoria Hotel, shall we," then the ever familiar voice of the late American President John F Kennedy came on:

The very word secrecy is repugnant in a free and open society; and we are as a people inherently and historically opposed to secret societies, to secret oaths and to secret proceedings.

We decided long ago that the dangers of excessive and unwarranted concealment of pertinent facts far outweighed the dangers which are cited to justify it. Even today, there is little value in opposing the threat of a closed society by imitating its arbitrary restrictions.

Even today, there is little value in ensuring the survival of our nation if our traditions do not survive with it. And there is very grave danger that an announced need for increased security will be seized upon by those anxious to expand its meaning to the very limits of official censorship and concealment. That I do not intend to permit to the extent that it is in my control. And no official of my Administration, whether his rank is high or low, civilian or military, should interpret my words here tonight as an excuse to censor the news, to stifle dissent, to cover up our mistakes or to withhold from the press and the public the facts they deserve to know.

For we are opposed around the world by a monolithic and ruthless conspiracy that relies primarily on covert means for expanding its sphere of influence—on infiltration instead of invasion, on subversion instead of elections, on intimidation instead of free choice, on guerrillas by night instead of armies by day. It is a system which has conscripted vast human and material resources into the building of a tightly knit, highly efficient machine that combines military, diplomatic, intelligence, economic, scientific and political operations.

Its preparations are concealed, not published. Its mistakes are buried, not headlined. Its dissenters are silenced, not praised. No expenditure is questioned, no rumour is printed, no secret is revealed…"

JFK's voice faded now and the female's returned: "So, do you believe, as some people do, that such rhetoric was the reason why he was murdered?" she asked the male who in turn, chuckled at her straightforwardness.

"Vell, I think there ver potentially several reasons as to vhy Jack Kennedy vas assassinated," he said somewhat reticently. "Of course," he continued, "I do remember that speech and I think that that, along vith his later address on a strategy ov peace at the American University in Washington DC, back in 63, vere two ov the most thought-provoking speeches ov John Kennedy's presidency," he dodged the question.

Monty had never heard this speech before, and he was taken aback by the relevance of it now, so much so that he had still not taken a bite of his toast yet; which was duly noted by the observing dog. Just then, his phone rang; he picked it up from the table—it was Charnley. He got up, toast in hand, and turned the radio off before leaning backwards against the kitchen worktop.

"Morning Ronnie, bit early, aren't you?" he said before stealing a bite of the toast.

"Morning Monty, I was eager to hear about your special guest," replied Charnley, far too merrily for Monty at this time of the morning.

"Just turned up, brought dinner and a wine from antiquity, we got along well enough and he explained a bit about the background of a client I will soon be representing," he took another bite of toast, "and whom is accused of a murder that he did not commit," he said whilst chewing.

"Antiquity?"

"Ancient times," explained Monty.

"Ah okay, well, they do travel through wormholes, don't they."

"Guess so, mate," replied Monty who now tried sipping his green tea but it was too hot.

"So, who is this poor fellow who has been wrongly accused then?" Charnley wanted to know.

"Not sure yet, but apparently a fallen angel, who was once worshiped as a god on Orkney is going to be leading the Crown case against us." Shrugged Monty as he tried running some cold water into the cup.

"Orkney? Sounds complicated then, not to mention demanding," exhaled Charnley with an obvious lack of enthusiasm. "Do you need my help?" He offered.

"Thanks Ronnie," replied Monty, "but not yet." He now forced himself to take a small sip of tea. "Nothing has begun yet, but I shall call you and let you know as soon as it all kicks off at this end," he promised before taking another bite of toast.

"Right, well, I'm just a call or text away should you need me," assured Charnley—secretly relieved as he was also feeling a tad rough this morning.

"Thanks Ronnie, I'll call you as soon as something transpires, but in the meanwhile that is my bath running, mate," fibbed Monty.

"Understood Monty, have a nice Boxing Day, mate," replied Charnley and Monty envisioned him saluting before hanging up.

Monty's tea was still too hot to do anything more than sip, so he went out into the garden with the dog for a moment to let it cool. The snow no longer covered the ground, instead there was more of an icy thaw between patches which revealed the green grass beneath. There were no footprints upon the lawn, he was glad to note, but it was still icy cold and so he returned inside and settled down on the sofa to watch tv with the patio door slightly ajar for the dog.

There was a festive sports show on with a compilation of football happenings from across 2014. Monty watched it for a while noting that it was all English games, which of course he was well used to. He fancied nipping through to the bedroom though and getting the Bible for another exploration, but just at that moment the phone rang again. This time the number was withheld.

"Hello, Stephen Montgomery?" he answered wearily.

"Good morning, Mr Montgomery." It was a middle-aged Scottish male and Monty's heart sank in anticipation.

"Morning?" He knew it was the police.

"This is Sergeant Bell in the custody suite at St Leonards, sir," revealed the caller.

"Yes?" Monty's heart began to pound now, and he sat up straight just as the dog came back.

"We have had a gentleman by the name of Christopher Forsyth in custody for three days now and who is charged with murder. He has, only this morning, asked us to notify your firm," declared Bell.

"Three days?" Monty wondered why Forsyth hadn't requested a solicitor sooner, and also, wasn't he the cop Dai had mentioned?

"Yes sir, he was residing in Tenerife and was detained before then willingly returning with a couple of our officers on a flight that arrived late on the 23rd. He was charged shortly thereafter but did not ask for a solicitor to be informed initially," explained the cop.

"So, he has been charged then?" Monty just wanted to confirm that particular detail.

"Yes sir, and he will be appearing at court on the 5th of January," confirmed the cop.

"Right, I'm on my way then," said Monty whilst walking over to close and lock the patio door.

This is it then.

"I will let him know then, sir," agreed the cop.

There was no chance of the cops bailing anyone on a murder charge, and next to no chance of the court doing so either. Monty rushed through to the bedroom to find some clothes—heart now beating fast, as a nervous excitement momentarily engulfed him.

"We will get our walk in a bit, son," he promised the dog, but the pooch was not listening, it was too busy eating the half-eaten toast which Monty had left on the sofa.

He hated driving through the city—it was consistently full of sporadic roadworks and strangely placed bus stops which usually had three or four buses lined up creating tail backs. A parking space was about as rare as a friendly smile and God forbid any unlucky drivers who happened to break down in the midst of all this madness; for then the evil eyes of some people and their vindictive car horns would be enough to push a person into a William Foster scenario[86]. There was no other option for him today however since the buses were limited and the taxi meters had been on time-and-a-half, since midnight on the 23rd.

---

[86] A fictional character in the 1993 movie, *Falling Down*, by Ebbe Roe Smith, who was brilliantly played by Michael Douglas.

There was a crisp chill to the air this morning but the weather was improving as he drove up Easter Road. He found himself giving off a few controlled revs on the throttle in his haste to get the car to warm up though. Leith was quiet today—with little traffic on the road. Boxing Day was traditionally associated with packing up gift boxes, but nowadays television and leftovers still tended to keep many people indoors.

It had been the tradition in his family to take a family walk with the dogs on what his mother had always referred to as—St Stephen's Day, but they had lived in the countryside back then, and here in the city that was not always the wisest notion. Monty tended to remain on his sofa now like the rest of his neighbours who were still enjoying the conviviality. It was a different story up in the city of course, where the many were out and about at the sales.

Monty hated all that, much preferring to read a book or watch a film during the lull. Fortunately today he was able to drive up to the southside in around ten minutes and cheekily park outside the revolving front door of St Leonards. There would surely be no traffic wardens out punishing the good burghers on the Feast of Stephen?

Though with this council, you never knew—the bloodsuckers were now active on Sundays and in the evenings too, these days.

He decided to run the gauntlet nonetheless. The desk sergeant had been expecting him. This was not the bloke who had telephoned earlier. This one was quite young for a sergeant, thought Monty, who had cross-examined enough of them in court. He was friendly enough sure, but he couldn't help but have a moan about not being at home today for a family get together with his kids who were over from Montreal. Monty humoured him a little by expressing sympathy at his predicament as they descended the old stairway down to the custody suite, which had some Christmas tinsel hanging here and there.

Bet the guests appreciate it.

As always, the stench of disinfectant and coffee hit Monty like a slap in the face as they entered and signed in the book. There were shouts and curses coming from the male cells and an agonising scream from one of the female ones. "A drunken mother caught driving with her three-year-old who wasn't wearing a seatbelt," explained the sergeant who sensed Monty's curiosity. Monty forced a half smirk back as he finished signing in, before then being handed Forsyth's chargesheet by another uniformed officer with blonde hair and moustache. He took a quick glance at it as the sergeant led him on down the main corridor—"Murder."

"Been screaming since she came in and tried to attack one of the custody officers," the cop went on as they turned down another little corridor which led to a single white door.

Allegedly.

The cop unlocked the door and ushered Monty into the little agents' room where solicitors met with their clients behind a reinforced plastic screen. It had not always been like this though. Once upon a time he would have met his client in a consultation room with only a table and an ashtray between them. Back then, lawyers were expected to bring cigarettes with them, which they would light for their clients as well as several newspapers for them to read when they returned to their cells.

Family members had even been allowed to send in food, books, and clean clothes for an accused person back in the day, but it was all changed now of course thanks to a minority who had abused the privilege by setting fire to their cells—having had drugs smuggled inside their food. "I'll get the turnkey to send your client along shortly," the cop duly informed him before then closing and locking him in the little room. There was a panic bell on the wall on Monty's side of the thick reinforced partition. Otherwise, it was just a plain, bright, concrete box. Monty went over the short and sweet chargesheet as he waited.

"That you Christopher Forsyth, of no fixed abode, did conspire to and did murder Yvonne Kidd at 2 Queens Park Avenue, Edinburgh, between the hours of 1500 and 1700 on Tuesday 8 July 2014 along with one Charles Kean (now deceased) of 14 Marlborough Street, Portobello, and by striking her throat with a knife to her severe injury and subsequent death."

Allegedly, and he does have an abode?

Monty sighed and leaned back onto the uncomfortable plastic seat which was bolted down onto the floor. 'They must have the murder weapon and a witness then?' He considered as he stared up at the camera on the ceiling. Just then he heard footsteps approaching from somewhere and the familiar sound of jingling keys. The noise increased as the door on the opposite side of the screen to Monty opened.

A tall bald turnkey appeared and frowned at Monty before ushering Forsyth in with a flick of a wrist. He then closed the door more gently than he usually closed the cell doors and walked away whistling. The sound of which echoed eerily throughout the underground complex and was quite disagreeable to Monty's delicate head.

"Hello Mr Forsyth." Monty got on with things regardless as his new client sat down opposite him. "I'm Stephen Montgomery of Hendry & Co solicitors." Forsyth nodded back, his brown hair was roughed up and he had a four-day stubble on him. He was wearing beige cargo shorts and looked slim in a yellow Hawaiian t-shirt. He appeared tired when Monty smiled at him but the poor distorted fellow managed a smile back, as he scratched his head and crossed his tanned legs.

"You asked for me in particular to represent you in this matter?" Monty pressed the chargesheet up against the screen with the palm of his hand.

"That's correct, Stephen." Nodded Forsyth again. His impassive face looked somewhat ghostly now. Monty sensed that this drama had taken a toll on him already, and immediately suspected that he may not be a suitable witness to place on the stand.

"It's a big allegation, you'll need to shower and shave for court," said Monty. "Did they fly you back in the clothes that you are wearing?"

Forsyth nodded back and ran his hands through his hair again. Monty scanned his face as Forsyth read the chargesheet, for any indication of contrition. Regardless of his belief in the intelligence relayed to him by the angels, Monty knew that he had to set about this task in the same manner with which he would approach any other case. He would first assess both the client and the charge at this first meeting. Seeking to note whether Forsyth would make a good witness or not, and whether he came across as reliable. These were the initial factors in determining how the next thirty years of the man's life would pan out.

"They are saying that you murdered this young female," said Monty, seeking a response.

"I'm innocent." Assured Forsyth. Monty saw that he was quite clear on this.

Monty had represented clients who had lied through their teeth when firmly stating—"I'm innocent—you have to believe me," but who had later forgot their story and fallen apart in the stand. Traditionally, he felt that most people who say—"believe me", tended to be lying. Forsyth however came across, at this initial stage, as sincere. He looked too skinny though, thought Monty.

The time passed since Forsyth's resignation as a DS in the Drug Squad, had perhaps been telling upon him. Monty nodded. — "Yes that's fine." He smiled, and both men sat through an ominous silence for a brief moment. Then the irritating whistling in the corridor started up again like a baby's cries on a plane. Monty pressed on and fired-off the usual questions regardless:

1)   Did Forsyth have any savings to fund his defence or did he seek legal aid?

2)   Apart from his Tenerife property, did he have a fixed abode in this country with which to at least try for bail?

3)   Would he sign this Scottish Legal Aid form please?

Monty handed it through the space underneath the screen along with a pen. Forsyth signed and Monty noticed nicotine stains upon his fingers. He probably either smoked untipped cigarettes or roll-ups. Forsyth then wrote down a mobile telephone number for an ex-partner and passed it back.

"So, you resigned from the drug squad then went to Tenerife to stay with your sister." Monty accepted it and took a gander, "and your ex-partner will agree to us using her address?" he asked.

Forsyth nodded. "Yes, Audrey Parks. Her address is 128 Carrick Gardens in Corstorphine."

"Is that where you resided with her before you moved to Tenerife then?" asked Monty whilst writing the address and telephone number down in his own notebook.

"No." Forsyth sighed through his nose; he seemed exhausted. "We rented a place in Newhaven, but we split shortly before I left for Tenerife." There was a hint of regret noticeable in his tone.

"That's fine," Monty didn't bother raising his head from his notebook as he continued writing, "But she will let us use her address?"

"I hope so, at least I will pray that she might," replied Forsyth.

Monty could see the anguish on the man's face. There was not the slightest pang of remorse though, nor was there any arrogance or suggestion of any plan out of this mess. Monty knew already that Forsyth was innocent, of course, and that he was probably still in shock, but he did wonder about the guy's faith since he mentioned prayer.

"May I ask why did you decide to contact myself?" he asked.

"It just came to me." Shrugged Forsyth again, whilst looking down at his side of the screen.

Monty didn't doubt that it had been angelic magic behind it. "I have met Dai," he said quietly.

Forsyth suddenly looked up at this, his eyes lit up like flamed gas. "What?" He beamed.

"He came to me and asked me to help you. You know him, I believe?"

"Really?" gasped Forsyth.

"Really." Nodded Monty with a knowing smile. "And he told me all about you and Chuck Kean and your investigation into the claims made by the late lawyer—Leo Frazier," confirmed Monty.

"Did he take you anywhere?" asked Forsyth with more curiosity than suspicion.

"No, but another angel did over in Fife, and I saw scenes from the past." Monty smiled faintly.

"Me too, I saw Christ," replied Forsyth. They both sat looking and smiling at one another for another lingering moment; both still trying to come to terms with the reality of their experiences.

"Has he abandoned me?" exclaimed Forsyth finally with what appeared to be the outset of tears forming.

"He hasn't. That is why you requested me, and why I have been briefed to help you," insisted Monty.

"Thank God then," sighed Forsyth.

"Yep, guess so. Now let's prepare. They are not going to take you up to court until the New Year, so let's go over this now and then I shall go visit Audrey Parks and see if she will support you, and if we can get you a change of clothes." Urged Monty. This was slightly uplifting for Forsyth; it had been the first sign of any hope since he had been arrested.

"Thanks Stephen." He smiled.

"Call me Monty."

Forsyth nodded in appreciation. This had been unexpected and was a comforting little piece of respite. "I'm Chris," he said.

"Okay. So what are the cops up to then, Chris?" asked Monty.

Forsyth took a deep breath and puffed his cheeks out before exhaling as if he were blowing up a balloon. "Well, thanks to Dai and other intel we received, it became clear that our investigation into Frazier's claims was opening a can of worms," Forsyth said before then looking up at the camera.

"Right." Monty thought that it might not be safe to really go into that side of events here. "Okay, well, because the stakes at play here are, in fact, the rest of your life, I don't need to know what, how and where, at this stage, rather just why?"

"Don't worry, they don't have microphones in here," assured Forsyth with a faint smile.

"Yes, but they might have lip readers," Monty pointed out.

"The camera only captures an image from an above angle looking down." Assured Forsyth. "It is focused upon our hands and what is being passed through the gap in the screen," he winked—"It cannot make out full lip movement."

They might have changed that since you were working.

"They haven't changed the system." Forsyth read his concerns and Monty met his gaze now. "I know exactly where it has always been positioned," guaranteed Forsyth.

"Well anyway, they might try to kill you once you are convicted and, in a prison serving a sentence," Monty used his notebook to cover his lips regardless, "because at which point, it can be blamed on another prisoner" he suggested.

"Well, where there is a will, there is a way, mate." Shrugged Forsyth.

Monty nodded. Forsyth was the victim here; he probably knew about as much as the whistling turnkey did about the modus operandi of this group of hybrids, or TIC group, as Dai had referred to them last night, and whom dead brief—Leo Frazer had supposedly brought to the equally dead Chuck Kean's attention. "Well, we can go over it all later, and you can tell me your thoughts on all of that then," he replied.

"Take it you know all about the allegations that Leo Frazer made to my murdered DI— Chuck Kean, then?" Sensed Forsyth.

Monty nodded that he did, having been filled in last night. "About *The Inner Circle*, yep." He nodded. "I also know how it all panned out but I don't know the details of what occurred in between."

"Okay." Nodded Forsyth with the first sense of relief he had experienced since landing.

For Monty though, the priority here was to try to establish ways to derail the murder charge. There would be a chance to talk to the Fiscal in court soon enough and to read the case against Forsyth, which could then be picked apart with any luck. In the meantime it was normal to establish a first line of defence, but often when it came to innocent clients, it is best to do nothing other than to wait to see the false evidence being relied upon by Crown. Monty did want to hear about the deniable investigation that Chuck Kean had undertaken and so opted to indulge his curiosity.

"Just give me an outline of things prior to Kean's death please."

"Well, after Chuck interviewed Frazer here at St Leonards, he called a sit-down with myself, Joe Roxburgh, who was a DS on our squad, and the other DI—Sharon Adams, at her place over in Baberton," explained Forsyth.

"Were you with Chuck when he interviewed Frazer here, then?"

"No. Joe was, but they brought the intel straight over to the sit-down at Adams place to decide what to do with it," said Forsyth.

"Why?" Monty pretty much knew the answer though.

"Because it was so sensitive, that to even be in possession of it, should it be of sound intelligence, which it was, was dangerous," replied Forsyth.

"Because it included cops?"

"Yes, among others," nodded Forsyth. "Frazer had intimated that senior cops and other powerful figures within the establishment were involved."

"Holyrood?"

"Potentially," smirked Forsyth.

"Frazer was murdered shortly afterwards, so in effect, he had only given Chuck a smell of the pie, as opposed to a bite, then?" Monty had heard the gist of it all from Dai, so was just confirming.

"Yep. No names before he got a deal to be released from custody," he nodded again. "Sharon Adams went to brief our squad gaffer DSI Wong and myself, while Chuck went back to get a deal done with Frazer at St Leonards."

"What deal?"

Forsyth shrugged his shoulders again. "We didn't have one as such. Frazer had wanted a deal before giving us the names, and this was what we discussed over at Adam's house. You see, he wanted out of a pickle, but despite knowing that he might be under threat should he be remanded in prison, we were unlikely to get him a deal from any Fiscal."

"So, you were just buying time then?" Frowned Monty, who had previously seen such tactics used upon clients of his.

"Yes, we were offering a bullshit deal. Names and evidence in return for a promise to persuade the Fiscal at court to spring him." Smirked Forsyth.

"Okay, I follow. So, before Chuck got back to the station, Frazer had been unbelievably released from custody and then shot dead up at the Queens Park?" Monty continued to take notes,

"And our boss—Wong, then authorised a deniable op into Frazier's allegations for a few days or so thereafter," confirmed Forsyth.

"And who was on that op?"

"Myself, Joe Roxburgh, Gav Caine, and watching on from the touch line—Sharon Adams," replied Forsyth.

"And are they all still working with the squad now?" asked Monty.

"No, Joe supposedly committed suicide by taking some sort of overdose shortly after they forced him to resign from the force, as they had myself" revealed Forsyth.

So not content to destroy a career, the conspirators whacked him?

"How did they make him resign?" Monty could see that he was in a real spider's web already.

"Not sure, he cut all contact with myself after I was suspended a few days after Chuck's murder," shrugged Forsyth.

"Okay, let's get back to the deniable operation then." Monty reminded himself that he needed to focus upon Forsyth's situation and not get too tangled up into the connected hearsay, at least not yet. "And the others?" he queried.

"Gav Caine is now a DS, having been promoted from DC soon after he grassed our deniable op in to a separate department."

"Which department?" Monty just couldn't help himself though.

"Fuck knows." Shrugged Forsyth scratching his elbow now.

"So, do you think he may have sold the operation out to someone involved with the TIC?" Monty was stating the obvious.

"I have no doubts about that." Sighed Forsyth. "And as for Sharon Adams, I'm not sure if she is still on the squad, but as I say, no one talks to me now and nor do I have any sources to pass on to you—I am persona non grata."

"Quite a cutthroat brigade then," said Monty.

"Yes and not all of them human," whispered Forsyth.

"So I hear."

"Yep, a couple of the bastards jumped Chuck and I when we were tailing a lead—a TIC puppet by the name of Philip Trevelen," said Forsyth matter-of-factly.

"Isn't he the wine guy?" Monty had met Trevelen once at a wedding at the Crieff Hydro hotel. The groom had been a solicitor friend from another firm. Monty had been seated at a large circular table with eight other guests and could recall hearing Trevelen and his foreign wife, who were both seated opposite, talking about wine with some old bloke who ran a restaurant up by Loch Venacher. They had exchanged greetings etc, but Trevelen had not been on the courtesy bus there from Edinburgh and presumably must have stayed over at the Hydro.

"Yes, that's him," confirmed Forsyth.

"Okay." Monty wrote all of this down.

"We fought back, of course, and I got knocked out by a kung fu style kick from one of the things, thankfully Chuck killed it in defence of his life with a weapon he had been given by Dai," explained Forsyth.

Monty did not mention that he too had one. "Killed it?" he asked.

Forsyth closed his eyes and nodded. "It apparently just disintegrated into nothing and disappeared."

"So, you did not see it happen then?"

"Well, not the death part as I had just been knocked out by the fucker."

"Okay, continue then please," urged Monty, feeling a tad safer.

Forsyth saw that Monty was not in the least bit shocked by any of this. "I take it Dai filled you in on everything?"

"Yeh, pretty much." Monty looked up again and met his gaze. "But I believe you anyway, after what I have been through recently, I don't doubt any of it." He smiled knowingly at the tousled man before him.

"Well, after that incident we knew that Trevelen was dodgy, and we also suspected that Frazer had most likely been on his way to meet him when he had been murdered," explained Forsyth. "We suspected that Trevelen was involved with TIC, and that he had been sprung from custody and lured into an ambush," he continued. "We then sniffed out some intel on an Irvine Stroker through another teenage victim of Lionel Frazer's, and both Chuck and I approached Stroker at the property he shared with an Alban Dudley in Musselburgh."

"Paedophiles?"

"Yes." Nodded Forsyth.

"We twisted Stroker's arm and he gave us the details of the head of Edinburgh City Council, who he claimed to be an associate of Frazer's and who had similar sexual preferences," he said. "We then got the name of a Yvonne Kidd from Stroker, after admitting that he had previously arranged for her to be abused by Frazer and his chums."

"And was Stroker's intel reliable?" Monty looked up from his notes again.

"Well, they killed him didn't they mate." Forsyth allowed the connotation to answer the question.

"And then what?" Monty got the point.

"And so myself and Chuck decided to doorstep Yvonne Kidd and see what names she might give us, and so we took Stroker with us because he knew her, and also because we did not want him to disappear or alert Trevelen."

"Did Stroker know Trevelen?"

"Oh yes. Trevelen had found him a job in a French restaurant up the Royal Mile."

"A bit unorthodox though, wasn't it?" Monty frowned now.

"You have to understand how hot this had all become," argued Forsyth. "We suspected that we were well out of our depth by this point, or at least I did, and that our own employers, as well as—the head of Midlothian Regional Council, and even the head coroner for Edinburgh—Esther Faulkner, whose car we spotted, along with several others at Trevelen's estate in Fife, were all involved," he mitigated.

"Bloody hell!" Exclaimed Monty. It really was a thick web this, which he was slowly but surely becoming more and more entangled within. One thing was for sure, none of this was going to be any help whatsoever to Forsyth's defence. Claiming a big institutional conspiracy as part of the defence, would probably make things much worse, particularly if the judge and prosecutor were involved.

"You see why we opted for unorthodoxy then." Smirked Forsyth.

"Yep." Nodded Monty.

"Anyway, so the three of us then turn up at Yvonne's place, and she answers the door, and despite being uncomfortable with Stroker's presence, she lets us in and takes us through to the lounge," revealed Forsyth.

"Is anyone else home, or are you seen by any neighbours?"

"We don't know about witnesses other than that her mother was supposedly terminally ill and in her bed."

"So, she could have seen or heard you?"

"Well, she answered the door earlier when we had first visited, but Yvonne had been at work then and the mother had been stinking of booze."

"So, you had been up earlier?"

"Yep, but Yvonne was at work," confirmed Forsyth.

"That might be a problem." Monty could see the mother being a potential false witness, for if she was a drunk she was just as likely to confuse the two occasions and claim she witnessed Forsyth being there at the time of the murder. "She didn't see you guys when you returned later that day?" He asked.

Forsyth shook his head, "I don't think so."

"Okay, continue please."

"Yvonne got us some drinks and then the doorbell went," sighed Forsyth, "we stayed put, as she mentioned something about expecting a delivery, and so she got up and went out into the hall to answer the door."

Monty straightened up again, then leaned back into the uncomfortable plastic chair as he listened. "After a few minutes when she hadn't returned, Chuck went out to see what was keeping her," said Forsyth.

"Right?" Monty knew this was where things got tasty.

"He was away less than a minute before he called me through and so I got up, went out and there was Yvonne laying on the hall floor." Forsyth allowed this to sink in for a brief moment before continuing, "Her legs were sticking out of the open front door entrance and Chuck bent down and turned her over. She had a stab wound to the heart and her throat had been slashed."

"Was there any sign of anyone else?"

"No, not in the hallway anyway, but we heard the downstairs communal entrance door slam shut."

Monty wrote that down. "There was, as you can imagine, a lot of blood flowing, and the carpet, a dark brown carpet, was soaked in it," explained Forsyth.

"Did you guys get any of it on you?"

"Nope," assured Forsyth.

"Okay, then what?"

"Then we got Stroker and the three of us exited by stepping over the scene and we went down the stairs and left the tenement."

"Were you seen?"

"We thought not, and Dai said we would have nothing to worry about when we saw him afterwards. I also think that if we had been seen, we would have been called in to Fettes the same day, and asked to explain why we were at the scene of a murder," suggested Forsyth.

"And also asked why you both left the scene of a murder without calling it in yourselves," said Monty with head back in his notes. He knew the answer by now, of course, but he had to ask why, for the Crown prosecutor certainly would. "Why did you not call it in then?"

Forsyth shook his head. He had been arguing this with himself for long enough and always came up with the same answer. "The killer, or killers, obviously knew that we were there speaking to Yvonne and had potentially seen us arrive. Either that or they were aware that we had received intel from Leo Frazer, which had led us to both Trevelen and to Stroker, so they murdered her."

"Wasn't that all the more reason to call it in?"

"No because if they were prepared to commit such an act whilst we were in the next room, and on top of the recent Frazer hit, we may have been set up, i.e., the murder weapon could have been found in Chuck's care, etc," reasoned Forsyth.

"And then Stroker was found dead?" considered Monty, leaving his notes again momentarily.

"And then Chuck and Joe!" Forsyth shook his head despondently.

"And now they are dealing with you." Sighed Monty.

"To be expected. After all, they killed everyone else, not to mention Cairns, and Yvonne too."

And me next?

"Cairns?" Monty asked.

"He was a cocaine player who was also Frazer's client," replied Forsyth with a hint of contempt.

Still a Drug Squad cop by nature.

Monty had known Lionel Frazer of course, not particularly well, other than having been introduced a few times when Frazer was a solicitor running child custody cases on the upper floor of Edinburgh Sheriff Court. A hopeless snob, but Monty had never taken him to be a pervert or Satanist though.

"Frazer told us that Cairns had recently been initiated into TIC," explained Forsyth.

"Okay?"

"Well, after Yvonne's murder, Cairns turned up in custody here for something or other and was facing a long sentence so Chuck went along to his cell and tried to negotiate a deal with him."

"For?"

"Intel on the membership list of TIC."

"Okay, and?" Monty continued to scribble notes.

"And they killed him here in his cell, and we suspected the coroner was about to play a part in the cover-up."

"Based on any evidence?"

Forever the lawyer.

"Nope, but I caught some suits wheeling his dead carcass out of the back door here and got into a brawl with them."

"A brawl?" Monty looked up at him again.

"Well, I confronted them, and they jumped me," insisted Forsyth. "Then I was frog marched out onto the street and the bastards made a complaint about me to my guvnor—Wong."

"And Wong then did what?"

"He called off our op, but Chuck and I agreed to keep going with it behind his back for a little while longer," said Forsyth.

"Why?"

"Because we sensed that we were quite close to the crown jewels, mate, and it was a serious conspiracy after all, which involved a multitude of crimes from hard drug running to child abuse," argued Forsyth. Monty nodded that he understood.

"Sharon Adams covered for us, and we drafted in Joe, Gav Caine and Stroker, then we went over to Crail Caravan Park in Fife where we knew that a retired police inspector was going to be in his caravan," continued Forsyth.

"Uh huh?"

"We took some unorthodox photos of him with Stroker," said Forsyth.

"How did you manage that?"

"Don't ask, mate, but they ended up using that to force my resignation thereafter." Sighed Forsyth.

"Okay, we can discuss that later if we need to then."

"Then we recorded Trevelen having dinner with the owner of the French restaurant in the old town where Stroker had been found a job by Trevelen."

"This is nuts, Chris." Monty shook his head as he tried to get a grasp of the plot here. "Why on earth was Trevelen using Stroker?"

"We recorded them discussing training Stroker in cookery and obtaining him a position within the Bute House residence of the Scottish First Minister," whispered Forsyth, despite there apparently being no reason to whisper.

"To what end?" Monty was astonished.

"We came to the conclusion that it was to use him as a patsy who would poison the First Minister and potentially others, in order to instigate a coup."

Shrugged Forsyth. "But then before we could sit down with Sharon Adams and decide on our next move, Gav Caine grassed us all up."

Monty just sat there thinking…unless Dai and Co step in, he was going to struggle with this case.

"Then Chuck was murdered on Portobello High Street and Stroker forced to take a heroin overdose in his flat the next day."

"And then you were pushed out, so you leave the country to go and live in Tenerife, while Joe Roxburgh apparently commits suicide here and both Gav Caine and Sharon Adams do okay out of it all," Monty thought aloud.

"Correct." Forsyth slapped his bare thigh with his right hand.

"Okay, well, how are we on evidence? Do you have the recording of the French Restaurant?" asked Monty.

"Nope, I gave the laptop to Wong but he suspended me and now I'm sitting in here facing this bullshit," snapped Forsyth angrily.

"So that will explain why they are gunning for you now then."

"Chuck had a phone with video evidence on it but I haven't a clue what happened to that," said Forsyth. "There were also photos taken by a freelance photographer named Dewar, of a golf course that we suspected had high-ranking masons as members, but your guess is as good as mine as to where they, or he, is now."

"Did you discover that TIC players were members of the golf course?"

"Not sure, I think Chuck was just fishing initially but it was also the golf course that the retired Inspector with the caravan in Crail frequented. So I guess Chuck was just sniffing the place out in order to corner him into giving us the low down on any other members of interest?"

"Okay. Chuck sounds as if he was a very resourceful bloke. So, what have you said to the cops who arrested and charged you?"

"Zilch."

"Good." Monty was glad to hear some good news, no matter how minor. "Don't say a word. If they want to interview you again, refuse until they have arranged with myself to attend and be present, okay?" he insisted.

Forsyth nodded, he knew the routine as well as any lawyer or villain does.

"In the meanwhile, you're not going to be up to court until after the New Year, so you will need to get your head down and I will try and make contact with your ex and establish a bail address at least."

"Any chance of bail?" asked Forsyth.

"Almost none but you are a former cop with no criminal record, so still worth a punt."

"I'm gagging on a smoke; can you hand in some nicotine patches?" asked Forsyth.

"Sure. I'll certainly try but they might tell me to fuck off out of spite, but I will try, and I'll hand in some newspapers and come back to see you before court," promised Monty. He now returned his trusted notepad and pen back into his bag before asking, "Why didn't you guys just pass all of this on to MI5?"

It seemed a fair point, both Forsyth and Kean had been up to their knees against it all and at best, they were in for a long dirty fight with a clique of people who were obviously intent upon playing dirty and who had considerable resources in their toolbox.

Forsyth had obviously either been thinking about this too or had anticipated the question. It was certainly likely that any prosecutor would hit him with it at trial. Particularly if the defence was going to be based around a claim that an evil and rogue masonic group embedded within the upper echelons of society, had really murdered Yvonne Kidd. "It wasn't my operation, Monty," sighed Forsyth, and Monty could tell that he was being honest.

"Good answer!" He replied with an encouraging smirk as he slowly stood up.

"Will you ask Dai to come and see me in my cell please?" Asked Forsyth now. For he believed that the angel had the ability to appear at will without going through the same procedure that Monty had to.

Monty had to think about this a moment though as he gently swung his bag back and forth. He knew that he was the only human friend that Forsyth had. It was important to keep his chin up at this stage of the game, "Yes, if I see him. I promise you, Chris, I will defend you on this with ferocity and I will make sure that at the very least, the rule of law is followed to the latter in that court room," he promised him.

"I believe you." Replied Forsyth, scraping his chair back across the thick rubber lino floor as he too stood up, but with an obvious physical toll which was duly noted by Monty. The man was clearly being drained of his mental and physical reserves, and it was possible that Forsyth did not realise it yet.

"I just hope that I don't commit suicide in the meantime." Forsyth raised his hands now and curled both index fingers to make the quotation sign. At least he can smirk, thought Monty with as much optimism as he could muster. He observed Forsyth sympathetically for a moment. He knew he needed to instigate some sort of deterrent to those who might wish him harm, so he knocked loudly upon the door on his side and gave his new client an encouraging wink. Within a few seconds, a new female officer opened the door and led Monty out and back along the way he had come earlier without as much as a word of pleasantry, leaving Forsyth to wait behind for the whistling turnkey.

"I would like a word with your duty inspector before I leave, please Constable," Monty said to the back of her pony-tailed head, which was in line with his throat as they walked. Cops had been a lot taller when Monty had been younger, and he reflected on the ever-changing development of the police service as they ascended the stairs.

"Fine," she replied pleasantly enough and without turning around.

Ten minutes later, he was standing waiting in a carpeted corridor beside a fake Yucca plant about the same height as himself. There was a hanging print of a 1930's London North Eastern train travel poster of Edinburgh opposite and he over-studied it as he waited. It was a brightly painted image of shoppers going about their business on Princess Street whilst grey mounted, and red tunicked cavalry trotted along on the main road. A door somewhere behind him opened, Monty stretched his neck out to see a man in the old styled white shirted uniform of the 1990's appear along the corridor. He was a tall, thin, grey-haired man in his fifties, with a thick salt and pepper moustache. Monty thought he resembled Neville Chamberlin, though he may have been influenced somewhat by the LNE poster.

"Mr Montgomery?" asked the man curtly. He sounded more like the Scottish version of Dick Dastardly than Neville Chamberlain however.

"Yes." Monty walked towards him; when the man never moved nor smiled, it became clear to Monty that a cup of tea was out of the question and that this chat was going to be a brief one in the corridor.

"What can I do for you?" enquired Neville as Monty approached him.

"Who am I speaking with?" smiled Monty with artificial pleasantry as he offered his hand.

"Inspector Arthur," replied Neville cautiously, as he wearily accepted it.

Monty took a breath and put his bag down on the rust-coloured carpet. "I represent Chris Forsyth," he said cheerily whilst meeting the man's gaze. There was no recognition in the grey eyes, simply suspicion and a hint of impatience.

Monty pressed on, "He is a former Drug Squad detective and is looking at spending the rest of his life in prison," he pointed out.

Neville stood there motionless.

"He is unable to smoke, but I want him to be given nicotine patches because I believe that he is in the early stages of an emotional breakdown, due to the fact that he is a fifty per day man," said Monty firmly now.

Neville considered this a moment, the prisoners were not permitted to smoke, and the fact that this was often highly uncomfortable for many of them was not relevant to the police. After all, when they had allowed it once upon a time, it had been abused, so it was just tough titty. However, no lawyer had ever pulled this out of the bag before; nicotine patches for medicinal purposes? And there was no precedent—at least not that Neville was aware of—which he could refer to when rejecting such a request.

"I could drag a private GP in to support my suspicion, but I am asking one cop to grant this request for another without the drama," urged Monty, sensing Neville's confusion.

"Forsyth is a former cop actually," Neville slowly but quite coldly replied. He could not see how any legal aid funded brief would be able to do any of this, but he was also aware that this could be a Jean Marc Bosnan moment[87], and that just because he had his doubts, he could see little reason to object. He just did not care enough on a Boxing Day, to come off the fence as it were.

"Indeed, but a cop all the same." Monty pointed out.

"A disgraced one," smiled Neville contemptuously.

"Not what he says," Monty returned the smile.

Both of them stared at each other for a rather awkward second or two, fathoming what each other actually knew about why Forsyth was really in custody.

"Fine." Neville blinked first. "If you're paying for them then, as he has no money in his property."

"Not a problem and thank you." Monty nodded his appreciation. Perceptive to the fact that because an inspector knew what was or was not in the property of a prisoner, offered various suggestions, such as, did Neville have an interest in Forsyth? But then, Forsyth was a former cop, wasn't he, so the gossip would be all around the station by now he supposed, and there would be obvious interest.

---

[87] A former Belgian professional footballer whose landmark judicial ruling (The Bosman Ruling) lead to changes to football regulations in Europe in 1995.

Neville was about to turn and walk away when Monty made his follow up move.

"Actually, Inspector Arthur," Monty spoke up just as the cop was reversing back into his office, "additionally, I would also like to request that my client be placed on suicide observation immediately."

Neville sighed, placed his hands on his hips and gave Monty the once over, "Why?" he sighed in obvious frustration.

Monty knew that by instigating hourly checks in an observation cell, Forsyth would be on 24-hour camera and that any plot to murder him would be checked, at least in the short term. It would not have done to have pulled this card beforehand, as then Neville may have rejected the request to provide the poor guy with nicotine patches, out of spite.

Neville grinned at him now. "Well, if you feel it necessary, I shall see to that then." He raised his eyebrows now, "Will there be anything else, Mr Montgomery?"

"No thank you, Inspector." Smiled Monty. "And Happy Christmas." He collected his bag as Neville turned and disappeared.

Maybe he's not a Christian then.

Monty had to find an open store in Marchmont that sold the patches; he grabbed the strongest ones they had and several newspapers that were two days old. When he returned to St Leonards, an unpleasant blonde woman with curly hair took them from him and gave him a scunner of a look.

"Will he receive them straight away?" he asked her.

"When we're ready," she snapped, before turning her back on him and walking away.

Fuck you too then, dear.

He promptly exited back through the revolving doors and into the cold air and drove back home via the Queens Park. The route was still relatively quiet but there were several people visiting the swans. He wondered if he should have pressed Forsyth into elaborating more about the plot to assassinate the First Minister? Or whether any names, other than Cairns and Frazer, had come up during the course of the investigation. He impulsively sensed however that it would not do for him to entangle himself into any conspiracy web though, as he would only become obsessed with it, and his brief was to stop Forsyth going down for a murder after all.

His phone rang as he was driving, he looked down at the passenger seat and saw that it was Sadie. He did not pick up, instead he now drove with both hands on the steering wheel in the nervous manner he used to when he had just passed his test many years previously. Then Ally Blyth rang, Monty blanked him too. Back at the house, the file was back laying on the porch floor again. Monty froze the moment he saw it and wondered if there had been something he had missed in it. The dog was pleased to see him so he leaded his friend up and set off for a walk first before settling down to read it over a brew.

They walked over and on to the eastern Links, which was full of dog walkers all wrapped up in their new scarfs, coats and shoes, that they had received for Christmas. He recognised some of the faces but focused on the dog by letting him of the lead and throwing sticks for him to chase. All the while Monty scanned the terrain for anything out of place. The fact that he pretty much knew what he was up against now, had him on full security alert.

Most people seemed to be enjoying the fresh air after yesterday's feasts, but Monty knew he could never relax fully now. The dog was now playing with a couple of basset hounds, the owners of which were standing idly nearby chatting. Monty had chatted to one of them in the past, a red-bearded and conceited know-it-all, whom he usually avoided with no more than a cheery wave.

Thankfully, Monty's phone rang again, so he quickly fetched it out, saw that it was an old school friend from his childhood who often kept in touch, and so accepted the call. The guy's wife had left him and Monty knew only too well that he would be sitting alone, drinking and seeking a shoulder to lean on. Of course, he couldn't be arsed playing Samaritans, but considering the season, he felt obliged and besides, it was either that or the basset hound owners who were now smiling over to encourage him to approach and hear all about a new house extension.

"Hi Kenny, how's it going?" He leisurely strolled over to a bench and sat down alone. The dog was within view and so was everyone else who were enjoying the fresh air.

"Hi Monty, how's it going, mate?" came the dreary reply that had as much festivity in it as the poor fellow bugger could scrape up.

Monty was still taking in the scene of people, couples, families and dogs of course; it felt as if he was observing a scene from a bygone era, something that seemed at home within an L.S. Lowry painting. Were it not for some kids with remote controlled 4X4 Trucks and cars, which were tearing through the melting snow like jet skis, he might have felt like he had travelled back in time again.

When he had been a kid, all his mates would be out eager to play football in their new strips and training gear that they had all received for Christmas. Kenny had always received goalie gloves, which everyone would share when taking their turn between the coats on the snow; changed days now of course, but still, Lowry would have noted little change here, at least not today.

"Aye not so bad, Kenny, just out with the dog."

"Know anything about marketing on the Internet, Monty?" Kenny wanted to know.

"Not really, bud, not quite my thing to be honest. How come?"

"I'm trying to flog a pair of trousers that my dad scrounged from Jimi Hendrix," stated Kenny.

Eh? As far as Monty recalled, Kenny's father had been a publican up in Fort William. "How on earth did your old boy come across those?" he asked.

"He had been a merchant seaman in the sixties and spent a year shacked up with a Cuban bird in New York," explained Kenny.

"Wow, really? I hadn't known that."

"Yeh, he was always going on about it and claimed that he used to see Hendrix play in that Café Wha place in Greenwich Village. One time dad ended up going back to a party somewhere with some pianist who was a student friend of the Cuban bird."

"Wow." Monty believed every word—Kenny didn't lie.

"Yeh, so anyway, Hendrix went to the party too and gave him his trousers."

"Some party by the sounds of it." Chuckled Monty—causing Kenny to laugh too.

"Anyway, the only problem is, Dad had them cut shorter so that he could wear them," insisted Kenny, which caused Monty to laugh even more as Kenny's father had been nicknamed 'titch'.

They chatted for a while and then when Monty's feet were beginning to feel cold, so he headed home but continued chatting all the way back. They went over the old days of course, and the football results as always, before they said their goodbyes. Monty liked Kenny, but he knew that he was weak, and he suspected things would get worse for him soon.

Back in the house, he put his Crocs on and hurried through to the kitchen to make a brew and get some lunch on the go. Then he heard the television in the lounge playing. He had turned it off before leaving earlier. He could hear no barking from the dog however so he grabbed the cork and touched it…voom…the celestial cutlass appeared and so he walked gamely through to investigate the noise with it held upwards in his hand as if he was bearing the Olympic torch.

Dai was sitting there cross-legged upon the sofa with the dog on his lap, tail wagging with happiness as it lapped up the petting. "Sorry to give you a fright, old boy." He smiled and at that moment a wave of well-being and happiness overwhelmed Monty. He immediately withdrew the weapon and put it back in his pocket.

"Don't you knock?" He smiled back—taking the armchair.

"I only arrived after you returned home, I would not come if you were not home and were not happy to welcome me," explained Dai, who was wearing a blue single-breasted suit with open blue shirt and fine black handmade shoes. "Also, I will never turn up when you are sleeping, etc," he promised.

"Oh it's fine, Dai, but I could have been in the shower." Smirked Monty.

"In which case, I would not have appeared until you were finished and dried," guaranteed Dai, somewhat amused.

"Fair enough. I'm making a cuppa and some food, are you staying?" offered Monty cheerfully whilst flicking a thumb towards the kitchen.

"No, I can't, I have to travel somewhere else very shortly, but I wanted to pop in and ask how your meeting with your new client went today?"

"Yeh not bad. He knows the score and is good to go but he is naturally drained, and probably still a little in shock."

"Well, you did well and got him put on a suicide watch; clever move." Grinned Dai mischievously.

"Was that wrong?" Monty asked open-mouthed—a tad worried that he shouldn't have.

"On the contrary," Dai smiled at him, "that is precisely why you have been selected. There are not many others who would have thought of that move." He nodded appreciatively.

Monty relaxed again. "It was just common sense, nothing more." He shrugged.

"Which is not something that everyone else possesses though." Shrugged Monty again.

"Not many others would also have ensured that he also received soothing nicotine into his system," Dai pointed out too.

Monty nodded; he had wanted to help him relax.

"And your instant acceptance of my presence here in your living room too, you did not get a fright or a surprise, rather you simply accepted what is in effect, a supernatural phenomenon, just like that." Dai clicked his fingers.

"I guess it's like taking LSD or magic mushrooms, Dai," Monty attempted to reason, "no matter how strange things become, you must either accept things and savour the experience, or you fight it and take a bad trip."

"And how would you know about that then?" Asked Dai curiously.

"I tried them both as a teenager," confessed Monty, half wondering if the angel already knew this.

Dai appeared to think about this for a moment before asking, "You know why they refer to it as a trip, don't you?"

"Because you go to a different place for a little while?" replied Monty whilst noting the considerable irony of Gene Wilder on the TV who was observing the singing Oompa Loompas in *Charlie and the Chocolate Factory*.

"Sort of yes, they enable teleportation to other dimensions," replied Dai telepathically.

"Dimensions? As in like the portal at the stones in Fife that I travelled through?"

"Not an entirely dissimilar process, but not quite." Dai seemed to think about this for a further moment before then deciding to change the subject. "What is your plan now then regarding Christopher Forsyth?"

Monty had to think about this for a second before answering. "Well, I will be trying to find him a bail address and dealing with his initial appearance at court in the New Year. Then I guess I shall approach Mark Dailly."

"And go over the file again too. Make sure that you read it all and take in everything as you are up against it here," urged Dai.

"Yeh I know, and frankly, if I didn't know that Forsyth had you guys on his side, I would be sensing an irreversible shit fuck oncoming."

Dai clicked his fingers again. "Don't swear in my presence. I do not like it and I will not tolerate it, okay?" he insisted in a calming and non-aggressive tone.

"Understood. I'm sorry," offered Monty, regretting the faux pas.

"Splendid." The angel beamed back at him warmly.

"Can I ask you something?" asked Monty.

"Yes?" replied Dai telepathically whilst continuing to gently stroke the contented dog.

"Forsyth said that you assured him and Kean that they would not be accused of Yvonne's murder back at the time?"

"True." Sighed Dai. "No one saw them at her flat that day and at that point, there was no indication that they would ever be accused of having been there. However, since then, the opposition has conspired to set them up for it," he revealed.

Monty had to think about this for a moment. "So you're saying that they didn't actually know that Chris was ever at Yvonne's place, and just fabricated these allegations against him then?"

"Well, they knew he attended earlier that day and spoke to the mother, when Yvonne was at work, but not that they had returned later with Stroker." Nodded Dai.

"But Yvonne's mother? Is she not being called as a witness?" asked Monty.

"If she is, then it is only after being shown photographs of Forsyth and Chuck and having it drilled into her head as, and I say this with genuine sympathy, she is intoxicated most of the time to the point wherein she doesn't have much recollection of whomever she encounters," explained Dai.

"Not the best witness then," considered Monty optimistically.

"As you say." Smirked Dai as he gently lifted the dog off his lap and placed it down upon the floor before then standing up himself.

"That you away then?" asked Monty.

"Yes, regrettably. You two enjoy your steaks and we shall chat again in due course. Call for me if you need me and I shall attend to you. Otherwise, I will call you before I next visit you."

Monty then walked him down the corridor and out into the front hall where he shook the angel's hand before opening the door for him.

"Am I safe here in my own home, Dai? And is my dog safe when I am not home?" He felt compelled to ask.

Dai turned around and smiled at him. "Your guardian angel will protect your home and our friend here should any non-human entities attack or enter," promised Dai whilst gazing down affectionally at the dog who had followed to come and see him off. "Though not all spirits or beings will ring the doorbell and await your convenience before entering a human home," he pointed out. "Rules are not always obeyed, of course, so I cannot say what mischief will be thrown in your direction, Stephen, but if anything comes here or threatens this dog, they will be confronted by your guardian angel and potentially others of my choir too," he assured. "Elsewhere though, on the street, who can tell?" He shrugged. "Which, of course, is why you have been given a weapon, Stephen," he reminded Monty whilst meeting his gaze.

There was such a comfort relayed from the angel's gaze that Monty just believed him and was instantaneously relaxed. This being's sheer radiance and trustworthiness was evident from the projected mystical energy that seeped into Monty's emotions and which provided instant relief from unease and worry. He was in fact automatically relieved in a manner comparable to that of a woman who, having been followed home at night by a shadowy figure, hears the sound of her door locking behind her.

"I just don't want to worry about my dog, he has nothing to do with this." Shrugged Monty.

"I know, and I am also here for you both, as best I can be. So, call my name if threatened," urged Dai. The angel then patted him affectionately upon his shoulder before turning and stepping outside into the coldness.

"Goodbye Dai," said Monty.

"God bless, Stephen," replied Dai as he walked east in the direction of Queen Charlotte Street.

When Monty had closed and locked the door again, he paused and wondered if Dai had been in the fridge. Otherwise, how else had he known that there were two steaks sitting there?

"I can smell them," came the telepathic reply from along the street.

Soon afterwards, Monty cooked the two steaks and gave one, slightly rare, to the dog. He cut it up with scissors and added a handful of kibbles which the dog loved. Then he sat on the sofa and eat his one—very well-done, along with some fried onions, a microwaved jacket potato and a cup of green tea. The evening news was on TV, so he watched it while he ate. SLP frontman Colin Anderson-Forbes was taking part in a festive dip in the river Tay at Broughty Ferry harbour along with a couple of hundred other lunatics. He was then shown being interviewed nearby wearing a green Northface fleece and with a towel round his neck.

"Is this the new face of Scottish politics?" An unseen male voice enquired of him.

"Well, I am visiting friends near here who take part in this local community event, and so I felt obliged to play a supporting role as it were." Chuckled Forbes to the camera before adding, "I'm not sure if Miss Sturgeon participated in her local Loony Dook at South Queensferry, or whether the newly appointed Scottish Labour leader Jim Murphy has considered jumping in the Clyde or not, but I certainly wanted to join in with this local tradition," he insisted.

Monty reached over and picked up the remote control and flicked the channel over to a documentary of sorts which he left on whilst he finished his steak. The programme was about some English physicist called Francis Crick who had apparently come to a ground-breaking conclusion on the structure of human DNA in the 1950s[88]. Monty couldn't be bothered turning it over again however and so ate on regardless. At that moment the dog reappeared, having polished off his festive meal, and opted to sit still like an alabaster statue of the Egyptian jackal god Anubis, at the coffee table, its eyes firmly upon the remaining steak on Monty's plate.

"Go and lie down," commanded Monty, and so it did, but in a corner of the lounge where it could still maintain a watchful vigilance over Monty's dwindling sirloin.

The American narrator of the documentary relieved the tension: "Crick, an atheist and critic of Christianity, had resigned his fellowship of Churchill College, Cambridge, because it had decided to establish a chapel on site." Monty had little choice but to listen, though he had even less interest in science.

"Crick speculated that the complexity of DNA suggested that it cannot have been developed by chance." The sound of Monty's knife upon the plate was more interesting to the dog though. "He then went on to speculate that perhaps what had originally been a simple code with a few amino acid types and an ability to self-replicate, evolved into a more complex code.

"So, what was this development process?" The narrator sounded east coast American, he reckoned..

"Well, Crick proposed the possibility that the production of living systems from molecules, was not of this earth, and that the event must have originally been universally rare. Though he also surmised that DNA had developed and

---

[88] Francis Crick was a British molecular biologist, neuroscientist, humanist and connoisseur of LSD who won the Nobel prize for Physiology or Medicine in 1962, before then declining an OBE in 1963. He was later awarded the Royal and Copley medals of the Royal Society in 1972 and 1975.

was spreadable via intelligent life forms who may have used space travel technology, a process he referred to as 'direct panspermia'."

You're not getting any of my steak boy.

"For Crick understood that one DNA particle is a magical mystery. Indeed one that could be described as of being the equivalent of a collection of medical journals that had been shredded into thousands of individual words and then mixed up and scattered randomly upon the wind from the top of a mountain, only to regather themselves in perfect order, becoming whole again upon landing," construed the narrator.

And this guy Crick, understood that there was a non-earthly creator of DNA, yet he was an atheist?

It seemed more probable to Monty, in his newly enlightened state, of course, that Crick was batting for the dark side and thus touting to the uninitiated. Regardless, Monty had heard enough so he polished off his last bite of steak and switched off the box. He then went into the kitchen and deposited his plate in the sink; he would wash it later, he promised himself. He then fetched a dental chew for the dog and the Orcadian file. He chucked the dog his chew and then settled down to finish his brew and have a read with his feet up. Just then his phone went. It was in the kitchen on the worktop; he sighed as he placed the file on the coffee table and dragged himself up again. It was a withheld number again.

"Hello?"

"Am I speaking to Stephen Montgomery, solicitor of Hendry & Co?" asked a polite male voice, though it was not the same police officer who had rung him earlier.

"Yep, that's me."

"It's PS Petrie calling from St Leonards here."

"Evening."

Manners cost nothing.

"Evening Sir. It is just to let you know that we have a Julie Boyd here who has been apprehended on an outstanding warrant for non-payment of a two-hundred and fifty pound fine."

"Right." Monty almost sighed but restrained the urge. "Has she no one who can pay it?"— to ask a silly question.

"Apparently not, sir," replied Petrie.

"Okay so she is appearing at court in January then?"

"That is correct, sir," confirmed Petrie.

"Okay, duly noted, officer. Please inform her that someone from my firm will be there to represent her."

"Will do sir, goodbye."

"Bye."

Monty knew her, of course; he had represented the teenager a few times and had seen her jailed twice for breaches of probation and a community service order. She was another lost soul who was addicted to heroin and had a string of convictions for shop lifting. He shook his head despondently, '*Merry Christmas Jules*' and fetched his briefcase with his notes. He wrote down her name and reason for her court appearance and then went back through to the lounge, taking his phone with him this time.

The reopening of the courts in January was always a hectic and stressful occasion, what with the general after-Christmas downer amongst lawyers and clients, of whom there were usually a few who had been locked up throughout the holidays. Monty traditionally dreaded it. He settled down again now, took a swig of tea and with the dog now beside him on the sofa with its dental chew, he relaxed and began reading the Orcadian file again.

Chapter Twelve

If ignorant both of your enemy and yourself, you are certain to be in peril.
Sun Tzu

Monty awoke on the sofa yet again. A quick glance at his watch confirmed that it was 23.15. Match of the Day was on the TV, he remembered, as he sat up and yawned, causing the dog, which was on his ankles to groan. He stretched and groaned too—another reminder that he wasn't getting any younger, and flicked the TV on with the remote. The Chelsea V West Ham highlights were on. Chelsea were winning 1-0 but the Hammers were having a right go at them he gathered. He wanted to get up and make a brew but instead just lay there on one elbow, watching the game. After a few seconds, however, Chelsea's Costa scored a second goal causing Monty to sigh disappointedly and get up to go and make that cuppa.

He had read the Orcadian file earlier for an hour or so before then dosing off. There had been a note attached to it this time that had not been there previously:

"We are standing at an old crossroad. We sense something coming down the road before we can visually identify it. Even the blind sense it. Retrospection is pointless to the blind. Sadly, their belief system is entrenched so deeply within their consciousness that their alertness would attempt to override the data contained within this file and so they would refuse to process it. You must not fall at this first barrier, Stephen, and so read up on your adversary."

When Monty then reviewed the file again, he found that there had been a small section at the bottom of a page that he had obviously just flicked past the first couple of times around. How Dai had known this, still amazed Monty. The section itself had covered the Orcadian's philosophical beliefs and how they consumed him in his dealings with humans. Apparently, as per all the seraphic rebels, the Orcadian is committed to seeing order out of chaos. The rebel's intention is to open, what the file described as, *"An occult Pandora's Box"*.

Enabling mankind to access to such things as quantum physics, hyper cognition and astral projection. The section also explained that this Pandora's box is now slightly ajar and that the Orcadian and his kind are now engaged in a bitter conflict to open it further.

It was hard to appreciate the fine details of it all, but Monty understood that the Orcadian was obviously a fanatical devote of a very ancient and dark ideology. As with most fanatics of course, the Orcadian was bitter. Monty thought about this a little before he finished off the file. Was this bitterness a weakness? The file described him as being both talented and learned. It also said that he was more than able to swoon a jury, but that he was a narcissist, who can breathe under water apparently? Monty supposed that this would have been an advantage when involved in a love affair with the sea creature—Ceto.

He was also as sturdy as a stag, and quite brilliant in most human matters-he wore his human Hellenic skin well and cannot be overcome by violence at the hands of men; however, he is unable to enter a place of worship without becoming extremely uncomfortable. He is haughty, and profoundly arrogant; which Monty had already taken for granted considering the fallen ones had all told God to go and whistle. If he is arrogant though, that is a weakness that the Orcadian surely cannot control then, considered Monty.

At least that's how it works with men?

If so, and the Orcadian does not quite understand the depth of his problem, then he might additionally suffer from other typical symptoms, such as being unable to prevent himself from being the centre of attention and a desire to be adored? The section concluded by revealing that the fallen ones had long since lost their purpose due to their devotion to a graceless, unpoetic degeneration which sought the overthrow of heaven. This however, regardless of whether he suffers from all the other symptoms, does provide at least one little chink in the Orcadian's armour—the fact that he cannot continuously control himself.

The lingering section on the page read itself out again loud and clear in Monty's mind as he made the brew:

Remember what it is that the Orcadian cannot admit to himself, that behind enmity, whether it be an angel's or a human's, there will be disappointment and often jealousy at the root of certain things. Therefore, enmity is an uninvited reaction, which can, if incited by an adversary, give the adversary control over you. The Orcadian, as per most haughty spirits, is blinded to the fact that an incensed foe, no matter how superior, can become vulnerable.

When he returned to the lounge, Monty considered this. The dog had moved onto the armchair now where it was curled up and snoozing again. It opened an eye to see if the master had foraged any snacks, then quickly closed it again when it smelled the green tea instead. Monty sunk back down onto the sofa and watched a little of the football whilst blowing on the tea.

What was the Orcadian so annoyed about then? he wanted to know. Instinctively, Monty desired to know more; to question and to understand the true cause of this angelic struggle which he now found himself in the thick of. There was little evidence as to why the Orcadian hated humans enough to have rebelled against God. Monty already knew that kindness can often wound hatred momentarily, and he was already considering this as a possible counter to the Orcadian's offensive in court, but he wanted to know what it is that drives this being on against mankind. He needed to know his enemy, in order to receive him properly, etc, and surely that is was best achieved by understanding the anger in the Orcadian.

He put the cup down and got up again and nipped through to the bedroom. Returning a few seconds later with the Bible. He sunk back into the sofa again and began flicking through and instantly he arrived at Revelation 12:7, which he read through to 12:9:

Then war broke out in heaven. Michael and his angels fought against the dragon, and the dragon and his angels fought back. But they were not strong enough, and they lost their heavenly estates. The great dragon was hurled down—that ancient serpent called the devil, or Satan, who leads the whole world astray. He was hurled to the earth, and his angels with him.

Monty thought about this a moment, then he felt the urge to read up online in order to try and reach an informed guess on the origins of this hatred of men. He used his smartphone to research for a while; mainly the first book of Enoch which, strangely enough, he was led to by his search engine. He read about the fallen ones there. After which, he then came across and read 53: 2.3-5 of the somewhat bizarre Urantia:

It is exceedingly difficult to point out the exact cause or causes which finally culminated in the Lucifer rebellion. We are certain of only one thing, and that is: whatever these first beginnings were, they had their origin in Lucifer's mind. There must have been a pride of self that nourished itself to the point of self-deception, so that Lucifer for a time really persuaded himself that his contemplation of rebellion was actually for the good of the system, if not of the universe.

Monty was then directed by the search engine to the Bible and to the Book of Zechariah 3:1-7, which describes Satan as a prosecutor of Joshua in a trial being judged by God. Then on to the Book of Job, wherein God highlights the loyalty of his creation—Job, causing Satan to point out that Job is only pious because God has permitted him to prosper. A resulting challenge between God and Satan supervenes, wherein Satan is permitted to attempt to test Job's faith. Monty looked up at the ceiling and considered this for a while.

Maybe this suggests that Satan has a strong belief that people are controlled mainly by material prosperity. He read on and quickly came to 12.1 of the Book of Adam. After a while, he leaned his head back into the sofa again and looked up at the ceiling and sighed. Why and what was all this madness about?

Is that why Satan and his rebels had refused to bow to the first human—Adam? The rebels regard humans in a similar manner as many humans regard rats?

When he finished his tea, he gave the thinking a rest. He was aware that he had not heard back from his son regarding the following day's football. Celtic were playing Ross County, though he did not expect they would miss much. He would catch the match on the radio no doubt. He was quite bushed now and so he went about checking that all the doors and windows were secured before turning on the alarm and placing the file back on the front porch tiles, as before. He then brushed his teeth and went to bed. As he lay there, he wondered if his guardian angel was watching him now.

The cork rested in his hand as he finally dozed off. In the morning, he was up, showered and out with the dog again by the back of ten. The snow was melting because, despite there being a sharp bite in the air, the sun was out. He took another call as they reached the Seafield bridge and so turned to head back. It was the police again, this time Liberton CID. They had arrested another of the firm's clients, on charges of driving without insurance and without a driving licence. The teenage client was being released so Monty instructed the cop to tell him to make an appointment with the office in the new year. He would email all the notes over the office girls on the 2nd of January.

They then took a leisurely stroll back to the house, where he chucked the dog another dental chew, before then taking a drive over to Carrick Knowe in order to doorstep Forsyth's ex-girlfriend. Once more, the city centre was busy due to the sales, and he soon found himself stuck in traffic on York Place and from thereon he progressed at a crawl westwards along Queen Street. He occasionally felt for the cork in his jacket pocket. Considering that at any moment someone or something may appear from any direction and attack him.

He was listening to the radio—two American females were discussing something or other about banking microchips that could be implanted into a human wrist and which could be used as a contactless means of credit. Both females were opposed to the notion and one was quite passionate about it and was banging on about how they had been testing the idea in dog identification chips for a while now.

"And of course, that will lead to your passport details and driving licence being on it and voila—we have the draconian mass control scenario," the other exclaimed in a north Atlantic coast accent—not quite New York, more Atlantic city, guessed Monty.

"Which is precisely what the Scottish owner of the low-cost budget airline, Alba - Andy Friggieri, is advocating for his customers, and he is even offering reduced fares based upon it," pointed out a male with an Edinburgh accent.

"An Orwellian nightmare," agreed one of the other females.

"Is that something you fear might affect painters like yourself then, Julieta?" asked the male.

Monty turned it over. The build-up to the football was on and so he located the station and left it on. Of course, all this congestion could have been avoided, he believed, should the council, who were hell-bent on destroying Edinburgh, he felt, not have banned cars from driving along Princess Street. That and endless one-way streets with their newly installed bollards and barriers which cut off all the old short-cuts and other crannies—being the cause of this endless congestion.

God forbid he ever needed to travel this way on a weekday, when it seemed that half of Scotland were in their cars heading west for the M8 or the Forth Bridge. This was the reason Princess Street was no longer the great shopping street it had once been, reckoned Monty. Well, that and the parking Gestapo who nailed anyone who did not have the right coinage on them.

He remembered when people could just drive onto Princess Street and enjoy views of the castle or the Greek themed monument, with its tall Doric columns on Calton Hill. Most Edinburgers only saw these views on calendars for sale in their local post offices nowadays. Monty was one of those who avoided the city centre like the plague now, if he could. He remembered stopping and parking up on it one night on a date years previously with a girl named Angela. They had parked freely and walked round to Bar Roma for a meal before then driving off again.

Edinburgh had been the best city in the world back then. By the time the traffic got moving again, it was early afternoon and he had been thinking again about the reasoning behind his involvement in this whole case—he just couldn't help himself. Sure, he knew he had the bowels for a confrontation with a demonic being who was obviously going to be a million times better than he was at everything, but there had to be deeper logic behind it all.

Even this trip now to doorstep Forsyth's ex, was surely not going to work out. She will probably slam the door in his face, he measured with growing doubt. Was he just a lone fisherman casting pointless bait into gloomy waters long poisoned by pollution? A kind of celestial civil servant? Monty laughed aloud now.

Just get on with it and stop bloody thinking pal.

He was attracted to the notion of a hot cup of tomato soup and a sausage roll, but then he reminded himself that at his age, it was no longer a clever idea to fill up on junk. However when he passed a sandwich shop he had to fight the urge to pull over and run the parking Gestapo gauntlet for something warm and savoury. He gradually felt better once he was past Roseburn though. There seemed to be something deep within the human psyche, he considered, a connection between food and morality.

Guilty treats and all that jazz.

A bizarrely applied moralistic value seemed to have been placed upon food by creating a correlation between it and the idea of fighting temptation and defeating indulgence. It was certainly a struggle for Monty because he found it easier to buy warm junk food as opposed to cooking after a busy day at work.

The football craic on the radio was all about Celtic versus Ross County at the Park. He listened in to an ex Celtic player discussing the current team as he turned left down Pinkhill and into the Carrick Knowe estate. Carrick Knowe was a privately owned 1930's four-in-a-block villa suburb which was bordered to the south by the Aberdeen/Glasgow railway, a golf course to the east, and a main road with row of shops to the west. To the north, the suburb bordered Corstorphine, and many Carrick Knowe owners listed their properties for sale as "Corstorphine," for obvious financial reasons.

Good on them, thought Monty; after all, they had all been built upon what had once been the dried-out marsh of the old Corstorphine loch. A momentary gust of wind arrived up on the road from the old and deserted 1940's train station which had once served Edinburgh Zoo. It made the young pines along the lower walkway curve like fencing swords while snowflakes began drifting soundlessly downwards upon them before then being shaken off as the trees recoiled. These snowflakes swirled around like white midges. Some landed upon the car's warmish windscreen now but were soon turned into water again from the engine heat.

He slowed down as the sound of the slush splattering beneath the wheels, combined with the wind to draw his attention away from the radio. He sluggishly turned into the suburbs and used sat nav to locate the property. Three minutes later he was parked up outside the address that Forsyth had given him, so he put his scarf on and then walked up and rang the doorbell. An attractive olive-skinned female with short, highlighted hair in her mid-thirties answered the door in jeans and bare feet. She looked surprised initially and then disappointed when he produced his solicitor's card from his pocket.

"Hello, I'm looking for Audrey Parks?" he said cheerily.

"Are you police?" she asked suspiciously.

"No, I'm Chris's lawyer."

"Ah," she sighed and leaned back behind the half ajar door, revealing only one foot as if she were a lap dancer teasing her crowd. "Is he in Edinburgh?"

"Yes, and he has been charged with murder," Monty could see that she had been expecting this news so guessed that the police had been at her prior to Forsyth's arrest. "You don't seem surprised?" he forced another smile.

"Well, the police sort of said that he was probably going to be charged with murder and that should I hear from him, I should contact them," she said.

"Are you a witness against him?" Monty was obliged to ask.

"No," she shook her head. "I was visited by them a couple of times, just asking questions about our separation."

"Well, he says he didn't do it and I believe him." Monty continued to stand there smiling. She was clearly not going to invite him in, he gathered, and her feet would be getting cold soon, so he had to work fast here.

"Me too," she insisted. "If there is one thing he is not, that is a murderer, and I told the police that."

"Good, well, I'm glad you agree. Can I ask you if you would be prepared to help him, Audrey?"

"In what way?" She jerked her chin defensively now.

"By saying precisely that in court?" He continued to give off his friendliest salesman act.

She thought about this a moment then shook her head. "I will need to think about that," she told him inflexibly.

"And in the meantime, would you help me get him bail by letting him use your address as he has no home now in Edinburgh and the court require—"

She cut him off, "I can't do that as the police officer warned me that if I let him use my address then they might have to put surveillance on here." She sounded disappointed.

What on earth were they noising her up like that for in order to sever his only route into the slight possibility of freedom? They had certainly gone way and above their remit by putting the shitters in her, that was for sure. "That is a load of crap, Audrey, I will go now and see them and tell them their heads will spin if they try that again, if you agree to let him stay here?" He pressed home on her now. He had cause to be optimistic when she bit her lower lip and drummed her expertly done clear fingernails upon the blue-painted door.

"Okay then, if you can guarantee that they won't bother me for doing so." She forced a concerned smile in agreement—She wasn't bad looking considering the state Forsyth had appeared to have become.

Monty sighed and thanked her.

"Well, I have a two-bedroom place here so it will be fine," she told him. Monty wondered if she wanted to rekindle something with Forsyth? One thing was for sure, if Forsyth did get bail, he would be mad not to accept the offer to keep this one toasty on these cold winter nights.

"Okay great, well, he isn't up at court until the new year sadly but in the meanwhile, here is my card." He handed her his business card with his mobile number on it. "Can you give me the details of the police officers who said that to you?"

"Yes, sure, they left a card, I think it's on my fireplace, hold on and I'll fetch it," she said and he watched her ascend the carpeted stairs again. She was very shapely, and her jeans revealed an impressive arse which he followed as she climbed every step.

What's happening to me, this monastic life needs to end soon.

She soon returned and handed him a yellow incident card with 'DI Calvin Bennett' handwritten upon it.

"Right Audrey, can you also give me a contact number please?" he asked, whilst fetching a pen from an inside pocket. Which, when she recited hers off by heart, he wrote down on the same yellow calling card. "Thanks very much." He smiled and made to leave. "I will be in touch regarding how I get on with the police, hopefully in the next few days or so," he promised her.

"Thank you, Mr Montgomery." She beamed back at him. Monty thought that she might have a distant Mediterranean background. Her eyes were smoky and she had the whitest teeth he thought he had ever seen. "Will I be able to go and see him?" she asked. "I work nights mostly, I'm a nurse but free during the day, Mr Montgomery."

"Call me Stephen,"

Oh aye.

"but no, no visitors allowed Audrey. It's for the best anyway until I sort this particular cop out," he said before then turning and walking down the garden path. Then he heard the door close behind him, checked the street out to see if there was any company—seemed safe enough, so he jumped back in the car with renewed optimism. He would go over to Fettes now and instigate a tug on this DS Bennett's collar then, he sighed.

He drove over to Fettes thinking about why the cops would be setting Forsyth up and why on earth they had put the shits on his ex? They must have known that the chances of him getting bail, even if the First Minister was offering him digs in Bute House, would be lower than low. It was a relatively short drive back over Ravelston and down through Craigleith. The snow had stopped now, and the route was relatively traffic-free.

He put the football on the radio again; it sounded like Celtic were probing Ross Country but were unable to unlock their stubborn defence:

"Spaniard Reguero is pulling off some top-drawer saves here to deny Celtic," roared the commentator.

This is what happens when there are games on Boxing and St Stephen's Days, thought Monty, the players are full up with Turkey, he smirked. He wondered if players did actually have a drink on Christmas Day when they were playing the following day. He suspected one or two former players who might have done so. He certainly knew he would have. The best game he had ever played as a teenager had been on the back of a night out, and with a donor kebab still inside him— he had scored a hat-trick.

He smirked just as Virgil Van Dijk came close for Celtic with a header. When he arrived at police headquarters at Fettes, he had to pay for parking, which frustrated him. This council certainly didn't miss a trick, did they, he considered contemptuously as he raked around for pound coins to feed the meter. They had cleverly removed the 10p coin option too from the meters and so considering he only had £3 in 10p coins, and a further £4 in one-pound coins, he had to chuck all the pound coins in just to be on the safe side. Inside Fettes, he was met by someone on the main desk who advised him that no one from professional standards was available today.

Four quid wasted then.

So he identified himself to the elderly chap and asked him to have an email sent to this DI Calvin Bennett. The bloke agreed and took a note of what Monty wanted to pass on.

"Give him my name and firm please and advise that I represent former DS Christopher Forsyth." Monty handed him another one of his cards. "And please advise him that it has come to my attention that he attended the Carrick Knowe address of my client's former partner, and that he advised her that should she allow my client to reside with her, he will install surveillance on her and her property."

The older man wrote this down quite fast without raising his head.

"And that I should like to discuss this with him, so ask him to give me a call and should he not do so, I shall instigate a complaint to profession standards," promised Monty. He knew that the old guy would probably also include the fact that Monty had actually attempted to raise matters with professional standards here today, but had been quite unable to do so due to the holidays. Monty guessed that this guy Bennett may consider himself somewhat fortunate on that score and either call him soon to backtrack or even just go away.

Either or, job done.

"I shall pass that through now, Sir, and have it emailed to him today," promised the bloke.

"Much obliged. Merry Christmas," offered Monty as he turned to leave.

"Merry Christmas Sir," replied the bloke as he too turned to go and pass his notes on to someone.

Monty walked slowly back to the car; there was no rush after all, he had paid for it and he doubted that the Celtic were likely to have achieved much in the ten minutes or so that he had been inside police HQ. The sun was out again, though there was still a chill in the air, four seasons in one day was the traditional Edinburgh outlook, he reminded himself as he took in the stunning Fettes collage ahead[89]. The private school with its layered landscape and large gates, had always looked beautiful from whatever angle of the city it was viewed from. By contrast, the state-run Broughton High School which stood directly ahead of him to the east, had the look of a 1980s council estate library. Monty much preferred the architecture of the old city fathers, such as the old Edwardian Broughton school building on Broughton Road, which was now a primary school.

They will destroy this city's beauty in the end.

Anyway, that was him for the day now, so he headed eastwards through Stockbridge with the football on. "Well, Celtic are huffing and puffing here, folks, but the Ross County house is refusing to blow over." The commentator was saying before he was interrupted by a sudden roar from the crowd beneath his gantry. "And Callum McGregor has just rattled the Ross County crossbar with a wonderfully placed effort," he bellowed.

"It was the first touch that set up the elevated, and as you say, well-placed shot onto the woodwork, that was clever," exclaimed the co-commentator.

Monty could hardly hear himself think from the noise of the crowd, so he turned the volume down and drove on; thinking instead about the whole angelic angle again. He wondered about heaven; was it like a metropolis or something out of the old 2000AD comics? He was then interrupted by further roars from the crowd and excited shouts from both commentators: "And Ross County have just hit the post after brilliantly hitting Celtic on the break." Gasped one.

---

[89] The fee-paying school was originally opened in 1870 and follows the English, as opposed to the Scottish education system, and has nine houses. In the 1960s, the school was pressed into selling land to allow Telford Collage, Fettes Police HQ and Broughton High School, to be built. In fiction, Ian Fleming stated in his 1964 novel, Y*ou Only Live Twice*, that James Bond had been a pupil.

Monty instinctively slowed down at Hectors Bar to turn left but then he remembered that the council had struck again here too, by putting bollards up blocking access onto Glenogle Road.

I bet that has done the old Victorian baths a great turn financially.

Just how many businesses and drivers careers had this council destroyed with their endless vanity projects, he wondered. He drove on now but there was considerable congestion eastwards on Henderson Row as a consequence, so he continued southwards and up into the city.

"Van Dyke just smashed a rasping drive across the County goal mouth but there were no takers there, Jim," shouts the commentator. Monty saw a baker's shop to his right and felt his stomach rumble now. He turned the match off and headed east via Queen Street and York Place. As he rolled into Leith via Picardy Place, he turned left at the grand old roundabout which had once homed an impressive Edwardian clock. The council had taken down the old ticker and dug the whole thing up to run their trams down and into Leith, but the Leith route had not materialised. The labour costs had been wasted and there remained now nothing more than a tarmac patch with concrete kerbing and no sign of the old clock?

Their incompetence is destroying this town piece by piece.

He drove along London Road with the intention of entering Leith via Easter Road, however there were the usual barriers and "Road Closed." signs which forced him to continue on into Abbeyhill, but the route into Leith down Alva Place was also closed off now so he had no choice but to press on into Meadowbank. The former commonwealth games stadium came into view ahead to his left. He could recall when top-level football had been played there back in the 80s, and also having seen Prince perform live there from the flat window of a party on Wishaw Terrace in the 90s[90].

The council had faced protests when they had sought to sell the stadium to property developers around the same time the old clock had disappeared from the London Road roundabout, but the "Save Meadowbank" group had taken a stand against them, he recalled as he finally found a cut-off into Leith via Marionville.

He stopped at a small shop on Lochend Road and picked up some tins of tuna and a couple of baking potatoes. On the television behind the shop counter, there

---

[90] The late artist known as Prince played an evening gig at Meadowbank Stadium in July 1993.

was news coming in about an exodus of migrants into Europe via Turkey. The volume was turned down but a few customers were quietly watching it whilst waiting to be served. There was an elderly gent serving who looked tired. Monty noted that one or two people were shaking their heads at the scenes of the women with infants trudging across snowy roads in the Balkans on their way to Germany and then potentially on to France and Britain. There were also images of improvised tents and blow-up dinghies abandoned across a Turkish shingle beach.

"Five twenty please," the old shop keeper asked someone.

Monty wondered why these people were being allowed to travel like this in such extreme conditions. The lawyer in him questioned both the morality and legality of forcing babies, to cross the Aegean Sea from Turkey to Greece, and then to further force them to endure a long journey into Germany? He was aware that most of them were fleeing from wars in Afghanistan, Iraq and Syria, but wondered why they were not told to stay in the safe haven that is Turkey, instead of this all this insanity that he was viewing?

Then separate images of David Cameron and a fag smoking Nigel Farage appeared on the screen regarding something else entirely. Monty paid for his stuff and headed back to the car. He quickly turned the radio on again to hear the final results and discovered that County had held Celtic to a draw, which caused him to shake his head in despair.

Things were just getting worse everywhere.

Then he heard that Hibs had tanked Rangers 4-0 and so he cheered up slightly. He soon arrived on his street to discover that the parking space which he had previously occupied, outside his front door, was still available.

Not so bad then.

As he stepped out onto the pavement, he could feel a frosty chill in the air now. The sludge was starting to freeze again he noticed as he stepped onto the pavement. Then he heard something approaching to his left, he instantly tensed up and turned to see a young dark-haired male approaching him on the pavement. Monty quickly checked behind him and then to his right, but there was no one else in the vicinity. Sensing danger however, he turned to face the male with the instinct of an antelope that catches the scent of the lion upon the breeze?

"Hello there," said the man who appeared to have a trace of oriental about him—mixed race perhaps, thought Monty. There had been no mistaking his twang though—Edinburgh. "You are Stephen Montgomery the lawyer, are you not?" asked the man with one of those fake smiles that was betrayed by the lack of any movement of his orbicularis oculi muscle.

"No, I am his brother," replied Monty swiftly enough to force the man's advance towards him to momentarily halt. "And you are?" Monty forced a smile of his own—hand in pocket he released his car keys and instantly found the cork. With his thumb and forefinger—pause now. The man was about 5.10 in height with an athletic frame, which was evident thanks to the fashionably tight jacket he was wearing.

"I don't think so." He eventually grinned after a moment.

"And you are?" Monty dropped his fake smile now and repeated the question.

The man stood there smiling as if he were taking Monty in.

Dai, thought Monty, but the man read his thought and understood.

"Who are you?" Monty demanded to know.

"I'm a man like you, so no one will come to help you."

"And what do you want?"

"To ask you why it is that you are making non-standard efforts for a murderer in a police station, but having just learned your thought, I see whose teat it is that you are drawing from," replied the man.

"And whose teat would that be?" Monty raised his chin in contempt.

Instead of replying however, the man turned towards Monty's front door and sniffed twice in short succession, "Nice doggy," he said before turning back to meet Monty's furious gaze.

"Touch my dog and you'll die—it's that simple," assured Monty in a softly yet chilling manner. His anger was brewing and he stood ready to strike out first.

The best way to defend is to attack.

The man smiled at him to tempt more of a reaction and it was touch and go for a moment. "Amusement is superior to rage because the greatest fighter is never angry," whispered an unknown voice in Monty's ear now.

"Where are you?" He stirred and looked around but he couldn't see anyone.

The man was confused now too and obviously had not heard the voice , so he impulsively also looked around in panic. "Touch my dog and I'll kill you," Monty promised again, before whipping out the cork which he expanded into the curved weapon, and drew back over his shoulder as if to strike down upon the no longer smiling man.

"Where are you?" he shouted now, which alarmed the man even more so and he continued to look around whilst taking a step back.

"Here," replied the guardian angel who suddenly appeared alongside Monty on the pavement in a long black overcoat and grey leather boots. His eyes were emerald green and his red hair was long. He was tall, about 6.1, and when he set his piercing gaze upon the man instead of Monty, he was looking down upon him. Suddenly, the man raised both his hands up into the air as if someone was pointing a gun at him, and then began walking slowly backwards along the pavement.

"It was just a probe," he nodded at the angel who in turn did not respond. Both Monty and the angel remained still, allowing the man to retreat along the pavement.

"He was trying to intimidate you, but he had no authority to attack either you or yours," assured the angel without taking his gaze from the man who now got into a blue VW van parked a few yards along the road and who then reversed it backwards on to Academy Street instead of driving forward past Monty and the angel. Then the sound of the car window coming down...

"They will marshal all the media powers of darkness to hound his credibility to the point of assisted suicide," the man shouted back at the angel before then doing a three-point turn manoeuvre and recklessly accelerating away.

"Well, if he is a man, how come he can hear my thoughts and knew what you were?" asked Monty.

"Just because he claimed to be a man does not mean that he was, nor that he spoke the truth," replied the angel.

"So, what was he then?" asked Monty, turning for the first time to look at the being beside him.

"Another hybrid," smirked the angel whose radiance caused Monty to look away again for a moment. When he then looked back again, the angel had vanished. Monty's heart was pounding now, he quickly let himself into the house and locked the door again before checking that the dog was alright, which of course it was. The file was gone too and one quick check later—the house seemed secure. He removed his coat but kept the cork in his trouser pocket and fetched an old hockey stick from the hall cupboard and placed it within reach upon a spare chair in the lounge. His phone began ringing, it was an unknown number: "Hello?" He sank down upon the sofa beside the tranquil dog.

"Well done." It was Dai.

"Thanks, but I'm really freaking out here, Dai. I mean, will he come back and hurt the dog?" Monty's heart was still pounding.

"He might try," admitted Dai, "However, he saw that your guardian angel revealed himself in your defence, as well as your weapon, which was duly noted I assure you, so unlikely, I would say."

"And will that stop him returning?" Monty wanted to hear it.

"Not necessarily but it is unlikely, as he is only a scout," explained Dai.

"As in just checking me out?"

"Sure," agreed Dai. "You must have made an impression with that little manipulation of the duty Inspector at St Leonards," he revealed with an inner smirk which Monty could sense.

"Why didn't you turn up?" Monty asked him.

"I didn't need to because of the reasons I just mentioned," assured Dai.

"Not because, when it is a man threatening me, you won't intervene?" asked Monty.

"No, because that scout was not a man, in that he had a 3% Nephilim bloodline and so he is to me, an abomination. Nothing protects him from my kind other than the rules; if he attacks you or your dog, he breaks the rules and it is up to me then," promised the angel now and as before, his honesty seemed copiously palpable again.

"But also take comfort from the fact that your guardian angel has shown his preferred response to such thuggery too. The scout knows that you are favoured now, Stephen," Dai pointed out. "So, the chance of any violence against you or yours, is very unlikely," he assured, "but if it were to happen, either you will deal with the threat yourself with your weapon, or, failing that, either myself and/or your guardian angel will step in to protect either you or the dog," he promised.

"Okay." Monty relaxed a little now, for he believed him 100%. "Why are these things allowed to exist, Dai? I mean, why doesn't society know what the hell is going on here?" He shook his head.

"Society is too busy following the trendsetters," replied Dai.

"But if they knew the truth, they would be appalled," insisted Monty.

"Like I say, they are otherwise engaged, Stephen," smirked the angel. "Regrettably, the society you live in is rapidly becoming an Orwellian one. As the dark hoard force their version of reality upon mankind. They are doing this by eradicating the free flow of opinion and of debate, whilst replacing them with chic sentiments and a disdain for morality," he explained.

"When you were a child, Stephen, you wanted to be a policeman didn't you?"

"Yes." Monty recalled wanting to be a police highway patrol officer like the guys from the *CHIPS* TV show.

"Then you wanted to be a lawyer. Many people of your generation also wanted to do likewise, or indeed to grow up to be doctors, firemen, nurses and vets, etc. whilst now, more and more people just crave to be famous and publicly adored. Whether people achieve this by becoming famous, or in the case of the majority, just spend their energy polishing and maintaining a social media image that they hope will create adoration, they are relentless in their commitment to getting there."

"Yes but if they knew what I now know.."

"No Monty," Dai cut him off. "If they did, they would seek to research the ways in which it could propel them to glory. For sure they would play around with the bloodlines and seek to mate with both the Nephilim and even the rebels," he stated confidently.

"It's all just a mess," sighed Monty flippantly.

"You did well though," assured the angel cheerily.

"You think? I was crapping it mate, honestly," admitted Monty.

"Regardless, you were still quite brave," insisted Dai. Both of them chuckled at this but Monty did so through nervousness.

"I expected you to come, that was all," he said.

"Yet even when I did not, you did not take one step backward and drew your weapon to advance forward," Dai pointed out.

"Momentary lapse of reason, I suppose."

"Listen, it is important to understand your enemy, Stephen, which is why I urged you to re-read the file, but it is just as important to know yourself," insisted Dai in the familiar warm, friendly and patient tone that once again reassured Monty.

"Well, they obviously know me now after my visits to both St Leonards and Fettes, so they might send men to jump me next time, now that they know that angels will step in only if it is not a man attacking me," hawed Monty regardless, which caused Dai to chuckle again.

"I seriously doubt they will approach you again after today, Stephen," he assured.

"Because they are haughty and conceited scumbags who believe they will win this trial at a canter?" Monty couldn't help being a tad sarcastic.

"Oh, they know they won't canter the judicial process, which is why they have called upon the Orcadian," Dai felt a need to point out.

"Well, that's just dandy then!" Sighed Monty mockingly. "Next time I will do more than just show them the weapon," he vowed. "In the meantime, if you would excuse me, I need to go and change my underwear." He then hung up, leant his head back, closed his eyes and put his feet up on the coffee table.

That's the spirit, lad, know yourself.

Chapter Thirteen

With cunning they conspire against your people.
Psalm 83:3

August 2015

It... had been an unusually warm evening for August apparently, Calògiru Profaci's neighbour—Holly, had informed him a few hours ago from across the irritatingly small garden fence. It was one of those cheaper woven-panelled jobs which had come with the house, and only encouraged her regular, "yoo-hooing".

Does she think I just sailed into Leith on a banana boat?

Having resided in Edinburgh for several years now, Profaci liked to think he knew the score on many aspects of life in Auld Reekie. He also preferred to be known as 'Charlie', these days, however Holly—a retired school teacher, who was all jolly hockey sticks and chatty, did tend to speak to him as if he were a newly arrived refugee—with an intentionally slow tone which many natives reserve for migrants with a poor grasp of English. Profaci knew how hot it had been today though; it was still warm now as he sat here upon the old fold up deck chair in the back of the stuffy little Berlingo van. He checked his watch—23:58. The air outside was thick with the unpleasant and chaotic fragrance of old shit from the Seafield sewage centre two miles away. Shit which had been steamed by the earlier sunshine and then wafted into the community to blend with the traffic emissions.

He couldn't turn the engine on for the air conditioning however, this would draw attention to the van. Instead, he quietly slid open the side door from time to time, regardless of the stench, and cooled himself. He looked up at the flickering branches of the tall elm trees which lined the badly lit pavement. The shadows of which performed with the streetlights to resemble exotic dancers upon the pavement. On the grass links beyond, there was less light, and so the shadows appeared more ominous; like a living forest. It seemed to Profaci that

310

people were a little like shadows, it just depended upon which side of the light they chose to dance.

He was receiving regular texts now, most of which referred to him as 'Charlie', unlike the Emilia-Romagnans who worked for Jimmy Lazarini, they still called him 'Carlo'. The text sender was a friend, a publican who, in Profaci's absence, was standing in to guest-host the lucrative monthly poker school that he laid on once a month in a flat on the Southside. The place was leased by a prostitute originally from Hull, who earned her coin out of one of the Outfit's saunas in Leith. She had a boyfriend who worked in an Outfit connected restaurant in Bruntsfield—a waiter named Tommy Puleo.

Tommy was a Sicilian like Profaci, and they had been casual friends for a while now. Puleo's texts were always in Sicilian, such as: "Dda", as opposed to "La"; or "Bunu", instead of "Bene", etc. Neither the Outfit nor the Lazarini crew had any interest in Profaci's poker enterprise; it was purely his gig and Puleo was his wingman.

The girl happily stays over at her Puleo's flat one night a month, and when she returns the following day, there is £500 in cash and some other unused goodies waiting for her. Profaci had a cleaner go over the flat, emptying the bins etc before the girl got home, but the half full bottles of booze, and top-class cuisine, were all left for her. The cleaner also doubled as a waiter throughout the evening too, serving the players the pricey food and booze—and it was becoming a much sought after sitting, as well as a lucrative little earner for Profaci.

Officially, Profaci was helping to run the Lazarini floral chain and the websites, whilst unofficially he was forced to do the sort of thing he was doing now— sitting here in a van, sipping coffee from a flask whilst twiddling his thumbs in the middle of the night.

"Just watch the lawyer's house for a few nights this week and don't let anyone see you," had been Jimmy Lazarini's instructions. "Ivan will take over during the day and then go home again at 8pm when you will return and sit it out in the van again until morning."

Profaci had agreed, of course. He would receive extra coin for doing so, as well as additionally not having to do his day job in the florists; so apart from the boredom, it had been a no-brainer. Deep down, however, he resented being the Sicilian grunt for Lazarini, and it was this resent which was whispering in his ear now, telling him that he had been sold a lemon. He watched the dancing shadows a little longer before sliding the door closed again. There were hardly any

Sicilians in Edinburgh, and many of those who were resident, were students and/or seasonal workers. Most of the established Italians in the city came from the towns of Filignano, Casino and Piccinisco in the Valle Latina south of Rome. Whereas Glasgow's Italian community tended to originate from the Tuscan towns of Barga and Lucca.

Whilst the funny speaking Emilia-Romagni in Lazarini's crew who had persuaded Profaci to give up his future plans in return for a generous employment contract in their floral/narcotics business, thought that they could just click their fingers and give him these shitty little errands because he was a Sicilian.

Profaci had not been involved in any criminality prior to his acquaintance with the Lazarini crew, though his grandfather had been a fence back in Sicily during WWII. The old timer had told him romanticised stories of his days fencing black market sugar and gasoline rations on behalf of a powerful cosca[91] in Trapani. His grandfather's kid brother—Gaspare, had been learned in the art of explosives having started work as a quarry blaster. Gaspare had been involved in two Mafiosi car bombs which had killed individuals in the 1960's[92]. Apparently he had visited America in the 1970's wherein he is thought to have passed on his skills to certain parties who intended using them against informers[93].

Here in Edinburgh however, Profaci's criminal experiences were quite different; his employers were narcotic merchants and the stakes couldn't have been any higher financially. The Lazarini crew were in the Ivy League of Scottish crime by 2014. Jimmy Lazarini ran a sophisticated and highly effective operation for sure, but the risk factor involved suggested to Profaci that the venture lacked longevity. They had lost two deliveries in the past eighteen months and Profaci

---

[91] Cosca: (pronounced koska) in Italian, (Plural cosche in Italian, and coschi in Sicilian) means clan. A cosca is also the crown of spiny, closely folded leaves found on artichokes and thistles, which represents a closeness of relationship between the members of Sicilian Mafiosi clans.

[92] In the 1960s, the Sicilian Mafia, unlike their American associates, escalated reciprocal murders by replacing the traditional lupara (sawn-off shotgun) with bomb-making equipment. Notably the car bombings of Ciaculli in 1963, Pizzolungo in 85, Capaci in 92 and Via D'Amelio also in 1992— were high-profile examples.

[93] In 1977 in Evansville, Indiana, an American millionaire Oil magnet and hotelier_Ray Ryan, died from a car bomb explosion. The bomb was connected to the ignition of his Lincoln Mark V coupe. Ryan had previously testified against the American Mafia. His murder remains unsolved.

was aware that with rapidly developing technology, the whole thing would be nothing more than a deck of cards once any of the Lazarini grunts got pinched for something serious—because there simply weren't enough buffers between the grunts and the higher echelons of the firm. Profaci knew that most of them would roll over in custody and create a wind that would blow the rotten house down quickly. It seemed logical to suggest that there should be more buffers between the grunts and the organ grinder.

There fucking would be if I were running the show.

For some reason Jimmy Lazarini had taken a liking to Profaci and placed him under his wing. In return Profaci ran the computer network for the floral chain as well as other business that Lazarini owned. Or at least those were Profaci's official roles, as Lazarini was using him more and more as a wheelman[94] and transporter these days. Of course, this unexpected career twist had provided money in the bank for Profaci, which he was grateful for, but it was a life wherein he was now constantly looking over his shoulder for cops, other villains and informers.

There was not a day went by that he did not contemplate the dangers that accompanied the commerce he was neck deep in, and so he was forced to live his life accordingly—with passport and cash on standby in case of an emergency. This perpetual threat prevented Profaci from relaxing and enjoying his life; which seemed to him to defeat the purpose of having money at all.

The sentiment was growing on him. He possessed a general lack of appreciation towards the Scottish weather and lifestyle, too. Perhaps more irritating to him however, was the Emilia-Romagni and their distasteful habit of bringing in East European guys as associates. Despite having no active history with the Sicilian Mafia, Profaci understood all the old Sicilian traditions of running a crime organisation—which had once been—honour, tradition, and omerta. These were the principles which went back to the old Black Hand (*La Mano Nera*) who had thrived on the old rackets of extortion, shylocking and gambling.

---

[94] Driver.

When the old Moustache Petes[95] had first gone to the States and packed their traditions into their suitcases, they had come up against the Young Turks[96], who had wanted to bring non-Sicilians, such as Italians, Jews and Irish, into the rackets. This had resulted in a war between the youngsters and the old guard in New York City, which the old Sicilians lost. Profaci believed that the subsequent ruin of omerta within La Cosa Nostra[97] in America today, was down to this.

He had once heard that in New York, the original Bonanno family had tried to restrict membership to their family to Castelammarese Sicilians, in the belief that blood relations with a Sicilian upbringing were least likely to break omerta. Despite Scotland offering much smaller financial pickings of course, Profaci instinctively felt that similarly, men who would not turn, when picked up by the police, were still a necessity for any criminal organisation that sought to avoid the proverbial stack of cards scenario.

He had tried talking to Jimmy about this from time to time, and of turning the direction of his venture away from narcotics towards other lucrative targets, such as stock market fraud, construction, and fixing sporting events. Both men had become close and so Jimmy had encouraged Profaci to talk freely about business when they were alone, and despite Profaci being Sicilian.

Jimmy had listened to him, and at one point even showed an enthusiasm for the notion of rigging boxing matches. Profaci had pointed out that it was nearly impossible to put any heavy action on a fight these days because the bookies now encouraged online betting, which is all electronically traceable, and so street bookies won't accept cash bets over £5-10k. So, it was hard to put any heavy action on an event unless it was on the specific minute of a knockout or of a goal being scored.

---

[95] Moustache Petes—nickname of the Sicilian Mafiosi who immigrated to America at the beginning of the last century and who mostly committed their first murders in Sicily. The old guard, as they were also known, favoured the traditions of the old country such as targeting the Italian community only for extortion as opposed to the entire American population.

[96] The Young Turks—nickname given to the young Italian/American mafia members led by Lucky Luciano and Vito Genovese, who opposed the old guard (Moustache Pete's), who they believed to have been too set in their ways because of their refusal to branch out and work with Irish and Jewish criminals.

[97] American mafia.

Profaci suggested that the serious money was now in the purses these days, and not in the fixing, so the concentration should be in getting a piece of a fruitful boxer. At one point he had wanted to fix fights between a couple of British heavyweights—Kelso Walters and Ryan McTurk, against Belgian/Italian—Sergio Marini who had been an Olympic Bronze and who was the number two contender for the European heavyweight title. Marini had begun his professional career on a tear, with 18 consecutive victories over limited opposition. Eventually he defeated a former European champion on a cut, and then limped past a former American Olympic gold medal winner on points in New York City.

The scam Profaci proposed was to bypass the European route by getting both Walters and McTurk's ratings up and then getting them to take falls against Marini which would then get Marini's ratings up and set him up nicely for an early challenge to the current undisputed heavyweight champion of the world. Jimmy had gotten somewhat lost in the translation of all of this however, and so had just laughed Profaci off.

Fucking northern inbred couldn't understand.

"What if either of those two fucking idiots accidently put Marini on the canvas?" Jimmy had wanted to know. "After all, mistakes happen, Charlie boy," he had chuckled.

"If they did, they would pick the fucker up," promised Profaci with straight face, which had caused Jimmy to roar with laughter.

At the end of the day though, Jimmy wasn't really interested in anything other than that which he already knew—the tried and tested smack game. This stance had only further persuaded Profaci that Lazarini and his whole crew were a car crash waiting to happen. The drug business, as per the reasoning of the American Young Turks, just didn't sit well with Profaci and it was becoming clear to him that his employers had no intention of ever steering course away from what he regarded to be a dangerous enterprise.

The Armenians were also rising in Scotland and they would soon present a competitive challenge, along with various other crews. This would lead to messy disputes and these Lazarini *Cafoni*[98], it seemed to Profaci, would intend wiping their bloody knives upon his sleeve at that time. Such were the concerns weighing upon Charlie Profaci's mind as he sat there now in the back of the florist van, playing babysitter to this lawyer. It was so easy to feel contempt, but he persisted in resisting such sentiment. Clearly he knew deep down that he was

---

[98] Sicilian slang (plural) meaning peasants.

better than this shit. He should be in his bed enjoying the slumber of the virtuous, as opposed to sitting here like a fucking spare prick watching shadows on pavements with the smell of shit in his nostrils. He felt like a murderer at his victim's wake, what was he going to do anyway if anyone did come along and try to break into this brief's house?

"Just call Ivan and then set about whoever it is threatening the lawyer, with that crowbar in the back of the van," had been his instructions.

That's potentially a murder charge, and for some fucking brief that I don't even know—while you inbred sheep-shaggers remain in the shadows.

There had previously been an opportunity to escape from all of this. Profaci. He had been invited to go into partnership with another Sicilian in Manchester named Sergio "Joe Pesto" Prestogiacomo, who owned a few B&B businesses down there. Profaci believed they could be developed into small hotels with bars and restaurants. He knew Pesto through a female friend from his student days whom he had always kept in touch with. Both men got along well and Profaci trusted him; the key factors being that they were both from the same part of Sicily and had similar dry senses of humour.

Pesto was a Don Rickles type who was remarkably similar in both appearance and in his mannerisms. He had Rickles wittiness about him which always brought a smile to Profaci whenever they met; so it was clear that should they work alongside each other, there would be endless banter on tap.

Whenever he considered his position in Edinburgh, Profaci found that he missed the simplicity of the life he had back in Trapani too. The son of a struggling photographer yes, but a warm climate where he had been surrounded by proper speaking paisanos[99]. He had not minded the first couple of years in Edinburgh, though. He had been introduced to tax-free cash, and comfortable lifestyle. Like all young bulls, he had assumed that he was invulnerable and so the risk factors had not concerned him in his earlier pursuit of coin.

Money was the language of youth after all.

He realised now however that when men are young the penalties of crime seem almost immaterial because youth misleads so many into considering themselves to be either too clever or too lucky to ever get pinched. Profaci now

---

[99] The plural of Paisano (Sicilian, Neopolitan, and Spanish) and Paesano (Italian)—meaning, a person from the same part of Italy as oneself. Though notably there is also Paysan (France) and Paisanos in America, which relates to a person from California with mixed Native American and Spanish ancestry.

recognised this folly and noted that many other young bulls didn't see the reality of their susceptibility until they became either old men, being told what time is lights out by some random carer, or banged up in a tiny cell for an exceedingly long time.

He was becoming drawn to leaving his life here with Jimmy Lazarini, who, he did like and had been loyal toward. The money was still intoxicating though, and Profaci wouldn't have to risk screwing the personal savings he had accumulated, should he decide to remain here a little longer.

Money talks, after all.

He had thought that one day he might buy a property near Palermo where he could live and hopefully teach computers and English. He would have considerable savings in the bank in say, five years from now, if he played his hand well enough here and stuck it out. He sighed; these conflicting musings were almost an everyday occurrence these days and when combined with the constant looking over his shoulder, contributed to a stressful life.

Money talks though.

This had not been the only miserable task they had placed him on, of course. Every Christmas he had to lead a team of ten guys for a month, whose entire purpose was to steal and flog Nobel Fir trees for Lazarini. This required four large vans to travel up north to various locations such as Tentsmuir forest, in order to find and extract these trees without alerting the Forestry Commission. This meant petrol chainsaws weren't an option and neither were headlights; so, it was always an arduous ninja style operation. Followed thereafter by a panicky retreat back across the Forth Bridge to Edinburgh before various return trips over the next few nights until they had accumulated a vast stockpile of trees that they stored at an old Edwardian factory in Leith.

Then they had been ordered to set up various unlicensed street stalls flogging said trees each day in the run up to Christmas between Musselburgh and Corstorphine. There had been some close calls, frozen feet from standing in snow all day, and plenty of wasted money on hot junk-food such as chips and curry sauce, and watered-down soups, from bakers etc; as the men tried to avoid hyperthermia.

Then in the end, all Profaci got for this risky enterprise was a poxy three grand to put in his tail on Christmas Eve—in exchange for what could have otherwise ended up as a prison sentence. He now looked at himself in the van's rear-view mirror—"*Sceccu*"[100] he sighed. He was tired and a little hungry too now, so he lit up a cigarette and leaned out of the sliding door again. Running along the top of Monty's street was the busier Duke Street with its pubs and takeaways. Profaci could see them from where he was parked. He now watched the East End Bar staff pulling down the noisy metal shutters next door to Spicuzza's meat store.

He read the hand-painted signs upon the store whilst slowly exhaling tobacco smoke: Salsiccia Pizzaiola, Capicola, Sopressata, Prosciutto, Cacciatorini, Provolone and Toscano. His mouth watered as he imagined some veal served with lupine or ceci beans in a sweet marsala sauce. No Italian restaurant in Edinburgh served such Sicilian delicacies sadly, so he sighed again and pinged his cigarette away before leaning back inside and fishing out a packet of chewing gum from his coat pocket. He then lay back into the deck chair chewing and watching Monty's house for a while.

The shadows of the tree branches continued to dance like the spirits of long dead cobras across the windscreen glass; the street eerily silent as neither people nor cars ventured passed. There was something comforting about this and he could imagine what the foxes felt like, hidden in their dens, observing the dangerous world of men beyond, only too aware that to reveal themselves in daylight would create vulnerability. He dozed off to this thought with his phone on his lap and the crowbar at his heel. He stirred five or six times during the night whenever a car or voice came into earshot. Placing one tired eye upon his phone and the other on Monty's doorway, before then closing them again for another little while.

It was 6am when he started hearing the familiar sound of the heavy diesel bus engines roaring their way along Duke Street behind him. He yawned and got up and hauled himself over into the front driver's seat where he opened the window and lit up a cigarette. As usual, it tasted as shit as every other early morning smoke he had ever taken before brushing his teeth, so he only had a couple of drags on it before pinging it into the gutter.

The UK general election was approaching in the next few days and many of the flats across the road on Profaci's left, had SNP signs on the windows with the odd Labour and SLP ones peppered here and there too; behind which there were lights coming on and signs of an awakening city. Profaci watched as a couple of women appeared now from a stairway door then promptly walked their

---

[100]Sceccu (Italian, "Asino") is Sicilian slang for donkey.

dogs across the road to the Links for the loo. before they got ready for work. A taxi appeared and dropped off a fat bloke with orange hair who was carrying a green rucksack and wearing what may have been a security guard's uniform.

Just then, a small female jogger flashed by the driver's window. Profaci initially got a fright but he was soon close to laughter as the baseball capped and Lycra-wearing jogger had been farting like a trooper as she trotted along the pavement. He wanted to roll down his window and call out some smart-arse remark to let her know she had been heard, but it had been a long watery fart that had sounded like a duck drowning, and so he preferred not to catch a waft of it. After a while, his stomach began rumbling; he had forgotten to eat prior to driving down to Leith last night for this shit and he could do with more coffee. He stretched over into the back to check the flask he had brought, but alas it was empty.

He settled back into the seat; it was going to be another warm one today he could tell. He turned the radio on and searched for some music, it was the usual political madness being discussed on almost every station, however, in the end, he left one on for some company. It was a recording of the British Labour leader Ed Miliband, who sounded like he was talking through his nose as usual. Miliband was having a go at Prime Minister—David Cameron's Conservative Party, whom, he claimed, was receiving dodgy donations from even dodgier donors.

Then another man came on: "With me now are the Labour MP Philip Townsend, Lib Dem MP Susan Bell, and our Election analyst Louise Wright. Good morning all. Erm what do we make of that then, Philip Townsend MP for Merseyside West?" he asked in a South-West Irish accent.

"Well, it is obviously Ed raising justifiable concerns about who is funding the Tory party, as well as the revolving door between them and the Swiss branch of HSBC," replied Townsend.

"More cronyism then?" enquired the young Irishman.

"Precisely, Anthony. But look, this is nothing new is it, we saw it with Cameron's appointment of Coulson, and then more recently—Stephen Green," confirmed the vaguely Scouse-sounding Townsend.

"And Susan Bell, your party, who are in a coalition with the Tories, are avoiding this tit-for-tat between Labour and your coalition partners and are instead focusing upon an election campaign which promotes your party as a future coalition partner to either Mr Miliband or Mr Cameron?" teased Anthony.

319

"Well no, Anthony," insisted the Lib Dem from Leith, "what the Liberal Democrat Party is focussing upon, is our own hymn book throughout this campaign, and we feel that because we have shown that we will make less cuts than the Conservatives, whilst borrowing considerably less than Labour, the British public now find themselves with a third option to lean on in these strenuous financial times," she declared overly gayly.

"So you do not feel that by stating to a Labour-inclined or Tory-inclined audience that your party is offering a clear head to a coalition with Labour, and some empathy to a coalition with the Conservatives, that you are in actual fact telling them that their parties are brainless and cold?" asked Anthony.

There was group chuckling now but Profaci turned it off; he was sick of it all. Naturally he took an interest in British politics but it had all been so crazy with Indyref last year, which he couldn't help getting dragged into—he just wanted some peace now. He had been quite relieved when it had all ended last year, but now there was this UK General Election to contend wherein the SNP were being challenged for their Westminster seats not only by Labour and the Lib-Dems, but by the other pro-independence party—the SLP.

He yawned. He had had enough of politics and instead trained his thoughts upon breakfast; but even now he found himself at another cross-border debate—A full English or Scottish fry-up on nearby Leith Walk[101]. Profaci suspected that a lot of the public would secretly vote for the Tories but not publicly admit it to friends or family. Mainly because he sensed that people had faith in Cameron continuing to lead the country out of the financial deficit.

The Tories had at least successfully begun cleaning up the mess and voters may well consider it to be a work in progress, and thus back them again to conclude the mop up job. Letting anyone else in now to govern, particularly Labour again, just wouldn't seem palatable to the majority of voters who now resented the present pinch. As for Scotland, it was probably a case of who between the SLP and the Lib-Dems would come second to the SNP, judging by what Profaci had seen and heard.

His spirits lifted again momentarily as he recalled something Jimmy had said to him a month or so back. His boss had been as vague as usual, but had hinted that there may be a "big job" coming up soon, wherein Profaci could possibly

---

[101] The English fry-up breakfast usually includes black pudding whereas the Scottish equivalent traditionally has haggis, tattie scones, and in some cases—fruit and suet dumpling.

earn big bucks for a just few hours work; whatever that meant. Regardless, if anything ever came to fruition and turned out to be a big enough earner, he could potentially take the money and leave this place. Then again, nothing had been said again about it for a few weeks now, so it could just as easily come to nothing.

Hunger was getting the better of him now and he was thinking that he needed to go eat soon. Then he noticed an old grey BMW arriving and pulling up on the opposite side of the road. From out of which, he was delighted to see Ivan carrying two polystyrene cups of coffee. Ivan was a tall, stocky, and ugly looking type, who had worked the doors for the Outfit in their brothels back in the day prior them beginning the winding down their interests. Jimmy Lazarini had noted that Ivan needed work, so chucked him a bone every now and then. The dayshift bodyguard gig on Monty, was yet another one of them.

Ivan, who was apparently just back from a weekend in Dubai with a lap-dancer called Inga, was wearing a black suit with open red shirt. He had probably been told to look sharp as he spent the day shadowing Monty around the courts. Profaci however, reckoned that he looked more like a caged fighter who was impersonating a Flamenco dancer up town on a Saturday night. He couldn't have cared less however, whether Ivan suited the suit or not, for Ivan was always polite to him and so Profaci liked the big Russian. He gazed over at him now as excitedly as if Ivan were Monica Bellucci—naked on roller skates—bearing a tray of bacon rolls and a hot coffee.

"Morning Charlie." Ivan crouched into the front passenger seat and handed Profaci a cup.

"Morning Ivan and thanks." Profaci was delighted.

Ivan slurped at his before asking, "So how was the night?" His complexion was flushed from his desert jollies with Inga.

"Quiet. How was Dubai?" Shrugged Profaci.

"Very hot," smirked the Russian before taking another sip. "We should get something going over there you know, some sort of lottery or something as there is a lot of money to be had," he suggested.

A numbers racket in Dubai?

"Yeh right, like fucking Sam Giancana[102]," sneered Profaci.

---

[102] Salvatore "Sam" Giancana was head of the Chicago faction of the American/Italian commission known as La Cosa Nostra from the late 1950s until the early 1970s. Originally a driver for Al Capone back in the 1920s, Giancana climbed to the top due to his ability to make money for the Chicago mob. It had been under Giancana's watch that

"Who?"

"Nobody."

Money talks.

At that, they both looked over to see Monty now leaving his house with the dog and heading over towards the Links. "Right, that's me then," said Ivan.

"See you tonight Ivan." Nodded Profaci—raising his cup.

"See you," replied the big man as he crouched to exit the vehicle, before then casually following Monty and his dog at a distance—continuing to sip at his coffee.

Across the city in an office occupied by the higher strata of the Crown Prosecution Service, on the top floor of an old edifice on Ramsey Lane, the Orcadian sat at a desk reading the file on the accused Christopher Forsyth. There was no one else around at this time of the morning except a security guard who had let him in and who was now downstairs watching TV. He had been provided with a luxury property in Cramond by one TIC member, and to use as his own throughout his time in Edinburgh. His kind did not sleep much, resolved to press on with this irritating matter before he could then enjoy the short time he would have left before returning to his incarceration.

He glanced up at the old ticking clock on the mantelpiece above the even older fireplace opposite—it was almost 7am—he would have peace for another hour or so before the talking monkeys began turning up for work. He had been in this iteration of Scotland for a while now since his assent from the Caves of Drach. His role this time was that of Deputy Advocate Oliver Farquharson QC. This time he was a tall, dark-haired and slim man with deep green eyes that appeared to see through those whom they focused upon. His mission was to ensure a conviction of the accused within the confines of Scottish criminal law.

A simple enough proposition; it was all Latin-based after all. Why he had been sent in, he could not be quite sure? An order was an order and he was thankful of it regardless. He suspected that it was must have been because of

---

Chicago had become the most influential crew on the Las Vegas hotel strip as well as owning casinos in pre-Castro Cuba. Following the fall of Cuba to Fidel Castro, Giancana sought to establish a Persian Vegas in pre-Islamic revolution Iran where he opened a lucrative casino in the early 1970's. He was murdered in his Chicago home in 1976. There has been some suggestion that he was killed for not sharing the profits of the Iranian casino with his friends in Chicago.

some concern about the talking monkeys inability to conclude matters satisfactorily.

He had gone through all the ceremonial crap on the day that he had arrived in Edinburgh—a tedious process. The self-absorbed monkeys had laid on all the pomp and glad rags at a celebratory gathering at a remote property outside of the city, wherein they had banged on about astrological and geometrical alignments that they all presumed to understand. The selected monkeys of TIC had also been in attendance and had covered the place in hieroglyphical images which they believed reflected the side they thought they were batting for. The medieval robes that they had all been wearing, almost caused him to laugh but he had never been one to mock a monkey for its traditions.

To him, there was no honour in arsing things up and pleading for support from his kind, but he could hardly grumble as he was after all, free again to a certain extent. Still, he had little time for these mortals at the best of times. They had sacrificed a female baby Orangutan in his honour. Frankly he always found that kind of stuff barbaric and he had wanted to behead every single one of them for it. It was them that he despised, and not the animal, but he was too old in the claw now to forget that he must let them have their silly rituals.

In the end, it is their acts of rebellion that count, regardless of whether or not his choir take pleasure from them. He had asked some of them if they had any knowledge as to why he had been ordered here to see out this job for them, but none had the foggiest idea. They had however described to him how one of their lower-level brethren had talked a little to Forsyth's boss whilst in custody, but that they had contained the conundrum and murdered the traitor as well as said boss. They then explained that instead of taking out Forsyth, they had set him up for a legal fall because they had not fancied drawing more attention to matters. "We have no idea why the dark lord has honoured us with your presence, but we are most honoured and delighted to receive you my lord," insisted one of the monkeys.

"Well, you failed in your plan because this Forsyth now has an opportunity to speak openly in a court," he had informed them.

He could sense an angelic touch to all of this right from the off, and he pointed out to another of the monkeys—a so-called 'Knight of the Sun' who appeared to be in charge of all of them, that the fact that a son of God was having to appear here now in this cold and shitty dimension before such lesser beings, was nothing more than a consequence of human ineptitude. Also, that it seemed clear that they had obviously not sufficiently contained matters, and had in actual fact, lost control of the situation. "You should all be ashamed of yourselves as opposed to celebrating," he had snapped at them.

The head honcho dared not to argue the contrary, instead he had simply stood there like a child caught with its hands in the cookie jar. "I would like you all to shit into your own hands and then bring your hands up to your chests and clap as enthusiastically as you clapped my arrival here a few minutes ago," he had then demanded of them all.

He waited a few moments to watch the majority of them attempt this, but the sight of one old man with his trousers around his ankles, tripping and then collapsing onto his knees in a puddle of his own piss, was enough, and the Orcadian had departed and was driven by a male Nephilim to the house in Cramond they had provided for him. It was an above average property, with an indoor pool and gymnasium yet within a few hours he had the driver take him into the city to his office on the Mound; where he had remained since.

He was now one of several Deputy Advocates who led criminal prosecutions on behalf of the Lord Advocate of Scotland—Maggie Boutellier QC. His role as Farquharson fitted in nicely with his mission—as a Lord Advocate would not be running Forsyth's trial, rather she allocates her deputies to run prosecutions. Farquharson, however, did not truly exist in human form. At least not in this dimension, and was an entirely made-up character who had been spell-formed for this particular mission.

Oliver Farquharson QC, being a temporary device of the Kertamen— he was though recognised within the conscious awareness of. not only Boutellier, but everyone else of relevance within the Scottish judicial system. To them, he was a long serving and well-respected QC with a history in overseas finance—though none knew any more about him than that. Once the trial was closed however, Farquharson would be nothing more than a memory carried away upon the Autumn wind. He was restricted to manoeuvring and researching as a human being might, and so had been stuck here researching the case. The office was wood panelled and resembled a captain's cabin on an eighteenth century two-masted brig. He had done his homework on the lead defence counsel—Mark Dailly QC, and deduced that there was nothing angelic about him nor for that matter, would he be much of a problem.

The answer as to why he was here however, remained evasive, so he had been reading up on the suitcase of paperwork regarding the case, while hoping to confirm his earlier suspicions about monkey incompetence. He paused after another hour or so, and spun his chair away from the desk towards a window with a view down over the Mound and the old Playfair steps. He stood up, hands in pockets, and looked down at the city spread out below that was pressed against the sea beyond. He hated this town, always had. It was a septic tank dressed up to appear as a dolls house for tourists.

It was bright and the sun was to be felt today he knew. There were some gulls hovering above the New Town, like vultures searching for scraps or little rodents they could try to lift then drop to kill, then pick at. He could smell the salty estuary from his side of the window despite all the pollution that the talking monkeys created. He wanted to climb out now and fly down to the water to call for her.

"Ceto"—his breath formed a condensed fog which stained the glass as he mouthed her name. He knew that if he did so of course, he would forfeit the mission and be castigated for it. The last time he had absconded had been during the trial of the Groupe du musée de l'Homme[103] back in February 1942. They had tortured him for that despite him only having been there in an advisory role to the lead prosecutor. His inner anger began to awaken now so he turned away and poured himself a glass of mineral water which he necked in one go—a technique he had applied over the centuries to try to cool the rage.

He paused a while to calm down before then turning around and sitting down to think on the legal case in his head. After another couple of hours passed, he smelled a female approaching outside his door before she lightly knocked it. "Yes?" he replied.

A well-shaped Chinese female in flats, popped her head around. "A message from Maggie, will you brief her on the Forsyth trial at some point today please, Sir?" She had a distinctly west of Edinburgh twang and was in her mid-thirties—not his type then.

"Yes," he dismissed her by lowering his gaze into his papers. He hated their stupidity. Boutellier could have called him without sending her toady along to interrupt him.

---

[103] French group (Group of the Museum of Man), who were an early WWII resistance movement created by intellectuals and academics who, through the disguise of being a literature society, opposed the German occupation. The group was infiltrated in late 1941, and arrests followed which led to a trial by Nazi court. Ten capital punishments and three prison sentences followed.

By professing that they have become wise, they have made themselves fools.

The door closed again. He looked up now at the framed picture beside the clock on the wall above the fireplace which he had turned around. He could see the image of Jack Kennedy upon it regardless, because it was imprinted in his memory as were the words typed beneath:

The great enemy of the truth is very often not the lie, deliberate, contrived and dishonest, but the myth, persistent, persuasive and unrealistic.

Oh what the hell, he was ready because he was the enemy of truth—he picked up the phone on his desk and typed in the three-number extension which automatically came to mind.

"Hello, Lord Advocate's office," the same Chinese female replied.

"Olly Farquharson here. Put me through to Maggie," he demanded coldly.

"One moment Sir." Bach began playing—he hated Bach for his damned cheerfulness.

Then there was a click followed by: "Good morning, Olly." It was the smooth-talking Boutellier.

"Aye Maggie. The case is ready to run," he cut straight to the chase whilst leaning back and putting his feet up upon the desk—black brogues shiny and new.

"Good stuff. Does that mean that you will have some time to help Andrea out with her historic abuse case?" she asked.

"Yes boss," he lied.

"Great, well, I just wanted to confirm that your one was ready to run Olly."

"Thanks. Toodle-oo." He hung up. She did not feel anything of consequence at him having done so, for she was charmed by his enchantment and so instantly forgot and moved on to other matters. He then removed his feet from the desk and began sorting out the case. He could see that they had provided false witnesses and one in particular—who didn't know his arse from his nose. He was considering this when his phone rang:

"Yes?" he snapped again.

"A Philip Trevelen calling for you, sir." An older female now, perhaps late fifties, informed him.

"Fine." He sighed down his nose. He knew who Trevelen was, knew everything about him, he had been at the ceremony yesterday and had been one

326

of the few who had successfully clapped his own shit into his face. Despite having little interest in him, the Orcadian was aware that Trevelen was TIC and probably part of the reason he was having to mop up their mess. Therefore, he decided to allow the arrogant chimp a brief moment.

"Hello, Mr Farquharson." Trevelen sounded excited but the Orcadian saw immediately that the thrill was fuelled by fear. "My name is Philip Tre—"

"What say you then, Trevelen?" he cut him off to ask with a dash of brogue for eminence.

"My lord, I am your servant throughout your stay and humbly wanted to invite you to have dinner at my home this evening," said Trevelen ever so politely.

The Orcadian considered this for an awkwardly long moment before snapping back: "Breakfast in one hour and twenty minutes, Trevelen." He then hung up, leaned back in his chair again and placed his feet back upon the desk. "Wannabe," he whispered to himself in a New York accent. He had seen clearly that the purpose of this telephone call from Trevelen was to attempt to do as Trevelen always tended to do—piggy-back ride on others' karma. Trevelen had done this with regard to his in-laws' wine business and intended now to connect himself to the arrival of a rebel angel who had dropped into his manor to tidy up the incompetence of his idiot brethren.

"Arrogant ape," he hissed. He could see Trevelen running out his door now and hear him swearing as he slipped on his gravel driveway, whilst frantically rushing to go and buy some food. He hated men so much, always had. He then stood up again and returned to the view of the sea from the window which drew him in like a beast upon it's pray. He gazed at the coastline a little more. Then he forced himself to consider the various Scottish Saltires and Union Jack flags which fluttered atop many of the buildings below. Oh yes, that's right, they are spiralling into a period of political chaos here aren't they, he sneered.

He now closed his eyes and used his superior sensitivity to review the intel on the election aspirants and the interpretations any of them had of arcane knowledge. Cameron, Miliband, Clegg and Bennett. All of them arguing that they will lead the pond-life better than the other monkeys. One or two of them might even have done so, should they not all have to resign soon. "Fasten your seatbelts chimps."

He grinned and opened his eyes again—bored with the subject now. Again, his gaze dropped out to the sea beyond the chimp hive. He stood there for a while

327

remembering, before then abruptly turning on his heels and striding out of his office and down along the carpeted corridor, also with wooden panelled walls, to a doorway which descended down a stone stairway that he positively glided down.

Upon reaching the main foyer, there were several people sat at desks who were either taking calls or reading emails, and he swept past them all like an ice dancer and then on past the fat security guard at the entrance, and who did not notice him. Then he was out upon the timeworn cobbles which wound down towards the Mound. Across the road, his hybrid driver was sat at the wheel of a Mercedes reading the Scottish political magazine—Manifesto.

The Orcadian could sense that it was a piece on the SLP's pledge to bring in national community service for all 16-21-year-olds who were not in either employment or further education. "They will be a great help in repairing Scotland's roads, buildings and natural countryside." It quoted another talking chimp as saying. He also knew that his hybrid driver was carrying a loaded Browning BDA in a holster under his blazer. When he got into the back of the car, he telepathically asked the driver if he knew Philip Trevelen.

"I know of him, my lord."

"Good. Take me to the Cramond house then go and arrange to have him punished for telephoning my office on a whim," he softly demanded.

"May I ask how severe, my lord?" The hybrid had the balls to ask, whilst knowing that Trevelen was both TIC brethren and a well-connected one at that.

"Nose, jaw, maybe an eye socket and a few ribs, but not his life."

"And then shall I return to Cramond, my lord?"

The Orcadian needed a break from the idiots in the office already and would return in the evening when they had all gone home. "No. I will alert you when I require you again."

"Yes, my lord, do you need my phone numb—"

"No!"

The engine started and the hybrid drove the car without another thought.

As the car crept down the cobbles towards the red traffic light on the Mound, something piqued the Orcadian's interest over to his right-hand side. There at an old stone archway which lead into that citadel of conscience and theological buffoons—New Collage—appeared a small thin teenage female, looking slightly confused. She was Jewish, no wait…he put his window down and attempted to catch her scent but it was no use, this place was riddled with monkeys and most of them tourists from all corners of the dimension, and he was overwhelmed with aromas.

"Stop and wait," he used his mind to tell the driver. Then he got out, hands in suit pockets, and curtly crossed the road towards her. She was about eighteen, slim, blue eyes, olive-coloured skin and long brown hair which was brushed over to one side and reached down to her elbows. Her face was beautiful, Jewish he believed. She wore black dungarees and a red and white polka dot long-sleeved top and new white Converse on her feet. And she was carrying a bag that she was now attentively rummaging through as he approached his pickings.

He caught her scent now, there was a distant twang of the Levi tribe somewhere from down her ancestry, fused with French and Viking stock. He slowed his pace momentarily in the way a good footballer does when reading a move, and just as she raised her head to read a sheet of paper she had found, he timed it flawlessly and intercepted her. "Hello," he said gently in a southern Idaho drawl. "You look mighty lost there." He beamed at her gaily.

Her lovely blue eyes took him in now as he stood before her. He was stunningly beautiful to her now and looked exceptionally dapper in his suit too. "I erm, well I…" She was an English Yah.

"You are new to the city, an undergraduate, who has arrived early before freshers week in order to settle in and who has come here to look around before you meet the only other person you know in this city—your flatmate, for lunch nearby but you can't figure out the photocopied map they sent you in the post last month," he told her smugly.

"Gosh, how did you know all that?" She grinned from ear to ear, for she was not only stunned by his knowledge, but was also overwhelmingly attracted to him and wanted to kiss him.

"I'm a lecturer here and I've seen this scenario many times," he smiled back at her. "Hi, I'm Professor Ralph Peterson and I teach Hebrew here." He offered his hand to her while gesturing towards the archway with the other one. She was beginning to slow down now, stunned and light-headed.

She was unable to remove her eyes from his gaze, nor stop smiling either— "I…I am Imogen and I…am…going to study Hebrew here next month," she replied as she slowly reached out a limp wrist and let him shake her hand.

The moment she touched him, everything changed. She now felt him in her head and had no power to move or to speak freely. "You can skip lunch and come to my place instead, it is not very far." He smirked.

329

"But what?"

"Don't speak, child, just get in my rig there," he transmitted the order into her mind whilst gesturing with a curt and over-magnanimous flick of his wrist. She did not want to now, but her brain directed her legs to walk over to the car where she then got in without any fuss. The hybrid neither spoke nor looked in the rear-view mirror. The Orcadian followed her in and then commanded him to drive to the house in Cramond. It was only when sitting at lights on Queensferry Road that the hybrid sneaked a peek at her in the rear-view mirror.

He could see that she was young and beautiful. Her blue eyes betrayed her inner terror however. The hybrid smiled, excited by her fear. If the Orcadian maintained the bewitching charm, he could have had her easily enough, but instead he had invaded her mind and was now controlling her actions. The hybrid understood this too and had no sympathy for her. He knew that there were few humans who were able to comprehend their own destruction. Then the lights changed and he put his foot down.

Chapter Fourteen

My courage always rises at every attempt to intimidate me.
Jane Austen

Charnley and Monty sat at the kitchen table eating toast and marmalade with their morning coffees. Charnley had been staying in the spare room ever since a strange female in a burgundy velvet coat and hat had purposely stalked Monty home a few weeks previously. She had somehow reached her hand through his front door as a ghost might, and attempted to pull him back out through it onto the street. She had lost her hand for her trouble and her hideous screams had been heard by people as far away as Abbeyhill,

Then she had gone but her high-pitched screeching still rung in some people's ears for at least an hour thereafter. There had been some mention of this high-pitched screeching on a local radio station the following day, just as rumours began developing about it having been some sheet metal work which was being carried out at nearby Leith docks.

It had been a terrifying experience for Monty but his weapon had worked and when Dai had arrived he found him sitting upon the hall tiles with his back against the wall, weapon—upright and still in his hand. The dog was sat beside him, anxious and on full alert. He was, as per his master, panting and drizzled in the female's blood. Dai patted the loyal beast before calming Monty down and slowly taking the weapon from his hand and returning it to its cork-like state.

"A beast of some sort," he had smelt her scent still. Her blood was red, like a man's, and there was enough of it as Monty had severed her hand and then the dog had punctured her wrist a few times before she had retreated to that awful scream. "Not human nor hybrid, and certainly not angelic," explained Dai, sniffing the air.

"I felt…I felt a hand reach through the door and pull at my collar." Monty was close to tears and clearly shaken.

"And then you turned around and cut part of her vessel off," replied Dai.

"Her vessel?" Monty had gradually got up.

"Yes, her human form," replied Dai.

Still confused, Monty asked: "Was she a demon spirit then? I mean her wrist was on the ground right here." He pointed at the tiles. "Then it just vanished?"

"She was an entity, let us just say that, and one aligned to the Orcadian," said Dai. "The body part you are referring to no longer exists and has simply faded from consequence," he told him.

"So, it is not dead then?"

"Nope. She is a spirit who shape-shifts, Stephen…but she has felt pain here today," Dai assured him as he looked down at the tiles. "Pain like nothing she has ever experienced before—human pain. She won't be back," he promised.

"She?"

"Yes, quite." Nodded Dai.

"And how do you know she won't return?"

"Because it was an attempt to frighten you, nothing more," insisted Dai convincingly. "She is also now painfully aware that you have been given a divinely forged weapon, which I assure you, will check not only her, but others too, in their tracks." He smirked. "Besides," he now patted the dog again, "your guardian angel would have stepped in again if you had not reacted so promptly." Dai's radiance had lit up the darkened porch like a warming blaze in a frosty cave—"I'm cleansing the area."

Regardless, shortly after, Charnley had moved into the house and Jimmy Lazarini had provided twenty-four hour leaches to stick on Monty. One big guy had been his shadow on a daily basis for months now, whilst another unknown person was apparently pitched up in a van outside the house during the night— life had changed—big time.

Charnley was clean, quiet, and good company most of the time. He got along well with the dog too but Monty was accustomed to his own space after so long alone, and just wanted this all to be over. There had been many occasions over the last few months, particularly when he was tired, when Monty would question his own sanity and whether or not this was really happening. He tried not to fret mostly, nor question things as much as before—instead committing himself to preparing Forsyth's defence as best you could.

"Is that QC—whatever his name is—ready for the trial then?" asked Charnley as they breakfasted.

"Mark Dailly, yes," replied Monty between mouthfuls of toast. "There are one or two more things for me to still check up on, but yes, we are getting there." He nodded.

"To check up on today?" Charnley was glad that he wasn't having to shadow Monty when out and about door-stepping potential witnesses. He was far more content being on dog protection duty most days. He also had a cork of his own now which he had collected from the standing stones again after another text. Charnley had never met Dai but he had been impressed by the mystical weapon and was far more relaxed about having it to hand after Monty's recent incident.

"Yep." Monty took another bite of his toast and nodded again. He was reading Dailly's notes on the case file that the QC had prepared thus far. The man's handwriting was atrocious and required Monty's full concentration. So he could do without the chit chat from Charnley, but just couldn't bring himself to be rude to his guest and friend, who had given up everything in his life to come over here and help out.

To be fair, Monty had become fairly used to Dailly's scribbles over the summer, but it was still a tricky and time demanding process reading them. He got along well with Dailly and found him to be, like Charnley, a funny, honest and quite modest man. He knew that he would make a fine judge one day because of his fairness. Dailly was west coast and working class, which Monty liked. Educated at Strathclyde and then afterwards at Balliol, Dailly had been a fine defence solicitor who had then become a Procurator Fiscal. before then taking silk and returning to practice as a defender.

Monty raised his head now and smiled at the chomping Charnley before sipping some more coffee. He recalled a previous meeting he had at Dailly's upmarket office on Great King Street. It had been around six in the evening when they had sat on the vintage leather sofas sipping nips of the Macallan and first went over the brief[104]. Dailly had been optimistic about the case from the start and this had raised Monty's spirits. Dailly had smiled thoughtfully whilst swirling his whiskey around in a glass. "There is something extra ordinary about all of this," the wily advocate had thought aloud.

"Totally," Monty had agreed.

---

[104] A brief (Old French from the Latin "brevis") is a written legal document used in various legal adversarial systems and is incorporated into Scots law here by the author, which is presented to a court arguing why one party should prevail.

"No…" Dailly paused and stared straight at him then. He was about the same age as Monty, perhaps a few years older, but he had a cheerful cheeky face, and a gregarious persona which Monty had taken to straight away. "Shortly before Forsyth was suspended from the police, I received an email from his late boss—Detective Inspector Chuck Kean," Dailly revealed.

"Did you?" Monty straightened up then and placed his glass on the table between them. He had spent years watching Dailly when the man had been a fiscal. On a weekly basis, most new criminal solicitors in Edinburgh would have encountered Dailly in both the district and Sheriff courts back in those days. Many of whom would loiter around the Clerk of Court in order to get their cases called and then have to hang around waiting their turn. Some would spend ages waiting and watching Dailly prosecute a variety cases—Monty had often been one of the watchers.

What he remembered of Dailly from those days, was his approachability. Dailly was a decent guy without the attitude found among many of the other fiscals who had prowled the marble corridors of the Sheriff Court. Monty now began to understood why the angels' had picked him to lead the defence; for not only was Dailly a highly a competent operator, but he was known as being a fair and decent man.

"Then soon after I received the email, I learned that Chuck Kean had been murdered," said Dailly.

"What did the email say?" asked Monty, studying Dailly's face. He had always thought the man was a ringer for Captain Darling in the British TV show—*Blackadder*[105].

"Well, it confirmed Forsyth's story, which I subsequently believed—that they were on a deniable investigation into the intelligence presented to them by the late Lionel Fraser," replied Dailly.

"What did you do?" Monty was wondering whether Dailly had informed any of his colleagues in the Crown Office, for if he had and it had been ignored, then that might have instigated the further backlash against Forsyth. Which suggests that the spider's web extends throughout the judiciary as well as the police.

"I passed it on to an associate in the Fiscal's office, a person I know and trust there from my time as a PF," confirmed Dailly.

Well, well, well.

---

[105] Tim McInnerny played the role of Captain Darling in *Blackadder Goes Fourth*.

"And now you are a defender of villains again," said Monty before sipping his malt.

"And innocents," smirked Dailly playfully.

Monty had always been impressed with Dailly, he had forgotten how sharp and articulate the guy was. Learned and classy in the court room, but one of the boys too. Monty had always found him to be a direct and personal prosecutor, which was why he wanted ammunition now from Monty, so that he could fight back on Forsyth's behalf. Dailly was prone to a well-reasoned defence and Monty knew that he more than fulfilled the prerequisite of a skilled defender for Forsyth; the bonus obviously being that he was also cheery, warm, and not barren of ethical conscious.

Monty's concern however, was that despite Dailly's obvious attributes, would he be able to out-fox a being such as the Orcadian? He had seen what the opposition could do when that bitch had extended her arm through the timber of his front door and tried to get him—they had powers beyond human comprehension.

"Here's to innocents." Monty had raised his glass.

"Aye." Smirked Dailly optimistically. His light reddish-brown sideburns giving him an almost Victorian appearance. All that was missing was a long wooden pipe and a pocket watch.

"And so your chum did nothing about it then?" asked Monty.

"Either that or someone made a call or two and motivated the cops to go after Forsyth at a later date," considered Dailly. "Technically, this could compromise my position for the defence, you see?"

Monty remained silent. He realised this but wanted to see where Dailly was going with it first. "Of course, the individual who I passed it over to in the Fiscal's office most likely did zilch with it, and has been six feet under from cancer since last November." Dailly shrugged, winked, then took another sip of his malt.

"Old Henry." Monty recalled a fiscal who had passed on not so long ago.

"The very man." Nodded Dailly—raising his glass.

"What if the emails are still about though?" Monty wanted to know.

"They did not mention Forsyth, nor the victim in this case—Yvonne Kidd, so unless we were going down the road of presenting the whole truth to the jury," Dailly paused and took yet another sip, "I can't see how it is relevant." He shrugged.

"The whole truth being?" Monty grinned at him impishly.

"That a secret group, let's call them the sons of favouritism," sighed Dailly whilst waving his hand theatrically, "murdered Yvonne Kidd, Irvine Stroker. Leslie Cairns, and Lionel Frazer, because Messrs Kean and Forsyth were on to their paedo antics." Shrugged Dailly impassively. Monty knew they couldn't go down that route obviously, for a start they had zero evidence and would likely be tagged as crazy by all and sundry within the fraternity.

"So...?" He queried.

"In which case we would lose, and a large tide would be raised against us Monty," smirked Dailly.

"So, carry on regardless then?"

"Indeed." Nodded Dailly who leaned back, crossed his legs and polished off his drink.

At that early meeting, Dailly had just come off the back of trial at the High Court in Glasgow where his legal aid client had been accused of a series of complex ATM raids across Scotland. It had been a demanding couple of days, and he was tired. His car had packed up on the M8 on the drive back to Edinburgh, so he had been towed back by the AA to a garage in Balgreen Road from where he had caught a fast-black to his office. Edinburgh taxi rates being second only to London of course, combined with the tormenting rush hour traffic—and ridiculous sum of £34.80 sought by the overly chatty and bonnet wearing driver, had made things even worse.

Monty had not been idling himself either over the last seven months, and had appeared at two pleading diets followed by an afternoon trial that particular day at the Sheriff Court which had run until 4pm before it had then been adjourned until the following morning. He had also endured something of a battering by an infamous limping old Fiscal—Kenny Allison, who looked more like the country and western singer—Kenny Rodgers.

After court, Monty had walked back to the office where he had another ding-dong with Russel Cuthbert about the Forsyth case in the second-floor printing room. It hadn't lasted long before he had walked straight back out again and made his way by foot down into the New Town for his meeting with Dailly. "Cuthbert's an arrogant wanker," groaned Dailly. "He wouldn't have appreciated you giving me this case, I'll wager." He had grinned at the time.

Monty had shrugged indifferently but with a telling grin. He made an effort to study Dailly's book shelve. It was modern, like the rest of the place, and so he was somewhat pleasantly surprised to note the entire *Flashman* series, and a couple of Dickens classics. On the wall behind Dailly, there were some children's drawings of houses and families. One had "Grandad and Granny with me and Mummy" scribbled upon it, and Monty realised that the artist was most probably Dailly's grandchild.

Over at the business end of the room, behind the man's desk, were some framed legal qualifications and an image of Dailly running in a charity run of some sort, while next to that was a black and white framed picture of the Lisbon Lions running along the pavement of London Road in Glasgow in the 1960's—presumably on their way back to Celtic Park from Barrowfield. There was a window to the left of the desk with a large Yucca beneath it and a colourful image of a matador murdering a bull above which had a large "No!" written across the impact wound on the bull, and "The shame of Spain" as a heading. Clearly, Dailly had a tenderness about him then, which complemented the cold professional sharpness that he was known for within legal circles.

"Lisbon Lions?"

"1969." Smiled Dailly. He knew Monty was a Celtic man too and they both glanced up at the picture briefly.

"Sorry Mark, you were saying about Russell Cuthbert?"

"Aye," exhaled Dailly, "I worked with the bugger back in the days when legal aid was to lawyers, what gold was to conquistadors." He gave Monty a naughty smirk.

Monty had been a student back in those days when lawyers brought several packs of cigarettes and twice as many Legal Aid application forms to visits with signature-happy clients in court cells. Indeed, if all the old stories were true, even the court cleaners could have signed the forms in order for a lawyer to get paid back then. "When old George Moore was the best defence solicitor in town, and Gordon Thompson the nicest?" He recalled.

Dailly chuckled. "Indeed. Gordon was a pleasant man, yes." He looked at the ceiling a moment as he recalled some of the old legal faces of the past, "And Dundee's Chris Sharp was the main man from Fife to Aberdeen." He raised his glass again.

"Yes Sharpy had done well back then," agreed Dailly.

"Where did you work with Russell?" asked Monty.

"Hood & Co in Moodiesburn."

"Right, I didn't know that." Nodded Monty. If truth be told, all he knew about Cuthbert was that he supported Rangers, voted Tory and wore cheap shoes. He had certainly never socialised with the man and had always found him to be quite standoffish.

"Aye, we both ended up there after university, and well," Dailly recollected, "Hoodies was a busy wee firm with loads of Sheriff and District court stuff going on around the Lanarkshire circuit," he explained. "I did Coatbridge court mostly for a year or so while Cuthbert did Airdrie, but we met up weekly at either Hamilton or Motherwell JP courts— he wasn't liked there either."

"Nothing changes." Smirked Monty.

"Eventually they had us both doing pleadings and amendments at Glasgow District and Sheriff courts," said Dailly.

"Not a favourite of yours then?" probed Monty with a grin of anticipation.

"Aye well, he was no pal-o-mine." Dailly shook his head. "He looked down his nose at not only myself, but everyone else, and he had a short fuse to go with his rather unjustified air of superiority." He chuckled.

"Tell me about it." Monty grinned back knowingly. Cuthbert was the type of bumptious boss who never smiled and who fancied himself as a gentrified right-winger, though he had gone to a state-run school and lacked enough class to purchase a decent pair of shoes. He was, like so many others in life, just another wannabe.

"He is everything I'm not, Monty," proclaimed Dailly.

"Well, he certainly isn't a friendly guy, but I just throw him a deaf ear and get on with my cases—he tends to leave me alone," agreed Monty sympathetically.

"He knows your good at your job, that's why," insisted Dailly.

Monty raised his glass to that. "Well, you have a point," he joked, and both men laughed.

"Anyway, regarding their offer of manslaughter, you should advise Forsyth that we feel he ought to reject it, and that instead we prefer to see their hand." Dailly had then gotten down to business. The Crown office had rung him earlier that day and made an offer of a reduced charge of manslaughter in return for a quick guilty plea, which had been the reason for Monty popping in at that time.

"Well, they can't prove murder can they, so no big surprise really." Nodded Monty. After all, anything they had on Forsyth was hearsay. Proving that he was at the scene of the crime, at the moment it occurred, was one thing, but arguing that Forsyth went there with an intention to commit murder, was something else entirely. "Self-defence?" he asked Dailly. It was always a last gasp option if the Crown produced witnesses or God forbid—DNA.

"If we raise the possibility of self-defence, it is up to them to prove otherwise," nodded Dailly in part agreement, but he was thinking something else and Monty sensed it. "It won't be wise to try to convince a jury that two experienced detectives defended themselves from a murderous young girl by slitting her throat then doing a bunk and not calling it in thereafter."

"Yep, the knife suggests premeditation, of course." Monty shook his head in agreement.

"Not quite so." Dailly had raised his hand as a referee might do to a mouthy footballer. "He could still have found a knife on the premises in the process of being attacked, of course," he pointed out. He was covering every angle but both men knew that such a tale would be unlikely to convince a jury. "Well, one thing is for sure," he persisted, "I can't defend him on an unsubstantiated claim that a paedophile cult is in existence and who are behind a conspiracy to frame our guy," he asserted.

"Soooo?" Monty was only too well aware that the task for any lawyer charged with getting an innocent person's head of the chopping block should be one of enthusiasm and endurance. Yet back at this early meeting with Dailly, he had sensed that they had little option but to accept that it was, park-the-bus-time, and try to shield Forsyth by arguing that any evidence against him was unreliable at best and circumstantial at worst.

Even then, upon reflection, that in itself seemed naive when Monty contemplated who was leading the prosecution case against them. Dailly had known little about the Orcadian of course, other than that he thought that he had heard that this Farquharson fellow had once worked in offshore finance and had practiced civil law for corporate fat-cats, before then moving into the criminal corridors.

"Apparently, he was once with some upmarket offshore firm based in the usual tax-free havens. He specialised in tax avoidance, not evasion, and is thought to have made a fortune out of it before then finding his calling in criminal law; my guess being that he is going after a well thought out path into government," considered Dailly.

If only you knew.

"Multi-talented then?" Monty had said thoughtfully.

"Aye, quite handy by all accounts," agreed Dailly, which left Monty wondering how all these people could just be calibrated into imagining that they somehow knew, or had heard, all about the Crown's talented new Advocate Depute.

"Magic." Sighed Monty glumly.

Dailly had sensed the despondency. "Never fear, there are some discrepancies in the evidence against Forsyth," he had insisted. "If we can attack their notion of corroboration and show that there is nothing connecting our guy to the murder, other than their cowboy witnesses, then our decent defence becomes a strong defence." He shrugged again with an obvious optimism which Monty had not encountered within himself in a while. It had not been arrogance with Dailly though, no, rather this was confidence.

"What about these two witnesses then?" Monty had felt the need to bring up the Crown's witnesses.

"Well, the old dear is a piss-artist to the point of no return apparently, so I fancy that we can get past her," jested Dailly.

"As for this so-called eyewitness – George Phillipson, who they claim saw Forsyth leaving the building in a rush," he continued, "well, considering he is essentially at the foundation of their case, our goal is to damage him," he declared.

"We know that this witness has a criminal record, so at this stage Monty, if you can rustle up anything else on him, we can make an effort to have the jury view him as shady at worst and as a compulsive lying satanic pervert at best," shrugged Dailly again. "Give me enough, and I'll have them comparing him to bloody Caligula[106]," he promised.

"I'll try," Monty wrote this down.

"That should see us across the line," Dailly said whilst stretching to pour them both top ups.

"I don't know, Mark." Monty had shaken his head at the time and raised his eyebrows. "Forsyth is quite keen to tell the truth at trial," he pointed out. He had visited Forsyth on remand twice a week over the previous few months—the

---

[106] Gaius Augustus Germanicus Caesar, known as Caligula, was emperor of Rome from AD 37-41 before he was murdered at the age of 29. Quite insane, Caligula had a habit of murdering on a whim. He was also utterly delusional and outrageously sexually perverted towards the nobility. This led to the assassination of himself, and his wife and child by his own friends and guards.

attempt to get him bail had, as expected, been unsuccessful, and he had been remanded, initially for further examination on a petition—then seven days later was fully committed until the trial date.

One thing that was made clear to Monty throughout these meetings with Forsyth was that the guy wanted the truth to be heard in court. Partly, Monty suspected, because he was bitter about his treatment which amounted not only to the obliteration of his career and domestic relationship, but also partly because the guy still believed in justice. The fact that neither Dai nor any other living being had tried to persuade him to the contrary, was also noted by Monty who now wondered if Dailly was onto a lemon with his tactic.[107]

Forsyth had been dumped in an isolated protection wing in Saughton Prison. As a former Drug Squad cop, he was deemed to be in serious danger from the rest of the prison population. What Monty was not sure about was whether the prison authorities knew that Forsyth was in even more danger from the conspirators than he was from any convicted drug dealers. So, it had taken Monty only a little persuasion to get Forsyth to agree to being isolated. The only problem with that had been that whilst in isolation, Forsyth was housed with informers and sex offenders as well as those at risk of self-harm, consequently they were all locked up in their cells almost twenty-three hours a day.

Dailly had recoiled at a follow-up meeting with Monty in Spring, when informed that Forsyth wanted to tell all in court. "Well, you need to convince him that the priority now is for him not to spend the rest of his life locked up in an isolation wing."

"Okay Mark, I'll speak to him again tomorrow and tell him how you want to run things. I'll also keep digging around one or two other former clients of mine who might know something spicy about this false witness of theirs." Monty had failed to dig anything up on Phillipson since their last meeting, but who was he to question the tactics of the one human being who had been divinely selected to defend Forsyth against this Satanic Goliath and his false witnesses anyway?

"Good." Dailly had winked.

George Phillipson was an unemployed homosexual male aged fifty-eight, who claimed to have been visiting his 19-year-old lover—a refugee from Syria, on the day of Yvonne Kidd's murder. Phillipson had a criminal record for cannabis possession with intent to supply, but apart from that, very little else was known about him. Phillipson's police statement read, that at about an hour or so

---

[107] Edinburgh slang for a bitter or disappointing experience.

after visiting his teenage lover, he had been walking back home again when he claimed to have seen Forsyth, Stroker, and Kean, as they were allegedly fleeing the scene of the murder at Queens Park Avenue.

In the months since Forsyth's arrest, Monty had worked furiously from getting Dailly onboard, arguing with Russell Cuthbert about the use of Dailly, and to prepare the case. Yet other than Phillipson's testimony, there was no persuasive evidence to tie Forsyth to the scene. No trace of blood, no DNA and no fingerprints. But they did have the victim's mother who placed Forsyth there at some point earlier on the day of the murder, as well as some circumstantial evidence including Gav Caine's statement. Dailly was quite right then, Monty realised—they should dismantle Phillipson in the dock in order to provide Forsyth with a clear path to a Not Proven verdict.

Since that initial meeting with Dailly, Monty had, after considerable persuasion, persuaded Forsyth to go along with Dailly's way of thinking. It had not been easy but both of them had prayed on a couple of occasions together at the prison visits, and Monty guessed that other powers had perhaps opened Forsyth's eyes to Dailly's strategy—an acquittal being the priority over any notion of exoneration. "Evil often defeats good, Chris," Dailly had told Forsyth at another visit. "Very often pawns are wiped out in the process though," he had also pointed out. "You should consider yourself a pawn here."

It had been such logic that made Monty wonder what, if indeed anything, Dailly actually understood about this whole Kertamen thing. Part of him intuitively felt that Dailly might even understand all the heaven and hell stuff, but then again at other times, he could not see how Dailly could possibly understand all of this. All that seemed to matter however, was that together, they would paint the jury a picture of an innocent cop with an excellent background.

One who does not understand why all this is happening to him, because he knows nothing about who killed Yvonne Kidd, nor did he have any motive to kill anyone.

As Monty sat now in his kitchen having breakfast with Charnley, he felt confident that the witness George Philipson would be seen as a poor witness by the jury and that the pile of circumstantial evidence which the Crown had listed against Forsyth, such as allegations of professional misconduct and violence, were precisely that—circumstantial, and therefore irrelevant.

After breakfast, Monty walked along in the sunshine carrying a briefcase containing two small files and a larger third—the Forsyth file, which took up the majority of the old and tattered case that he had owned for years. The tall East Slavic looking guy in grey suit and black shirt tailed him as usual. Monty knew that his shadow was Jimmy Lazarini's guy, and from the build and look of him, Monty could be forgiven for thinking that he was living in a John le Carré novel.

The fact was that for the entire summer, Monty had been overwhelmed by this whole experience. His life had changed in all ways, in every corner of his head he had been doing little more than reading and working on Forsyth's defence, as well as constantly looking over his shoulder for whatever else might appear. Everything had changed: he had been reading the Bible, praying and discussing theology with Charnley most evenings over dinner. He now tried to display compassion and patience towards others, much more than he ever had done previously—part of which was listening more and offering supportive advise to anyone who sought his ear.

Just then, a boy racer in a supped-up Ford Fiesta roared past him as he walked along Duke Street, almost knocking over a woman who was crossing in the process. There were a few frowns and head shakes from other commuters on the pavement, and a cry of "Arsehole!" rang out from one bloke attempting to cross over from the opposite side of the road. Monty usually would have mentally uttered something too, but now he simply hoped that the kid would rapidly grow up without ever having to suffer an injury or accident.

One thing he had noticed since his enlightenment had begun, was that everywhere he looked, be it here in the city. on the television, or at work in the court, the world was riddled with psycho-social venom and a multitude of egotistical and selfish people. He now grasped how this was a contagious conundrum, not just for adults but also among kids. Whenever there was a fight up town on a weekend, people were automatically drawn to watch and scream around it as flying insects are to a lightbulb.

If two groups of men were fighting in the street on a Saturday night, and one of the groups took to heels and left one of their comrades behind to take the fall, many of the opposition group would be drawn to putting the boot in to this last man standing with animalistic snarls and chants. Monty had often had to represent such people on the following Monday mornings. Mostly they regrated their behaviour and recognised it to have been an infectious flaw in their natures. *I'm not usually like that— honestly.*

All that seemed clearer to Monty now as he soaked up this new awareness of mankind, its nature, and of divinity. It was through both research and from talking with Dai, that he now realised that faith, empathy and selflessness musters a resistance to this flaw. "How can we expect God to forgive us if we cannot forgive those who have crossed us?" Charnley had pointed out only the other day.

Monty usually caught the bus from the bus stop at the Mermaid fish and chip shop, up to the Bridges. Today he boarded and sat downstairs as usual with his back to the front wherein he crossed a leg and read the Independent that he always picked up from the newsagents next door to the chippy. The newsagents had stopped providing change for the multitude of bus commuters as far back as the early 1990s and now did a roaring trade in matches and chewing gum as a direct result.

He usually tried to sit with his back to the driver in order to avoid the repertoire of clients who might get on his bus on route to the same Sheriff Court. Such occurrences were generally a nightmare whenever they did occur because some clients tended to want to become his mate, and to chat with him.

Another reason he preferred to avoid some of these individuals, particularly at that time of the day when he was never traditionally one of the cheeriest of bunnies, was that some of them lacked personal hygiene and stunk. The last one who had planted her unwelcome arse down beside him, had clearly not been anywhere near a tooth brush or floss for the majority of her middle-aged life, and had stunk of a vile combination of urine and cheap whiskey. Monty had endured it, as he had known that she was probably beyond recognising what she had become, and so he had pitied her. Though he had put on an all-purpose and incomprehensible smile before then purposely making all the other passengers aware of the fact that she was not his friend, but rather a client—a pauper that he would be doing all he could to spring from an unjust allegation of theft because he was her lawyer.

He momentarily recalled the scenario now for a moment and considered that he would have no need to behave this way for the benefit of any other passengers ever again. He no longer cared about the opinions of any other passengers, he realised. He also suspected that the entities above, who may be observing his actions and thoughts, also knew that his thinking had changed. Other people's opinions were not a justifiable reason for disassociating himself from a booze drenched and very lonely client. "Don't worry, mistakes are understandable, Monty," Dai had assured him on one visit. "Had not Peter the apostle denied that he knew Jesus three times, despite stating that he would never do such a thing

344

only hours earlier?" he had pointed out. "Even Peter the Rock had momentarily responded accordingly to the estimation of other people whom he had not known."

Monty had concluded reading the bible by the end of June and so understood only too well the point that Dai had made, but Peter had acted out of self-preservation and fear of his life. Monty had acted this way with the client on the bus simply through awkwardness, but it had been nice to hear an angel compare his transgressions to that of an apostle's of course. Still, he sat with his back to the front now and busied himself in his newspaper.

No one is perfect, he reminded himself before starting an article on Labour's election hopes. His minder had also boarded the bus and was sat a couple of seats towards the front. Who knows what he would do should another freak attack occur, Monty sometimes wondered, but he was a sturdy enough big lad with an impassive face and it seemed likely that he would at least put up a good enough fight to enable Monty sufficient time to draw his weapon. He felt for it now inside his suit packet with his right hand as he read more crap about the pending general election. It was there and this comforted him.

The noisy bus engine roared as it pulled away up the Walk towards the city. He couldn't really get into the entertainment rag formerly known as a newspaper though, and kept people watching and taking in the variety of summer fruits on display along Leith Walk. Melons the size of basket balls from Africa, and Pakistani mangos as well as Sicilian peaches were everywhere at this time of year. There was as diverse an assortment of people at the bus stops too, Italians, Poles, Orientals and Africans all hopping off and on the bus as it pulled into the many stops along Leith Walk.

The Fringe was starting up too and so most of these bus shelters had colourful posters upon them which Monty also took in. Not that he would be taking in a show this year, however. There were a few people handing out fliers for both the SNP and Labour Party too, he noted, but no sign of any SLP fascists? They wouldn't last five minutes in Leith he supposed, before going back to the political article in the Independent.

The UK general election was now upon them, and Labour appeared to be attempting to gain the undecided teenage vote with a pledge to raise student bursaries and provide grants for unemployed 16-18-year-olds seeking to start their own businesses. They were talking the talk for sure, but the hour was late, thought Monty who was not sure that the public would believe anything that

Labour said. The Iraq and Afghan wars were still raw, as was the consequent recession, but perhaps more importantly to the youth of Scotland was the fact that Labour had stood hand in glove with the Tories in the previous year's referendum, which Monty suspected may well hurt them at the ballot next week.

The reality was that under devolution, Scotland only had 59 seats in the House of Commons, so the real test for the Scottish political parties wouldn't really be until next year when the 2016 Scottish general election came around. In truth, Monty had not really focussed much upon the balloting stuff as it all approached its climax; he had of course more important matters to concern himself with.

Everything was now so utterly surreal – similar perhaps to falling in love or losing a loved one, in that it was all consuming and oddly surreal. Every action he undertook now mattered only in the eyes of his creator; a being he had not worshipped nor believed in until his trip to Lundin Links.

He repeatedly asked himself: *Why me? Why am I special? I never went to church, never even preyed unless I was desperate—had even tried hating God when my parents had died—why me?*

But then, he would remind himself of what Dai once said: "Why not you? Some men, even those of favoured lines, regularly display ignorance as well as a vast amount of self-deception. Man's nature is to assist not only other people, but every other creature beneath him in the pecking order. He subconsciously desires to be compassionate, to provide sanctuary and aid to those who really need it. But man has been misguided from infancy by those who long to see him obliterated by God."

Regardless, everything still seemed dreamlike now though. Perhaps this was also down to the fact that Monty had not been sleeping properly. Merely grabbing superficial uneasy slumbers from time to time, which lasted only an hour or so before he was twisting and turning himself awake again. He sometimes dreamed of his parents and of the accident. Sometimes they spoke to him, he knew this, but he could never recollect what they had said to him when he awoke. It was inspiration though, he sensed that much, but then he would lay away awake with the cork in his hand thinking about how their deaths had affected him and how he had then surrounded himself with a wall thereafter. A wall that kept his true feelings out of his daily life, but which also prevented anyone else from penetrating and either giving or receiving feelings from him. He had thought that loneliness had been his friend, until now—now he resented it.

He looked up at the tenement windows above the shops outside as the bus trundled onwards. There were SNP and Labour posters evident on windows now. He remembered driving through Cramond to run the dog on the beach the previous Sunday morning and all the Conservative and SLP ones were up on display there. There was a young female in her late teens sitting opposite him now. She was spotty and blonde with NHS spectacles and wore a mustard blouse and dark tweed skirt, neither of which went with her white leather handbag. She was probably late for work in some retail outlet, he widely guessed, though he tried not to stare at her. She was obviously not well paid he considered, as she was wearing far too much of an older woman's perfume, possibly her mother's— Oscar de la Renta perhaps. Which, combined with the warm weather and lack of air on the bus, was making him feel slightly nauseous now.

Along to her right at the opposite window, sat a fat popcorn haired male in his late fifties who was on the phone to someone who was causing him to continually sigh in frustration. He had a white t-shirt and khaki cargo shorts on and had a crumpled up high visibility vest sticking out from one of the large pockets of his shorts. There was a younger female sitting opposite him wearing a cheap black nylon suit with stains on it and signs of wear and tear at the trouser hems. Her bushy black hair was brushed, but looked scruffy and rough. Monty wondered if she was on her way to court too.

"Aye well, I'll see how I feel this afternoon, but I doubt it as it was a heavy sesh last night," Popcorn was mumbling into his phone. His nose was pink from the drink and his eyes reddened from last night's vodka and orange binge. "Nah, I'm not sure yet but I'm not voting for those cunts like, they lost the fucking referendum and now we are being told we need to pay for garden waste to be collected, nah fuck that." Popcorn sighed again before thankfully ending the call. "Right cheerio then Darren, call you later, mate."

He then blew his fat pink nose into a used McDonald's napkin which he found in yet another pocket. He took a wee glance at it to see if anything noteworthy had been deposited, before then having a quick glimpse around to see if anyone had been observing...*Ah, a tad of self-pride left in you yet then, Popcorn?* thought Monty as he reverted his gaze just in time.

Popcorn then dropped the thing at his feet and yawned to reveal dark yellow teeth. Behind them all, two older women with Leith accents were chattering away about the election and seemed oblivious to the fact that everyone was probably listening to them. "Well, Brian has always voted Labour, but he voted

YES last year and now he says he is going to vote Labour again the morn because he doesnie like that wee Nicola Sturgeon, eh," said one.

Monty did not turn around and instead tried to get back into his paper, but he couldn't help but tune into this soap opera scene like every other passenger.

"Aye, she reminds me of that wee Jimmy Krankie character fae the telly, Bette." Laughed the other woman.

Just then the retail the female sitting opposite stood up and rang the bell to get off. She stepped over Popcorn's dirty napkin on the ground as if it were the size of a bedside cabinet and gave him a scunner of a stare as she did so. Popcorn was oblivious as he was now scrolling through his phone like the majority of people standing outside at yet another bus stop. Shortly after the bus drove on, they arrived on the South Bridge just as one young male voice started having a go at the two old dears. "You two are full of shite, I'm sorry but it's true," he exclaimed. "Wee Nicola has done amazing things for Scotland," he insisted.

"I beg your pardon?" gasped one of the women.

"Who do you think you are, son?" demanded the other, but the male merely appeared to snigger.

"Such as?" shouted someone else—another female somewhere.

"It's people like you that put me off voting SNP," snapped one of the Leith dearies.

Monty had had enough and decided to get up and get off a couple of stops early and just walk the rest of the way to court. Popcorn wasn't interested, Monty noted; instead, he was having a good pick at his nose with his index finger, presumably to find something or other up there for breakfast. Deep probe— another sneaky glance at the findings, then an even sneakier swipe of finger upon the seat fabric, before returning to his phone.

"Ah fuck off, the pair of you." The youth raised his tone now.

Monty went along the aisle with his case in one hand and newspaper under his arm and stopped dead at where the youth was sitting. He was a blonde stoner type about twenty years of age and wearing a Tesco uniform. Monty reached into the inside pocket of his suit and pulled out his wallet. It had to be a quick movement here for the bluff to work, otherwise things could get messy. he was only too well aware. "Right, you," he flashed the now open wallet down at the kid to reveal his lawyer's card which he was always required to show to the security guys at the court in order to skip the metal detector queue. "I'm a Procurator Fiscal and you're on the bus camera committing a breach of the peace, pal." He quickly closed the wallet again and replaced it in his inside pocket. "And you obviously work at Tesco," he shrewdly pointed out. "So, unless you want to be arrested at work, then charged and facing me in a courtroom, I suggest you quieten down and show these two ladies the respect they deserve," he suggested firmly.

He had gambled upon the kid having at least enough knowledge of the criminal biosphere to know that a Fiscal was the Texas Ranger of bus confrontation nightmares and that it would be wise to immediately stand down here; though there was no accounting for egotism and stupidity when it came to the possibilities, Monty knew. The kid sized him up a moment and saw that he seemed to be as he claimed and so simply nodded compliance before turning to the women and nodding at them too. "I'm sorry I was rude, ladies."

Phew, another wannabe. A real ned might not have cared. The saloon piano started playing again and it was time to get out of Dodge.

On the pavement, Monty wasted no time in quickly crossing over and making his way to work without looking back at the bus in case the kid gave him the coward's verbal's from behind the glass. Instead he strode confidently up Chambers Street towards the court, enjoying for a brief moment the morning sunshine upon his face. His Russian shadow followed behind him with a slim grin of esteem at his style. Monty didn't think anything of it of course, it had not been too much of a gamble really.

Since he had been a kid, he had always had this faint, unexplainable ability to read a man by his face. He wasn't always bang on the money mind, but often enough he was able to tell a baddie just from his face. Or perhaps it was the other way around and he could place a good guy? He wasn't sure. Sometimes it was just the eyebrows or frown, other times it was the eyes. The eyes say a lot about a person. Other clues such as dress sense, posture, and habits, all contributed but mostly it was just the face itself that motivated Monty's inner instinct.

The knack seemed much weaker on females for some reason, perhaps because they tended to use make-up, he could never be as sure. In this case, he had sensed that the Tesco guy had a chip on his shoulder but was not so bad deep down; and Monty supposed that the lad's reaction confirmed this.

Usually, he could hear the soles of his black brogues tapping along the pavement as he covered Chambers Street to the court building every day but they were quieter now and he reminded himself that he may need to either re-sole them or buy a new pair. Few people bothered going to a cobbler's these days, instead they just bought another pair in town or more commonly—online. It was the easy option, and this generation preferred the easy option.

As he neared the court, he had a strange feeling on the back of his neck. Like a breath upon his skin. He felt watched and slowed his pace to look around accordingly. The area was busy as usual with cars trying to find a much-sought parking spot next the court. Across the road at the museum there were two queues of schoolchildren being kept in orderly lines by sheep dog-like teachers. Monty turned and glanced behind him—no one stood out other than a female with a pram who was walking too slowly whilst texting. Next to her was his shadow Ivan, who seemed unalarmed.

Then Monty realised that he was outside of the Crown Prosecution Offices and he instinctively looked up at the windows but couldn't make anything out—there was something though, he sensed it. He walked on again and then he remembered what the file had said:

"The Orcadian can view your thoughts from short range if you allow him."

Monty immediately tried to change his thoughts now—*Faither, Craig, Cesar, Gemmil, Murdoch, Ten-Thirty, Jinky, Stevie Chalmers, Buzz-bomb, and Wallace…*

A minute or so later he waltzed past the security boys at the court metal detector, who gave him the usual nod to pass. Ivan hung about outside the entrance with all the fag smokers who were grabbing a last gasp before the butterflies in their stomachs drove them mad.

There was no point of him following Monty inside, the court should be safe enough with all the security staff and cameras on the go. Besides, Ivan was carrying a knuckle duster and a Stanley knife in his suit pocket and wasn't keen to start looking for a hiding place for them.

Inside, Monty took the stairs straight up to the lawyers' room on the top floor. There were a couple of out-of-town lawyers getting changed and his own boss Russell Cuthbert was sitting underneath an open locker sipping coffee and eating a square sausage roll. Beyond yonder was the passageway with the Roman style alcoves, which lead down to the library with all the tacky sculptures and a common room.

"Morning," Monty acknowledged him but Cuthbert remained seated and merely gave him his usual cold stare whilst chewing his breakfast. He was a frosty-faced individual at the best of times, with a general lack of gaiety regardless of who he was talking to, and so Monty was more than used to it. The door then suddenly opened and in came two giggling younger solicitors who Monty was unfamiliar with. There were always new kids on the block and plenty who were just appearing from out of town. One of these kids had his hair greased back into an overly long ponytail whilst the other was wearing a shirt and tie that Monty thought may have been better suited to a night out on George Street.

"What have you got?" Monty asked Cuthbert whilst placing his phone, bag and newspaper in a locker opposite before then fiddling around for a pound coin for the lock. Cuthbert who was pissed off at him for giving Mark Dailly the Forsyth brief, thought about ignoring him, as they had quarrelled badly about that a few months back, but thought better of it and sighed as he first checked his pocket watch before finally replying: "A big Sheriff and Jury," he said indifferently.

A case of non-payment of a TV licence then—pedantic bastard.

"Good luck with that then—have a nice day," Monty replied with his back to him whilst he located a coin and deposited it into the slot. He then removed the key and coolly exited onto the main landing again. He paused for a moment to put his robe on; he had been unable to stand another second in Cuthbert's company.

"Aye-aye, morning all."—unwelcome, yet familiar voice, causing Monty to frown and look down at the polished floor as he wriggled into the robe. If he had bothered looking up he would have come face to face with another little orange-haired rodent standing before him—one with a smile that pleaded to be punched. It was none other than little Blair Bingham, a cockeyed, yellow toothed pain in the arse, and quite frankly the worst civil law solicitor in town. Bingham hailed from Hawick originally but now lived in Peebles, and was notoriously always late for court, so this was clearly a unique moment.

He did however tend to frequent the upper levels of the court a lot. Bingham was about 5ft4 and seemed to Monty to be going through some sort of midlife crisis wherein he had cut his hair in the 1960's Mod/wings style, in a reaction to his discomfort with his age.

He was stood now before Monty, wearing a green parka over his suit and a silk paisley patterned cravat. "Morning." Monty nodded before then walking away without further pleasantries—they had a history. The treacherous little bastard had drunkenly gotten lippy with Monty at a Christmas do in the Scotsman Hotel a couple of years back after Monty had suggested, perhaps somewhat indelicately, that Bingham had been a childhood glory hunter for claiming to "support" Liverpool FC, despite him having been raised in Hawick nor rarely ever travelling to Anfield.

They had both ended up having to be separated by Cuthbert of all people, and later on in the evening, someone had then taken a photo of Monty on a hotel balcony smoking a joint with an unknown female, who had snuggled on up to him and made, lit, then passed him the thing.

The photo had then found its way to the Law Society of Scotland along with an anonymous allegation that Monty had been smoking drugs. The LSS in turn, contacted him and told him that an unnamed person had made the claim that he had been smoking cannabis in front of other lawyers, and so they were obliged to invite him to comment. Monty knew it had been Bingham, and so had simply denied that it had been anything other than a rolled-up cigarette which he had cadged from the unknown female.

"I tend to have a puff when drinking, a habit that goes back to my student days," he had claimed. As a result of the complainant having been anonymous, and without there being any palpable evidence to the contrary, the LSS had left it at that but Monty had grabbed Bingham the next time he encountered him at court and had made it quite clear that he knew it was him behind the drama. Naturally, and with significant ease, Bingham had lied through his yellow teeth by denying any knowledge of the dirty deed, before then scurrying away to the civil court.

For Monty, regardless of the obliged present-day civility, there was forever no love lost between himself and the man. He knew that Bingham was a rodent—everyone did. It was common knowledge among the legal fraternity that the man was two-faced, dishonest, and that he associated with even dodgier clients. The guy had a long list of complaints filed against him from clients whom he had misrepresented. Monty knew though, that the only thing separating the little shit from disbarment was time. He was content to exchange a curt hello with him until then. After all, he had been raised to believe that manners cost nothing.

Downstairs, and outside of court six, where villains, neds and scratching junkies hung around waiting on their state funded defenders, Monty located his client—one Kevin Rafferty a forty-one-year-old traffic warden accused of flashing himself at a thirteen-year-old schoolboy in King George V park. Today was just a pleading diet and the highly nervous and agitated Rafferty, who had no prior convictions, was pleading not guilty. Rafferty was short, fat, slightly balding, and wore a black suit, white shirt and silly purple tie with gold trumpets on it. Monty confirmed a few things with him such as his address and date of birth etc whilst an elderly tea lady wheeled an annoyingly squeaky tea trolly around touting for business.

"I have been suspended and my wife still doesn't know about any of this, Mr Montgomery, I'm so worried..." he was whining away needlessly whilst Monty scribbled down the notes.

"Never mind all that today, Kevin. We are just going to plead Not Guilty to the Sheriff today and then the clerk of court will give us a date for the trial, and then you can get yourself home," he explained with a trace of compassion.

"Right, but will I still be on bail?"

"Yes, your bail will be continued but you will need to ring my office and make an appointment to come in and see me in a week or so to go over everything, alright?" confirmed Monty.

"Right okay, but do you think I will go to jail?" Rafferty asked. They had been through this before, both face to face and over the phone.

"As I have already explained to you before, Mr Rafferty"—*it was Mr Rafferty now then*—"if convicted, there may be a possibility of that; however, because you are a first offender, that is not the only option open to the court and a community service order seems more likely." Monty again provided the hope that was sought. Rafferty nodded now like a child who was being called in from his play but who had been told that he could go back out again after his dinner for a short while.

"But that is only if you are found to be guilty and I'm confident that we have a reasonable case," Monty also pointed out to him. The truth was that he didn't quite think that the guy was guilty, but he couldn't be quite sure. The evidence against him was flimsy and the kid had been previously exposed to a similar type of abuse from his stepfather and had also cried wolf once upon a time on a teacher too, before then retracting his complaint. There was apparently no question about whether or not Rafferty was circumcised or not in the police report either. The cops had just gone with the two adult witnesses, whose statements were somewhat conflicting and one of whom had a rap sheet three pages long for dishonesty. So, Monty just wasn't sure, but that was never important in his job anyway.

"Right, so just go and sit in the court and then wait until they call your name. Then when they do, go and stand in the dock and remain standing until they confirm your name, and then only sit down when the clerk tells you to do so; I'll do the rest, okay?" he told Rafferty who nodded enthusiastically. Monty then wandered off in search of another client of Arty Llewellyn's, who had asked him to stand in and do a pleading diet for him whilst he attended to another matter up at Perth Sheriff Court.

"Hayden Duffy?" Monty called out to all the ants busying themselves around the marble pillars and tea trolly. Quick glance at the second file that he was holding again, yep… "Hayden Duffy?"

"That's me," a teenager in a grey hoody and joggers, who had been leaning casually against a pillar whilst texting on his phone, acknowledged haughtily.

"Hello Hayden, I'm Stephen Montgomery." Monty strode over towards him. "I'm filling in for Mr Llewellyn today," he explained without offering his hand. This little shit was guilty however, guilty of threatening a female Swiss tourist with a knife and stealing her bag containing her passport, purse and credit cards at the previous New Year's street party. He was banged to rights due to various witnesses, and despite wearing a hood, he was caught running away on three cameras which revealed his face.

This facial recognition was decent enough, though the bag and its contents had not been found for eight weeks, but when they were, they were covered in Duffy's fingerprints.

Llewellyn had urged him to plead guilty but the little bastard wanted to drag things out as long as possible before being sent to a young offender's institution. This meant that the victim, who had already endured a nightmare during a holiday period when everything in Scotland was closed for the festivities, and without any money, passport, or flight home, had now to travel back to Scotland to give evidence against the little shit.

"Aye, where the fuck's your boss like?" snarled the kid.

"He has been called away to a serious case out of town and as this is only a pleading diet then for you, and you'll be away in no time, I'll be pleading on your behalf today, okay?" Monty wanted to knock the little bastard out but was experienced enough not to arse up Llewellyn's client and face a complaint.

Forgiveness, remember.

That really would have seen Cuthbert blowing yet another fuse as he would then be forced to juggle his prized Sheriff and jury case in order to stand in and plead on behalf of this low-life. "Aye well, ah better be eh." The kid eyeballed Monty now, who smiled back and passed him the pen and legal aid form to sign. Duffy did so slowly and with his tongue appearing from the corner of his mouth due to the intense mental effort required in the process.

"Perfect, Hayden. If you just go into court six then and wait on your name being called, I'll see to things for you," urged Monty without advising Duffy to turn his phone off in the courtroom.

If it goes off, hell mend the little bastard.

Ten minutes later, Monty entered court six which was full of accused persons awaiting their turn to be called. He noted that both Rafferty and Duffy were seated on the same row as he glided past security and into the official area where the fiscal was sat at a long oval table opposite four other solicitors who were awaiting their cases being called by the clerk. The clerk was sat at a computer at the head of the table and underneath the Sheriff's bench. There were also five other solicitors casually loitering along the wall behind those seated, likewise they were waiting and ready to pounce upon the next available seat.

Monty noted that there were a couple of local regulars standing there— Aurelia Myerscough of Bannerman & Wick, who was yawning but who gave him a knowing wink as he approached. And old Davie Cunningham—another wanker who was handshake brigade. Not to mention a golfing chum of Cuthbert's. Cunningham wore a blue pinstripe job and was pretending to flick through his files when in actual fact he was trying not to get caught eyeing up the fledgling female Fiscal—a Miss Heung, who was addressing the Sheriff regarding some miserable looking bloke sat in the dock who had just plead guilty to stealing £28.00 from a parked car outside the university on Buccleuch Place.

It was Sheriff Kelvin sitting today, a fair female with a pointy nose, and who tended to hit hard. Duffy was lucky that it only a pleading diet today. Monty could smell Aurelia's perfume—a dark and intense affair, which he liked but was not entirely convinced that it went with her blonde Heidi pleats and student-y personality.

"Gosh, she's nippy," she whispered to him.

"Who, the new fiscal or Kelvin?" Monty sought ever so quietly to confirm.

"Fiscal," replied Aurelia. "I just asked her to chuck a shoplifting case." She turned to look up at Monty now with an expression of confusion. "A Mars Bar from Sainsbury by a despo addict," she shook her head, "and she looked at me as if I had just skooshed mustard on her salmon."

"New generation of fiscals, Aurelia," whispered Monty whilst taking in a good look at Heung. There had been a time when a few Edinburgh-based court lawyers could regularly get cases binned—*pro loco et tempore*[108]—after a quiet word across the oval table with the fiscal on pleading day, but Monty knew that those days were long gone now. He recollected that one of the best fiscals to approach for a *pro loco* had been Mark Dailly. Eventually, Heung finished her push for punishment, then one of the seated solicitors got up and argued for three minutes for forgiveness for his homeless, alcoholic, opportunistic client. Sheriff Kelvin, an attractive looking lady in her late forties, eventually told the guilty chap to stand up with a charming smile.

"Angus Rennie, you have pled guilty to opening an unlocked car and stealing £28.00. I have heard what your solicitor has said on your behalf and I take on board the fact that you have a serious drink problem which most probably influenced this act. I see that you are a first offender too, and so I am prepared to dispose of this matter by imposing a repayment order upon you as well as a fine of £200.00," she informed him. "Are you prepared to agree to this proposal, Mr Rennie?"

The guy nodded and mumbled that he was. Monty wondered how that would affect the guy's ability to buy alcohol and whether or not he would be back in front of the court on a non-payment warrant sooner rather than later. Suddenly, the guy's solicitor, a slim dark-haired man whom Monty had not seen before, and with a Glaswegian accent, scurried over to confer with his client and then scurried back and addressed Kelvin. "M'lady, Mr Rennie receives a benefit living allowance of £57,00 per week which is paid monthly. He proposes instalments of £5.00 per month?" he pleaded.

Kelvin was looking down at the paperwork in front of her now and there was an intense sense of anticipation around the court; even old Cunningham had stopped ogling the fiscal and was looking over at the Sheriff now. The defending solicitor sat back down now and played with a pen between his fingers whilst Heung took a sip of mineral water from a small plastic bottle opposite him. The only sound was that of the Clerk of Court typing on her computer. Monty knew the clerk well, another old-school female who had been around since the old days

---

[108] To desert a legal case *pro loco et tempore* means to stop the indictment or summary proceeding further without the facts being determined.

when the Sheriff Court had once occupied what was now the High Court building on the Royal Mile.

Blonde Betty had a cartoon character's face not entirely unlike that of Bart Simpson's sister—Lisa, Monty often thought. However, her voice was more akin to that of Jean Broadie[109].

Eventually, Kelvin spoke: "Oh I think he can do better than that; £15.00 per month," she declared and of course, there was no complaint. As the convicted client was leaving the dock, Monty popped over and whispered sweet nothings in the old clerk's ears and received a cartoonish smile from her which reminded him of a duckbilled platypus. Consequently, his two cases were called after Aurelia's shoplifter—whom she pled Not Guilty for. Fifteen minutes later, Monty had collected his stuff from his locker upstairs and left the building.

It had heated up outside now and there was a bright glare coming down from above. He stopped to rumble around his briefcase for his sunglasses and when he found them, paused for a moment and noted that Ivan had a pair on too now; which made him seem even more like a KGB agent. Monty then headed up Chambers Street and on to George IV Bridge, or Lawyers Avenue, as he referred to it. He called it this because he nearly always bumped into one of the many solicitors or advocates who commuted up and down it on their route between the Court of Session, High Court and Sheriff Court buildings.

There was warm sunshine, tourists and their coaches everywhere, whilst tacky touristy shops thrived; even the newsagents had tartan trinkets on display in their windows. The aroma of Italian food and coffee mingled with French patisseries and Turkish menemen[110] to fill the air with a continental vibe.

Monty loved this street usually, but today there was something different about it. Something not quite right, he sensed. He slowed his pace to try to figure it out, scanning both sides of the road as well as up ahead. He couldn't make anything out though, but once again, he felt watched. At that moment, he had an image of his parents pop up in his head. It was not of any warm family memory however, rather it was an image that he had never seen before—that of their mangled bodies covered both in blood and smashed windscreen glass.

---

[109] A 1930s Edinburgh teaching character from the Muriel Spark novel—*The Prime of Miss Jean Broadie,* who was played by Maggie Smith in the 1969 film of the same name.
[110] A traditional Turkish breakfast of scrambled eggs and sautéed vegetables served with toast.

He knew that had been how they had been discovered by police after the crash, but he had not seen either of them until the funeral when only his Mother had an open coffin; his father's face having apparently been beyond the talent of the undertaker. He stopped now for a moment and pretended to stand in a queue at a bus stop; just to take a breath and understand what had just flashed up in his mind. He knew he had not created the images—he was sure of that much. He felt fear now though—real fear. Ivan stopped a few feet behind him and wondered if they were about to get on another bus somewhere and so was looking for his day saver ticket that he had purchased earlier.

Monty knew that someone had placed these images in his mind; it had to be the Orcadian. He removed his shades a moment and looked around again. There were plenty of people passing by but no one in particular stood out as a threat. Ivan now saw that Monty was sketching the area and wondered what was up— what had he heard or seen? He instinctively began doing likewise. Then Monty started walking again, faster and then faster, not because he sensed any threat pursuing him, but because it just felt better to do so. Confusion and panic arrived now, and he was aware that the Orcadian's office was nearby.

As he zig-zagged along and through the endless flow of people heading in the opposite direction, Monty tried to apply reason to his suspicions in order to smooth this out. He wondered if it had just been his imagination, but his heart was going like the clappers and his mouth felt parched and unpleasant. He knew better though—this was something applying tension. The images of his parents had been vivid and detailed, his father's crooked yet silent squeal of fear had been blasted into his brain by some unseen, nonverbal channel. Then everything appeared to be normal again for the next few yards with no more visions springing to mind, but his heart rate continued to pound. He now felt a trickle of sweat on his temple.

When he came to be opposite the Central Library building, he impulsively looked over at the library's upper facade, which appeared to have two stone gargoyles upon it. One of which appeared to be looking directly down at him. Aware that the original sculptor had probably intend this, he quickly looked away and continued walking but could not prevent himself from looking back up again.

It had moved, clearly it had moved—No doubt about it.

It was now smiling at him and so he stopped dead in his tracks. He could clearly see that it was moving slowly upon its stone carved legs along the frieze, then it stepped down upon a window ledge where it proceeded to sit like a dog and grinned an evil looking grin right down at him.

Monty looked around now in fear, yes—fear, which now engulfed him, but also to see if anyone else was observing this—no one was though. People simply hurried past or chatted on their phones and so he searched through the crowd for Ivan, and quickly located him about three yards behind. The big Russian was watching him curiously and didn't even glance over at the library building. Monty himself was witnessing this phenomena, he realised. He instinctively touched the cork in his pocket now, whilst gazing up at the beast which continued to smile down at him. Then below, underneath another window ledge, he saw a sculpted Edinburgh coat of arms.

The design was that of a long-haired woman and a doe. These two sculptures also began moving now. Monty gasped and was close to crying out but his eyes were still glued to the stone carvings and so he instead did nothing but stand there breathing heavily and twiddling the cork in his pocket. The stone woman now began strangling the doe upon the library wall and not one of at least two-hundred people on either side of the road looked up to witness the doe's helpless kicking. There was a motto in Latin upon the coat of arms, and the grinning gargoyle was pointing a long-nailed reptilian finger at it—*Nisi Dominus Frustra*.

"Except the Lord in vain?" Monty suddenly found that he could translate the Latin.

Then a voice appeared in his head now, a mysterious and severe voice, but not unlike that of a man who was being strangled: "Accept the Lord in vain." It mocked callously. "I'm entertained by the fact that someone with your old bloodline, Stephen, cannot read it properly."

Terror filled Monty now and so he turned and began walking faster again towards the Royal Mile. "So you see, by accepting him now at this late hour, it will be of absolutely no use to you," assured the voice in his head.

"Get out of my head," Monty replied timidly…sweat now pouring down his face and along the inside rim of his sunglasses which were steaming up, but he did not remove them and continued to march on. He tried to remember what the file had said about this kind of mind-playing routine. Then he accidently shouldered into a big body builder type bloke, who was wearing a white vest and shorts.

"Hey watch out, mate," the guy complained in a strong Aussie accent.

"And they are dragons, my boy, not fucking gargoyles," hissed the voice in his head.

The temperature seemed to go up even further and from somewhere, Bananarama's *Cruel Summer* now began playing in his head, but Monty pressed on and around the corner onto the Royal Mile. He glanced over at the seated bronze statue of philosopher John Hume outside the High Court building as he passed. Hume was naked except for his Greek-styled Archaic himation. The statue's face was also now smiling at him and there was a flicking movement under its robe which suddenly opened to reveal a bronze hand masturbating a thick circumcised penis.

Monty looked around again to see if anyone else was noticing this, but the tourists were all standing watching a silver-painted street performer doing a levitating act and had not noticed the sex act being performed by the statue. Then Monty remembered what the file had said now about such magic—"The artful Orcadian reacts sharply to criticism."

Monty thought about this then dug deep mentally and mockingly asked, "What seventeenth-century Scottish philosopher such as Hume would be circumcised, I ask you?" before then promptly turning and continuing across towards Parliament Square.

No reply.

"You wouldn't pass any history exams with that pathetic display. Not quite as clever as you think then, are you? Is that why you were only given the role of the Lord Advocate's deputy then, as opposed to the Lord Advocate position?" he now mentally shouted at the voice in his head.

"What the fuck did you say, you talking chimp?" came the thunderous response which was so deafening and painful that Monty had to drop his suitcase and hold his forehead in both hands for a brief moment as if he had an unbearable migraine.

"Not quite good enough to be the Lord Advocate himself because that role is reserved for yet another talking chimp," Monty continued to shout back regardless of the painful echo between his ears.

And then just like that, the pain was gone. He now felt a hand upon his shoulder which startled him and caused him to quickly turn around. His heart was in his mouth as he came face to face with a concerned-looking Ivan.

"Are you okay?" he asked, quite surprised at the amount of sweat visible on Monty's face.

Monty looked past him and back towards the now still statue of Hume and then up to the rooftops beyond. There was no sign of the gargoyles nor anything for that matter—thank Christ. He blessed himself and nodded excitedly, "Yes…yes, I think so. Okay I, well I,…let's just go," he got the words out between somewhat laboured breaths as he stooped to pick up his case. He then took a deep breath and pressed on to his prearranged meeting. He took a few hurried strides forward before pausing again to squirt a little dry foamy spittle from his mouth down upon the heart-shaped mosaic on the cobbles—the Heart of Midlothian.

Chapter Fifteen

Justice will overtake fabricators of lies and false witnesses.
Heraclitus

Monty sat down beside a tall, but overweight man on the bench outside the former district court building. Ivan loitered beneath a statue of Adam Smith nearby—smoking and watching the festival crowds while the sun slow cooked his shaved head. The bench Monty was sat upon was warm beneath his trousers—too warm actually. He was still on edge and quite tense too, so he couldn't be sure whether it was this, or the heat, that was making him sweat.

"You said you had something for me?" he turned to the man sat to his left and said. The bloke had thinning blond hair, blue eyes and a roundish pink face. From what Monty could see, he also had a set of crooked and badly stained teeth.

"Malky said that you would give me something for my time?" the man looked at Monty and replied. He was dressed as though he was on holiday with dark blue and white Aloha short-sleeved shirt and cream cargo slacks. On his feet, which appeared to be surprisingly small for a man of his size, were a pair of well-worn and scuffed brown leather brogues.

"What can you tell me about George Phillipson?" Monty wanted to know first. He had been attempting to dig up any salacious gossip on Phillipson for a while now in order to provide Dailly with something to chuck at him in court. So far nothing had popped up until recently when an old client—a hash selling bloke in his sixties from Gilmerton named Malky, had finally come up with the name of a cokehead—Donnie McDuff.

McDuff was a 45-year-old unemployed wastewater engineer who had previously been in India for several years, but who was now back living in Edinburgh with his third wife—a Nigerian who married him for a visa. Monty had not had the pleasure of meeting Mrs McDuff but judging by her husband's appearance here, it was not too hard to presume that she hadn't married him entirely for his good looks. Apparently, her two predecessors had been from

Rwanda and Vietnam and both divorced him as soon their citizenships had come through.

Some people never learn.

"I used to hang about in a group of around ten pals back in the early nineties in the Corstorphine area," explained McDuff, whilst fanning himself with a Fringe flyer that someone had handed him on his way here.

"And was Phillipson one of the group?" asked Monty whilst looking straight ahead at the old walls of St Giles cathedral.

"No he was older than us, oh and a poof," replied McDuff. "He wormed his way in by firstly smoking blow with us from time to time, but he wasn't like us," he shook his head. "George was always bit of a tramp who came from a skanky council flat up Broomhouse where he still lived with his patents. We were mainly all middle class in the sense that the majority of us lived in private homes whereas his folks didn't even have carpets or double glazing in their flat."

"So?" Monty wanted to get to the nitty gritty of things and was eager to get away from the nearby David Hume. There were throngs of tourists around them now, some taking photos and others just resting upon nearby benches with ice creams and cold drinks. An elderly woman was stood by their bench with three carrier bags full of tourist tack from a nearby Sikh owned shop. Monty guessed that she had relieved herself of hundreds of pounds in the process of filling them. These businesses absolutely thrived here and have provided their owners with palatial homes that would shame a sultan.

Good luck to them.

However, Monty was focussing more upon the surrounding buildings and had noted the stone carved coat of arms upon the city chambers building. He wondered whether it too would begin moving or if the statue of Alexander and Bucephalus[111], which stood beneath, might suddenly come to life and charge at him as they had Darius at Gaugamela?

"So, we all used to go down to Cramond Island and smoke hash, play guitar etc, that kind of thing," continued McDuff now. "George would turn up and have a smoke with us, but he had been a drinker prior to that so I guess he was just a loner who stumbled upon us," he explained.

---

[111] An 1883 bronze statue of Alexander the Great taming his horse, Bucephalus, by Sir John Steel stands in the courtyard of Edinburgh city chambers. Interestingly, there has been a suggestion that Steel, having been short-changed on his fee by the city council, gave Bucephalus pig's ears.

"Like a cat among the pigeons," considered Monty. "Were any of your group homosexual too?"

"No, not at that point but George would work on that that over time." McDuff shook his head and scrunched his mouth up distastefully as if he has something unpleasant in it.

"Why welcome him then?" Why would a group of teenagers indulge an older loaner who had very little in common with them and who was a homosexual?

"I guess initially because cannabis is a social drug and we were all just discovering our own thoughts and processes at that time; it was good to talk to others about such things as music and just life in general." McDuff shrugged, "I guess we also welcomed him in as he could afford to provide the hash regularly."

Monty was aware that he was relaxing more now and may even become comfortable in this sunshine despite his pale pinkish skin, because he had quit fidgeting.

What the hell?

"Various people would come and sit down around our beach fires and smoke blow with us," insisted McDuff. Monty had been no different in his own youth and so understood the scene. "We had a few beach parties before George appeared on the scene, and there had always been plenty of birds around too, which was another learning experience for most of us." McDuff grinned unpleasantly to show more of his disfigured and decaying teeth.

"And?" Monty pressed impatiently; he still wanted to hurry-up however.

"And after that first summer, I think it had been 1988, I can't be sure, but when winter came around, George got a council flat up Wester Hailes and invited us all up for a free smoke," said McDuff. "This was for two reasons—firstly, it was getting colder and we all needed somewhere to go—two, because George was still buying all the hash."

"I see. So, presumably he had a job then as he was older than you lot?"

"Yeh. George was a street sweeper with the council, and we had all just left school back then. It was either that or hang around the beach till it got freezing, as I said, or in each other's parents houses." Nodded McDuff.

"So, are you saying that Phillipson was borderline grooming you all?"

"No, not us all but maybe our leader Ryan Speedie," replied McDuff.

"Right, and?"

"Well, George gradually established himself as the dominant leader of our group and then began imposing his rules and regulations on us."

"Such as?" asked Monty, who was still scanning the city chambers beyond all the sightseers who were commuting up and down the Royal Mile to the sound of drums being played somewhere in the background.

"At first it was small stuff like the music being played in his flat, for example we weren't allowed to put anything on his hi-fi, and he played stuff like Shirley Bassey and Barbara Streisand." McDuff shook his head distastefully. "We weren't allowed to watch football or Eurotrash on the TV either. Once George had established these initial ground rules, he then banned girls from the group, and began regulating the topic of conversation most evenings—if he didn't like the lads discussing something he knew little about, such as football, boxing or even people we knew from school, he raised his voice and targeted his least favourites into changing the subject—which was a clear message to the rest of us . Then he moved on to what the lads could eat or drink etc—he was just a control freak with an agenda."

"Such as?" Monty had stopped sweating but would love to continue the conversation in a cool building though, but he needed to hear more from this guy first.

"He had a particular fancy for introducing vodka to us, which didn't sit well with most of us because we were all stoners, you know—into to early Floyd, Harper, Marley, etc—few of us enjoyed drinking much."

"Did he have a sexual agenda?" Monty was groping for the ammo now.

"Yes, for sure, but first he had to establish dominance over our group, which gradually did by ostracising us all one by one, and then after that, he began targeting the few lads that remained—including the one he had an interest in," replied McDuff glumly.

"And so, he targeted this lad Speedie?"

"Yep, after he had pushed some of us away, which he achieved simply by banning certain people from his flat one after another."

"So they didn't come to his door anymore?"

"If they did they either didn't get any answer or he would tell them they were banned," said McDuff. "Within a few months George had trimmed us down to three or four and this was all tolerated because our so-called leader—Speedie was okay with that."

"Why was he okay with that?"

"Well, initially we all thought it was because Speedie had always been a bit of a user," replied McDuff.

Monty shrugged now and looked suitably mystified.

"Well, despite being our unofficial leader before George had infiltrated our group, Speedie had been a bit financially hard up, in the sense that he wasn't working, and lived with his old man who was just getting by as a bar man."

"Speedie lived in the same street as George, in a council house," continued McDuff, "but he had previously lived in Corstorphine years previously, and so still hung out with us—obviously."

"Fallen on hard times then?"

"That's what we thought but none of us discussed any of it with him. Anyway, he left school a year or so before the rest of us—without any GCSEs and was too lazy to get a job. He was always asking the rest of us if he could borrow our clothes or trainers, whenever our parents bought us new designer gear," explained McDuff. "He was also always asking us to buy him a sweet from the shop too, or bag of chips when he went in a chippy etc, and he could be a bit of a psychological bully in a way too, I guess. So, I think because George was showering him with hash, booze and Chinese takeaways etc, we all just thought that Speedie was taking advantage of him."

"But?"

"But it turned out to be more than that, and in the end—Speedie and George began having a sexual relationship while the rest of us, just moved on and started career paths."

"And what did you do?" Monty was curious.

"I gave up smoking blow and went off to study engineering and then got a job over in Saudi Arabia by the time I was twenty. Then I ended up in India for seven years where I worked in waste management," revealed McDuff with a smugness which was not quite lost on Monty.

"And what do you do now, Donnie?" asked Monty with a mind now to putting this guy on the stand in the case of Her Majesty V Forsyth.

"I'm not working at the moment but I have a few things in the pipeline," assured McDuff, with all the exuberance of a guy on the phone to a relative who needed to be told that all was well.

"So, do you see Phillipson these days?"

"Nope. None of the old group have any time for him. Not even Speedie who is now married and who still denies the true nature of their relationship." McDuff shook his head again distastefully.

"So, the gist of what you're saying is that Phillipson was a sneaky old queen—a manipulator and a control freak?" Monty put it to him.

"A fox in amongst the chickens."

"Well, that's fair enough but it is only your opinion, Donnie, and hardly enough to discredit him," insisted Monty with a distant 'if only' expression upon his now partly dry face.

"It's an accurate opinion though, and the fact that in later life George became a loaner on the dole, who borrowed money from everyone he knew including his relatives, before then bumping them, proves it!" insisted McDuff with obvious derision.

Not in a court of law, sadly.

Malky boy had obviously filled McDuff in on Monty's desire to discredit Phillipson in an outstanding legal matter. Was the guy simply scraping the barrel with hearsay? "Okay," conceded Monty after a moment. "Is there anything else you can tell me about him?"

Still digging.

"He is a serial failure who has failed his driving test a few times—has never travelled abroad, and has no qualifications or achievements," insisted McDuff in the hope of earning the promised coin.

"Hmm," Monty scratched his head now.

"He likes young boys, and is on benefits," offered McDuff in what seemed to be a desperate last throw of a dice. "He has always been jealous of the achievements of others, even his own family who have all done better than him with their lives," he assured. "Let me tell you how treacherous he was, one of our crew, having been ostracised by George, started dealing a little bit of hash, nothing much mind, just a little bit to the rest of us, but suddenly he was grassed up and we all strongly suspected that it had been George because he feared us straying and hanging out elsewhere," he alleged.

Well, I can't give that to a jury obviously.

"And apparently, he is now pretending that he has converted to Islam and is hanging around mosques because he is targeting young refugee lads," Added McDuff.

"How do you know that if you haven't seen him in years?"

"Word of mouth and besides, his Facebook page is riddled with a combination of young Asian lads and Islamic propaganda."

Well, that fitted with the young refugee in Philipson's statement at least.

"So, he has a taste for guys-that isn't really going to help my client. " Monty thought aloud.

"Suppose not," agreed McDuff. "He is a horrible sleazeball though; the type of guy who will never take his parents out to dinner even if he lives to be 100 years old."

"Okay, look," said Monty, tired of sitting here exposed to the elements and whatever else might be lurking upon the roof tops, "here's the fifty quid you were promised for meeting up with me." He slipped the cash to McDuff. "Would you be prepared to come to my office now and give me a statement on Philipson's character and then appear in court for me to be questioned about it, if I needed you to?"

McDuff looked surprised at this and was clearly unsure about it, but he discretely took the cash and slipped it into his shorts. "There will be another grand on top of that for you after the trial if you do help, but it must be completely between us and if you repeat what I have just said to anyone, even Malky, I'll deny it," assured Monty very firmly.

"So, I won't get the grand until after the court case?" asked McDuff with a pang of disappointment.

"You'll get it if and when you give evidence in court," pledged Monty.

McDuff was silent now for what seemed like an eternity. Nearby the drums were replaced by bagpipes and cheers—Monty could hear Japanese accents nearby. He could not speak Japanese, but he knew it was not Chinese or Korean. "And I'll slip you another hundred too, once we do the initial statement at the office," he chucked in another sweetener and gave McDuff a friendly nod. For it was clear that the man was in need of cash right now.

"Where is your office?" McDuff was on the verge of biting his hand off.

"Two minutes away." It was closer to ten in these crowds but who was counting?

McDuff sighed, his mouth watering at the bait. He checked his watch and considered things for a second or two—if he accepted then he could pick up a bag of coke on his way home afterward and still pay the dreaded gas bill—no brainer. He slowly nodded his agreement and offered Monty his hand.

"Right, let's go then." Monty shook it firmly and stood up.

The crowds on the Royal Mile had thickened and there were several street performers on the go with English accents and colourful props who were attracting even more observers from the main drag. Monty ushered McDuff, who hadn't even noticed Ivan, around to the back of the crowd between tables of drinkers and diners on the pavement, and like a secret service agent on a protection assignment. Despite the pressure to get this witness down to the office without him being tempted to bolt down one of the various alleyways which led off from the main drag, or from being flame throwed by a monstrous stone gargoyle from above, Monty was able to wade a path for them both easily enough.

Anyone used to jinking in and out of large crowds at football matches would manage this and so this was a relatively simple process now. Within a couple of minutes or so, Monty had the asset out of the throng and onto the Bridges—wherein it was a relatively calmer stroll down to the office. A quick look behind however revealed that big Ivan was having less luck and who was now simply resorting to barging a group of teenagers out of his way before finally emerging like an explorer who had just cut his way through some dense jungle.

Eight minutes later, they arrived at the office and so Ivan sat on someone's red car outside and smoked another cigarette; becoming a tad fed-up off with this role and was wishing that he had worn trainers instead of a suit and formal shoes today. At that moment, a couple of Labour Party canvassers approached him and offered him a flyer. "Fuck off!" he snarled at them and so they then duly scampered away in the direction of Waverly without so much as a backward glance.

Inside, old Trisha was slouched on the reception desk wearing a blouse as accessible as an open prison and which seemed to be twenty years too young for her. Consequently, her wrinkly fake-tanned former assets were on full display. Both Monty and McDuff took in the view for a second whilst she blew on her freshly painted nails before eventually noticing them. At which point she gave Monty her genuinely pleased to see you smile, which rapidly became a come-to-mama, smile. "Trish, I'm going to quickly take a statement from this gentleman, can you get it typed up pronto so he can sign it and get himself home please?" He gave her the puppy dog eyes routine.

As if I've not got enough on my plate here with my nails, sweetie.

"Sure." She clenched her teeth and gave McDuff the once over.

"Thanks." Monty winked at her and then led McDuff upstairs to his office.

"Right, Mr McDuff, have a seat please," he insisted as he filled them both cups of chilled water from the standing cooler which Llewellyn had recently installed in everyone's offices. "So, I'll read into this." He then produced a small silver handheld dictation device from his desk drawer and inserted a miniature cassette into it.

McDuff nodded as Monty sat down now and loosened his tie. There were noises outside of the office door and one or two doors shutting. "I'll just skirt over things and leave out the grassing up of the drug dealer part, as that won't help me much, then I'll get Trisha downstairs to quickly type it up— then you're away…okay?" he stated cheerily. McDuff just nodded and placed both his hands under his thighs. Just then there was a knock on the door and Ally Blyth popped his head in,

"Oh, sorry, I'm away to Polmont Young Offenders for a visit so I will catch you later." He winked at Monty, who promptly nodded back at him with the machine held up to his mouth. "Right Al," he replied as Blyth quietly closed the door again. "I'll begin then."

He went over things, giving a slight twist here and there and stopping to confirm things such as McDuff's date of birth and address as well as some rough dates and locations.

Monty was focussed primarily upon attacking Phillipson's character by painting him to be a manipulative homosexual control freak who was a serial failure and who spent his life borrowing and failing to repay his friends. He also homed in on the drug use, as he was aware that Phillipson had a minor conviction for drugs. Twenty minutes later there were two typed copies of the statement on the desk before McDuff who barely read them before signing them both. Monty casually pretended to be sending a text to another lawyer as McDuff was in the process of signing the statements but was in fact secretly recording him—just in case McDuff forgot that he had signed them.

"Right, here is your bus fare." Monty handed him another £100.

"Thanks, so when will the court case be, do you think?" The greedy little bugger wanted to know.

"Starts next week, so you'll probably get a citation sent to you tomorrow," Monty told him.

You hadn't seen that one coming, had you.

McDuff looked stunned for a brief second and then his eyelids began to flicker like a bat's who was being exposed to daylight, before he then remembered the money and quickly collected himself. He then shrugged, hoping to display significantly more composure than he felt. "Fine, suits me then. How long do you think I'll be needed?" he queried.

Money talks.

"Probably just a half a day or so, mate," assured Monty enthusiastically.

"Fine okay, see you next week then."

Certainly does.

McDuff then stood up and left the room with the look of a man who had adjourned the dreadful hour. Once the door was shut, Monty smirked and refilled his cup and sat down again to go over the statements. A copy would remain here in Forsyth's file and in a minute, he would fire around to Mark Dailly's office and personally deliver a second copy. The hour was late—true, but this was damning character evidence against Phillipson and it may well lead a jury to take him with a pinch of salt.

Once he had finished reading, Monty nipped out for a piss in the toilets along the corridor. As he stood there peeing, he could still hear the bagpipes from up the road and a loudspeaker which seemed closer— the female voice coming from it was endorsing the Tories and referring to what she regarded as SNP negligence across the board since they had first swept to power in 2007:

"Under the SNP in the past eight years, your NHS has deteriorated. In the quarter to the end of March this year, 47,390 outpatients waited more than twelve weeks before being seen while 21,987 waited more than sixteen weeks. As for outpatients still waiting after twelve weeks, the previous three quarters have seen the highest numbers since the existing measurement scheme was established".

The speaker must have been coming from a vehicle as it soon faded away and Monty was suddenly conscious of how tired he felt. Not only tired of the politics but tired physically too. It must be the sun, he reasoned. It had a habit of overpowering everyone and this heat was not normal for Scotland.

Climate change?

He re-zipped— washed his hands in the sink and thought about those stone gargoyles earlier. What the fuck were they? The images of his parents had been brutal and would probably stay in his head until he died now. He would be talking to Dai about this for sure. He wanted to cry now but knew it wasn't possible— not here.

When he returned to his office, he was surprised to find Cuthbert sitting upon his desk reading McDuff's statement with his legs crossed.

"Hi Stevie, what do you make of all this election stuff then?" he asked in an unusually friendly tone of voice whilst gesturing a hand towards the window, but without taking his eyes from the statement—his overly wide smile being the obvious evidence of his disingenuousness.

Monty was not cuckolded by his gentle tenor, however. "When it comes to that lot, Russell, I find the truth to be elusive until they start formally refuting it," he replied.

Cuthbert couldn't help but look up at him in a totally conspiratorial manner—breaking out the remnants of a leer. Monty suspected that he had been eavesdropping on McDuff giving his statement. "I thought you had a big case today?" he asked him as he took a seat.

Cuthbert returned his gaze back to the statement and began reading again: "It was adjourned until next week, as one of the crown witnesses has been delayed at Gatwick," he mumbled.

"I see." Monty wanted to snatch the papers from him.

"I've got another big trial next week though, so we shall have to see how things develop," sighed Cuthbert.

A parking on a pelican crossing at the district court then, is it?

"A new witness in your murder trial then is it?" asked Cuthbert without lifting his gaze.

Did he just read my thought?

"Talking of the truth, what are you doing here, Russell?" Monty had just about enough of him.

Cuthbert looked up—his voice back to normal. "Reading this statement, as is abundantly obvious," he replied as cold as ever.

"Why?"

"Because I want to and because I am a senior partner at this firm which employs you." The chill remained.

Monty snatched the papers from his hand. "Fuck off," he mouthed at him.

Cuthbert stood up now. "What did you just say?" He swung around accusingly and frowned.

"Just fuck off, Russell." Monty turned his back on him by swinging his chair around and searched for a stapler.

"You're on thin ice, mister." Cuthbert waved a finger at him now. "You have spent the last few months trying to milk our clients for info on a Crown witness in this Forsyth case, and now at this late hour you have conjured up that pish," he pointed to the statements.

I always disliked your habit of putting on a colloquial accent when being aggressive. Not only is it not effective, but it makes you seem comical, Russell.

"How do you know what I have or have not asked my clients?" snapped Monty as he finally found a stapler.

"The firm's clients. Get it right," Cuthbert corrected him with the same unconvincing smile. "And this McDuff character just happens to appear at the last minute and gifts you a futile statement before then walking out of here counting a handful of cash?" He stared at Monty for a moment before adding an overbearing, "Well?"

There was a prolonged silence between then now. "Fishing around for mud to sling at the Crowns witness for months on end?" Cuthbert eventually shook his head in mock despair. "Is that the only defence open to the great Dailly?" he asked.

"It's my job." Sighed Monty, stapling the two statement papers and placing them in his briefcase.

"No," snarled Cuthbert. "Your job is to pass the brief over and advise—and to make sure we get our legal aid payment—that's all!"

Monty ignored him, locked the case and started to put his suit jacket back on. "You're going overboard with these desperate attempts to create a defence witness here, Stevie." Cuthbert pointed at the briefcase. Monty sighed, but said nothing despite having an inner smirk.

Your mask is coming off.

Refusing to sheath his sword however, Cuthbert continued, "First you give the Forsyth brief to Dailly, without as much as a discussion with myself, despite knowing only too well that we don't use his chambers for high court matters," he pointed out with a look of excruciating contempt across his face. "And now you're swearing at me and refusing to let me view the case?" He was obviously rehearsing the hymn he intended singing to Llewellyn when arguing for Monty's sacking. "Well, I tell you what," frowned Cuthbert now, clearly on the verge of losing his temper—*there goes the mask*—"you can come in and see myself and Arty next week and we shall discuss exactly what your job is, as well as your future in this firm—right?" He insisted with the left side of his upper lip now coiled into a snarl.

At this, Monty exhaled deeply from his nostrils and spun around slowly on his heels, case in one hand, mobile phone in the other, whilst meeting Cuthbert's pallid coldblooded stare, and replied: "Whatever you say, boss!" He then winked and made for the door.

"You're pissing off a lot of influential people with this, Stevie, and it's about time you understood just how detrimental it could be to your career." Cuthbert cast his line after him but then instantly wished that he had not.

Monty stopped and about-turned again. "By providing a defence for an accused person?" He grinned back cynically. Cuthbert stood there, right foot tapping, and stared hard at him for a moment.

"And who precisely am I pissing off, Russell, hmm?"

"Don't be so fucking naïve, Stevie." Cuthbert's control finally cracked.

"Well, enlighten me, Russell. Some of your handshake brigade pals perhaps? Or some more sinister ego-driven individuals?"

Cuthbert sneered disapprovingly but then dismissed him with a flick of his wrist.

"If it is, then do say so, Russell, as I'd like to know. Because Christopher Forsyth is innocent and has been set up and if you know something about that then now is the time to say," insisted Monty—refusing to retreat.

Cuthbert continued to stare, his cold eyes radiating defiance. "Are you completely off your trolly, Stevie?" he finally demanded to know.

"So, you know what I'm talking about then?" nodded Monty knowingly.

Cuthbert composed himself now and straightened his thin black tie before changing tact: "Look, you're digging a hole for yourself here and you need to stop watching certain movies and get your priorities in order," he now said followed by that disturbing grin again.

"Is this what you put to all the other lawyers that you have run out of this firm then, Russell?" Monty asked him.

Cuthbert waved the question away. "Get your arse out of here and be in on Monday at 8am sharp to see myself and Arty," he said before turning away with hands behind his back and slowly strolling over towards the little round window which looked down upon Waverly Station, as if he were Hitler at the Berghof.

"Yep, you don't like that, do you, Russell—being reminded that lawyer after lawyer, have been railroaded out of this firm because of you?" Monty was lowering himself into goading him now.

"END OFF!" snapped Cuthbert without turning around. Monty utterly despised Cuthbert's persistent use of that turn of phrase, particularly when he used it in court, but he bit his lip now and turned and exited the room without closing the door behind him.

You're a horrible little shit Cuthbert and you're destined for hell where I hope you get a red-hot poker shoved up your Japs eye for an eternity—End Off!

He walked downstairs and straight out of the building without acknowledging old Trisha. It was still sweltering outside and the heat blasted him as he hit the pavement. Regardless, he walked at pace towards the taxi rank at Waverly and jumped in the first fast black that he came across without looking up to see if Herr Cuthbert was still admiring the view.

"Where to, pal?" asked the female cabbie wearing shades and who had a raspy smoker's voice.

"Fettes Row please, driver, and I'm just waiting on someone," replied Monty whilst leaning over and holding the door ajar. A few seconds later, Ivan turned up and jumped in without a word. "Going to the New Town and in a hurry, so save you following in another cab," Monty told him. Today being the first time they had ever spoken.

"You're busy today," smiled the big Russian as he settled into one of the small chairs opposite. Monty forced a smile back at him and then closed the door shut. The car swung around and off they went. Just then his phone beeped, and so he fetched it from his inside jacket pocket and swiped it open. It was a text message from his son.

Fancy the football next Wed night dad? Hearts were hosting Celtic next week, Monty now remembered. He looked at Ivan, who was engrossed in his own phone now. Tynecastle would be a perfect place for a murder, wouldn't it, and he would have to get a third ticket for whomever was shadowing him that night too.

Reply:

Don't know son, I have a murder trial all next week so could be late finishes most nights as lots of homework to do. We could get a takeaway and watch it at mine instead if you fancy?

Sent.

The journey down to Mark Dailly's chambers took around ten minutes, despite the traffic. On Hanover Street they pulled up behind a big red transit van that was, as per the Tory vehicle, blasting out political waffle from a loudspeaker. There were several teenagers in red t-shirts leaning out of the windows waving little handheld union jack flags and smiling cheerily at passers-by.

"*Whilst the Scottish Liberation Party promote racial segregation and blame all your problems on outsiders, the SNP have also mastered this strategy by blaming everything on London and the Union. Yet neither party can answer the key questions put to them on either the economy, or crime. The SNP have centralised the police service, creating serious issues with crime, whilst the SLP propose to go a step further and introduce a totalitarian police state where the police are armed with lethal weapons in order to enforce an authoritarian administration who pursue the destruction of both our demographic diversity and Scotland's political pluralism,*" insisted a posh sounding male who was singing the hymn.

"Ah wouldnie vote Labour again if they were giving away free fish suppers," insisted the cabbie—she was obviously looking for a chat.

Neither Monty nor Ivan took her up on it however.

Ping...a text:

Okay Dad can we have a beer too lol?

Monty replied just as the lights changed and they got moving again: *We'll see. Text you Tuesday night to see where we are at.*

Sent.

When they finally arrived at Dailly's chambers, Monty gave the cabbie a tenner and jumped out. "I will be about twenty minutes," he called back to Ivan without turning around. Ivan did not respond and slowly got out and took a slow walk along the street and back, wherein he would consume at least two more cigarettes and continue to check up on his Facebook messages.

Monty walked in through an elegant Georgian Palladian archway which was crudely adorned with framed contemporary modern art. Clearly someone had redecorated their house and brought all these ugly prints here instead. "Mark Dailly please?" He smiled at a young female seated behind a panelled wooden desk, and who was, by the sound of it, casually flicking through a glossy magazine.

"May I have your name please sir?" She looked up at him with a sweet poker face. She was evidently West Coast American.

"I'm Stephen Montgomery, his advising solicitor." Monty knew that most Fridays, Dailly would be in his office from midday onwards and that today he would most certainly be in working on the Forsyth trial.

The girl picked up a green handset and called upstairs then relayed the information to Dailly before smiling and politely hanging up again. "Just go on up, Mr Montgomery." She smiled at him now before returning to whatever engrossing mag she had been reading—*Cosmopolitan, judging by the pile of used copies on a nearby table.*

"Come in, Monty," smiled Dailly. He too was sat down working, but behind his colonial-period desk where he was going over some files. Monty chucked one copy of the signed statement down before him. "Manna from heaven." He grinned.

"Yummy." Dailly smiled and picked it up to take a gander whilst motioning Monty to take a pew opposite. As Dailly read, Monty rubbed his temples. The sunshine followed by that little drama with Cuthbert was starting to pall on him now. He had always taken Cuthbert for a mason of course, everyone had, but a Satanist? Now that was something else entirely.

Wasn't it?

The guy celebrated Christmas just like everyone else, Monty new. Then again, he considered, so did most atheists, Muslims, Hindus and Sikhs. Maybe it was simply a case of power from above being pressed down upon the grunts, and as Cuthbert had himself suggested, there were people getting pissed off somewhere or other?

"I caught Cuthbert in my office reading it," he told Dailly.

Dailly looked up curiously. "Really?"

"Yep. He wasn't happy and told me in a veiled way to bin it as I was pissing certain people off by my efforts, as well as having given you the original brief."

Dailly sighed. "Well, no surprise there really, is there. We always knew he was batting for the dark side, but he is just a small fry, so let's not concern ourselves with such arseholes, Monty." He smiled and returned to the statement.

So you know who the dark side is?

"Well, he is hauling me in on Monday for some sort of bullshit disciplinary so I think after this trial, I'll be inclined to walk away from the firm." Sighed Monty.

Dailly looked up again for a moment and appeared to consider this before then coming out of his reverie. "Fine, I'll call up Bobby Ainsley at Ainsley &

Rioch tonight and let him know that you might be available, as he was telling me recently that he was on the lookout for a bit more experience," he declared. Ainsley had a busy firm based in Tollcross, and Monty got along well enough with the old Hibs supporter, so much so in fact, that they usually had a banter about the football whenever they bumped into each other.

Monty had not seen him in a while as his partner—Jim Rioch did most of the firm's criminal stuff in Edinburgh these days. Rioch was more withdrawn and less approachable but he was a damn fine operator who had once had a well-known clash with Cuthbert in the court loo regarding something or other. "I would appreciate that, Mark, thanks."

"Nae bother. Right," Dailly put the statement down again, "well, it's hardly steak or salmon, Monty, but yes…manna it surely is." He smiled.

"Useful?"

"Well…" Dailly paused and gave it a quick look over again. "It doesn't suggest Phillipson is full of unreliable spite mind, but along with his previous drugs conviction, we can use it to paint him as both a manipulator and a generally untrustworthy character." He nodded.

"Which is surely all we really have to do to get a Not Proven across the line?" suggested Monty.

"Well, we still have the police verbals, as in the cops claiming our man admitted his guilt to them in Tenerife, to deal with, but yes, this McDuff statement can be useful if handled correctly," agreed Dailly.

"Good." Monty exhaled and leaned back on the chair.

"Our advantage here is that despite said verbals usually being enough to get the Crown to raise murder charges; in this case, they lack any serious supporting evidence," assured Dailly.

"So, all set for trial then?" asked Monty.

"Sure," nodded Dailly with a default expression across his face.

"Okay-dokay, well, I'll call Kenny and have him cite this McDuff guy just now, then get a copy of this statement faxed over to him pronto. I'll see you there on Tuesday, but Kenny might bell you on Monday just to see if anything else needs done." Dailly nodded hearteningly and picked up the phone to the junior counsel for the trial—Kenny Mercer.

Monty took his cue and got up to leave. He spotted the bottle of Macallan over on a table by the window and felt a sudden urge for a drink now. He could head around the corner to the Cumberland Bar and sink a couple of glasses of

Cote du Niddrie; perhaps his big Russian Shadow might also participate? Outside he approached the big Russian who was now on his third cigarette and walking towards him. "I'm going to go for a drink on my way home, do you fancy joining me?" he asked.

Ivan took him in for a moment before nodding. "I'll go in for a lemonade and sit away from you at the bar, it is best that we are not seen together," he insisted. Fair enough. And so, they walked a yard or two apart to the Cumberland. Once there, Monty ordered two glasses of Cote du Niddrie and took a private booth alone whilst Ivan entered a few minutes later and discretely chose to sit at the bar with his pint of lemonade and copy of a local rag.

Monty supped deeply at the plonk; it had been a draining day thus far and he wanted a cold shower. He was worried about the trial too and this eat at him now. He saw himself as a competent lawyer, if not a good one, but Dailly was certainly a good one. Yet he couldn't help asking himself whether this was going to be anywhere near enough. Forsyth had left the selection of junior counsel down to Monty, who in turn had asked Dailly to pick someone. Mercer wasn't a QC, but he was canny enough advocate, and certainly from the handful of emails and calls Monty had exchanged with him, Mercer seemed handy enough.

But was this three-man team going to be enough?

Some lawyers read law at university in the hope of perhaps taking silk or becoming a judge; others are interested in political power. Whereas Monty had chosen criminal law because he wanted nothing more than to be a day to day, court lawyer. Perhaps he wouldn't experience any of the so-called fascinating points of law in the criminal courts, but since joining his present firm, he had stumbled into manly maturity and come into his own as a defence lawyer. He had experienced some wonderful victories in recent times, as well as learning from the odd miscalculation too.

All he really had to go on, though, was retrospection and talent, but he had learned well from his mistakes. The good results had come from skill and old-fashioned research, as opposed to the conveniency of the internet. He was, he supposed, an old-fashioned type of guy who felt that it was more important to protect innocence than it was to punish guilt. He had initially been naïve about the law, whereas he now knew that automatic justice for a falsely accused person was not always mandatory, and even if a good defender fought for it, they were often outnumbered and out-played in the process. All a defence lawyer could do was his best, and hope for good luck.

Had he done enough research here though? Could he have unearthed anything else on the witness Phillipson? Or even the cop witnesses? He sighed to himself now as he polished off the first glass of wine and then dragged the second over with the tip of his finger. Any mistakes he had made in his career had only intensified his readings thereafter, and so traditionally, the two main ingredients that he went with in criminal law were impulse and skill.

Neither of which were providing much positivity to him presently however. He had always wanted to win cases on his own terms, and not as others, such as Cuthbert, dictated. In a way then, he had always been a lone fisherman throwing his net into mucky streams long discarded by others. It had been evident to him that there was never any automatic justice within his profession—true.

Good men have to fight to see justice.

If no one fights however, it is thus unlikely to occur. Fighting for justice, as even people outside of the judiciary will confirm, is never an effortless process either. Monty knew only too well that it was always a stressful and demanding struggle for all involved. He understood too, that it was only normal then that he should be fatigued, anxious, and freaked out by his recent experiences.

It was still demanding and draining, regardless of Dai's appearances. He sensed now that he may not have enough mud to sling at Phillipson or the alcoholic mother either. The whole process had been hard enough so far, and he felt like a blind man with a key pottering around an unfamiliar street looking for a door.

Justice was going to be hard to achieve here, and how would defeat be accepted by God, he wondered? This well-established dark force, with their excessive power, desire an autocratic system of justice and intend to get it. His notion of a fair and impartial justice system however, presents a threat to their autocracy. So, in order to make justice exist, it is unfortunately necessary to have to fight it out with them. They were stronger, more cunning and utterly sneakier for sure. Yet he could not sheath the sword nor bend the knee to them. He still believed in the real spirit of justice for all. To him it is the judgment of the people that counts—It is the panel of people on the jury system, regardless of the appalling effort by the dark side to suppress the truth.

He necked the majority of the second glass now. Emboldened by it somewhat, he concluded his thoughts by reminding himself that, in the question of The People V Excessive Power, he would side with the people every time regardless of the cost. Suddenly, part fatigued, part in love—for just an instant, with the notion of judicial martyrdom, he emptied the glass and was jerked out of his brooding by the sound of a TV from above the bar. It was reporting comments that the SNP leader had made whilst being interviewed beside the ever-familiar fireplace of her Bute House residence. Monty noted that she was apparently having another go at the Tories and declaring David Cameron to be on borrowed time.

Another rush of dread overpowered him for a moment as he remembered it was election time on Monday, but he consoled himself by deciding here and now, not to participate. If anything, he would have voted for any party, including the SNP, if it meant keeping out the SLP. A nasty streak of racism had taken root in Scotland now through them, the seeds of which had apparently originated elsewhere. He ruminated that a generation prior to his, that of the 1980's, had possessed a far more enlightened view of race relations, and that the SLP had seized upon the demographical changes to raise unwarranted concerns.

Anyone can see how they champion the old working-class football casuals—who secretly seek a return to mob street violence. Fuck it, maybe he would vote Green then.

He stood up now and returned his empty glasses to the bar—thanked the barman and left without giving Ivan a glance. He decided to walk in the direction of home until a fast black appeared, wherein he would again offer Ivan a ride back to his car, which would presumably be baking hot by the time the big Russian returned to it.

He would send Charnley out with a cold drink for him.

Chapter Sixteen

Correction does much, but encouragement does more.
Johann Wolfgang von Goethe

It was late and the smell of the Indian food they had eaten earlier still lingered in the air as they sat watching the election results floating in. Charnley had ordered it for them when he returned from spending the afternoon with his Mrs at the botanical gardens. She appeared to be supportive of him and understanding of the strange situation; at least that was what Charnley said. She tended to travel over to Edinburgh on a Sunday afternoon, or occasionally on a Monday when Monty was working so she and Charnley had the house to themselves.

Having attended the early morning meeting at the firm's office with Cuthbert and Llewellyn, which had not lasted particularly long, Monty was tired. Cuthbert had accused him of leading the witness McDuff into giving a questionable statement, and then of being abusive thereafter when confronted about it. Monty had told him where to go, yet again, and then turned to Llewellyn and offered his resignation. Llewellyn, well aware that too many decent lawyers had been lost to the firm as a result of Cuthbert, refused to accept it.

Instead, he had calmly told Monty to go away and think about things, and that he would call him later. Cuthbert had contemptuously scanned Monty like a hawk as he left. He had failed to strike the fatal blow, and so Forsyth's defence would continue regardless. Monty had left the meeting relieved that it had been cut short and with a spring in his step.

I'm still leaving after the Forsyth trial.

He then walked over to the Sheriff Court and did three custody weekenders. One was for a shoplifter, the next—one of Jimmy's crew who had been pinched with a small amount of heroin in a car that was not his, and finally—a female prostitute who had allegedly stabbed her client on the head with a pen. Monty had, as per his agreement with Jimmy, waved any fee for the driver. Afterwards, as he was leaving the court building, he had received a call from Malky the old pusher from Gilmerton—he had a little more info on Phillipson. "He was apparently pinched for working in a pub in Leith—The Bass Rock, whilst claiming benefits back in 2009," he revealed.

"What happened?" Monty wanted to know if Phillipson had been charged or not.

"He got pinched by the dole, that's all I know," replied Malky.

Monty knew it would be hard going to look into this at this late hour, what with the trial kicking off tomorrow, however he was also aware that Dailly could just ask Phillipson straight out whilst under oath in the dock, whether this was true or not, and thus potentially force an admission from him.

How was Philipson to know whether they had checked up or not?

If on the other hand, Phillipson lied, and they were to later confirm that he had—even better. The jury could then be informed that the main Crown witness had lied under oath, thus painting him as an erroneous witness.

"Are you sure of this?" asked Monty.

"Ninety-nine percent sure—it is from a good source," insisted Malky.

"Right thanks for chucking me another bone Malky." Monty had represented him for several years and always received a bottle of malt dropped off at the office every time he got him off the hook. The relationship was not quite a friendship however, but Monty trusted him more than most. So he sent emails to both Dailly and Mercer from his phone accordingly—filling them in on the new intel and his thoughts on potential questioning.

By the time he arrived at the office and dropped the three custody files off to Trisha, he had received a reply from Mercer, whose wife had apparently been a Job Coach at Wester Hailes Jobcentre until recently, and who: "still had chums there." Mercer hoped they would be able to confirm the facts regarding Phillipson's previous benefit fraud by the end of the day. Monty had then gone home early to prepare for the trial.

Charnley and his wife had been quite understanding and appropriately swanned off to walk among the petunias at the botanic gardens. Monty had some tomato soup which he spooned away at it whilst going over the trial material. Occasionally he would lean back and stare up at the ceiling whilst mentally recalling the content of the Orcadian file.

"His weakness is his arrogance and it can be used against him to instigate his rage."

Monty had progressed through everything that had been chucked at him to date, but he did wonder whether twisting the thumb screws on the Orcadian, in order to activate a potential lapse in control of his temperament, was a wise move?

Hell hath no wrath, and all that jazz.

After lunch he had taken the dog for a run around the Links and then up the old walkway for an hour or so. He noticed Ivan following behind as he proceeded up the old walkway. He soon found his thoughts drifting back to the Orcadian again though and he couldn't help going over it all in his head again throughout the stroll.

"He had loved a sea entity named Ceto who had provided sustenance for his disciples on Orkney. In the end, he had been torn apart from her and still pines for her presently."

Assortative mating did not appear to be a practice that the fallen angels cared much about then, he considered as he headed back home— fingers upon the cork at all times. He had never experienced love, he thought now, at least not in that way. There had been a girl at university but that had not been love. "It's the French way," she would exclaim whenever he stopped her from flicking her tongue in his ear.

So is cruelty to geese and eating snails, so kindly spare me the saliva rinse, sweetie.

Mehreen had not been in touch again since her card last Christmas. He had returned the bible when he had known that she had not been in the office. She was nothing like him, and cultural boundaries require too much effort, should they have started something. Despite this, he was always aware that when two bodies fuse, class and cultural division seem quite irrelevant—at least momentarily.

Perhaps it had been the same for the Orcadian with his sea entity?

After his walk, Monty showered and then took out a cold drink for big Ivan who had been ever present throughout the day and who was now sitting in his car filling out a football coupon. The big man thanked him with a nod, but it was clear that the Russian did not want to get too close and would rather that Monty refrained from such gestures. Regardless, Monty felt obliged because he appreciated every minute that Jimmy's goons put in babysitting him. He then went back inside and text Charnley to ask him to collect the glass from Ivan on his way back. Then he re-took his seat at the kitchen table, sighed, and delved back into the paperwork in search of anything he might have missed. After a while, he stopped as something that he had read in the Orcadian file came to mind again.

"This son of disobedience specialises in all the laws both of the heavens and of the earths, yet he does not respect nor abide by them, as he has no respect for them. He is the enemy of truth— arrogant and haughty, and he has no humility. What he does dread, is prayer. When men pray to God, not only does he, but also all of his choir, tremble with fear. It is therefore in their interests that men abandon prayer."

As well as:

"He enters this realm from his incarceration only through the inter dimensional gates opened to him by God, and even then, only for a specific period of time. His last entrance was in January 1969 when he entered at Aramu Muru[112]. He is only permitted to act according to his mission, and even then only for a specifically sanctioned period. Should he deviate from the rules of the Kertamen, his mission shall be forfeited and he shall be incarcerated once again."

Monty thought about this for a while before Charnley finally returned. Could the Orcadian be provoked into anger—causing him to damage his case? If so, what could provoke such an anger? Short of wrapping up a fish in a pair of suspenders and writing "Ceto" upon it in thick felt tip pen, what could get him going?

Prayer?

When Charnley got back they discussed the previous drama with the moving gargoyle and David Hume statue again. In fact, they had discussed it all weekend as Charnley would urged him to go over it all again and again. "If they appear again cut right through them with this." He pressed his cork to reveal the stunning weapon given to him and which they knew could sever stone.

---

[112] A strangely carved stone doorway in Peru known by locals as *Puerta de Hayu Marca* (*Gate of the Gods*).

"I'll tell you what though, Ronnie," exclaimed Monty. "Once you see something like that your heart pounds and you bowels loosen mate, regardless of who is minding you, or whatever weapon that you might have in your pocket," he assured.

"Well, I still think the bugger was in breach of the rules Monty. He was playing with your mind." Charnley had shaken his head before fetching the takeaway menu of a curry house on Leith Walk. Now as they sat with full bellies—watching the election updates on TV, it was clear that the Tories were romping home nationally, but that both the SNP and SLP were doing well in Scotland. Monty found himself yawning now but still wishing that Dai would turn up for an encouraging pre-trial chat. Neither himself nor Charnley had bothered voting, nor had they discussed where their political inclinations traditionally lay either.

"And news coming in now from Strathkelvin and Bearsden, is that…well…I'm not sure, do we have an update? Well, we think that the SLP candidate Anna Hillis has taken the seat from the SNP," said a posh female presenter whom they both recognised.

Charnley turned to Monty despairingly. "Hate the SLP," he said and Monty nodded in tired agreement. Up until now though, and the count was still relatively young tonight, the SNP had won 27 of the Westminster votes, the SLP—5, and the Scottish Greens—1. This was just a rehearsal for next year's real battle between Scotland's two independence parties, and it was then that Anderson-Forbes and Nicola Sturgeon would commence the real battle for the keys to Bute House. Monty hoped Sturgeon would have a plan to deal with the SLP threat, as this UK election seemed to him to be little more than a side-line for the Scottish political parties.

"I'm away to bed, Ronnie. I've had enough of this crap and I've got the trial tomorrow," said Monty as he dragged himself up from the sofa. Charnley gave him an absent wave, his thoughts towards polishing off the remaining pakoras and poppadoms in the kitchen.

Monty flossed then brushed his teeth in the bathroom, staring at himself in the small oval mirror for a while after. He was aging, that much was clear, and he was stressed out with all of this drama too which didn't help. He sighed and then went through to his bedroom where his black pinstripe single breasted suit was hanging up with ironed white shirt and light grey tie for the morning.

He looked over at his briefcase on the green armchair beside the window and considered flicking through his notes again, but then decided not to. He fetched his phone from his coat pocket which was hanging up behind the door and considered turning it back on again. He had turned it off to avoid Arty Llewellyn's call earlier whilst eating and had not bothered turning it back on. He pressed the on button and then got undressed and placed the cork on the bedside cabinet. It was warm tonight in his room, so he switched on the tall fan which stood in a far corner and which was powerful enough to keep the whole room cool on nights like this. His phone beeped; it was a text from Kenny Mercer which confirmed the following:

"Phillipson was caught working in a pub in May 2009 and initially had his benefit suspended by the benefit agency and then had to repay them over £3000.00."

Monty took a deep breath then exhaled…*Gotcha*!
Then the expected text came through from Llewellyn:

"Tried to call but phone off. Look, we will go over things next week when your murder trial is wound up. Don't worry about Rus, I know he can be a twat but he is a good friend to have."

Monty scoffed at this, and the dog looked up at him in confusion. "May God protect me from my friends," he looked down and said to it, "as I can just about cope with my enemies." Then he went down onto his knees and said the Lord's prayer. He had learned it quite quickly since all of this drama had begun and had added a few reflections of his own. He thanked the Lord for the luxuries in his life, and his meals, as well as for the escape from Cuthbert's dreaded kangaroo court hearing earlier. Then he prayed for success and protection in court tomorrow.

Please Lord, give us a neutral jury at least.

Once he had finished, he sat on the edge of the bed for a moment. He could smell curry being heated up despite his room door being closed. Surprisingly he then thought about the rise of the SLP in Scotland. The charming Anderson-Forbes and his intuitive grasp of the importance of both journalism and broadcasting, which had propelled him into contention with the main political parties.

Monty began to dread the election results in the morning. He could hear Forbes' voice now, his peculiar yet smooth delivery ringing in his ears as clear as day. Just then there was a light knock on his bedroom door. The dog got up and went over, tail wagging excitedly. Half expecting Charnley to appear with a midnight feast on a tray, he called out, "Come in."

The door opened and in walked Dai. "Evening all." He beamed.

There was a soft ethereal light or energy which came from him and which appeared abstract in the lampshade. Monty was transfixed by it. It seemed to place a calmness over both himself and the dog. He could feel the calmness shifting through him like a stiff drink -it was pleasant, though he was quite sure that the sensation could not exist anywhere on this planet. "Thought you would always text first?" he laughed before adding, "I'm glad you came."

Dai smiled back at him and gently moved Monty's briefcase onto the floor before taking a seat on the chair; causing the dog to spring over and jump up onto his lap. He seemed pleased by this and stroked the hound affectionately, "Hello my friend, are you looking after your dad here for us?" he thought to the dog. Monty heard the thought in his head but was surprised to see some recognition in the dog's eyes as it panted away joyfully.

Dai then looked over at Monty. "Are you ready for tomorrow then?" he asked.

"Worried." Monty shrugged his shoulders and smiled. He only had his boxer shorts and a t-shirt on, so he got into bed and sat up under the duvet.

"I know." Nodded Dai.

"You know what happened to me with the gargoyle and the brass statue then?" asked Monty.

Dai nodded again.

"Freaked me out a bit, Dai."

"It was only spell craft." Shrugged the angel.

"Spell craft? It looked pretty real to me." Monty raised his eyebrows at this.

"Precisely. An astral projection of both the stone and the brass statue which only your inner soul could experience," explained Dai. "The fact that no one else saw what you saw is always a clue," he pointed out.

"Is he allowed to do that? I mean, isn't that against the rules?" Monty shook his head.

"You have a favoured bloodline," explained Dai. "He knows that. Only favoured bloodlines can experience astral projections and he communicated with you because of that connection."

"I don't understand, Dai." Monty still didn't grasp how he was any different from everyone else.

"You have a hereditary ability which enables you to experience such illusions. Indeed, your bloodline goes back to a chosen select whose offspring attended the first council of Nicaea, but who remained in the shadows of the proceedings, whilst they noted the disciples of hell who were in attendance[113]."

"Chosen by whom, by you?"

"I am just a messenger, Stephen." Winked Dai.

"As ambiguous as always." Sighed Monty despondently.

"That is all you need to know at present," assured Dai. "We will discuss this further after this Forsyth business is over." He promised.

"Thing is, I'm no warrior, you know." Monty felt the need to point out again.

"Most modern-day battles take place within court and cabinet rooms Stephen, and you will best champion our cause in a very important skirmish tomorrow," promised Dai.

"In times of war, the law falls silent." Monty quoted Cicero.

"Not this war," promised Dai with a serious look now in his otherwise tranquil eyes.

Monty believed him—impossible not to. He did not know how or why—he just did. "Okay." He nodded.

"I do without being ordered what some are constrained to do by their fear of the law." Dai smirked back at him.

"Aristotle?" Laughed Monty and Dai nodded that he was correct.

"You have light in you, Stephen, and you were well chosen."

---

[113] The First Council of Nicaea was the first ecumenical council of the Christian church which was convened by the Roman Emperor Constantine in the Bithynian city of Nicaea (now Iznik in Turkey). It was intended to define unity of beliefs for the whole of Christendom but entailed much arguing between factions. The conclusive result was the first uniformed Christian doctrine called—The Nicene Creed. Notably, Constantine attended whilst wearing a robe made of gold and jewels which glittered as if rays of divine light were present. He did this in order to present himself as a divine messenger of God.

Monty thought about things for a moment whilst Dai continued to stroke the dog. "What if I just blew the whistle in court about him not actually being the crown prosecutor, I mean, he prob doesn't even have a degree, does he?" suggested Monty nervously.

"The court would respond in a similar manner as they would if you suddenly stood up and declared him to be a block of cheese, Stephen, and further down the line, you would end up in the Royal Edinburgh Hospital under a short-term psychological assessment order." Smiled the angel. He allowed this to sink in for a moment before adding, "And the nastier side of the gutter press would then target you thereafter."

"Men are evil, Dai. You know what Cuthbert has been up to this week?" He felt sure the angel would be aware. Dai nodded that he was.

"So, you know that I found another witness then?"

Dai nodded again: "Yes, so a new vegetable has hopped into the stew; well done you."

"So many people are involved in this unholy conspiracy, Dai, I feel it deep down—so many. I felt I had to try to strengthen our hand," Monty mitigated.

"Are you surprised?" Asked Dai. "Regardless of his accomplishments and wisdom, man has fashioned a highly treacherous and perilous world here on earth where all of his attainments may well end up being obliterated by himself."

Dai shrugged his shoulders to indicate this was not necessarily going to happen, just that it could. "So is mankind's destruction inevitable then?" Monty sought reassurance.

"No, there is still time. There are still good people in this dimension who are waging war upon the dark side Stephen, but the warnings of another good man— Daniel Webster, have been ignored over the last century or so and his was an accurate omen." Shrugged the angel.

"Daniel Webster?" Monty had never heard of him.

"Who he was doesn't matter, Stephen, it is what he said that is relevant," clarified Dai.

"Which was?" Monty held in a yawn now.

"If we abide by the principles taught in the Bible, our country will go on prospering and to prosper; but if we and our posterity neglect its instructions and authority, no man can tell how sudden a catastrophe may overwhelm us and bury all our glory in profound obscurity."

Dai thought the quote over to him in a New Hampshire accent, strangely reminiscent of Victorian English but he pronounced the words that ended in 'r' as 'ah', and 's' as 'sh'.

There was a silence between them both now. The only sound was that of the dog's heavy breathing which indicated it was in a snooze. "Did the Orcadian fight against you in the war in heaven?" Monty suddenly asked.

Did seemed surprised. "Yes," he replied thoughtfully.

"Did you lose anyone you cared for?"

It was obvious that Dai did not want to discuss it, but he replied nonetheless, "There were casualties on both sides; I mourned for them all."

"Did you have friends on the side of the fallen angels?"

"I had brothers." Confirmed Dai.

The momentary silence returned and Monty listened to the dogs breathing . "Were you injured?" He had been thinking a lot about the angelic realm since this all begun and wanted to know more about it as well as about God.

"Yes; I lost a limb," replied the angel.

"But you obviously got it back?" Monty motioned to the fact that he was sat there with all his limbs apparently intact.

"In the form you see me in now, which is intended for this dimension and to make you comfortable, I lost an arm, yes, and you are correct—it was replaced."

"Can I ask how it was replaced—presumably more spell craft?" Monty was keen to learn.

Dai sighed. "No—hologram regeneration."

"Hologram regeneration?"

They looked at each other and both smiled.

"Okay." Dai chose to relent and explain the procedure to the ever-curious life-form before him. "When your body has a wound such as a deep cut, the body regenerates from either side of the wound to heal and to replace the lost matter and tissue by forming a scab, yes?"

"Okay yes?" Nodded Monty.

"But if you have your finger cut off in an accident, the body can only seal the wound at best, as it is unable to regrow the tissue or bone because one side is missing, right?"

Monty replied very slowly… "Riiiiight?"

"So, when my earthly arm was severed, a holographic projector was applied to manipulate the body into thinking that the wound was situated between two tissue matters on either side," clarified Dai.

"But how does that work?" Monty couldn't quite picture the procedure. "I mean, is it like a machine?"

"Yes," nodded Dai. "A projector which uses the genetic code for the tissue which has been severed, and then projects an artificial cellular light, which is, as I said, a forgery of the actual limb, against the wound. This then connects to the cells on the remaining wound and fools the body into beginning both tissue and matter regrowth."

"Wow." Monty was stunned. "Why can't mankind have such a machine then?"

"The same reason it could not have smartphones back in 1950, Stephen; because it prefers to busy itself with warhead technology as opposed to devoting itself to more fitting aptitudes." Replied Dai shrewdly.

"So, the technology is there to be discovered then?"

"Quite," confirmed Dai. "Anyway, I came to let you know that I shall be in court tomorrow to make you feel somewhat more relaxed and confident." He announced as he gently lifted the sleeping dog without awakening it, which surprised Monty considerably as he couldn't even tip-toe to the loo without the hound waking-up.

"That's fantastic, Dai, I have been really uncomfortable and worried about facing this creature." He sighed in relief.

"I know. So, let it be so." Said Dai as he now gently stood up.

"I will feel a lot safer."

"You were always going to be safe, Stephen." Dai nodded reassuringly down at him. "I can't get involved in what is said or thought between you but, rest assured that I will step in if he breaks any rules or attempts to injure you; which is your main concern, I think?"

Monty nodded.

"And try not to show him any fear when you are in court tomorrow, for it is his preferred nourishment." Warned the angel.

"Easier said than done."

"Okay then. Good luck and remember what you read in his file," urged Dai. "Goodnight and God bless, my friend." He then walked out of the door and gently closed it behind him.

Monty knew that there was no point in following him through to lock the front door behind him; for it had been done—angels don't require keys. He called the dog up onto the bed and it responded immediately as if awoken from a trance, and then curled up at his feet. Monty wondered for a moment who it was that was outside in the florist's van watching the front door courtesy of Lazarini tonight, and whether or not they would witness an angel passing through his front door. He turned the bedside lamp off and lay back into his pillow. He felt enthusiastic now and an appetite for the battle. Then his thoughts began to float as tiredness overcame him.

Holographic regeneration, eh.

Chapter Seventeen

To be able to bear provocation is an argument of great reason, and to forgive it of a great mind.
John Tillotson

The Orcadian walked the short distance from the office to the high court building on the Royal Mile in a new black pinstripe double breasted suit and white shirt. He carried a sports bag containing his fall[114], court jacket, wig and robe; all of which he had found in the Cramond house. He was also carrying a briefcase containing the case file. He felt as confident as always and strode purposely and assertively towards his destination. He soon began to feel an instinctive alarm which irritated him as much as the odour of oranges did. He was unsure as to the cause of it, only that he sensed something peculiar which increased the closer he got to court.

He had not experienced anything like this since back at the Tipperary trial in 1895[115], where he had appeared again purely in an advisory capacity. Unlike Ireland back then, it was hot today and the sunlight warmed him as he cut through the old nooks and crannies of the old town, which in a way, reminded him of old Jerusalem in summertime. He could visualise himself on a particular morning leaning upon the cool brick wall of the praetorium beneath the Tower of David, whilst picking at Jerusalem bread dipped in hyssop as he awaited the kangaroo trial of the Nazarene—Jesus Christ.

---

[114] In Scotland, QCs and judges wear long scarf-like white ties known as falls. Whereas advocates wear white bow ties.

[115] Michael Cleary was convicted of murdering his wife, Bridget, with the help of some of his relatives in Ballyvadlea, County Tipperary, in 1895. Cleary alleged that his wife had been abducted by fairies and that a changeling had been left in her place—claiming only to have killed the changeling. Mr Justice O'Brien preceding stated that the case had demonstrated an evil religious darkness among several culprits.

The Orcadian had experienced a similar troubling sensation back then too; partly due to other entities having been in the vicinity to witness the blockbuster event. He recalled being uncomfortable at the time and was feeling likewise now.

The high court was busy as usual. As per most courts in the land, there were the usual crowd of accused persons hanging about outside, smoking nervously and leaning against the exterior brickwork like a brazen national scaffolding. There were also one or two reporters floating about, he noticed when he arrived. Two overweight security guards were checking people at the entrance; however he simply waved his hand at them which caused them to focus upon other people as he waltzed through and into the old foyer.

He intended heading directly for the robing room but he had cause to stop dead in his tracks. The air and atmosphere alerted his mystical senses to the presence of another non-human entity.

Yes that was it.

He scanned the square-shaped foyer which resembled an American courthouse more than a Scottish one, with its marble floor and Corinthian pillars. There were people scurrying about everywhere, many of them wearing old, stained wigs and black robes—some of them gathered in little huddles, whispering and conferring, whilst others hung about looking anxious.

He sniffed the air, using an extrasensory perception that humans call clairalience. There it was—a smooth and energetic smell of roses. There was an angel here somewhere. Why? Why were they interfering again? He felt anger rousing within him now and so lowered his gaze towards the ground and walked off at pace towards the glass doors leading onto the corridor and the stairway which led to the robing rooms. In court four, sitting together upon the old dark public benches, were Dailly and the witness, Donnie McDuff.

Dailly was running him through the questions he would be asking as well as alerting him to the inevitable hostility to be expected from the prosecution. There were three other people already sitting in the court room behind them, one was Forsyth's former partner, who was being called by the defence to account for his movements at the time of the murder. The other two were officers from Forsyth's former unit—the Drug Squad.

Downstairs in the old and overly confined holding area, Monty was sat at a table with Forsyth drinking tea from a foam cup that he had purchased and brought down from the canteen. They had been going over the questions that Dailly intended asking Forsyth under oath, for the last fifteen minutes. "You need to be very careful when the prosecutor questions you, Chris, he is quite devious and will obviously be looking to trip you up," warned Monty.

He had chosen not to inform him that the prosecutor was in fact a fallen entity. Forsyth merely nodded despondently. He was scared. He had been separated from all the other prisoners on the drive into court from the prison, but neither that fact nor the diesel engine of the transportation lorry, had prevented him from hearing the threats and abuse being hollered at him on the journey. The threats had continued here in the holding area where the cells contained up to ten men who could all see him being escorted past, due to the American styled bars which penned them in. Forsyth had been spat at after the turnkey had stupidly hollered out his name to have him brought over to see Monty.

"Do you think you could broadcast it any louder?" Monty pulled the young turnkey up. In recent years, the judiciary had stopped using police to run the court cells and had instead replaced them with private security firms who were full of cowboys like this kid.

"Shouldn't be a beast then eh," replied the guard,

"He isn't a beast, you fucking idiot, he's a cop, so watch yourself or I'll see that you never work in this court again and are instead manning building sites for the rest of your career," Monty had whispered in the lad's ear. The youngster nodded his compliance after that and then apologised.

Sensing the weight upon Forsyth's shoulders now, Monty patted him upon the shoulder: "Your sister Sadie was on the phone to me this morning from Tenerife, said to tell you that she is right behind you and has been praying for you mate."

Forsyth looked up with a sadness in his eyes that moved Monty. "She isn't here though, is she." He shrugged. "Pus she has no credit with God, I suspect." He gave a shy half smile.

"She couldn't leave the pub but she told me that if we were to lose today, she will come over and see you as well as support you through the appeal process," insisted Monty with as much enthusiasm as he could muster.

"Do you think we will win?" asked Forsyth. His eyes looking into Monty's. It was the dreaded question that all lawyers were trained to evade in case of getting it spectacularly wrong. It was a question Forsyth had never asked before either.

"Yes, I do, Chris." Monty found himself being honest. Did he now believe that they would win? That they would defeat this unholy alliance?

Forsyth suddenly smiled for the first time this morning and took a sip of his tea. "You're a modern-day Don Quixote, mate," he then said.

"Nope." Monty grinned and shook his head. "I'm an eternal optimist, mate."

"Well, I lack your buoyancy." Shrugged Forsyth dejectedly again.

Emotions like a rollercoaster.

"Dai is here," declared Monty.

Forsyth suddenly perked up again. "Really?"

"Yes. He's wandering about the court. He is here to back us up, so don't you dare give up, mate."

Forsyth seemed alive and bright again. "Right." He nodded.

Upstairs, the Orcadian was now making his way to the courtroom fully robed and wigged. His horse-hair wig, as was the preferred fashion of learned advocates, looked old and tobacco-stained. It would not do at all for him to have one which, on appearance, seemed appeared new and white as all the young devils wore[116]. Then, just as he approached the final step down to the corridor, he detected the presence of an angel once again. He grinned now for he had soothed himself and composed his anger. He walked slowly and with caution however—through the glass doors and across the busy foyer. There was no sign of the entity whose mere presence had shaken, but not quite broken his applecart. He politely and quite elegantly danced around lawyers and their clients as he made his way to court four; knowing that he was probably being watched.

"Show yourself," he thought.

Then as he approached the thick wooden court doors, Dai showed himself. Both entities stared at each other for a brief instant, as Jacob and Esau perhaps had when Jacob crossed the Jabbok river[117]. They both then stood aside with an acrimonious graciousness to permit the other entry into the court room. Both of them remained still however, waiting on the other to make the first move.

"I see that you still prefer to wear monkey clothes, such as you wore at that little picnic back in Mamre," grinned the Orcadian in Akkadian.

---

[116] In Scotland, a prospective advocate who intends to be admitted to the Courts of Scotland via the Faculty of Advocates, is termed to be a "devil", and is subsequently placed under the care of a devil master who traditionally must not be a Queens Counsellor. Hence, the term—"devil's advocate".

[117] In Genesis 33:1, brothers Jacob and Esau first approached each other having not spoken since quarrelling twenty years previously.

"Indeed, and I see that your human form continues to fluctuate as frequently as your faithfulness," replied Dai.

"Bit below the wings, that." Said the Orcadian—smile gone.

"It is perhaps an improvement on your au natural look however," added Dai in English now.

The Orcadian gave the angel a piercing stare. "Why are you here?" He thought back at him in Sumerian. His high aquiline nose raised momentarily like an eagle ready to take its prey. If anyone else cared to look over at them both, it would have seemed quite a peculiar scene—these two impressive figures standing there silently staring at one another.

"Just making sure that you don't overstep the mark again." Dai winked at him.

"Again?" snapped the Orcadian in verbal English now, conscious of how busy the foyer was.

"Well, when you're not busy brutalising your own disciples, or young girls, you're projecting illusions at the defence lawyer, aren't you," replied Dai curtly.

"Just killing time," replied the Orcadian in Aramaic, his beautiful smile back. Which in turn triggered a smile back from Dai. Yet as he gazed into this serpent's eyes before him, all that they radiated back was bitterness and defiance.

"As you will soon be again elsewhere," Dai promised him and then ditched the smile before gently pushing him backwards on the chest with the palm of his hand and entered the courtroom.

"Keep your halo on," purred the Orcadian as he patiently followed.

Dailly looked up at the two men who just entered the court and felt a flash of fear for the first time in a long time. The one at the front with the shoulder-length straight hair and interesting green eyes slid into an aisle behind where he was sat with McDuff and nodded over at him. He could not help but feel that this man was a friend somehow, and a good one at that, but he had no comprehension of why this might be. He then found himself staring at the Orcadian as he descended down towards the court table beneath the judge's bench.

He possessed a lean, hawk-like nose and a prominent chin which cried out resolve and self-belief. He was lanky, but because he was slim, he seemed even lankier. His face smooth and extended—like a statue of Akhenaten, it was tanned and different. Dailly saw that his eyes were also green. They seemed crafty, and deeply penetrating. There was also an obvious air of vigilance about him too— Dailly sensed a deep darkness about him.

"Right, come on, Donald." He turned to McDuff. "I'll take you to the witness room," eager to usher the hen away from the fox. As both of them left the court, Dai nodded at Dailly again and dispatched a calming ambience over him. Once they had exited, the Orcadian, who was now seated at the table, looked up at the angel and tutted. "That's interfering." He sneered.

"Just killing time," thought Dai back down at him in Aramaic.

"Touché," chuckled the Orcadian, head down flicking through his notes.

"Monty, a word with you please." Dailly, despite the calmness, appeared to be in some sort of urgency ten minutes later when he located Monty in the bowels of the building talking to junior counsel Kenny Mercer.

"What's up?"

"Have you seen that bugger?"

"Who?" Monty and Mercer exchanged confused glances.

"Oliver fucking Farquharson QC?" Dailly whispered patiently as if passing on a password to a military sentry.

"The Deputy Advocate?" asked Mercer leaning forward.

Monty understood now. "Why, what happened?" he whispered.

Dailly looked around to see if anyone else was listening, but only another lawyer who was trying to calm down his client—a skinny little man, were in the immediate vicinity.

"He's a right creepy bastard. He just waltzed into court and gave me the shivers," insisted Dailly. Monty and Mercer exchanged yet another glance but refrained from commenting.

"Then some other guy, entered the court and nodded at me and calmed me down with his eyes somehow," he looked at both of them to see if they thought he had completely lost the plot. "Honestly—it was seriously weird." He insisted.

"Fuck him, Mark," urged Monty. "Let's just wipe the floor with the bastard." He knew that the other bloke that Dailly was referring to must have been Dai, and so his confidence was up.

"How's Forsyth?" Dailly began focussing again.

"Confident," lied Mercer lied who first glanced at Monty then back at Dailly.

"And have all the Crown witnesses turned up?" Dailly asked.

"Yep, a neighbour, the victim's mother, Phillipson, their pathologist, mortuary technician, several cops and Alban Dudley," confirmed Mercer from his notes.

"Fine." Nodded Dailly.

"We have McDuff, and Forsyth's ex—Audrey Parks," added Mercer.

And Dai ,don't forget Dai.

"Right well, let's go up then, boys, as we are only around a few minutes away from kick-off time," suggested Dailly.

"Right, best turn your phone off, gents," said Monty as he fetched his from his pocket. This was it; eight stressful and demanding months were about to close with a bang now. During which time he had been theologically enlightened, put under pressure from his firm, attacked in his hall, forced to share his home with a stranger, and freaked-out by stone dwelling gargoyles and statues. He was however, glad that things were coming to a head now; though there was much nervousness and apprehension building up in him too.

The courtroom had begun to fill up with public observers, the odd press person and the clerks who were sat on desks elevated slightly higher than the lawyers table which were all beneath the judge's bench. The clerks wore white bow ties and black robes and spent most of their time glued to computer monitors.

Dailly, Monty, and Mercer all took their seats at said long table beneath the clerk's bench and directly opposite the Orcadian who did not bother looking up at them. On the table before them lay several folders, various piles of paperwork and a multitude of highlighting pens. Dailly poured out three glasses of water from a carafe and then scanned through his own personal notes for the umpteenth time.

Monty had butterflies in his stomach now. He could not help but stare at the Orcadian across the table regardless. The fallen one appeared to be reading from a police document and Monty noticed that he had thin olive-skinned fingers with manicured nails. Then the creature looked up and directly across at him. Monty experienced a shiver, but he quickly recovered and stared back defiantly. The Orcadian smiled at him, seemingly amused at this stubborn, yet brave little ape. "You're a game one, aren't you," he thought. Monty heard him loud and clear but ignored him and just maintained his expressionless gaze.

"Yet so full of pain and emotion," added the Orcadian. "In my experience, trust me, I have a lot of it, young man—when bravery and emotion collide, emotion tends to fuck everything up."

"Why would I ever trust a word that comes out of your mouth," replied Monty telepathically.

The Orcadian lowered his gaze to a folder back upon the desk and then withdrew another sheet of paper from it which he started to read. "Why? Because I walked the earth with Dumuzid[118]." He was somehow still able to think across to Monty regardless.

"Repeat—why would I ever trust you?" repeated Monty. "I wouldn't trust you to tell me the time in a room full of clocks."

"Because I walked the earth when the bards sang tales of Troy and I have seen monarchs anointed and slain, empires sprout and crumble, just as your pathetic hopes efforts shall here today." Smirked the Orcadian without lifting his gaze.

"Again, why does any of that merit my trust?" Monty was unmoved.

The Orcadian finally looked up at him now with those piercing green eyes which had the ability to see right through his head. "The same reason you put your trust in that old seraph sitting yonder." He looked up at Dai and for a brief second Monty thought that he could glimpse sharp white teeth that seemed as unhuman as a piranha's.

"My faith is in God." He replied.

"And Jesus of Nazareth?" The Orcadian sighed and returned to his paperwork.

"Yes."

"And his chums too?"

"Chums?"

The Orcadian impatiently looked up at him again. "The apostles, boy." He sighed.

"You better believe it," snarled Monty—finding confidence now from Dai's presence.

"And that blessed little fisherman Peter?" The Orcadian was clearly leading, but Monty was hooked.

"Yes!"

"Then consider this," smirked the Orcadian, "When Jesus said that Peter was going to be his rock upon which he would build his church, how was it that he then did also say onto him, 'Get thee behind me, Satan, thou art an offence unto me'?"

---

[118] A Mesopotamian deity in Sumerian mythology. The earliest known mention of this deity come in texts from the early dynastic period (2600-2334 BC).

Monty was now familiar with the dialogue in Matthew 16, having studied the Bible, but he could only guess at why Christ had said certain things. One thing he had learned was that Christ had often spoken in riddles and so any opinion he might form from of these riddles, was merely that—an opinion.

In this case, he presumed that Satan may have been present when Christ had made the remark, and had probably somehow put words in Peter's mouth? The very fact that Monty was unsure prompted him to respond accordingly, "Who are you to question the Lord, Job?[119]"

"Quite the contrary, I am a being who knows the answers," assured the Orcadian who was gradually becoming irritated by Monty's cockiness.

"Enough!" Dai's thought rang loud and clear to them both.

At that moment, Forsyth entered the court from a door off to the rear of the defence team. He was led between two security guards wearing white shirts and black ties, on either side of him, to the accused persons dock on Monty's left. The Orcadian looked up at the accused for a brief second before then turning back to now look at images of the murder scene upon a computer screen.

Forsyth was dressed in a dark blue single-breasted suit, light blue shirt and blue tie with little white polka dots, which his ex-had brought for him. He now noticed Dai and smiled and waved keenly up at him. Dai winked back at him and mentally beckoned him to remain calm and polite throughout proceedings. At this point, Dailly scurried over to the dock to whisper to Forsyth not to stare either at the judge, nor the prosecutor in the eye throughout proceedings. "Has the jury been selected?" enquired Forsyth.

"All done earlier this morning, and hopefully the judge will be instructing them to produce a Not Guilty verdict, Chris," confirmed Dailly.

"Can I just ask finally, Mr Dailly," Forsyth then hesitated a moment—"are you confident?"

Traditionally, Dailly would refrain from committing himself to telling a client that they were going to win, but this was a slightly different question. "Yes," replied Dailly who then gave Forsyth a reassuring pat upon the shoulder. Shortly after this, the jury filed in and took their seats—all fifteen of them. Monty turned around to steal a quick glance at them once they were all settled. There were both men and women, young and old, black, white, yellow, brown

---

[119] In Job 38-41, God asks Job who he thinks he is by questioning his creator, as well as sarcastically enquiring what it is that Job presumes to comprehend about various matters.

and olive. He then turned and looked over at the Orcadian to see if he was displaying a familiarity with any of them. "I won't need them," thought the Orcadian—reading Monty's mind again.

Monty then leaned down and took a cereal bar from his briefcase which he opened and took a bite from. He was nervous and uncomfortable, and he always nibbled when nervous. He looked up at Dai who was smiling down at him knowingly, which relaxed him a little more. Suitably heartened, he took another bite and looked over at the Orcadian again. He certainly looked the part, like some kind of mature model. The Orcadian was still looking at something on a computer monitor whilst expertly flicking a Parker pen between his neatly manicured fingers—which Monty knew were long since stained with injustice.

"Warm today," Monty turned and said to Mercer who nodded back that it was. "We get a sea breeze in Leith but what with the pollution and stuff at Seafield—tends to stink a bit," blethered Monty who then turned and smirked at the Orcadian.

The Orcadian looked up now. He sensed provocation and stared at Monty a moment, his head leaning slightly to the side as he considered this reference to the sea.

"Yeh, the marine life must be poisoned these days," added Monty. This was mostly lost on Mercer who simply nodded politely and returned to his own computer screen where he had been viewing the police pathology report again.

The Orcadian grinded his teeth together now: *Who is this fucking talking monkey to think he can sit there and poke fun at me?* Both he and Monty exchanged cold stares for what seemed like an awfully long time, during which time fear suddenly returned to Monty. "Have a care, youngster, it would not be prudent to play your hand so early in the game," thought the Orcadian condescendingly. Monty felt a chill inside his chest at the tone and so he sounded the retreat and duly withdrew his gaze. He had been successful in baiting him though, that much was for sure.

This sea-dwelling bitch—Ceto, was certainly a touchy subject then.

For a few more minutes, everyone sat in silence. A combination of fear, tiredness and dreamy thoughts were where Monty was at. He thought about God and why all of this was happening, again. The end times scenario that every generation since Christ's crucifixion had thought that they were living in had been something he had thought a lot about in 2015. What was this Kertamen game really all about? An innocent man's life was on the line here today and surely God could prevent all this with just a simple click of his divine fingers?

"Who says he is innocent?" Thought the Orcadian, reading his thoughts again.

Then a door opened behind the judge's bench. "All rise," a male voice called out now, and so everyone stood up.

A female judge—Lady Flora Plumptre-Carr—entered the court, her bleached blonde hair showing beneath her wig as she bowed to the court. Both the Orcadian and the defenders bowed back as she took her seat and eyed everyone as an owl might an empty barn. She wore a red- and white-faced robe with little red crosses across the white, and Monty noticed a gold wedding ring on her left hand. She was probably in her late fifties but looked more mid-forties. Her brown glasses were designer, and she frowned behind them like a librarian with a hangover. There was a further moment of silence as everyone else sat down again and while she looked over some paperwork before her. During which time, Dailly and the Orcadian exchanged another glance. Finally, she motioned to the bench beneath her and to her clerk who then addressed the court.

"Call the diet of Her Majesty's Advocate versus Christopher Forsyth." Dailly now motioned for Forsyth to stand up again.

"Are you Christopher Forsyth?" Asked the clerk.

"I am," replied Forsyth firmly and with surprising confidence, noted Monty.

"Please be seated, Mr Forsyth." Replied the clerk.

The judge then turned to address the jury: "Ladies and gentlemen of the jury, the charge against Mr Forsyth is one of murder." She explained in what Monty guessed to be an Edinburgh accent. "To my right is the defence counsel—Mr Dailly, and directly to his left is junior defence counsel—Mr Mercer, who will both be representing the accused.

"Next to Mr Mercer, is the instructing solicitor—Mr Montgomery, who also represents the accused. To my left," she gestured with her right hand, "the Lord Advocate has allocated one of her deputies to prosecute the Crown case on her behalf—Mr Farquharson; therefore, we shall refer to him as the Advocate Depute.

"The Crown have brought an allegation of murder against the accused; it is therefore necessary for the Advocate Depute to prove the allegation. However, you should all note that the accused is presumed to be innocent until, and if, the charge against him is proven.

"In a trial in Scotland, there are no opening speeches, so I am now going to invite the Advocate Depute to directly present his case to you." She smiled kindly at them.

The Orcadian now very swiftly and gracefully pushed his chair backwards, stood up, flicked his robe back slightly and nodded up at her. "Obliged M'lady. The Crown calls PC Adam Harfield," he said ever so courteously. Shortly afterwards, a young dark-haired cop in police uniform entered the court and stood on the witness stand.

"Please raise your right hand and repeat after me," Plumptre stood up and said—the cop followed suit.

"I swear by almighty God to tell the truth, the whole truth and nothing but the truth," she ordered.

The cop repeated the oath, and satisfied by this, Plumptre sat back down again.

"Are you PC Adam Harfield?" asked the Orcadian politely.

"I am, sir," replied the eager beaver.

"And are you a Police Constable with Police Scotland?"

"Yes sir."

"And how long have you been a police officer?"

"Three years, sir."

"And what station are you based at?"

"Wester Hailes, sir."

"And would I be right in saying that in August of last year, 2014, you were based at Gayfield Square police station?"

"That is correct, sir."

"And on 28th August 2014, were you called to an incident at Queens Park Avenue in Edinburgh?" asked the Orcadian.

"Yes sir." Nodded the cop.

"Can you tell the court about that please?"

"May I refer to my notebook, sir?" asked the cop, as he produced one of the new electronic varieties.

"You may." Nodded the Orcadian, chest out and one hand behind his back.

Monty studied him again now that the Orcadian's eyes were focused upon the stand. He was in his element here—a canny one for sure.

"I was on patrol in a car with my colleague WPC Pasha De Grout, heading east along London Road at 17:36 hours when a call came through from dispatch asking us to attend to a suspected murder at 17/flat 10, Queens Park Avenue," stated the cop.

"Were you aware of who had called in to report this incident?" asked the Orcadian—cool as you like.

"Dispatch stated that it was a Mrs Ruby Kidd, the tenant of the address, and that she had awoken to find her daughter lying in the corridor and that there was much blood and no obvious sign of life."

"And did Mrs Kidd state that she thought her daughter was dead?"

"Yes sir, that was the information relayed to us, as well as that an ambulance was also on route to the location."

"I see," said the Orcadian. "And can you tell the court what happened when you arrived please?"

"Yes sir. Well, we attended and found Mrs Kidd kneeling beside the body of a young female who was on her back, face up, with a deeply cut throat and a bloody puncture wound in the vicinity of her heart, which had leaked a lot of blood so that the entire area was a big puddle of it."

"Can you describe the exact position of where the body was please, constable?"

"Well, the front door was open and she was in the corridor but it was as if she had opened the front door and then been attacked and fallen down in such a way that it would have been impossible to have closed the door unless a body was blocking the door from closing," explained the cop.

"So it seemed to you that the victim had been assaulted at the location wherein her body was situated when you arrived?"

"Yes sir, and I checked her pulse and could not find one."

"So she was presumed to be deceased on arrival then?"

"Yes sir, she was not breathing, and then the paramedics arrived three or four minutes after us and proceeded to confirm this."

"And am I right in thinking that it is your opinion that the scene you discovered suggested that Yvonne had potentially opened the house door to her murderer before being assaulted where she stood, in the doorway?"

"Yes, well that is what I suspected sir, yes."

The Orcadian then moved over to the computer on his side of the lawyer's desk and tapped a keyboard. "If it will please the court, M'lady, I will now show the court a photograph taken from the scene by the police shortly after PC Harfield's arrival." An image then appeared upon a large screen on the wall opposite the jury as well as on the computer monitors in front of the defence and the judge. "We see here that the victim is laying on her back with signs of a throat wound and a further wound to her chest area, with the flat door open to her left-hand side," he explained. Then he turned again to the cop. "Is this the scene which you came upon when you first attended, PC Harfield?"

"Yes, that is correct," replied the cop.

"And did you then take a statement from a Mrs Ruby Kidd?"

"Yes, and then CID arrived with a forensic team and as soon as I finished taking the statement, they ordered us to go around all the other properties in the stair and make enquiries in order to determine whether or not any of the other residents had seen or heard anything."

"Yes constable, we will come to that. First can you tell me what Mrs Kidd said to you in her statement please?"

The cop checked his electronic notebook again. "Well, only that she had been sleeping and had awoken to go to the toilet and found her daughter, Yvonne Kidd, there."

"So Mrs Kidd confirmed that the victim was her daughter, Yvonne Kidd?"

"Yes sir."

"And how did Mrs Kidd seem?"

"Very upset, sir, she had to be helped by the paramedics as I think she had become dizzy and was in a state of shock."

"And so, when you pursued enquiries amongst the neighbours, did you discover anything helpful initially?"

"Yes, we took a statement from a Mrs Bette Kurtz in flat 3, who claimed to have heard men's voices upstairs and then shortly afterwards, the sound of various people running down the stairs and out of the main door."

"Thank you, constable. No further questions, M'Lady." The Orcadian smiled at the cop and then returned to his seat.

The judge then motioned for Dailly to cross-examine the witness.

"Thank you, M'lady." Dailly slowly stood up and turned towards the cop now. "Constable, did you examine the rest of the flat at any point?"

"No sir, I think CID did all that."

"You think?" Dailly looked surprised.

"Yes sir, and Mrs Kidd told us that no one else was in the house with her at the time."

"But isn't it your evidence that upon taking Mrs Kidd's statement, that she informed you that she had woken up to go to the loo wherein she had discovered the body of her daughter in said position, and then rushed back into her bedroom to telephone 999?" Dailly smiled at him and waved a copy of Mrs Kidd's statement at him.

"Well, yes."

"And then you also suggested to us that Mrs Kidd was dizzy and required assistance from paramedics, presumably down to the shock of finding her child dead and covered in blood?"

"Er…yes."

"And you did not feel compelled to search the property to see if anyone else was hiding in it, or if there was any evidence that there had been visitors, and/or a struggle elsewhere?"

"Well, we were busy comforting Mrs Kidd."

"Where did you comfort Mrs Kidd?"

"We took her back through to her bedroom."

"Both you and your partner did this?"

"Yes."

"So, you left the hallway and doorway unattended?"

"Only momentarily."

"So, you left the doorway momentarily unattended?"

"Well, for a second or two, yes."

"I see." Dailly shook his head and turned to face the jury. "And did you see anyone else in the vicinity of Mrs Kidd's flat at any time during your attendance there?"

"No sir," replied the cop.

"So someone could have left the property in the period wherein you were in Mrs Kidd's bedroom, correct?"

"Well…I…suppose…so."

"And despite the reports of voices being heard by a neighbour, which is hardly irregular in a tenement stair that houses ten flats, nor indeed footsteps, did you come across any witnesses who claimed to see a person whose description fitted that of the accused, either inside or outside of the common stairway?"

"No sir," confirmed the cop.

"None at all?"

"No sir."

"Thank you, constable," said Dailly to him before then returning to his seat at the table.

"Advocate Depute?" queried the judge.

"The Crown calls WPC Pasha De Grout, M'lady." Nodded the Orcadian, standing up again.

This time a small blonde female in a grey suit and pink blouse entered the court and took the stand. The fact that she was not in uniform made Monty wonder if she was on a day off. She was really small however, and Monty could remember when he had been a kid and most British cops had been quite tall.

Now they were recruiting hobbits by the look of it.

The Orcadian led De Grout through a tantamount routine to the one he had PC Harfield, and she was just as obliging towards him as Harfield had been.

"Yes sir, no sir, three bags full sir", etc.

She made one mistake however, when she revealed that she had smelled alcohol from the victim's mother upon finding her crouched down in the corridor.

"Perfect, that sets us up very nicely." Mercer turned and assured Dailly and then Monty *sotto voce.*

Just before Dailly was about to cross-examine her however, Monty scribbled a note down upon a piece of paper and passed it to Mercer who then handed it to Dailly who read it:

Forsyth said he ordered a Chinese that night having been dropped off at home at around 18.05, so if they didn't check the other rooms, can you get her to agree that it was then possible that someone else might still have been in the flat?

He looked towards Monty slightly puzzled and then slowly got up and walked over to where Forsyth was sat in the dock and leaned over and had a fleeting *sotto voce* exchange with him. "When you bought a Chinese that night, did you get a delivery?"

Forsyth also seemed confused for a moment before responding, "Yes...I think, yes, I ordered online and paid by card to have it delivered," he confirmed.

"Right, we need to get the credit card details and—"

Forsyth interrupted him, "I can give you my digital online banking sign-in details and you can print it out here," he suggested, still slightly confused.

"Right, two secs." Dailly then skipped back over to the desk, apologised to the judge for the delay and then quickly returned with a pen and paper which he then handed to Forsyth.

"I know them off by heart as I needed them often enough in Tenerife," whispered Forsyth as he scribbled down his sign-in details.

"RBS Online Banking Account—ForsythChris3333@yahoo.co.uk Password-JimBaxterWembly67"

Then promptly handed the pen and paper back to Dailly. Dailly then returned to the table and leaned down to whisper in Monty's ear, "Right, get into his account and back to the 28th of August and see if he ordered a Chinese that evening." Monty immediately got going on the computer whilst Daily turned to the witness stand again. "Constable De Grout, when you said to the court that you and PC Harfield helped Mrs Kidd back along the corridor and into her bedroom, you mentioned her smelling of alcohol, I believe?"

"Yes, that is correct sir," replied De Grout.

"Uh huh, and was it your opinion that she was drunk?"

De Grout had to think about this for a moment. "Well, it's hard to say because she was all over the shop due to finding her daughter in the state she was in, and she was dizzy on her feet anyway."

"She smelled of alcohol, was all over the shop, as you put it, and was dizzy on her feet; okay, I think we see, constable." Smiled Dailly.

De Grout was about to add something when he quickly jumped in again, "Was there any alcohol visible in Mrs Kidd's bedroom when you helped her into it?"

"I think there was a bottle of vodka on a bedside table."

"You think?"

De Grout needed a second or two now to reply but Dailly dived in again, "Not particularly observant, are you, constable?" he suggested with a cheery smirk.

Again, De Grout was not instantly sure how to reply, and required another couple of seconds thought time, however Dailly, as sharp as a razor, was in again: "Your colleague PC Harfield told the court that neither he nor yourself did a sweep of the property upon arrival at the scene, and left the victim's body unattended at the front door area whilst you were both in Mrs Kidd's bedroom?"

De Grout was lost now but instinctively she sensed that she had fucked up and so looked over towards the Orcadian who was watching Monty intently.

Suddenly, the clerk of court handed down an A4 sheet of paper to Mercer that Monty had just printed off. Mercer read it; the Orcadian tried to also do so, though he was wary of reading Mercer's mind due to Dai's presence, and so was now focussing up Monty's face which he attempted to read.

"Well, it was only momentarily, sir," De Grout finally replied.

Dailly then turned to see Monty waving the printout at him and so walked back over to receive it. As he walked back across to De Grout, he read the transaction on 28 August 2014 that Monty had circled in green highlight pen.

"Meekee Chinese Takeaway, Ferry Road, Edinburgh. 18.26 hours= £24.89."

"I understand." He now turned and smiled again at De Grout. "Would you agree then that it is possible that there could have been someone else in the house and that they might have sneaked out when you were in the bedroom?" he asked her quite casually.

"It would have been unlikely, sir."

"Yet quite possible though, yes?" he pressed her.

She was silent again for a moment as she considered the possibility, so he helped her along again. "Considering that you were in another room assisting a woman who was, by your own words, 'all over the shop' and who, I presume, both yourself and PC Harfield were trying to calm down at the time, it is possible is it not, constable?"

De Grout looked paler now than she actually was and simply nodded.

"Can you speak up please, Constable?" Dailly had her by her tail.

"Yes," she almost whispered.

"Then I put it to you again, constable, it is possible that the murderer could have been in the flat and then eloped in the period wherein you were trying to calm down Mrs Kidd in her bedroom, is it not?"

De Grout nodded again. "I suppose it is possible if they were really quiet and moved quickly," she replied. "But why would a murder remain in the flat so long after killing the victim?"

"I'm asking the questions," replied Dailly. He then looked at the printout again, walked over and handed it to the judge before turning back to De Grout. "Your evidence here today is that you turned up on the scene at around 17:56 hours, correct?"

De Grout checked her electronic notebook again and then concurred that it was.

"And so, what time would you say that it had been when you were in Mrs Kidd's bedroom?"

"Perhaps five past six, or thereabouts." Shrugged De Grout.

"Uh huh." Nodded Dailly. "And so if you agree that it is possible that there could have been a murderer in the property who may have slipped out at the back just after 18:00, then would you also agree that it would then be difficult for the murderer to be ordering a Chinese meal online at 18:26 from an address in Newhaven?" he asked her.

De Grout looked like a rabbit in the headlights now. "Unless the traffic was abnormally light at that time of night, yes, it would be difficult." She nodded slowly.

"And so, just to confirm, it is your evidence that it is possible that someone other than the accused, could have still been hiding in the flat when you failed to check the other rooms, correct?"

"As I said, it is possible, yes, but also unlikely in my opinion."

"Let us both agree on that then." Smiled Dailly. "No further questions, M'Lady." He then about turned and retrieved more printouts from the clerk who had just made copies to list as evidence, a copy of which he then duly handed down to the Orcadian who read it and then laid it aside contemptuously.

Now there was extraordinarily little in this point of Dailly's regarding the murderer still potentially having been in the property after Forsyth and co were supposedly seen leaving, but when a Not Proven verdict is the target, any doubts, regardless of flimsiness, must be sought out and stored away. The fact that a cop was now supporting this flimsy straw, would lend a gram of weight to it if used later on.

The defence would need a hell of a lot more than a flimsy straw, any suggestion that the murderer may have hung around for a snooze on the sofa for two or three hours after committing the ghastly deed, was as likely to be accepted by the jury as any suggestion that the Loch Ness Monster was the culprit before then escaping from the *locus in quo* down the loo.

Yet the point, when it comes to a Not Proven verdict, is to place reasonable doubt upon the Crown case which in turn could result in an inconclusive prosecution. Dailly knew only too well that in some cases, it was necessary to lay the first stone and then press on; this little pyrrhic victory was nothing more than that then—a first stone. The defence knew that they were tiptoeing here with their noses just above the water, but a fight was a fight and Dailly intended fighting for every inch of ground.

The Orcadian read the strategy, smiled and now stood up to further examine De Grout. "Constable, would you say that it is possible that Scotland could win the next football world cup?" he asked her with a dazzling smile that made her quiver all over. He then shrugged before she could reply. "Is it not a physical possibility, Constable?"

She beamed back at him as she hooked up on his point. "Well yes sir, it is a possibility, but highly unlikely I'd say," she replied cheerily. There were also one or two sniggers from the public benches.

"I'm asking the questions," the Orcadian replied in a parody of Dailly, causing even the judge to smile now. "No further questions, M'Lady." He nodded in servility at her before returning to his side of the desk, where he gave the jury a delectably all-eloquent beam of those teeth of his. He then sipped some water and spoke: "I call the next witness, Detective Inspector Calvin Bennett," he announced.

Bennett had led the murder squad which investigated Yvonne Kidd's death. He had not however, attended the murder scene until the day after she had been discovered—and had only inspected the cadaver the following morning at the mortuary in the presence of the police pathologist and her assistant. The Orcadian got all the stuff out from him regarding the wounds and then his later visit to the flat, before then intricately draining from him his notes on Ruby Kidd's statement, which of course included a claim that she witnessed Forsyth and Chuck Kean door stepping her earlier on the day of the murder.

"And then, would I be right in saying that you were directly contacted by another witness several weeks after the murder?" he asked Bennett who was an overweight, grey-haired and pink-faced type, who was wearing a light blue short-sleeved shir. Over which, he proudly wore his Police Scotland ID card from a royal blue lanyard.

"That is correct." There was no brown-nosing from Bennett then, noted Monty.

"Okay, can you tell the court about this please?" asked the Orcadian.

"Well, I was telephoned by one George Phillipson on 7th December 2014," said Bennett.

"And how do you know this individual?"

413

"He was someone who had relayed me with information of a criminal nature in the past and who had my personal mobile number," replied Bennett.

Monty, Dailly and Mercer all leaned forward and scribbled down notes now. Monty wrote only one word—Grass.

"And pray enlighten us, Detective Inspector, what did Mr Phillipson have to say?"

"Well, he said that he had heard on the radio that there had been a murder at the location where Yvonne Kidd's body had been found, which was 17/flat 10, Queens Park Avenue, and that he had seen three men leaving the property on the day of the murder," explained Bennett.

"And how did he come to speak to you about this?"

"He had apparently made enquiries and learned that I was running the murder squad investigation," replied Bennett.

"I see. Go on?" The Orcadian was smiling again.

That's not going to do Mr Farquharson—who is just going to Phillipson Bennett's number? Wouldn't the main switchboard just take notes of his contact details and pass it on to one of Bennett's underlings to chase up?.

"And so, myself and my colleague—Detective Sergeant Anna Clarke, went around to visit him at his flat on Bingham Broadway that afternoon."

"Ah hah?" Nodded the Orcadian as if he were being told an old story in a tavern.

"Well, we took a statement from him and showed him some photographs," explained Bennett.

"And would this be Mr Phillipson's statement here?" The Orcadian waved a printout in the air as Chamberlain had when he landed back in England after his infamous meeting with Adolf Hitler in 1938. He then duly handed it to Bennett in the dock and stood back—both hands behind his back.

"Yes, this appears to be an accurate cop." Bennett replied after a moment, and slowly handed it back.

"Fine." Nodded the Orcadian. "Now, you may refer to your notebook," he said, and Bennett got his electronic gadget out and started looking for the statement of George Phillipson. "George Phillipson says here," the Orcadian pretended to be eyeing the document intensely despite knowing precisely where and what he was about to quote, "and I quote, 'I saw the vehicle that the three

414

men got into, it was an old gold-coloured Volvo and the registration number was RX54YZF'."

"That is correct," agreed Bennett.

"And did you investigate this registration number?"

"I did, and I discovered that the car was owned by a Detective Inspector Charles Kean of Police Scotland."

"I see. And did Mr Phillipson say at what time he witnessed these three gentlemen leaving the building and driving off in said vehicle?" asked the Orcadian.

"Yes, at 15.30 hours."

"And you said that you showed Mr Phillipson some photographs?"

"Yes, of DI Charles Kean, his colleague DS Chris Forsyth and one Irvine Stroker," agreed Bennett quite ardently.

"And why did you show Mr Phillipson photographs of these men in particular?" The Orcadian—arms still behind him—rocked childishly back and forth on his heels.

"Well, the vehicle belonged to DI Kean, and upon further investigation I learned that DI Kean had been on duty that day in the field with DS Forsyth, and that they had in their custody, at approximately the time Mr Phillipson stated he had seen them—one Irvine Stroker."

"I see." The Orcadian returned to his side of the desk now and produced three mugshots of Kean, Forsyth and Stroker on the large screen. "And were these the images you took along with you to Mr Phillipson's house that day?" Bennett nodded that they were.

"And so, DI Bennett, did Mr Phillipson identify any of these images?"

"Yes, he identified all three as the men that he saw leaving Yvonne Kidd's stairway," confirmed Bennett.

The Orcadian then removed the images from the screen. Finally, he now raised a printed copy of Forsyth's image and asked, "And this image here of Detective Sergeant Christopher Forsyth," he slowly turned to smile again at the jury, "do you see this person here today in this court?"

"Yes, that is him there." Bennett pointed over towards Forsyth in the dock.

"Thank you, Detective Inspector." The Orcadian turned back to smirk at the cop before casually returning to his side of the table. "No further questions, M'lady."

At which point Dailly slid his chair back and stood up again to begin the task of chiselling away at Bennett's testimony. "DI Bennett, what time exactly did you receive the telephone call from George Phillipson?" He asked.

"After lunch, I think, I can't truly recall." Bennett appeared surprised by this.

"You cannot remember."

"No," confirmed Bennett.

"I see, so do you remember what you were wearing that day?"

"No." Bennett appeared duly baffled now.

"Or whether it was raining or sunny that day?" asked Dailly.

The Orcadian stood up now. "Relevance, M'lady?"

"Yes, I'm unsure as to how the weather is pertinent to the case, Mr Dailly, and if the questioning is not relevant, then it becomes insolvent." Grinned Flora who then had a cheeky look at her watch to ram her point home.

"Just establishing the witness' ability to recollect events reliably, M'lady," insisted Dailly.

"Very well, carry on then." She gave him a—*don't mess with me*—nod before returning again to her notes.

"So, just to confirm," he returned to Bennett, "you cannot recall what time you received this call from Mr Phillipson?"

"No, after lunch though." Bennett's memory appeared to be slowly returning.

"I see." Smiled Dailly. "And so, in the afternoon then?"

"Yes." Nodded Bennett.

"What time do you usually finish your lunch then, Detective Inspector?"

Bennett looked up at the judge now, who was still in her notes, and then unenthusiastically back at Dailly again. "Around 2 pm-ish?" He shrugged.

"Okay. And here," Dailly too now waved a copy of Phillipson's statement, "in Mr Phillipson's statement, you state that you took his statement at 15.20 hrs on 7th December 2014 at his home address at Bingham Broadway?"

A couple of months after the murder?

"Yes." Bennett realised he had cut his timings slightly fine now.

"And so you received a call from Mr Phillipson at your office at Moredun Police Station after 2 pm, wherein you chatted with him, and then after your chat you decided to check out the vehicle registration number which he passed on to you?"

"Yes," agreed Bennett.

"You then discovered that the vehicle in question belonged to a DI Charles Kean. You then did some further digging, leading to your claim here in this court today—that you allegedly discovered precisely where DI Kean was at the time Mr Phillipson claims to have seen him exiting the property of 17 Queens Park Avenue?"

"That is correct." Bennett sounded quite unsure.

Monty studied the jury who were all studying Bennett. Dailly then spun around to face them now. "But not 17, flat 10, Queens Park Avenues," he pointed out.

"Sorry?" asked Bennett.

"Flat ten's door is on the interior top floor," declared Dailly to the jury before then turning his attention back to Bennett who was now squirming slightly in the dock. "So, this witness of yours, DI Bennett, he does not claim to have seen who left the murder scene at flat ten, does he?" Dailly toyed with him now, hands held behind his back like an Edwardian house master questioning a boy with a mouthful of stolen cake.

"Then you found and printed out photographs of three people, before then driving across the city to the Bingham neighbourhood, where you would have climbed the stairs to Mr Phillipson's flat, which I note is also on a top floor," smirked Dailly, "and where you then presumably had a chat with your mate?"

The Orcadian was out of his seat in a flash now, to object but Flora required no convincing. "Watch yourself, Mr Dailly." She half smirked over her glasses. "Ladies and gentlemen of the jury, please ignore that facetious remark by Mr Dailly, who knows better."

"Obliged, M'lady," nodded the Orcadian who retook his seat again.

Dailly pressed on regardless, "You then then presumably showed Mr Phillipson these photographs," he too produced print outs of the same images which the Orcadian had shown the court. "Then had a discussion, and then began taking his statement?"

"Yes, well yes," agreed Bennett.

"And all within an approximate one-hour time frame?" asked Dailly.

Bennett again looked at the judge before shrugging and then turning back to face Dailly. "I am not sure of the time of the phone call then." He sighed.

"Clearly, Detective Inspector." Smirked Dailly. He then questioned the fellow on the fingerprinting process of the crime scene, the pathology process and the later search of Forsyth's former home in Newhaven. "So, I am correct in saying, DI Bennett, that throughout the course of your investigation into the murder of Yvonne Kidd, you discovered no evidence to link my client to the murder?" He sought to confirm.

"Well, apart from the witnesses' account—no," conceded Bennett.

"Apart from the witnesses—no," echoed Dailly, well aware that these sources would be attacked in due course. "No further questions, M'lady."

As soon as Flora had excused Bennett, the Orcadian stood up and called Bennett's assistant, a DS Anna Clarke. Clarke was a drinker and she wore a black nylon suit, probably from Next or somewhere and a blue blouse that matched Bennett's shirt. She had short wiry brown hair, blue eyes and a face and scalp that shone as if they had been polished. The Orcadian went through the same routine with her, confirming everything that Bennett had provided for the prosecution previously, including the intelligence regarding the vehicle registration and Phillipson's eyewitness statement.

"So it was Ruby Kidd's position that she had seen DI Kean and DS Forsyth at her door earlier on the day of the murder, and George Phillipson's position that he witnessed the same two officers leaving the building later in the afternoon at around the suspected time of the murder?" he asked her.

"That is correct sir, yes," agreed Clarke precipitously. She had either a North East Fife or a Dundonian accent, reckoned Monty. When it came to Dailly, however, he simply homed in on the timing issues between Bennett supposedly having received the call from Phillipson and then him turning up to take the statement in Phillipson's flat.

"I'm not one hundred percent sure of the precise time of the call or when we followed up the investigation," admitted Clarke.

"You are aware, Detective Sergeant, that this is a murder trial and that a man is on trial for his life here today?" he curtly asked her.

"I am, sir, but I just received a request from DI Bennett to join him on a visit to Phillipson's flat." She shrugged.

"I see, so DI Bennett took the phone call alone and did his investigating alone too?"

"Well yes, but he filled me in on the way over to—"

"That's fine!" snapped Dailly. "So just to confirm, when you and DI Bennett arrived at George Phillipson's flat on Bingham Broadway," he now turned to the jury, "at whatever time that was?" before then turning back to Clarke, "Am I correct in saying that at no point whatsoever did Mr Phillipson claim to see the accused exiting the murder scene at flat ten, and only claimed to have witnessed him leaving the main tenement entrance door?"

"Yes," confirmed Clarke quietly. Which prompted Flora to lift her head momentarily.

"And would I also be correct in saying that apart from Mr Phillipson's statement, you did not discover any other evidence linking my client to the scene of the murder, and at the time that the murder is believed to have taken place?"

"Well, the victim's mother claimed she had seen him there earlier asking about her daughter," Clarke pointed out.

"That was, as you point out, DS Clarke, was earlier in the day. So, I ask you again, apart from Mr Phillipson's statement, did you uncover any evidence linking my client to the scene of the murder at the supposed time of the murder?"

"No sir," nodded Clarke.

"No further questions, M'Lady." Dailly about turned and walked back to the table.

The Orcadian stared hard at him as he rose again. "The Crown calls Detective Constable Reece Hutton," he announced.

Hutton was a tall woman with long wavy red hair and pale skin which was covered in rusty freckles. She sounded polite—friendly, and was the final member of what had been a relatively small murder squad investigating Yvonne Kidd's death. She had apparently just joined the squad the day after the murder and so the Orcadian merely went through the formalities with her now. The key to her evidence being that she had tracked down and located the main suspect—Forsyth, in Tenerife after Bennett had declared him to be his prime suspect.

"And so, what did you learn from your enquiries into the Drug Squad?" he asked her.

"Only that DS Forsyth had resigned from the force following an investigation into his conduct," revealed Hutton.

"So, he was facing potential disciplinary proceedings by Police Scotland?"

"That was my understanding, yes, but he had apparently resigned and moved to Tenerife," confirmed Hutton.

"And were you made aware of what these proceedings entailed?"

"I was informed that he had been investigated for intimidating witnesses in an ongoing investigation and that this had led to his suspension."

"And when was he suspended?"

Hutton checked her notebook without requesting permission to do so, for a few seconds. "On 19th October 2014," she finally confirmed.

"And the cause of DS Forsyth's suspension was due to this investigation?"

"Yes."

"And were the allegations which were being investigated related to another investigation wherein DS Forsyth and his superior, the late DI Charles Kean, had cause to interview a person by the name of Irvine Stroker?"

"That was my understanding—yes."

"And would I be right in saying that this investigation which DS Forsyth and DI Kean were involved in, and which involved this Irvine Stroker person, was ongoing on the day that Yvonne Kidd was discovered murdered by her mother Ruby Kidd?"

"Yes, that is the information that the Drug Squad relayed to me."

"And so, were you given an address in Tenerife for DS Forsyth?"

"Initially no, we obtained it former partner."

"Can I ask you, DC Hutton, would you say it was normal procedure, in your experience, for a serving undercover officer to resign whilst being investigated?" The Orcadian turned to give the jury a staged expression of mystification whilst everyone awaited her response.

Hutton took a moment to consider her answer again; when she did finally reply, it was slow and cautious. "Well...I have known of other occasions when someone has agreed to resign in return for an investigation against that individual being dropped," she said with an almost naughty expression.

"I see. No further questions, M'lady," he said whilst continuing to smirk at the jury.

Flora also smiled over at the jury now and Monty wouldn't have been surprised should she have tapped a finger knowingly upon her nose, but she refrained, thankfully. "Mr Dailly, your witness." She cracked at him before reverting to her notes again.

Dailly stood up and walked over towards Hutton, hands in pockets. "Tell me, officer, my learned friend enquired of you as to your opinion of police investigations and resignations, what exactly is your experience within Police Scotland?"

"Six years," responded Hutton whilst looking duly confused.

"Ah, I see." Dailly took a sidestep now. "And how many internal investigations have you been involved in?"

"None," she admitted.

"I see, so anything you think you know about any previous investigations, is based upon the old grapevine then?"

"Well, I heard, well, okay yes," she conceded.

"I see. Moving on then from your unqualified opinion on internal investigations, officer, can I now ask you; at any point in your communication with the Drug Squad, did you hear that my client resigned from the police as a direct consequence of him being investigated?"

"Well, not officially…no, but—"

"And would it also be, in your experience, fair to surmise that the investigation into DS Forsyth was dropped because there was no evidence against him and that he then subsequently resigned his job for other reasons before then starting a new life abroad?"

Hutton appeared to wince now but then answered politely, "I suppose so, but I don't know all the facts other than that he resigned and that we had to obtain an international warrant for his arrest."

"Quite so, Detective," agreed Dailly. "And so, if my client was to state here today that he resigned his post and moved abroad because he was disillusioned with the police service, would it be reasonable to accept this as a possibility?"

Hutton scratched her temple with long blue fingernails and looked up at Flora who stopped taking notes for a moment to look back down at her. For a moment, Monty thought that Hutton might ask her what to do next but thankfully, she merely turned back to Dailly again and replied, "I would not disagree with that but I do not know all the facts."

"Quite. No further questions, M'lady," declared Dailly who returned to his chair at the table with a content look upon his face, which was primarily for the benefit of the jury.

Capital.

Flora then looked over towards the jury and smiled seductively at them. Monty considered whether she was worth a romp in the hay…well, anyone would in his current position, he supposed. Then he remembered the Orcadian and saw him smirking over the table at him and so channelled his thoughts to the jury instead.

Most of whom were studying Forsyth, they had been doing this throughout proceedings, particularly when one of the witnesses mentioned either him or the murder. Clearly, they were searching for clues within his demeanour, such as did he smirk, was he frowning, or even sad? Monty reckoned that he must have come across as quite sad.

"Right well, I think we shall break for lunch then," Flora informed them before rising. Which in turn caused everyone at the table to jump to attention and curtsy. She would be well fed in her chambers now, as would the jury members, whilst Forsyth would get a sandwich and a cup of watery tea in his cell.

"Pint?" suggested Dailly. Monty nodded, the Castle Arms did a fine bar lunch and his kind were always made welcome by the chatty Persian owners.

"Right, I'll pop down and see Forsyth to clarify a couple of things and then meet you both up there," agreed Mercer. "Make mine a fish and chips and a half pint of John Smith please," he added as he packed up his papers.

"The bugger did that so we have to pay for his lunch," laughed Dailly as he strode resolutely up towards the Lawn market with Monty.

"We?" exclaimed Monty. "This is your pay day, Mark, so you're getting them in," he insisted. The weather was starting to warm up again and the area was busy with tourists however there appeared to be a calm vibe due to the conclusion of last night's General Election.

Gone were the loudspeakers blaring from vehicles and gone were the blue t-shirt wearing nationalists trying to slap yellow stickers on unwitting Japanese tourists. Dailly smiled and nodded back as they rounded on their destination. "Fair enough. Anyway, I want to get back to get a word with Forsyth too before the second half kicks off," he said.

In the pub, Monty had scampi and fries and a pint of diet coke whilst Dailly opted for steak pie—colcannon—pint of Guinness. Presumably to help scuttle any nerves the Orcadian might be creating.

"Chris is adamant that Yvonne Kidd had been a sex slave at some point and then a prostitute, who just knew too much," insisted Mercer when he joined them twenty minutes later.

"Hmm," considered Dailly. "I still don't want to get into the whole clandestine investigation thing, as it will make our man look like he is off his trolly," he reasoned. Monty could see how this was probably a fair presumption. It could turn the jury against Forsyth and there was no need to go down that alley as the case was going reasonably well enough. Over in a corner beside a window which looked down onto the Grassmarket, sat Ivan. Monty noticed him now for the first time, but Ivan was too busy looking around the pub and sipping a glass of orange juice to make eye contact.

"But it does provide us with a plausible scenario regarding why all these witnesses are conspiring against him," thought Mercer aloud as he began his lunch—the noise of laughter, glass and cutlery upon ceramics almost drowning him out.

"No, they would look at him as if he was David Icke on trial for tunnelling into Area 51." Dailly shook his head now as he scooped up the last of his mash in a fork dripping with gravy.

"We are doing alright though, wouldn't you say, Mark?" asked Monty.

Dailly sat back and wiped his lips with a paper napkin. "That bugger hasn't made his move yet, gentlemen," He shook his head and then supped deeply at his pint. "He is just laying down the foundation for his *pièce de résistance*," he gasped as he replaced his glass on the table and wiped his lips with a paper napkin.

"Phillipson and Alban Dudley." Nodded Monty, pushing his plate with the remaining chips away.

"Aye," agreed Dailly. "And this Gav Caine character too. All we have done thus far is to continually check him— it's when he really gets going with those three that he will really come on to us," he warned.

"Well, regarding Ruby Kidd," offered Mercer, "Forsyth is positive that she is an alcoholic and so it might be worth the risk in attacking her regarding this, as well as noising her up about her daughter's promiscuous past," he suggested before burping loudly and promptly excusing himself. "Sorry, beer always gives me jip," he smiled.

"Aye well, we shall play that by ear and see how she is on the stand," thought Dailly.

"Did you speak to Forsyth about giving evidence?" Monty asked Mercer.

"Yep," nodded Mercer, "he is keen, of course, but I said you would pop in after lunch as Mark will make a final decision over lunch." He looked at Dailly invitingly.

"I'm not sure about that yet, guys." Shrugged Dailly just as a female arrived to take both his and Monty's plates. "So far, we are on track for an acquittal and I'm inclined not to put him on the stand because that bastard Farquharson will only turn the jury him," he predicted.

That's a hell of a presumption for someone who isn't supposed to know the true identity of the Orcadian.

423

Both Mercer and Monty were silent now. "Of course, depending on how damaging the other witnesses are to us, it's possible that we may have to, so I'll pop down and fill him in on how I want him to play out such a scenario," added Dailly.

The jury will want to hear from him before acquitting him, surely?

"Right, let us return to the lion's den then, gents." Dailly wiped his mouth again, stood up and took an old grey wallet from his back trouser pocket and removed three crisp ten-pound notes—left them under his now glass on the table. "Avanti." He grinned and confidently strolled out onto the street.

The walk back was more laboured. The food and the sun combined to slow down them down like a virus to a computer hard drive. None of them mentioned the election results—all three glad that it was over, and none were too disappointed that David Cameron had won the right to complete the tidying up job he had half completed.

At last, after Indyref and now this, they can finally put politics behind them for a few months of peace before the Scottish elections came around.

Monty accompanied Dailly downstairs to see Forsyth, whom they found to be quite pale and sullen. A new guard told them that he had been "Getting it tight," verbally from the other prisoners. Monty had seen to this earlier, but the holding area was tight and Forsyth was being subjected to all sorts of threats from the other cages.

"Is it going well, Mr Dailly?" He asked in the little windowless meeting room.

"It's not going badly, Chris." Smiled Dailly.

"They need to score a goal to get their noses in front, so far they are just recycling the ball around the midfield zone whilst probing," added Monty, feeling the need for an analogy. Forsyth smiled now, as an ex-footballer, this seemed to be a good way of describing things.

Dailly looked at Monty and then smiled and nodded in agreement. "That's correct." He then turned to Forsyth. "And we are pressing at their heels as they do so; however, we can expect them to go for it in the second half," he warned. Forsyth nodded to show that he understood.

"Now, Chris, are you sure that Ruby Kidd is an alcoholic because we just have your word for it and if I attack her based on that observation, well, put it this way, if they have sobered her up, she could deny it and we might look like bullies in the eyes of some of the jury," asked Dailly.

"I'm positive. She was shaking, and we could just tell, I would bet her GP is well aware of her drink issues," assured Forsyth confidently.

"And Alban Dudley, are you sure that he was investigated by both police and social work as you have previously said to Mr Montgomery here?" asked Dailly.

"Certain." Nodded Forsyth.

"Right. Look, about calling you as a witness," Dailly leaned back in his chair and simulated the familiar posturing of a man deep in evaluation by gently massaging his chin with his fingers, "you need to understand that despite the fact that the jury will expect to hear from you before they make their minds up, I won't make the call on that until the time comes," he explained.

"That is because if they still have not proven their case against you, it might be risky to put you on the stand as sometimes a witness, no matter how innocent he or she might be, can turn the jury in the wrong direction," explained Monty.

"Quite so," agreed Dailly, leaning forward again now.

"Yeh, I understand, guys," insisted Forsyth. "I've seen it happen enough times myself."

"Of course, you have." Smiled Dailly. "The other thing to remember is that should we put you on the stand, it is vitally important that you try to just answer yes or no when the Deputy Advocate cross-examines you. If he sees you going on and on, he will instantly detect your doing so to be a weakness and then lead you into a cobweb of confusion, clear?"

"Yes, Mr Dailly, don't worry about me, I'm a practised inquisitor and so won't let myself down on the stand," promised Forsyth.

"Right you are then." Dailly shook his hand and the three of them stood up.

"Have faith, Chris." Monty patted Forsyth on the shoulder.

Upstairs, the Orcadian was waiting patiently at the table as the three defenders arrived and resumed their seats. Both himself and Dailly exchanged swift nods of professional recognition before he then turned and exchanged a look with Monty, which was more mutual contempt as opposed to any professional courtesy.

When Forsyth was brought back up into court by the two security guards, Monty noticed Dai, who seemed to appear from nowhere, exchange a smile with him; it was nice to see Forsyth smile. Behind Dai were two suited men. They were staring down intently towards the lawyers' table and Monty sensed something untoward about them, however he was not sure exactly what it was. He had no time to worry about this though, as the clerk of court then appeared and declared that Flora was entering the room to referee the second half of the first day's action.

"All rise." Once again, they all rose to their feet as she sauntered back in as slowly and as gracefully as a lioness who had just had a bellyful of Zebra. Straight away the Orcadian got back down to business again, calling firstly a spectacled homicide and forensic pathologist from the Royal College of Pathologists—Dr Paula Curran, who informed everyone that Yvonne Kidd had been around five weeks pregnant. She then proceeded to explain the manner of her death and her wounds. Monty watched as the jury studied Forsyth for his reaction, but he looked just as shocked as everyone else, thankfully.

"I would suggest that the murder weapon was potentially an eight-to-ten-inch kitchen knife," stated Curran softly.

"Suggest?" The Orcadian wanted an explanation from her for the benefit of the jury.

"Yes, well, attempts to measure most knifes from a wound only, are traditionally fraught with inaccuracies because the human skin, being somewhat similar to elastic, tends to shrink somewhat on the blade being withdrawn from it by as much as two millimetres," explained Curran.

"So, how do you presume that said blade was potentially an eight-to-ten-inch kitchen knife?" he enquired of her.

"Because it entered under there," and she used the power point laser he had given her, to highlight an enlarged diagram of a female body upon the mounted screen—highlight the sixth rib down of eight on Kidd's left-hand side, "and nicked the rib—causing a splinter, and then penetrating up into the heart and puncturing it.

"I believe that the blade itself, as with a kitchen knife, started off thin as it went through the skin and flesh but then became wider by perhaps by two inches towards the handle, and consequently the thicker part of the blade nicked the bone here." She shot the laser upon the rib.

The Orcadian then presented some images of Yvonne Kidd's autopsy and had Dr Curran confirm her theory from the grizzly images of chipped rib bone and a measurement between the rib and heart location. He then brought up mortuary photographs of a couple of carving knives taken from the flat Forsyth had formerly shared in Newhaven with Audrey Parks. "In your opinion, Dr Curran, would you say that the murder weapon was likely to look something like these?" He appeared disturbingly playful.

At this, Dailly was up on his feet sharper than a football supporter at a potential penalty claim. "I must object, M'Lady," he insisted.

"To?" queried Flora.

"To showing the witness these images from my client's former home address, M'lady—To suggest that either of these basic kitchen utensils might be the actual missing murder weapon, is just bad form," protested Dailly.

The Orcadian, stood now, hands on waist—grinning and shaking his head at Dailly. "I am unawares that I have suggested anything of the sort yet, M'lady," he pointed out.

"Well, Mr Dailly," Flora addressed the defence, "the advocate depute knows well enough to tread carefully on this but the witness may give her opinion."

"M'lady, then would it not be just as reasonable to present an image of the kitchen knives which the advocate depute keeps in his own kitchen, or indeed that the majority of other citizens of this country, to the witness?" retorted Dailly as he retreated back upon his chair.

Flora looked down at him again with a smirk and shook her head in disregard. "That is a matter for later argument, Mr Dailly, and in the meantime, please also tread carefully," she warned.

Curran then confirmed that it was possible that the weapon would have been similar to the two images being displayed. Monty shook his head for the benefit of the jury, hoping that most of them would comprehend his disappointed at the Crown's suggestion. When it was the defence's turn to cross examine the witness, Dailly rose to his feet and asked only two questions of the good doctor. "Can you tell the court whether or not any evidence was presented to, or discovered by you, which suggested that my client, Christopher Forsyth, committed this murder?"

"No, none." Curran seemed to have anticipated this.

"I see, and did you determine who the father of the child that Yvonne Kidd was carrying, was?"

"No. DNA is only recognisable in a foetus after ten weeks so it would be quite impossible to trace the father," explained Curran.

"No further questions." Dailly smiled at her politely and gave her a dismissive nod.

Up next was Curran's sidekick, one assistant mortuary technician called Park Hye-Ri, who had assisted in the autopsy by undressing the cadaver, assisting in the removal then weighing of the organs, foetus and toxicology specimens. She told the Orcadian that she had stored the personal inventories such as Kidd's clothes, watch and shoes, etc, as well as additionally taking the photographs which had just been displayed to the court.

Again, Dailly asked her the same questions that he had asked her superior.

"No nothing," she replied civilly.

"Thank you, no further questions." Dailly turned and smiled knowingly at the jury.

Then came the turn of the police crime scene investigators and a forensic biologist who all informed the court that they had examined the crime scene, Forsyth's then home address, and Chuck Kean's Volvo that Kean and Forsyth had been using on the day of Yvonne Kidd's murder. No blood nor DNA of any person had been discovered at the crime scene. While none of the victim's blood was found either in Forsyth's home nor in Chuck Kean's Volvo. "So, we use luminol to detect blood as it reacts to any traces of haemoglobin within blood," explained a ginger-bearded and middle-aged Oxbridge biologist named Coughlan, to Mercer now.

"And so, Mr Coughlan, did you detect any traces of blood, or the victim's DNA, upon any of the items that the investigating officers presented to you?" asked Mercer courteously,

"No, we did not," replied Coughlan.

"No further questions." Nodded Mercer to Flora, who then dismissed the witness.

Next up, the Orcadian called the victim's mother—Ruby Kidd.

When Kidd appeared, Monty studied her intently as she shuffled into the witness stand. She was a small, frail-looking woman who was probably in her early fifties but who, because of the booze, looked more late sixties. The Orcadian took her in now too.

Their capacity for self-destruction never ceases to amaze even after all these years.

He could smell the whiskey that she kept in her tattered handbag and which she had supped at like a hungry calf, in the witness room along the corridor. She was wrinkly, and her overgrown hair was grey, wiry, and unkept. She had hastily tied it back today for the occasion, but it was still untidy and some of the grey was becoming brownish yellow due to nicotine staining. He could see that she was on two to three litres of booze a day from when she awoke in the early morning from liver pains, pausing only to vomit the first few mouthfuls up along with the green phlegm which formed every night in her throat as a result of her constantly chain smoking rolled-up cigarettes. He had viewed a replay of her decline over the years, with some curiosity last night. He had felt obliged to put more revision into this shit case he had been lumbered with due to the effort being put in by the opposition.

He had seen her gradual loss of friends and family right through to her current loss of personal hygiene and self-respect. He could smell the stale urine stains on her now too, that no one else in the court could detect under her clean clothes except Dai; but like Dai, the Orcadian blocked it out. She didn't have long now he knew, but today she was sober enough thankfully and had made an effort for the trial which was all that mattered. Afterwards she could lay in a pool of boozy piss for all he cared. She was a little shaky though, and so he mentally urged her to place her scrawny hands upon the smooth curved witness stand before her in order to steady herself—she duly applied.

Influence, not interference. He looked over towards Dai and smiled.

Monty noticed the dark yellow nicotine stains upon Kidd's fingers. Her eyes, which were dark like little shrivelled raisins, seemed too small for her face, and they darted up at Flora and then back down and over towards the public gallery which they then combed nervously until finally resting upon another elderly woman who was sat looking back at her. This lady was a plumper, cleaner and better presented version of Kidd herself; her sister perhaps, thought Monty.

So that was how she had made it up the road this morning. An otherwise distant sister who was sympathetic to her loss, and who wanted to see justice done for her niece?

"Good afternoon, Mrs Kidd," opened the Orcadian softly and tactfully. "I know this must be a difficult experience for you today but thank you for coming along." He smiled at her affectionately.

He would make some womaniser, thought Monty.

"I am," thought the Orcadian back at him.

"Yet you prefer fish, I hear," thought Monty.

429

"Be cautious now, little monkey, didn't your puppeteers tell you that it would be dangerous to overplay your hand this early in the game?" thought the Orcadian right back.

Arrogant little bastard.

"Enough, both of you." Dai—referee and Kertamen authority, interceded once again.

"It's fine," whispered Kidd in reply as Flora looked down at her with both interest and pity.

"And would I be right in saying that you live at 17/flat 10, Queens Park Avenue in Edinburgh, Mrs Kidd?"

"Aye." Kidd was uncomfortable but there was still a bit of bite in her tone yet.

"And can I ask how old you are, Mrs Kidd, and what you do for a living?"

"I'm fifty-three and I'm unemployed." She seemed proud of this.

"And who do you live with?"

"Well, I've been divorced for fifteen years so it was just me and my daughter." The pride and bite faded now and she began softly shaking.

"And would I be right in saying that your daughter was Yvonne Kidd?"

"Yes."

"And that Yvonne sadly passed away on 28 August 2014?"

"Yes." She began to sob.

"Can I get you a glass of water, Mrs Kidd?" The Orcadian played his role perfectly, even collecting a couple of tissues from the box he had brought with him for this very purpose and taking them over to the stand with a glass of mineral water. After she had been given a minute to compose herself, he then asked her, "And did you discover Yvonne after she had passed away on that day Mrs Kidd?"

She replied that she had and then proceeded to describe the scene and the impact it had had upon her thereafter. The Orcadian had her discuss how Yvonne was the bread winner through her job as a cleaner, her working hours and how her loss was not only devastating emotionally due to the manner of how she died, but also financially. Then he made his first attack of the trial: "And can you tell us about earlier on that day, Mrs Kidd; did you have some visitors at your door?" he enquired nonchalantly.

The first twist of the thumbscrew then.

"Aye." The bitterness was back now—she practically snarled in reply. "Around lunchtime, two men were at the door asking for Yvonne."

"I see." The Orcadian looked down at the floor now as he leaned casually upon the stand. "And were these gentlemen in police uniforms or were they plain clothed?"

"No, they were in plain clothes," she told him. "They said they were from the council but a few weeks later when the police showed me their pictures, they told me that they were police officers."

"Ah yes, of course." Smirked the Orcadian. "So then when the police later showed you a selection of photographs you picked out the two men?"

"Aye, that's right."

"And can you see one of those men here in the court today, Mrs Kidd?"

"That's him there." She pointed over towards Forsyth.

"Let it be noted that the witness is pointing directly at the accused." Smirked the Orcadian. "And what did these two men say?" He asked her.

"Well, they said they worked for the council and asked for Yvonne. I told them that she worked from 5 am until around 1 pm," she said.

"And then?"

"And then they left? They said they wanted to speak to her regarding council tax, I think."

"And did they ever come back to your knowledge?"

"I don't know as I went to my bed as I had been feeling unwell that day."

"I see. And so, you went to your bed and did not get up again until when?"

"Around 4 pm," she replied.

"And was that when you discovered your daughter lying partially in the hallway?"

"Yes, and she was dead," said Kidd.

"Was it your interpretation that the men would be returning when they expected Yvonne to be home from work?" He led her in.

"Well, yes, I think so." She looked down and considered this.

"Thank you, Mrs Kidd, no further questions."

"Mr Dailly?" said Flora, her eyes scanning him from over the rim of her spectacles.

This was a chance for the defence to begin dismantling the Orcadian's attack, but Monty knew that Dailly needed to take it easy on the old women for fear of alienating the jury. Dailly rummaged a moment in his papers until he came across

431

Monty's background bullet points on Yvonne Kidd, which he scanned over for a moment before turning to face Kidd. Addressing the witness in the tone of a compassionate vicar, he asked her first, "Can I get you some more water, Mrs Kidd?"

She looked at her glass a moment then shook her head and forced a smile. Dailly nodded and smiled back. "Mrs Kidd, I know this is a difficult process for you but I am going to ask you a few questions on behalf of my client who is also under considerable stress here today," he explained, and she nodded back. "Mrs Kidd, you have been divorced for a number of years now, you told the court?" He sought to confirm.

Again, she nodded. "My man, Tam, left me seventeen years ago to go and lives with a barmaid from Leith but we have been divorced fifteen years—aye," she confirmed.

"I'm sorry to hear that," Dailly commiserated. "That cannot have been easy for you."

"No."

"And so, did you have to raise Yvonne on your own?"

"Yes, and it was hard going."

She was biting, this one feels sorry for herself and like most drinkers, has long established someone else to blame for her collapse into the barrel.

"No doubt difficult both financially as well as emotionally?" Dailly began to reel her in.

"Aye well, she was hard work and we had our problems."

The dam was beginning to open.

"And I see that Yvonne was suspended from school a couple of times and ended up spending a short time in a care home for children."

"Aye, she blocked a sink up at the school and ran the taps—causing a flood," replied Kidd.

"Why do you think she did that?" asked Dailly as delicately as possible.

The Orcadian was out of his seat in an attempt to scupper him however. "M'Lady, do we really have to endure my learned friend's petty attempt to discredit the victim?"

Flora required little persuading. "I presume you are coming to a significant juncture, Mr Dailly?" She raised her recently manicured eyebrows at him.

"Indeed, M'Lady. If you would oblige me a few more moments." Smiled Dailly back up at her. Flora appeared to consent without reply by simply returning to her notes.

"Why do you think she blocked the sink up, Mrs Kidd?" Dailly repeated the question as if he and Kidd were friends enjoying a drink in the pub.

"She was always mischievous. The social workers said she wanted attention as she didn't have her dad in her life but she was just a tomboy who was always doing stupid stuff," she insisted. Monty had half expected her to block him and take offence at the line of questioning; however, it slowly dawned upon him that there may be a deep underlying contempt within Ruby Kidd towards her late daughter.

"I see, and when she returned home after her time in care, did things improve?"

"Aye well, she was still not coming home on time and was staying out later than I told her she could. She thought she was a model and left a mess around the house."

So that was it, Ruby, she was young—good-looking and popular with men, and you resented her because of what you had become.

"And what about boyfriends? Did she have any?" asked Dailly tactfully.

"Well aye, plenty like. That was always another issue we had and she had to get an abortion when she was fifteen; the social workers invaded my life again after that;" complained Kidd frowningly.

Dailly had not been aware of this, of course; Monty hadn't come across it in his research, but both men knew that it would be a tad risky to home in on any notion that Yvonne had put it about. Female jurors might resent that particular angle. "What about now, or in more recent times; had Yvonne been seeing anyone?" he instead asked her.

"I don't know, I haven't been very well lately and so I stay in my bed a lot but she had been seeing a Turkish guy from the kebab shop around the corner from the house, but he was much older and married and was just using her. I told her that had to end, or I'd put her out," revealed Kidd.

"And when was that exactly, can you remember, Mrs Kidd?"

"Last summertime I think but I can't be sure of dates or anything."

"And did this chap from the kebab shop ever fall out with Yvonne or perhaps show any aggression towards her?"

"He used to demand that she meet him after he closed the shop and they had the odd argument over the phone if she was tired or didn't want to go out, but I never heard of him hitting her, no."

"And how did he take it when Yvonne ended the relationship?"

"I don't know and don't care!" She shook her head and frowned.

Dailly took a deep breath and exhaled. "So, you haven't had it easy, what with having to raise Yvonne alone and her childhood behaviour, as well as her relationships, and now her untimely passing, have you, Mrs Kidd?" suggested Dailly benevolently.

"No, it's not been easy," conceded Kidd.

Dailly made his move now: "Would you say that she was a bit of a firecracker then?"

"Well, she was hard work, as I said," agreed Kidd.

"And were you aware that Yvonne was pregnant?"

"Only after the police told me after the biopsy." She seemed to be snarling now.

Dailly nodded. "That also must have been hard to hear, Mrs Kidd, I'm sure; is it fair to say that you are a heavy drinker because of all the hard work that Yvonne has put you?"

She took a moment to consider the bait, but it was a hard ask for any alcoholic not to lay the blame for their own demise at the door of someone else. "Well aye, I suppose so," she replied with a touch more anger in her tone.

"Is that what you had been doing before you discovered Yvonne in the hallway that day—drinking?" He pressed her now with the tone that a compassionate social worker might press a naughty child for the truth.

Again, Kidd was hesitant, before she then suddenly began crying. "It's what I do every day." She sobbed.

Gotcha!

Dailly dashed back to the table and accepted a tissue from Mercer which he returned and offered to her. "There, there, Mrs Kidd, I'm sorry to ask you such a question but I just need to confirm something before you can leave and get yourself home," he told her as gently as he could. "Had you been drinking before the two men from the council turned up looking for Yvonne that day?"

She composed herself now and blew her nose into the tissue before replying, "Well yes."

"How much would you say you had drunk?"

"Well, from morning until midday, probably a quarter bottle and a can or two of cider." She shrugged.

"I see," nodded Dailly. "And just to confirm, at no point thereafter did you see or hear these two men returning again that day?"

"No." She shook her head before then blowing her nose.

"Yet despite the drink you consumed, you remembered their faces when detectives later came around and showed you their photographs?"

Kidd seemed confused now by this. "Well, I think so, yes."

"You think so? So you can't be sure?"

"Well, I thought I remembered them when I saw the photographs."

"And can I just confirm, Mrs Kidd, had you had a drink before the detectives visited you and showed you the photographs?"

"I told you, I drink every day," she snapped—impatience building.

"I understand, Mrs Kidd." Smiled Dailly. "What I am trying to establish is that, with you having had a substantial amount of alcohol prior to answering the door to the two gentlemen, and then again thereafter, is it possible that you might not have been quite so about the photographs, and consequently the police pointed out which ones to say were the men you had seen?"

Kidd rubbed her head with her hands now, she was confused and didn't like how this was going. She desperately needed a drink and her chest was pounding in the manner it usually did when she was running dry. "Oh, I don't know, it's possible but I really can't remember, it just looked like them when I saw them." She sighed and shook her head.

"It's possible?" Dailly looked at her now. She didn't answer and instead just shrugged.

"Thank you, Mrs Kidd, no further questions." He turned away from her and returned to his seat at the table.

Mercer thought that he should have gone in for more blood but Monty could see that the dam had burst and that apart from not seeing the murderer, Kidd's claim to have seen Forsyth at her door a few hours prior to the murder could be exposed in the closing speech as the non-credible ramblings of an unsure alcoholic. And one who thought it possible that she had been guided by the investigating officers. Besides, whether Forsyth had or had not been at Kidd's door prior to the murder was immaterial at this point.

The Orcadian thought about standing up and leading her back into the firm conviction that was evident within her original statement, but he could see that she was exhausted and on the edge. To work her further may be seen as overbearing and she may not respond favourably and could even worsen his case. Like lawyers who had been on their feet all day, witnesses are more alert in the mornings and can be exhausted by the afternoon; particularly those who are in desperate need of whiskey.

"Thank you, Mrs Kidd, you are free to go now." Flora gave her the best smile she could muster. "And I think we shall adjourn now for the rest of the day and return tomorrow," she declared. Monty exchanged a glance with Dai who smiled at him. Dailly had certainly raised the required doubts in the jury's eyes, regarding the credibility of Ruby Kidd as an eyewitness.

"Pub?" whispered Mercer. At which point Flora reminded the jury not to discuss the trial with anyone else and to return to court early the following day.

Where they will be fed like royalty.

"A quick jar then, yes." Nodded Monty.

They all stood to attention now as Flora rose and then gracefully glided out of court. "Let's pop down as see our guy in the cells first then pop over to the Castle Arms then," urged Dailly whilst gathering his notes. As they were leaving, Monty noticed that Dai was nowhere to be seen but that the two men wearing bland grey suits remained seated at the back of the public benches. They were staring down at Forsyth as he was being led away by the guards. There seemed something strange about them and for a moment Monty wondered if they were cops, but then he noticed them exchanging glances with the Orcadian who remained seated at the centre table under the pretence of also gathering up his papers.

Chapter Eighteen

This is a court of law, young man, not a court of justice.
Oliver Wendell Holmes Jnr

The pub was much busier than it had been at lunch time. Tourists were piling in from overpriced tours of Edinburgh Castle across the road and Monty counted fourteen whiskies being supped over the bar by Japanese people who appeared to have a taste for Johnnie Walker. The three of them chose to stand at the end of the bar this time. Monty was supping a cold pint of cider as he had gained a thirst under the hot afternoon sunshine during the walk up from the court. Both Mercer and Dailly were on Guinness. "That kebab shop guy angle, and Yvonne Kidd having had a childhood abortion etc, was a handy turn up for the books," considered Mercer.

Monty had rummaged up the dirt on both the witnesses Phillipson and Dudley but little had been available on the victim herself. "At least you managed to get the mother to admit that Yvonne was a wildcat." He submitted in mitigation to Dailly.

"Aye, he's a canny man," echoed Mercer.

"The jury could see that the mother was an alcoholic, but thanks to her honesty, they should now see that her kid was a long-term nightmare who, down to poverty or ambition etc, was shagging older blokes. This enables us to construct a plausible argument for there being other men who could have had a motive for killing her," insisted Dailly before necking quarter of his pint.

"We won't even need to go down that route once Phillipson and Dudley are destroyed," suggested Monty.

"A fair assessment, Monty." Mercer clinked his glass with Monty's and beamed confidently.

"Aye well, I'll concede that we have checked Farquharson's case thus far and should rightfully fancy our chances against his *piece de resistance* witness to follow but let us not count our chickens just yet, gents," warned Dailly before necking some more of the black stuff whilst signalling the barmaid to line up another round.

Farquharson?

Monty had always thought of him as the Orcadian. "Well you did well today Mark, Forsyth is fortunate in that respect." He raised his glass.

"And on top of that, I have you." Dailly raised his too.

"Babe," added Monty and they clinked glasses.

Over at a table behind them, sat the solicitor advocate Rozina Aslam and two other females whom Monty did not recognise. Aslam was wearing her customary hijab and sipping orange juice while her companions were on gin and tonics. "Think she'll ever take silk?" asked Mercer, who was eyeing her up.

"Possibly," considered Dailly, "unless she has an arranged marriage to a control freak who is covertly intimidated by her career."

"Which could be a reason why she hasn't married yet," suggested Mercer.

"Apparently, she is looking online for an arranged marriage and has been for years." Monty had overheard the locker room gossip a year or so back.

"Precisely, she is picky. So yes, if she stays single, she will go for silk," offered Mercer thoughtfully. It seemed clear to Monty that Mercer fancied Aslam, but the fact that she was obviously quite religious offered the poor chap optimism.

"Never mind." Monty patted him on the shoulder. "You could always search online yourself," he teased.

"Very good, Monty." Mercer grinned just as the fresh round of drinks appeared on the bar before them.

A television was on above a window ledge, with more reporting on the general election result. The SLP leader was talking from a rooftop somewhere, about the rise of his party and its leapfrogging of Scottish Labour at the polls. "The target for our party now is next year's Scottish election where we would hope to take seats from the SNP." He was coming across as cool as a cucumber despite his obvious delight in taking various Labour and some SNP seats.

"Our next king?" said Monty.

"Nah, his party will never be accepted by the majority of Scots," considered Mercer between sips of Guinness.

Dailly stared up at the screen for a moment before shaking his head. "He has rebranded fascism for marketing purposes sure, but you're right, he will never come to power here," he assured.

Just then Monty's phone rang, it was the office. He felt a pang of disappointment as he saw the number and considered turning it off but did not and instead took the call. It was the firm's clerk, Matty Wishart. He wanted to know when the trial was expected to end. "Day after tomorrow I expect, Matty, why?"

"Just that Russell asked me to call you as Ally Blyth now has a trial to do in Livingston on Friday and so his case at Jedburgh is now free," explained Wishart. There was an overly long pause and Monty wondered if Cuthbert was listening in on another line. "What is it?" he asked.

"It's a big fat fraud by credit card," replied Wishart overly enthusiastically.

"Well, hopefully, we will finish up here tomorrow and get a verdict by Wednesday, but I'll be better placed to say tomorrow," was about all that Monty could offer him.

"Magic. Okay, I'll put you down for it and if you can update me tomorrow."

"Fine, cheers, Matty." Monty hung up. He had intended quitting straight after the trial but knew it was best to say nothing until after Forsyth's case was finished. Besides, one final day out in the borders wouldn't be so bad, at least he would not have to step foot in Edinburgh Sheriff Court and endure Cuthbert's cold stare.

"Right, drink up, lads, then get your arses home and reading up on these police verbals[120] and witness statements again," ordered Dailly as he set about necking his second velvety pint of Guinness. Monty had a go at his fresh pint but too much cider didn't agree with him due to its gassy content. He only ever drank it with food or on a hot day to quench a thirst, and if he was out on a session, he tended to have something smooth such as an IPA.

"That's me then, I'll get down the road and go over the statements again for tomorrow guys," he said before burping loud enough to startle the Japanese tourists.

"Right Monty, text me if anything comes to mind and I'll see you in the morning then," chuckled Dailly as he turned his gaze away from a couple of repulsed sunhat-wearing Japanese females.

---

[120] Police verbals, otherwise known within the judiciary as the "Vaudeville routine", were particularly common in the 1970s but have, in the main, been stamped out in the modern policing era. Invariably, they tended to be associated with an accused person having either assaulted a police officer, or having confessed to committing a crime.

"Night then, guys." Monty then made his way out and back into the sunshine followed by big Ivan. There were the usual crowds spilling out from the castle and around the trinket shops which always frustrated him. He was tired, and the drink had made him want to relax. Once he got down onto George IV Bridge though, he managed to hail a taxi easily enough and waited for Ivan to jump in.

"Leith please, driver."

They did not talk on the journey, though the driver nattered away about the election. Both Monty and Ivan were soon frustrated at the traffic on Waterloo Place. Ivan sighed deeply as he scrolled over his phone while Monty leaned his head on the window and thought of the Orcadian file. The Orcadian had controlled his anger well enough today, he considered. He would press him more tomorrow. The booze had given him an appetite so he texted Charnley: *Fancy homemade fish and chips, Ronnie, I'll stop in at the fishmongers?*

They were halfway down Leith Walk when he received a reply:

"Aye, that would be braw, I'm just back from a dog walk, do you want me to cut the chips if you're bringing the fish"?

So Monty got the driver to pull over at Kelly's fishmonger on the Walk. There weren't many of these little businesses left nowadays sadly, but he still preferred Kelly's for fish, and Cherrie's on Albert Street for butchery, as opposed to the large supermarket chains. Ivan was content to wait in the cab with the door open when they arrived at the shop. Fortunately there was no other customers inside and the staff were starting to clean up so Monty picked up some breaded haddock and one or two other treats for the dog and was back on the road again within a couple of minutes.

"I need to get some beer; can you please pull over at the Co-op?" he asked the cabbie. Ivan looked at him in the way any man would look at a woman who was dragging him unwillingly around the shops, but said nothing. The cabbie nodded and swung across the road to where the Co-op was located.

"Thanks; two minutes," said Monty as he hopped out onto the pavement and into the store. Returning a few minutes later with a plastic carrier bag. When the cab finally turned onto his street eight minutes later, Monty saw to it that the driver—a cheery enough youngster, pulled up outside his front door because he didn't want to be seen by Mehreen. He had been avoiding her since all of this kicked-off, and because of the crimbo card—obviously. This looking over his shoulder routine, and stress regarding the firm, had left him way too weary for any "yoo-hoo" dynamics.

He gave the driver a twenty and handed Ivan a wrapped package of haddock. "I got you some breaded haddock, my friend, thanks for looking after me. Have a good night," he said cheerily to him. Ivan smiled for the first time at this and nodded his appreciation before exiting the cab and walking over towards a florist van a few yards up the street.

"Honey, I'm home," said Monty as he unlocked the door and went inside. Thankfully, Charnley had got things ready and was in the process of opening up a tin of peas, as Monty entered the kitchen. The house was warm despite the patio door being open—the summer sunshine having penetrating throughout the day as it usually did.

"You've got plenty of beer in the fridge," said Charnley curiously, pointing to the two cans of Grolsch which Monty had in the Co-op bag.

"Reckon we needed them in this weather, mate, and just in case you run low." Smiled Monty who shrugged. This was a problem he had much of the time—picking up crap and wasting money whenever he just popped into a shop.

"Dai was here half an hour ago," said Charnley as he put the fryer on.

"Really? What did he say?"

"Nought much, lad, ended up chumming me on the dog walk but did say that this would all be over soon and that I would be heading home in due course," said Charnley.

"Did he say when?" Monty handed him the fish and took out some tinned mackerel for the dog.

"Nope—just said soon."

Monty sighed. "He is as vague as Jesus Christ apparently was," he said whilst putting the cans in the fridge.

"He certainly is." Chuckled Charnley who began frying the chips whilst whistling merrily. Monty went in his room and placed the plastic bag inside another old carrier bag and then carefully put it in his wardrobe. The dog had followed his master through and lay down on the floor beside his feet as Monty began to get changed into a t-shirt and jeans. It could smell the fishmonger's bag and was sniffing around the wardrobe.

Smell something nice, boy, hmm?

Shortly afterward, whilst sitting at the kitchen table sipping hot tea, Monty read his notes on the witnesses Phillipson and Dudley. A friend of his—Louise, was a social worker and she had kindly provided him with a copy of a two-year-old report on Alban Dudley. It was completely inadmissible as evidence, of course, and she had made Monty swear that he would destroy it after reading it and never tell a soul that she had broken all her codes of practice by giving it to him. Nevertheless, it made for an interesting read.

Apparently, Dudley had been arrested a few times between 2010 and 2012 for stealing children's underwear from washing lines—the court ordered a social enquiry report to determine his suitability for community service. There was also a reference to a previous assessment back in 2006 wherein his estranged partner and mother of his teenage daughter had expressed serious concerns about him having unsupervised access to the daughter.

Monty recalled that Forsyth had said that both Alban Dudley and his late flat mate Irvine Stroker, had been paedophiles who were involved with the cult that Chuck Kean and Forsyth had been investigating. Monty read an old report by a social worker named Pete Dysart. He thought he could recall a social worker with that name from another case— a friendly fedora wearing chap who had also been, If Monty recalled correctly, a singer in a Van Morrison tribute act. He sipped at his tea and looked up to see how Charnley was getting on. "Won't be a minute, just buttering the bread," insisted Charnley, noticing.

Monty read the report —philosophical trappings—wild but overly sensitive and not naturally a social person—blurred boundaries between fantasy and reality—charming—character suggests a highly developed melodic sensibility—claims to be an artist and musician— tremendously protean.

There was a second report from Dysart:

"Met Mr Dudley for our follow up meeting at his home address in Musselburgh. Was surprised to find him answering the door in torn jeans that had felt tip pen writing all over them. He was barefooted with his toenails all painted black, and a Syd Barrett t-shirt with food stains all over it. The property, which is a two-bedroom flat that he shares with his friend—Irvine Stroker, is in receipt of benefit, as is Mr Dudley himself who claims not to be making any money from painting nor Uber now.

Mr Dudley comes across as quirky and eccentric, an oddball even. He claims that he is a cannabis addict and a talented musician in limbo. It is at this point that I noticed the scribbled writing on his jeans which appeared to be Morrissey quotes. He also claims to be an artist and the walls are covered in his erratic drawings. Upon close inspection however, these images appear to be the produce of amalgamated and an overly sensitive personality that is locked between a realm of fantasy and sadness. There does seem to be a developed artistic sensibility however, but not a sophisticated one. Rather these drawings seem pasticheur and quite dark.

Mr Dudley has recently been diagnosed as desultory and depressed by his GP and has been proscribed Prozac, he tells me. However, on a trip to his toilet, I discover several weeks of untouched prescriptions. I sense that his efforts to come across as an incoherent musical recluse, are precisely that, a concerted effort to portray himself as a copycat Syd Barrett figure. There is a 1960's Fender Telecaster guitar with attached mirror discs mounted upon a wall with what would appear to be a forged autograph of Mr Barrett's, dedicated to "my friend Alby." written upon it in crayon. Considering Mr Barrett had been in seclusion since the 1970's and no longer used the name "Syd", it would seem to be simply a fantasy trophy.

There may well be an underlying mental health issue, however he does come across as having a charming character, as well as protean, manipulative and insincere side. I suspect that he is deliberately using his issues to maintain a fully funded lifestyle on benefits. The rent on his property is, as is to be expected with any sea view in the area, considerably high, and when I pointed out that should he ever return to work, he might struggle to afford such a property, he immediately changed the subject and asked me if I wanted to hear some music?

When I said that I did not, he stood up and put on Mr Barrett's "Arnold Layne" and turned it up so that we could no longer continue our conversation. Notably, "Arnold Layne" is a song about a sinister individual who stole washing from washing lines in Cambridge back in the early sixties.

When I insisted that Mr Dudley turn the music off, he did so but then became evasive and attempted to talk about what he considered to be his "band" and his "music". Though upon enquiry, he admitted that he has no band and has never recorded any music. Consequently, I sense that Mr Dudley is something of a modern-day Don Quixote, and in my view, may be suffering from potential Machiavellianism.

My initial thoughts are that he is depressed but that he may not only be playing the benefit system by portraying himself as withdrawn and hermitic, but also attempting to play myself regarding this social enquiry report, by avoiding the question of his guilt and frequently attempting to distract me from the purpose of this report.

He does comes across as energetic, excited and keen to assist with the report initially, but his mood suddenly drops if he does not like a particular question. His thought process and articulation then become hard to follow thereafter as he is unpredictable and I detected increasing boredom within his responses thereafter. On the question of remorse, or even guilt, I found him to be dissembled, evasive and remorseful merely of getting caught as opposed to the committing of the offence itself.

Mr Dudley's property is, like himself, something of a curiosity, with scribbles as well as drawings covering all the walls—graffiti-like. The effect is perhaps intended to project a childlike simplicity, or a regression into childhood, however it seemed to me to project poignancy. I feel he would benefit from a psychological valuation, if only for the possibility that he may desire to portray himself as mentally ill in order to shield the real reasons behind his crime.

Mr Dudley claims to be a paranoid recluse, however there is considerable evidence of people having recently visited, such as the multiple XBOX control pads, photographs of cannabis parties and various dirty plates and glasses. Reclusive when it comes to non-cannabis smokers perhaps, and paranoid due to his drug intake, but a lost and eccentric artistic musical genius he does not appear to be,, or if he is, he has landed himself into an indeterminate state wherein he is not producing music or creative art. Also notable are books and pictures of another "lost" musician—Pete Docherty, all over Mr Dudley's flat.

Monty had read enough; Dudley was clearly far from a credible source when it came to his statement which states that he had witnessed both Forsyth and Chuck Kean mentally leaning upon Irvine Stroker shortly before Strokers apparent suicide. His credibility was clearly always going to be flimsy in the dock. However, the part where he stated that he had overheard Forsyth, Kean and Stroker all agreeing to go and pay Yvonne Kidd a visit "after 1 pm and closer to 3 pm-ish" on the day of the murder was an inconvenient obstacle that Dailly would need to overcome. This historical social enquiry background report by Pete Dysart was going to be helpful on that score however. Monty now emailed both Dailly and Mercer with his thoughts on this just as Charnley served up supper.

After they had eaten, the two of them went through to the lounge and relaxed. Monty now sprawled out on the sofa and reread through George Phillipson's statement whilst Charnley watched a report on the SLP and SNP's sweeping aside of what remained of Scottish Labour. Labour leader Jim Murphy, his former deputy Anas Sarwar, Douglas Alexander and Margaret Curran, had all lost their seats and were all being interviewed. Murphy was delivering a blistering assault on Unite the Union general secretary—Len McCluskey, in addition to accusing the Scottish Labour party executive of disregarding party democracy, whilst also imploring them to reform the party's policy making rules.

"It's not the union's fault, Jim, it was Blair's opening of the immigration flood gates and two daft wars that destroyed Labour," hissed Charnley with the dog curled up on his lap.

"We have to draw the poison out of some of the personalities," insisted Murphy. "Sometimes people see it as a badge of honour to have Mr McCluskey's support. I kind of see it as a kiss of death to be supported by that type of politics."

"I've had enough of politics to last me a life time, that's Labour starting an internal election now that will finish the part off once and for all in Scotland." Charnley used the remote control to turn the channel over to a Japanese film with English subtitles. Monty lowered Phillipson's statement a moment and took a look at the film, it looked decent enough but he had to read this statement as well as the statement of his counter witness—Donnie McDuff.

"Did the Orcadian give you any problems apart from the mind games today then?" asked Charnley.

"Nope, but no doubt he will try something tomorrow." Sighed Monty as he got back into Phillipson's statement. An hour later, he received a call from Cuthbert, which he ignored and then he took a shower before texting his son to see how he was. Similarly, he did not receive a reply. He then went to bed early and read a little of Matthew 27-28 before praying. At which point he received a reply by means of a text from Dailly.

"Perfect. Tomorrow he chucks Phillipson and Dudley at us and we shall raise this question about the quality of these witnesses. See you tomorrow." It read.

Unless the fallen on has another trick up his robe?

Monty leaned into his bedside drawer and scrambled about until he found his old iPod. He turned it on—thankfully with some battery available—quickly finding what he was looking for—Pachelbel—Canon in D Major. Usually Pachelbel made him remember the past, but tonight he simply leaned back onto his pillow and closed his eyes to listen. He was too tired to think any more—so he just listened and smiled internally; before drifting off. When he awoke around 7 am, he hadn't a clue what he had dreamed about, only that he had indeed dreamed of something.

The three lawyers met briefly at a cafe on the Bridges at 9 am. Ivan shadowed them by standing across the road at a busy bus stop where he smoked and pretended to check his phone. The social work report on Alban Dudley was discussed, as was George Phillipson. Dailly was somewhat concerned about the police verbal's that were expected this morning, as the Orcadian had summoned a list of police witnesses, but by the time he had polished of his square sausage on a roll, Monty had persuaded him that they were nothing more than that— police verbals which placed little weight on placing Forsyth as the murderer of Yvonne Kidd. "He's right, Mark, the only danger is coming from the two arresting officers who claim that on the flight back from Tenerife, Forsyth admitted to the murder," concurred Mercer dismissively.

"Hmm." Dailly was thoughtful as he sipped at his latte.

"And he obviously didn't admit to it thereafter in St Leonards, and so they don't have anything on tape." Mercer, who had opted for a small bowl of Alpen, which he had merely picked at, pointed out.

Monty agreed, "So, it's the "It's a fair cop, Guv" scenario, then Mark, and all you have to do is sprinkle a little doubt on their lies."

"Yes but getting the jury to accept that a couple of cops are fibbing is one thing, but we also have four detectives claiming that Forsyth attacked them in the St Leonards custody suite last year." Dailly sat back to let his breakfast settle.

"Yeh but none of them can place Forsyth at the murder scene, so that seems irrelevant at best—he is charged with murder and not brawling in St Leonards with those four detectives." Shrugged Monty.

Dailly was still considering things further though. Eventually he sighed through his nostrils and nodded to himself— "Fine. Let us commence battle then, gents." He then slid his chair back and stood up.

Her Majesty V Forsyth - Round Two

The scene at court was no different from the previous day, except that the two strange men who had been in the public seats yesterday were now three strange men. Dai was present and winked at both Monty and Forsyth upon their separate arrivals. Forsyth had a different suit on today, a dark grey one that Audrey Parks had purchased and handed in to the prison for him. The Orcadian was seated at the desk as they had arrived, wearing what appeared to be the same suit under his robe as the previous day.

"Morning." He smiled at Dailly who nodded back at him.

Then he turned and stared at Monty. "I like Pachelbel too." He smirked. "Did it help you sleep?" he mentally asked. Then at that moment, there was a mental exchange between himself and Dai that Monty was not privy too, but it was obvious because the Orcadian gazed up at the angel and then retreated into his notes. Dailly went over to talk with Forsyth for a moment before returning and shuffling his papers around in the manner of a clerk of court.

At which point, the clerk himself stood up as a door opened and a spectacled gentleman with old horse guard whiskers declared that Flora was on her way. "ALL RISE," he bellowed with childlike enthusiasm.

Most likely keeps him going every day.

Bizarrely, classical music now blared in Monty's head: Mozart's Requiem Mass—*Rex Tremendae Majestatis*—with its stunningly brilliant female vocals ringing out just at the moment Flora entered and sauntered over to her throne.

"Just kidding." Monty heard the Orcadian saying to Dai as the music stopped.

"Good morning, Advocate Depute, would you care to proceed?" asked Flora with a glowing smile.

The Orcadian stood up: "Obliged M'lady. The Crown calls DCS Jordan Kavanagh," he said. Kavanagh turned out to be the new head of the drug squad in Edinburgh but he had had no prior dealings with Forsyth, so the Orcadian only able to touch the subject matter with him. "And so your predecessor advised you that DS Forsyth was being investigated for being involved in an unauthorised investigation involving Yvonne Kidd?" he enquired of him.

"As I said, I was informed that DS Forsyth had resigned from the force after we received various complaints against him regarding intimidation of both witnesses and suspects," replied the tall moustached man on the stand with the salt and pepper hair.

"And was it explained to you that DS Forsyth and DI Kean had both been approaching witnesses in respect to an unknown line of enquiry?" The Orcadian was displaying breath-taking confidence again, hand on hip and a smile that could melt any heart.

"It was," replied Kavanagh.

"And at any point in this process, were you informed that DS Forsyth and DI Kean had intended interviewing Yvonne Kidd as part of their enquiries?" asked the Orcadian.

"Well, I was only briefly advised about DS Forsyth's resignation and that there had been various complaints against him leading up to his decision to resign; it was only after I settled into my new post that I became aware from a member of the squad that DS Forsyth had stated that he had intended door-stepping Miss Kidd," stated Kavanagh.

"Forgive me, Detective Chief Superintendent, but when you say door-stepping, what is it you mean by that?"

"Paying a visit to her home address," replied Kavanagh.

"Thank you, no further questions."

"Mr Dailly?" said Flora.

"Yes M'lady, just a couple of questions." He smiled as he stood up and slowly walked over to where Kavanagh was stood. The new DCI was a tall skinny man and he looked uncomfortable as Dailly approached him.

"Ah, good morning, I won't keep you long, officer." Smiled Dailly with hands behind his back. "So let me understand. Your predecessor Colin Wong did not feel the need to state to you that DS Forsyth had intended visiting Miss Kidd's home address; however, at a later date, someone else within the drug squad told you this?"

Kavanagh didn't like the line of questioning and briefly looked over at Flora for clarity; however, he hit a brick wall as she did not raise her head from her notes. "Well, the team was probably better informed that he was," mitigated Kavanagh.

"Probably is not a word that this jury can rely upon, DCI Kavanagh, so I ask you again, did your predecessor not mention anything of this alleged visit to Yvonne Kidd's house?"

"No," conceded Kavanagh.

"And then you claim to have heard a rumour of it from someone else on the squad?"

"Yes."

"But that is all it was, a rumour that was never noted nor officially logged?" enquired Dailly.

"I think so, yes." Shrugged Kavanagh.

"Now let us consider this source then, was it officer Gavin Caine who informed you over a pint perhaps?"

"As it happens it was, but I cannot recall where it was that he mentioned it." Shrugged Kavanagh apologetically.

"But probably it was in the pub, no?" Dailly pressed clumsily.

"The witness has already answered that question, Mr Dailly." Flora looked up with a cheeky grin and shook her head in disapproval.

"Okay dokey, I withdraw the question." Smirked Dailly.

"Moving on then, did officer Caine also mention that he had evidence that DS Forsyth either sought to or did murder Yvonne Kidd?"

"No," confirmed Kavanagh.

"No further questions, M'lady." Dailly then swooped his robe to put a hand in his pocket and returned triumphantly to his seat.

Up next was former drug squad DI Sharon Adams. Fortunately, she played a fair game and praised Forsyth for his professionalism throughout his career in the squad. However, when the Orcadian asked her about the unauthorised investigation that Chuck and Forsyth had been on, she became uncomfortable, which would not have been missed by the sharper eyes among the jury. "I don't really know," she lied under oath. "Other than to say that DI Kean was calling me from time to time to do background checks on various individuals of interest to him." She skipped around the truth.

"Well, was one of those persons of interest a Yvonne Kidd?" The Orcadian was well aware of what she was doing but wasn't interested, he had his end-game in sight and was focussing on that.

Adams couldn't lie now, she knew, for there was a record of all person checks done by officers. "I think so, yes."

"Which suggests DI Kean and DS Forsyth intended speaking to Miss Kidd regarding something or other, does it not?"

"Possibly, but I really couldn't comment because I am unaware as to why DI Kean sought a check on Yvonne Kidd and he certainly did not discuss her with me at any point thereafter," insisted Adams.

"Come, come, Inspector!" Smirked the Orcadian, "Is it not the case that whenever an officer seeks a person check on an individual, he or she can just radio it through to control and would not require to telephone yourself, another busy senior officer, in order to achieve this?"

Adams was up against a wall now, her career potentially under siege. "Well, there are sometimes reasons why an officer might do this, such as regarding informers or delicate information." She was obviously still trying to help Forsyth out though, which was not missed on Monty.

"And also if the officers were involved in something they wanted to keep under wraps, wouldn't you say?"

Adams remained silent however.

"Or if they were involved in a criminal offence and were using you as an accessory?"

Again, she remained silent.

"Precisely. No further questions."

"Mr Dailly?" asked Flora.

Dailly motioned for Mercer to lead the questioning, and he was up and over at the stand faster than a whippet. "So, DI Adams, did DS Forsyth ever call you asking for a person check on Yvonne Kidd or was it only DI Kean?" he asked her.

"As far as I recall, it was only DI Kean," she lied again.

"And at any point did either DI Kean or DS Forsyth state to yourself that they intended visiting Yvonne Kidd?"

"No, not that I can recall." She was being completely honest now.

"I see, and did either of your colleagues ever suggest that they intended murdering Yvonne Kidd?"

"No!" Conscious of the three suited men in the public gallery watching events, she fell slightly short of adding—"Absolutely not!"

"And finally, did you ever feel that DS Forsyth was capable of murder?" Mercer went for it now.

A gamble, Alex.

"No, I had not seen anything like that in him."

"Thank you, Detective Inspector, no further questions."

There was the sound of shuffling around the court as Adams left and people adjusted their seating. Monty felt that Adams had done Forsyth a favour and so turned and winked at him. Forsyth smiled back then lowered his gaze again.

"The Crown now calls DS Gavin Caine," declared the Orcadian.

Dailly, Mercer and Monty huddled up. "Right, take notes, Monty, and let's get ready to unsheathe our swords," whispered Dailly.

Caine was a small fellow with dirty brown curly hair which was cut short enough to give the impression that it may be straight. He had some freckles and a few lines sprouting from his grey eyes and broad cheekbones. He was well presented in a sharp blue suit though his tie was mismatched, but he proudly wore his police Scotland ID around his neck. Monty noticed him stealing a glance down at Forsyth just before the Orcadian began leading him.

Caine was soon explaining that he was now a member of Drylaw CID having been promoted to DS and transferred from the drug squad a few months back. He described how he had worked with both Chuck Kean and Forsyth the previous summer and how they had roped him into an unauthorised investigation into the owner of a French restaurant on the Royal Mile where the late Irvine Stroker had worked at the time as a chef.

"DI Kean was my boss and DS Forsyth was my superior, so despite my reservations, I felt obliged because they assured me that the surveillance on the restaurant was for the greater good," explained Caine.

"And what was the extent of this surveillance?" asked the Orcadian whilst neatly twirling a pen between his fingers and thumb.

"Stroker had placed a microphone under a table in the restaurant where the target regularly ate and met with associates. Myself, DI Kean and DS Forsyth listened in around the corner in DI Kean's vehicle."

"And would that be this vehicle?" The Orcadian showed him an image of Kean's Volvo upon a screen, whilst continuing to twirl the pen; Caine nodded that it was.

"And who was this target?"

"I cannot recall; I think it was a suspected drug mule," lied Caine with considerable ease.

The Orcadian then got him to confirm that this eavesdropping operation occurred shortly after the date of Yvonne Kidd's murder and that nothing of any significance nor interested had come from the surveillance. "And was there just the three of you sitting in DI Kean's car?"

"Yes," lied Caine again.

"And did Irvine Stroker seem to you to be a willing participant in all of this?"

"Yes, but DS Forsyth had mentioned to me in the car that both himself and DI Kean had threatened him with trumped up charges of drug possession in order to get him to play along, but he had not elaborated any further on that," lied Caine again.

Well, that fits in nicely with what Alban Dudley will be saying next—rogue cops place poor old Stroker under duress and force him to take them to where Yvonne Kidd lives, which of course then connects to what Phillipson will then claim that he witnessed.

"And what happened next?" The Orcadian leaned on one leg now, one hand in trouser pocket, the other still twirling the pen around with such skill that Monty considered that he could well have led an Orange Walk should he have fancied. Monty then looked around at the jury, they were all watching Caine intently with only a couple looking over at Forsyth to study his reaction to what Caine was saying.

Up on the public seats, the three suited men were staring down at the jury too, whilst Dai seemed to be watching the Orcadian very closely. Up on the bench, Flora was studying Caine. Monty stared up at her for a moment, she was looking hotter today for some reason, and he mentally undressed her now for a brief moment before snapping out of it.

What am I doing here?

Why was he here in this bizarre charade again, with a fallen angel and those potential Satanists sitting up in the public gallery? He rubbed his temple and sighed quietly. As if in a dream, he felt as if he could be in the court room scene from *The Wind in the Willows*. He had always been fantastically perceptive of people's real characters in court, but this scenario was utterly wacky.

He could do with another drink, a large glass of Barolo perhaps, just to help things along. Following his recent theological enlightenment, he had decided that it would be an affront to a generous God, to decline one of his most wonderous inventions—wine, at least to participate in moderation. "We waited until Stroker returned to the car and then we drove over to Fife," explained Caine.

"And what happened then?"

"We drove to Crail on the East Neuk. I had been led to believe that we were going to question a suspect called Dave, who was somehow connected to the case, but when we arrived at a caravan site, DS Forsyth and DI Kean attached a hose pipe to the exhaust of DI Kean's vehicle and then fed it into the site and extracted exhaust fumes into an air vent on a caravan," revealed Caine.

"Why, and what did you do?"

"To knock out the inhabitant of the caravan, and I did nothing. I was too shocked and frozen to my seat in the car."

"I see. Then can you describe to us what happened next?"

"Well, DI Kean and DS Forsyth told Irvine Stroker to strip off and then the three of them broke into the caravan and took some compromising photographs of Stroker beside a male who was apparently knocked out by the fumes," explained Caine.

"And?"

"And then they returned, and we drove back to Edinburgh and DI Kean dropped me off at my home address. The next day, I felt that I had no choice but to report the incident to my superior at Fettes," insisted Caine.

"Did they tell you what had gone on in the caravan?"

"Yes."

"And this led to DS Forsyth eventually resigning from the police and making a new life abroad?"

"So, I believe." Nodded Caine.

"No further questions." The Orcadian turned and waltzed back to his chair confidently.

"Your witness, Mr Dailly," stated Flora as she began scribbling down something.

Dailly got up slowly and forced a smile now, which seemed to unsettle Caine who half-smiled back but then thought better of it.

"DS Caine, you said that my client led a hose pipe from a car into a caravan park?"

"Yes," replied Caine cautiously.

"Was it far?"

"What?" Caine seemed lost, but he was far from lost, suspected Monty.

"The distance between the caravan and the car?"

"No, well, a few metres I think beyond a fence and some trees and shrubbery."

"I see. And what time would that have been?"

"Around 2 am."

"I see. You also said that you had been frozen to your seat in the car throughout proceedings?" asked Dailly.

"That's right."

"Then pray tell us all, DS Caine, sorry it is Detective Sergeant now, is it not?"

"Yes." Caine looked quite unsettled and tightened the knot on his tie.

"As opposed to Detective Constable, which was your rank at the time of this incident?"

"Yes."

"So, you have been promoted to what was my client's rank prior to his resignation?"

Caine clicked now what Dailly was implying and sighed—"Yes."

"Well, pray tell the court Detective Sergeant, how did you witness the break in to the caravan and the staged photography session that you claim occurred, from your position in the car on a dark night at 2 am, beyond the fence, the trees, and the shrubbery?"

"Well, erm, I heard what happened once they returned," admitted Caine.

"Ah, so you claim that three people returned to the car and told you that they had done all of what you have just described witnessing here to the court?"

"Yes, that is correct." Caine was on the defensive now.

"Yet there was never any official complaint made by any persons regarding this, was there?"

"I don't know." Caine knew better than to explain that the victim had been a former cop and that it had all been kept internal in order to push Forsyth into his resignation.

"I see. And the only three witnesses to your story then are my client, who denies your allegation, Irvine Stroker and DI Kean?" asked Dailly.

"Yes."

"So only your word for it then, detective sergeant?"

"Well, the other two are deceased," replied Caine.

"Precisely." Nodded Dailly, "Let you and I agree upon that unfortunate detail at least."

Dailly took a moment now to let the odour of his pissing upon Caine's evidence waft around the court and looked over a sheet of paper with some of his handwritten notes upon it. "Let us move on to more relevant matters." He sighed without looking up. "Did you witness the murder of Yvonne Kidd?"

"No!" Caine firmly shook his head.

"Are you claiming that my client told you that he murdered Yvonne Kidd or that you saw evidence to suggest that he did murder Yvonne Kidd?"

"No!" Again Caine shook his head.

"No further questions!" snapped Dailly as he retook his seat, put his notes down and looked straight over at the Orcadian, who surprisingly enough grinned at him.

"That will be all, thank you, Detective Sergeant," said Flora to Caine before then looking down at the Orcadian invitingly.

"The Crown now calls Alban Dudley, M'lady," he said whilst standing up and looking down at all three defence lawyers somewhat mischievously.

Dudley soon appeared wearing a white t-shirt with red hoops across it. He appeared to be in his late forties with plenty of wrinkles and an old tan that had refused to abandon its host. He had a classic mod hairstyle and Monty reckoned that he resembled a cross between Ronnie Wood of the Rolling Stones and an older Paul Weller. When Dudley began telling the court his name and age, etc., Monty thought he had an Essex accent but could not be quite sure.

"And your occupation, Mr Dudley?" asked the Orcadian.

"Erm, musician," replied Dudley.

"Am I right in saying that you once shared a flat with an Irvine Stroker?"

"Yeh, we lived together in Musselburgh for a few years until last year when he died." Grinned Dudley playfully.

"I see. Would I also be right in saying that in August of last year, yourself and Mr Stroker received some visitors from Police Scotland?" The Orcadian asked him.

"Yeh, two cops turned up early one morning and started roughing us up." Shrugged Dudley.

"Really? Can you tell the court what happened?"

"Well, there were two of them and they were banging the door around about 7 am, I think, and Irvine let them in." Dudley knew his lines well enough.

"I see?"

"And well, they started kicking Irvine and threatening to plant cocaine on us both and then nick us for intent to supply, they says."

"Right, and did they have cocaine in their possession?"

"Yeh and they says that we would get remanded in custody and that they knew people inside who would slash us and stuff." Grinned Dudley with an earie oddness.

"Go on please," urged the Orcadian with even more of an eerie grin.

"Well, they says they wanted Irvine to give 'em some information on some bird called Yvonne," lied Dudley.

"I see."

"Irvine knew her from meeting her at a some party or other, I think." Dudley shrugged again.

"Did they say why they were interested in her?"

"No, just that they wanted her address and Irvine couldn't remember it but said that he would take them there instead."

"Okay, and then?"

"Then they returned a few hours later and Irvine said that they had visited Yvonne and been sitting in her living room but that the two cops had gone out into the corridor with her and then returned without her and told Irvine to leave with them, and that on the way out he saw her laying on the floor at her front door and that..." Dudley paused. "Well, that she seemed to be dead?" He shrugged again.

"I see. And did Mr Stroker elaborate further?"

"No. He said the cops dropped him off and threatened him not to tell anyone or else they would plant the coke on him and make sure he went to prison for a long time," said Dudley.

"And were you home when the three of them returned?"

"No, Irvine told me later what had happened. He also said that DS Forsyth had been sleeping with Yvonne and that she was saying that she was pregnant with his kid and asking for cash from him."

"And did he tell you that DS Forsyth had told him that?"

"Yeh, he said both of the officers had been discussing it in the car," said Dudley.

"Can you recognise any of those two police officers here in the court today, Mr Dudley?"

"Erm yes, that's one of them there." Dudley pointed with what appeared to be considerable effort at Forsyth in the dock, who in turn shook his head back at him.

"No further questions, M'lady," said the Orcadian as he sat back down again.

"Mr Dailly?" Flora smiled at all of the defence team.

Monty noticed Forsyth nodding over at him so he creeped over to the dock and leaned his head over.

"One moment please to confer with my client, M'lady," pleaded Dailly at which Flora nodded her consent.

Forsyth whispered in Monty's ear, "We were questioning Stroker, yes, that is true, and Dudley was there but we already knew Kidd's address, as her mother has claimed, when she said we had already door stepped her prior to visiting Stroker's house when Yvonne had been at work earlier that day."

"Okay." Nodded Monty.

"Then when we returned later that afternoon to Stroker's house, Dudley wasn't there and considering we then had a surreal time-travelling experience with Dai, which reduced Stroker to tears, I doubt very much that he would then have told Dudley anything after that night or in the days following?" Forsyth shook his head.

"Right, so our learned friend has given him a script to enact." Nodded Monty who then returned to the table and similarly crouched over Dailly and relayed part of it, missing out the stuff about time-travel and angels.

"Right, well, not to worry," responded Dailly aloud, partly for the benefit of jury and partly to coerce Dudley. He then stood up, hands clasped behind his back again and slowly approached Dudley. "Mr Dudley, you have advised my learned friend here that you are a musician?" He pointed out with a grin.

"That's right." Dudley was already on the defensive.

Touchy subject then.

"Do you have any material on vinyl, CD or available for the public to buy?"

Dudley did not like the question and so sighed, leaned his neck to one side and partly groaned, "No."

"Do you perform publicly then?"

"No!" The tone becoming sharper.

"So, you do not earn financially from music then?"

"No!" And yet sharper still.

"And yet you told the court that you are a musician."

Dudley remained silent for a moment and both men stared at each other. "I write music and work on it from home," Dudley finally responded through gritted teeth.

"So, it is a hobby then, Mr Dudley, and not a vocation," stated Dailly.

Dudley just stared back at him.

If looks could kill, eh.

"Which is why you have been in receipt of benefit for several years now, is it not?" Dailly now handed him a photocopy of confirmation of this from the Department of Work and Pensions which Monty had acquired.

"So?" snapped Dudley.

"So, you were either fibbing to my learned friend when he asked you your vocation, or you are perhaps delusional?"

"Objection," thundered the Orcadian. "The witness is not on trial."

Flora grinned and looked down at Dailly.

"His ability to respond honestly and coherently matters profoundly when the jury is being asked to consider him as a reliable source of evidence, M'lady." Shrugged Dailly, returning her grin. "If he cannot be honest about such a simple matter as his vocation, is he to then be taken seriously when he claims he heard from a deceased person that my client did this or that?" argued Dailly.

"I'll allow it," said Flora before turning back to her notes.

Dailly nodded at her then walked back to the table where he picked up another collection of paperwork which Monty had given him this morning. He then walked back over towards Dudley. "Which is it then, Mr Dudley, are you simply being dishonest because you wish you were a musician, or are you delusional?" he asked him casually.

Dudley sighed again. "What?" He cranked his neck to look up and stare at the ceiling lights momentarily, as if half expecting a divine wink or a nod in acknowledgment of this unjust harassment by learned counsel.

"Are you hard of hearing, Mr Dudley?" Dailly pressed on. "Or are you simply endeavouring to acquire time with which to create a response?"

Dudley did not respond. Dailly saw no need to ask Flora to press him either, for the jury had now gotten the point. "I have here a copy of a social enquiry report in relation to your conviction of stealing children's underwear from washing lines." Dailly let this revelation sink in for a moment before continuing. "Which suggests that not only are you mentally ill," he turned to look at the jury whilst waving the report, "but also a fantasist. A modern-day Don Quixote. And that you are a manipulator, Mr Dudley."

Dudley remained silent and looked down at the floor now. "So, either/or, Mr Dudley, your account of what the late Irvine Stroker allegedly told you should be taken with a pinch of salt, wouldn't you agree?" Dailly smirked at his prey now.

"That's your opinion," snapped Dudley without looking up. He was seriously uncomfortable now with all of this and struggled to prevent himself from breaking out and singing Shirley and Company's *Shame, Shame, Shame*, which was really the only tune he could play on guitar.

"On the contrary, Mr Dudley." Dailly searched through the paperwork for what was an agonising few moments for Dudley. "This is the opinion of the author of this social work report, who also states that you appeared to have no remorse for your crime, and so states here that you should be considered untrustworthy and, I quote, 'an individual whose words should be taken with a pinch of salt'. However, let us now move on to the person who you claim told you that my client was at the scene of Yvonne Kidd's murder—Irvine Stroker." By moving on, Dailly released his grip momentarily. "How did Irvine Stroker die?" he asked.

Dudley recovered slightly, now that it appeared that Dailly had relaxed his grip on him. "Well, the police said that he had overdosed on heroin, but he didn't do heroin."

"So, the official verdict was that he had overdosed on heroin?"

"Yeh." Dudley was like a child in a huff now.

"And you say that he didn't do heroin because usually both Mr Stroker and yourself only participated in smoking cannabis?" Dailly waved the report at him again, "Am I right?" He smirked.

"Yes," conceded Dudley with a look of sheer hatred upon his face.

"So, even if it was the first time Mr Stroker had taken heroin, which we only have your word for, you do admit that you were both regular cannabis smokers?"

"Yes." Dudley conceded again but now with a strange and monstrous grin.

"And we all know that one of the side effects of cannabis abuse is memory loss," stated Dailly. Dudley neither contested nor confirmed this.

"So, we only have your word, Mr Dudley, a convicted criminal with a background of dishonesty, who is a known fantasist, and who tells us that you heard a rumour from a dead heroin user who was, like yourself, also a regular cannabis abuser." Smirked Dailly.

"It's the truth," insisted Dudley derisively.

"Somehow I doubt that, Mr Dudley. No further questions." Dailly casually turned his back on him.

"Thank you, Mr Dudley, you are free to go," declared Flora. "I think we shall break for lunch now then," she added cheerily.

"I'm going to pop down and see Forsyth in the cell area, shall we nip to the pub for lunch?" asked Dailly to both Monty and Mercer. Both men gestured that they would follow him down but Monty wanted to grab a quick pee first. Upon leaving the courtroom, Monty noticed that Dai had disappeared. He frequently did this so he was not alarmed; however, he could feel the eyes of the three suited men upon him as he exited at the top of the stairs.

The toilets were busy. Two lawyers were talking as they took turns drying their hands on the blowing machine whilst three other men were all debating the election results whilst relieving themselves at the urinals. He quickly relieved himself too, washed his hands and opted for a paper towel in order to escape the ongoing election debate, and promptly exited.

Upon re-entering the court foyer, he found himself face to face with the two of the three suited men from the public benches. "Hello Monty lad," said the taller of the two with the thick ginger moustache.

"Can I help you?" Monty tensed up and faced them both.

Just then, they all had to take a step aside as a wig-wearing lawyer excused himself in order to access the toilets. "Is your trial going well then?" asked the moustache whilst the smaller, plumper of the two, continued to eyeball him as if he were about to unleash a head butt.

"Well, you should know, pal; you have been in attendance since it began," replied Monty curtly.

"Yes, but I'm interested in your take on it." Smiled the moustache.

"Who are you?" Monty looked around; the area was busy enough.

"Well, you might be mistaken." Shrugged the moustache.

Monty took a deep breath. "Really?" he then exhaled through his nose.

"Yes." The moustache continued to smirk. "Just as you are mistaken about your client's innocence," he pointed out rather smugly.

"Are you two guys cops then?" Monty looked at them both questioningly.

"Why do you waste your time and energy on such a small fry?" asked the plump one now.

"Same reason you, and the whole fucking police force, are using your power to hunt down and destroy him," replied Monty. "You're like fucking huntsmen who dig out fox dens for no other reason than to satisfy a lust for blood, aren't you?" He leaned forward so that his nose was almost touching the moustached guy's nose, before then taking a step back and turning to walk away.

"I don't know what your beef is with the police service, Monty lad, but we aren't cops," insisted the moustache.

"Besides, who would you call if you saw an armed intruder in your house looking to cut your dog's throat, mate?" asked the chubby one.

At this, Monty turned around and took a couple of steps back towards them. "Well, it wouldn't be Police Scotland, as they would already fucking be there, wouldn't they," he snapped. The two men chuckled at this before Monty spoke again, "I don't know, nor do I care who you are, other than that you enforce the will of faceless power," he whispered, "but if that is a veiled threat, know this, if anyone or anything comes near my home, family or my dog, then I'll personally hunt you two puppets down and stalk you both until I find an opportunity to kill you," he promised them.

"Calm down, Monty," insisted the moustache. "No one is ever going to harm you or yours, that has been agreed."

"Fuck off, the pair of you, or I'll have you both thrown out onto the street," Monty snapped at them before then turning away from them again and striding off.

The Afternoon Sitting

The three defence lawyers agreed that so far, the Orcadian had failed to prove zilch and that unless anything dramatically changed with Phillipson's evidence—there would be no need to call Forsyth to give evidence. Forsyth appeared seemed to comprehend this and had been well briefed on the possibility that he may still be required.

The Orcadian called up his next witness—Philipson was a small dark-skinned man with cropped greying hair and Freddie Mercury moustache. He wore a cheap grey used car salesman's suit, white shirt, and mismatched orange tie which was as garish as a pink poodle. His skin was so tanned that it was at the point of appearing almost black on his hands which he placed on the wooden stand. He scanned the courtroom now, his face oily and littered with tiny skin tags.

Once the Orcadian had greeted him and led him through the formalities, he got straight down to business by bringing him to the date, time and scene of the murder: "Mr Phillipson, can you explain to us where you were headed that afternoon?"

"I had been to meet my boyfriend, Imad Al-Wassouf, at his house on Loganlea Terrace," explained Phillipson in a somewhat camp voice.

"I see." Nodded the Orcadian. "And so, you had walked through the Queens Park?"

"Yes, I always walk that way from my home at Dumbiedykes," confirmed Phillipson. "And then at around about the back of 3 pm, I started walking back home again."

"And did you take the same route home?"

"Yes, and I found myself back at Queens Park Avenue at around 3:30 pm," stated Phillipson.

"Can you tell the court what you saw there?"

"Well, once I turned onto Queens Park Avenue, I saw three men coming out from number 17 and getting into a gold-coloured Volvo car," said Phillipson.

"And did you by any chance get the registration number of this Volvo car?" asked the Orcadian.

"No." Phillipson shook his head in obvious regret.

"Was it a Volvo that looked like this one up here on the screen?" the Orcadian then projected an image of Chuck Kean's car for everyone to see.

"Yes, exactly the same." Nodded Phillipson enthusiastically.

"Exactly the same," echoed the Orcadian for the benefit of the jury. "And what were these three men doing?"

"They all appeared a bit panicked and one of them, the one who then went on to drive the car away, put something in the boot which I could not make out properly and then they all got in the car and drove off," said Phillipson.

"I see, and then what happened?"

"Then I continued home. It was several weeks later that I heard about the murder which had occurred at 17 Queens Park Avenue on the day that I had been passing, and that the police requesting anyone with any information to come forward and help them with their enquiries," explained Phillipson.

"And so, you made contact?"

"Yes, and I was shown some photographs and I identified the three men." Monty noted that Phillipson was modifying his working-class accent into what he regarded to be a middle-class Edinburgh brogue.

"And am I correct in saying that these were the three men who you identified?" The Orcadian now projected photographs of Forsyth, Chuck Kean and Irvine Stroker onto the screen again for all to see.

"Yes, that's them." Nodded Phillipson.

"And can you see any of these men here today in the courtroom?" asked the Orcadian.

"Yes, that is one of them there." Phillipson pointed to Forsyth.

"Let the record show that the witness has identified the accused." Smirked the Orcadian. "No further questions." He then sat down again and eyeballed Monty.

"Mr Dailly?" Flora looked down at the defence team again.

"Yes M'lady." Dailly stood up now and turned towards Phillipson.

"You are a man in your fifties, Mr Phillipson; tell me, how old is your boyfriend?"

"Objection," trumpeted the Orcadian. "I see no relevance—"

"Merely establishing the witness's character, M'lady," insisted Dailly.

"Not relevant, Mr Dailly, move on please," ordered Flora.

"Okey-dokey. Are you a convicted criminal?" asked Dailly now.

"Yes." Phillipson recoiled, and Monty saw that the jury were quite spellbound.

"Convicted of what, precisely?"

"Three possessions of cannabis."

"And you plead not guilty to all three offences and were, nevertheless, after three trials, found guilty, were you not?"

"Yes." Philipson stuck his chest out arrogantly.

"So, hardly an honest man, are you, Mr Phillipson?" suggested Dailly—forcing him back upon the ropes.

"We all make mistakes, even you, I'm sure," replied Phillipson fearlessly.

"So, you are a reformed character then? And no longer an aficionado of dishonesty?" teased Dailly with a playful grin that betrayed the fact that he was enjoying this spar.

"I never was." Phillipson was not quite sure what aficionado meant but he got the gist of it.

"Would you say that you were a treacherous person then, Mr Phillipson?"

"Nope. I don't know what you mean."

"Do you borrow money from your oldest friends and then refuse to repay them even when you are able to do so?" asked Dailly.

Phillipson panicked a bit now and looked up at Flora and then over towards the Orcadian.

No one had mentioned this!

"Erm, no, what do you mean?" He shook his head.

"So, you are not regarded to be a two-faced liar who is jealous of your friends and family because they have done better than you in life?" Dailly pressed.

"No. What do you mean?" repeated Phillipson with a little gasp now.

"So you do not pretend to be a Muslim who hangs around the central Mosque in Edinburgh so that you can prey upon young male refugees such as your teenage boyfriend?" asked Dailly which caused Phillipson looked up at Flora as if she had burped.

"When in reality, you eat pork, drink alcohol, and practice homosexual sex, do you not, Mr Phillipson?"

The Orcadian was up creating a hullaballoo now—demanding that Flora reel Dailly in. "Just establishing the witness's honesty and integrity, M'lady," mitigated Dailly but Flora was having none of it, so he respectfully withdrew the question. "So, are you or are you not an honest person?" he asked Phillipson again.

"Look you," Phillipson pointed his finger at Dailly, "now wait a minute, I'm a good person who volunteers three hours a week with homeless teenagers in a hostel in the Cowgate," he insisted scornfully.

"I see, so you are a cultural island in an otherwise sea of chaviness, Mr Phillipson?" mocked Dailly, which again earned him a rap on the knuckles from Flora.

"Mr Phillipson, are you a police informer?" asked Dailly now.

There was a moment's silence where Phillipson did not know what to say.

"I remind you that you are under oath."

"Yes," Phillipson finally replied, and gasps could now be heard from the public seating area.

"And so, I put it to you that you did not contact police Scotland in order to respond to a plea for eye witnesses to the murder of Yvonne Kidd, but rather that you had a discussion in a private with the officer who handles your information; am I correct?"

"Well, yes, I told him what I had seen," acknowledged Phillipson, too scared to risk lying when he knew there was a fair chance that his handler could be called to contradict him.

"Yet earlier you told my learned friend here that you had responded to a public request for information?"

"Same sort of thing," insisted Phillipson.

"I think not, Mr Phillipson." Dailly shook his head despondently. "I put it to you that your police handler is one DI Calvin Bennett, and that he asked you to say that you had witnessed my client outside number 17 Queens Park Avenue on the day in question?"

"Yes, Calvin is my handler," admitted Phillipson.

"And he persuaded you to identify my client, did he not?"

"No." Phillipson rustled his hair and then shook his head. "I did see him, or I think I did."

"You think you did?" Dailly was onto this in a flash.

"I think so; look, it is hard to tell from where I was walking at the other side of the road."

"It was hard to tell from where you were situated. Yes, of course, it was. And despite this, you claim to know it was number 17 you saw these men exit from; tell me, how could you read the door number then?"

"I just did." Mumbled Phillipson

"I think now, Mr Phillipson," smirked Dailly. "I put it to you that your handler-DI Bennett, took photos up to your flat and put pressure on you to pick out my client, isn't that the truth?"

"I don't know, no look, I can't remember." Phillipson seemed close to tears now and Monty sensed a complete collapse coming.

"Can't remember seeing my client there because, as you correctly stated, it was hard to tell from where you were located, or can't remember being pressurised to pick him out by the police at a later date?"

"I don't know, both I think." Phillipson was sighing and shaking his head.

GOAL!

Dailly decided to cash in. "No further questions, M'lady." He casually walked back to the table and sat down again.

Monty thought that he could have reeled Phillipson in further—causing him to totally shatter. They were past the worst now though, both Dudley and Philipson had been the main hurdles to endure and Dailly had pretty much blown the pair of them away. The Orcadian now called on the two detectives who had gone over to Tenerife to arrested Forsyth—one DS Kyle Bowie and a DI Ross Turner. Turner came in first, and went through the motions of explaining the arrest warrant, flights, and bureaucratical procedure with the Spanish Guarda Civil, before then claiming that Forsyth admitted to him that he had indeed murdered Kidd whilst they on the flight back.

"Did he tell you why and how he murdered her?"

"No sir, he just whispered it in my ear and then closed his eyes and went to sleep."

Mercer then got up and played the police verbals card by accusing Turner of making it all up. "You are simply making it all up, detective inspector, in an attempt to destroy this man's life." He pointed at Forsyth who had been shaking his head at Turner's claim. "And for no other reason than that he was investigating your colleagues on corruption." He snapped and raised his voice angrily at the cop.

"That is not correct," replied Turner. Monty saw that Turner had gone red in the face—not a blush as such, but with anger at being spoken to in this manner.

This fucker knew the drill and was no weakling like Phillipson.

"Was your colleague within earshot when you heard this so-called confession then?" asked Mercer contemptuously.

"No. He was in the lavatory, I believe," replied Turner—solid in his stance.

"Don't you consider it strange then that my client admitted to a murder when only one officer was present but then maintained his innocence thereafter and throughout the interview process in Edinburgh, detective?"

"I cannot presume to know what his thinking was," retorted Turner.

"I put it to you that you are lying, detective?" Mercer went for it.

"That is not correct." Turner stuck to his guns.

Later, when the Orcadian questioned Turner's sidekick—DS Bowie, all he was able to squeeze out of him was an admission that DI Turner had informed him back at the station in Edinburgh that Forsyth had admitted to the murder on the plane. "And you did not find it strange that DI Turner did not mention this great revelation to you either on the flight, when it allegedly occurred, nor in the transport from Edinburgh airport back to St Leonards?" Mercer followed up.

"I did not think about that, no," was Bowie's reply.

"No further questions, M'lady."

At which point, the Orcadian declared that the Crown now rested. He knew only too well now that he had not quite proven the case against Forsyth and he saw little use in calling the cops who had been involved in the punch up with him at St Leonard's either; if anything that would only draw attention to the mysterious death of Leslie Cairns in police custody. This had always been a weak case that the monkeys had lumbered him with from the outset thanks to their blasted incompetence.

He was angry at them now more than ever and wanted out of here as soon as possible. His key witnesses had been bashed by that shit Dailly, and all that was left to point to Forsyth's guilt were the questionable police verbals. Even if the defence didn't call their two witnesses now—Parks and McDuff—the jury would be inclined to go with a Not Proven at best, he suspected; unless he intervened with their reasoning.

Which wasn't worth the price.

"Mr Dailly?" asked Flora.

Dailly turned to the other two now. "Don't think we need McDuff, guys; shall we just run with Parks and possibly Forsyth, then end this charade," he whispered to them.

Mercer shrugged. "Sounds about right. It's good that he isn't calling his St Leonard witnesses to try and dent our chap's character," he agreed. "We don't really need McDuff to dent Phillipson's either—he did a good job on his own credibility himself.".

"We will probably get a result now even if we don't call any witnesses; so yes, agreed?" Monty leaned over and whispered. "I do think that the jury needs to hear from Forsyth though, yes" he added.

"Oh goodie," thought the Orcadian to him now. Monty sat back and turned to meet his gaze.

He is going to try something?

"Mr Dailly?" Flora was becoming impatient.

"Apologies, M'lady. The Defence calls Audrey Parks."

Chapter Nineteen

Speak when you are angry, and you will make the best speech you will ever regret.

Ambrose Bierce

Audrey Parks entered the courtroom wearing a dark blue trouser suit over a pink t-shirt and a pair of white Converse. Her intention was to display respect for the court but contempt at what she regarded to be farcical proceedings—smart but casual then. Flora went through the swearing in procedure as she had done with all the others, while everyone else studied Parks, including the Orcadian, who could smell her vagina and who made it obvious to both Monty and Dai that he was doing precisely that.

Dailly was all charm with her, asking her to confirm her age, address and occupation. "I'm a nurse at the Western General hospital," she told him assuredly.

"What department?"

"Chemotherapy at the moment." She forced a smile.

"And do you know Christopher Forsyth?" he asked her.

"Yes, he is my ex-boyfriend," she confirmed.

"I see. How long were you in a relationship with him?"

"Well, from 2005 until last year." She appeared a tad sad about it, considered Monty.

Good girl, keep it up.

"And did you live together?"

"Yes, we moved into a rented property in Newhaven in 2008." She nodded then gave her nose a little scratch.

"And was Christopher working for the police in the Drug Squad throughout this period?"

"First, he was in the CID and then later the Drug Squad, yes."

"Can I ask you if it was a good relationship?"

"Mostly. It was normal, I'd say."

"Why did you split up?" Dailly got down to it now.

"Well, Chris had some difficulties with his job and had decided to quit. We struggled a bit thereafter and decided to have a temporary break just to see where we were at, and then Chris was offered a job opportunity by his sister who has a business in Tenerife," explained Parks without going too much into detail as she had previously been advised by Monty.

"And so, he decided to go out to Tenerife and you chose not to go with him?"

"Well, I had my NHS contract and I don't speak Spanish so yes, it was a difficult time for us but he needed to take some time out over there," explained Parks.

"I see. And you mentioned that Christopher had been under some sort of pressure at work, can you tell me more about that?"

"Only that he had been involved in investigating police corruption, and that certain people were not being very nice to him as a result. I guess he wanted away from it all." She shrugged. "His colleague Chuck Kean had recently been murdered and I think that changed him." She looked down and considered this briefly. "He seemed scared that he might get hurt too, and he had said he was worried, but had not really explained why," she said thoughtfully.

"Scared and worried that something might happen to him?" Dailly asked her.

Monty saw that Forsyth was watching her intently.

He still loved her.

"Yes, but more that something could happen to myself, I think." Nodded Parks.

"Was Christopher ever violent towards you in the relationship?"

The jury were all staring at her too. She seemed sincere and saddened by Forsyth's plight.

"No never, he was always very loving and my best friend."

"Do you think he was capable of murder?" Dailly made his end-move now.

Parks had been well briefed however. "No, no way, he was a good man and an honest cop," she insisted.

Monty noticed two women on the jury looking at each other before taking notes down.

"Did he ever give you cause to suspect that he had been involved in a murder?"

"No, never!" Parks was quite clear.

"Do you recall where you were on 28 August 2014 at around 6 pm?"

"Ever since Chris's arrest, I have been unable to forget—yes. I was working until 2 pm and then went home and stayed home all night."

"And can you recall what time Christopher came home that day?"

She didn't need to think about it. "About 6 pm, I think."

"And how did he seem?"

"Just as normal. He ordered Chinese and we had a couple of glasses of wine." She sounded believable.

"So, he did not come home with any blood on him then?"

"No, definitely not." She shook her head vehemently.

"And can I ask you, did you ever notice any kitchen knives missing from your property around that time?"

"No. I would notice that as they are all really expensive these days, aren't they?"

"And is it the case that should Christopher be released from custody by this court, that he will be moving in with you into your new home in Carrick Knowe?" Dailly sought to confirm.

"Yes." Parks forced an optimistic smile.

She must love him too.

"And presumably, if you even suspected for one second that Christopher was capable of murdering anyone you would not be welcoming him into your home?"

"No chance!" assured Parks.

"And can I ask you, were you ever visited by any police officers regarding Christopher?"

"Yes. In January this year, the CID turned up and told me that Chris might be in trouble and may try to use my address as a bail address and that if I agreed to that, I would get dragged into the trouble."

"And is this the card with contact details that a detective left with you?" Dailly handed her back the yellow contact card which she had previously passed on to Monty with DI Calvin Bennett's details on it. Once she confirmed that it was, Dailly then retrieved it and walked back over to the table and placed it doen before the Orcadian who simply gazed at it before then returning his gaze back up at Parks.

"For the record, let it be known that the name and contact details on this card are that of Detective Inspector Calvin Bennett who was the investigating officer into Yvonne Kidd's unfortunate murder, as well as the handler of police informer—George Phillipson," declared Dailly. "Were you intimidated by DI Bennett?" he then asked Parks.

"Yes, very much so. I didn't want any trouble as it could affect my job and all that."

"Ah yes, of course, that is understandable. So, as a consequence, you were inclined not to offer your home to Christopher?"

"Yes. Until his solicitor—Mr Montgomery complained to the police at Fettes and assured me that I could let Chris stay with me if I wanted to," explained Parks

"I see. Well, thank you, Miss Parks, no further questions." Daily gave her a brief smile of appreciation.

Flora then turned to the Orcadian. "Advocate Depute?"

"Yes M'lady" He gradually rose from his seat with poise, then slipped his hands in his pockets and casually strolled over towards the stand.

Dailly leaned over to Mercer and Monty and whispered to them: "By my calculations, we have at the very least, secured reasonable doubt, gentlemen."

At which both nodded in agreement. "I even think we will get an acquittal as things stand," speculated Mercer.

"Which is why I am not convinced that we should call Forsyth," suggested Dailly.

Monty wasn't quite sure; on one hand, he sensed that the jury needed to hear from Forsyth, but on the other, he had to agree with Dailly that they had successfully presented a defence which should ensure that Forsyth walked out of court a free man. Of course, he was additionally mindful too that by putting Forsyth upon the stand now, there was a slim possibility that they might jeopardise this achievement, particularly when up against the Orcadian and his tricks.

The Orcadian had his back to the rest of the court as he grinned at Parks. His radiance appeared visible to her momentarily, and she blinked twice before instinctively leaning back slightly. "Why did you and Mr Forsyth split up?" he softly enquired.

"Well…well, he was under a lot of pressure so we felt it was a good idea for him to go out to the Canaries and earn some money, as well as to sort his head out," replied Parks, somewhat spellbound by his wonderful almond-shaped eyes which only she could see now.

"Ah yes, of course," he repeated sarcastically. "Presumably, something was affecting his head then?" he asked with feigned interest.

"Yes. The death of a colleague and his decision to leave his chosen vocation."

She's still fighting.

"Hmm, and you mentioned there to my friend that you regarded Mr Forsyth to have been a good police officer?"

"Yes," she wearily confirmed.

"Did you ever accompany him on one of his shifts then?" he asked, whilst turning momentarily to beam his beautiful smile towards the jury.

"No." She appeared somewhat confused by this angle and scared of him. Except it was not quite fear that she was experiencing, rather she felt bashful when under his gaze. This was unexpected and confused her even more.

"How do you know he was a good police officer then?" He took a slow step towards her now.

She continued to look down and took a moment to find her voice before replying, "Well, I was being conjectural."

"Ah, I see now. Well, we are only interested in the facts here, Miss Parks." He leered and she seemed slightly shaken by this. "And because you did not join Mr Forsyth on his shifts, nor were you privy to the business of an undercover detective, you could not possibly know what was going on professionally between your partner and his colleagues," he half told her, half pointed out.

"Not really no." She looked down now and her voice seemed much lower. He had softened her defences merely by placing his ephemeral features at her.

"In which case, is it not reasonable to presume that his colleagues, who were privy to what was or was not going on with him at work, and who have given evidence here in this court, are more reliable witnesses regarding whether or not Mr Forsyth was a good police officer?"

She shook her head in partial uncertainty. "I don't know," she muttered just loud enough for him to hear, which in turn prompted Flora to direct her to speak louder.

He went for the kill now: "And is it fair to say that if a person is prone to hiding the darker side of their job, which in this case involved various unsavoury characters and events, from a partner, then that person may have little problem in concealing a darker side to their personal life too?" he asked her as if they were simply friends having lunch.

"Not necessarily no, I would not say so." She shook her head defiantly.

Good girl—strong girl.

"I suggest that it would be straightforward for such an individual to extend such a tried and tested practice of secrecy, into say, the covering up of an affair." He very slowly and gently gestured with open hands, as if he were a magician producing a dove. "Or a murder even." He then stared at her again. His face relaxed and barren of any feeling, as he slowly placed his hands in his trouser pockets.

"No. Chris is not a murderer. I would know that as I am a good judge of character," she insisted.

"You are being conjectural again, Miss Parks." He turned and slowly walked back around to his side of the table and then faced her again from there. "Christopher Forsyth had something wrong with his head when he chose to remove himself from what was apparently a difficult and worrying situation, correct?"

Don't answer; he is leading you.

"Yes but—"

"And you could not possibly understand the true nature of what the situation was that he was leaving behind," he told her.

"He is not a murderer," she maintained.

"But you cannot know that for sure, can you, Miss Parks?"

"I sense it," she insisted.

"Alas, yet more conjecture." He removed a clenched right fist from his pocket, raised it up and then opened it out as if to reveal something, before then returning to his seat. "No further questions."

"Thank you, Miss Parks, you may leave now." Flora gave her one of her gentle smiles.

Dailly leaned over again now, "Strike that, I'm calling him up," he whispered to both Monty and Mercer. Mercer remained still but Monty nodded enthusiastically.

"Mr Dailly?" asked Flora now—smile gone.

"The defence calls Christopher Forsyth," announced Dailly.

Monty looked over at Forsyth with his best, *go canny* expression, which Forsyth read accurately. They had all gone over the procedure again at lunch time and so he knew not to talk too much when being questioned.

"Mr Forsyth," stated Dailly after Forsyth opted to swear upon the bible, "can you please tell us your name, age and occupation?" Forsyth replied that he was a barista in his sister's pub in Tenerife.

"Why did you resign from Police Scotland?" Dailly got straight to the point.

"I had been involved in an investigation into police corruption and things had become quite difficult for those involved," replied Forsyth.

No mention of a child abusing cult then? thought the Orcadian to both Dai and Monty.

"Who were the officers involved in the investigation?" asked Dailly.

"Myself, Detective Inspector Chuck Kean, Detective Constable Joe Roxburgh and Detective Constable Gavin Caine," replied Forsyth, leaving Sharon Adams out of it.

"And where are they now?"

"Well, DI Kean was shot dead by assailants unknown during the investigation, and DC Roxburgh is also dead though I am unsure precisely how he died; only that the police are claiming it was suicide."

"And DS Caine was the whistle-blower of what was otherwise a clandestine investigation?"

"In the end, yes. At the beginning, someone up the command ladder instructed DI Kean to commence the investigation on a strict denial basis. I do not know who, and I just did my job as a surveillance officer."

"I see. Please explain how things were after DI Kean was killed," urged Dailly.

"Well, after DI Kean was murdered, attitudes changed towards me at work. In the end, I decided to quit the service and take some time out. I decided to go abroad for a break and help my sister out for a short while until I decided what to do with my life."

"And this meant leaving your long-term partner behind?" Dailly pointed out.

"Yes, she was tied down with the NHS and couldn't speak Spanish, plus we had not been getting on so well, so it just made sense short term to take time out," agreed Forsyth.

"So, you did not run away because you had committed a crime then?"

"No. If that had been the case, I wouldn't have left my Tenerife contact details with Audrey," affirmed Forsyth.

"You say that you and Miss Parks were not getting on, why was that?"

"We had been trying for a child which had not happened and so I think we were both feeling a little stress regarding that."

"Not because of any other reason?"

"Well, we were both busy in our jobs working long hours, and we probably needed to spend more time together, so like Audrey said, we just needed a break to re-evaluate the relationship."

"Were you or have you ever been romantically involved with Yvonne Kidd?" Dailly asked him.

"No, not ever," assured Forsyth steadfastly.

"Did you murder Yvonne Kidd?"

"Certainly not!" Forsyth replied and then looked straight at the jury. "No way!" He shook his head.

"Did you tell DI Turner on the flight back from Tenerife that you had murdered Yvonne Kidd?"

"No!"

"Why do you think that George Phillipson gave evidence to the court that he had witnessed yourself, DI Kean and Irvine Stroker, leaving Yvonne Kidd's tenement on Queens Park Avenue on the day of the murder?"

"I do not know; I've never met the guy."

"So, you were not at Yvonne Kidd's house in the late afternoon with DI Kean and Irvine Stroker that day?"

"I attended the address earlier, before lunch, with DI Kean, but not with Irvine Stroker, as Yvonne's mother confirmed here under oath. However, Yvonne was out and so we left."

"And did you return later in the afternoon?"

"No."

"Why were you looking for her?" Dailly had to ask.

"She had apparently been connected to an individual whom we were interested in, and we wanted to speak to her as part of the investigation into that person," replied Forsyth.

"So, you had her address?"

"Yes."

"So, you did not require Irvine Stroker to take you to her address then?"

"Correct," agreed Forsyth.

That's it, short and sweet replies.

"Why do you think Alban Dudley would say that Irvine Stroker told him that you were involved in Yvonne Kidd's murder?"

"Perhaps for some sort of deal with the same police officers who persuaded George Phillipson to lie too? After all, Dudley is suspected by police as being an active paedophile, and his flatmate Irvine Stroker had been investigated and cautioned in relation to similar offences," Forsyth pointed out.

"Thank you, Mr Forsyth, no further questions."

Flora looked down at the Orcadian now who was smirking at Monty.

Let's see if I can make him admit to murdering the bitch then.

Monty however was rummaging through his briefcase for something which he found and placed down upon the table behind a computer monitor so that it was only visible to the Orcadian. It was a parcel of white paper—within which was a raw channel catfish with a netted ladies stocking wrapped around its tail end and "Ceto" written in marker pen on a slip of yellow note paper sticking from its open mouth.

The Orcadian gazed down momentarily before Monty then replaced it in his briefcase as if he had simply been looking for something else. The pen in the Orcadian's hand suddenly broke into fragments and he knocked a water glass off the table which smashed and also broke, with one very swift flick of his fingers.

Temper, temper.

"Advocate Depute...are you alright?" enquired a stunned Flora who, along with everyone else, had missed Monty's little lure.

Everyone in the court turned to take in the scene. "YOU!" the Orcadian raised his voice in ire at the ceiling, before then calming down and nodding up at Flora. "Quite alright now, M'lady, just a sudden sharp pain in my head, but perfectly fine now. I apologise for the fright I may have given the court," he assured her as he recomposed himself.

"It's quite alright but are you sure you would not prefer a short adjournment to get checked out?" suggested Flora.

"No, I'm quite fine, M'lady, I perhaps stood up too quickly, all good now to continue." He forced a smile but Monty could see his fists were still clenched and that a trickle of blood was appearing from one of them due to his nails digging into his flesh. Monty now felt for the cork in his pocket and was poised to quickly produce it and slash wildly at him should he make a move towards him.

"Pray continue then, but if you feel any more pain, we shall adjourn in order for you to see an expert," insisted Flora.

"Obliged, M'lady." Nodded the Orcadian courteously before then looking down at Monty and telepathically hollering at him.

You audacious little ape, you'll be lucky if it is not your... but then he sensed Dai looking down at him and stopped himself. He now turned to face Forsyth with both fists still clenched in fury.

"Right," he barked at him, which caused Flora to jerk her head slightly in surprise again.

"You claim that you quit your job, severed your relationship, gave up the property you were renting with Audrey Parks and just sailed off into the sunset because of pressure at work?" he spoke quickly and sharply.

"Yes," replied Forsyth. A little taken aback.

"That is a lie, isn't it?" He was not mincing his words now—gone was any courtesy or "I suggest", etc.

"Nope." Forsyth shook his head.

"You conspired to pervert the course of justice by sending Irvine Stroker into a caravan in Fife so that yourself and DI Kean could take compromising photographs of an unnamed retired police officer, as your colleague, DS Gavin Caine, told the court."

"Not true," contended Forsyth.

"Consequently, you were urged to jump before you were shoved, weren't you?" insisted the Orcadian angrily, before instantly wishing he had not phrased it this way.

Need to calm down, to relax, but no time, the prey is before me and the anger burns.

"No," replied Forsyth with a sarcastic smirk.

"What is so funny?" the Orcadian demanded to know.

"Your absurd allegations," replied Forsyth.

"And you were only too happy to run away because you had indeed slaughtered Yvonne Kidd in cold blood, and because she was threatening to reveal to both your partner and your employers that in all likelihood, you were the father of her unborn child."

Forsyth chortled. "That is preposterous."

"It is not preposterous," roared the Orcadian, on the verge of losing all control.

Flora sat back; she was on the verge of adjourning and having a doctor called when the Orcadian realised that he could not control his anger and needed a few seconds to calm down.

"No further questions, M'lady." He turned and stormed back to the table and promptly poured himself some water into a spare glass; which he then sat down and sipped at slowly with his slightly bloody hand.

A couple of jury members began shaking their heads and both Dailly and Mercer looked as if a topless streaker had just run across the courtroom. Monty, however, remained still and on edge.

"Right, please return the accused to the dock." Flora instructed the security officers who were as stunned by events as everybody else was. "Mr Dailly?" She looked at the defence with slight confusion across her face.

"No further witnesses, M'lady." Dailly shook his head.

"Right, well, if the Advocate Depute is feeling himself again, we can proceed to closing speeches, gentlemen?" She raised a wary eyebrow at the Orcadian.

The Orcadian was sipping the water and eyeballing Monty over the glass with an active malevolence, but he now calmly put it back down upon the table, took a deep breath and nodded up at her. "Quite refreshed, M'lady," he assured.

Outmanoeuvred by a talking monkey. Who told him about Ceto anyway? Dai, you old seraph?

He looked up at Dai now, the rage finally under control.

My hands were always tied with your presence here anyway.

He now turned to face the jury. All was lost, he knew this now, but one thing was for sure, a shitty closing speech certainly wouldn't change the situation. He decided to be short and sharp with his.

"Ladies and gentlemen of the jury, thank you for your patience. Now that you have heard all of the evidence, I suggest to you that any evaluation of it will bring you to only one possible conclusion," he paused to look all of them in the eyes before continuing, "and that is that Christopher Forsyth murdered Yvonne Kidd with Charles Kean and quite possibly Irvine Stroker." He continued to meet the gazes of those who were able to look into his beautiful celestial eyes. "In the course of your deliberations, you may well consider the alternative scenarios.

Was it a burglary that went wrong?" He shrugged. "Well, she was killed on her doorstep and there was nothing found to be missing from the house. Nor did it appear to have been ransacked. So Yvonne had answered the door to her killer," he reminded them.

"Was it a random door to door salesperson who happened to be carrying a large kitchen knife? Or was it someone who knew Yvonne and had a reason to kill her? I suggest that you know that the killer must have known the victim." He nodded knowingly at each of them. "Did the killer go to her door with the intention of speaking with her? Then, unhappy with the dialogue, did the killer then lash out and take that poor young girl's life out of anger or even desperation?"

He questioned them now. "The accused has admitted going to the house that day, and he has offered this court no explanation as to why he went there and pretended to Yvonne's mother that he was not a police officer?

"Why lie? You lie when you have something to hide or you want to cover up something" He shrugged again. "You must weigh this up and review the evidence that you have heard before coming to your conclusion ladies and gentlemen," he contended. "And what evidence is there against the accused?" he queried.

"Yvonne Kidd's mother said that Forsyth and Kean, two officers who were, we are told by a serving police officer, operating without the authority of their employer, and who apparently have no qualms whatsoever about risking a person's life in order to blackmail them, turned up on her doorstep a couple of hours prior to the murder looking for her daughter," he softly reminded them. "And both men disguised their professions before being duly informed that Yvonne would be home from work later that afternoon." He paused and turned to look at Monty.

I should have roasted Forsyth about that under cross-examination but you played your little trick.

He turned his back to the jury now. "Makes sense that they would return later then don't you think?" He turned around again and gestured towards Forsyth. "They left no calling card as police generally tend to do when looking to establish contact or make an appointment with someone."

"Why do you think that might have been?" He shook his head. "Because they intended to come back after lunch when they knew that Yvonne would be home, and obviously because they did not want to wait for a telephone call from her." He looked around and smiled knowingly at Forsyth now, who was gently shaking his head. "Because their business with her was both urgent and surreptitious." He raised his voice as he stared at him before then turning back to the jury again. "Then we have a witness who swears under oath that thereafter, both Kean and Forsyth turned up at the home of Irvine Stroker and press-ganged him into joining them for a second visit to Yvonne's house that afternoon; which fits with the time frame of the murder." He let this sink in for a few seconds.

"This also fits with the evidence of another witness, George Phillipson, who saw the three of them leaving Yvonne's tenement in a hurry whilst looking anxious, and at the estimated time of the murder," he continued. "How else would George Phillipson know what type of car Mr Kean drove unless he had seen it that day?"

Because the cops showed him a photo of it.

"Then we have another serving officer who swears under oath that Forsyth admitted murdering Yvonne Kidd whilst under arrest for her murder." He nodded eloquently to the jury. "So, ladies and gentlemen, when you consider all of this and weigh it up with the circumstantial evidence, which suggests that the accused removed himself from his guilt and responsibility by abandoning his long-term partner and home by fleeing the country. As well as showing a history of violence towards both Irvine Stroker and police officers, then I suggest that you can only arrive at one logical conclusion," he contended.

"Therefore, I ask you to deliver justice to Yvonne Kidd and her family by finding Christopher Forsyth guilty of her murder. I thank you again for your time and patience." He nodded at them and then gracefully and leisurely walked back to his seat at the table. He wanted to leave now. Under the table, he dabbed his bloody palm with a tissue and glared over at Forsyth ominously.

It had always been a shit case. It should have been simple enough for a speck of Kidd's blood to have been deposited upon an item of clothing in the flat Forsyth had shared with Parks. These primitive monkeys were useless beings fit only for servitude, and now they had dragged him down into their ineptness.

"Mr Dailly?" Flora looked down at the defence team now.

Dailly nodded and got up from his seat. He casually approached the jury with both hands behind his back. He had done this many times before and knew only too well that a poor closing speech could sway a jury. Some of whom may still be wavering at this stage, some might even change their minds; so the closing speech is key. However, in this instance, as per the Orcadian, he felt that a short delivery was all that was required, and so he checked his watch—14:22 pm.

They might even come back with a verdict today; this case is so cut and dry.

He knew he would do well not to over-season it now. The Orcadian was not looking up at him. Instead, he continued to stare at Monty, who refrained from returning the stare and followed his adversary's movements from the corner of his eye. The Orcadian now very quietly passed classical music into Monty's head—Karl Jenkins *Sanctus*. Thankfully, it was not loud enough to prevent him from hearing Dailly's closing speech; nonetheless, it was loud enough.

Dai could hear it too up in the public gallery and mentally thought down to Monty not to be alarmed by it, but rather to just enjoy the music as opposed to being intimidated. Daily adjusted his wig now and gave the jury a respectful nod and one of his best smiles.

"Ladies and gentlemen, you have endured what has become a relatively short murder trial, and for that I thank you. The reason it has been such a short trial, however, is because there is very little evidence to show us who killed Yvonne Kidd.

"My learned friend has urged you to analyse the little evidence that the almighty Crown Office have managed to rustle up for you and to come to a conclusion based upon nothing more than sheer presumption and scuttlebutt.

"Indeed, like my learned friend, I too urge you to review the little evidence there is in this case, but also to consider the source of this evidence. For only then will you come to the only plausible conclusion open to you, which is that this man," he pointed over towards Forsyth in the dock, "is innocent of this vile crime," he proclaimed.

"For the very foundation of the Crown's case was to argue that my client had impregnated Miss Kidd and then roped his superior officer, as well as the civilian Irvine Stroker, in to a conspiracy to murder her as a butcher might slaughter a lamb.

"And what evidence do they provide for this motive, hmm?" He extended his hands out to either side of him now to highlight confusion. "None whatsoever!" He shook his head. "On the contrary, we have heard that the unfortunate victim was, by her own mother's admission, quite a firecracker from an early age, who had a history of promiscuous relationships."

A moment to allow this to sink in.

"While Mr Forsyth has explained that it was Yvonne Kidd's connection to a person of interest which had caused both himself and DI Kean to seek her out earlier on, on the day of the murder. They had hoped to discuss this with her but when they were informed by her mother that Yvonne was not at home, they left. This was confirmed by the testimony of Ruby Kidd," he pointed out.

"So, the fact is that Yvonne Kidd appeared to have secrets, lovers, and there has been no evidence presented to this court which proves that she had ever met Christopher Forsyth. Which, of course, opens the door to the distinct possibility that another person, or persons, may have impregnated her and/or wanted to kill her.

"These are the only certainties that we can take from the evidence presented to this court by the Crown. Was Yvonne Kidd murdered? Sadly yes, there can be no doubt. At which point we reach the end of certainty, and the trail goes cold thereafter.

"For it is at the untimely ending of Yvonne Kidd's life that we come to the end of the facts, ladies and gentlemen. Thereafter, we only have the Crown's appalling sequence of presumptive hypotheses, which are supported by questionable police verbals and some even more questionable witness claims.

"The main police claim being this so-called admission on the flight back from Tenerife to Edinburgh, which is, of course, both unverified and unrecorded.

"Then we have the two civilian witnesses. Please consider these two sources, ladies and gentlemen. Both convicted criminals, one with mental health problems and some very abnormal habits, and the other a known police informer who admitted in the dock that he may have been pressurised into identifying Christopher Forsyth as being outside Yvonne's stairway by his police handler. A police handler who also just happens to be the officer investigating Yvonne Kidd's murder?"

Dailly leaned back upon the table now, crossed his legs and placed his hands in his trouser pockets. "Can you seriously conclude that these witnesses are credible enough for you to take away a man's life for a crime that otherwise, there is zero evidence to connect him with?" He gazed at them all now.

"Even if Alban Dudley and George Phillipson were law-abiding pillars of society and as pure as the driven snow, there would still clearly be room for reasonable doubt here, as the entire Crown case is based upon circumstantial evidence and wishful thinking.

"The man had just resigned, and there is no evidence that he had been pushed to do so as my learned friend is implying. He was also traumatised from the recent murder of his friend and colleague. It made sense to go to his last remaining family, get some sunshine, and try to come to terms with it all as both Mr Forsyth and Miss Parks have stated.

"And did he contest his extradition back to Scotland? No, he did not because he had nothing to hide, and naturally he wanted to clear his name when he was first informed of the allegations being made against him.

"Ladies and Gentlemen, there is no requirement by law for my client to prove that he did not commit this crime. By doing so, he would relieve the Crown of its burden of presenting proof to the contrary." He stood up straight again and placed his hands behind his back.

"You see, a criminal trial is a search for the truth. But in order for this process to work, there requires a willingness to see the truth, and the burden of proof here is—beyond any reasonable doubt," he gently informed them.

"Beyond any reasonable doubt!" he repeated whilst staring straight at them.

"And so," he shifted his weight from one leg to another, "has my learned friend provided proof without a reasonable doubt that Christopher Forsyth murdered Yvonne Kidd? No. I suggest to you that he has depended entirely upon hindsight and said wishful thinking, as a structure for a profoundly flimsy case that he has erected against my client.

"It is unjust to make assumptions or to accept an allegation against any person without there being conclusive evidence. Conclusive evidence. Not insufficient evidence or hearsay," he cautioned.

"There was no blood, nor any DNA found in DI Kean's car. No blood nor DNA evidence found in Christopher Forsyth's home. No murder weapon with his prints nor DNA upon it either. And we are supposed to believe that having murdered Yvonne Kidd, he went at the speed of a flying crow back to his house, didn't bother cleaning up, or disposing of any murder weapon, and simply ordered a Chinese takeaway?

"I suggest that you are all well aware that more than a reasonable doubt is evident here, and so consequently it is your duty to acquit Christopher Forsyth and allow him to put all the ambiguity and stress behind him, and to get on with the remainder of his life in peace," he proposed. "Thank you. The defence rests."

He smiled firstly at the jury, and then up at Flora whom he nodded at before then returning to his seat.

Flora then addressed the jury: "Ladies and gentlemen, you have heard the argument of both the Crown and the defence. You now have three options open to you—Not guilty, Guilty or Not Proven."

Monty needed the loo and Dai must have understood as he stood up and thought over to him that it was alright to leave. Monty excused himself just as the jury were getting up to leave and hurried out in order to avoid any potential backlash from the Orcadian. "It's alright. He won't harm you, nor will his human followers," promised Dai in the foyer outside the courtroom.

"Have we won then?" Monty wanted to know. "Is it over?"

"Almost. Why don't you just go home and relax now, I'll visit you soon," urged Dai.

"Am I going to be safe walking down the road? I need the air right enough, but am I safe from moving statues, etc.?" Monty was worried about the Orcadian; the viciousness in his eyes had been intense and quite nerve-racking.

"Yes, I promise you will not be harmed, nor will your home be touched now either. Ronnie will stay on for a while longer though. I've spoken with him so don't stress, and you and I will talk more later, okay?" Dai's vibe was as reassuring as ever and Monty just exhaled all his tension out with his breath and smiled back at him.

Thank you.

He then he walked over to Dailly and Mercer who were just exiting the courtroom.

"You okay?" asked Mercer.

"Yeh, just a bit tired, think I might be coming down with something. Do you mind if I just go home and I'll see you back here tomorrow for the verdict?" asked Monty.

"Hopefully, not the same condition that Farquharson came down with; did you see his breakdown there?" smirked Dailly.

Monty nodded. "I thought your closing speech was good, Mark."

Dailly smiled and looked at his watch. "Well, we might get a verdict today, but if so, I'll call you so go on, get yourself home and I'll see you in the morning."

Monty nodded and nipped to the loo before then heading off out into the sunshine and down the Royal Mile which was mobbed with performers and crowds. He didn't bother looking up or worrying about gargoyles and statues

484

however, he had faith in Dai's assurances. Though he carried his briefcase in one hand and kept the other on the cork inside his pocket. When he reached North Bridge, he stopped at a bin and fetched the trout he had purchased the previous day in the fishmonger's, with the stockings he had found in the Co-Op, from his briefcase and binned them.

Temper, temper.

He smiled to himself in the process and then proceeded to walk down to Waterloo Place and on to Leith with Ivan following slowly behind him. Once they were half way down Leith Walk, Monty stopped at the new Sainsbury's, where the old Shrubhill House had once stood; a soviet styled monstrosity that had been pulled down and replaced with a superstore. He purchased an ice lolly to cool him for the remainder of the walk home.

When he did finally arrive home, he made a note to himself to search for a Panama hat as the sunshine had caused him to feel quite tired and drained. He filled Charnley in on all the day's drama at court later on as they shared a large pepperoni pizza and bottle of Sangiovese. Monty mentioned that if a verdict was returned tomorrow, he intended just handing in his resignation now, as opposed to the end of the week as he had contemplated. Charnley suggested that he sleep on it and pray for guidance before he acted, which Monty conceded, made sense.

"Aye, you're a wise head, Ronnie; look, I really appreciate you being my flatmate these last few months, and for supporting me through these strange times, mate." He raised his half empty glass to toast him. Charnley just shrugged it off though and headed outside with a flask of coffee and slice of pizza for big Ivan who now appeared to be doing a double shift as he was sat outside in his car.

Monty then received a call from Mercer, he checked his watch—17.03 pm. "We just got called back into court ten minutes ago with a verdict," gasped Mercer down the line excitedly.

"What? Okay, that was quick." Monty took a deep breath which felt as if his lungs were filling up with dread. Such a short deliberation usually meant the worst for a defence; the jury having possibly made up their minds from early on in the trial.

"Not Proven!" exclaimed Mercer with a deliberate trace of disappointment now.

"Really?" Monty exhaled and suddenly felt massive relief. "That's, well, okay." He was surprised, and needed a second. Forsyth was free. "Was it a

485

majority?" he heard himself ask, his emotions all over the place. He had gone from expecting a Not Guilty verdict, to sudden panic just now at the jury's short deliberation, to instant relief. However, a gradual disappointment was slowly seeping into his mind.

"Yep, a majority," confirmed Mercer. "Look, job done, eh."

"Sure."

"Mark says if you're feeling perkier tomorrow, you should join us both in his chambers for breakfast and a chin-wag around 10.30 am?"

"Right, okay. Look, give him my congratulations," urged Monty, still somewhat in shock.

Not Guilty had seemed inevitable just five minutes ago; where did they get a Not Proven from?

"Will do, Monty. Oh and Forsyth asked me to pass on his warmest regards to you and said he will make an appointment with you in a few days," said Mercer. "I think they are going to let him out of a side door in order to give the press the slip."

"Okay. Thanks mate, chat tomorrow." Monty doubted he would be around the firm long enough to have a meeting with Forsyth; his feet were itching now more than ever and he had probably been needing a break for a while, not only from all of this stuff, but from the judiciary too.

"Goodnight, Monty," said Mercer.

Monty sat down at the kitchen table and took this in before declaring the good news to Charnley when he returned. "Let's crack open another bottle of plonk then, Ronnie," he suggested.

"Thought you'd never ask." Laughed the ever-jolly Charnley who had intended mentioning that the ever-present floral van, which had been sat outside most nights, was nowhere to be seen this evening.

Next morning, Monty awoke around 9 am and took the dog out for a run. He noticed Ivan still sitting in his BMW and exchanged a wave with him. Half an hour later, he was making coffee in the kitchen whilst the dog ate its breakfast and Charnley snored away on the chair he had crashed out in after sinking yet another bottle of wine.

Llewellyn then rang but Monty did not pick up; instead, he made a brew for Charnley and himself. He then gently woke Charnley up and urged him to come and have it at the table. Just then Monty received another call, this time from Audrey Parks. He sighed and considered whether or not to take it. He wanted all of this to be over and knew that he should have turned the phone off.

"You not going in today?" yawned Charnley. Monty shook his head as he answered.

"Hello?"

"Mr Montgomery, its Audrey Parks here." She sounded distraught.

"Hi, yes, what's wrong, Audrey?"

"It's Chris...he's...he's dead," she stuttered before then bursting into an agonising whine.

"Oh my God, how?" Monty felt his heart sink and his eardrum being tickled.

"I don't know." She was barely comprehensible now.

"Audrey, Audrey," He tried to get through to her and she gradually stopped whining and began sniffing as she calmed down again.

"Calm down. Where are you? Have you called the emergency services?" Monty needed to establish the situation first.

"Yes. The police and ambulance people are all here." She began to cry again, softly this time as if her and Forsyth had merely had an argument and she was calling her girlfriend.

"Where? At your house in Carrick Knowe?"

"Yes." She paused now to reply and then began sniffing again.

"Right." Monty looked at Charnley alarmingly, who was now leaning against the hall wall blowing up his brew whilst listening in intently.

"I was on night shift last night so I left my spare key with Mr Dailly just in case Chris was released, which, of course, he was." She now slowly stopped sobbing.

"It's alright, Audrey, go on; you're doing really well, sweetie. Then what happened?"

Momentarily in control again, she explained: "Well, Chris called me on my mobile phone from my house around the back of 7 pm and we chatted for a while; he was so happy, Mr Montgomery."

"I know, I know, but then what, Audrey?" Monty looked at Charnley and mouthed to him that Forsyth was dead. Charnley responded by sliding down the wall and sitting on the hall floor, shaking his already partially hung-over head despondently.

"Well, I told him there was a chicken casserole in the oven and that I had a couple of bottles of champagne in the fridge as I had been hoping he might get out in the next couple of days, so he said he would have some and that he would see me in the morning," explained Parks between sniffs and the odd groan.

"And then what?"

"Well, I got home around 9 am as I had to pop in on my mum in Clermiston with some messages, and I found Chris naked on the living room floor with the two empty champagne bottles, an empty bottle of vodka and two empty containers of pills that I had never seen before," she revealed.

"What pills?" Monty knew nothing about any medication that Forsyth had been on. Charnley suddenly lifted his head up at this.

"Nembutal," replied Parks. "I mean, Nembutal is pentobarbital and that is a barbiturate that is used as a sedative or to treat insomnia and both containers were prescribed in his name, so he must have received them in prison, no?" she reasoned before beginning to break down again.

"Miss Parks, if you don't mind, could you turn your phone off just now as we need to ask you some questions?" asked a female voice in the background.

"Is that the police, Audrey?" asked Monty.

"No, it's the paramedic. The police are all in the house." She was crying again.

"And where is Chris?"

"About to be moved into the ambulance where I am." She seemed really confused and judging by the fading volume of her voice, was doing a lot of turning around and lowering her phone.

"Audrey...Audrey?"

"Yeh?"

"I'll come over, it will take me about half an hour okay, so if you go anywhere, call or text me to let me know," insisted Monty.

"Erm okay, I've got to go now," she replied—the line then went dead.

"Suicide?" Charnley looked up suspiciously.

Monty just shook his head and joined him in the corridor. "Apparently."

"Doesn't make any sense though? Why would you celebrate winning the trial by topping yourself?" Charnley thought aloud.

"Fuck knows." Monty leaned against the wall opposite him, sighed and then slid down until he was sat on the floor opposite him.

Neither of them spoke for almost three minutes. It was not down to having nothing to say, for both their heads were buzzing with thoughts. Monty stared up at a photo of himself with his parents on the wall above Charnley. He now recalled the time when he had given up playing football, perhaps when he was in his early twenties or something. He had instead started playing football tennis on the council run tennis courts on the Meadows with his friend Louie Moretti who had been a bank manager with the TSB. Louie had been an average footballer, nothing special, who had never played for a boys club nor anything like that, but he was fit and energetic and was the type of player who would chase a crisp packet about on a windy day.

Monty, on the other hand, was a little older than him and considerably less fit; however, he made up for that in ability. He could just about place the ball anywhere on the court, due to having a naturally good first touch. He had always seen the smart move as a footballer, and so simply applied this vision to football tennis. The two friends had played out a few real Borg V McEnroe style sets over the summer months, even seen the tennis lovies, who had initially grumbled at two guys kicking a football ball across their sacred courts, had ended up applauding some of their rallies. Monty recalled now that there had always been a dark side to Louie however, in that he cheated consistently and always disputed when Monty had either served an ace or he had been out played—often to the point of screaming and shouting like McEnroe used to do too.

Monty had never understood Louie's desire to win based upon cheating. The murderers of Forsyth however were cut from a similar cloth he now realised. They had lost the trial, despite having the Orcadian prosecuting it for them, and so now they had lashed out. Charnley stared at his cup of coffee until the dog arrived and showed him some affection. He was thinking about lots of possible scenarios and outcomes to this news. Such as who was next to be targeted? Eventually, Monty spoke: "All that hard work and then they fucking whack him, Ronnie."

"They must have," agreed Charnley without lifting his gaze from the cup.

Just then, Monty's phone rang again. His phone now informed him that it was "Dai" despite him never having stored any number for the angel in it.

"Yeh?" He placed it on speaker so Charnley could hear.

"You're right," said the angel.

"About?"

"Them killing him."

489

"So, they forced him to take an overdose then?" guessed Monty.

"The autopsy will, of course, examine his stomach, blood and other organs. Here, they will see the cause of death and declare it to be the Nembutal," confirmed Dai.

"An examination of his liver will show a level of 16% of Nembutal. For it is here that the Nembutal is broken down. If the liver has a 16% level of the drug, this suggests that it was unhurriedly soaked up over a considerable period of time before Christopher died," explained Dai. "If he had consumed such a dose orally, there would be obvious evidence of it in his stomach, such as a clearly visible yellow dye stain in his duodenum," he also pointed out.

"And there will be no such stains?" asked Monty whilst exchanging a telling glance with Charnley.

"No. It will be obvious to the examiner that if Christopher lived long enough to accumulate 16% Nembutal in his liver, where cleansing ends after death, that he was slowly absorbing it for a protracted period before he died."

"So, the killers were injecting him whilst he was out cold from the vodka and champagne?" proposed Monty.

"An injection would leave a fingerprint, or to be more precise, a pin prick on the cadaver. So, no," corrected Dai.

"Also, the killer was aware that if he injected him, he would have passed away well before any liver breakdown could have transpired," he added.

"He?" asked Monty.

"Yes," replied Dai before continuing, "Nembutal is intestinally absorbable yes; it is even marketed by human medical experts as an optional rectal suppository. However, the liver reading at 16% will be far too high to support any suppository assertion. However, Nembutal does easily dissolve in water," he pointed out mysteriously to see if either of them had cottoned on yet.

When he concluded from their silence that they had not, he relieved them of their suspense. "The assassin found Christopher very drunk and almost out cold due to him having consumed two bottles of champagne and three quarters of a 1.75 litre bottle of vodka," he revealed. Monty and Charnley stared at each other again.

"He was given chloroform to assure that he was completely out cold before a considerable amount of dissolved Nembutal was administered by enema. As the drug was unhurriedly absorbed, the fleshy tissue of Christopher's large intestine responded to the distress by producing a marked lavender colouring as opposed to a yellow one. This obvious internal congestion and the tell-tale lavender colouring will be clearly evident at the autopsy."

"Right…"

"However, despite all of this, the final conclusion of the examiner will be of an oral overdose fused with alcohol," Dai confirmed both their suspicions.

"So, they put it up his arse?" asked Charnley.

"Quite," confirmed Dai.

"Why weren't you protecting him, Dai?" Monty wanted to know.

"My brief was to ensure that he was well represented at trial and that you, Mark Dailly and young Mercer were protected," replied the angel.

There was a prolonged silence. "What about Forsyth's guardian angel?" Monty finally asked.

"He had the right to decide for himself and although I have not spoken to him yet, I suspect the fact that Christopher was intoxicated may have played a part in that decision process."

"How did the killer get in the house?" asked Monty.

"Forsyth had been drinking in the garden until late and then left his key in the door when he went back inside."

Monty gritted his teeth. "He should have known better than to let his guard down." He sighed.

"So, what now, Dai?" asked Charnley.

"Well, I shall visit you both this evening and we shall discuss everything. As much as I know that this has come as a shock to you both, please try to relax for the remainder of the day," replied the angel.

"Was it the Orcadian?" asked Monty.

"No," replied Dai firmly. "He has left. He knew nothing about it," he assured.

"Then who?" Monty had to know.

"Just another human puppet. It is who ordered the contract that is of relevance," insisted the angel.

"And who was that?" asked Monty.

"The usual circle of old associates but let us talk tonight; I must go. God bless," insisted Dai. The phone then went dead.

"What now?" repeated Charnley.

"I need to ring Mark Dailly, then call my firm and resign. Then who knows?" Shrugged Monty, still stunned.

"We could call the press?" suggested Charnley.

"Eh?"

"From a call box outside." Smiled Charnley mischievously.

"And say what?"

Charnley put on his best Les Patterson impersonation[121]: "I'll explain that a cop who was secretly investigating a paedophile ring involving some pommy big-wigs, and whose fellow team members all turned up dead, won a murder trial yesterday and then was himself murdered last night," suggested Charnley, which caused Monty to smile.

"Then I'll explain all about this autopsy mischief and see if we can't get something stirred up about it and get them to start calling the coroner before the bad guys have time to impose their cover-up." Smirked Charnley.

"Excellent." Laughed Monty. "Right, you get on to that then and I'll make some calls here before I drive over to Audrey Parks' place."

"Do you think that's a good idea, Monty? Maybe better to wait for Dai to come around and not get too involved just yet, Monty?"

Monty considered this; Charnley was right, it might endanger him if he just turned up in the lion's den before a press investigation into the autopsy process began: "Fine I'll speak to Mark Dailly first, then I'll text Audrey Parks and tell her to call me later on when things calm down."

"Good thinking, Monty. Right, I'll walk a couple of miles up to Piershill and use a pay phone there; got any change?"

Palermo Airport

Profaci had enjoyed his view of the sea as he landed at Falcone-Borsellino, but it was the view of the towering cliffs which shielded the airport, that now gave him a deep sense of safety. He was home again, and he was glad of it. He had to wait a while to collect his luggage—two suitcases and two large bags; his life in Scotland all crammed into them. He had even brought a haggis from Tesco for his sister who wanted to try stuffing it into ravioli. He looked at his watch—18:42pm, the Palermitani would all be unwinding before dinner, he would make it too if his brother-in-law were on time and the thirty-minute drive into town was not hindered by traffic.

---

[121] "Sir Leslie Colin Patterson" is a brilliantly uncouth, lecherous and offensive comedy character from Sydney, Australia, created by the comedian Barry Humphries.

Once outside the terminal, he wheeled his luggage out to the P2 carpark facing the main terminal and there, standing with his back to him and wearing his black legal robe with Recupero Crediti written upon the back, was his brother-in-law Enzo Quidaciolu. Enzo was an arsehole who never took his debt agent's robe off because, like some people with tattoos who tend to wear t-shirts or shorts in the colder months, Enzo thought it made him look cool.

"Ciao Enzo, how about you put your phone down and help me with these bags?" Profaci greeted him.

"Eh, certo." The tall, bearded Enzo quickly turned his phone off, shook Profaci's hand, and quickly placed the luggage in both the boot and back seat of an adjacent green Alpha. Fortunately, the drive along the E90 was congestion free. Profaci didn't mind at all anyway because of the views of the Mediterranean that he had missed. The sun was still beaming down and so he put his sunglasses on, leaned back in the passenger seat and finally relaxed. His sister would be making his favourite tonight—penne con sarde, and there would be Brioscia's gelato for dessert too.

Served in a brioche bun no doubt.

"So, you're home to stay then?" asked Enzo, offering him one of his cigarettes.

"Yep." Profaci took one.

"So, what are your plans?"

"Buy a property, who knows but, in the meantime, I'll stay with you for a while if you don't mind?" replied Profaci whilst lighting the cigarette.

"No problem, we have two spare rooms now, so you are welcome," assured Enzo.

Profaci did not want to talk about money or anything else, so he leaned over and turned the car radio on and rolled his window down. Enzo understood.

The view was stunning, the bluest sea to their left—lightly tinted by the sun, and dark imposing hills to their right.

Safe here on this ancient island of assassins.

The song playing was Leonard Cohen's *Everybody Knows*. Profaci smirked as he listened to the lyrics.